classics

CW01651756

H. Rider Haggard

2 Books in 1

She

&

Ayesha The Return of She

A Wilco Book

Outstanding works of universal interest

This Omnibus edition printed in 2007

ISBN NO.: 81-8252-287-0

H. Rider Haggard

She &
Ayesha The Return of She

Complete and Unabridged

Published by
Wilco
PUBLISHING HOUSE
ITTS House, 33, Sri Saibaba Marg,
Kalaghoda, Mumbai - 400 023. INDIA
Tel: (91-22) 22041420 / 22842574
Fax: (91-22) 22041429
E mail: wilcos@vsnl.com
Website: www.wilcobooks.com

About the Author

H. RIDER HAGGARD

(1856-1925)

Henry Haggard was born in Norfolk England, as the eighth son of William Haggard, a barrister and a country squire, and Ella Haggard who was an upcoming writer. His father doubted his intelligence and regarded him as a slow-learner. Haggard therefore had to attend private schools in London. When he failed to join the coveted army, he took up a secretarial job in the Natal colony in South Africa, and rose to a high post in the Transvaal province. The overseas exposure acquainted him with the British colonial policy. He firmly believed in the adverse impact of European intrusion on their colonies.

On his return to England, he married Mariana Louisa Margitson, a heiress to Norfolk. As the Haggards moved to Transvaal to tend their ostrich farm, the territory was ceded to the Dutch, which forced them to come back to England. Haggard then joined the Bar in 1884 after graduating in law. In 1891 Haggards lost their son, a tragedy that cast a heavy shadow of gloom on the family.

Haggard thereafter retired to Norfolk country and pursued serious writing. It is said that Haggard, unimpressed by the success of *Treasure Island* by R.L. Stevenson, made a five-shilling bet that he could write a better book. The result was *King Solomon's Mines* (1885) – a tale of treasure hunt for a diamond mine in a strange land. The book became a runaway success. Haggard briskly followed up with three more novels set in Africa – *She*, *Jess*, and *Allan Quatermain*, all published within a span of two years.

Haggard's brilliance at fantasy and myth later inspired several film directors: 'King Solomon's Mines' alone was put on the celluloid by six different Producers!

After a flurry of successful novels, Haggard contested for, and was elected as an MP in 1895. For the next two decades he travelled frequently in the British colonies, becoming an expert on social conditions and in agriculture, bringing out valuable works such as *The Farmer's Year Book, Rural England, Rural Denmark,* and others such as *The Poor And The Land* (1905). For his social and literary contributions he was knighted in 1912, and was made the 'Knight Commander of the British Empire' five years later. Haggard died in London, in May 1925.

Chapter 1

My Visitor

THERE ARE some events of which each circumstance and surrounding detail seems to be graven on the memory in such fashion that we cannot forget it, and so it is with the scene that I am about to describe. It rises as clearly before my mind at this moment as though it had happened yesterday.

It was in this very month something over twenty years ago that I, Ludwig Horace Holly, was sitting one night in my rooms at Cambridge, grinding away at some mathematical work, I forget what. I was to go up for my fellowship within a week, and was expected by my tutor and my college generally to distinguish myself. At last, wearied out, I flung my book down, and, going to the mantelpiece, took down a pipe and filled it. There was a candle burning on the mantelpiece, and a long, narrow glass at the back of it; and as I was in the act of lighting the pipe I caught sight of my own countenance in the glass, and paused to reflect. The lighted match burned away till it scorched my fingers, forcing me to drop it, but still I stood and stared at myself in the glass, and reflected.

"Well," I said aloud, at last, "it is to be hoped that I shall be able to do something with the inside of my head, for I shall certainly never do anything by the help of the outside."

This remark will doubtless strike anybody who reads it as being slightly obscure, but I was in reality alluding to my physical deficiencies. Most men of twenty-two are endowed at any rate with some share of the comeliness of youth, but to me even this was denied. Short, thick-set, and deep-chested almost to deformity, with long sinewy arms, heavy features, deep-set gray eyes, a low brow half overgrown with a mop of thick black hair, like a deserted clearing on which the forest had once more begun to encroach; such was my appearance nearly a quarter of a century ago, and such, with some modification, is it to this day. Like Cain, I was branded – branded by Nature with the stamp of abnormal ugliness, as I was gifted by Nature with iron and abnormal strength and considerable intellectual powers. So ugly was I that the spruce young men of my college, though they were proud enough of my feats of endurance and physical prowess, did not even care to be seen walking with me. Was it wonderful that I was misanthropic and sullen? Was it wonderful that I brooded and worked alone, and had no friends – at least, only one? I was set apart by Nature to live alone, and draw comfort from her breast, and hers only. Women hated the sight of me. Only a week before I had heard one call me a "monster" when she thought I was out of hearing, and say that I had converted her to the monkey theory. Once, indeed, a woman pretended to care for me, and I lavished all the pent-up affection of my nature upon her. Then money that was to have come to me went elsewhere, and she discarded me. I pleaded with her as I have never pleaded with any living creature before or since, for I was caught by her sweet face, and loved her; and in the end by way of answer she took me to the glass, and stood side by side with me, and looked into it.

"Now," she said, "if I am Beauty, who are you?" That was when I was only twenty.

And so I stood and stared, and felt a sort of grim satisfaction in the sense of my own loneliness; for I had neither father, nor mother, nor brother; and as I did so there came a knock at my door.

I listened before I went to open it, for it was nearly twelve o'clock at night, and I was in no mood to admit any stranger. I had but one friend in the college, or, indeed, in the world – perhaps it was he.

Just then the person outside the door coughed, and I hastened to open it, for I knew the cough.

A tall man of about thirty, with the remains of great personal beauty, came hurrying in, staggering beneath the weight of a massive iron box which he carried by a handle with his right hand. He placed the box upon the table, and then fell into an awful fit of coughing. He coughed and coughed till his face became quite purple, and at last he sank into a chair and began to spit up blood. I poured out some whisky into a tumbler, and gave it to him. He drank it, and seemed better; though his better was very bad indeed.

"Why did you keep me standing there in the cold?" he asked pettishly. "You know the drafts are death to me."

"I did not know who it was," I answered. "You are a late visitor."

"Yes; and I verily believe it is my last visit," he answered, with a ghastly attempt at a smile. "I am done for, Holly. I am done for. I do not believe that I shall see tomorrow!"

"Nonsense!" I said. "Let me go for a doctor."

He waved me back imperiously. "It is sober sense; but I want no doctors. I have studied medicine, and I know all about it. No doctors can help me. My last hour has come! For a year past I have only lived by a miracle. Now listen to me as you never listened to anybody before; for you will not have the opportunity of getting me to repeat my words. We have been friends for two years; now tell me how much do you know about me?"

"I know that you are rich, and have had a fancy to come to college long after the age that most men leave it. I know that you have been married, and that your wife died; and that you have been the best, indeed almost the only friend I ever had."

"Did you know that I have a son?"

"No."

"I have. He is five years old. He cost me his mother's life, and I have never been able to bear to look upon his face in consequence. Holly, if you will accept the trust, I am going to leave you that boy's sole guardian."

I sprang almost out of my chair. "*Me!*" I said.

"Yes, you. I have not studied you for two years for nothing. I have known for some time that I could not last, and since I realized the fact I have been searching for someone to whom I could confide the boy and this," and he tapped the iron box. "You are the man. Holly; for, like a rugged tree, you are hard and sound at core. Listen; the boy will be the only representative of one of the most ancient families in the world, that is, so far as families can be traced. You will laugh at me when I say it, but one day it will be proved to you beyond a doubt, that my sixty-fifth or sixty-sixth lineal ancestor was an Egyptian priest of Isis, though he was himself of Grecian extraction, and was called Kallikrates.[1] His father was one of the Greek mercenaries raised by Hak-Hor, a Mendesian pharaoh of the twenty-ninth dynasty, and his grandfather, I believe, was that very Kallikrates mentioned by Herodotus.[2] In or about the year 339 before Christ, just at the time of the final fall of the Pharaohs, this Kallikrates (the priest) broke his vows of celibacy and fled from Egypt with a princess of royal blood who had fallen in love with him, and was finally wrecked upon the coast of Africa, somewhere, as I believe, in the neighborhood of where Delagoa Bay now is, or rather to the north of it, he and his wife being saved, and all the remainder of their company destroyed in one way or another. Here they endured great hardships, but were at last entertained by the mighty queen of a savage people, a white woman of peculiar loveliness, who, under circumstances which I cannot enter into, but which you

1 The Strong and Beautiful, or, more accurately, the Beautiful in Strength.

2 The Kallikrates here referred to by my friend was a Spartan, spoken of by Herodotus (Herod, ix.72) as being remarkable for his beauty. He fell at the glorious battle of Plataea (September 22, B.C. 479), when the Lacedaemonians and Athenians under Pausanias routed the Persians, putting nearly 300,000 of them to the sword. The following is a translation of the passage: "For Kallikrates died out of the battle, he came to the army the most beautiful man of the Greeks of that day – not only of the Lacedaemonians themselves, but of the other Greeks also. He when Pausanias was sacrificing was wounded in the side by an arrow; and then they fought, but on being carried off he regretted his

(contd. on the next pg.)

will one day learn, if you live, from the contents of the box, finally murdered my ancestor, Kallikrates. His wife, however, escaped, how I know not, to Athens, bearing a child with her, whom she named Tisisthenes, or the Mighty Avenger. Five hundred years or more afterwards the family migrated to Rome under circumstances of which no trace remains, and here, probably with the idea of preserving the idea of vengeance which we find set out in the name of Tisisthenes, they appear to have pretty regularly assumed the cognomen of Vindex, or Avenger. Here, too, they remained for another five centuries or more, till about 770 A.D., when Charlemagne invaded Lombardy, where they were then settled, whereon the head of the family seems to have attached himself to the great Emperor, and to have returned with him across the Alps, and finally to have settled in Brittany Eight generations later his lineal representative crossed to England in the reign of Edward the Confessor, and in the time of William the Conqueror was advanced to great honor and power. From that time till the present day I can trace my descent without a break. Not that the Vinceys – for that was the final corruption of the name after its bearers took root in English soil – have been particularly distinguished – they never came much to the fore. Sometimes they were soldiers, sometimes merchants, but on the whole they have preserved a dead level of respectability, and a still deader level of mediocrity. From the time of Charles II till the beginning of the present century they were merchants. About 1790 my grandfather made a considerable fortune out of brewing, and retired. In 1821 he died, and my father succeeded him, and dissipated most of the money. Ten years ago he died also, leaving me a net income of about two thousand a year. Then it was that I undertook an expedition in connection with *that*" – and he pointed

death, and said to Arimnestus, a Plataean, that he did not grieve at dying for Greece, but at not having struck a blow, or, although he desired so to do, performed any deed worthy of himself." This Kallikrates, who appears to have been as brave as he was beautiful, is subsequently mentioned by Herodotus as having been buried among the *lpÝνεs* (young commanders), apart from the other Spartans and the Helots. – L. H. H.

to the iron chest – "which ended disastrously enough. On my way back I traveled in the South of Europe, and finally reached Athens. There I met my beloved wife, who might well also have been called the 'Beautiful,' like my old Greek ancestor. There I married her, and there, a year afterwards, when my boy was born, she died."

He paused awhile, his head sunk upon his hand, and then continued, "My marriage had diverted me from a project which I cannot enter into now. I have no time, Holly – I have no time! One day, if you accept my trust, you will learn all about it. After my wife's death I turned my mind to it again. But first it was necessary, or, at least, I conceived that it was necessary, that I should attain to a perfect knowledge of Eastern dialects, especially Arabic. It was to facilitate my studies that I came here. Very soon, however, my disease developed itself, and now there is an end of me." And as though to emphasize his words he burst into another terrible fit of coughing.

I gave him some more whisky, and after resting he went on: "I have never seen my boy, Leo, since he was a tiny baby. I never could bear to see him, but they tell me that he is a quick and handsome child. In this envelope" – and he produced a letter from his pocket addressed to myself – "I have jotted down the course I wish followed in the boy's education. It is a somewhat peculiar one. At any rate, I could not entrust it to a stranger. Once more, will you undertake it?"

"I must first know what I am to undertake," I answered.

"You are to undertake to have the boy, Leo, to live with you till he is twenty-five years of age – not to send him to school, remember. On his twenty-fifth birthday your guardianship will end, and you will then, with the keys that I give you now" – and he placed them on the table – "open the iron box, and let him see and read the contents, and say whether or no he is willing to undertake the quest. There is no obligation on him to do so. Now, as regards terms. My present income is two thousand two hundred a year. Half of that income I have secured to you by will for life contingent on your undertaking the guardianship – that is, one thousand a year remuneration to yourself, for you will have to give up your life to it, and one hundred a year to pay for the board of the boy. The rest is to accumulate till Leo is twenty-five, so that there may be a sum in hand should he wish to undertake the quest of which I spoke."

"And suppose I were to die?" I asked. "Then the boy must become a ward of Chancery and take his chance. Only be careful that the iron chest is passed on to him by your will. Listen, Holly, don't refuse me. Believe me, this is to your advantage. You are not fit to mix with the world – it would only embitter you. In a few weeks you will become a fellow of your college, and the income that you will derive from that combined with what I have left you will enable you to live a life of learned leisure, alternated with the sport of which you are so fond, such as will exactly suit you."

He paused and looked at me anxiously, but I still hesitated. The charge seemed so very strange.

"For my sake. Holly. We have been good friends, and I have no time to make other arrangements."

"Very well," I said, "I will do it, provided there is nothing in this paper to make me change my mind," and I touched the envelope he had put upon the table by the keys.

"'Thank you, Holly, thank you. There is nothing at all. Swear to me by God that you will be a father to the boy, and follow my directions to the letter."

"I swear it," I answered solemnly.

"Very well, remember that perhaps one day I shall ask for the account of your oath, for though I am dead and forgotten, yet shall I live. There is no such thing as death, Holly, only a change, and, as you may perhaps learn in time to come, I believe that even here that change could under certain circumstances be indefinitely postponed," and again he broke into one of his dreadful fits of coughing.

"There," he said, "I must go. You have the chest, and my will will be found among my papers, under the authority of which the child will be handed over to you. You will be well paid, Holly, and I know that you are honest, but if you betray my trust, by heaven I will haunt you."

I said nothing, being, indeed, too bewildered to speak.

He held up the candle, and looked at his own face in the glass. It had been a beautiful face, but disease had wrecked it. "Food for the worms," he said. "Curious to think that in a few hours I shall be stiff and cold – the journey done, the little game played out. Ah me, Holly, life is not worth the trouble of life, except when one is in love – at least, mine has not been; but the boy Leo's may be if he has the courage and the faith. Good-by, my friend!" and with a sudden access of tenderness he flung his arm about me and kissed me on the forehead, and then turned to go.

"Look here, Vincey," I said, "if you are as ill as you think, you had better let me fetch a doctor."

"No, no," he said earnestly. "Promise me that you won't. I am going to die, and, like a poisoned rat, I wish to die alone."

"I don't believe that you are going to do anything of the sort," I answered. He smiled, and, with the word "Remember" on his lips, was gone. As for myself, I sat down and rubbed my eyes, wondering if I had been asleep. As this supposition would not bear investigation I gave it up, and began to think that Vincey must have been drinking. I knew that he was, and had been, very ill, but still it seemed impossible that he could be in such a condition as to be able to know for certain that he would not outlive the night. Had he been so near dissolution surely he would scarcely have been able to walk, and carry a heavy iron box with him. The whole story, on reflection, seemed to me utterly incredible, for I was not then old enough to be aware how many things happen in this world that the common sense of the average man would set down as so improbable as to be absolutely impossible. This is a fact that I have only recently mastered. Was it likely that a man would have a son five years of age whom he had never seen since he was a tiny infant? No. Was it likely that he could foretell his own death so accurately? No. Was it likely that he could trace his pedigree for more than three centuries before Christ, or that he would suddenly confide the absolute guardianship of his child, and leave half his fortune, to a college friend? Most certainly not. Clearly Vincey was either drunk or mad. That being so, what did it mean? And what was in the sealed iron chest?

The whole thing baffled and puzzled me to such an extent that at last I could stand it no longer, and determined to sleep over it. So I jumped up, and having put the keys and the letter that Vincey had left away into my dispatch box, and stowed the iron chest in a large portmanteau, I turned in, and was soon fast asleep.

As it seemed to me, I had only been asleep for a few minutes when I was awakened by somebody calling me. I sat up and rubbed my eyes; it was broad daylight – eight o'clock, in fact.

"Why, what is the matter with you, John?" I asked of the gyp who waited on Vincey and myself. "You look as though you had seen a ghost!"

"Yes, sir, and so I have," he answered, "leastways I've seen a corpse, which is worse. I've been in to call Mr. Vincey, as usual, and there he lies stark and dead!"

Chapter 2

The Years Roll By

Of course, poor Vincey's sudden death created a great stir in the college; but, as he was known to be very ill, and a satisfactory doctor's certificate was forthcoming, there was no inquest. They were not so particular about inquests in those days as they are now; indeed, they were generally disliked, as causing a scandal. Under all these circumstances, as I was asked no questions, I did not feel called upon to volunteer any information about our interview of the night of Vincey's decease, beyond saying that he had come into my rooms to see me, as he often did. On the day of the funeral a lawyer came down from London and followed my poor friend's remains to the grave, and then went back with his papers and effects, except, of course, the iron chest which had been left in my keeping. For a week after this I heard no more of the matter, and, indeed, my attention was amply occupied in other ways, for I was up for my fellowship, a fact that had prevented me from attending the funeral or seeing the lawyer. At last, however, the examination was over, and I came back to my rooms and sank into an easy chair with a happy consciousness that I had got through it very fairly.

Soon, however, my thoughts, relieved of the pressure that had crushed them into a single groove during the last few days, turned to the events of the night of poor Vincey's death, and again I asked myself what it all meant, and wondered if I should hear anything more of the matter, and if I did not, what it would be my duty to do with the curious iron chest. I sat there and thought and thought till I began to grow quite disturbed over the whole occurrence: the mysterious midnight visit, the prophecy of death so shortly to be fulfilled, the solemn oath that I had taken, and which Vincey had called on me to answer to in another world than this. Had the man committed suicide? It looked like it. And what was the quest of which he spoke? The circumstances were almost uncanny, so much so that, though I am by no means nervous, or apt to be alarmed at anything that may seem to cross the bounds of the natural, I grew afraid, and began to wish I had had nothing to do with it. How much more do I wish it now, over twenty years afterwards!

As I sat and thought, there was a knock at the door, and a letter, in a big blue envelope, was brought in to me. I saw at a glance that it was a lawyer's letter, and an instinct told me that it was connected with my trust. The letter, which I still have, runs thus:

> Sir,
>
> Our client, the late M. L. Vincey, Esq., who died on the 9th instant in — College, Cambridge, has left behind him a Will, of which you will please find copy enclosed, and of which we are the executors. By this Will you will perceive that you take a life interest in about half of the late Mr. Vincey's property, now invested in Consols, subject to your acceptance of the guardianship of his only son, Leo Vincey, at present an infant, aged five. Had we not ourselves drawn up the document in question in obedience to Mr. Vincey's clear and precise instructions, both personal and written, and had he not then assured us that he had very good reasons for what he was doing, we are bound to tell you that its provisions seem to us of so unusual a nature, that we should have felt bound to call the attention of the Court of Chancery to them, in order that such steps might be taken as seemed desirable to it, either by contesting the capacity of the testator or otherwise, to safeguard the interest of the infant. As it is, knowing that the testator was a gentleman of the highest intelligence and acumen, and that he has absolutely no relations living to whom he could have confided the guardianship of the child, we do not feel justified in taking this course.

Awaiting such instructions as you please to send us as regards the delivery of the infant and the payment of the proportion of the dividends due to you,

We remain, Sir, faithfully yours.

Geoffrey and Jordan

I put down the letter, and ran my eye through the will, which appeared, from its utter unintelligibility, to have been drawn on the strictest legal principles. So far as I could discover, however, it exactly bore out what my friend had told me on the night of his death. So it was true after all. I must take the boy. Suddenly I remembered the letter which he had left with the chest. I fetched it and opened it. It only contained such directions as he had already given to me as to opening the chest on Leo's twenty-fifth birthday, and laid down the outlines of the boy's education, which was to include Greek, the higher Mathematics, and Arabic. At the bottom there was a postscript to the effect that if the boy died under the age of twenty-five, which, however, he did not believe would be the case, I was to open the chest, and act on the information I obtained if I saw fit. If I did not see fit, I was to destroy all the contents. On no account was I to pass them on to a stranger.

As this letter added nothing material to my knowledge, and certainly raised no further objection in my mind to undertaking the task I had promised my dead friend to undertake, there was only one course open to me – namely, to write to Messrs. Geoffrey and Jordan, and express my readiness to enter on the trust, stating that I should be willing to commence my guardianship of Leo in ten days' time. This done I proceeded to the authorities of my college, and, having told them as much of the story as I considered desirable, which was not very much, after considerable difficulty succeeded in persuading them to stretch a point, and, in the event of my having obtained a fellowship, which I was pretty certain I had done, allow me to have the child to live with me. Their consent, however, was only granted on the condition that I vacated my rooms in college and took lodgings. This I did, and with some difficulty succeeded in obtaining very good apartments quite close to the college gates. The next thing was to find a nurse. And on this point I came to a determination. I would have no woman to lord it over me about the child, and steal his affections from me. The boy was old enough to do without female assistance, so I set to work to hunt up a suitable male attendant. With some difficulty I succeeded in hiring a most respectable round-faced young man, who had been a helper in a hunting stable, but who said that he was one of a family of seventeen and well accustomed to the ways of children, and professed himself quite willing to undertake the charge of Master Leo when he arrived. Then, having taken the iron box to town, and with my own hands deposited it at my banker's, I bought some books upon the health and management of children, and read them, first to myself, and then aloud to Job – that was the young man's name – and waited.

At length the child arrived in the charge of an elderly person, who wept bitterly at parting with him, and a beautiful boy he was. Indeed, I do not think that I ever saw such a perfect child before or since. His eyes were gray, his forehead broad, and his face, even at that early age, clean cut as a cameo, without being pinched or thin. But perhaps his most attractive point was his hair, which was pure gold in color and tightly curled over his shapely head. He cried a little when his nurse finally tore herself away and left him with us. Never shall I forget the scene. There he stood, with the sunlight from the window playing upon his golden curls, his fist screwed in one eye, while he took us in with the other. I was seated in a chair, and stretched out my hand to him to induce him to come to me, while Job, in the corner, was making a sort of clucking noise, which, arguing from his previous experience, or from the analogy of the hen, he judged would have a soothing effect, and inspire confidence in the youthful mind, and running a wooden horse of peculiar hideousness backwards and forwards in a way that was little short of inane.

This went on for some minutes, and then all of a sudden the lad stretched out both his little arms and ran to me.

"I like you," he said. "You is ugly, but you is good."

Ten minutes afterwards he was eating large slices of bread and butter, with every sign of satisfaction; Job wanted to put jam on them, but I sternly reminded him of the excellent works we had read, and forbade it.

In a very little while (for, as I expected, I got my fellowship) the boy became the favorite of the whole college – where, all orders and regulations to the contrary notwithstanding, he was continually in and out – a sort of chartered libertine, in whose favor all rules were relaxed. The offerings made at his shrine were simply without number, and I had a serious difference of opinion with one old resident Fellow, now long dead, who was usually supposed to be the crustiest man in the university, and to abhor the sight of a child. And yet I discovered, when a frequently recurring fit of sickness had forced Job to keep a strict lockout, that this unprincipled old man was in the habit of enticing the boy to his rooms and there feeding him upon unlimited quantities of brandy balls, and making him promise to say nothing about it. Job told him that he ought to be ashamed of himself, "at his age, too, when he might have been a grandfather if he had done what was right," by which Job understood had got married, and thence arose the row.

But I have no space to dwell upon those delightful years, round which memory still fondly hovers. One by one they went by, and as they passed we two grew dearer and yet more dear to each other. Few sons have been loved as I love Leo, and few fathers know the deep and continuous affection that Leo bears to me.

The child grew into the boy, and the boy into the young man, as one by one the remorseless years flew by, and as he grew and increased so did his beauty and the beauty of his mind grow with him. When he was about fifteen they used to call him Beauty about the college, and me they nicknamed the Beast. Beauty and the Beast was what they called us when we went out walking together, as we used to do every day. Once Leo attacked a great strapping butcher's man, twice his size, because he sang it out after us, and thrashed him, too – thrashed him fairly. I walked on and pretended not to see, till the combat got too exciting, when I turned round and cheered him on to victory. It was the chaff of the college at the time, but I could not help it. Then when he was a little older the undergraduates got fresh names for us. They called me Charon and Leo the Greek god! I will pass over my own appellation with the humble remark that I was never handsome, and did not grow more so as I grew older. As for his, there was no doubt about its fitness. Leo at twenty-one might have stood for a statue of the youthful Apollo. I never saw anybody to touch him in looks, or anybody so absolutely unconscious of them. As for his mind, he was brilliant and keen-witted, but not a scholar. He had not the dullness necessary for that result. We followed out his father's instructions as regards his education strictly enough, and on the whole the results, especially so far as the Greek and Arabic went, were satisfactory. I learned the latter language in order to help to teach it to him, but after five years of it he knew it as well as I did – almost as well as the professor who instructed us both. I always was a great sportsman – it is my one passion – and every autumn we went away somewhere shooting or fishing, sometimes to Scotland, sometimes to Norway, once even to Russia. I am a good shot, but even in this he learned to excel me.

When Leo was eighteen I moved back into my rooms, and entered him at my own college, and at twenty-one he took his degree – a respectable degree, but not a very high one. Then it was that I, for the first time, told him something of his own story, and of the mystery that loomed ahead. Of course he was very curious about it, and of course I explained to him that his curiosity could not be gratified at present. After that, to pass the time away, I suggested that he should get himself called to the bar; and this he did, reading at Cambridge, and only going up to London to eat his dinners.

I had only one trouble about him, and that was that every young woman who came across him, or, if not every one, nearly so, would insist on falling in love with him. Hence arose difficulties which I need not enter into here, though they were troublesome enough at the time. On the whole, he behaved fairly well; I cannot say more than that.

And so the time went by till at last he reached his twenty-fifth birthday, at which date this strange and, in some ways, awful history really begins.

Chapter 3

The Sherd of Amenartas

ON THE day preceding Leo's twenty-fifth birthday we both proceeded to London, and extracted the mysterious chest from the bank where I had deposited it twenty years before. It was, I remember, brought up by the same clerk who had taken it down. He perfectly remembered having hidden it away. Had he not done so, he said, he should have had difficulty in finding it, it was so covered up with cobwebs.

In the evening we returned with our precious burden to Cambridge, and I think that we might both of us have given away all the sleep we got that night and not have been much the poorer. At daybreak Leo arrived in my room in a dressing gown, and suggested that we should at once proceed to business. I scouted the idea as showing an unworthy curiosity. The chest had waited twenty years, I said, so it could very well continue to wait until after breakfast. Accordingly at nine – an unusually sharp nine – we breakfasted; and so occupied was I with my own thoughts that I regret to state that I put a piece of bacon into Leo's tea in mistake for a lump of sugar. Job, too, to whom the contagion of excitement had, of course, spread, managed to break the handle off my Sèvres china teacup, the identical one I believe that Marat had been drinking from just before he was stabbed in his bath.

At last, however, breakfast was cleared away, and Job, at my request, fetched the chest, and placed it upon the table in a somewhat gingerly fashion, as though he mistrusted it. Then he prepared to leave the room.

"Stop a moment. Job," I said. "If Mr. Leo has no objection, I should prefer to have an independent witness to this business, who can be relied upon to hold his tongue unless he is asked to speak."

"Certainly, Uncle Horace," answered Leo; for I had brought him up to call me uncle – though he varied the appellation somewhat disrespectfully by calling me "old fellow," or even "my avuncular relative."

Job touched his head, not having a hat on.

"Lock the door, Job," I said, "and bring me my dispatch box."

He obeyed, and from the box I took the keys that poor Vincey, Leo's father, had given me on the night of his death. There were three of them: the largest a comparatively modern key, the second an exceedingly ancient one, and the third entirely unlike anything of the sort that we had ever seen before, being fashioned apparently from a strip of solid silver, with a bar placed across to serve as a handle, and some nicks cut in the edge of the bar. It was more like a model of some antediluvian railway key than anything else.

"Now are you both ready?" I said, as people do when they

are going to fire a mine. There was no answer, so I took the big key, rubbed some salad oil into the wards, and after one or two bad shots, for my hands were shaking, managed to fit it, and shoot the lock. Leo bent over and caught the massive lid in both his hands, and with an effort, for the hinges had rusted, leaned it back. Its removal revealed another case covered with dust. This we extracted from the iron chest without any difficulty, and removed the accumulated filth of years from it with a clothes brush.

It was, or appeared to be, of ebony, or some such close-grained black wood, and was bound in every direction with flat bands of iron. Its antiquity must have been extreme, for the dense heavy wood was actually in parts commencing to crumble away from age.

"Now for it," I said, inserting the second key.

Job and Leo bent forward in breathless silence. The key turned, and I flung back the lid, and uttered an exclamation, as did the others; and no wonder, for inside the ebony case was a magnificent silver casket, about twelve inches square by eight high. It appeared to be of Egyptian workmanship, for the four legs were formed of Sphinxes, and the dome-shaped cover was also surmounted by a Sphinx. The casket was of course much tarnished and dinted with age, but otherwise in fairly sound condition.

I drew it out and set it on the table, and then, in the midst of the most perfect silence, I inserted the strange-looking silver key, and pressed this way and that until at last the lock yielded, and the casket stood open before us. It was filled to the brim with some brown shredded material, more like vegetable fiber than paper, the nature of which I have never been able to discover. This I carefully removed to the depth of some three inches, when I came to a letter enclosed in an ordinary modern-looking envelope, and addressed in the handwriting of my dead friend Vincey: '*To my son Leo, should he live to open this casket.*' I handed the letter to Leo, who glanced at the envelope, and then put it down upon the table, making a motion to me to go on emptying the casket. The next thing that I found was a parchment carefully rolled up. I unrolled it, and seeing that it was also in Vincey's handwriting, and headed "Translation of the Uncial Greek Writing on the Potsherd," put it down by the letter. Then followed another ancient roll of parchment, that had become yellow and crinkled with the passage of years. This I also unrolled. It was likewise a translation of the same Greek original, but into black-letter Latin this time, which at the first glance appeared to me from the style and character to date from somewhere about the beginning of the sixteenth century. Immediately beneath this roll was something hard and heavy, wrapped up in yellow linen, and reposing upon another layer of the fibrous material. Slowly and carefully we unrolled the linen, exposing to view a very large but undoubtedly ancient potsherd of a dirty yellow color! This potsherd had in my judgment once been a part of an ordinary amphora of medium size. For the rest, it measured ten and a half inches in length by seven in width, was about a quarter of an inch thick, and densely covered on the convex side that lay towards the bottom of the box with writing in the later uncial Greek character, faded here and there, but for the most part perfectly legible, the inscription having evidently been executed with the greatest care, and by means of a reed pen, such as the ancients often used. I must not forget to mention that in some remote age this wonderful fragment had been broken in two, and rejoined by means of cement and eight long rivets. Also there were numerous inscriptions on the inner side, but these were of the most erratic character, and had clearly been made by different hands and in many different ages, and of them, together with the writings on the parchments, I shall have to speak presently.

"Is there anything more?" asked Leo, in a kind of excited whisper.

I groped about, and produced something hard, done up in a

little linen bag. Out of the bag we took first a very beautiful miniature done upon ivory, and, secondly, a small chocolate-colored composition scarabaeus, marked thus:

symbols which, we have since ascertained, mean "Suten se Râ," which is being translated the "Royal Son of Râ or the Sun." The miniature was a picture of Leo's Greek mother – a lovely, dark-eyed creature. On the back of it was written, in poor Vincey's handwriting, "My beloved wife."

"That is all," I said.

"Very well," answered Leo, putting down the miniature, at which he had been gazing affectionately; "and now let us read the letter," and without further ado he broke the seal, and read aloud as follows:

My Son Leo,

When you open this, if you ever live to do so, you will have attained to manhood, and I shall have been long enough dead to be absolutely forgotten by nearly all who knew me. Yet in reading it remember that I have been, and for anything you know may still be, and that in it, through this link of pen and paper, I stretch out my hand to you across the gulf of death, and my voice speaks to you from the unutterable silence of the grave. Though I am dead, and no memory of me remains in your mind, yet am I with you in this hour that you read. Since your birth to this day I have scarcely seen your face. Forgive me this. Your life supplanted the life of one whom I loved better than women are often loved, and the bitterness of it endureth yet. Had I lived I should in time have conquered this foolish feeling, but I am not destined to live. My sufferings, physical and mental, are more than I can bear, and when such small arrangements as I have to make for your future well being are completed it is my intention to put a period to them. May God forgive me if I do wrong. At the best I could not live more than another year."

"So he killed himself," I exclaimed. "I thought so."

"And now," Leo went on, without replying, "enough of myself. What has to be said belongs to you who live, not to me, who am dead, and almost as much forgotten as though I had never been. Holly, my friend (to whom, if he will accept the trust, it is my intention to confide you), will have told you something of the extraordinary antiquity of your race. In the contents of this casket you will find sufficient to prove it. The strange legend that you will find inscribed by your remote ancestress upon the potsherd was communicated to me by my father on his deathbed, and took a strong hold upon my imagination. When I was only nineteen years of age I determined, as, to his misfortune, did one of our ancestors about the time of Elizabeth, to investigate its truth. Into all that befell me I cannot enter now. But this I saw with my own eyes. On the coast of Africa, in a hitherto unexplored region, some distance to the north of where the Zambesi falls into the sea, there is a headland, at the extremity of which a peak towers up, shaped like the head of a Negro, similar to that of which the writing speaks. I landed there, and learned from a wandering native, who had been cast out by his people because of some crime which he had committed, that far inland are great mountains, shaped like cups, and caves surrounded by measureless swamps. I learned also that the people there speak a dialect of Arabic, and are ruled over by a *beautiful white woman* who is seldom seen by them, but who is reported to have power over all things living and dead. Two days after I had ascertained this the man died of fever contracted in crossing the swamps, and I was forced by want of provisions and by symptoms of an illness which afterwards prostrated me to take to my dhow again.

"Of the adventures that befell me after this I need not now speak. I was wrecked upon the coast of Madagascar, and rescued some months afterwards by an English ship that brought me to Aden, whence I started for England, intending to prosecute my search as soon as I had made sufficient preparations. On my way I stopped in Greece, and there, for *Omnia vincit amor*, I met your beloved mother, and married her, and there you were born and she died. Then it was that my last illness seized me, and I returned hither to die. But still I hoped against hope, and set myself to work to learn Arabic, with the intention, should I ever get better, of returning to the coast of Africa, and solving the mystery of which the tradition has lived so many centuries in our family. But I have not got better, and, so far as I am concerned, the story is at an end.

"For you, however, my son, it is not at an end, and to you I hand on these the results of my labor, together with the hereditary proofs of its origin. It is my intention to provide that they shall not be put into your hands until you have reached an age when you will be able to judge for yourself whether or no you will choose to investigate what, if it is true, must be the greatest mystery in the world or to put it by as an idle fable, originating in the first place in a woman's disordered brain.

"I do not believe that it is a fable; I believe that if it can only be rediscovered there is a spot where the vital forces of the world visibly exist. Life exists; why therefore should not the means of preserving it indefinitely exist also? But I have no wish to prejudice your mind about the matter. Read and judge for yourself. If you are inclined to undertake the search, I have so provided that you will not lack for means. If, on the other hand, you are satisfied that the whole thing is a chimera, then, I adjure you, destroy the potsherd and the writings, and let a cause of troubling be removed from our race forever. Perhaps that will be wisest. The unknown is generally taken to be terrible, not as the proverb would infer, from the inherent superstition of man, but because it so often is terrible. He who would tamper with the vast and secret forces that animate the world may well fall a victim to them. And if the end were attained, if at last you emerged from the trial ever beautiful and ever young, defying time and evil, and lifted above the natural decay of flesh and intellect, who shall say that the awesome change would prove a happy one? Choose, my son, and may the Power who rules all things, and who says 'thus far shalt thou go, and thus much shalt thou learn,' direct the choice to your own happiness and the happiness of the world, which, in the event of your success, you would one day certainly rule by the pure force of accumulated experience. – Farewell!"

Thus the letter, which was unsigned and undated, abruptly ended.

"What do you make of that, Uncle Holly?" said Leo, with a sort of gasp, as he replaced it on the table. "We have been looking for a mystery, and we certainly seem to have found one."

"What do I make of it? Why, that your poor dear father was off his head, of course," I answered testily. "I guessed as much that night, twenty years ago, when he came into my room. You see he evidently hurried his own end, poor man. It is absolute balderdash."

"That's it, sir!" said Job solemnly. Job was a most matter-of-fact specimen of a matter-of-fact class.

"Well, let's see what the potsherd has to say, at any rate," said Leo, taking up the translation in his father's writing, and commencing to read:

> "I, Amenartas, of the Royal House of the Pharaohs of Egypt, wife of Kallikrates *(the Beautiful in Strength)*, a Priest of Isis whom the gods cherish and the demons obey, being about to die, to my little son Tisisthenes *(the Mighty Avenger)*. I fled with thy father from Egypt in the days of Nectanebes,[1] causing him through love to break the vows that he had vowed. We fled southward, across the waters, and we wandered for twice twelve moons on the coast of Libya *(Africa)* that looks towards the rising sun, where by a river is a great rock carven like the head of an Ethiopian. Four days on the water from the mouth of a mighty river were we cast away, and some were drowned and some died of sickness. But us wild men took through wastes and marshes, where the sea fowl hid the sky, bearing us ten days' journey till we came to a hollow, mountain, where a great city had been and fallen, and where there are caves of which no man hath seen the end; and they brought us to the Queen of the people who place pots upon the heads of strangers, who is a magician having a knowledge of all things, and life and loveliness that does not die. And she

1 Nekht-nebf, or Nectanebo II, the last native Pharaoh of Egypt fled from Ochus to Ethiopia, B.C. 339. – EDITOR.

cast eyes of love upon thy father, Kallikrates, and would have slain me, and taken him to husband, but he loved me and feared her, and would not. Then did she take us, and lead us by terrible ways, by means of dark magic, to where the great pit is, in the mouth of which the old philosopher lay dead, and showed to us the rolling Pillar of Life that dies not, whereof the voice is as the voice of thunder; and she did stand in the flames, and come forth unharmed, and yet more beautiful. Then did she swear to make thy father undying even as she is, if he would but slay me, and give himself to her, for me she could not slay because of the magic of my own people that I have, and that prevailed thus far against her. And he held his hand before his eyes to hide her beauty, and would not. Then in her rage did she smite him by her magic, and he died; but she wept over him, and bore him thence with lamentations: and being afraid, me she sent to the mouth of the great river where the ships come, and I was carried far away on the ships where I gave thee birth, and hither to Athens I came at last after many wanderings. Now I say to thee, my son, Tisisthenes, seek out the woman, and learn the secret of Life, and if thou mayest find a way slay her, because of thy father Kallikrates; and if thou dost fear or fail, this I say to all of thy seed who come after thee, till at last a brave man be found among them who shall bathe in the fire and sit in the place of the Pharaohs. I speak of those things, that though they be past belief, yet I have known, and I lie not."

"May the Lord forgive her for that," groaned Job, who had been listening to this marvelous composition with his mouth open.

As for myself, I said nothing, my first idea being that my poor friend, being demented, had composed the whole thing, though it scarcely seemed likely that such a story could have been invented by anybody. It was too original. To solve my doubts I took up the potsherd and began to read the close uncial Greek writing on it; and very good Greek of the period it is, considering that it came from the pen of an Egyptian born. Here is an exact transcript of it:

ΑΜΕΝΑΡΤΑΣΤΟΥΒΑΣΙΛΙΚΟΥΓΕΝΟΥΣΤΟΥΑ
ΙΓΥΓΤΙΟΥΗΤΟΥΚΑΛΛΙΚΡΑΤΟΥΣΙΣΙΔΟΣΙΕΡ
ΕΩΣΗΝΟΙΜΕΝΘΕΟΙΤΡΕΦΟΥΣΙΤΑΔΕΔΑΙΜΟ
ΝΙΑΥΓΟΤΑΣΣΕΤΑΙΗΔΗΤΕΛΕΥΤΩΣΑΤΙΣΙΣ
ΘΕΝΕΙΤΩΓΑΙΔΙΕΓΙΣΤΕΛΛΕΙΤΑΔΕΣΥΝΕΦΥΓΟ
ΝΓΑΡΓΟΤΕΕΚΤΗΣΑΙΓΥΓΤΙΑΣΕΓΙΝΕΚΤΑΝΕΒ
ΟΥΜΕΤΑΤΟΥΣΟΥΓΑΤΡΟΣΔΙΑΤΟΝΕΡΩΤΑΤΟ
ΝΕΜΟΝΕΓΙΟΡΚΗΣΑΝΤΟΣΦΥΓΟΝΤΕΣΔΕΓΡΟ
ΣΝΟΤΟΝΔΙΑΓΟΝΤΙΟΙΚΑΙΚΔΜΗΝΑΣΚΑΤΑΤΑ
ΓΑΡΑΘΑΛΑΣΣΙΑΤΗΣΛΙΒΥΗΣΤΑΓΡΟΣΗΛΙΟΥ
ΑΝΑΤΟΛΑΣΓΛΑΝΗΘΕΝΤΕΣΕΝΘΑΓΕΡΓΕΤΡΑ
ΤΙΣΜΕΓΑΛΗΓΛΥΓΤΟΝΟΜΟΙΩΜΑΑΙΘΙΟΓΟΣ
ΚΕΦΑΛΗΣΕΙΤΑΗΜΕΡΑΣΔΑΓΟΣΤΟΜΑΤΟΣΓΟ
ΤΑΜΟΥΜΕΓΑΛΟΥΕΚΓΕΣΟΝΤΕΣΟΙΜΕΝΚΑΤΕ
ΓΟΝΤΙΣΘΗΜΕΝΟΙΔΕΝΟΣΩΙΑΓΕΘΑΝΟΜΕΝΤ
ΕΛΟΣΔΕΥΓΑΓΡΙΩΝΑΝΘΡΩΓΩΝΕΦΕΡΟΜΕΘΑ
ΔΙΑΕΛΕΩΝΤΕΚΑΙΤΕΝΑΓΕΩΝΕΝΘΑΓΕΡΓΤΗΝ
ΩΝΓΛΗΘΟΣΑΓΟΚΡΥΓΤΕΙΤΟΝΟΥΡΑΝΟΝΗΜ
ΕΡΑΣΙΕΩΣΗΛΘΟΜΕΝΕΙΣΚΟΙΛΟΝΤΙΟΡΟΣΕΝ
ΘΑΓΟΤΕΜΕΓΑΛΗΜΕΝΓΟΛΙΣΗΝΑΝΤΡΑΔΕΑΓ
ΕΙΡΟΝΑΗΓΑΓΟΝΔΕΩΣΒΑΣΙΛΕΙΑΝΤΗΝΤΩΝΞ
ΕΝΟΥΣΧΥΤΡΑΙΣΣΤΕΦΑΝΟΥΝΤΩΝΗΤΙΣΜΑΓΕ
ΙΑΜΕΝΕΧΡΗΤΟΕΓΙΣΤΗΜΗΔΕΓΑΝΤΩΝΚΑΙΔ
ΗΚΑΙΚΑΛΛΟΣΚΑΙΡΩΜΗΝΑΓΗΡΩΣΗΝΗΔΕΚΑ
ΛΛΙΚΡΑΤΟΥΣΤΟΥΣΟΥΓΑΤΡΟΣΕΡΑΣΘΕΙΣΑΤ
ΟΜΕΝΓΡΩΤΟΝΣΥΝΟΙΚΕΙΝΕΒΟΥΛΕΤΟΕΜΕΔ
ΕΑΝΕΛΕΙΝΕΓΕΙΤΑΩΣΟΥΚΑΝΕΓΕΙΘΕΝΕΜΕΓΑ
ΡΥΓΕΡΕΦΙΛΕΙΚΑΙΤΗΝΞΕΝΗΝΕΦΟΒΕΙΤΟΑΓΗ
ΓΑΓΕΝΗΜΑΣΥΓΟΜΑΓΕΙΑΣΚΑΘΟΔΟΥΣΣΦΑΛ
ΕΡΑΣΕΝΘΑΤΟΒΑΡΑΘΡΟΝΤΟΜΕΓΑΟΥΚΑΤΑΣ
ΤΟΜΑΕΚΕΙΤΟΟΓΕΡΩΝΟΦΙΛΟΣΟΦΟΣΤΕΘΝΕ
ΩΣΑΦΙΚΟΜΕΝΟΙΣΔΕΔΕΙΞΕΦΩΣΤΟΥΒΙΟΥΕΥ
ΘΥΟΙΟΝΚΙΟΝΑΕΛΙΣΣΟΜΕΝΟΝΦΩΝΗΝΙΕΝΤ
ΑΚΑΘΑΓΕΡΒΡΟΝΤΗΣΕΙΤΑΔΙΑΓΥΡΟΣΒΕΒΗΚ
ΥΙΑΑΒΛΑΒΗΣΚΑΙΕΤΙΚΑΛΛΙΩΝΑΥΤΗΕΑΥΤΗΣ
ΕΞΕΦΑΝΗΕΚΔΕΤΟΥΤΩΝΩΜΟΣΕΚΑΙΤΟΝΣΟ

ΝΓΑΤΕΡΑΑΘΑΝΑΤΟΝΑΓΟΔΕΙΞΕΙΝΕΙΣΥΝ
ΕΙΝΟΙΒΟΥΛΟΙΤΟΕΜΕΔΕΑΝΕΛΕΙΝΟΥΓΑΡ
ΝΑΥΤΗΑΝΕΛΕΙΝΙΣΧΥΕΝΥΓΟΤΩΝΗΜΕΔΑΙ
ΝΗΝΚΑΙΑΥΤΗΕΧΩΜΑΓΕΙΑΣΟΔΟΥΔΕΝΤΙ
ΛΛΟΝΗΘΕΛΕΤΩΧΕΙΡΕΤΩΝΟΜΜΑΤΩΝΓΡ
ΣΧΩΝΙΝΑΔΗΤΟΤΗΣΓΥΝΑΙΚΟΣΚΑΛΛΟΣΜ
ΟΡΩΗΕΓΕΙΤΑΟΡΓΙΣΘΕΙΣΑΚΑΤΕΓΟΗΤΕΥΣΕ
ΕΝΑΥΤΟΝΑΓΟΛΟΜΕΝΟΝΜΕΝΤΟΙΚΛΑΟΥ
ΚΑΙΟΔΥΡΟΜΕΝΗΕΚΕΙΘΕΝΑΓΗΝΕΓΚΕΝΕΜΙ
ΕΦΟΒΩΙΑΦΗΚΕΝΕΙΣΣΤΟΜΑΤΟΥΜΕΓΑΛΟ
ΟΤΑΜΟΥΤΟΥΝΑΥΣΙΓΟΡΟΥΓΟΡΡΩΔΕΝΑΥ
ΝΕΦΩΝΓΕΡΓΛΕΟΥΣΑΕΤΕΚΟΝΣΕΑΓΟΓΛΕ
ΑΣΑΜΟΛΙΣΓΟΤΕΔΕΥΡΟΑΘΗΝΑΖΕΚΑΤΗΓ
ΟΜΗΝΣΥΔΕΩΤΙΣΙΣΘΕΝΕΣΩΝΕΓΙΣΤΕΛΛ
ΗΟΛΙΓΩΡΕΙΔΕΙΓΑΡΤΗΝΓΥΝΑΙΚΑΑΝΑΖΗΤ
ΝΗΝΓΩΣΤΟΤΟΥΒΙΟΥΜΥΣΤΗΡΙΟΝΑΝΕΥΙ
ΣΚΑΙΑΝΑΙΡΕΙΝΗΝΓΟΥΓΑΡΑΣΧΗΔΙΑΤΟΝ
ΝΓΑΤΕΡΑΚΑΛΛΙΚΡΑΤΗΝΕΙΔΕΦΟΒΟΥΜΕΝ
ΣΗΔΙΑΑΛΛΟΤΙΑΥΤΟΣΛΕΙΓΕΙΤΟΥΕΡΓΟΥΙ
ΣΙΤΟΙΣΥΣΤΕΡΟΝΑΥΤΟΤΟΥΤΟΕΓΙΣΤΕΛΛ
ΩΣΓΟΤΕΑΓΑΘΟΣΤΙΣΓΕΝΟΜΕΝΟΣΤΩΓΥΡ
ΟΥΣΑΣΘΑΙΤΟΛΜΗΣΕΙΚΑΙΤΑΑΡΙΣΤΕΙΑΕΧ
ΒΑΣΙΛΕΥΣΑΙΤΩΝΑΝΘΡΩΓΩΝΑΓΙΣΤΑΜΕΝ
ΗΤΑΤΟΙΑΥΤΑΛΕΓΩΟΜΩΣΔΕΑΑΥΤΗΕΓΝ
ΑΟΥΚΕΨΕΥΣΑΜΗΝ

For general convenience in reading, I have here accurately transcribed this inscription into the cursive character:

'Αμενάρτας, τοῦ βασιλικοῦ γένους τοῦ Αἰγυπτίου, ἡ τοῦ Καλλικράτους Ἴσιδος ἱερέως, ἣν οἱ μὲν θεοὶ τρέφουσι τὰ δὲ δαιμόνια ὑποτάσσεται, ἤδη τελευτῶσα Τισισθένει τῷ παιδὶ ἐπιστέλλει τάδε· συνέφυγον γάρ ποτε ἐκ τῆς Αἰγυπτίας ἐπὶ Νεκτανέβου μετὰ τοῦ σοῦ πατρός, διὰ τὸν ἔρωτα τὸν ἐμὸν ἐπιορκήσαντος. φυγόντες δὲ πρὸς νότον διαπόντιοι καὶ κ΄δ΄ μῆνας κατὰ τὰ παραθαλάσσια τῆς Λιβύης τὰ πρὸς ἡλίου ἀνατολὰς πλανηθέντες, ἔνθα πέτρα τις μεγάλη, γλυπτὸν ὁμοίωμα Αἰθίοπος κεφαλῆς, εἶτα ἡμέρας δ΄ ἀπὸ στόματος ποταμοῦ μεγάλου ἐκπεσόντες, οἱ μὲν κατεποντίσθημεν, οἱ δὲ νόσῳ ἀπεθάνομεν· τέλος δὲ ὑπ' ἀγρίων ἀνθρώπων ἐφερόμεθα διὰ ἑλέων τε καὶ τεναγέων ἔνθαπερ πτηνῶν πλῆθος ἀποκρύπτει τὸν οὐρανόν, ἡμέρας ί, ἕως ἤλθομεν εἰς κοῖλόν τι ὄρος, ἔνθα ποτὲ μεγάλη μὲν πόλις ἦν, ἄντρα δὲ ἀπείρονα· ἤγαγον δὲ ὡς βασίλειαν τὴν τῶν ξένους χύτραις στεφανούντων, ἥτις μαγείᾳ μὲν ἐχρῆτο ἐπιστήμῃ δὲ πάντων καὶ δὴ καὶ κάλλος καὶ ῥώμην ἀγήρως ἦν· ἡ δὲ Καλλικράτους τοῦ σοῦ πατρὸς ἐρασθεῖσα τὸ μὲν πρῶτον συνοικεῖν ἐβούλετο ἐμὲ δὲ ἀνελεῖν· ἔπειτα, ὡς οὐκ ἀνέπειθεν, ἐμὲ γὰρ ὑπερεφίλει καὶ τὴν ξένην ἐφοβεῖτο, ἀπήγαγεν ἡμᾶς ὑπὸ μαγείας καθ' ὁδοὺς σφαλερὰς ἔνθα τὸ βάραθρον τὸ μέγα, οὗ κατὰ στόμα ἔκειτο ὁ γέρων ὁ φιλόσοφος τεθνεώς, ἀφικομένοις δ' ἔδειξε φῶς τοῦ βίου εὐθύ, οἷον κίονα ἑλισσόμενον φώνην ἱέντα καθάπερ βροντῆς, εἶτα διὰ πυρὸς βεβηκυῖα ἀβλαβὴς καὶ ἔτι καλλίων αὐτὴ ἑαυτῆς ἐξεφάνη, ἐκ δὲ τούτων ὤμοσε καὶ τὸν σὸν πατέρα ἀθάνατον ἀποδείξειν, εἰ συνοικεῖν οἱ βούλοιτο ἐμὲ δε ἀνελεῖν, οὐ γὰρ οὖν αὐτὴ ἀνελεῖν ἴσχυεν ὑπὸ τῶν ἡμεδαπῶν ἣν καὶ αὐτὴ ἔχω μαγείας. ὁ δ' οὐδέν τι μᾶλλον ἤθελε, τὼ χεῖρε τῶν ὀμμάτων προίσχων ἵνα δὴ τὸ τῆς γυναικὸς κάλλος μὴ ὁρῴη· ἔπειτα ὀργισθεῖσα κατεγοήτευσε μὲν αὐτόν, ἀπολόμενον μέντοι κλάουσα καὶ ὀδυρομένη ἐκεῖθεν ἀπήνεγκεν, ἐμὲ δὲ φόβῳ ἀφῆκεν εἰς στόμα τοῦ μεγάλου ποταμοῦ τοῦ ναυσιπόρου, πόρρω δὲ ναυσίν, ἐφ' ὧνπερ πλέουσα ἔτεκόν σε, ἀποπλεύσασα μόλις ποτὲ δεῦρο 'Αθηνάζε κατηγαγόμην. σὺ δέ, ὦ Τισίσθενες, ὧν ἐπιστέλλω μὴ ὀλιγώρει· δεῖ γὰρ τὴν γυναῖκα ἀναζητεῖν ἤν πως τὸ τοῦ βίου μυστήριον ἀνεύρῃς. καὶ ἀναιρεῖν, ἤν που παρασχῇ, διὰ τὸν σὸν πατέρα Καλλι-

κράτην. εἰ δὲ φοβούμενος ἢ διὰ ἄλλο τι αὐτὸς λείπει τοῦ ἔργου, πᾶσι τοῖς ὕστερον αὐτὸ τοῦτο ἐπιστέλλω, ἕως ποτὲ ἀγαθός τις γενόμενος τῷ πυρὶ λούσασθαι τολμησει καὶ τὰ ἀριστεῖα ἔχων βασιλεῦσαι τῶν ἀνθρώπων· ἄπιστα μὲν δὴ τὰ τοιαῦτα λέγω, ὅμως δὲ ἃ αὐτὴ ἔγνωκα οὐκ ἐψευσαμην.

The English translation was, as I discovered on further investigation, and as the reader may easily see by comparison, both accurate and elegant.

Besides the uncial writing on the convex side of the sherd at the top, painted in dull red, on what had once been the lip of the amphora, was the cartouche already mentioned as being on the scarabaeus, which we had also found in the casket. The hieroglyphics or symbols, however, were reversed, just as though they had been pressed on wax. Whether this was the cartouche of the original Kallikrates,[1] or of some Prince or Pharaoh from whom his wife Amenartas was descended, I am not sure, nor can I tell if it was drawn upon the sherd at the same time that the uncial Greek was inscribed, or copied on more recently from the Scarab by some other member of the family. Nor was this all. At the foot of the writing, painted in the same dull red, was the faint outline of a somewhat rude drawing of the head and shoulders of a Sphinx wearing two feathers, symbols of majesty, which, though common enough upon the effigies of sacred bulls and gods, I have never before met with on a Sphinx.

Also on the right-hand side of this surface of the sherd, painted obliquely in red on the space not covered by the uncial, and signed in blue paint, was the following quaint inscription:

IN EARTH AND SKIE AND SEA
STRANGE THYNGES THER BE.

HOC FECIT

DOROTHEA VINCEY

1 The cartouche, if it be a true cartouche, cannot have been that of Kallikrates, as Mr. Holly suggests Kallikrates was a priest and not entitled to a cartouche, which was the prerogative of Egyptian royalty, though he might have inscribed his name or title upon an *oval*. – EDITOR.

Perfectly bewildered, I turned the relic over. It was covered from top to bottom with notes and signatures in Greek, Latin, and English. The first, in uncial Greek, was by Tisisthenes, the son to whom the writing was addressed. It was, "I could not go. Tisisthenes to his son, Kallikrates." Here it is in facsimile with its cursive equivalent:

ΟΥΚΑΝΔΥΝΑΙΜΗΝΓΟΡΕΥΕCΘΑΙΤΙCΙCΘΕΝΗ
CΚΑΛΛΙΚΡΑΤΕΙΤΩΙΓΑΙΔΙ

οὐκ ἂν δυναίμην πορεύεσθαι.
Τισισθένης Καλλικράτει τῷ παιδί.

This Kallikrates (probably, in the Greek fashion, so named after his grandfather) evidently made some attempt to start on the quest, for his entry, written in very faint and almost illegible uncial, is, "I ceased from my going, the gods being against me, Kallikrates to his son." Here it is also:

ΤΩΝΘΕΩΝΑΝΤΙΣΤΑΝΤΩΝΕΓΑΥΣΑΜΗΝΤΗΣ
ΓΟΡΕΙΑΣΚΑΛΛΙΚΡΑΤΗΣΤΩΙΓΑΙΔΙ

τῶν θεῶν ἀντιστάντων ἐπαυσάμην τῆς πορείας.
Καλλικράτης τῷ παιδί.

Between these two ancient writings – the second of which was inscribed upside down and was so faint and worn that, had it not been for the transcript of it executed by Vincey, I should scarcely have been able to read it, since, owing to its having been written on that portion of the tile which had, in the course of ages, undergone the most handling, it was nearly rubbed out – was the bold, modern-looking signature of one Lionel Vincey, "Aetate sua 17," which was written thereon, I think, by Leo's grandfather. To the right of this were the initials "J. B. V.," and below came a variety of Greek signatures, in uncial and cursive character, and what appeared to be some carelessly executed repetitions of the sentence "ôϖ παιδι" (to my son), showing that the relic was religiously passed on from generation to generation.

The next legible thing after the Greek signatures was the word "ROMAE, A.U.C.," showing that the family had now migrated to Rome. Unfortunately, however, with the exception of its termination (cvi), the date of their settlement there is forever lost, for just where it had been placed a piece of the potsherd is broken away.

Then followed twelve Latin signatures, jotted about here and there, wherever there was a space upon the tile suitable to their inscription. These signatures, with three exceptions only, ended with the name "Vindex" or "the Avenger," which seems to have been adopted by the family after its migration to Rome as a kind of equivalent to the Grecian "Tisisthenes," which also means an avenger. Ultimately, as might be expected, this Latin cognomen of Vindex was transformed first into De Vincey, and then into the plain, modern Vincey. It is very curious to observe how the idea of revenge, inspired by an Egyptian before the time of Christ, is thus, as it were, embalmed in an English family name.

A few of the Roman names inscribed upon the sherd I have actually since found mentioned in history and other records. 'They were, if I remember right:

MVSSIVS. VINDEX
SEX. VARIVS. MARVLLVS
C. FVFIDIVS. C. F. VINDEX

and

LABERIA POMPEIANA. CONIVX. MACRINI. VINDICIS

the last being, of course, the name of a Roman lady.

The following list, however, comprises all the Latin names upon the sherd:

C. CAECILIVS VINDEX
M. AIMILIVS VINDEX
SEX. VARIVS. MARVLLVS
Q. SOSIVS PRISCVS SENECIO VINDEX
L. VALERIVS COMINIVS VINDEX
SEX. OTACILIVS. M. F.
L. ATTIVS. VINDEX
MVSSIVS VINDEX
C. FVFIDIVS. C. F. VINDEX
LICINIVS FAVSTVS
LABERIA POMPEIANA CONIVX MACRINI VINDICIS
MANILIA LVCILLA CONIVX MARVLLI VINDICIS

After the Roman names there is evidently a gap of very many centuries. Nobody will ever know now what was the history of the relic during those dark ages, or how it came to have been preserved in the family. My poor friend Vincey had, it will be remembered, told me that his Roman ancestors finally settled in Lombardy, and when Charlemagne invaded it, returned with him across the Alps, and made their home in Brittany, whence they crossed to England in the reign of Edward the Confessor. How he knew this I am not aware, for there is no reference to Lombardy or Charlemagne upon the tile, though, as will presently be seen, there is a reference to Brittany. To continue: the next entries on the sherd, if I may except a long splash of either blood or red coloring matter of some sort, consist of two crosses drawn in red pigment, and probably representing Crusaders' swords, and a rather neat monogram ('D. V.') in scarlet and blue, perhaps executed by that same Dorothea Vincey who wrote, or rather painted, the doggerel couplet. To the left of this, inscribed in faint blue, were the initials A. V., and after them a date, 1800.

Then came what was perhaps as curious an entry as anything upon this extraordinary relic of the past. It is executed in black letter, written over the crosses or Crusaders' swords, and dated fourteen hundred and forty-five. As the best plan will be to allow it to speak for itself, I here give the black-letter facsimile, together with the original Latin without the contractions, from which it will be seen that the writer was a fair medieval Latinist. Also we discovered what is still more curious, an English version of the black-letter Latin. This, also written in black letter, we found inscribed on a second parchment that was in the coffer, apparently somewhat older in date than that on which was inscribed the medieval Latin translation of the uncial Greek of which I shall speak presently. This I also give in full:

Facsimile of Black-Letter Inscription on the Sherd, of Amenartas

Ista reliq̄ia est valde misticū et myrificv op̄s q̄d maiores mei ex Armorica sc Brittania miore secū cōvehebāt et q̄dm scs clerīcs sēper p̄ri meo in manv ferebat q̄d pēitus illvd destrueret affirmās q̄d esset ab ipso sathana cōflatū prestigiosa et dyabolica arte q̄re p̄ter mevs cōfregit illvd ī dvas p̄tes q̄s q̄dm ego Johs̄ de Vīceto salvas servavi et adaptavi sicvt ap̄paret die lūe p̄x post fest beate Mrie virḡ anni grē mccccxlv

Expanded Version of the above Black-Letter Inscription

ISTA reliquia est valde misticum et myrificum opus, quod majores mei ex Armorica, scilicet Britannia Minore, secum convehebant; et quidam sanctus clericus semper patri meo in manu ferebat quod penitus illud destrueret, affirmans quod esset ab ipso Sathan conflatum prestigiosa et dyabolica arte, quare pater meus confregit illud in duas partes, quas quidem ego Johannes de Vinceto salvas servavi et adaptavi sicut apparet die lune proximo post festum beate Marie Virginis anni gratie MCCCCXLV.

Facsimile of the Old English Black-Letter Translation of the above Latin Inscription from the Sherd of Amenartas found inscribed upon a parchment

Thys rellike ys a ryghte mistycall worke & a marveylous ye whyche myne aunceteres afore tyme dyd conveighe hider wt ym ffrom Armoryke which ys to seien Britayne ye lesse & a certayne holye clerke shoulde allweyes beare my ffadir on honde yt he owghte utterly ffor to ffrusshe ye same affermynge yt yt was fformed & conflatyd off sathanas hym selffe by arte magike & devellysshe wherefore my ffadir dyd take ye same & to brast yt yn tweyne but I Johan de Vincey dyd save whool ye tweye ptes therof & topeecyd ym togydder agayne soe as yee se on ys daye mondaye next ffolowynge after ye ffeeste of seynte Marye ye blessed vyrgyne yn ye yeere of salvacioun ffowertene hundreth & ffyve & ffowrti.

Modernized Version of the above Black-Letter Translation

Thys rellike ys a ryghte mistycall worke and a marvaylous, ye whyche myne aunceteres aforetyme dyd conveigh hider with them from Armoryke which ys to seien Britaine ye Lesse and a certayne holye clerke should allweyes beare my fadir on honed that he owghte uttirly for to frusshe ye same, affyrmynge that yt was fourmed and conflatyd of Sathanas hym selfe by arte magike and dyvellysshe wherefore my fadir dyd take ye same and tobrast yt yn tweyne, but I, John de Vincey, dyd save whool ye tweye partes therof and topeecyd them togydder agayne soe as yee se, on this daye mondaye next followynge after ye feeste of Seynte Marye ye Blessed Vyrgyne yn ye yeere of Salvacioun fowertene hundreth and fyve and fowerti.

The next and, save one, last entry was Elizabethan, and dated 1564, 'A most strange historie, and one that did cost my father his life; for in seekynge for the place upon the east coast of Africa, his pinnace was sunk by a Portuguese galleon off Lorenzo Marquez, and he himself perished.' – John Vincey.

Then came the last entry, apparently, to judge by the style of writing, made by some representative of the family in the middle of the eighteenth century. It was a misquotation of the well-known lines in *Hamlet*, and ran thus:

"There are more things in Heaven and earth man are dreamt of in your philosophy, Horatio."[1]

And now there remained but one more document to be examined – namely, the ancient black-letter translation into medieval Latin of the uncial inscription on the sherd. As will be seen, this translation was executed and subscribed in the year 1495, by a certain "learned man," Edmundus de Prato (Edmund

1 Another thing that makes me fix the date of this entry at the middle of the eighteenth century is that, curiously enough, I have an acting copy of *Hamlet*, written about 1740, in which these two lines are misquoted almost exactly in the same way, and I have little doubt but that the Vincey who wrote them on the potsherd heard them so misquoted at that date. Of course, the lines really run:

There are more things in heaven and earth, Horatio,
Than are dreamt of in your philosophy. – L. H. H.

Pratt) by name, licentiate in Canon Law, of Exeter College, Oxford, who had actually been a pupil of Grocyn, the first scholar who taught Greek in England.[1] No doubt on the tame of this new learning reaching his ears, the Vincey of the day, perhaps that same John de Vincey who years before had saved the relic from destruction and made the black-letter entry on the sherd in 1445, hurried off to Oxford to see if perchance it might avail to solve the secret of the mysterious inscription. Nor was he disappointed, for the learned Edmundus was equal to the task. Indeed, his rendering is so excellent an example of medieval learning and Latinity that, even at the risk of sating the learned reader with too many antiquities, I have made up my mind to give it in facsimile, together with an expanded version for the benefit of those who find the contractions troublesome. The translation has several peculiarities on which this is not the place to dwell, but I would in passing call the attention of scholars to the passage '*duxerunt autem nos ad reginam advenaslasaniscoronantium*,' which strikes me as a delightful rendering of the original:

"ἠγαγον δὲ ὡς βασίλειαν τὴν τῶν ξένους χυτραις στεφανουντων"

Medieval Black-Letter Latin Translation of the Uncial Inscription on the Sherd of Amenartas

Amenartas e gen. reg. Egyptii uxor Cal-
licratis sacerdot̄ Isidis quā dei fovēt
demonia attēdūt filiol' suo Tisisthen iā mori-
būda ita mādat: Effugi quōdā ex Egypto
regnāte Nectanebo cū patre tuo, p̄pter mei

1 Grocyn, the instructor of Erasmus, studied Greek under Chalcondylas the Byzantine at Florence, and first lectured in the Hall of Exeter College, Oxford, in 1491. – EDITOR.

amorē pejerato. Fugiētes autē v'sus Notū trans mare et xxiiij mēses p'r litora Libye v'sus Oriētē errant ubi est petra quedā magna sculpta instar Ethiop̄ capit̄, deinde dies iiij ab ost̄ flum̄ magni eiecti p'tim submersi sumus p'tim morbo mortui sum̄: in fine autē a fer̄ hōibs portabamur p̄r palud̄ et vada. ubi aviū m'titudo celū obūbrat dies x. donec advenim̄ ad cavū quedā montē, ubi olim magna urbs erat, caverne quoq̄ imēse: duxerūt autē nos ad reginā Aducnaslasaniscoronātiū que magic̄ utebaīr et peritia omniū rer̄ et saltē pulcrit̄ et vigore īsēescibil' erat. Hec magno patr̄ tui amore p̄culsa p'mū q'dē ei conubiū michi mortē parabat. postea v'ro recusāte Callicrate amore mei et timore regine affecto nos p̄r magicā abduxit p'r vias horribil' ubi est puteus ille p̄fūdus, cuius iuxta aditū iacebat senior̄ philo-sophi cadaver, et advēiētib mōstravit flamā Vite erectā, īstar columne volutātis, voces emittēte q̄si tonitrus: tūc p̄r ignē īpetu nocivo expers trāsiit et iā ipa sese formosior visa est.

Quib fact̄ iuravit se patrē tuū quoq̄ imor-talē ostēsurā esse, si me prius occisa regine cōtuberniū mallet; neq̄ eni ipsa me occidere valuit, p̄pter nostratū magicā cuius egomet p̄tem habeo Ille vero nichil huius gen̄ maluit, manib ante ocul̄ passis ne mulier̄ formositatē adspiceret: postea eū magica pcussit arte, at mortuū efferebat inde cū fletib et vagitib, me pr timorē expulit ad ostiū magni fluminis velivoli porro in nave in qua te peperi, uix post dies huc Athenas invecta sū. At tu, O Tisisthenē, ne q'd quorū mādo nauci fac necesse enī est mulierē exquirere si qua Uite mysteriū īpetres et vīdicare, quātū in te est, patrē tuū Callicratē in regine morte. Sin timore seu aliq causa rē reliquis īfectā, hoc ipsū oīb posterī mādo dū bonus qs inveniatur qui ignis lavacrū nō pḥorrescet et ptentia dignū dōiabit hoīm.

Talia dico incredibilia qdē at minime ficta de reb michi cognitis.

Hec Grece scripta Latine reddidit vir doctus Edmūds de Prato, in Decretis Licenciatus e Coll. Exon · Oxon · doctissimi Grocyni quondam e pupillis, Id Apr A° Dni. MCCCCLXXXXV°.

Expanded Version of the above Medieval Latin Translation

Amenartas, e genere regio Egyptii, uxor Callicratis, sacerdotis Isidis, quam dei fovent demonia attendunt, filiolo suo Tisistheni jam moribunda ita mandat: Effugi quondam ex Egypto, regnante Nectanebo, cum patre tuo, propter mei amorem pejerato. Fugientes autem versus Notum trans mare, et viginti quatuor menses per litora Libye versus Orientem errantes, ubi est petra quedam magna sculpta instar Ethiopis capitis, deinde dies quatuor ab ostio fluminis magni ejecti partim submersi sumus partim morbo mortui sumus: in fine autem a feris hominibus portabamur per paludes et vada, ubi avium multitudo celum obumbrat, dies decem, donec advenimus ad cavum quendam montem, ubi olim magna urbs erat, caverne quoque immense; duxerunt autem nos ad reginam Advenasla-saniscoronantium, que magica utebatur et peritia omnium rerum, et saltem pulcritudine et vigore insenescibilis erat. Hec magno patris tui amore perculsa, primum quidem ei connubium michi mortem parabat; postea vero, recusante Callicrate, amore mei et timore regine affecto nos per magicam abduxit per vias horribiles ubi est puteus ille profundus, cujus juxta aditum jacebat senioris philosophi cadaver, et advenientibus monstravit flammam Vite erectam, instar columne volutantis, voces emittentem quasi tonitrus: tunc per ignem impetu nocivo expers transiit et jam ipsa sese formosior visa est.

Quibus factis juravit se patrem tuum quoque immortalem ostensuram esse, si me prius occisa regine contubernium mallet; neque enim ipsa me occidere valuit, propter nostratum magicam cujus egomet partem habeo. Ille vero nichil hujus generis malebat, manibus ante oculos passis, ne mulieris formositatem adspiceret: postea illum magica percussit arte, at mortuum efferebat inde cum fletibus et vagitibus, at me per timorem expulit ad ostium magni fluminis, velivoli, porro in nave, in qua te peperi, vix post dies huc Athenas vecta sum. At tu, O Tisisthenes, ne quid quorum mando nauci fac: necesse enim est mulierem exquirere si qua Vite mysterium impetres et vindicare, quantum in te est, patrem tuum Callicratem in regine morte. Sin timore seu aliqua causa rem relinquis infectam, hoc ipsum omnibus posteris mando, dum bonus quis inveniatur qui ignis lavacrum non perhorrescet, et potentia dignus dominabitur hominum.

Talia dico incredibilia quidem at minime ficta de rebus michi cognitis.

Hec Grece scripta Latine reddidit vir doctus Edmundus de Prato, in Decretis Licenciatus, e Collegio Exoniensi Oxoniensi doctissimi Grocyni quondam e pupillis, Idibus Aprilis Anno Domini MCCCCLXXXXV°.

"Well," I said, when at length I had read out and carefully examined these writings and paragraphs, at least those of them that were still easily legible, "that is the conclusion of the whole matter, Leo, and now you can form your own opinion on it. I have already formed mine."

"And what is it?" he asked, in his quick way.

"It is this. I believe that potsherd to be perfectly genuine, and that, wonderful as it may seem, it has come down in your family from since the fourth century before Christ. The entries absolutely prove it, and therefore, however improbable it may seem, it must be accepted. But there I stop. That your remote ancestress, the Egyptian princess, or some scribe under her direction, wrote that which we see on the sherd I have no doubt, nor have I the slightest doubt but that her sufferings and the loss of her husband had turned her head, and that she was not right in her mind when she did write it."

"How do you account for what my father saw and heard there?" asked Leo.

"Coincidence. No doubt there are bluffs on the coast of Africa that look something like a man's head, and plenty of people who speak bastard Arabic. Also, I believe that there are lots of swamps. Another thing is, Leo, and I am sorry to say it, but I do not believe that your poor father was quite right when he wrote that letter. He had met with a great trouble, and also he had allowed this story to prey on his imagination, and he was a very imaginative man. Anyway, I believe that the whole thing is the most unmitigated rubbish. I know that there are curious things and forces in nature which we rarely meet with, and, when we do meet them, cannot understand. But until I see it with my own eyes, which I am not likely to, I never will believe that there is any means of avoiding death, even for a time, or that there is or was a white sorceress living in the heart of an African swamp. It is bosh, my boy, all bosh! What do you say, Job?"

"I say, sir, that it is a lie, and, if it is true, I hope Mr. Leo won't meddle with no such things, for no good can't come of it."

"Perhaps you are both right," said Leo very quietly. "I express no opinion. But I say this. I am going to set the matter at rest once and for all, and if you won't come with me I will go by myself."

I looked at the young man, and saw that he meant what he said. When Leo means what he says he always puts on a curious look about the mouth. It has been a trick of his from a child. Now, as a matter of fact, I had no intention of allowing Leo to go anywhere by himself, for my own sake, if not for his. I was far too much attached to him for that. I am not a man of many ties or affections. Circumstances have been against me in this respect, and men and women shrink from me – or at least I fancy they do, which comes to the same thing – thinking, perhaps, that my somewhat forbidding exterior is a key to my character. Rather than endure this, I have, to a great extent, secluded myself from the world, and cut myself off from those opportunities which with most men result in the formation of relations more or less intimate. Therefore Leo was all the world to me – brother, child, and friend – and until he wearied of me, where he went there I should go too. But, of course, it would not do to let him see how great a hold he had over me; so I cast about for some means whereby I might let myself down easy.

"Yes, I shall go, Uncle; and if I don't find the 'rolling Pillar of Life,' at any rate I shall get some first-class shooting."

Here was my opportunity, and I took it.

"Shooting?" I said. "Ah, yes; I never thought of that. It must be a very wild stretch of country, and full of big game. I have always wanted to kill a buffalo before I die. Do you know, my boy, I don't believe in the quest, but I do believe in big game, and really, on the whole, if, after thinking it over, you make up your mind to go, I will take a holiday, and come with you."

"Ah," said Leo, "I thought that you would not lose such a chance. But how about money? We shall want a good lot."

"You need not trouble about that," I answered. "There is all your income that has been accumulating for years, and besides that I have saved two-thirds of what your father left to me, as I consider, in trust for you. There is plenty of cash."

"Very well, then, we may as well stow these things away and go up to town to see about our guns. By the way, Job, are you coming too? It's time you began to see the world."

"Well, sir," answered Job stolidly, "I don't hold much with foreign parts, but if both you gentlemen are going you will want somebody to look after you, and I am not the man to stop behind after serving you for twenty years."

"That's right, Job," said I. "You won't find out anything wonderful, but you will get some good shooting. And now look here, both of you. I won't have a word said to a living soul about this nonsense," and I pointed to the potsherd "If it got out, and anything happened to me, my next of kin would dispute my will on the ground of insanity, and I should become the laughingstock of Cambridge"

That day three months we were on the ocean, bound for Zanzibar.

Chapter 4

The Squall

How DIFFERENT is the scene that I have now to tell from that which has just been told! Gone are the quiet college rooms, gone the wind-swayed English elms and cawing rooks, and the familiar volumes on the shelves, and in their place there rises a vision of the great calm ocean gleaming in shaded silver lights beneath the beams of the full African moon. A gentle breeze fills the huge sail of our dhow, and draws us through the water that ripples musically against our sides. Most of the men are sleeping forward, for it is near midnight, but a stout swarthy Arab, Mahomed by name, stands at the tiller, lazily steering by the stars. Three miles or more to our starboard is a low dim line. It is the eastern shore of Central Africa. We are running to the southward, before the Northeast Monsoon, between the mainland and the reef that for hundreds of miles fringes that perilous coast. The night is quiet, so quiet that a whisper can be heard fore and aft the dhow; so quiet that a faint booming sound rolls across the water to us from the distant land.

The Arab at the tiller holds up his hand, and says one word: "*Simba* [lion]!"

We all sit up and listen. Then it comes again, a slow, majestic sound that thrills us to the marrow.

"Tomorrow by ten o'clock," I say, "we ought, if the Captain is not out in his reckoning, which I think very probable, to make this mysterious rock with a man's head, and begin our shooting."

"And begin our search for the ruined city and the Fire of Life," corrected Leo, taking his pipe from his mouth, and laughing a little.

"Nonsense!" I answered. "You were airing your Arabic with

that man at the tiller this afternoon. What did he tell you? He has been trading (slave-trading probably) up and down these latitudes for half of his iniquitous life, and once landed on this very "man" rock. Did he ever hear anything of the ruined city or the caves?"

"No," answered Leo. "He says that the country is all swamp behind, and full of snakes, especially pythons, and game, and that no man lives there. But then there is a belt of swamp all along the East African coast, so that does not go for much."

"Yes," I said, "it does – it goes for malaria. You see what sort of an opinion these gentry have of the country. Not one of them will go with us. They think that we are mad, and upon my word I believe that they are right. If ever we see old England again I shall be astonished. However, it does not greatly matter to me at my age, but I am anxious for you, Leo, and for Job. It's a Tom Fool's business, my boy."

"All right. Uncle Horace. So far as I am concerned, I am willing to take my chance. Look! What is that cloud?" and he pointed to a dark blotch upon the starry, sky, some miles astern of us.

"Go and ask the man at the tiller," I said.

He rose, stretched his arms, and went. Presently he returned.

"He says it is a squall, but it will pass far on one side of us."

Just then Job came up, looking very stout and English in his shooting suit of brown flannel, and with a sort of perplexed appearance upon his honest round face that had been very common with him since he got into these strange waters.

"Please, sir," he said, touching his sun hat, which was stuck on to the back of his head in a somewhat ludicrous fashion, "as we have got all those guns and things in the whaleboat astern, to say nothing of the provisions in the lockers, I think it would be best if I got down and slept in her. I don't like the looks" – here he dropped his voice to a portentous whisper – "of these black gentry; they have such a wonderful thievish way about them. Supposing now that some of them were to slip into the boat at night and cut the cable, and make off with her? That would be a pretty go, that would."

The whaleboat, I may explain, was one specially built for us at Dundee, in Scotland. We had brought it with us, as we knew that this coast was a network of creeks, and that we might require something to navigate them with. She was a beautiful boat, thirty feet in length, with a center-board for sailing, copper-bottom to keep the worm out of her, and full of water-tight compartments. The captain of the dhow had told us that when we reached the rock, which he knew, and which appeared to be identical with the one described upon the sherd and by Leo's father, he would probably not be able to run up to it on account of the shallows and breakers. Therefore we had employed three hours that very morning, while we were totally becalmed, the wind having dropped at sunrise, in transferring most of our goods and chattels to the whaleboat, and placing the guns, ammunition, and preserved provisions in the water-light lockers specially prepared for them, so that when we did sight the fabled rock we should have nothing to do but step into the boat, and run her ashore. Another reason that induced us to take this precautionary step was that Arab captains are apt to run past the point that they are making, either from carelessness or owing to a mistake in its identity. Now, as sailors know, it is quite impossible for a dhow which is only rigged to run before the monsoon to beat back against it. Therefore we got our boat ready to row for the rock at any moment.

"Well, Job," I said, "perhaps it would be as well. There are lots of blankets there, only be careful to keep out of the moon, or it may turn your head or blind you."

"Lord, sir! I don't think it would much matter if it did; it is that turned already with the sight of these blackamoors and their filthy, thieving ways. They are only fit for muck, they are; and they smell bad enough for it already."

Job, it will be perceived, was no admirer of the manners and customs of our dark-skinned brothers.

Accordingly we hauled up the boat by the tow rope till it was right under the stern of the dhow, and Job bundled into her with all the grace of a falling sack of potatoes. Then we returned and sat down on the deck again, and smoked and talked in little gusts and jerks. The night was so lovely, and our brains were so full of suppressed excitement of one sort and another, that we did not feel inclined to turn in. For nearly an hour we sat thus, and then, I think, we both dozed off. At least I have a faint recollection of Leo sleepily explaining that the head was not a bad place to hit a buffalo, if you could catch him exactly between the horns, or send your bullet down his throat, or some nonsense of the sort.

Then I remember no more; till suddenly – a frightful roar of wind, a shriek of terror from the awakening crew, and a whiplike sting of water in our faces. Some of the men ran to let go the halyards and lower the sail, but the parrel jammed and the yard would not come down. I sprang to my feet and hung on to a rope. The sky aft was dark as pitch, but the moon still shone brightly ahead of us and lit up the blackness. Beneath its sheen a huge white-topped breaker, twenty feet high or more, was rushing onto us. It was on the break – the moon shone on its crest and tipped its foam with light. On it rushed beneath the inky sky, driven by the awful squall behind it. Suddenly, in the twinkling of an eye, I saw the black shape of the whaleboat cast high into the air on the crest of the breaking wave. Then – a shock of water, a wild rush of boiling foam, and I was clinging for my life to the shroud, ay, swept straight out from it like a flag in a gale.

We were pooped.

The wave passed. It seemed to me that I was under water for minutes – really it was seconds. I looked forward. The blast had torn out the great sail, and high in the air it was fluttering away to leeward like a huge wounded bird. Then for a moment there was comparative calm, and in it I heard Job's voice yelling wildly, "Come here to the boat."

Bewildered and half drowned as I was, I had the sense to rush aft. I felt the dhow sinking under me – she was full of water. Under her counter the whaleboat was tossing furiously, and I saw the Arab Mahomed, who had been steering, leap into her. I gave one desperate pull at the tow rope to bring the boat alongside. Wildly I sprang also, and Job caught me by one arm and I rolled into the bottom of the boat. Down went the dhow bodily, and as she did so Mahomed drew his curved knife and severed the fiber rope by which we were fast to her, and in another second we were driving before the storm over the place where the dhow had been.

"Great God!" I shrieked, "where is Leo? *Leo! Leo!*"

"He's gone, sir. God help him!" roared Job into my ear; and such was the fury of the squall that his voice sounded like a whisper.

I wrung my hands in agony. Leo was drowned, and I was left alive to mourn him. "Look out!" yelled Job. "Here comes another." I turned; a second huge wave was overtaking us. I half hoped that it would drown me. With a curious fascination I watched its awful advent. The moon was nearly hidden now by the wreaths of the rushing storm, but a little light still caught the crest of the devouring breaker. There was something dark on it – a piece of wreckage. It was on us now, and the boat was nearly full of water. But she was built in air-tight compartments – heaven bless the man who invented them! – and lifted up through it like a swan. Through the foam and turmoil I saw the black thing on the wave hurrying right at me. I put out my right arm to ward it from me, and my hand closed on another arm, the wrist of which my fingers gripped like a vice. I am a very strong man, and had something to hold to, but my arm was nearly torn from its socket by the strain and weight of the floating body. Had the rush lasted another two seconds I must either have let go or gone with it. But it passed, leaving us up to our knees in water.

"Bail out! Bail out!" shouted Job, suiting the action to the word.

But I could not bail just then, for as the moon went out and left us in total darkness, one faint, flying ray of light lit upon the face of the man I had gripped, who was now half lying, half floating in the bottom of the boat.

It was Leo. Leo brought back by the wave – back, dead or alive, from the very jaws of death.

"Bail out! Bail out!" yelled Job. "Or we shall founder." I seized a large tin bowl with a handle to it, which was fixed under one of the seats, and the three of us bailed away for dear life. The furious tempest drove over and round us, flinging the boat this way and that; the wind and the storm wreaths and the sheets of stinging spray blinded and bewildered us; but through it all we worked like demons with the wild exhilaration of despair, for even depair can exhilarate. One minute! Three minutes! Six minutes! The boat began to lighten, and no fresh wave swamped us. Five minutes more, and she was fairly clear. Then, suddenly, above the awful shriekings of the hurricane came a duller, deeper roar. Great heavens! It was the voice of breakers!

At that moment the moon began to shine forth again – this time behind the path of the squall. Far out across the torn bosom of the ocean shot the ragged arrows of her light, and there, half a mile ahead of us, was a white line of foam, then a little space of open-mouthed blackness, and then another line of white. It was the breakers, and their roar grew clearer and yet more clear as we sped down upon them like a swallow. There they were, boiling up in snowy spouts of spray, smiting and gnashing together like the gleaming teeth of hell.

"Take the tiller, Mahomed!" I roared in Arabic. "We must try and shoot them." At the same moment I seized an oar, and got it out, motioning to Job to do likewise. Mahomed clambered aft and got hold of the tiller and with some difficulty Job, who had sometimes pulled a tub upon the homely Cam, got out his oar. In another minute the boat's head was straight on to the ever nearing foam, towards which she plunged and tore with the speed of a racehorse. Just in front of us the first line of breakers seemed a little thinner than to the right or left – there was a gap of rather deeper water. I turned and pointed to it.

"Steer for your life, Mahomed!" I yelled. He was a skillful steersman, and well acquainted with the dangers of this most perilous coast, and I saw him grip the tiller and bend his heavy frame forward, and stare at the foaming terror till his big round eyes looked as though they would start out of his head. The send of the sea was driving the boat's head round to starboard. If we struck the line of breakers fifty yards to starboard of the gap we must sink. It was a great field of twisting, spouting waves. Mahomed planted his foot against the seat before him, and, glancing at him, I saw his brown toes spread out like a hand with the weight he put upon them as he took the strain of the tiller. She came round a bit, but not enough. I roared to Job to back water, whilst I dragged and labored at my oar. She answered now, and none too soon.

Heavens, we were in them! And then followed a couple of minutes of heartbreaking excitement such as I cannot hope to describe. All I remember is a shrieking sea of foam, out of which the billows rose here, there, and everywhere like avenging ghosts from their ocean grave. Once we were turned right round, but either by chance, or through Mahomed's skillful steering, the boat's head came straight again before a breaker filled us. One more – a monster. We were through it or over it – more through than over – and then, with a wild yell of exultation from the Arab, we shot out into the comparatively smooth water of the mouth of sea between the teeth-like lines of gnashing waves.

But we were half full of water again, and not more than half a mile ahead was the second line of breakers. Again we set to and bailed furiously. Fortunately the storm had now quite gone by, and the moon shone brightly, revealing a rocky headland running half a mile or more out into the sea, of which this second line of breakers appeared to be a continuation. At any rate, they boiled around its foot. Probably the ridge that formed the headland ran out into the ocean, only at a lower level, and made the reef also. This headland was terminated by a curious peak that seemed not to be more than a mile away from us. Just as we got the boat pretty clear for the second time, Leo, to my immense relief, opened his eyes and remarked that the clothes had tumbled off the bed, and that he supposed it was time to get up for chapel. I told him to shut his eyes and keep quiet, which he did without in the slightest degree realizing our position. As for myself, his reference to chapel made me reflect, with a sort of sick longing, on my comfortable rooms at Cambridge. Why had I been such a fool as to leave them? This is a reflection that has several times recurred to me since, and with ever increasing force.

But now again we were drifting down on the breakers, though with lessened speed, for the wind had fallen, and only the current or the tide (it afterwards turned out to be the tide) was driving us.

Another minute, and with a sort of howl to Allah from the Arab, a pious ejaculation from myself, and something that was not pious from Job, we were in them. And then the whole scene, down to our final escape, repeated itself, only not quite so violently. Mahomed's skillful steering and the air-tight compartments saved our lives. In five minutes we were through, and drifting – for we were too exhausted to do anything to help ourselves except keep the boat's head straight – with the most startling rapidity round the headland which I have described.

Round we went with the tide, until we got well under the lee of the point, and then suddenly the speed slackened, we ceased to make way, and finally appeared to be in dead water. The storm had entirely passed, leaving a clean-washed sky behind it; the headland intercepted the heavy sea that had been occasioned by the squall, and the tide, which had been running so fiercely up the river (for we were now in the mouth of a river), was sluggish before it turned, so we floated quietly, and before the moon went down managed to bail out the boat thoroughly and get her a little shipshape. Leo was sleeping profoundly, and on the whole I thought it wise not to wake him. It was true he was sleeping in wet clothes, but the night was now so warm that I thought (and so did Job) that they were not likely to injure a man of his unusually vigorous constitution. Besides, we had no dry ones at hand.

Presently the moon went down and left us floating on the waters, now only heaving like some troubled woman's breast, giving us leisure to reflect upon all that we had gone through and all that we had escaped. Job stationed himself at the bow, Mahomed kept his post at the tiller, and I sat on a seat in the middle of the boat close to where Leo was lying.

The moon went slowly down in chastened loveliness, she departed like some sweet bride into her chamber, and long veil-like shadows crept up the sky through which the stars peeped shyly out. Soon, however, they too began to pale before a splendor in the east, and then the quivering footsteps of the dawn came rushing across the newborn blue, and shook the planets from their places. Quieter and yet more quiet grew the sea, quiet as the soft mist that brooded on her bosom, and covered up her troubling, as the illusive wreaths of sleep brood upon a pain-racked mind, causing it to forget its sorrow. From the east to the west sped the angels of the dawn, from sea to sea, from mountain top to mountain top, scattering light with both their hands. On they sped out of the darkness, perfect, glorious, like spirits of the just breaking from the tomb; on, over the quiet sea, over the low coastline, and the swamps beyond, and the mountains beyond them; over those who slept in peace, and those who woke in sorrow; over the evil and the good; over the living and dead; over the wide world and all that breathes or has breathed thereon.

It was a wonderfully beautiful sight, and yet sad, perhaps from the very excess of its beauty. The arising sun; the setting sun! There we have the symbol and the type of humanity, and all things with which humanity has to do. The symbol and the type, yes, and the earthly beginning, and the end also. And on that morning this came home to me with a peculiar force. The sun that rose today for us had set last night for eighteen of our fellow-voyagers! – had set forever for eighteen whom we knew!

The dhow had gone down with them, they were tossing about now among the rocks and seaweed, so much human drift on the great ocean of death! And we four were saved. But one day a sunrise will come when we shall be among those who are lost, and then others will watch those glorious rays, and grow sad in the midst of beauty, and dream of death in the full glow of arising life!

For this is the lot of man.

Chapter 5

The Head of the Ethiopian

AT LENGTH the heralds and forerunners of the royal sun had done their work, and, searching out the shadows, had caused them to flee away. Then up he came in glory from his ocean bed, and flooded the earth with warmth and light. I sat there in the boat listening to the gentle lapping of the water and watched him rise, till presently the slight drift of the boat brought the odd-shaped rock, or peak, at the end of the promontory which we had weathered with so much peril, between me and the majestic sight, and blotted it from my view. I still continued to stare at the rock, however, absently enough, till presently it became edged with the fire of the growing light behind it, and then I started, as well I might, for I perceived that the top of the peak, which was about eighty feet high by one hundred and fifty thick at its base, was shaped like a Negro's head and face, whereon was stamped a most fiendish and terrifying expression. There was no doubt about it; there were the thick lips, the fat cheeks, and the squat nose standing out with startling clearness against the flaming background. There, too, was the round skull, washed into shape perhaps by thousands of years of wind and weather, and, to complete the resemblance, there was a scrubby growth of weeds or lichen upon it, which against the sun looked for all the world like the wool on a colossal Negro's head. It certainly was very odd; so odd that now I believe that it is not a mere freak of nature but a gigantic monument fashioned, like the well-known Egyptian Sphinx, by a forgotten people out of a pile of rock that lent itself to their design, perhaps as an emblem of warning and defiance to any enemies who approached the harbor. Unfortunately we were never able to ascertain whether or not this was the case, inasmuch as the rock was difficult of access from both the land and the water side, and we had other things to attend to. Myself, considering the matter by the light of what we afterwards saw, I believe that it was fashioned by man, but whether or not this is so, there it stands, and sullenly stares from age to age out across the changing sea – there it stood two thousand years and more ago, when Amenartas, the Egyptian princess, and the wife of Leo's remote ancestor Kallikrates, gazed upon its devilish face – and there I have no doubt it will still stand when as many centuries as are numbered between her day and our own are added to the year that bore us to oblivion.

"What do you think of that, Job?" I asked of our retainer, who was sitting on the edge of the boat, trying to get as much sunshine as possible, and generally looking uncommonly wretched, and I pointed to the fiery and demoniacal head.

"Oh Lord, sir," answered Job, who now perceived the object for the first time, "I think that the Old Gentleman must have been sitting for his portrait on them rocks."

I laughed, and the laugh woke up Leo.

"Hullo," he said, "what's the matter with me? I am all stiff –

where is the dhow? Give me some brandy, please."

"You may be thankful that you are not stiffer, my boy," I answered. "The dhow is sunk, and everybody on board her is drowned, with the exception of us four, and your own life was only saved by a miracle"; and while Job, now that it was light enough, searched about in a locker for the brandy for which Leo asked, I told him the history of our night's adventure.

"Great heavens!" he said, faintly. "And to think that we should have been chosen to live through it!"

By this time the brandy was forthcoming, and we all had a good pull at it, and thankful enough we were for it. Also the sun was beginning to get strength, and warm our chilled bones, for we had been wet through for five hours or more.

"Why," said Leo with a gasp, as he put down the brandy bottle, "there is the head the writing talks of, the 'rock carven like the head of an Ethiopian.' "

"Yes," I said, "there it is."

"Well, then," he answered, "the whole thing is true."

"I don't at all see that that follows," I answered. "We knew this head was here, your father saw it. Very likely it is not the same head that the writing talks of; or if it is, it proves nothing."

Leo smiled at me in a superior way. "You are an unbeliever, Uncle Horace," he said. "Those who live will see."

"Exactly so," I answered, "and now perhaps you will observe that we are drifting across a sandbank into the mouth of the river. Get hold of your oar, Job, and we will row in and see if we can find a place to land."

The river mouth which we were entering did not appear to be a very wide one, though as yet the long banks of steaming mist that clung about its shores had not lifted sufficiently to enable us to see its exact width. There was as is the case with nearly every East African river, a considerable bar at the mouth, which, no doubt, when the wind was on shore and the tide running out, was absolutely impassable even for a boat drawing only a few inches. But as things were it was manageable enough, and we did not ship a cupful of water. In twenty minutes we were well across it, with but slight assistance from ourselves, and being carried by a strong though somewhat variable breeze, well up the harbor. By this time the mist was being sucked up by the sun, which was getting uncomfortably hot, and we saw that the mouth of the little estuary was here about half a mile across, and that the banks were very marshy, and crowded with crocodiles lying about on the mud like logs. About a mile ahead of us, however, was what appeared to be a strip of firm land, and for this we steered. In another quarter of an hour we were there, and making the boat fast to a beautiful tree with broad shining leaves, and flowers of the magnolia species, only they were rose-colored and not white,[1] which hung over the water, we disembarked. This done we undressed, washed ourselves, and spread our clothes and the contents of the boat in the sun to dry, which they very quickly did. Then, taking shelter from the sun under some trees, we made a hearty breakfast off a "Paysandu" potted tongue, of which we had brought a good quantity with us, from the Army and Navy Stores, congratulating ourselves loudly on our good fortune in having loaded and provisioned the boat on the previous day, before the hurricane destroyed the dhow. By the time that we had finished our meal our clothes were quite dry, and we hastened to get into them, feeling not a little refreshed. Indeed, with the exception of weariness and a few bruises, none of us were the worse for the terrifying adventure which had been fatal to all our companions. Leo, it is true, had been half-drowned, but that is no great matter to a a vigorous young athlete of five-and-twenty.

After breakfast we started to look about us. We were on a strip of dry land about two hundred yards broad by five hundred long, bordered on one side by the river, and on the other three by endless desolate swamps that stretched as far as the eye could

1 There is a known species of magnolia with pink flowers. It is indigenous in Sikkim, and known as Magnolia Campbellii – EDITOR.

reach. This strip of land was raised about twenty-five feet above the plain of the surrounding swamps and the river level: indeed, it had every appearance of having been made by the hand of man.

"This place has been a wharf," said Leo dogmatically.

"Nonsense," I answered. "Who would be stupid enough to build a wharf in the middle of these dreadful marshes in a country inhabited by savages, that is if it is inhabited at all?"

"Perhaps it was not always marsh, and perhaps the people were not always savage," he said drily, looking down the steep bank, for we were standing by the river. "Look there," he went on, pointing to a spot where the hurricane of the previous night had torn up one of the magnolia trees, which had grown on the extreme edge of the bank just where it sloped down to the water, by the roots, and lifted a large cake of earth with them. "Is not that stonework? If not, it is very like it."

"Nonsense," I said again, and we clambered down to the spot, and got between the upturned roots and the bank.

"Well?" he said.

But I did not answer this time. I only whistled. For there, laid bare by the removal of the earth, was an undoubted facing of solid stone laid in large blocks and bound together with brown cement, so hard that I could make no impression on it with the file in my shooting knife. Nor was this all; seeing something projecting through the soil at the bottom of the bared patch of walling, I removed the loose earth with my hands, and revealed a huge stone ring, a foot or more in diameter, and about three inches thick. This fairly staggered me.

"Looks rather like a wharf where good-sized vessels have been moored, does it not, Uncle Horace?" said Leo with an excited grin.

I tried to say "Nonsense" again, but the word stuck in my throat – the ring spoke for itself. In some past age vessels had been moored there, and this stone wall was undoubtedly the remnant of a solidly constructed wharf. Probably the city to which it had belonged lay buried beneath the swamp behind it.

"Begins to look as though there were something in the story after all, Uncle Horace," said the exultant Leo; and reflecting on the mysterious Negro's head and the equally mysterious stonework, I made no direct reply.

"A country like Africa," I said, "is sure to be full of the relics of long dead and forgotten civilizations. Nobody knows the age of the Egyptian civilization, and very likely it had offshoots. Then there were the Babylonians and the Phoenicians, and the Persians and all manner of people, all more or less civilized, to say nothing of the Jews, whom everybody 'wants' nowadays. It is possible that they, or any one of them, may have had colonies or trading stations about here. Remember those buried Persian cities that the consul showed us at Kilwa."[1]

"Quite so," said Leo, "but that is not what you said before."

"Well, what is to be done now?" I asked, turning the conversation.

As no answer was forthcoming we proceeded to the edge of the swamp, and looked over it. It was apparently boundless, and vast flocks of every sort of waterfowl came flying from its recesses, till it was sometimes difficult to see the sky. Now that the sun was getting high it drew thin sickly-looking clouds of poisonous vapor from the surface of the marsh and from the scummy pools of stagnant water.

"Two things are clear to me," I said, addressing my three companions, who stared at this spectacle in dismay: "first, that we can't go across there" – I pointed to the swamp – "and, secondly, that if we stop here we shall certainly die of fever."

"That's as clear as a haystack, sir," said Job. "Very well,

1 Near Kilwa, on the east coast of Africa, about four hundred miles south of Zanzibar, is a cliff which has been recently washed by the waves. On the top of this cliff are Persian tombs known to be at least seven centuries old by the dates still legible upon them. Beneath these tombs is a layer of debris representing a city. Further down the cliff is a second layer representing an older city, and further down still a third layer, the remains of yet another city of vast and unknown antiquity. Beneath the bottom city were recently found some specimens of glazed earthenware, such as are occasionally to be met with on that coast to this day I believe that they are now in the possession of Sir John Kirk – EDITOR.

then; there are two alternatives before us. One is to 'bout ship, and try and run for some port in the whaleboat, which would be a sufficiently risky proceeding, and the other to sail or row on up the river, and see where we come to."

"I don't know what you are going to do," said Leo, setting his mouth, "but I am going up that river."

Job turned up the whites of his eyes and groaned, and the Arab murmured, "Allah," and groaned also. As for me, I remarked sweetly that as we seemed to be between the Devil and the deep sea, it did not much matter where we went. But in reality I was as anxious to proceed as Leo. The colossal Negro's head and the stone wharf had excited my curiosity to an extent of which I was secretly ashamed, and I was prepared to gratify it at any cost. Accordingly, having carefully fitted the mast, restowed the boat, and got out our rifles, we embarked. Fortunately the wind was blowing on shore from the ocean, so we were able to hoist the sail. Indeed, we afterwards found out that as a general rule the wind set on shore from daybreak for some hours, and off shore again at sunset, and the explanation that I offer of this is that when the earth is cooled by the dew and the night the hot air rises, and the draft rushes in from the sea till the sun has once more heated it through. At least that appeared to be the rule here.

Taking advantage of this favoring wind, we sailed merrily up the river for three or four hours. Once we came across a school of hippopotami, which rose, and bellowed dreadfully at us within ten or a dozen fathoms of the boat, much to Job's alarm, and, I will confess, to my own. These were the first hippopotami that we had ever seen, and, to judge by their insatiable curiosity, I should judge that we were the first white men that they had ever seen. Upon my word, I once or twice thought that they were coming into the boat to gratify it. Leo wanted to fire at them, but I dissuaded him, fearing the consequences. Also we saw hundreds of crocodiles basking on the muddy banks, and thousands upon thousands of waterfowl. Some of these we shot, and among them was a wild goose, which, in addition to the sharp curved spurs on its wings, had a spur about three-quarters of an inch long growing from the skull just between the eyes. We never shot another like it, so I do not know if it was a "sport" or a distinct species. In the latter case this incident may interest naturalists. Job named it the Unicorn Goose.

About midday the sun grew intensely hot, and the stench drawn up by it from the marshes which the river drains was something too awful, and caused us instantly to swallow precautionary doses of quinine. Shortly afterwards the breeze died away altogether, and as rowing our heavy boat against the stream in the heat was out of the question, we were thankful enough to get under the shade of a group of trees – a species of willow – that grew by the edge of the river, and lie there and gasp till at length the approach of sunset put a period to our miseries. Seeing what appeared to be an open space of water straight ahead of us, we determined to row there before settling what to do for the night. Just as we were about to loosen the boat, however, a beautiful waterbuck, with great horns curving-forward, and a white stripe across the rump, came down to the river to drink, without perceiving us hidden away within fifty yards under the willows. Leo was the first to catch sight of it, and being an ardent sportsman, thirsting for the blood of big game, about which he had been dreaming for months, he instantly stiffened all over, and pointed like a setter dog. Seeing what was the matter, I handed him his express rifle, at the same time taking my own. "Now then," I whispered, "mind you don't miss."

"Miss!" he whispered back contemptuously. "I could not miss it if I tried."

He lifted the rifle, and the roan-colored buck, having drunk his fill, raised his head and looked out across the river. He was standing right against the sunset sky on a little eminence, or ridge of ground, which ran across the swamp, evidently a favorite path for game, and there was something very beautiful about him. Indeed, I do not think that if I live to a hundred I shall ever forget that desolate and yet most fascinating scene: it is stamped upon my memory. To the right and left were wide stretches of lonely, death-breeding swamp, unbroken and unrelieved so far as the eye could reach, except here and there by ponds of black and peaty water that, minor-like, flashed up the red rays of the setting sun. Behind us and before stretched the vista of the, sluggish river, ending in glimpses of a reed-fringed lagoon, on the surface of which the long lights of the evening played as the faint breeze stirred the shadows. To the west loomed the huge red ball of the sinking sun, now vanishing down the vapory horizon, and filling the great heaven, high across whose arch the cranes and wild fowl streamed in line, square, and triangle, with flashes of flying gold and the lurid stain of blood. And then ourselves – three modern Englishmen in a modern English boat – seeming to jar upon and looking out of tone with that measureless desolation; and in front of us the noble buck limned out upon a background of ruddy sky.

Bang! Away he goes with a mighty bound. Leo has missed him. Bang! right under him again. Now for a shot. I must have one, though he is going like an arrow, and a hundred yards away and more. By Jove! Over and over and over! "Well, I think I've wiped your eye there, Master Leo," I say, struggling against the ungenerous exultation that in such a supreme moment of one's existence will rise in the best-mannered sportsman's breast.

"Confound you, yes," growled Leo; and then, with that quick smile that is one of his charms lighting up his handsome face like a ray of light, "I beg your pardon, old fellow. I congratulate you; it was a lovely shot, and mine were vile."

We got out of the boat and ran to the buck, which was shot through the spine and stone dead. It took us a quarter of an hour or more to clean it and cut off as much of the best meat as we could carry, and, having packed this away, we had barely light enough to row up into the lagoon-like space, into which, there being a hollow in the swamp, the river here expanded. Just as the light vanished we cast anchor about thirty fathoms from the edge of the lake. We did not dare to go ashore, not knowing if we should find dry ground to camp on, and greatly fearing the poisonous exhalations from the marsh, from which we thought we should be freer on the water. So we lighted a lantern, and made our evening meal off another potted tongue in the best fashion that we could, and then prepared to go to sleep, only, however, to find that sleep was impossible. For, whether they were attracted by the lantern, or by the unaccustomed smell of a white man, for which they had been waiting for the last thousand years or so, I know not; but certainly we were presently attacked by tens of thousands of the most bloodthirsty, pertinacious, and huge mosquitoes that I ever saw or read of. In clouds they came, and pinged and buzzed and bit till we were nearly mad. Tobacco smoke only seemed to stir them into a merrier and more active life, till at length we were driven to covering ourselves with blankets, head and all, and sitting to slowly stew and continually scratch and swear beneath them. And as we sat, suddenly rolling out like thunder through the silence came the deep roar of a lion, and then of a second lion, moving among the reeds within sixty yards of us.

"I say," said Leo, sticking his head out from under his blanket, "lucky we ain't on the bank, eh. Avuncular?" (Leo sometimes addressed me in this disrespectful way.)

"Curse it! A mosquito has bitten me on the nose," and the head vanished again.

Shortly after this the moon came up, and notwithstanding every variety of roar that echoed over the water to us from the lions on the banks, we began, thinking ourselves perfectly secure, to gradually doze off.

I do not quite know what it was that made me poke my head but of the friendly shelter of the blanket; perhaps I did so because I found that the mosquitoes were biting right through it.

Anyhow, as I did so I heard Job whisper, in a frightened voice, "Oh, my stars, look there!"

Instantly we all of us looked, and this was what we saw in the moonlight. Near the shore were two wide and ever widening circles of concentric rings rippling away across the surface of the water, and in the heart and center of the circles were two dark moving objects.

"What is it?" asked I.

"It is those damned lions, sir," answered Job, in a tone which was an odd mixture of a sense of personal injury, habitual respect, and acknowledged fear, "and they are swimming here to *h*eat us," he added, nervously picking up an "h" in his agitation.

I looked again, there was no doubt about it; I could catch the glare of their ferocious eyes. Attracted either by the smell of the newly killed waterbuck or of ourselves, the hungry beasts were actually storming our position.

Leo already had his rifle in his hand. I called to him to wait till they were nearer, and meanwhile grabbed my own. Some fifteen feet from us the water shallowed on a bank to the depth of about fifteen inches, and presently the first of them – it was the lioness – got onto it and shook herself and roared. At that moment Leo fired, and the bullet went right down her open mouth and out at the back of her neck, and down she dropped, with a splash, dead. The other lion – a full-grown male – was some two paces behind her. At this second he got his forepaws onto the bank, when a strange thing happened. There was a rush and disturbance of the water, such as one sees in a pond in England when a pike takes a little fish, only a thousand times fiercer and larger, and suddenly the lion gave a most terrific snarling roar and sprang forward onto the bank, dragging something black with him.

"Allah!" shouted Mahomed. "A crocodile has got him by the leg!" And sure enough he had. We could see the long snout with its gleaming lines of teeth and the reptile body behind it.

And then followed an extraordinary scene indeed. The lion managed to get well onto the bank, the crocodile half standing and half swimming, still nipping his hind leg. He roared till the air quivered with the sound, and then, with a savage, shrieking snarl, turned round and clawed hold of the crocodile's head. The crocodile shifted his grip, having, as we afterwards discovered, had one of his eyes torn out, and slightly turned over, and instantly the lion got him by the throat and held on, and then over and over they rolled upon the bank struggling hideously. It was impossible to follow their movements, but when next we got a clear view the tables had turned, for the crocodile, whose head seemed to be a mass of gore, had got the lion's body in his iron jaws just above the hips, and was squeezing him and shaking him to and fro. For his part the tortured brute, roaring in agony, was clawing and biting madly at his enemy's scaly head, and fixing his great hind claws in the crocodile's, comparatively speaking, soft throat, ripping it open as one would rip a glove.

Then, all of a sudden, the end came. The lion's head fell forward on the crocodile's back, and with an awful groan he died, and the crocodile, after standing for a minute motionless, slowly rolled over onto his side, his jaws still fixed across the carcass of the lion, which we afterwards found he had bitten almost in halves.

This duel to the death was a wonderful and a shocking sight, and one that I suppose few men have seen – and thus it ended.

When it was all over, leaving Mahomed to keep a look-out, we managed to spend the rest of the night as quietly as the mosquitoes would allow.

Chapter 6

An Early Christian Ceremony

NEXT MORNING, at the earliest blush of dawn, we rose, performed such ablutions as circumstances would allow, and generally made ready to start. I am bound to say that when there was sufficient light to enable us to see each other's faces I, for one, burst out into a roar of laughter. Job's fat and comfortable countenance was swollen out to nearly twice its natural size from mosquito bites, and Leo's condition was not much better. Indeed, of the three I had come off much the best, probably owing to the toughness of my dark skin, and to the fact that a good deal of it was covered by hair, for since we started from England I had allowed my naturally luxuriant beard to grow at its own sweet will. But the other two were, comparatively speaking, clean shaved, which of course gave the enemy a larger extent of open country to operate on, though as for Mahomed the mosquitoes, recognizing the taste of a true believer, would not touch him at any price. How often, I wonder, during the next week or so did we wish that we were flavored like an Arab!

By the time that we had done laughing as heartily as our swollen lips would allow, it was daylight, and the morning breeze was coming up from the sea, cutting lanes through the dense marsh mists, and here and there rolling them before it in great balls of fleecy vapor. So we set our sail, and having first taken a look at the two dead lions and the dead crocodile, which we were of course unable to skin, being destitute of means of curing the pelts, we started, and, sailing through the lagoon, followed the course of the river on the farther side. At midday, when the breeze dropped, we were fortunate enough to find a convenient piece of dry land on which to camp and light a fire, and here we cooked two wild duck and some of the waterbuck's flesh – not in a very appetizing way, it is true, but still, sufficiently. The rest of the buck's flesh we cut into strips and hung in the sun to dry into "biltong," as I believe the South African Dutch call flesh thus prepared. On this welcome patch of dry land we stopped till the following dawn, and, as before, spent the night in warfare with the mosquitoes, but without other troubles. The next day or two passed in similar fashion, and without noticeable adventures, except that we shot a specimen of a peculiarly graceful hornless buck, and saw many varieties of water lilies in full bloom, some of them blue and of exquisite beauty, though few of the flowers were perfect, owing to the prevalence of a white water maggot with a green head that fed upon them.

It was on the fifth day of our journey, when we had traveled, so far as we could reckon, about one hundred and thirty-five to a hundred and forty miles westwards from the coast, that the first event of any real importance occurred. On that morning the usual wind failed us about eleven o'clock, and after pulling a little way we were forced to halt more or less exhausted at what appeared to be the junction of our stream with another of a uniform width of about fifty feet. Some trees grew near at hand – the only trees in all this country were along the banks of the river, and under these we rested, and then, the land being fairly dry just here, walked a little way along the edge of the river to prospect, and shoot a few waterfowl for food. Before we had gone fifty yards we perceived that all hopes of getting further up the stream in the whaleboat were at an end, for not two hundred yards above where we had stopped were a succession of shallows and mudbanks, with not six inches of water over them. It was a watery *cul-de-sac*.

Turning back, we walked some way along the banks of the other river, and soon came to the conclusion, from various indications, that it was not a river at all, but an ancient canal, like the one which is to be seen above Mombasa, on the Zanzibar coast, connecting the Tana River with the Ozy, in such a way as to enable the shipping coming down the Tana to cross to the Ozy, and reach the sea by it, and thus avoid the very dangerous bar that blocks the mouth of the Tana. The canal before us had evidently been dug out by man at some remote period of the world's history, and the results of his digging still remained in the shape of the raised banks that had no doubt once formed towing-paths. Except here and there, where they had been hollowed out or fallen in, these banks of stiff binding clay were at a uniform distance from each other, and the depth of the water also appeared to be uniform. Current there was little or none, and, as a consequence, the surface of the canal was choked with vegetable growth, intersected by little paths of clear water, made, I suppose, by the constant passage of waterfowl, iguanas, and other vermin. Now, as it was evident that we could not proceed up the river, it became equally evident that we must either try the canal or else return to the sea. We could not stop where we were, to be baked by the sun and eaten up by the mosquitoes, till we died of fever in that dreary marsh.

"Well, I suppose that we must try it," I said; and the others assented in their various ways – Leo as though it were the best joke in the world; Job in respectful disgust; and Mahomed with an invocation to the Prophet and a comprehensive curse upon all unbelievers and their ways of thought and travel.

Accordingly, as soon as the sun got low, having little or nothing more to hope for from our friendly wind, we started. For the first hour or so we managed to row the boat, though with great labor; but after that the weeds got too thick to allow it, and we were obliged to resort to the primitive and most exhausting resource of towing her. For two hours we labored, Mahomed, Job, and I, who was supposed to be strong enough to pull against the two of them, on the bank, while Leo sat in the bow of the boat, and brushed away the weeds which collected round the cutwater with Mahomed's sword. At dark we halted for some hours to rest and enjoy the mosquitoes, but about midnight we went on again, taking advantage of the comparative cool of the night. At dawn we rested for three hours, and then started once more, and labored on till about ten o'clock, when a thunderstorm, accompanied by a delude of rain, overtook us, and we spent the next six hours practically under water.

I do not know that there is any necessity for me to describe the next four days of our voyage in detail, further than to say that they were, on the whole, the most miserable that I ever spent in my life, forming one monotonous record of heavy labor, heat, misery, and mosquitoes. All the way we passed through a region of almost endless swamp, and I can only attribute our escape from fever and death to the constant doses of quinine and purgatives which we took, and the unceasing toil which we were forced to undergo. On the third day of our journey up the canal we had sighted a round hill that loomed dimly through the vapors of the marsh, and on the evening of the fourth night, when we camped, this hill seemed to be within five-and-twenty or thirty miles of us. We were by now utterly exhausted, and felt as though our blistered hands could not pull the boat a yard further, and that the best thing that we could do would be to lie down and die in that dreadful wilderness of swamp. It was an awful position, and one in which I trust no other white man will ever be placed; and as I threw myself down in the boat to sleep the sleep of utter exhaustion, I bitterly cursed my folly in ever having been a party to such a mad undertaking, which could, I saw, only end in our death in this ghastly land. I thought, I remember, as I slowly sank into a doze, of what the appearance of the boat and her unhappy crew would be in two or three months' time from that night. There she would lie, with gaping seams and half filled with fetid water, which, when the mist-laden wind stirred her, would wash backwards and forwards through our moldering bones, and that would be the end of her, and of those in her who would follow after myths and seek out the secrets of nature.

Already I seemed to hear the water rippling against the desiccated bones and rattling them together, rolling my skull against Mahomed's, and his against mine, till at last Mahomed's stood straight up upon its vertebrae, and glared at me through its empty eyeholes, and cursed me with its grinning jaws, because I, a dog of a Christian, disturbed the last sleep of a true believer. I opened my eyes, and shuddered at the horrid dream, and then shuddered again at something that was not a dream, for two great eyes were gleaming down at me through the misty darkness. I struggled up, and in my terror and confusion shrieked, and shrieked again, so that the others sprang up too, reeling, and drunken with sleep and fear. And then all of a sudden there was a flash of cold steel, and a great spear was held against my throat, and behind it other spears gleamed cruelly.

"Peace," said a voice, speaking in Arabic, or rather in some dialect into which Arabic entered very largely. "Who are ye who come hither swimming on the water? Speak or ye die," and the steel pressed sharply against my throat, sending a cold chill through me.

"We are travelers, and have come hither by chance," I answered in my best Arabic, which appeared to be understood, for the man turned his head, and, addressing a tall form that towered up in the background, said, "Father, shall we slay?"

"What is the color of the men?" said a deep voice in answer.

"White is their color."

"Slay not," was the reply. "Four suns since was the word brought to me from *'She-who-must-be-obeyed,'* 'White men come; if white men come, slay them not.' Let them be brought to the land of '*She-who-must-be-obeyed.*' Bring forth the men, and let that which they have with them be brought forth also."

"Come," said the man, half leading and half dragging me from the boat, and as he did so I perceived other men doing the same kind office to my companions.

On the bank were gathered a company of some fifty men. In that light all I could make out was that they were armed with huge spears, were very tall, and strongly built, comparatively light in color, and nude, save for a leopard skin tied round the middle.

Presently Leo and Job were bundled out and placed beside me.

"What on earth is up?" said Leo, rubbing his eyes.

"Oh, Lord, sir here's a rum go," ejaculated Job; and just at that moment a disturbance ensued, and Mahomed came tumbling between us, followed by a shadowy form with an uplifted spear.

"Allah! Allah!" howled Mahomed, feeling that he had little to hope from man. "Protect me! Protect me!"

"Father, it is a black one," said a voice. "What said *'She-who-must-be-obeyed'* about the black one?"

"She said naught; but slay him not. Come hither, my son."

The man advanced, and the tall shadowy form bent forward and whispered something.

"Yes, yes," said the other, and chuckled in a rather blood-curdling tone.

"Are the three white men there?" asked the form.

"Yes, they are there,"

"Then bring up that which is made ready for them, and let the men take all that can be brought from the thing which floats."

Hardly had he spoken when men came running up, carrying on their shoulders neither more nor less than palanquins – four bearers and two spare men to a palanquin – and in these it was promptly indicated we were expected to stow ourselves.

"Well!" said Leo. "It is a blessing to find anybody to carry us after having to carry ourselves so long."

Leo always takes a cheerful view of things.

There being no help for it, after seeing the others into theirs I tumbled into my own litter, and very comfortable I found it. It appeared to be manufactured of cloth woven from grass fiber, which stretched and yielded to every motion after the body, and, being bound top and bottom to the bearing pole, gave a grateful support to the head and neck.

Scarcely had I settled myself when, accompanying their steps with a monotonous song, the bearers started at a swinging trot. For half an hour or so I lay still, reflecting on the very remarkable experiences that we were going through, and wondering if any of my eminently respectable fossil friends down at Cambridge would believe me if I were to be miraculously set at the familiar dinner table for the purpose of relating them. I don't want to convey any disrespectful notion or slight when I call those good and learned men fossils, but my experience is that people are apt to fossilize even at a university if they follow the same paths too persistently. I was getting fossilized myself, but of late my stock of ideas has been very much enlarged. Well, I lay and reflected, and wondered what on earth would be the end of it all, till at last I ceased to wonder, and went to sleep.

I suppose I must have slept for seven or eight hours, getting the first real rest that I had had since the night before the loss of the dhow, for when I woke the sun was high in the heavens. We were still journeying on at a pace of about four miles an hour. Peeping out through the mistlike curtains of the litter, which were ingeniously fixed to the bearing pole, I perceived to my infinite relief that we had passed out of the region of eternal swamp, and were now traveling over swelling grassy plains towards a cup-shaped hill. Whether or not it was the same hill that we had seen from the canal I do not know, and have never since been able to discover, for, as we afterwards found out, these people will give little information upon such points. Next I glanced at the men who were bearing me. They were of a magnificent build, few of them being under six feet in height, and yellowish in color. Generally their appearance had a good deal in common with that of the East African Somali, only their hair was not frizzed up, and hung in thick black locks upon their shoulders. Their features were aquiline, and in many cases exceedingly handsome, the teeth being especially regular and beautiful. But notwithstanding their beauty, it struck me that, on the whole, I had never seen a more evil-looking set of faces. There was an aspect of cold and sullen cruelty stamped upon them that revolted me, and which in some cases was almost uncanny in its intensity.

Another thing which struck me about them was that they never seemed to smile. Sometimes they sang the monotonous song of which I have spoken, but when they were not singing they remained almost perfectly silent, and the light of a laugh never came to brighten their somber and evil countenances. Of what race could these people be? Their language was a bastard Arabic, and yet they were not Arabs; I was quite sure of that. For one thing they were too dark, or rather yellow. I could not say why, but I know that their appearance filled me with a sick fear of which I felt ashamed. While I was still wondering another litter came up alongside of mine. In it – for the curtains were drawn – sat an old man, clothed in a whitish robe, made apparently from coarse linen, that hung loosely about him, who, I at once jumped to the conclusion, was the shadowy figure who had stood on the bank and been addressed as "Father." He was a wonderful-looking old man, with a snowy beard, so long that the ends of it hung over the sides of the litter, and he had a hooked nose, above which flashed out a pair of eyes as keen as a snake's, while his whole countenance was instinct with a look of wise and sardonic humor impossible to describe on paper.

"Art thou awake, stranger?" he said in a deep and low voice.

"Surely, my father," I answered courteously, feeling certain that I should do well to conciliate this ancient Mammon of Unrighteousness.

He stroked his beautiful white beard, and smiled faintly.

"From whatever country thou camest," he said, "and by the way it must be from one where somewhat of our language is known, they teach their children courtesy there, my stranger son. And now wherefore comest thou unto this land, which scarce an alien foot has pressed from the time that man knoweth? Art thou and those with thee weary of life?"

"We came to find new things," I answered boldly. "We are tired of the old things; we have come up out of the sea to know that which is unknown. We are of a brave race who fear not death, my very much respected father – that is, if we can get a little fresh information before we die."

"Humph!" said the old gentleman. "That may be true; it is rash to contradict, otherwise I should say that thou wast lying, my son. However, I dare say that '*She-who-must-be-obeyed*' will meet thy wishes in the matter."

"Who is '*She-who-must-be-obeyed*'?" I asked curiously.

The old man glanced at the bearers, and then answered, with a little smile that somehow sent my blood to my heart, "Surely, my stranger son, thou wilt learn soon enough, if it be her pleasure to see thee at all in the flesh."

"In the flesh?" I answered. "What may my father wish to convey?"

But the old man only laughed a dreadful laugh, and made no reply.

"What is the name of my father's people?" I asked.

"The name of my people is Amahagger" (the People of the Rocks).

"And if a son might ask, what is the name of my father?"

"My name is Billali."

"And whither go we, my father?"

"That shalt thou see," and at a sign from him his bearers started forward at a run till they reached the litter in which Job was reposing (with one leg hanging over the side). Apparently, however, he could not make much out of Job, for presently I saw his bearers trot forward to Leo's litter.

And after that, as nothing fresh occurred, I yielded to the pleasant swaying motion of the litter, and went to sleep again. I was dreadfully tired. When I woke I found that we were passing through a rocky defile of a lava formation with precipitous sides, in which grew many beautiful trees and flowering shrubs.

Presently this defile took a turn, and a lovely sight unfolded itself to my eyes. Before us was a vast cup of green from four to six miles in extent, of the shape of a Roman amphitheater. The sides of this great cup were rocky, and clothed with bush, but the center was of the richest meadow land, studded with single trees of magnificent growth, and watered by meandering brooks. On this rich plain grazed herds of goats and cattle, but I saw no sheep. At first I could not imagine what this strange spot could be, but presently it flashed upon me that it must represent the crater of some long-extinct volcano, which had afterwards been a lake, and was ultimately drained in some unexplained way. And here I may state that from my subsequent experience of this and a much larger, but otherwise similar spot, which I shall have occasion to describe by and by, I have every reason to believe that this conclusion was correct. What puzzled me, however, was that, although there were people moving about herding the goats and cattle, I saw no signs of any human habitation. Where did they all live? I wondered. My curiosity was soon destined to be gratified. Turning to the left the string of litters followed the cliffy sides of the crater for a distance of about half a mile, or perhaps a little less, and then halted. Seeing the old gentleman, my adopted 'father,' Billali, emerge from his litter, I did the same, and so did Leo and Job. The first thing I saw was our wretched Arab companion, Mahomed, lying exhausted on the ground. It appeared that he had not been provided with a litter, but had been forced to run the entire distance, and, as he was already quite worn out when we started, his condition now was one of great prostration.

On looking round we discovered that the place where we had halted was a platform in front of the mouth of a great cave, and piled upon this platform were the entire contents of the whaleboat, even down to the oars and sail. Round the cave stood groups of the men who had escorted us, and other men of a similar stamp. They were all tall and all handsome, though they varied in their degree of darkness of skin, some being as dark as

Mahomed, and some as yellow as a Chinese. They were naked, except for the leopard skin round the waist, and each of them carried a huge spear.

There were also some women among them, who, instead of the leopard skin, wore a tanned hide of a small red buck, something like that of the oribé, only rather darker in color. These women were, as a class, exceedingly good-looking, with large, dark eyes, well-cut features, and a thick bush of curling hair – not crisped like a Negro's – ranging from black to chestnut in hue, with all shades of intermediate color. Some, but very few of them, wore a yellowish linen garment, such as I have described as worn by Billali, but this, as we afterwards discovered, was a mark of rank, rather than an attempt at clothing. For the rest, their appearance was not quite so terrifying as that of the men, and they sometimes, though rarely, smiled. As soon as we had alighted they gathered round us and examined us with curiosity, but without excitement. Leo's tall, athletic form and clear-cut Grecian face, however, evidently excited their attention, and when he politely lifted his hat to them, and showed his curling yellow hair, there was a slight murmur of admiration. Nor did it stop there; for, after regarding him critically from head to foot, the handsomest of the young women – one wearing a robe, and with hair of a shade between brown and chestnut – deliberately advanced to him, and, in a way that would have been winning had it not been so determined, quietly put her arm round his neck, bent forward, and kissed him on the lips.

I gave a gasp, expecting to see Leo instantly speared; and Job ejaculated, "The hussy – well, I never!" As for Leo, he looked slightly astonished; and then, remarking that we had got into a country where they clearly followed the customs of the early Christians, deliberately returned the embrace.

Again I gasped, thinking that something would happen; but to my surprise, though some of the young women showed traces of vexation, the older ones and the men only smiled slightly. When we came to understand the customs of this extraordinary people the mystery was explained. It then appeared that, in direct opposition to the habits of almost every other savage race in the world, women among the Amahagger are not only upon terms of perfect equality with the men, but are not held to them by any binding ties. Descent is traced only through the line of the mother, and while individuals are as proud of a long and superior female ancestry as we are of our families in Europe, they never pay attention to, or even acknowledge, any man as their father, even when their male parentage is perfectly well known. There is but one titular male parent of each tribe, or, as they call it, 'household,' and he is its elected and immediate ruler, with the title of 'father.' For instance, the man Billali was the father of this 'household,' which consisted of about seven thousand individuals all told, and no other man was ever called by that name. When a woman took a fancy to a man she signified her preference by advancing and embracing him publicly, in the same way that this handsome and exceedingly prompt young lady, who was called Ustane, had embraced Leo. If he kissed her back it was a token that he accepted her, and the arrangement continued till one of them wearied of it. I am bound, however, to say that the change of husbands was not nearly so frequent as might have been expected. Nor did quarrels arise out of it, at least among the men, who, when their wives deserted them in favor of a rival, accepted the whole thing much as we accept the income tax or our marriage laws, as something not to be disputed, and as tending to the good of the community, however disagreeable they may in particular instances prove to the individual.

It is very curious to observe how the customs of mankind on this matter vary in different countries, making morality an affair of latitude, and what is right and proper in one place wrong and improper in another. It must, however, be understood that, as all civilized nations appear to accept it as an axiom that ceremony is the touchstone of morality, there is, even according to our canons, nothing immoral about this Amahagger custom, seeing that the interchange of the embrace answers to our ceremony of marriage, which, as we know, justifies most things.

Chapter 7

Ustane Sings

WHEN THE kissing operation was finished – by the way, none of the young ladies offered to pet me in this fashion, though I saw one hovering round Job, to that respectable individual's evident alarm – the old man Billali advanced, and graciously waved us into the cave, whither we went, followed by Ustane, who did not seem inclined to take the hints I gave her that we liked privacy.

Before we had gone five paces it struck me that the cave that we were entering was none of Nature's handiwork, but, on the contrary, had been hollowed by the hand of man. So far as we could judge it appeared to be about one hundred feet in length by fifty wide, and very lofty, resembling a cathedral aisle more than anything else. From this main aisle opened passages at a distance of every twelve or fifteen feet, leading, I supposed, to smaller chambers. About fifty feet from the entrance of the cave, just where the light began to get dim, a fire was burning, which threw huge shadows upon the gloomy walls around. Here Billali halted, and asked us to be seated, saying that the people would bring us food, and accordingly we squatted ourselves down upon the rugs of skins which were spread for us, and waited. Presently the food, consisting of goat's flesh boiled, fresh milk in an earthenware pot, and boiled cobs of Indian corn, was brought by young girls. We were almost starving, and I do not think that I ever in my life before ate with such satisfaction. Indeed, before we had finished we literally ate up everything that was set before us.

When we had done, our somewhat saturnine host, Billali, who had been watching us in perfect silence, rose and addressed us. He said that it was a wonderful thing that had happened. No man had ever known or heard of white strangers arriving in the country of the People of the Rocks. Sometimes, though rarely, black men had come here, and from them they had heard of the existence of men much whiter than themselves, who sailed on the sea in ships, but for the arrival of such there was no precedent. We had, however, been seen dragging the boat up the canal, and he told us frankly that he had at once given orders for our destruction, seeing that it was unlawful for any stranger to enter here, when a message had come from *"She-who-must-be-obeyed,"* saying that our lives were to be spared, and that we were to be brought hither.

"Pardon me, my father," I interrupted at this point; "but if, as I understand, *'She-who-must-be-obeyed'* lives yet farther off, how could she have known of our approach?"

Billali turned, and seeing that we were alone – for the young lady, Ustane, had withdrawn when he had begun to speak – said, with a curious little laugh, "Are there none in your land who can see without eyes and hear without ears? Ask no questions; *She* knew."

I shrugged my shoulders at this, and he proceeded to say that no further instructions had been received on the subject of our disposal, and this being so he was about to start to interview *"She-who-must-be-obeyed,"* generally spoken of, for the sake of brevity, simply as "Hiya" or *She*, who he gave us to understand was the Queen of the Amahagger, and learn her wishes.

I asked him how long he proposed to be away, and he said that by traveling hard he might be back on the fifth day, but there were many miles of marsh to cross before he came to where *She* was. He then said that every arrangement would be made for our comfort during his absence, and that, as he personally had taken a fancy to us, he sincerely trusted that the answer he should bring from *She* would be one favorable to the continuation of our existence, but at the same time he did not wish to conceal from us that he thought this doubtful, as every stranger who had ever come into the country during his grandmother's life, his mother's life, and his own life, had been put to death without mercy, and in a way that he would not harrow our feelings by describing; and this had been done by the order of *She* herself, at least he supposed it was by her order. At any rate, she never interfered to save them.

"Why," I said, "but how can that be? You are an old man, and the time you talk of must reach back three men's lives. How therefore could *She* have ordered the death of anybody at the beginning of the life of your grandmother, seeing that she herself would not have been born?"

Again he smiled – that same faint, peculiar smile – and with a deep bow departed, without making any answer; nor did we see him again for five days.

When he had gone we discussed the situation, which filled me with alarm. I did not at all like the accounts of this mysterious Queen, *"She-who-must-be-obeyed,"* or more shortly *She*, who apparently ordered the execution of any unfortunate stranger in a fashion so unmerciful. Leo, too, was depressed about it, but proceeded to console himself by triumphantly pointing out that this *She* was undoubtedly the person referred to in the writing on the potsherd and in his father's letter, in proof of which he advanced Billali's allusions to her age and power. I was by this time so overwhelmed with the whole course of events that I had not even got the heart left to dispute a proposition so absurd, so I suggested that we should try and go out and get a bath, of which we all stood sadly in need.

Accordingly, having indicated our wish to a middle-aged individual of an unusually saturnine cast of countenance, even among this saturnine people, who appeared to be deputed to look after us now that the father of the hamlet had departed, we started in a body – having first lit our pipes. Outside the cave we found quite a crowd of people evidently watching for our appearance, but when they saw us come out smoking they vanished this way and that, calling out that we were great magicians. Indeed, nothing about us created so great a sensation as our tobacco smoke – not even our firearms.[1] After this we succeeded in reaching a stream that had its source in a strong ground spring, and taking our bath in peace, though some of the women, not excepting Ustane, showed a decided inclination to follow us even there.

By the time that we had finished this most refreshing bath the sun was setting; indeed, when we got back to the big cave it had already set. The cave itself was full of people gathered round fires – for several more had now been lighted – and eating their evening meal by their lurid light, and by that of various lamps which were set about or hung upon the walls. These lamps were of a rude manufacture of baked earthenware, and of all shapes, some of them graceful enough. The larger ones were formed of big red earthenware pots, filled with clarified melted fat, and having a reed wick stuck through a wooden disk which filled the top of the pot, and this sort of lamp required the most constant attention to prevent its going out whenever the wick burned down, as there were no means of turning it up. The smaller hand lamps, however, which were also made of baked clay, were fitted with wicks manufactured from the pith of a palm tree, or sometimes from the stem of a very handsome variety of fern. This kind of wick was passed through a round hole at the end of the lamp, to which a sharp piece of hard wood was attached wherewith to pierce and draw it up whenever it showed signs of burning low.

For a while we sat down and watched this grim people eating their evening meal in silence as grim as themselves, till at length, getting tired of contemplating them and the huge moving shadows

1 We found tobacco growing in this country as it does in every other part of Africa, and, although they are so absolutely ignorant of its other blessed qualities, the Amahagger use it habitually in the form of snuff, and also for medicinal purposes. – L. H. H.

on the rocky walls, I suggested to our new keeper that we should like to go to bed.

Without a word he rose, and, taking me politely by the hand, advanced with a lamp to one of the small passages that I had noticed opening out of the central cave. This we followed for about five paces, when it suddenly widened out into a small chamber, about eight feet square, and hewn out of the living rock. On one side of this chamber was a stone slab, about three feet from the ground, and running its entire length like a bunk in a cabin, and on this slab he intimated that I was to sleep. There was no window or air hole to the chamber, and no furniture; and, on looking at it more closely, I came to the disturbing conclusion (in which, as I afterwards discovered, I was quite right) that it had originally served for a sepulcher for the dead rather than a sleeping place for the living, the slab being designed to receive the corpse of the departed. The thought made me shudder in spite of myself; but, seeing that I must sleep somewhere, I got over the feeling as best I might, and returned to the cavern to get my blanket, which had been brought up from the boat with the other things. There I met Job, who, having been inducted to a similar apartment, had flatly declined to stop in it, saying that the look of the place gave him the horrors, and that he might as well be dead and buried in his grandfather's brick grave at once, and expressed his determination of sleeping with me if I would allow him. This, of course, I was only too glad to do.

The night passed very comfortably on the whole. I say on the whole, for personally I went through a most horrible nightmare of being buried alive, induced, no doubt, by the sepulchral nature of my surroundings. At dawn we were aroused by a loud trumpeting sound, produced, as we afterwards discovered, by a young Amahagger blowing through a hole bored in its side into a hollowed elephant tusk, which was kept for the purpose.

Taking the hint, we got up and went down to the stream to wash, after which the morning meal was served. At breakfast one of the women, no longer quite young, advanced, and publicly kissed Job. I think it was in its way the most delightful thing (putting its impropriety aside for a moment) that I ever saw. Never shall I forget the respectable Job's abject terror and disgust. Job, like myself, is a bit of a misogynist – I fancy chiefly owing to the fact of his having been one of a family of seventeen – and the feelings expressed upon his countenance when he realized that he was not only being embraced publicly, and without authorization on his own part, but also in the presence of his masters, were too mixed and painful to admit of accurate description. He sprang to his feet, and pushed the woman, a buxom person of about thirty, from him.

"Well, I never!" he gasped, whereupon, probably thinking that he was only coy, she embraced him again.

"Be off with you! Get away, you minx!" he shouted, waving the wooden spoon, with which he was eating his breakfast, up and down before the lady's face. "Beg your pardon, gentlemen, I am sure I haven't encouraged her. Oh, Lord! She's coming for me again. Hold her, Mr. Holly! Please hold her! I can't stand it; I can't, indeed. This has never happened to me before, gentlemen, never. There's nothing against my character," and here he broke off, and ran as hard as he could go down the cave, and for once I saw the Amahagger laugh. As for the woman, however, she did not laugh. On the contrary, she seemed to bristle with lury, which the mockery of the other women about only served to intensify. She stood there literally snarling and shaking with indignation, and, seeing her, I wished Job's scruples had been at Jericho, forming a shrewd guess that his admirable behavior had endangered our throats. Nor, as the sequel shows, was I wrong.

The lady having retreated. Job returned in a great state of nervousness, and keeping his weather eye fixed upon every woman who came near him. I took an opportunity to explain to our hosts that Job was a married man, and had had very unhappy experiences in his domestic relations, which accounted for his presence here and his terror at the sight of women, but my remarks were received in grim silence, it being evident that our retainer's behavior was considered as a slight to the 'household' at large, although the women, after the manner of some of their more civilized sisters, made merry at the rebuff of their companion.

After breakfast we took a walk and inspected the Amahagger herds, and also their cultivated lands. They have two breeds of cattle, one large and angular, with no horns, but yielding beautiful milk; and the other, a red breed, very small and fat, excellent for meat, but of no value for milking purposes. This last breed closely resembles the Norfolk red-pole strain, only it has horns which generally curve forward over the head, sometimes to such an extent that they have to be cut to prevent them from growing into the bones of the skull. The goats are long-haired, and are used for eating only, at least I never saw them milked. As for the Amahagger cultivation, it is primitive in the extreme, being all done by means of a spade made of iron, for these people smelt and work iron. This spade is shaped more like a big spear head than anything else, and has no shoulder to it on which the foot can be set. As a consequence, the labor of digging is very great. It is, however, all done by the men, the women, contrary to the habits of most savage races, being entirely exempt from manual toil. But then, as I think I have said elsewhere, among the Amahagger the weaker sex has established its rights.

At first we were much puzzled as to the origin and constitution of this extraordinary race, points upon which they were singularly uncommunicative. As the time went on – for the next four days passed without any striking event – we learned something from Leo's lady friend Ustane, who, by the way, stuck to that young gentleman like his own shadow. As to origin, they had none, at least, so far as she was aware. There were, however, she informed us, mounds of masonry and many pillars near the place where *She* lived, which was called Kôr, and which the wise said had once been houses wherein men lived, and it was suggested that they were descended from these men. No one, however, dared go near these great ruins, because they were haunted: they only looked on them from a distance. Other similar ruins were to be seen, she had heard, in various parts of the country, that is, wherever one of the mountains rose above the level of the swamp. Also, the caves in which they lived had been hollowed out of the rocks by men, perhaps the same who built the cities. They themselves had no written laws, only custom, which was, however, quite as binding as law. If any man offended against the custom, he was put to death by order of the rather of the "household." I asked how he was put to death, and she only smiled, and said that I might see one day soon.

They had a queen, however. *She* was their queen, but she was very rarely seen, perhaps once in two or three years, when she came forth to pass sentence on some offenders, and when seen was muffled up in a big cloak, so that nobody could look upon her face. Those who waited upon her were deaf and dumb, and therefore could tell no tales, but it was reported that she was lovely as no other woman was lovely, or ever had been. It was rumored also that she was immortal, and had power over all things, but she, Ustane, could say nothing of all that. What she believed was that the Queen chose a husband from time to time, and as soon as a female child was born this husband, who was never again seen, was put to death. Then the female child grew up and took the place of the Queen when its mother died, and had been buried in the great caves. But of these matters none could speak for certain. Only *She* was obeyed throughout the length and breadth of the land, and to question her command was certain death. She kept a guard, but had no regular army, and to disobey her was to die.

I asked what size the land was, and how many people lived in it. She answered that there were ten 'households,' like this that she knew of, including the big 'household,' where the Queen was, that all the 'households' lived in caves, in places resembling this stretch of raised country, dotted about in a vast extent of swamp, which was only to be threaded by secret paths. Often the "households" made war on each other until *She* sent word that it was to stop, and then they instantly ceased. That and the fever which they caught in crossing the swamps prevented their numbers from increasing too much. They had no connection with any other race, indeed, none lived near them, or were able to thread the vast swamps. Once an army from the direction of the great river (presumably the Zambesi) had attempted to attack them, but they got lost in the marshes, and at night, seeing the great balls of fire that move about there, tried to come to them, thinking that they marked the enemy's camp, and half of them were drowned. As for the rest, they soon died of fever and starvation, not a blow being struck at them. The marshes, she told us, were absolutely impassable except to those who knew the paths, adding, what I could well believe, that we should never have reached this place where we then were had we not been brought thither.

These and many other things we learned from Ustane during the four days' pause before our real adventures began, and, as may be imagined, they gave us considerable cause for thought. The whole thing was exceedingly remarkable, almost incredibly so, indeed, and the oddest part of it was that so far it did more or less correspond to the ancient writing on the sherd. And now it appeared that there was a mysterious queen clothed by rumor with dread and wonderful attributes, and commonly known by the impersonal but, to my mind, rather awesome title of *She*. Altogether, I could not make it out, nor could Leo, though of course he was exceedingly triumphant over me because I had persistently mocked at the whole thing. As for Job, he had long since abandoned any attempt to call his reason his own, and left it to drift upon the sea of circumstance. Mahomed, the Arab, who was, by the way, treated civilly indeed, but with chilling contempt, by the Amahagger, was, I discovered, in a great fright, though I could not quite make out what he was frightened about. He would sit crouched up in a corner of the cave all day long, calling upon Allah and the Prophet to protect him. When I pressed him about it, he said that he was afraid because these people were not men and women at all, but devils, and that this was an enchanted land; and, upon my word, once or twice since then I have been inclined to agree with him. And so the time went on, till the night of the fourth day after Billali had left, when something happened.

We three and Ustane were sitting round a fire in the cave just before bedtime, when suddenly the woman, who had been brooding in silence, rose, and laid her hand upon Leo's golden curls, and addressed him. Even now, when I shut my eyes, I can see her proud, imperial form, clothed alternately in dense shadow and the red flickering of the fire, as she stood, the wild center of as weird a scene as I ever witnessed, and delivered herself of the burden of her thoughts and forebodings in a kind of rhythmical speech that ran something as follows:

Thou art my chosen – I have waited for thee from the beginning!

Thou art very beautiful. Who hath hair like unto thee, or skin so white?

Who hath so strong an arm, who is so much a man?

Thine eyes are the sky, and the light in them is the stars.

Thou art perfect and of a happy face, and my heart turned itself towards thee.

Ay, when mine eyes fell on thee I did desire thee, –

Then did I take thee to me – thou, my Beloved,

And hold thee fast, lest harm should come unto thee.

Ay, I did cover thine head with mine hair, lest the sun should strike it;

And altogether was I thine, and thou wast altogether mine.

And so it went for a little space, till Time was in labor with an evil Day;

And then what befell on that day? Alas! my Beloved, I know not!

But I, I saw thee no more – I, I was lost in the blackness.

And she who is stronger did take thee; ay, she who is fairer than Ustane.

Yet didst thou turn and call upon me, and let thine eyes wander in the darkness.

But, nevertheless, she prevailed by Beauty, and led thee down horrible places,

And then, ah! then my Beloved –

Here this extraordinary woman broke off her speech, or chant, which was so much musical gibberish to us, for all that we understood of what she was talking about, and seemed to fix her flashing eyes upon the deep shadow before her. Then in a moment they acquired a vacant, terrified stare, as though they were striving to realize some half-seen horror. She lifted her hand from Leo's head, and pointed into the darkness. We all looked, and could see nothing; but she saw something, or thought she did, and something evidently that affected even her iron nerves, for, without another sound, down she fell senseless between us.

Leo, who was growing really attached to this remarkable young person, was in a great state of alarm and distress, and I, to be perfectly candid, was in a condition not far removed from superstitious fear. The whole scene was an uncanny one.

Presently, however, she recovered, and sat up with an extraordinary convulsive shudder.

"What didst thou mean, Ustane?" asked Leo, who, thanks to years of tuition, spoke Arabic very prettily.

"Nay, my chosen," she answered with a little forced laugh. "I did but sing unto thee after the fashion of my people. Surely, I meant nothing. How could I speak of that which is not yet?"

"And what didst thou see, Ustane?" I asked, looking her sharply in the face.

"Nay," she answered again; "I saw naught. Ask me not what I saw. Why should I fright ye?" And then, turning to Leo with a look of the most utter tenderness that I ever saw upon the face of a woman, civilized or savage, she took his head between her hands, and kissed him on the forehead as a mother might. "When I am gone from thee, my chosen; when at night thou stretchest out thine hand and canst not find me, then shouldst thou think at times of me, for of a truth I love thee well, though I be not fit to wash thy feet. And now let us love and take that which is given us, and be happy; for in the grave there is no love and no warmth, nor any touching of the lips. Nothing perchance, or perchance but bitter memories of what might have been. Tonight the hours are our own, how know we to whom they shall belong tomorrow?"

Chapter 8

The Feast, and After!

On the day following this remarkable scene – a scene calculated to make a deep impression upon anybody who beheld it, more because of what it suggested and seemed to foreshadow than of what it revealed – it was announced to us that a feast would be held that evening in our honor. I did my best to get out of it, saying that we were modest people, and cared little for feasts, but my remarks being received with the silence of displeasure, I thought it wisest to hold my tongue.

Accordingly, just before sundown, I was informed that everything was ready, and, accompanied by Job, went into the cave, where I met Leo, who was, as usual, followed by Ustane. These two had been out walking somewhere, and knew nothing of the projected festivity till that moment. When Ustane heard of it I saw an expression of horror spring up upon her handsome features. Turning, she caught a man who was passing up the cave by the arm, and asked him something in an imperious tone. His answer seemed to reassure her a little, for she looked relieved, though far from satisfied. Next she appeared to attempt some remonstrance with the man, who was a person in authority, but he spoke angrily to her, and shook her off, and then changing his mind, led her by the arm, and sat her down between himself and another man in the circle round the fire, and I perceived that for some reason of her own she thought it best to submit.

The fire in the cave was an unusually big one that night, and in a large circle round it were gathered about thirty-five men and two women, Ustane and the woman to avoid whom Job had played the role of another Scriptural character. The men were sitting in perfect silence, as was their custom, each with his great spear stuck upright behind him, in a socket cut in the rock for that purpose. Only one or two wore the yellowish linen garment of which I have spoken, the rest had nothing on except the leopard's skin about the middle.

"What's up now, sir?" said Job doubtfully. "Bless us and save us, there's that woman again. Now, surely, she can't be after me, seeing that I have given her no encouragement. They give me the creeps, the whole lot of them, and that's a fact. Why, look, they have asked Mahomed to dine, too. There, that lady of mine is talking to him in as nice and civil a way as possible. Well, I'm glad it isn't me, that's all."

We looked up, and sure enough the woman in question had risen, and was escorting the wretched Mahomed from the corner, where, overcome by some acute prescience of horror, he had been seated, shivering, and calling on Allah. He appeared unwilling enough to come, if for no other reason perhaps because it was an unaccustomed honor, for hitherto his food had been given to him apart. Anyway I could see that he was in a state of great tenor, for his tottering legs would scarcely support his stout, bulky form, and I think it was rather owing to the resources of barbarism behind him, in the shape of a huge Amahagger with a proportionately huge spear, than to the seduction of the lady who led him by the hand, that he consented to come at all.

"Well," I said to the others, "I don't at all like the look of things, but I suppose that we must face it out. Have you fellows got your revolvers on? Because, if so, you had better see that they are loaded."

"I have, sir," said Job, tapping his Colt, "but Mr. Leo has only got his hunting knife, though that is big enough, surely."

Feeling that it would not do to wait while the missing weapon was fetched, we advanced boldly, and seated ourselves in a line, with our backs against the side of the cave.

As soon as we were seated, an earthenware jar was passed round containing a fermented fluid, of by no means unpleasant taste, though apt to turn upon the stomach, made of crushed grain – not Indian corn, but a small brown grain that grows upon the stem in clusters, not unlike that which in the southern part of Africa is known by the name of Kafir corn. The vase in which this liquid was handed round was very curious, and as it more or less resembled many hundreds of others in use among the Amahagger I may as well describe it. These vases are of a very ancient manufacture, and of all sizes. None such can have been made in the country for hundreds, or rather thousands, of years. They are found in the rock tombs, of which I shall give a description in their proper place, and my own belief is that, after the fashion of the Egyptians, with whom the former inhabitants of this country may have had some connection, they were used to receive the viscera of the dead. Leo, however, is of opinion that, as in the case of Etruscan amphorae, they were placed there for the spiritual use of the deceased. They are mostly two-handled, and of all sizes, some being nearly three feet in height, and running from that down to as many inches. In shape they vary, but are all exceedingly beautiful and graceful, being made of a very fine black ware, not lustrous, but slightly rough. On this groundwork were inlaid figures much more graceful and lifelike than any others I have seen on antique vases. Some of these inlaid pictures represented love scenes with a child-like simplicity and freedom of manner which would not commend itself to the taste of the present day. Others again were pictures of maidens dancing, and yet others of hunting scenes. For instance, the very vase from which we were then drinking had on one side a most spirited drawing of men, apparently white in color, attacking a bull elephant with spears, while on the reverse was a picture, not quite so well done, of a hunter shooting an arrow at a running antelope, I should say from the look of it either an eland or a koodoo.

This is a digression at a critical moment, but it is not too long for the occasion, for the occasion itself was very long. With the exception of the periodical passing of the vase, and the movement necessary to throw fuel onto the fire, nothing happened for the best part of a whole hour. Nobody spoke a word. There we all sat in perfect silence, staring at the glare and glow of the large fire, and at the shadows thrown by the flickering earthenware lamps (which, by the way, were not ancient). On the open space between us and the fire lay a large wooden tray, with four short handles to it, exactly like a butcher's tray, only not hollowed out. By the side of the tray was a great pair of long-handled iron pincers, and on the other side of the fire was a similar pair. Somehow I did not at all like the appearance of this tray and the accompanying pincers. There I sat and stared at them and at the silent circle of the fierce moody faces of the men, and reflected that it was all very awful, and that we were absolutely in the power of this alarming people, who, to me at any rate, were all the more formidable because their true character was still very much of a mystery to us. They might be better than I thought them, or they might be worse. I feared that they were worse, and I was not wrong. It was a curious sort of a feast, I reflected, in appearance, indeed, an entertainment of the Barmecide stamp, for there was absolutely nothing to eat.

At last, just as I was beginning to feel as though I were being mesmerized, a move was made. Without the slightest warning, a man from the other side of the circle called out in a loud voice, "Where is the flesh that we shall eat?"

Thereon everybody in the circle answered in a deep measured tone, and stretching out the right arm towards the fire as he spoke: "*The flesh will come.*"

"Is it a goat?" said the same man.

It is a goat without horns, and more than a goat, and we shall slay it," they answered with one voice, and turning halt round they one and all grasped the handles of their spears with the right hand, and then simultaneously let them go.

"Is it an ox?" said the man again.

"*It is an ox without horns, and more than an ox, and we*

shall slay it," was the answer, and again the spears were grasped, and again let go.

Then came a pause, and I noticed, with horror and a rising of the hair, that the woman next to Mahomed began to fondle him, patting his cheeks, and calling him by names of endearment, while her fierce eyes played up and down his trembling form. I do not know why the sight frightened me so, but it did frighten us all dreadfully, especially Leo.

The caressing was so snakelike, and so evidently a part of some ghastly formula that had to be gone through.[1] I saw Mahomed turn white under his brown skin, sickly white with fear.

"Is the meat ready to be cooked?" asked the voice more rapidly.

"It is ready; it is ready."

"Is the pot hot to cook it?" it continued, in a sort or scream that echoed painfully down the great recesses of the cave.

"It is hot; it is hot"

"Great heavens!" roared Leo. "Remember the writing, *'The people who place pots upon the heads of strangers.'"*

As he said the words, before we could stir, or even take the matter in, two great ruffians jumped up, and, seizing the long pincers, plunged them into the heart of the fire, and the woman who had been caressing Mahomed suddenly produced a fiber noose from under her girdle or moocha, and, slipping it over his shoulders, ran it tight, while the men next him seized him by the legs. The two men with the pincers gave a heave, and, scattering the fire this way and that upon the rocky floor, lifted from it a large earthenware pot, heated to a white heat. In an instant, almost with a single movement, they had reached the spot where Mahomed was struggling. He fought like a fiend, shrieking in the abandonment of his despair, and notwithstanding the noose round him, and the efforts of the men who held his legs, the advancing wretches were for the moment unable to accomplish their purpose, which, horrible and incredible as it seems, was *to put the red-hot pot upon his head.*

1 We afterwards learned that its object was to pretend to the victim that he was the object of love and admiration, and so to soothe his injured feelings, and cause him to expire in a happy and contented frame of mind. – L. H. H.

I sprang to my feet with a yell of horror, and drawing my revolver fired it by a sort of instinct straight at the diabolical woman who had been caressing Mahomed, and was now gripping him in her arms. The bullet struck her in the back and killed her, and to this day I am glad that it did, for, as it afterwards transpired, she had availed herself of the anthropophagous customs of the Amahagger to organize the whole thing in revenge of the slight put upon her by Job. She sank down dead, and as she did so, to my terror and dismay, Mahomed, by a superhuman effort, burst from his tormentors, and, springing high into the air, fell dying upon her corpse. The heavy bullet from my pistol had driven through the bodies of both, at once striking down the murderess, and saving her victim from a death a hundred times more horrible. It was an awful and yet a most merciful accident.

For a moment there was a silence of astonishment. The Amahagger had never heard the report of a firearm before, and its effects dismayed them. But the next a man close to us recovered himself, and seized his spear preparatory to making a lunge with it at Leo, who was the nearest to him.

"Run for it!" I shouted, setting the example by starting up the cave as hard as my legs would carry me. I would have made for the open air if it had been possible, but there were men in the way, and, besides, I had caught sight of the forms of a crowd of people standing out clear against the skyline beyond the entrance to the cave. Up the cave I went, and after me came the others, and after them thundered the whole crowd of cannibals, mad with fury at the death of the woman. With a bound I cleared the prostrate form of Mahomed. As I flew over him I felt the heat from the red-hot pot, which was lying close by, strike upon my legs, and by its glow saw his hands – for he was not quite dead – still feebly moving. At the top of the cave was a little platform of rock three feet or so high by about eight deep, on which two large lamps were placed at night. Whether this platform had been left as a seat, or as a raised point afterwards to be cut away when it had served its purpose as a standing-place from which to carry on the excavations, I do not know – at least, I did not then. At any rate, we all three reached it, and, jumping on it, prepared to sell our lives as dearly as we could. For a few seconds the crowd that was pressing on our heels hung back when they saw us face round upon them. Job was on one side of the rock to the left, Leo in the center, and I to the right. Behind us were the lamps. Leo bent forward, and looked down the long lane of shadows, terminated in the fire and lighted lamps, through which the quiet forms of our would-be murderers flitted to and fro with the faint light glinting on their spears, for even their fury was silent as a bulldog's. The only other thing visible was the red-hot pot still glowing angrily in the gloom. There was a curious light in Leo's eyes, and his handsome face was set like a stone. In his right hand was his heavy hunting knife. He shifted its thong a little up his wrist, and then put his arm round me and gave me a good hug.

"Good-by, old fellow," he said, "my dear friend – my more than father. We have no chance against those scoundrels; they will finish us in a few minutes, and eat us afterwards, I suppose. Good-by. I led you into this. I hope you will forgive me. Good-by, Job."

"God's will be done," I said, setting my teeth, as I prepared for the end. At that moment, with an exclamation, Job lifted his revolver and fired, and hit a man – not the man he had aimed at, by the way: anything that Job shot *at* was perfectly safe.

On they came with a rush, and I fired too as fast as I could, and checked them – between us, Job and I, besides the woman, killed or mortally wounded five men with our pistols before they were emptied. But we had no time to reload, and they still came on in a way that was almost splendid in its recklessness, seeing that they did not know but that we could go on firing forever.

A great fellow bounded up upon the platform, and Leo struck him dead with one blow of his powerful arm, sending the knife right through him. I did the same by another, but Job missed his stroke, and I saw a brawny Amahagger grip him by the middle and whirl him off the rock. The knife, not being secured by a thong, fell from Job's hand as he did so, and, by a most happy accident for him, lit upon its handle on the rock, just as the body of the Amahagger, being undermost, hit upon its point and was transfixed upon it. What happened to Job after that I am sure I do not know, but my own impression is that he lay still upon the corpse of his deceased assailant, "playing 'possum" as the Americans say. As for myself, I was soon involved in a desperate encounter with two ruffians who, luckily for me, had left their spears behind them; and for the first time in my life the great physical power with which Nature has endowed me stood me in good stead, I had hacked at the head of one man with my hunting knife, which was almost as big and heavy as a short sword, with such vigor that the sharp steel had split his skull down to the eyes, and was held so fast by it that as he suddenly fell sideways the knife was twisted right out of my hand.

Then it was that the two others sprang upon me. I saw them coming, and got an arm round the waist of each, and down we all fell upon the floor of the cave together, rolling over and over. They were strong men, but I was mad with rage, and that awful lust for slaughter which will creep into the hearts of the most civilized of us when blows are flying, and life and death tremble on the turn. My arms were round the two swarthy demons, and I hugged them till I heard their ribs crack and crunch up beneath my grip. They twisted and writhed like snakes, and clawed and battered at me with their fists, but I held on. Lying on my back there, so that their bodies might protect me from spear thrusts from above, I slowly crushed the life out of them, and as I did so, strange as it may seem, I thought of what the amiable head of my college at Cambridge (who is a member of the Peace Society) and my brother fellows would say if by clairvoyance they could see me, of all men, playing such a bloody game. Soon my assailants grew faint, and almost ceased to struggle, their breath had failed them, and they were dying, but still I dared not leave them, for they died very slowly. I knew that if I relaxed my grip they would revive. The other ruffians probably thought – for we were all three lying in the shadow of the ledge – that we were all dead together; at any rate they did not interfere with our little tragedy.

I turned my head, and as I lay gasping in the throes of that awful struggle I could see that Leo was off the rock now, for the lamplight fell full upon him. He was still on his feet, but in the center of a surging mass of struggling men, who were striving to pull him down as wolves pull down a stag. Up above them towered his beautiful pale face crowned with its bright curls (for Leo is six feet two high), and I saw that he was fighting with a desperate abandonment and energy that was at once splendid and hideous to behold. He drove his knife through one man – they were so close to him and mixed up with him that they could not get at him to kill him with their big spears, and they had no knives or sticks. The man fell, and then somehow the knife was wrenched twin his hand, leaving him defenseless, and I thought the end had come. But no; with a desperate effort he broke loose from them, seized the body of the man he had just slain, and lifting it high in the air hurled it right at the mob of his assailants, so that the shock and weight of it swept some five or six of them to the earth. But in a minute they were all up again, except one, whose skull was smashed, and had once more fastened upon him. And then slowly, and with infinite labor and struggling, the wolves bore the lion down. Once even then he recovered himself, and felled an Amahagger with his fist, but it was more than man could do to hold his own for long against so many, and at last he came crashing down upon the rock floor, falling as an oak falls, and bearing with him to the earth all those who clung about him. They gripped him by his arms and legs, and then cleared off his body.

"A spear," cried a voice, "a spear to cut his throat, and a vessel to catch his blood."

I shut my eyes, for I saw the man coming with a spear, and myself, I could not stir to Leo's help, for I was growing weak, and the two men on me were not yet dead, and a deadly sickness overcame me.

Then suddenly there was a disturbance, and involuntarily I opened my eyes again, and looked towards the scene of murder. The girl Ustane had thrown herself on Leo's prostrate form, covering his body with her body, and fastening her arms about his neck. They tried to drag her from him, but she twisted her legs round his, and hung on like a bulldog, or rather like a creeper to a tree, and they could not. Then they tried to stab him in the side without hurting her, but somehow she shielded him, and he was only wounded.

At last they lost patience.

"Drive the spear through the man and the woman together," said a voice, the same voice that had asked the questions at that ghastly feast, "so of a verity shall they be wed."

Then I saw the man with the weapon straighten himself for the effort. I saw the cold steel gleam on high, and once more I shut my eyes.

As I did so I heard the voice of a man thunder out in tones that rang and echoed down the rocky ways: *"Cease!"*

Then I fainted, and as I did so it flashed through my darkening mind that I was passing down into the last oblivion of death.

Chapter 9

A Little Foot

WHEN I OPENED my eyes again I found myself lying on a skin mat not far from the fire round which we had been gathered for that dreadful feast. Near me lay Leo, still apparently in a swoon, and over him was bending the tall form of the girl Ustane, who was washing a deep spear wound in his side with cold water preparatory to binding it up with linen. Leaning against the wall of the cave behind her was Job, apparently uninjured, but bruised and trembling. On the other side of the fire, tossed about this way and that, as though they had thrown themselves down to sleep in some moment of absolute exhaustion, were the bodies of those whom we had killed in our frightful struggle for life. I counted them: there were twelve besides the woman, and the corpse of poor Mahomed, who had died by my hand, which, the fire-stained pot at its side, was placed at the end of the irregular line. To the left a body of men were engaged in binding the arms of the surviving cannibals behind them, and then fastening them two and two. The villains were submitting with a look of sulky indifference upon their faces which accorded ill with the baffled fury that gleamed in their somber eyes. In front of these men, directing the operations, stood no other than our friend Billali, looking rather tired, but particularly patriarchal with his flowing beard, and as cool and unconcerned as though he were superintending the cutting up of an ox.

Presently he turned, and perceiving that I was sitting up advanced to me, and with the utmost courtesy said that he trusted that I felt better. I answered that at present I scarcely knew how I felt, except that I ached all over.

Then he bent down and examined Leo's wound.

"It is a nasty cut," he said, "but the spear has not pierced the entrails. He will recover."

"Thanks to thy arrival, my father," I answered. "In another minute we should all have been beyond the reach of recovery, for those devils of thine would have slain us as they would have slain our servant," and I pointed towards Mahomed.

The old man ground his teeth, and I saw an extraordinary expression of malignity light up his eyes.

"Fear not, my son," he answered. "Vengeance shall be taken on them such as would make the flesh twist upon the bones merely to hear of it. To *She* shall they go, and her vengeance shall be worthy of her greatness. That man" – pointing to Mahomed – "I tell thee that man would have died a merciful death to the death these hyena men shall die. Tell me, I pray of thee, how it came about."

In a few words I sketched what had happened.

"Ah, so," he answered. "Thou seest, my son, here there is a custom that if a stranger comes into this country he may be slain by 'the pot,' and eaten."

"It is hospitality turned upside down," I answered feebly. "In our country we entertain a stranger, and give him food to eat. Here ye eat him, and are entertained."

"It is a custom," he answered with a shrug. "Myself I think it an evil one; but then," he added as an afterthought, "I do not like the taste of strangers, especially after they have wandered through the swamps and lived on wildfowl. When *'She-who-must-be-obeyed'* sent orders that ye were to be saved alive she said naught of the black man, therefore, being hyenas, these men lusted after his flesh, and the woman it was, whom thou didst rightly slay, who put it into their evil hearts to hot-pot him. Well, they will have their reward. Better for them would it be if they had never seen the light than that they should stand before *She* in her terrible anger. Happy are those of them who died by your hands.

"Ah," he went on, "it was a gallant fight that ye fought. Knowest thou, that thou, long-armed old baboon that thou art, hast crushed in the ribs of those two who are laid out there as though they were but as the shell on an egg? And the young one, the lion, it was a beautiful stand that he made – one against so many – three did he slay outright, and that one "there" – and he pointed to a body that was still moving a little – "will die anon, for his head is cracked across, and others of these who are bound are hurt. It was a gallant fight, and thou and he have made a friend of me by it, for I love to see a well-fought fray. But tell me, my son, the baboon – and now I think of it thy face, too, is hairy, and altogether like a baboon's – how was it that ye slew those with a hole in them? Ye made a noise, they say, and slew them – they fell down on their faces at the noise?"

I explained to him as well as I could, but very shortly – I was terribly wearied, and only persuaded to talk at all through fear of offending one so powerful if I refused to do so – what were the properties of gunpowder, and he instantly suggested that I should illustrate what I said by operating on the person of one of the prisoners. One, he said, never would be counted, and it would not only be very interesting to him, but would give me an opportunity of an installment of revenge. He was greatly astounded when I told him that it was not our custom to avenge ourselves in cold blood, and that we left vengeance to the law and a higher power, of which he knew nothing. I added, however, that when I recovered I would take him out shooting with us, and he should kill an animal for himself, and at this he was as pleased as a child at the promise of a new toy.

Just then Leo opened his eyes beneath the stimulus of some brandy (of which we still had a little) that Job had poured down his throat, and our conversation came to an end.

After this we managed to get Leo, who was in a very poor way indeed, and only half-conscious, safely off to bed, supported by Job and that brave girl Ustane, to whom, had I not been afraid she might resent it, I would certainly have given a kiss for her splendid behavior in saving my dear boy's life at the risk of her own. But Ustane was not the sort of young person with whom one would care to take liberties unless one were perfectly certain that they would not be misunderstood, so I repressed my inclinations. Then, bruised and battered, but with a sense of safety in my breast to which I had for some days been a stranger, I crept off to my own little sepulcher, not forgetting before I lay down in it to thank Providence from the bottom of my heart that it was not a sepulcher indeed, as were it not for a merciful combination of events that I can only attribute to its protection, it would certainly have been for me that night. Few men have been nearer their end and yet escaped it than we were on that dreadful day.

I am a bad sleeper at the best of times, and my dreams that night when at last I got to rest were not of the pleasantest. The awful vision of poor Mahomed struggling to escape the red-hot pot would haunt them, and then in the background, as it were, a veiled form was always hovering, which, from time to time, seemed to draw the coverings from its body, revealing now the perfect shape of a lovely blooming woman, and now again the white bones of a grinning skeleton, and which, as it veiled and unveiled, uttered the mysterious and apparently meaningless sentence: '*That which is alive hath known death, and that which is dead yet can never die, for in the Circle of the Spirit life is naught and death is naught. Yea, all things live forever, though at times they sleep and are forgotten.*'

The morning came at last, but when it came I found that I was too stiff and sore to rise. About seven Job arrived, limping terribly, and with his face the color of a rotten apple, and told me that Leo had slept fairly, but was very weak. Two hours afterwards Billali (Job called him "Billy-goat," to which, indeed, his white beard gave him some resemblance, or more familiarly "Billy") came too, bearing a lamp in his hand, his towering form reaching nearly to the roof of the little chamber. I pretended to be asleep, and through the cracks of my eyelids watched his sardonic but handsome old face. He fixed his hawklike eyes upon me, and stroked his glorious white beard, which, by the way, would have been worth a hundred a year to any London barber as an advertisement.

"Ah!" I heard him mutter (Billali had a habit of muttering to himself), "he is ugly – ugly as the other is beautiful – a very Baboon, it was a good name. But I like the man. Strange now, at my age, that I should like a man. What says the proverb – 'Mistrust all men, and slay him whom thou mistrustest overmuch; and as for women, flee from them, for they are evil, and in the end will destroy thee.' It is a good proverb, especially the last part of it: I think it must have come down from the ancients. Nevertheless I like this Baboon, and I wonder where they taught him his tricks, and I trust that *She* will not bewitch him. Poor Baboon! He must be wearied after that fight. I will go lest I should awake him."

I waited till he had turned and was nearly through the entrance, walking softly on tiptoe, and then I called after him.

"My father," I said, "is it thou?"

"Yes, my son, it is I; but let me not disturb thee. I did but come to see how thou didst fare, and to tell thee that those who would have slain thee, my Baboon, are by now well on their road to *She*. *She* said that ye also were to come at once, but I fear ye cannot yet."

"Nay," I said; "not till we have recovered a little; but have me borne out into the daylight, I pray thee, my father. I love not this place."

"Ah, no," he answered, "it hath a sad air. I remember when I was a boy I found the body of a fair woman lying where thou liest now, yes, on that very bench. She was so beautiful that I was wont to creep in hither with a lamp and gaze upon her. Had it not been for her cold hands, almost could I think that she slept and would one day awake, so fair and peaceful was she in her robes of white. White was she, too, and her hair was yellow and lay down her almost to the feet. There are many such still in the tombs at the place where *She* is, for those who set them there had a way I know naught of, whereby to keep their beloved out of the crumbling hand of Decay, even when Death had slain them. Ay, day by day I came hither, and gazed on her till at last – laugh not at me, stranger, for I was but a silly lad – I learned to love that dead form, that shell which once had held a life that no more is. I would creep up to her and kiss her cold face, and wonder how many men had lived and died since she was, and who had loved her and embraced her in the days that long had passed away. And, my Baboon, I think I learned wisdom from that dead one, for of a truth it taught me of the littleness of life, and the length of Death, and how all things that are under the sun go down one path, and are forever forgotten. And so I mused, and it seemed to me that wisdom flowed into me from the dead, till one day my mother, a watchful woman, but hasty-minded, seeing I was changed, followed me, and saw the beautiful white one, and feared that I was bewitched, as, indeed, I was. So half in dread, and half in anger, she took the lamp, and standing the dead woman up against the wall there, set fire to her hair, and she burned fiercely, even down to the feet, for those who are thus kept burn excellently well.

"See, my son, there on the roof is yet the smoke of her burning."

I looked up doubtfully, and there, sure enough, on the roof of the sepulcher, was a peculiarly unctuous and sooty mark, three feet or more across. Doubtless it had in the course of years been rubbed off the sides of the little cave, but on the roof it remained, and there was no mistaking its appearance.

"She burned," he went on in a meditative way, "even to the feet, but the feet I came back and saved, cutting the burned bone from them, and hid them under the stone bench there, wrapped up in a piece of linen. Surely, I remember it as though it were but yesterday. Perchance they are there if none have found them, even to this hour. Of a truth I have not entered this chamber from that time to this very day. Stay, I will look," and, kneeling down, he groped about with his long arm in the recess under the stone bench. Presently his face brightened, and with an exclamation he pulled something forth that was caked in dust; which he shook onto the floor. It was covered with the remains of a rotting rag, which he undid, and revealed to my astonished gaze a beautifully shaped and almost white woman's foot, looking as fresh and as firm as though it had but now been placed there.

"Thou seest, my son, the Baboon," he said, in a sad voice, "I spake the truth to thee, for here is yet one foot remaining. Take it, my son, and gaze upon it."

I took this cold fragment of mortality in my hand and looked at it in the light of the lamp with feelings which I cannot describe, so mixed up were they between astonishment, fear, and fascination. It was light, much lighter I should say than it had been in the living state, and the flesh to all appearance was still flesh, though about it there clung a faintly aromatic odor. For the rest it was not shrunk or shriveled, or even black and unsightly, like the flesh of Egyptian mummies, but plump and fair, and, except where it had been slightly burned, perfect as on the day of death – a very triumph of embalming.

Poor little foot! I set it down upon the stone bench where it had lain for so many thousand years, and wondered whose was the beauty that it had upborne through the pomp and pageantry of a forgotten civilization – first as a merry child's, then as a blushing maid's, and lastly as a perfect woman's. Through what halls of Life had its soft step echoed, and in the end, with what courage had it trodden down the dusty ways of Death! To whose side had it stolen in the hush of night when the black slave slept upon the marble floor, and who had listened for its stealing? Shapely little foot! Well might it have been set upon the proud neck of a conqueror bent at last to woman's beauty, and well might the lips of nobles and of kings have been pressed upon its jeweled whiteness.

I wrapped up this relic of the past in the remnants of the old linen rag which had evidently formed a portion of its owner's graveclothes, for it was partially burned, and put it away in my

Gladstone bag, which I had bought at the Army and Navy Stores – a strange combination, I thought. Then with Billali's help I staggered off to see Leo. I found him dreadfully bruised, worse even than myself, perhaps owing to the excessive whiteness of his skin, and faint and weak with the loss of blood from the flesh wound in his side, but for all that cheerful as a cricket, and asking for some breakfast. Job and Ustane got him onto the bottom, or rather the sacking of a litter, which was removed from its pole for that purpose, and with the aid of old Billali carried him out into the shade at the mouth of the cave, from which, by the way, every trace of the slaughter of the previous night had now been removed, and there we all breakfasted, and indeed spent that day, and most of the two following ones.

On the third morning Job and myself were practically recovered. Leo also was so much better that I yielded to Billali's often expressed entreaty, and agreed to start at once upon our journey to Kôr, which we were told was the name of the place where the mysterious *She* lived, though I still feared for its effects, upon Leo, and especially lest the motion should cause his wound, which was scarcely skinned over, to break open again. Indeed, had it not been for Billali's evident anxiety to get off, which led us to suspect that some difficulty or danger might threaten us if we did not comply with it, I would not have consented to go.

Chapter 10

Speculations

WITHIN AN HOUR of our finally deciding to start, five litters were brought up to the door of the cave, each accompanied by four regular bearers and two spare hands, also a band of about fifty armed Amahagger, who were to form the escort and carry the baggage. Three of these litters, of course, were for us, and one for Billali, who, I was immensely relieved to hear, was to be our companion, while the fifth I presumed was for the use of Ustane.

"Does the lady go with us, my father?" I asked of Billali, as he stood superintending things generally.

He shrugged his shoulders as he answered, "If she wills. In this country the women do what they please. We worship them, and give them their way, because without them the world could not go on; they are the source of life."

"Ah," I said, the matter never having struck me quite in that light before.

"We worship them," he went on, "up to a certain point, till at last they get unbearable, which," he added, "they do about every second generation."

"And then what do you do?" I asked with curiosity.

"Then," he answered with a faint smile, "we rise, and kill the old ones as an example to the young ones, and to show them that we are the strongest. My poor wife was killed in that way three years ago. It was very sad, but to tell thee the truth, my son, life has been happier since, for my age protects me from the young ones."

"In short," I replied, quoting the saying of a great man whose wisdom has not yet lightened the darkness of the Amahagger, "thou hast found thy position one of greater freedom and less responsibility."

This phrase puzzled him a little at first from its vagueness, though I think my translation hit off its sense very well, but at last he saw it, and appreciated it.

"Yes, yes, my Baboon," he said, "I see it now, but all the 'responsibilities' are killed, at least some of them are, and that is why there are so few old women about just now. Well, they brought it on themselves. As for this girl," 'he went on, in a graver tone, "I know not what to say. She is a brave girl, and she loves the Lion [Leo], thou sawest how she clung to him, and saved his life. Also, she is, according to our custom, wed to him, and has a right to go where he goes, unless," he added significantly, "*She* would say her no, for her word overrides all rights."

"And if *She* bade her leave him, and the girl refused?"

"What then?"

"If," he said with a shrug, "the hurricane bids the tree to bend, and it will not, what happens?"

And then, without waiting for an answer, he turned and walked to his litter, and in ten minutes from that time we were all well under way.

It took us an hour and more to cross the cup of the volcanic plain, and another half hour or so to climb the edge on the farther side. Once there, however, the view was a very fine one. Before us was a long steep slope of grassy plain, broken here and there by clumps of trees mostly of the thorn tribe. At the bottom of this gentle slope, some nine or ten miles away, we could make out a dim sea of marsh, over which the foul vapors hung like smoke about a city. It was easy going for the Bearers down the slopes, and by midday we had reached the borders of the dismal swamp. Here we halted to eat our midday meal, and then, following a winding and devious path, plunged into the morass. Presently the path, at any rate to our unaccustomed eyes, grew so faint as to be almost indistinguishable from those made by the aquatic beasts and birds, and it is to this day a mystery to me how our bearers found their way across the marshes. Ahead of the cavalcade marched two men with long poles, which they now and again plunged into the ground before them, the reason of this being that the nature of the soil frequently changed from causes with which I am not acquainted, so that places which might be safe enough to cross one month would certainly swallow the wayfarer the next. Never did I see a more dreary and depressing scene. Miles on miles of quagmire, varied only by bright green strips of comparatively solid ground, and by deep and sullen pools fringed with tall rushes, in which the bitterns boomed and the frogs croaked incessantly: miles on miles of it without a break, unless the fever fog can be called a break. The only life in this great morass was that of the aquatic birds, and the animals that fed on them, of both of which there were vast numbers. Geese, cranes, ducks, teal, coot, snipe, and plover swarmed all around us, many being of varieties that were quite new to me, and all so tame that one could almost have knocked them over with a stick. Among these birds I especially noticed a very beautiful variety of painted snipe, almost the size of woodcock, and with a flight more resembling that bird's than an English snipe's. In the pools, too, was a species of small alligator or enormous iguana, I do not know which, that fed, Billali told me, upon the waterfowl, also large quantities of a hideous black water snake, of which the bite is very dangerous, though not, I gathered, so deadly as a cobra's or a puff adder's. The bullfrogs were also very large, and with voices proportionate, to their size; and as for the mosquitoes – the 'musqueteers,' as Job called them – they were, if possible, even worse than they had been on the river, and tormented us greatly. Undoubtedly, however, the worst feature of the swamp was the awful smell of rotting vegetation that hung about it, which was at times positively overpowering, and the malarious exhalations that accompanied it, which we were of course obliged to breathe.

On we went through it all, till at last the sun sank in sullen splendor just as we reached a spot of rising ground about two acres in extent – a little oasis of dry in the midst of the miry wilderness – where Billali announced that we were to camp. The camping, however, turned out to be a very simple process, and consisted, in fact, in sitting down on the ground round a scanty fire made of dry reeds and some wood that had been brought with us. However, we made the best we could of it, and smoked and ate with such appetite as the smell of damp, stifling heat would allow, for it was very hot on this low land, and yet, oddly enough, chilly at times. But, however hot it was, we were glad enough to keep near the fire, because we found that the mosquitoes did not like the smoke. Presently we rolled ourselves up in our blankets and tried to go to sleep, but so far as I was concerned the bullfrogs, and the extraordinary roaring and alarming sound produced by hundreds of snipe hovering high in the air, made sleep an impossibility, to say nothing of our other discomforts. I turned and looked at Leo, who was next me; he was dozing, but his face had a flushed appearance that I did not like, and by the flickering firelight I saw Ustane, who was lying on the other side of him, raise herself from time to time upon her elbow, and look at him anxiously enough.

However, I could do nothing for him, for we had all already taken a good dose of quinine, which was the only preventive we had; so I lay and watched the stars come out by thousands, till all the immense arch of heaven was sewn with glittering points, and every point a world! Here was a glorious sight by which man might well measure his own insignificance! Soon I gave up thinking about it, for the mind wearies easily when it strives to grapple with the Infinite, and to trace the footsteps of the Almighty as he strides from sphere to sphere, or deduce His purpose from His works. Such things are not for us to know. Knowledge is to the strong, and we are weak. Too much wisdom would perchance blind our imperfect sight, and too much strength would make us drunk, and overweight our feeble reason till it fell, and we were drowned in the depths of our own vanity. For what is the first result of man's increased knowledge interpreted from Nature's book by the persistent effort of his purblind observation? Is it not but too often to make him question the existence of his Maker, or indeed of any intelligent purpose beyond his own? The truth is veiled, because we could no more look upon her glory than we can upon the sun. It would destroy us. Full knowledge is not for man as man is here, for his capacities, which he is apt to think so great, are indeed but small. The vessel is soon filled, and, were one-thousandth part of the unutterable and silent wisdom that directs the rolling of those shining spheres, and the force which makes them roll, pressed into it, it would be shattered into fragments. Perhaps in some other place and time it may be otherwise, who can tell? Here the lot of man born of the flesh is but to endure midst toil and tribulation, to catch at the bubbles blown by fate, which he calls pleasures, thankful if before they burst they rest a moment in his hand, and when the tragedy is played out, and his hour comes to perish, to pass humbly whither he knows not.

Above me, as I lay, shone the eternal stars, and there at my feet the impish marsh-born balls of fire rolled this way and that, vapor-tossed and earth-desiring, and me-thought that in the two I saw a type and image of what man is, and what perchance man may one day be, if the living Force who ordained him and them should so ordain this also. Oh, that it might be ours to rest year by year upon that high level of the heart to which at times we momentarily attain! Oh, that we could shake loose the prisoned pinions of the soul and soar to that superior point, whence, like to some traveler looking out through space from Darien's giddiest peak, we might gaze with the spiritual eyes of noble thoughts deep into Infinity!

What would it be to cast off this earthy robe, to have done forever with these earthy thoughts and miserable desires; no longer, like those corpse candles, to be tossed this way and that, by forces beyond our control; or which, if we can theoretically control them, we are at times driven by the exigencies of our nature to obey! Yes, to cast them off, to have done with the foul and thorny places of the world; and, like to those glittering points above me, to rest on high wrapped forever in the brightness of our better selves, that even now shines in us as fire faintly shines within those lurid balls, and lay down our littleness in that wide glory of our dreams, that invisible but surrounding good, from which all truth and beauty comes!

These and many such thoughts passed through my mind that night. They come to torment us all at times. I say to torment, for, alas, thinking can only serve to measure out the helplessness of thought. What is the use of our feeble crying in the awful silences of space? Can our dim intelligence read the secrets of that star-strewn sky? Does any answer come out of it? Never any at all, nothing but echoes and fantastic visions. And yet we believe that there is an answer, and that upon a time a new Dawn will come blushing down the ways of our enduring night. We believe it, for its reflected beauty even now shines up continually in our hearts from beneath the horizon of the grave, and we call it Hope. Without Hope we should suffer moral death, and by the help of Hope we yet may climb to Heaven, or at the worst, if she also prove but a kindly mockery given to hold us from despair, be gently lowered into the abysses of eternal sleep.

Then I fell to reflecting upon the undertaking on which we were bent, and what a wild one it was, and yet how strangely the story seemed to fit in with what had been written centuries ago upon the sherd. Who was this extraordinary woman, queen over a people apparently as extraordinary as herself, and reigning amidst the vestiges of a lost civilization? And what was the meaning of this story of the Fire that gave unending life? Could it be possible that any fluid or essence should exist which might so fortify these fleshy walls that they should from age to age resist the mines and batterings of decay? It was possible, though not probable. The indefinite continuation of life would not, as poor

Vincey said, be so marvelous a thing as the production of life and its temporary endurance. And if it were true, what then? The person who found it could no doubt rule the world. He could accumulate all the wealth in the world, and all the power, and all the wisdom that is power. He might give a lifetime to the study of each art or science. Well, if that were so, and this *She* were practically immortal, which I did not for one moment believe, how was it that, with all these things at her feet, she preferred to remain in a cave among a society of cannibals? This surely settled the question. The whole story was monstrous, and only worthy of the superstitious days in which it was written. At any rate I was very sure that I would not attempt to attain unending life. I had had far too many worries and disappointments and secret bitternesses during my forty-odd years of existence to wish that this state of affairs should be continued indefinitely. And yet I suppose that my life has been, comparatively speaking, a happy one.

And then, reflecting that at the present moment there was far more likelihood of our earthly careers being cut exceedingly short than of their being unduly prolonged, I at last managed to get to sleep, a fact for which anybody who reads this narrative, if anybody ever does, may very probably be thankful.

When I woke again it was just dawning, and the guard and bearers were moving about like ghosts through the dense morning mists, getting ready for our start. The fire had died quite down, and I rose and stretched myself, shivering in every limb from the damp cold of the dawn. Then I looked at Leo. He was sitting up, holding his hands to his head, and I saw that his face was flushed and his eye bright, and yet yellow round the pupil.

"Well, Leo," I said, "how do you feel?"

"I feel as though I were going to die," he answered hoarsely. "My head is splitting, my body is trembling, and I am as sick as a cat."

I whistled, or if I did not whistle I felt inclined to – Leo had got a sharp attack of fever. I went to Job and asked him for the quinine, of which fortunately we had still a good supply, only to find that Job himself was not much better. He complained of pains across the back, and dizziness, and was almost incapable of helping himself. Then I did the only thing it was possible to do under the circumstances – gave them both about ten grains of quinine, and took a slightly smaller dose myself as a matter of precaution. After that I found Billali, and explained to him how matters stood, asking at the same time what he thought had best be done. He came with me, and looked at Leo and Job (whom, by the way, he had named the Pig on account of his fatness, round face, and small eyes).

"Ah," he said, when we were out of earshot, "the fever! I thought so. The Lion has it badly, but he is young, and he may live. As for the Pig, his attack is not so bad; it is the 'little fever' which he has; that always begins with pains across the back, it will spend itself upon his fat."

"Can they go on, my father?" I asked.

"Nay, my son, they must go on. If they stop here they will certainly die; also, they will be better in the litters than on the ground. By tonight, if all goes well, we shall be across the marsh and in good air. Come, let us lift them into the litters and start, for it is very bad to stand still in this morning fog. We can eat our meal as we go."

This we accordingly did, and with a heavy heart I once more set out upon our strange journey. For the first three hours all went as well as could be expected, and then an accident happened that nearly lost us the pleasure of the company of our venerable friend Billali, whose litter was leading the cavalcade. We were going through a particularly dangerous stretch of quagmire, in which the bearers sometimes sank up to their knees. Indeed, it was a mystery to me how they contrived to carry the heavy litters at all over such ground as that which we were traversing, though the two spare hands, as well as the four regular ones, had of course to put their shoulders to the pole.

Presently, as we blundered and floundered along, there was a sharp cry, then a storm of exclamations, and, last of all, a most tremendous splash, and the whole caravan halted.

I jumped out of my litter and ran forward. About twenty yards ahead was the edge of one of those sullen peaty pools of which I have spoken, the path we were following running along the top of its bank, which, as it happened, was a steep one. Looking towards this pool, to my horror I saw that Billali's litter was floating on it, and as for Billali himself, he was nowhere to be seen. To make matters clear I may as well explain at once what had happened. One of Billali's bearers had unfortunately trodden on a basking snake, which had bitten him in the leg, whereon he had, not unnaturally, let go of the pole, and then, finding that he was tumbling down the bank, grasped at the litter to save himself. The result of this was what might have been expected. The litter was pulled over the edge of the bank, the bearers let go, and the whole thing, including Billali and the man who had been bitten, rolled into the slimy pool. When I got to the edge of the water neither of them was to be seen, and, indeed, the unfortunate bearer never was seen again. Either he struck his head against something, or got wedged in the mud, or possibly the snake bite paralyzed him. At any rate, he vanished. But though Billali was not to be seen, his whereabouts was clear enough from the agitation of the floating litter, in the bearing cloth and curtains of which he was entangled.

"He is there! Our father is there!" said one of the men, but he did not stir a finger to help him, nor did any of the others. They simply stood and stared at the water.

"Out of the way, you brutes," I shouted in English, and throwing off my hat I took a run and sprang well out into the horrid slimy-looking pool. A couple of strokes took me to where Billali was struggling beneath the cloth.

Somehow, I do not quite know how, I managed to push this

free of him, and his venerable head, all covered with green slime, like that of a yellowish Bacchus with ivy leaves, emerged upon the surface of the water. The rest was easy, for Billali was an eminently practical individual, and had the common sense not to grasp hold of me as drowning people often do, so I got him by the arm and towed him to the bank, through the mud of which we were with difficulty dragged. Such a filthy spectacle as we presented I have never seen before or since, and it will perhaps give some idea of the almost superhuman dignity of Billali's appearance when I say that, coughing, half-drowned, and covered with mud and green slime as he was, with his beautiful beard coming to a dripping point, like a Chinaman's freshly oiled pigtail, he still looked venerable and imposing.

"Ye dogs," he said, addressing the bearers, as soon as he had sufficiently recovered to speak, "ye left me, your father, to drown. Had it not been for this stranger, my son the Baboon, assuredly I should have drowned. Well, I will remember it," and he fixed them with his gleaming though slightly watery eye, in a way I saw they did not like, though they tried to appear sulkily indifferent.

"As for thee, my son," the old man went on, turning towards me and grasping my hand, "rest assured that I am thy friend through good and evil. Thou hast saved my life: perchance a day may come when I shall save thine."

After that we cleaned ourselves as best we could, fished out the litter, and went on, minus the man who had been drowned. I do not know if it was owing to his being an unpopular character, or from native indifference and selfishness of temperament, but I am bound to say that nobody seemed to grieve much over his sudden and final disappearance, unless, perhaps, it was the men who had to do his share of the work.

Chapter 11

The Plain of Kôr

About an hour before sundown we at last, to my unbounded gratitude, emerged from the great belt of marsh onto land that swelled upwards in a succession of rolling waves. Just on the hither side of the crest of the first wave we halted for the night. My first act was to examine Leo's condition. It was, if anything, worse than in the morning. and a new and very distressing feature, vomiting, set in, and continued till dawn. Not one wink of sleep did I get that night, for I passed it in assisting Ustane, who was one of the most gentle and indefatigable nurses I ever saw, to wait upon Leo and Job. However, the air here was warm and genial without being too hot, and there were no mosquitoes to speak of. Also, we were above the level of the marsh mist, which lay stretched beneath us like the dim smoke pall over a city, lit up here and there by the wandering globes of fen fire. Thus it will be seen that we were, speaking comparatively, in clover.

By dawn on the following morning Leo was quite lightheaded, and fancied that he was divided into halves. I was dreadfully distressed, and began to wonder with a sort of sick fear what the termination of the attack would be. Alas! I had heard but too much of how these attacks generally terminate. As I was doing so Billali came up and said that we must be getting on, more especially as, in his opinion, if Leo did not reach some spot where he could be quiet, and have proper nursing, within the next twelve hours, his life would only be a matter of a day or two. I could not but agree with him, so we got him into the litter, and started on, Ustane walking by Leo's side to keep the flies off him, and see that he did not throw himself out onto the ground.

Within half an hour of sunrise we had reached the top of the rise of which I have spoken, and a most beautiful view broke upon our gaze. Beneath us was a rich stretch of country, verdant with grass and lovely with foliage and flowers. In the background, at a distance, so far as I could judge, of some eighteen miles from where we then stood, a huge and extraordinary mountain rose abruptly from the plain. The base of this great mountain appeared to consist of a grassy slope, but rising from this, I should say, from subsequent observation, at a height of about five hundred feet above the level of the plain, was a most tremendous and absolutely precipitous wall of bare rock, quite twelve or fifteen hundred feet in height. The shape of the mountain, which was undoubtedly of volcanic origin, was round, and of course, as only a segment of its circle was visible, it was difficult to estimate its exact size, which was enormous. I afterwards discovered that it could not cover less than fifty square miles of ground. Anything more grand and imposing than the sight presented by this great natural castle, starting in solitary grandeur from the level of the plain, I never saw, and I suppose I never shall. Its very solitude added to its majesty, and its towering cliffs seemed to kiss the sky. Indeed, generally speaking, they were clothed in clouds that lay in fleecy masses upon their broad and level battlements.

I sat up in my hammock and gazed out across the plain at this thrilling and majestic sight, and I suppose that Billali noticed it, for he brought his litter alongside.

"Behold the House of *'She-who-must-be-obeyed'*!" he said. "Had ever a queen such a throne before?"

"It is wonderful, my father," I answered. "But how do we enter? Those cliffs look hard to climb."

"Thou shalt see, my Baboon. Look now at the plain below us. What thinkest thou that is? Thou art a wise man. Come, tell me."

I looked, and saw what appeared to be the line of roadway running straight towards the base of the mountain, though it was covered with turf. There were high banks on each side of it, broken here and there, but fairly continuous on the whole, the meaning of which I did not understand. It seemed so very odd that anybody should embank a roadway.

"Well, my father," I answered, "I suppose that it is a road, otherwise I should have been inclined to say that it was the bed of a river, or rather," I added, observing the extraordinary directness of the cutting, "of a canal."

Billali – who, by the way, was none the worse for his immersion of the day before – nodded his head sagely as he replied, "Thou art right, my son. It is a channel cut out by those who were before us in this place to carry away water. Of this am I sure: within the rocky circle of the great mountain whither we journey was once a great lake. But those who were before us, by wonderful arts of which I know naught, hewed a path for the water through the solid rock of the mountain, piercing even to the bed of the lake. But first they cut the channel that thou seest across the plain. Then, when at last the water burst out, it rushed down the channel that had been made to receive it, and crossed this plain till it reached the low land behind the rise, and there, perchance, it made the swamp through which we had come. Then when the lake was drained dry, the people whereof I speak built a mighty city, whereof naught but ruins and the name of Kôr yet remaineth, on its bed, and from age to age hewed the caves and passages that thou wilt see."

"It may be," I answered; "but if so, how is it that the lake does not fill up again with the rains and the water of the springs?"

"Nay, my son, the people were a wise people, and they left a drain to keep it clear. Seest thou the river to the right?" and he pointed to a fair-sized stream that wound away across the plain, some four miles from us. "That is the drain, and it comes out through the mountain wall where this cutting goes in. At first, perhaps, the water ran down this canal, but afterwards the people turned it, and used the cutting for a road."

"And is there then no other place where one may enter into the great mountain," I asked, "except through the drain?"

"There is a place," he answered, "where cattle and men on foot may cross with much labor, but it is secret. A year mightest thou search and shouldst never find it. It is only used once a year, when the herds of cattle that have been fatting on the slopes of the mountain, and on this plain, are driven into the space within."

"And does *She* live there always?" I asked, "or does she come at times without the mountain?"

"Nay, my son, where she is, there she is."

By now we were well onto the great plain, and I was examining with delight the varied beauty of its semitropical flowers and trees, the latter of which grew singly, or at most in clumps of three or four, much of the timber being of large size, and belonging apparently to a variety of evergreen oak. There were also many palms, some of them more than one hundred feet high, and the largest and most beautiful tree ferns that I ever saw, about which hung clouds of jeweled honeysuckers and great-winged butterflies. Wandering about among the trees or crouching in the long and feathered grass were all varieties of game, from rhinoceros down. I saw rhinoceros, buffalo (a large herd), eland, quagga, and sable antelope, the most beautiful of all the bucks, not to mention many smaller varieties of game, and three ostriches which scudded away at our approach like white drift before a gale. So plentiful was the game that at last I could stand it no longer. I had a single-barrel sporting Martini with me in the litter, the express being too cumbersome, and espying a beautiful fat eland rubbing himself under one of the oaklike trees, I jumped out of the litter, and proceeded to creep as near to him as I could. He let me come within eighty yards, and then turned his head, and stared at me, preparatory to running away. I lifted the rifle, and taking him about midway down the shoulder, for he was side on to me, fired. I never made a cleaner shot or a better kill in all my small experience, for the great buck sprang right up into the air and fell dead. The bearers, who had all halted to see the performance, gave a murmur of surprise, an unwanted compliment from these sullen people, who never appear to be surprised at anything, and a party of the guard at once ran off to cut the animal up. As for myself, though I was longing to have a look at him, I sauntered back to my litter as though I had been in the habit of killing eland all my life, feeling that I had gone up several degrees in the estimation of, the Amahagger, who looked on the whole thing as a very high-class manifestation of witchcraft. As a matter of fact, however, I had never seen an eland in a wild state before. Billali received me with enthusiasm.

"It is wonderful, my son the Baboon," he cried; "wonderful! Thou art a very great man, though so ugly. Had I not seen, surely I would never have believed. And thou sayest that thou wilt teach me to slay in this fashion?"

"Certainly, my father," I said airily; "it is nothing."

But all the same I firmly made up my mind that when "my father" Billali began to fire I would without fail lie down or take refuge behind a tree.

After this little incident nothing happened of any note till about an hour and a half before sundown, when we arrived beneath the shadow of the towering volcanic mass that I have already described. It is quite impossible for me to describe its grim grandeur as it appeared to me while my patient bearers toiled along the bed of the ancient watercourse towards the spot where the rich brown-clad cliff shot up from precipice to precipice till its crown lost itself in cloud. All I can say is that it almost awed me by the intensity of its lonesome and most solemn greatness. On we went up the bright and sunny slope, till at last the creeping shadows from above swallowed up its brightness, and presently we began to pass through a cutting hewn in the living rock. Deeper and deeper grew this marvelous work, which must, I should say, have employed thousands of men for many years. Indeed, how it was ever executed at all without the aid of blasting powder or dynamite I cannot to this day imagine. It is and must remain one of the mysteries of that wild land. I can only suppose that these cuttings and the vast caves that had been hollowed out of the rocks they pierced were the state undertakings of the people of Kôr, who lived here in the dim lost ages of the world, and, as in the case of the Egyptian monuments, were executed by the forced labor of tens of thousands of captives, carried on through an indefinite number of centuries. But who were the people?

At last we reached the face of the precipice itself, and found ourselves looking into the mouth of a dark tunnel that forcibly reminded me of those undertaken by our nineteenth-century engineers in the construction of railway lines. Out of this tunnel flowed a considerable stream of water. Indeed, though I do not think that I have mentioned it, we had followed this stream, which ultimately developed into the river I have already described as winding away to the right, from the spot where the cutting in the solid rock commenced. Half of this cutting formed a channel for the stream, and half, which was placed on a slightly higher level – eight feet, perhaps – was devoted to the purposes of a roadway. At the termination of the cutting, however, the stream turned off across the plain and followed a channel of its own. At the mouth of the cave the cavalcade was halted, and, while the men employed themselves in lighting some earthenware lamps they had brought with them, Billali, descending from his litter, informed me politely but firmly that the orders of *She* were that we were now to be blindfolded, so that we should not learn the secret of the paths through the bowels of the mountains. To this I, of course, assented cheerfully enough, but Job, who was now very much better, notwithstanding the journey, did not like it at all, fancying, I believe, that it was but a preliminary step to being hot-potted. He was, however, a little consoled when I pointed out to him that there were no hot pots at hand, and, so far as I knew, no fire to heat them in. As for poor Leo, after turning restlessly for hours, he had, to my deep thankfulness, at last dropped off into a sleep or stupor, I do not know which, so there was no need to blindfold him. The blindfolding was performed by binding a piece of the yellowish linen – whereof those of the Amahagger who condescended to wear anything in particular made their dresses – tightly round the eyes. This linen I afterwards discovered was taken from the tombs, and was not, as I had at first supposed, of native manufacture. The bandage was then knotted at the back of the head, and finally brought down again and the ends bound under the chin to prevent its slipping. Ustane was, by the way, also blindfolded, I do not know why, unless it was from fear that she should impart the secrets of the route to us.

This operation performed, we started on once more, and soon, by the echoing sound of the footsteps of the bearers and the increased noise of the water caused by reverberation in a confined space, I knew that we were entering into the bowels of the great mountain. It was an eerie sensation, being borne along into the dead heart of the rock we knew not whither, but I was getting used to eerie sensations by this time, and by now was pretty well prepared for anything. So I lay still, and listened to the tramp, tramp of the bearers and the rushing of the water, and tried to believe that I was enjoying myself. Presently the men set up the melancholy little chant that I had heard on the first night when we were captured in the whaleboat and the effect produced by their voices was very curious, and quite indescribable on paper. After a while the air began to get exceedingly thick and heavy, so much so, indeed, that I felt as though I were going to choke, till at length the litter took a sharp turn, then another and another, and the sound of the running water ceased. After this the air got fresher again, but the turns were continuous, and to me, blindfolded as I was, most bewildering. I tried to keep a map of them in my mind in case it might ever be necessary for us to try and escape by this route, but, needless to say, failed utterly. Another half hour or so passed, and then suddenly I became aware that we were once more in the open air. I could see the light through my bandage and feel its freshness on my face. A few more minutes and the caravan halted, and I heard Billali order Ustane to remove her bandage and undo ours. Without waiting for her attentions I got the knot of mine loose, and looked out.

As I anticipated, we had passed right through the precipice, and were now on the farther side, and immediately beneath its beetling face. The first thing I noticed was that the cliff was not nearly so high here, not so high I should say by five hundred feet, which proved that the bed of the lake, or rather of the vast ancient crater in which we stood, was much above the level of the surrounding plain. For the rest, we found ourselves in a huge rock-surrounded cup, not unlike that of the first place where we had sojourned, only ten times the size. Indeed, I could only just make out the frowning line of the opposite cliffs. A great portion of the plain thus enclosed by nature was cultivated, and fenced in with walls of stone placed there to keep the cattle and goats, of which there were large herds about, from breaking into the gardens. Here and there rose great grass mounds, and some miles away towards the center I thought that I could see the outline of colossal ruins. I had no time to observe anything more at the moment, for we were instantly surrounded by crowds of Amahagger, similar in every particular to those with whom we were already familiar, who, though they spoke little, pressed round us so closely as to obscure the view to a person lying in a hammock. Then all of a sudden a number of armed men arranged in companies, and marshaled by officers who held ivory wands in their hands, came running swiftly towards us, having, so far as I could make out, emerged from the face of the precipice like ants from their burrows. These men as well as their officers were all robed in addition to the usual leopard skin, and, as I gathered, formed the bodyguard of *She* herself.

Their leader advanced to Billali, saluted him by placing his ivory wand transversely across his forehead, and then asked some question which I could not catch, and Billali having answered him the whole regiment turned and marched along the side of the cliff, our cavalcade of litters following in their track. After going thus for about half a mile we halted once more in front of the mouth of a tremendous cave, measuring about sixty feet in height by eighty wide, and here Billali descended finally, and requested Job and myself to do the same. Leo, of course, was far too ill to do anything of the sort. I did so, and we entered the great cave, into which the light of the setting sun penetrated for some distance, while beyond the reach of the light it was faintly illuminated with lamps which seemed to me to stretch away for an almost immeasurable distance, like the gas lights of an empty London street. The first thing that I noticed was that the walls were covered with sculptures in bas-relief, of a sort, pictorially speaking, similar, to those that I have described upon the vases: love scenes principally, then hunting pictures, pictures of executions, and the torture of criminals by the placing of a presumably red-hot pot upon the head, showing whence our hosts had derived this pleasant practice. There were very few battle pieces, though many of duels, and men running and wrestling, and from this fact I am led to believe that this people was not much subject to attack by exterior foes, either on account of the isolation of its position or because of its great strength. Between the pictures were columns of stone characters of a formation absolutely new to me; at any rate they were neither Greek, nor Egyptian, nor Hebrew, nor Assyrian – that I am sure of. They looked more like Chinese writings than any other that I am acquainted with. Near the entrance of the cave both pictures and writings were worn away, but further in they were in many cases absolutely fresh and perfect as the day on which the sculptor had ceased work upon them.

The regiment of guards did not come further than the entrance to the cave, where they formed up to let us pass through. On entering the place itself we were, however, met by a man robed in white, who bowed humbly, but said nothing, which, as it afterwards appeared that he was a deaf mute, was not very wonderful.

Running at right angles to the great cave, at a distance of some twenty feet from the entrance, was a smaller cave or wide gallery that was pierced into the rock both to the right and to the left of the main cavern. In front of the gallery to our left stood two guards, from which circumstance I argued that it was the entrance to the apartments of *She* herself. The mouth of the right-hand gallery was unguarded, and along it the mute indicated that we were to proceed. Walking a few yards down this passage, which was lighted with lamps, we came to the entrance to a chamber having a curtain made of some grass material, not unlike a Zanzibar mat in appearance, hung over the doorway. This the mute drew back with another profound obeisance, and led the way into a good-sized apartment, hewn, of course, out of the solid rock, but to my great delight lighted by means of a shaft pierced in the face of the precipice. In this room was a stone bedstead, pots full of water for washing, and beautifully tanned leopard skins to serve as blankets.

Here we left Leo, who was still sleeping heavily, and with him stopped Ustane. I noticed that the mute gave her a very sharp look, as much as to say, "Who are you, and by whose orders do you come here?" Then he conducted us to another similar room, which Job took, and then to two more that were respectively occupied by Billali and myself.

Chapter 12

'She'

THE FIRST care of Job and myself, after seeing to Leo, was to wash ourselves and put on clean clothing, for what we were wearing had not been changed since the loss of the dhow. Fortunately, as I think that I have said, by far the greater part of our personal baggage had been packed into the whaleboat, and was therefore saved – and brought hither by the bearers – although all the stores laid in by us for barter and presents to the natives were lost. Nearly all our clothing was made of a well-shrunk and very strong gray flannel, and excellent I found it for traveling in these places, because though a Norfolk jacket, shirt, and pair of trousers of it only weighed about four pounds, a great consideration in a tropical country, where every extra ounce tells on the wearer, it was warm, and offered a good resistance to the rays of the sun, and best of all to chills, which are so apt to result from sudden changes of temperature.

Never shall I forget the comfort of the "wash and brush-up," and of those clean flannels. The only thing that was wanting to complete my joy was a cake of soap, of which we had none.

Afterwards I discovered that the Amahagger, who do not include dirt among their many disagreeable qualities, use a kind of burned earth for washing purposes, which, though unpleasant to the touch till one gets accustomed to it, forms a very fair substitute for soap.

By the time that I was dressed, and had combed and trimmed my black beard, the previous condition of which was certainly sufficiently unkempt to give weight to Billali's appellation for me, the "Baboon," I began to feel most uncommonly hungry. Therefore I was by no means sorry when, without the slightest preparatory sound or warning, the curtain over the entrance to my cave was flung aside, and another mute, a young girl this time, announced to me by signs that I could not misunderstand – that is, by opening her mouth and pointing down it – that there was something ready to eat. Accordingly I followed her into the next chamber, which we had not yet entered, where I found Job, who had also, to his great embarrassment, been conducted thither by a fair mute Job had never got over the advances the former lady had made towards him, and suspected every girl who came near to him of similar designs.

"These young parties have a way of looking at one, sir," he would say apologetically, "which I don't call respectable."

This chamber was twice the size of the sleeping caves, and I saw at once that it had originally served as a refectory, and also probably as an embalming room for the Priests of the Dead; for I may as well say at once that these hollowed-out caves were nothing more or less than vast catacombs, in which for tens of ages the mortal remains of the great extinct race whose monuments surrounded us had been first preserved, with an art and a completeness that has never since been equaled, and then hidden away for all time. On each side of this particular rock chamber was a long and solid stone table, about three feet wide by three feet six in height, hewn out of the living rock, of which it had formed part, and was still attached to at the base. These tables were slightly hollowed out or curved inward, to give room for the knees of anyone sitting on the stone ledge that had been cut for a bench along the side of the cave at a distance of about two feet from them. Each of them, also, was so arranged that it ended right under a shaft pierced in the rock for the admission of light and air. On examining them carefully, however, I saw that there was a difference between them that had at first escaped my attention, viz., that one of the tables, that to the left as we entered the cave, had evidently been used, not to eat upon, but for the purposes of embalming. That this was beyond all question the case was clear from five shallow depressions in the stone of the table, all shaped like a human form, with a separate place for the head to lie in, and a little bridge to support the neck, each depression being of a different size, so as to fit bodies varying in stature from a full-grown man's to a small child's, and with little holes bored at intervals to carry off fluid. And, indeed, if any further confirmation was required, we had but to look at the wall of the cave above to find it. For there, sculptured all round the apartment, and looking nearly as fresh as the day it was done, was the pictorial representation of the death, embalming, and burial of an old man with a long beard, probably an ancient king or grandee of this country.

The first picture represented his death. He was lying upon a couch which had four short curved posts at the comers coming to a knob at the end, in appearance something like a written note of music, and was evidently in the very act of expiring. Gathered round the couch were women and children weeping, the former with their hair hanging down there back. The next scene represented the embalmment of the body, which lay nude upon a table with depressions in it, similar to the one before us; probably, indeed, it was a picture of the same table. Three men were employed at the work – one superintending, one holding a runnel shaped exactly like a port wine strainer, of which the narrow end was fixed in an incision in the breast, no doubt in the great pectoral artery; while the third, who was depicted as standing straddle-legged over the corpse, held a kind of large jug high in his hand, and poured from it some steaming fluid which fell accurately into the funnel. The most curious part of this sculpture is that both the man with the funnel and the man who poured the fluid are drawn holding their noses, either I suppose because of the stench arising from the body, or more probably to keep out the aromatic fumes of the hot fluid which was being forced into the dead man's veins. Another curious thing which I am unable to explain is that all three men were represented as having a band of linen tied round the face with holes in it for the eyes.

The third sculpture was a picture of the burial of the deceased. There he was, stiff and cold, clothed in a linen robe, and laid out on a stone slab such as I had slept upon at our first sojourning place. At his head and feet burned lamps, and by his side were placed several of the beautiful painted vases that I have described, which were perhaps supposed to be full of provisions. The little chamber was crowded with mourners, and with musicians playing on an instrument resembling a lyre, while near the foot of the corpse stood a man with a sheet, with which he was preparing to cover it from view.

These sculptures, looked at merely as works of art, were so remarkable that I make no apology for describing them rather fully. They struck me also as being of surpassing interest as representing, probably with studious accuracy, the last rites of the dead as practiced among an utterly lost people, and even then I thought how envious some antiquarian friends of my own at Cambridge would be if ever I got an opportunity of describing these wonderful remains to them. Probably they would, say that I was exaggerating, notwithstanding that every page of this history must bear so much internal evidence of its truth that it would obviously have been quite impossible for me to have invented it.

To return. As soon as I had hastily examined these sculptures, which I think I omitted to mention were executed in relief, we sat down to a very excellent meal of boiled goat's flesh, fresh milk, and cakes made of meal, the whole being served upon clean wooden platters.

When we had eaten, Job and I returned to see how poor Leo was getting on, Billali going to wait upon *She* and hear her commands. On reaching Leo's room we found the poor boy in a very bad way. He had woke up from his torpor, and was altogether off his head, babbling about some boat race on the Cam, and was inclined to be violent. Indeed, when we entered the room Ustane was holding him down. I spoke to him, and my voice seemed to soothe him; at any rate he grew much quieter, and was persuaded to swallow a dose of quinine.

I had been sitting with him for an hour, perhaps – at any rate I know that it was getting so dark that I could only just make out his head lying like a gleam of gold upon the pillow we had extemporized out of a bag covered with a blanket – when suddenly Billali arrived with an air of great importance, and informed me that *She* herself had deigned to express a wish to see me – an honor, he added, accorded to but very few. I think that he was a little horrified at my cool way of taking the honor, but the fact was that I did not feel overwhelmed with gratitude at the prospect of seeing some savage, dusky queen, however absolute and mysterious she might be, more especially as my mind was full of dear Leo, for whose life I began to have great fears. However, I rose to follow him, and as I did so I caught sight of something bright lying on the floor, which I picked up. Perhaps the reader will remember that with the potsherd in the casket was a composition scarabaeus marked with a round O, a goose, and another curious hieroglyphic, the meaning of which signs is "Suten se Râ," or 'Royal Son of the Sun.' This scarab, which is a very small one, Leo had insisted upon having set in a massive gold ring, such as is generally used for signets, and it was this very ring that I now picked up. He had pulled it off in the paroxysm of his fever, at least I suppose so, and flung it down upon the rock floor. Thinking that if I left it about it might get lost, I slipped it onto my own little finger, and then followed Billali, leaving Job and Ustane with Leo.

We passed down the passage, crossed the great aisle-like cave, and came to the corresponding passage on the other side, at the mouth of which the guards stood like two statues. As we came they bowed their heads in salutation, and then lifting their long spears placed them transversely across their foreheads, as the leaders of the troop that had met us had done with their ivory wands. We stepped between them, and found ourselves in an exactly similar gallery to that which led to our own apartments, only this passage was, comparatively speaking, brilliantly lighted.

A few paces down it we were met by four mutes – two men and two women – who bowed low and then arranged themselves, the women in front and the men behind of us, and in this order we continued our procession past several doorways hung with curtains resembling those leading to our own quarters, and which I afterwards found opened out into chambers occupied by the mutes who attended on *She*. A few paces more and we came to another doorway facing us, and not to our left like the others, which seemed to mark the termination of the passage. Here two more white, or rather yellow-robed guards were standing, and they too bowed, saluted, and let us pass through heavy curtains into a great antechamber, quite forty feet long by as many wide, in which some eight or ten women, most of them young and handsome, with yellowish hair, sat on cushions working with ivory needles at what had the appearance of being embroidery frames. These women were also deaf and dumb. At the farther end of this great lamp lit apartment was another doorway closed in with heavy Oriental-looking curtains, quite unlike those that hung before the doors of our own rooms, and here stood two particularly handsome girl mutes, their heads bowed upon their bosoms and their hands crossed in an attitude of the humblest submission. As we advanced they each stretched out an arm and drew back the curtains. Thereupon Billali did a curious thing. Down he went, that venerable-looking old gentleman – for Billali is a gentleman at the bottom – down onto his hands and knees, and in this undignified position, with his long white beard trailing on the ground, he began to creep into the apartment beyond. I followed him, standing on my feet in the usual fashion. Looking over his shoulder he perceived it.

"Down, my son; down, my Baboon; down onto thy hands and knees. We enter the presence of *She*, and, if thou art not humble, of a surety she will blast thee where thou standest."

I halted, and felt scared. Indeed, my knees began to give way of their own mere motion; but reflection came to my aid. I was an Englishman, and why, I asked myself, should I creep into the presence of some savage woman as though I were a monkey in fact as well as in name? I would not and could not do it, that is, unless I was absolutely sure that my life or comfort depended upon it. If once I began to creep upon my knees I should always have to do so, and it would be a patent acknowledgment of inferiority. So, fortified by an insular prejudice against kowtowing, which has, like most of our so-called prejudices, a good deal of common sense to recommend it, I marched in boldly after Billali. I found myself in another apartment, considerably smaller than the anteroom, of which the walls were entirely hung with rich-looking curtains of the same make as those over the door, the work, as I subsequently discovered, of the mutes who sat in the antechamber and wove them in strips, which were afterwards sewn together. Also, here and there about the room, were settees of a beautiful black wood of the ebony tribe, inlaid with ivory, and all over the floor were other tapestries, or rather rugs. At the top end of this apartment was what appeared to be a recess, also draped with curtains, through which shone rays of light. There was nobody in the place except ourselves.

Painfully and slowly old Billali crept up the length of the cave, and with the most dignified stride that I could command I followed after him. But I felt that it was more or less of a failure. To begin with, it is not possible to look dignified when you are following in the wake of an old man writhing along on his stomach like a snake, and then, in order to go sufficiently slowly, either I had to keep my leg some seconds in the air at every step, or else to advance with a full stop between each stride, like Mary Queen of Scots going to execution in a play. Billali was not good at crawling, I suppose his years stood in the way, and our progress up that apartment was a very long affair. I was immediately behind him, and several times I was sorely tempted to help him on with a good kick. It is so absurd to advance into the presence of savage royalty after the fashion of an Irishman driving a pig to market, for that is what we looked like, and the idea nearly made me burst out laughing then and there. I had to work off my dangerous tendency to unseemly merriment by blowing my nose, a proceeding which filled old Billali with horror, for he looked over his shoulder and made a ghastly face at me, and I heard him murmur, "Oh, my poor Baboon!"

At last we reached the curtains, and here Billali collapsed flat onto his stomach, with his hands stretched out before him as though he were dead, and I, not knowing what to do, began to stare about the place. But presently I clearly felt that somebody was looking at me from behind the curtains. I could not see the person, but I could distinctly feel his or her gaze, and, what is more, it produced a very odd effect upon my nerves. I was frightened, I do not know why. The place was a strange one, it is true, and looked lonely, notwithstanding its rich hangings and the soft glow of the lamps – indeed, these accessories added to, rather than detracted from its loneliness, just as a lighted street at night has always a more solitary appearance than a dark one. It was so silent in the place, and there lay Billali like one dead before the heavy curtains, through which the odor of perfume seemed to float up towards the gloom of the arched roof above. Minute grew into minute, and still there was no sign of life, nor did the curtain move, but I felt the gaze of the unknown being sinking through and through me, and filling me with a nameless terror, till the perspiration stood in beads upon my brow.

At length the curtain began to move. Who could be behind it? Some naked savage queen, a languishing Oriental beauty, or a nineteenth-century young lady, drinking afternoon tea? I had not the slightest idea, and should not have been astonished at seeing any of the three. I was getting beyond astonishment. The curtain agitated itself a little, then suddenly between its folds there appeared a most beautiful white hand (white as snow), and with long tapering fingers, ending in the pinkest nails. The hand grasped the curtain, and drew it aside, and as it did so I heard a voice, I think the softest and yet most silvery voice I ever heard. It reminded me of the murmur of a brook.

"Stranger," said the voice in Arabic, but much purer and more classical Arabic than the Amahagger talk, "stranger, wherefore art thou so much afraid?"

Now I flattered myself that in spite of my inward terrors I had kept a very fair command of my countenance, and was, therefore, a little astonished at this question. Before I had made up my mind how to answer it, however, the curtain was drawn, and a tall figure stood before us. I say a figure, for not only the body, but also the face was wrapped up in soft white, gauzy material in such a way as at first sight to remind me most forcibly of a corpse in its grave-clothes. And yet I do not know why it should have given me that idea, seeing that the wrappings were so thin that one could distinctly see the gleam of the pink flesh beneath them. I suppose it was owing to the way in which they were arranged; either accidentally, or more probably by design. Anyhow, I felt more frightened than ever at this ghostlike apparition, and my hair began to rise upon my head as the feeling crept over me that I was in the presence of something that was not canny. I could, however, clearly distinguish that the swathed mummy-like form before me was that of a tall and lovely woman, instinct with beauty in every part, and also with a certain snake-like grace which I had never seen anything to equal before. When she moved a hand or foot her entire frame seemed to undulate, and the neck did not bend, it curved.

"Why art thou so frightened, stranger?" asked the sweet voice again – a voice which seemed to draw the heart out of me, like the strains of softest music. "Is there that about me that should affright a man? Then surely are men changed from what they used to be!" And with a little coquettish movement she turned herself, and held up one arm, so as to show all her loveliness and the rich hair of raven blackness that streamed in soft ripples down her snowy robes, almost to her sandaled feet.

"It is thy beauty that makes me fear, O Queen," I answered humbly, scarcely knowing what to say, and I thought that as I did so I heard old Billali, who was still lying prostrate on the floor, mutter, "Good, my Baboon, good."

"I see that men still know how to beguile us women with false words. Ah, stranger," she answered, with a laugh that sounded like distant silver bells, "thou wast afraid because mine eyes were searching out thine heart, therefore wast thou afraid. But being but a woman, I forgive thee for the lie, for it was courteously said. And now tell me how came ye hither to this land of the dwellers among caves – a land of swamps and evil things and dead old shadows of the dead? What came ye for to see? How is it that ye hold your lives so cheap as to place them in the hollow of the hand of Hiya, into the hand of *'She-who-must-be-obeyed'*? Tell me also how come ye to know the tongue I talk. It is an ancient tongue, that sweet child of the old Syriac. Liveth it yet in the world? Thou seest I dwell among the caves and the dead, and naught know I of the affairs of men, nor have I cared to know. I have lived, O stranger, with my memories, and my memories are in a grave that mine own hands hollowed, for truly hath it been said that the child of man maketh his own path evil," and her beautiful voice quivered, and broke in a note as soft as any wood bird's. Suddenly her eye fell upon the sprawling frame of Billali, and she seemed to recollect herself.

"Ah! Thou art there, old man. Tell me how it is that things have gone wrong in thine household. Forsooth, it seems that these my guests were set upon. Ay, and one was nigh to being slain by the hot pot to be eaten of those brutes, thy children, and had not the others fought gallantly they too had been slain, and not even I could have called back the life which had been loosed from the body. What means it, old man? What hast thou to say that I should not give thee over to those who execute my vengeance?"

Her voice had risen in her anger, and it rang clear and cold against the rocky walls. Also, I thought I could see her eyes flash through the gauze that hid them. I saw poor Billali, whom I had believed to be a very fearless person, positively quiver with terror at her words.

"O Hiya! O *She*!" he said, without lifting his white head from the floor. "O *She*, as thou art great be merciful, for I am now as ever thy servant to obey. It was no plan or fault of mine, O *She*, it was those wicked ones who are called my children. Led on by a woman whom thy guest the Pig had scorned, they would have followed the ancient custom of the land, and eaten the fat black stranger who came hither with these thy guests the Baboon and the Lion who is sick, thinking that no word had come from thee about the black one. But when the Baboon and the Lion saw what they would do, they slew the woman, and slew also their servant to save him from the horror of the pot. Then those evil ones, ay, those children of the Wicked One who lives in the Pit, they went mad with the lust of blood, and flew at the throats of the Lion and the Baboon and the Pig. But gallantly they fought. O Hiya! They fought like very men, and slew many, and held their own, and then I came and saved them, and the evildoers have I sent on hither to Kôr to be judged of thy greatness, O *She*, and here they are."

"Ay, old man, I know it, and tomorrow will I sit in the great hall and do justice upon them, fear not. And for thee, I forgive thee, though hardly. See that thou dost keep thine household better. Go."

Billali rose upon his knees with astonishing alacrity, bowed his head thrice, and, his white beard sweeping the ground, crawled down the apartment as he had crawled up it, till he finally vanished through the curtains, leaving me, not a little to my alarm, alone with this terrible but most fascinating person.

Chapter 13

Ayesha Unveils

"THERE," SAID *She*, "he has gone, the white-bearded old fool! Ah, how little knowledge does a man acquire in his life. He gathereth it up like water, but like water it runneth through his fingers, and yet, if his hands be but wet as though with dew, behold a generation of fools call out, 'See, he is a wise man!' Is it not so? But how call they thee? 'Baboon,' he says," and she laughed; "but that is the fashion of these savages who lack imagination, and fly to the beasts they resemble for a name. How do they call thee in thine own country, stranger?"

"They call me Holly, O Queen," I answered. "Holly," she answered, speaking the word with difficulty, and yet with a most charming accent; "and what is 'Holly'?"

" 'Holly' is a prickly tree," I said. "So. Well, thou hast a prickly and yet a treelike look. Strong art thou, and ugly, but, if my wisdom be not at fault, honest at the core, and a staff to lean on. Also one who thinks. But stay, O Holly, stand not there, enter with me and be seated by me. I would not see thee crawl before me like those slaves. I am aweary of their worship and their terror; sometimes when they vex me I could blast them for very sport, and to see the rest turn white, even to the heart." And she held the curtain aside with her ivory hand to let me pass in.

I entered, shuddering. This woman was very terrible. Within the curtains was a recess, about twelve feet by ten, and in the recess was a couch and a table whereon stood fruit and sparkling water. By it, at its end, was a vessel like a font cut in carved stone, also full of pure water. The place was softly lit with lamps formed out of the beautiful vessels of which I have spoken, and the air and curtains were laden with a subtle perfume. Perfume too seemed to emanate from the glorious hair and white, clinging vestments of *She* herself. I entered the little room, and there stood uncertain.

"Sit," said *She*, pointing to the couch. "As yet thou hast no cause to fear me. If thou hast cause, thou shalt not fear for long, for I shall slay thee. Therefore let thy heart be light."

I sat down on the end of the couch near to the fontlike basin of water, and *She* sank down softly onto the other end.

"Now, Holly," she said, "how comest thou to speak Arabic? It is my own dear tongue, for Arabian am I by my birth, even 'al Arab al Ariba' [an Arab of the Arabs], and of the race of our father Yárab, the son of Kâhtan, for in that fair and ancient city Ozal was I born, in the province of Yaman the Happy. Yet dost thou not speak it as we used to speak. Thy talk doth lack the music of the sweet tongue of the tribes of Hamyar which I was wont to hear. Some of the words too seemed changed, even as among these Amahagger, who have debased and denied its purity, so that I must speak with them in what is to me another tongue."[1]

"I have studied it," I answered, "for many years. Also, the language is spoken in Egypt and elsewhere."

"So it is still spoken, and there is yet an Egypt? And what pharaoh sits upon the throne? Still one of the spawn of the Persian Ochus, or are the Achaemenians gone, for far is it to the days of Ochus?"

"The Persians have been gone from Egypt for nigh two thousand years, and since then the Ptolemies, the Romans, and many others have flourished and held sway upon the Nile, and fallen when their time was ripe," I said, aghast. "What canst thou know of the Persian Artaxerxes?"

She laughed, and made no answer, and again a cold chill went through me. "And Greece," she said; "is there still a Greece? Ah, I loved the Greeks. Beautiful were they as the day, and clever, but fierce at heart and fickle, notwithstanding."

"Yes," I said, "there is a Greece; and, just now, is it once more a people. Yet the Greeks of today are not what the Greeks of the old time were, and Greece herself is but a

1 Yarab the son of Kâhtan, who lived some centuries before the time of Abraham, was the father of the ancient Arabs, and gave its name Araba to the country. In speaking of herself as 'al Arab al Ariba,' *She* no doubt meant to convey that she was of the true Arab blood as distinguished from the naturalized

(contd. on the next pg.)

mockery of the Greece that was."

"So! The Hebrews, are they yet at Jerusalem? And does the Temple that the wise king built stand, and if so, what God do they worship therein? Is their Messiah come, of whom they preached so much and prophesied so loudly, and doth He rule the earth?"

"The Jews are broken and gone, and the fragments of their people strew the world, and Jerusalem is no more. As for the temple that Herod built – "

"Herod!" she said. "I know not Herod. But go on."

"The Romans burned it, and the Roman eagles flew across its ruins, and now Judea is a desert."

"So, so! They were a great people, those Romans, and went straight to their end – ay, they speed to it like Fate, or like their own eagles on their prey! – and left peace behind them."

"*Solitudinem faciunt, pacem appellant*," I suggested.

"Ah, thou canst speak the Latin tongue, too!" she said, in surprise. "It hath a strange ring in my ears after all these days, and it seems to me that thy accent does not fall as the Romans put it. Who was it wrote that? I know not the saying, but it is a true one of that great people. It seems that I have found a learned man – one whose hands have held the water of the world's knowledge. Knowest thou Greek also?"

"Yes, O Queen, and something of Hebrew, but not to speak them well. They are all dead languages now."

She clapped her hands in childish glee. "Of a truth, ugly tree that thou art, thou growest the fruits of wisdom, O Holly," she said, "but of those Jews whom I hated, for they called me 'heathen' when I would have taught them my philosophy. Did their Messiah come, and doth He rule the world?"

"Their Messiah came," I answered with reverence; "but He

Arabs, the descendants of Ismael, the son of Abraham and Hagar, who were known as 'al Arab al mostareba.' The dialect of the Koreish was usually called the clear or 'perspicuous' Arabic, but the Hamaritic dialect approached nearer to the purity of the mother Syriac. – L. H. H.

came poor and lowly, and they would have none of Him. They scourged Him, and crucified Him upon a tree, but yet His words and His works live on, for He was the Son of God, and now of a truth He doth rule half the world, but not with an Empire of the World."

"Ah, the fierce-hearted wolves," she said, "the followers of Sense and of many gods – greedy of gain and faction-torn. I can see their dark faces yet. So they crucified their Messiah? Well can I believe it. That he was a Son of the Living Spirit would be naught to them, if indeed He was so, and of that we will talk afterwards. They would care naught for any God if he came not with pomp and power. They, a chosen people, a vessel of Him they call Jehovah, ay, and a vessel of Baal, and a vessel of Astoreth, and a vessel of the gods of the Egyptians – a high-stomached people, greedy of aught that brought them wealth and power. So they crucified their Messiah because He came in lowly guise – and now are they scattered about the earth. Why, if I remember, so said one of their prophets that it should be. Well, let them go – they broke my heart, those Jews, and made me look with evil eyes across the world, ay, and drove me to this wilderness, this place of a people that was before them. When I would have taught them wisdom in Jerusalem they stoned me, ay, at the Gate of the Temple whose white-bearded hypocrites and rabbis hounded the people on to stone me! See, here is the mark of it to this day!" and with a sudden move she pulled up the gauzy wrapping on her rounded arm, and pointed to a little scar that showed red against its milky beauty. I shrank back horrified.

"Pardon me, O Queen," I said, "but I am bewildered. Nigh upon two thousand years have rolled across the earth since the Jewish Messiah hung upon His cross at Golgotha. How then canst thou have taught thy philosophy to the Jews before He was? Thou art a woman, and no spirit. How can a woman live two thousand years? Why dost thou befool me, O Queen?"

She leaned back on the couch, and once more I felt the hidden eyes playing upon me and searching out my heart.

"O man!" she said at last, speaking very slowly and deliberately, "it seems that there are still things upon the earth of which thou knowest naught. Dost thou still believe that all things die, even as those very Jews believed? I tell thee that naught really dies. There is no such thing as Death, though there be a thing called Change. See," and she pointed to some sculptures on the rocky wall. "Three times two thousand years have passed since the last of the great race that hewed those pictures fell before the breath of the pestilence which destroyed them, yet are they not dead. E'en now they live; perchance their spirits are drawn towards us at this very hour," and she glanced round. "Of a surety it sometimes seems to me that my eyes can see them."

"Yes, but to the world they are dead."

"Ay, for a time; but even to the world are they born again and again. I, yes I, Ayesha[1] – for that is my name, stranger – I say to thee that I wait now for one I loved to be born again, and here I tarry till he finds me, knowing of a surety that hither he will come, and that here, and here only, shall he greet me. Why, dost thou suppose that I, who am all powerful, I, whose loveliness is more than the loveliness of the Grecian Helen, of whom they used to sing, and whose wisdom is wider, ay, far more wide and deep than the wisdom of Solomon the Wise – I, who know the secrets of the earth and its riches, and can turn all things to my uses – I, who have even for a while overcome Change, that ye call Death – why, I say, O stranger, dost thou think that I herd here with barbarians lower than the beasts?"

"I know not," I said humbly.

"Because I wait for him I love. My life has perchance been evil, I know not – for who can say what is evil and what good? – so I fear to die even if I could die, which I cannot until mine hour comes, to go and seek him where he is; for between us there might rise a wall I could not climb, at least, I dread it. Surely easy would it be also to lose the way in seeking in those great spaces wherein the planets wander on forever. But the day will come, it

1 Pronounced *Assha*. – L. H. H.

may be when five thousand more years have passed, and are lost and melted into the vault of Time, even as the little clouds melt into the gloom of night, or it may be tomorrow, when he, my love, shall be born again, and then, following a law that is stronger than any human plan, he shall find me *here*, where once he knew me, and of a surety his heart will soften towards me though I sinned against him; ay, even though he know me not again, yet will he love me, if only for my beauty's sake."

For a moment I was dumfounded, and could not answer. The matter was too overpowering for my intellect to grasp.

"But even so, O Queen," I said at last, "even if we men be born again and again, that is not so with thee, if thou speakest truly" – here she looked up sharply, and once more I caught the flash of those hidden eyes – "thou," I went on hurriedly, "who hast never died?"

"That is so," she said; "and it is so because I have, half by chance and half by learning, solved one of the great secrets of the world. Tell me, stranger: life is – why therefore should not life be lengthened for a while? What are ten or twenty or fifty thousand years in the history of life? Why in ten thousand years scarce will the rain and storms lessen a mountain top by a span in thickness? In two thousand years these caves have not changed, nothing has changed, but the beasts and man, who is as the beasts. There is naught that is wonderful about the matter, couldst thou but understand. Life is wonderful, ay, but that it should be a little lengthened is not wonderful. Nature hath her animating spirit as well as man, who is Nature's child, and he who can find that spirit, and let it breathe upon him, shall live with her life. He shall not live eternally for Nature is not eternal, and she herself must die, even as the nature of the moon hath died. She herself must die, I say, or rather change and sleep till it be time for her to live again. But when shall she die? Not yet, I ween, and while she lives, so shall he who hath all her secret live with her. All I have not, yet have I some, more perchance than any who were before me. Now, to thee I doubt not that this thing is a great mystery, therefore I will not overcome thee with it now. Another time will I tell thee more if the mood be on me, though perchance I shall never speak thereof again. Dost thou wonder how I knew that ye were coming to this land, and so saved your heads from the hot pot?"

"Ay, O Queen," I answered feebly.

"Then gaze upon that water," and she pointed to the fontlike vessel, and then, bending forward, held her hand over it.

I rose and gazed, and instantly the water darkened. Then it cleared, and I saw as distinctly as I ever saw anything in my life – I saw, I say, our boat upon that horrible canal. There was Leo lying at the bottom asleep in it, with a coat thrown over him to keep off the mosquitoes, in such a fashion as to hide his face, and myself. Job, and Mahomed towing on the bank.

I started back aghast, and cried out that it was magic, for I recognized the whole scene – it was one which had actually occurred.

"Nay, nay, O Holly," she answered, "it is no magic; that is a fiction of ignorance. There is no such thing as magic, though there is such a thing as a knowledge of the secrets of Nature. That water is my glass; in it I see what passes if I care to summon up the pictures, which is not often. Therein I can show thee what thou wilt of the past, if it be anything to do with this country and with what I have known, or anything that thou, the gazer, hast known. Think of a face if thou wilt, and it shall be reflected from thy mind upon the water. I know not all the secret yet – I can read nothing in the future. But it is an old secret; I did not find it. In Arabia and in Egypt the sorcerers knew it centuries ago. So one day I chanced to bethink me of that old canal – some twenty centuries ago I sailed upon it, and I was minded to look thereon again. And so I looked, and there I saw the boat and three men walking, and one, whose face I could not see, but a youth of a noble form, sleeping in the boat, and so I sent and saved ye. And now farewell. But stay, tell me of this youth – the

Lion, as the old man calls him. I would look upon him, but he is sick, thou sayest – sick with the fever, and also wounded in the fray."

"He is very sick," I answered sadly; "canst thou do nothing for him, O Queen who knowest so much?"

"Of a surety I can. I can cure him; but why speakest thou so sadly? Doth thou love the youth? Is he perchance thy son?"

"He is my adopted son, O Queen. Shall he be brought in before thee?"

"Nay. How long hath the fever taken him?"

"This is the third day."

"Good; then let him lie another day. Then will he perchance throw it off by his own strength, and that is better than that I should cure him, for my medicine is of a sort to shake the life in its very citadel. If, however, by tomorrow night, at that hour when the fever first took him, he doth not begin to mend, then will I come to him and cure him. Stay, who nurses him?"

"Our white servant, him whom Billali names the Pig, also" – and here I spoke with some little hesitation – "a woman named Ustane, a very handsome woman of this country, who came and embraced him when first she saw him, and hath stayed by him ever since, as I understand is the fashion of thy people, O Queen."

"My people! Speak not to me of my people," she answered hastily; "these slaves are no people of mine, they are but dogs to do my bidding till the day of my deliverance comes; and as for their customs, naught have I to do with them. Also, call me not Queen – I am sick of flattery and titles – call me Ayesha; the name hath a sweet sound in mine ears, it is an echo from the past. As for this Ustane, I know not. I wonder if it be she against whom I was warned, and whom I in turn did warn? Hath she – stay, I will see," and, bending forward, she passed her hand over the font of water and gazed intently into it. "See," she said quietly, "is that the woman?"

I looked into the water, and there, mirrored upon its placid surface, was the silhouette of Ustane's stately face. She was bending forward, with a look of infinite tenderness upon her features, watching something beneath her, and with her chestnut locks falling onto her right shoulder.

"It is she," I said, in a low voice, for once more I fell much disturbed at this most uncommon sight. "She watches Leo asleep."

"Leo!" said Ayesha in an absent voice. "Why, that is 'lion' in the Latin tongue. The old man hath named happily for once. It is very strange," she went on speaking to herself, "very. So like – but it is not possible!" With an impatient gesture she passed her hand over the water once more. It darkened, and the image vanished as silently and mysteriously as it had risen, and once more the lamplight, and the lamplight only, shone on the placid surface of that limpid, living mirror.

"Hast thou aught to ask me before thou goest, O Holly?" she said after a few moments' reflection. "It is but a rude life that thou must live here, for these people are savages, and know not the ways of cultivated man. Not that I am troubled thereby, for, behold my food," and she pointed to the fruit upon the little table. "Naught but fruit doth ever pass my lips – fruit and cakes of flour, and a little water. I have bidden my girls to wait upon thee. They are mutes, thou knowest, deaf are they and dumb, and therefore the safest of servants, save to those who can read their faces and their signs. I bred them so – it hath taken many centuries and much trouble; but at last I have triumphed. Once I succeeded before, but the race was too ugly, so I let it die away; but now, as thou seest, they are otherwise. Once, too, I reared a race of giants, but after a while Nature would no more of it, and it died away. Hast thou aught to ask of me?"

"Ay, one thing, O Ayesha," I said boldly; but feeling by no means as bold as I trust I looked. "I would gaze upon thy face."

She laughed out in her bell-like notes. "Bethink thee, Holly," she answered; "bethink thee. It seems that thou knowest the old myths of the gods of Greece. Was there not one Actaeon who perished miserably because he looked on too much beauty? If I showed thee my face, perchance thou wouldst perish miserably also; perchance thou wouldst eat out thy heart in impotent desire; for know I am not for thee – I am for no man, save one, who hath been, but is not yet."

"As thou wilt, Ayesha," I said. "I fear not thy beauty I have put my heart away from such vanity as woman's loveliness, that passes like a flower."

"Nay, thou errest," she said; "that does *not* pass. My beauty endures even as I endure; still, if thou wilt, oh rash man, have thy will; but blame not me if passion mount thy reason, as the Egyptian breakers used to mount a colt, and guide it whither thou wilt not. Never may the man to whom my beauty hath been unveiled put it from his mind, and therefore even with these savages do I go veiled, lest they vex me, and I should slay them. Say, wilt thou see?"

"I will," I answered, my curiosity overpowering me. She lifted her white and rounded arms – never had I seen such arms before – and slowly, very slowly, withdrew some fastening beneath her hair. Then all of a sudden the long, corpselike wrappings fell from her to the ground, and my eyes traveled up her form, now robed only in a garb of clinging white that did but serve to show its perfect and imperial shape, instinct with a life that was more than life, and with a certain serpentlike grace that was more than human. On her little feet were sandals, fastened with studs of gold. Then came ankles more perfect than ever sculptor dreamed of. About the waist her white kirtle was fastened by a double-headed snake of solid gold, above which her gracious form swelled up in lines as pure as they were lovely, till the kirtle ended on the snowy argent of her breast, whereon her arms were folded. I gazed above them at her face, and – I do not exaggerate – shrank back blinded and amazed. I have heard of the beauty of celestial beings, now I saw it; only this beauty, with all its awful loveliness and purity, was *evil* – at least, at the time, it struck me as evil. How am I to describe it? I cannot – simply, I cannot! The man does not live whose pen could convey a sense of what I saw. I might talk of the great changing eyes of deepest, softest black, of the tinted face, of the broad and noble brow, on which the hair grew low, and delicate, straight features. But, beautiful, surpassingly beautiful as they all were, her loveliness did not lie in them. It lay rather, if it can be said to have had any fixed abiding place, in a visible majesty, in an imperial grace, in a godlike stamp of softened power, which shone upon that radiant countenance like a living halo. Never before had I guessed what beauty made sublime could be – and yet, the sublimity was a dark one – the glory was not all of heaven – though none the less was it glorious. Though the face before me was that of a young woman of certainly not more than thirty years, in perfect health, and the first flush of ripened beauty, yet it had stamped upon it a look of unutterable experience, and of deep acquaintance with grief and passion. Not even the lovely smile that crept about the dimples of her mouth could hide this shadow of sin and sorrow. It shone even in the light of the glorious eyes, it was present in the air of majesty, and it seemed to say:

"Behold me, lovely as no woman was or is, undying and half-divine; memory haunts me from age to age, and passion leads me by the hand – evil have I done, and with sorrow have I made acquaintance from age to age, and from age to age evil I shall do, and sorrow shall I know till my redemption comes."

Drawn by some magnetic force which I could not resist, I let my eyes rest upon her shining orbs, and felt a current pass from them to me that bewildered and half-blinded me.

She laughed – ah, how musically! – and nodded her little head at me with an air of sublimated coquetry that would have done credit to a Venus Victrix.

"Rash man!" she said. "Like Actaeon, thou hast had thy will; be careful lest, like Actaeon, thou too dost perish miserably, torn to pieces by the ban-hounds of thine own passions. I too, O

Holly, am a virgin goddess, not to be moved of any man, save one, and it is not thou. Say, hast thou seen enough?"

"I have looked on beauty, and I am blinded," I said hoarsely, lifting my hand to cover up my eyes.

"So! What did I tell thee? Beauty is like the lightning; it is lovely, but it destroys – especially trees, O Holly!" And again she nodded and laughed.

Suddenly she paused, and through my fingers I saw an awful change come over her countenance. Her great eyes suddenly fixed themselves into an expression in which horror seemed to struggle with some tremendous hope arising through the depths of her dark soul. The lovely face grew rigid, and the gracious, willowy form seemed to erect itself.

"Man," she half whispered, half hissed, throwing back her head like a snake about to strike, "man, where didst thou get that scarab on thy hand? Speak, or by the Spirit of Life I will blast thee where thou standest!" And she took one light step towards me, and from her eyes there shone such an awful light – to me it seemed almost like a flame – that I fell, then and there, on the ground before her, babbling confusedly in my terror.

"Peace," she said, with a sudden change of manner, and speaking in her former soft voice, "I did affright thee! Forgive me! But at times, O Holly, the almost infinite mind grows impatient of the slowness of the very finite, and I am tempted to use my power out of pure vexation – very nearly wast thou dead, but I remembered – But the scarab – about the scarabaeus!"

"I picked it up," I gurgled feebly as I got onto my feet again, and it is a solemn fact that my mind was so disturbed that at the moment I could remember nothing else about the ring except that I had picked it up in Leo's cave.

"It is very strange," she said, with a sudden access of womanlike trembling and agitation which seemed out of place in this awful woman, "but once I knew a scarab like that. It – hung

of such tremendous powers and the knowledge of a mystery that could hold off death, was certainly worth falling in love with, if ever woman was. But alas, it was not a question of whether or no she was worth it, for so far as I could judge, not being versed in such matters, I, a fellow of my college, noted for what my acquaintances are pleased to call my misogyny, and a respectable man now well on in middle life, had fallen absolutely and hopelessly in love with this white sorceress. Nonsense; it must be nonsense! She had warned me fairly, and I had refused to take the warning. Curses on the fatal curiosity that is ever prompting man to draw the veil from woman, and curses on the natural impulse that begets it! It is the cause of half – ay, and more than half – of our misfortunes. Why cannot man be content to live alone and be happy, and let the women live alone and be happy too? But perhaps they would not be happy, and I am not sure that we should either. Here was a nice state of affairs. I, at my age, to fall a victim to this modern Circe! But then she was not modem, at least she said not. She was almost as ancient as the original Circe.

I tore my hair, and jumped up from my couch, feeling that if I did not do something I should go off my head. What did she mean about the scarabaeus too? It was Leo's scarabaeus, and had come out of the old coffer that Vincey had left in my rooms nearly one-and-twenty years before. Could it be, after all, that the whole story was true, and the writing on the sherd was *not* a forgery, or the invention of some crack-brained, long-forgotten individual? And if so, could it be that *Leo* was the man that *She* was waiting for – the dead man who was to he born again? Impossible again! The whole thing was gibberish! Who ever heard of a man being born again?

But if it were possible that a woman could exist for two thousand years, this might be possible also – anything might be possible. I myself might, for aught I knew, be a reincarnation of some other forgotten self, or perhaps the last of a long line of ancestral selves. Well, *vive la guerre!* why not? Only, unfortunately, I had no recollection of these previous conditions. The idea was so absurd to me that I burst out laughing, and, addressing the sculptured picture of a grim-looking warrior on the cave wall, called out to him aloud, "Who knows, old fellow? Perhaps I was your contemporary. By Jove! perhaps I was you and you are I," and then I laughed again at my own folly, and the sound of my laughter rang dismally along the vaulted roof, as though the ghost of the warrior had uttered the ghost of a laugh.

Next I bethought me that I had not been to see how Leo was, so, taking up one of the lamps which was burning at my bedside, I slipped off my shoes and crept down the passage to the entrance of his sleeping cave. The draft of the night air was lifting his curtain to and fro gently, as though spirit hands were drawing and redrawing it. I slid into the vaultlike apartment and looked round. There was a light by which I could see that Leo was lying on the couch, tossing restlessly in his fever, but asleep. At his side, half-lying on the floor, half-leaning against the stone couch, was Ustane. She held his hand in one of hers, but she too was dozing, and the two made a pretty, or rather a pathetic, picture. Poor Leo! His cheek was burning red, there were dark shadows beneath his eyes, and his breath came heavily. He was very, very ill; and again the horrible fear seized me that he might die, and I be left alone in the world. And yet if he lived he would perhaps be my rival with Ayesha; even if he were not the man, what chance should I, middle-aged and hideous, have against his bright youth and beauty? Well, thank Heaven, my sense of right was not dead. *She* had not killed that yet; and, as I stood there, I prayed to the Almighty in my heart that my boy, my more than son, might live – ay, even if he proved to be the man.

Then I went back as softly as I had come, but still I could not sleep; the sight and thought of dear Leo lying there so ill had but added fuel to the fire of my unrest. My wearied body and overstrained mind awakened all my imagination into preternatural activity. Ideas, visions, almost inspirations, floated before it with startling vividness. Most of them were grotesque enough, some were ghastly, some recalled thoughts and sensations that had for years been buried in the debris of my past life. But behind and above them all hovered the shape of that awful woman, and through them gleamed the memory of her entrancing loveliness. Up and down the cave I strode – up and down.

Suddenly I observed what I had not noticed before, that there was a narrow aperture in the rocky wall. I took up the lamp and examined it; the aperture led to a passage. Now I was still sufficiently sensible to remember that it is not pleasant, in such a situation as ours was, to have passages running into one's bedchamber from no one knows where. If there are passages, people can come up them; they can come up when one is asleep. Partly to see where it went to, and partly from a restless desire to be doing something, I followed the passage. It led to a stone stair, which I descended; the stair ended in another passage, or rather tunnel, also hewn out of the bedrock, and running, so far as I could judge, exactly beneath the gallery that led to the entrance of our rooms, and across the great central cave. I went on down it: it was as silent as the grave, but still, drawn by some sensation or attraction that I cannot describe, I followed on, my stockinged feet falling without noise on the smooth and rocky floor. When I had traversed some fifty yards of space, I came to another passage running at right angles, and here an awful thing happened to me: the sharp draft caught my lamp and extinguished it, leaving me in utter darkness in the bowels of that mysterious place. I took a couple of strides forward so as to clear the bisecting tunnel, being terribly afraid lest I should turn up it in the dark if once I got confused as to the direction, and then paused to think. What was I to do? I had no match; it seemed awful to attempt that long journey back through the utter gloom, and yet I could not stand there all night, and, if I did, probably it would not help me much, for in the bowels of the rock it would be as dark at midday as at midnight. I looked back over my shoulder – not a sight or a sound. I peered forward down the darkness: surely, far away, I saw something like the faint glow of fire. Perhaps it was a cave where I could get a light – at any rate, it was worth investigating. Slowly and painfully I crept along the tunnel, keeping my hand against its wall, and feeling at every step with my foot before I put it down, fearing lest I should tall into some pit. Thirty paces – there was a light, a broad light that came and went, shining through curtains! Fifty paces – it was close at hand! Sixty – oh, great heaven!

I was at the curtains, and they did not hang close, so I could see clearly into the little cavern beyond them. It had all the appearance of being a tomb, and was lit up by a fire that burned in its center with a whitish flame and without smoke. Indeed, there, to the left, was a stone shelf with a little ledge to it three inches or so high, and on the shelf lay what I took to be a corpse; at any rate, it looked like one, with something white thrown over it. To the right was a similar shelf, on which lay some broidered coverings. Over the fire bent the figure of a woman; she was sideways to me and facing the corpse, wrapped in a dark mantle that hid her like a nun's cloak. She seemed to be staring at the flickering flame. Suddenly, as I was trying to make up my mind what to do, with a convulsive movement that somehow gave an impression of despairing energy, the woman rose to her feet and cast the dark cloak from her.

It was *She* herself!

She was clothed, as I had seen her when she unveiled, in the kirtle of clinging white, cut low upon her bosom, and bound in at the waist with the barbaric double-headed snake, and, as before, her rippling black hair fell in heavy masses down her back. But her face was what caught my eye, and held me as in a vice, not this time by the force of its beauty, but by the power of fascinated terror. The beauty was still there, indeed, but the agony, the blind passion, and the awful vindictiveness displayed upon those quivering features and in the tortured look of the upturned eyes, were such as surpass my powers of description.

For a moment she stood still, her hands raised high above her head, and as she did so the white robe slipped from her down to her golden girdle, baring the blinding loveliness of her form. She stood there, her fingers clenched, and the awful look of malevolence gathered and deepened on her face.

Suddenly, I thought of what would happen if she discovered me, and the reflection made me turn sick and faint. But even if I had known that I must die if I stopped, I do not believe that I could have moved, for I was absolutely fascinated. But still I knew my danger. Supposing she should hear me, or see me through the curtain, supposing I even sneezed, or that her magic told her that she was being watched – swift indeed would be my doom.

Down came the clenched hands to her sides, then up again above her head, and, as I am a living and honorable man, the white flame of the fire leaped up after them, almost to the roof, throwing a fierce and ghastly glare upon *She* herself, upon the white figure beneath the covering, and every scroll and detail of the rockwork.

Down came the ivory arms again, and as they did so she spoke, or rather hissed, in Arabic, in a note that curdled my blood, and for a second stopped my heart.

"Curse her, may she be everlastingly accursed."

The arms fell and the flame sank. Up they went again, and the broad tongue of fire shot up after them; then again they fell.

"Curse her memory – accursed be the memory of the Egyptian."

Up again, and again down.

"Curse her, the fair daughter of the Nile, because of her beauty."

"Curse her, because her magic hath prevailed against me."

"Curse her, because she kept my beloved from me."

And again the flame dwindled and shrank.

She put her hands before her eyes, and abandoning the hissing tone, cried aloud: "What is the use of cursing? She prevailed, and she is gone."

Then she recommenced with an even more frightful energy:

"Curse her where she is. Let my curses reach her where she is and disturb her rest.

"Curse her through the starry spaces. Let her shadow be accursed.

"Let my power find her even there.

"Let her hear me even there. Let her hide herself in the blackness.

"Let her go down into the pit of despair, because I shall one day find her."

Again the flame fell, and again she covered her eyes with her hands.

"It is no use – no use," she wailed; "who can reach those who sleep? Not even I can reach them."

Then once more she began her unholy rites.

"Curse her when she shall be born again. Let her be born accursed.

"Let her be utterly accursed from the hour of her birth until sleep finds her.

"Yea, then, let her be accursed: for then shall I overtake her with my vengeance, and utterly destroy her."

And so on. The flame rose and fell, reflecting itself in her agonized eyes; the hissing sound of her terrible maledictions – and no words of mine, especially on paper, can convey how terrible they were – ran round the walls and died away in little echoes, and the fierce light and deep gloom alternated themselves on the white and dreadful form stretched upon that bier of stone.

But at length she seemed to wear herself out, and ceased. She sat herself down upon the rocky floor, and shook the dense cloud of her beautiful hair over her face and breast, and began to sob terribly in the torture of a heart-rending despair.

"Two thousand years," she moaned, "two thousand years have I waited and endured; but though century doth still creep on to century, and time give place to time, the sting of memory hath not lessened, the light of hope doth not shine more bright. Oh, to have lived two thousand years, with my passion eating at my heart, and with my sin ever before me! Oh, that for me life cannot bring forgetfulness! Oh, for the weary years that have been and are yet to come, and evermore to come, endless and without end!

"My love! My love! My love! Why did that stranger bring thee back to me after this sort? For five hundred years I have not suffered thus. Oh, if I sinned against thee, have I not wiped away the sin? When wilt thou come back to me who have all, and yet without thee have naught? What is there that I can do? What? What? What? And perchance she – perchance that Egyptian doth abide with thee where thou art, and mock my memory. Oh, why could I not die with thee, I who slew thee? Alas, that I cannot die! Alas! Alas!" And she flung herself prone upon the ground, and sobbed and wept till I thought her heart must burst.

Suddenly she ceased, raised herself to her feet, rearranged her robe, and, tossing back her long locks impatiently, swept across to where the figure lay upon the stone.

"Oh Kallikrates," she cried, and I trembled at the name, "I must look upon thy face again, though it be agony. It is a generation since I looked upon thee whom I slew – slew with mine own hand," and with trembling fingers she seized the corner of the sheetlike wrapping that covered the form upon the stone bier, and then paused. When she spoke again, it was in a kind of awed whisper, as though her idea were terrible even to herself.

"Shall I raise thee," she said, apparently addressing the corpse, "so that thou standest there before me, as of old? I *can* do it," and she held out her hands over the sheeted dead, while her whole frame became rigid and terrible to see, and her eyes grew fixed and dull. I shrank in honor behind the curtain, my hair stood up upon my head, and whether it was my imagination or a fact I am unable to say, but I thought that the quiet form beneath the covering began to quiver, and the winding sheet to lift as though it lay on the breast of one who slept. Suddenly she withdrew her hands, and the motion of the corpse seemed to me to cease.

"What is the use?" she said gloomily. "Of what use is it to recall the semblance of life when I cannot recall the spirit? Even if thou stoodest before me thou wouldst not know me, and couldst but do what I bid thee. The life in thee would be *my* life, and not *thy* life, Kallikrates."

For a moment she stood there brooding, and then cast herself down on her knees beside the form, and began to press her lips against the sheet, and weep. There was something so horrible about the sight of this awe-inspiring woman letting loose her passion on the dead – so much more horrible even than anything that had gone before, that I could no longer bear to look at it, and, turning, began to creep, shaking as I was in every limb, slowly along the pitch-dark passage, feeling in my trembling heart that I had had a vision of a soul in Hell.

On I stumbled, I scarcely know how. Twice I fell, once I turned up the bisecting passage, but fortunately found out my mistake in time. For twenty minutes or more I crept along, till at last it occurred to me that I must have passed the little stair by which I descended. So, utterly exhausted, and nearly frightened to death, I sank down at length there on the stone flooring, and sank into oblivion.

When I came to I noticed a faint ray of light in the passage just behind me. I crept to it, and found it was the little stair down which the weak dawn was stealing. Passing up it I gained my chamber in safety, and, flinging myself on the couch, was soon lost in slumber or rather stupor.

Chapter 15

Ayesha Gives Judgment

THE NEXT THING that I remember is opening my eyes and perceiving the form of Job, who had now practically recovered from his attack of fever. He was standing in the ray of light that pierced into the cave from the outer air, shaking out my clothes as a makeshift for brushing them, which he could not do because there was no brush, and then folding them up neatly and laying them on the foot of the stone couch. This done, he got my traveling dressing case out of the Gladstone bag, and opened it ready for my use. First, he stood it on the foot of the couch also, then, being afraid, I suppose, that I should kick it off, he placed it on a leopard skin on the floor, and stood back a step or two to observe the effect. It was not satisfactory, so he shut up the bag, turned it on end, and, having rested it against the foot of the couch, placed the dressing case on it. Next, he looked at the pots full of water, which constituted our washing apparatus. "Ah," I heard him murmur, "no hot water in this beastly place. I suppose these poor creatures only use it to boil each other in," and he sighed deeply. "What is the matter, Job?" I said. "Beg pardon, sir," he said, touching his hair "I thought you were asleep, sir; and I am sure you look as though you want it. One might think from the look of you that you had been having a night of it."

I only groaned by way of answer. I had, indeed, been having a night of it, such as I hoped never to have again.

"How is Mr. Leo, Job?"

"Much the same, sir. If he don't soon mend, he'll end, sir; and that's all about it; though I must say that that there savage, Ustane, do do her best for him, almost like a baptized Christian. She is always hanging round and looking after him, and if I ventures to interfere, it's awful to see her; her hair seems to stand on end, and she curses and swears away in her heathen talk – at least I fancy she must be cursing from the look of her."

"And what do you do then?"

"I make her a perlite bow, and I say, 'Young woman, your position is one that I don't quite understand, and can't recognize. Let me tell you that I has a duty to perform to my master as is incapacitated by illness, and that I am going to perform it until I am incapacitated too,' but she don't take no heed, not she – only curses and swears away worse than ever. Last night she put her hand under that sort of nightshirt she wears and whips out a knife with a kind of a curl in the blade, so I whips out my revolver, and we walks round and round each other till at last she bursts out laughing. It isn't nice treatment for a Christian man to have to put up with from a savage, however handsome she may be, but it is what people must expect as is *fools* enough" – Job laid great emphasis on the 'fools' – "to come to such a place to look for things no man is meant to find. It's a judgment on us, sir – that's my opinion; and I, for one, is of opinion that the judgment isn't half done yet, and when it is done, we shall be done too, and just stop in these beastly caves with the ghosts and the corpseses for once and all. And now, sir, I must be seeing about Mr. Leo's broth, if that wildcat will let me; and, perhaps, you would like to get up, sir, because it's past nine o'clock."

Job's remarks were not of an exactly cheering order to a man who had passed such a night as I had; and, what is more, they had the weight of truth. Taking one thing with another, it appeared to me to be an utter impossibility that we should escape from the place where we were. Supposing that Leo recovered, and supposing that *She* would let us go, which was exceedingly doubtful, and that she did not 'blast' us in some moment of vexation, and that we were not hot-potted by the Amahagger, it would be quite impossible for us to find our way across the network of marshes which, stretching for scores and scores of miles, formed a stronger and more impassable fortification round the various Amahagger households than any that could be built or designed by man. No, there was but one thing to do – face it out; and, speaking for my own part, I was so intensely interested in the whole weird story that, so far as I was concerned, notwithstanding the shattered state of my nerves, I asked nothing better, even if my life paid forfeit to my curiosity. What man for whom physiology has charms could forbear to study such a character as that of this Ayesha when the opportunity of doing so presented itself? The very terror of the pursuit added to its fascination, and besides, as I was forced to own to myself even now in the sober light of day, she herself had attractions that I could not forget. Not even the dreadful sight which I had witnessed during the night could drive that folly from my mind; and alas, that I should have to admit it, it has not been driven thence to this hour.

After I had dressed myself I passed into the eating, or rather embalming chamber, and had some food, which was as before brought to me by the girl mutes. When I had finished I went and saw poor Leo, who was quite off his head, and did not even know me. I asked Ustane how she thought he was; but she only shook her head and began to cry a little. Evidently her hopes were small; and I then and there made up my mind that, if it were in any way possible, I would get *She* to come and see him. Surely she would cure him if she chose – at any rate she said she could. While I was in the room, Billali entered, and also shook his head.

"He will die at night," he said.

"God forbid, my father," I answered, and turned away with a heavy heart.

"'*She-who-must-be-obeyed*' commands thy presence, my Baboon," said the old man as soon as we got to the curtain; "but oh, my dear son, be more careful. Yesterday I made sure in my heart that *She* would blast thee when thou didst not crawl upon thy stomach before her. She is sitting in the great hall even now to do justice upon those who would have smitten thee and the

Lion. Come on, my son; come swiftly."

I turned and followed him down the passage, and when we reached the great central cave saw that many Amahagger, some robed, and some merely clad in the sweet simplicity of a leopard skin, were hurrying up it. We mingled with the throng, and walked up the enormous and, indeed, almost interminable cave. All the way its walls were elaborately sculptured, and every twenty paces or so passages opened out of it at right angles, leading, Billali told me, to tombs, hollowed in the rock by "the people who were before." Nobody visited those tombs now, he said; and I must say that my heart rejoiced when I thought of the opportunities of antiquarian research which opened out before me.

At last we came to the head of the cave, where there was a rock dais almost exactly similar to the one on which we had been so furiously attacked, a fact that proved to me that these daises must have been used as altars, probably for the celebration of religious ceremonies, and more especially of rites connected with the interment of the dead. On either side of this dais were passages leading, Billali informed me, to other caves full of dead bodies. "Indeed," he added, "the whole mountain is full of dead, and nearly all of them are perfect."

In front of the dais were gathered a great number of people of both sexes, who stood staring about in their peculiar gloomy fashion, which would have reduced Mark Tapley himself to misery in about five minutes. On the dais was a rude chair of black wood inlaid with ivory, having a seat made of grass fiber, and a footstool formed of a wooden slab attached to the framework of the chair.

Suddenly there was a cry of "Hiya! Hiya!" (*"She! She!"*), and thereupon the entire crowd of spectators instantly precipitated itself upon the ground, and lay still as though it were individually and collectively stricken dead, leaving me standing there like some solitary survivor of a massacre. As it did so a long string of guards began to defile from a passage to the left, and ranged themselves on either side of the dais. Then followed about a score of male mutes, then as many women mutes bearing lamps, and then a tall white figure, swathed from head to foot, in whom I recognized *She* herself. She mounted the dais and sat down upon the chair, and spoke to me in Greek, I suppose because she did not wish those present to understand what she said.

"Come hither, O Holly," she said, "and sit thou at my feet, and see me do justice on those who would have slain thee. Forgive me if my Greek doth halt a lame man; it is so long since I have heard the sound of it that my tongue it stiff, and will not bend rightly to the words."

I bowed, and, mounting the dais, sat down at her feet.

"How didst thou sleep, my Holly?" she asked.

"I slept not well, O Ayesha!" I answered with perfect truth, and with an inward fear that perhaps she knew how I had passed the heart of the night.

"So," she said with a little laugh. "I, too, have not slept well. Last night I had dreams, and methinks that thou didst call them to me, O Holly."

"Of what didst thou dream, Ayesha?" I asked indifferently.

"I dreamed," she answered quickly, "of one I hate and one I love," and then, as though to turn the conversation, she addressed the captain of her guard in Arabic: "Let the men be brought before me."

The captain bowed low, for the guard and her attendants did not prostrate themselves but had remained standing, and departed with his underlings down a passage to the right.

Then came a silence. *She* leaned her swathed head upon her hand and appeared to be lost in thought, while the multitude before her continued to grovel upon their stomachs, only screwing their heads round a little so as to get a view of us with one eye. It seemed that their queen so rarely appeared in public that they were willing to undergo this inconvenience, and even graver risks, to have the opportunity of looking on her, or rather on her garments, for no living man there except myself had ever seen her face. At last we caught sight of the waving of lights, and heard the tramp of men coming along the passage, and in filed the guard, and with them the survivors of our would-be murderers to the number of twenty or more, on whose countenances the natural expression of sullenness struggled with the terror that evidently filled their savage hearts. They were ranged in front of the dais, and would have cast themselves down on the floor of the cave like the spectators, but *She* stopped them.

"Nay," she said in her softest voice, "stand; I pray you stand. Perchance the time will soon be when ye shall grow weary of being stretched out," and she laughed melodiously.

I saw a cringe of terror run along the rank of the poor doomed wretches, and, wicked villains as they were, I felt sorry for them. Some minutes, perhaps two or three, passed before anything fresh occurred, during which *She* appeared from the movement of her head – for, of course, we could not see her eyes – to be slowly and carefully examining each delinquent. At last she spoke, addressing herself to me in a quiet and deliberate tone.

"Dost thou, O my guest, who art known in thine own country by the name of the Prickly Tree, recognize these men?"

"Ay, O Queen, nearly all of them," I said, and I saw them glower at me as I said it.

"Then tell to me, and this great company, the tale whereof I have heard."

Thus adjured, I, in as few words as I could, related the history of the cannibal feast, and of the attempted torture of our poor servant. The narrative was received in perfect silence, both by the accused and by the audience, and also by *She* herself. When I had done, Ayesha called upon Billali by name, and, lifting his head from the ground, but without rising, the old man confirmed my story. No further evidence was taken.

"Ye have heard," said *She* at length, in a cold, clear voice, very different from her usual tones – indeed, it was one of the most remarkable things about this extraordinary creature that her voice had the power of suiting itself in a wonderful manner to the mood of the moment. "What have ye to say, ye rebellious children, why vengeance should not be done upon you?"

For some time there was no answer, but at last one of the men, a fine, broad-chested fellow, well on in middle-life, with deep-graven features and an eye like a hawk's, spoke, and said that the orders that they had received were not to harm the white men; nothing was said of their black servant, so, egged on thereto by a woman who was now dead, they proceeded to try to hot-pot him after the ancient and honorable custom of their country, with a view of eating him in due course. As for their attack upon ourselves, it was made in an access of sudden fury, and they deeply regretted it. He ended by humbly praying that mercy might be extended to them; or, at least, that they might be banished into the swamps, to live or die as it might chance; but I saw it written on his face that he had but little hope of mercy.

Then came a pause, and the most intense silence reigned over the whole scene, which, illuminated as it was by the flicker of the lamps striking out broad patterns of light and shadow upon the rocky walls, was as strange as any I ever saw, even in that unholy land. Upon the ground before the dais were stretched scores of the corpselike forms of the spectators, till at last the long lines of them were lost in the gloomy background. Before this outstretched audience were the knots of evildoers, trying to cover up their natural terrors with a brave appearance of unconcern. On the right and left stood the silent guards, robed in white and armed with great spears and daggers, and men and women mutes watching with hard curious eyes. Then, seated in her barbaric chair above them all, with myself at her feet, was the veiled white woman, whose loveliness and awesome power seemed to visibly shine about her like a halo, or rather like the glow from some unseen light. Never have I seen her veiled shape look more terrible than it did in that space, while she gathered herself up for vengeance.

At last it came.

"Dogs and serpents," She began in a low voice that gradually gathered power as she went on, till the place rang with it. "Eaters of human flesh, two things have ye done. First, ye have attacked these strangers, being white men, and would have slain their servant, and for that alone death is your reward. But that is not all. Ye have dared to disobey me. Did I not send my word unto you by Billali, my servant, and the father of your household? Did I not bid you to hospitably entertain these strangers, whom now ye have striven to slay, and whom, had not they been brave and strong beyond the strength of men, ye would cruelly have murdered? Hath it not been taught to you from childhood that the law of *She* is an ever fixed law, and that he who breaketh it by so much as one jot or tittle shall perish? And is not my lightest word a law? Have not your fathers taught you this, I say, while as yet ye were but children? Do ye not know that as well might ye bid these great caves to fall upon you, or the sun to cease its journeying, as to hope to turn me from my courses, or make my word light or heavy, according to your minds? Well do ye know it, ye wicked ones. But ye are all evil – evil to the core – the wickedness bubbles up in you like a fountain in the springtime. Were it not for me, generations since had ye ceased to be, for of your own evil way had ye destroyed each other. And now, because ye have done this thing, because ye have striven to put these men, my guests, to death, and yet more because ye have dared to disobey my word, this is the doom that I doom you to. That ye be taken to the cave of torture,[1] and given over to the tormentors,

1 I afterwards saw this dreadful place, also a legacy from the prehistoric people who lived in Kôr. The only objects in the cave itself were slabs of rock arranged in various positions to facilitate the operations of the torturers. Many of these slabs, which were of a porous stone, were stained quite dark with the blood of ancient victims that had soaked into them. Also in the center of the room was a place for a furnace, with a cavity wherein to heat the historic pot. But the most dreadful thing about the cave was that over each slab was a sculptured illustration of the appropriate torture being applied. These sculptures were so awful that I will not harrow the reader by attempting a description of them. – L. H. H

and that on the going down of tomorrow's sun those of you who yet remain alive be slain, even as ye would have slain the servant of this my guest."

She ceased, and a faint murmur of horror ran round the cave. As for the victims, as soon as they realized the full hideousness of their doom, their stoicism forsook them, and they flung themselves down upon the ground, and wept and implored for mercy in a way that was dreadful to behold. I, too, turned to Ayesha, and begged her to spare them, or at least to mete out their fate in some less awful way. But she was as hard as adamant about it.

"My Holly," she said, again speaking in Greek, which, to tell the truth, although I have always been considered a better scholar of that language than most men, I found it rather difficult to follow, chiefly because of the change in the fall of the accent. Ayesha, of course, talked with the accent of her contemporaries, whereas we have only tradition and the modern accent to guide us as to the exact pronunciation. "My Holly, it cannot be. Were I to show mercy to those wolves, your lives would not be safe among this people for a day. Thou knowest them not. They are tigers to lap blood, and even now they hunger for your lives. How thinkest thou that I rule this people? I have but a regiment of guards to do my bidding, therefore it is not by force. It is by terror. My empire is of the imagination. Once in a generation mayhap I do as I have done but now, and slay a score by torture. Believe not that I would be cruel, or take vengeance on anything so low. What can it profit me to be avenged on such as these? Those who live long, my Holly, have no passions, save where they have interests. Though I may seem to slay in wrath, or because my mood is crossed, it is not so. Thou hast seen how in the heavens the little clouds blow this way and that without a cause, yet behind them is the great wind sweeping on its path whither it listeth. So is it with me, O Holly. My moods and changes are the little clouds, and fitfully these seem to turn; but behind them ever blows the great wind of my purpose. Nay, the men must die; and die as I have said."

Then, suddenly turning to the captain of the guard: "As my word is, so be it!"

Chapter 16

The Tombs of Kôr

AFTER THE PRISONERS had been removed Ayesha waved her hand, and the spectators turned round and began to crawl off down the cave like a scattered flock of sheep. When they were a fair distance from the dais, however, they rose and walked away, leaving the Queen and myself alone, with the exception of the mutes and the few remaining guards, most of whom had departed with the doomed men. Thinking this a good opportunity, I asked *She* to come and see Leo, telling her of his serious condition; but she would not, saying that he certainly would not die before the night, as people never died of that sort of fever except at nightfall or dawn. Also she said that it would be better to let the sickness spend its course as much as possible before she cured it. Accordingly, I was rising to leave, when she bade me follow her, as she would talk with me, and show me the wonders of the caves.

I was too much involved in the web of her fatal fascinations to say her no, even if I had wished, which I did not. She rose from her chair, and, making some signs to the mutes, descended from the dais. Thereupon four of the girls took lamps and ranged themselves two in front and two behind us, but the others went away, as also did the guards.

"Now," she said, "wouldst thou see some of the wonders of this place, O Holly? Look upon this great cave. Sawest thou ever the like? Yet was it and many more like it, hollowed by the hands of the dead race that once lived here in the city on the plain. A great and a wonderful people must they have been, those men of Kôr, but, like the Egyptians, they thought more of the dead than of the living. How many men, thinkest thou, working for how many years, did it need to the hollowing out this cave and all the galleries thereof?"

"Tens of thousands," I answered.

"So, O Holly. This people was an old people before the Egyptians were. A little can I read of their inscriptions, having found the key thereto – and, see thou here, this was one of the last of the caves that they hollowed," and, turning to the rock behind her, she motioned the mutes to hold up the lamps. Carven over the dais was the figure of an old man seated in a chair, with an ivory rod in his hand. It struck me at once that his features were exceedingly like those of the man who was represented as being embalmed in the chamber where we took our meals. Beneath the chair, which, by the way was shaped exactly like the one in which Ayesha had sat to give judgment, was a short inscription in the extraordinary characters of which I have already spoken, but which I do not remember sufficient of to illustrate. It looked more like Chinese writing than any other that I am acquainted with. This inscription Ayesha proceeded, with some difficulty and hesitation, to read aloud and translate. It ran as follows:

In the year four thousand two hundred and fifty-nine from the founding of the City of imperial Kôr was this cave [or burial place] completed by Tisno, King of Kôr, the people thereof and their slaves having labored thereat for three generations, to be a tomb for their citizens of rank who shall come after. May the blessing of the heaven above the heaven rest upon their work, and make the sleep of Tisno, the mighty monarch, the likeness of whose features is graven above, a sound and happy sleep till the day of awakening,[1] *and also the sleep of his servants, and of those of his race who, rising up after him, shall yet lay their heads as low.*

"Thou seest, O Holly," she said, "this people founded the city, of which the ruins yet cumber the plain yonder, four thousand years before this cave was finished. Yet, when first mine eyes beheld it two thousand years ago, was it even as it is now. Judge, therefore, how old must that city have been! And now, follow thou me, and I will show thee after what fashion this great people fell when the time was come for it to fall," and she led the way down to the center of the cave, stopping at a spot where a round rock had been let into a kind of large manhole in the flooring, accurately filling it just as the iron plates fill the spaces in the London pavements down which the coals are thrown. "Thou seest," she said. "Tell me, what is it?"

"Nay, I know not," I answered; whereon she crossed to the left-hand side of the cave (looking towards the entrance) and signed to the mutes to hold up the lamps. On the wall was something painted with a red pigment similar characters to those hewn beneath the sculpture of Tisno, King of Kôr. This inscription she proceeded to translate to me, the pigment still being quite fresh enough to show the form of the letters. It ran as follows:

I, Junis, a priest of the Great Temple of Kôr, write this upon the rock of the burying place in the year four thousand eight hundred and three from the founding of Kôr. Kôr is fallen! No more shall the mighty feast in her halls, no more shall she rule the world, and her navies go out to commerce with the world. Kôr is fallen! And her mighty works and all the cities of Kôr, and all the harbors that she built and

1 This phrase is remarkable, as seeming to indicate a belief in a future state. – EDITOR.

the canals that she made, are for the wolf and the owl and the wild swan, and the barbarian who comes after. Twenty and five moons ago did a cloud settle upon Kôr, and the hundred cities of Kôr, and out of the cloud came a pestilence that slew her people, old and young, one with another, and spared not. One with another they turned black and died – the young and the old, the rich and the poor, the man and the woman, the prince and the slave. The pestilence slew and slew, and ceased not by day or by night, and those who escaped from the pestilence were slain of the famine. No longer could the bodies of the children of Kôr be preserved according to the ancient rites, because of the number of the dead, therefore were they hurled into the great pit beneath the cave through the hole in the floor of the cave. Then at last, a remnant of this the great people, the light of the whole world, went down to the coast and took ship and sailed northwards; and now am I, the Priest Junis, who write this, the last man left alive of this great city of men, but whether there be any yet left in the other cities. I know not. This do I write in misery of heart before I die, because Kôr the Imperial is no more, and because there are none to worship in her temple, and all her palaces are empty, and her princes and her captains and her traders and her fair women have passed off the face of the earth.

I gave a sigh of astonishment – the utter desolation depicted in this rude scrawl was so overpowering. It was terrible to think of this solitary survivor of a mighty people recording its fate before he too went down into darkness. What must the old man have felt as, in ghastly terrifying solitude, by the light of one lamp feebly, illumining a little space of gloom, he in a few brief lines daubed the history of his nation's death upon the cavern wall? What a subject for the moralist, or the painter, or indeed for anyone who can think!

"Doth it not occur to thee, O Holly," said Ayesha, laying her hand upon my shoulder, "that those men who sailed north may have been the fathers of the first Egyptians?"

"Nay, I know not," I said; "it seems that the world is very old."

"Old? Yes, it is old indeed. Time after time have nations, ay, and rich and strong nations, learned in the arts, been and passed away and been forgotten, so that no memory of them remains. This is but one of several; for Time eats up the works of man, unless, indeed, he digs in caves like the people of Kôr, and then mayhap the sea swallows them, or the earthquake shakes them in. Who knows what hath been on the earth, or what shall be? There is no new thing under the sun, as the wise Hebrew wrote long ago. Yet were not these people utterly destroyed, as I think. Some few remained in the other cities, for their cities were many. But the barbarians from the south, or perchance my people, the Arabs, came down upon them, and took their women to wife, and the race of the Amahagger that is now is a bastard brood of the mighty sons of Kôr, and behold it dwelleth in the tombs with its fathers' bones.[1] But I know not: who can know? My arts cannot pierce so far into the blackness of Time's night. A great people were they. They conquered till none were left to conquer, and then they dwelt at ease within their rocky mountain walls, with their man servants and their maid servants, their minstrels, their sculptors, and their concubines, and traded and quarreled, and ate and hunted and slept and made merry till their time came. But come, I will show thee the great pit beneath the cave whereof the writing speaks. Never shall thine eyes witness such another sight."

Accordingly I followed her to a side passage opening out of the main cave, then down a great number of steps, and along an underground shaft which cannot have been less than sixty feet beneath the surface of the rock, and was ventilated by curious borings that ran upward, I do not know where. Suddenly the

1 The name of the race Amahagger would seem to indicate a curious mingling of races such as might easily have occurred in the neighborhood of the Zambesi. The prefix 'ama' is common to the Zulu and kindred races, and signifies "people," while "hagger" is an Arabic word meaning a stone. – EDITOR.

passage ended, and she halted and bade the mutes hold up the lamps, and, as she had prophesied, I saw a scene such as I was not likely to see again. We were standing in an enormous pit, or rather on the edge of it, for it went down deeper – I do not know how much – than the level on which we stood, and was edged in with a low wall of rock. So far as I could judge, this pit was about the size of the space beneath the dome of St. Paul's in London, and when the lamps were held up I saw that it was nothing but one vast charnel house, being literally full of thousands of human skeletons, which lay piled up in an enormous gleaming pyramid, formed by the slipping down of the bodies at the apex as fresh ones were dropped in from above. Anything more appalling than this jumbled mass of the remains of a departed race I cannot imagine, and what made it even more dreadful was that in this dry air a considerable number of the bodies had simply become desiccated with the skin still on them, and now, fixed in every conceivable position, stared at us out of the mountain of white bones, grotesquely horrible caricatures of humanity. In my astonishment I uttered an ejaculation, and the echoes of my voice ringing in the vaulted space, disturbed a skull that had been accurately balanced for many thousands of years near the apex of the pile. Down it came with a run, bounding along merrily towards us, and of course bringing an avalanche of other bones after it, till at last the whole pit rattled with their movement, even as though the skeletons were getting up to greet us.

"Come," I said, "I have seen enough. These are the bodies of those who died of the great sickness, is it not so?" I added, as we turned away.

"Yes. The people of Kôr ever embalmed their dead, as did the Egyptians, but their art was greater than the art of the Egyptians, for whereas the Egyptians disemboweled and drew the brain, the people of Kôr injected fluid into the veins, and thus reached every part. But stay, thou shalt see," and she halted at haphazard at one of the little doorways opening out of the passage along which we were walking, and motioned to the mutes to light us in. We entered into a small chamber similar to the one in which I had slept at our first stopping place, only instead of one there were two stone benches or beds in it. On the benches lay figures covered with yellow linen,[1] on which a fine and impalpable dust had gathered in the course of ages but nothing like to the extent that one would have anticipated, for in these deep-hewn caves there is no material to turn to dust. About the bodies on the stone shelves and floor of the tomb were many painted vases, but I saw very few ornaments or weapons in any of the vaults.

"Uplift the cloths, O Holly," said Ayesha, but when I put out my hand to do so I drew it back again. It seemed like sacrilege, and to speak the truth I was awed by the dread solemnity of the place, and of the presences before us. Then, with a little laugh at my fears, she drew them herself, only to discover other and yet finer cloths lying over the forms upon the stone bench. These also she withdrew, and then for the first time for thousands upon thousands of years did living eyes look upon the face of that chilly dead. It was a woman; she might have been thirty-five years of age, or perhaps a little less, and had certainly been beautiful. Even now her calm clear-cut features, marked out with delicate eyebrows and long eyelashes which threw little lines of the shadow of the lamplight upon the ivory face, were wonderfully beautiful. There, robed in white, down which her blue-black hair was streaming, she slept her last long sleep, and on her arm, its face pressed against her breast, there lay a little babe. So sweet was the sight, although so awful, that – I confess it without shame – I could scarcely withhold my tears. It took me back across the dim gulf of the ages to some happy home in dead Imperial Kôr, where this winsome lady girt about with beauty had lived and died, and dying taken her last-born with her to the tomb. There they were before us, mother and babe, the white memories of a forgotten human history speaking more eloquently

1 All the linen that the Amahagger wore was taken from the tombs, which accounted for its yellow hue. If it was well washed, however, and properly rebleached, it acquired its former snowy whiteness, and was the softest and best linen I ever saw. – L. H. H.

to the heart than could any written record of their lives. Reverently I replaced the grave-clothes, and, with a sigh that flowers so fair should, in the purpose of the Everlasting, have bloomed only to be gathered to the grave, I turned to the body on the opposite shelf, and gently unveiled it. It was that of a man in advanced life, with a long grizzled beard, and also robed in white, probably the husband of the lady, who, after surviving her many years, came at last to sleep once more for good and all beside her.

We left the place and entered others. It would be too long to describe the many things I saw in them. Each one had its occupants, for the five-hundred-odd years that had elapsed between the completion of the cave and the destruction of the race had evidently sufficed to fill these catacombs, numberless as they were, and all appeared to have been undisturbed since the day when they were placed there. I could fill a book with the description of them, but to do so would only be to repeat what I have said, with variations.

Nearly all the bodies, so masterly was the art with which they had been treated, were as perfect as on the day of death thousands of years before. Nothing came to injure them in the deep silence of the living rock: they were beyond the reach of heat and cold and damp, and the aromatic drugs with which they had been saturated were evidently practically everlasting in their effect. Here and there, however, we saw an exception, and in these cases, although the flesh looked sound enough externally, if one touched it it fell in, and revealed the fact that the figure was but a pile of dust. This arose, Ayesha told me, from these particular bodies having, either owing to haste in the burial or to other causes, been soaked in the preservative,[1] instead of its being injected into the substance of the flesh.

About the last tomb we visited I must, however, say one

1 Ayesha afterwards showed me the tree from the leaves of which this ancient preservative was manufactured. It is a low bush-like tree that to this day grows in wonderful plenty upon the sides of the mountains, or rather upon the slopes leading up to the rocky walls. The leaves are long and narrow, a vivid green in color, but turning a bright red in the autumn, and not unlike those of a laurel in general appearance. They have little smell when green, but if boiled the aromatic odor from them is so strong that one can hardly bear it. The best mixture,

(contd. on the next pg.)

word, for its contents spoke even more eloquently to the human sympathies than those of the first. It had but two occupants, and they lay together on a single shelf. I withdrew the grave-clothes, and there, clasped heart to heart, were a young man and a blooming girl. Her head rested on his arm, and his lips were pressed against her brow. I opened the man's linen robe, and there over his heart was a dagger wound, and beneath the girl's fair breast was a like cruel stab, through which her life had ebbed away. On the rock above was an inscription in three words Ayesha translated it. It was "*Wedded in Death.*"

What was the life history of these two, who, of a truth, were beautiful in their lives, and in their death were not divided?

I closed my eyelids, and imagination, taking up the thread of thought, shot its swift shuttle back across the ages, weaving a picture on their blackness so real and vivid in its detail that I could almost for a moment think that I had triumphed o'er the Past, and that my spirit's eyes had pierced the mystery of Time.

I seemed to see this fair girl form – the yellow hair streaming down her, glittering against her garments snowy white, and the bosom that was whiter than the robes, even dimming with its luster her ornaments of burnished gold. I seemed to see the great cave filled with warriors, bearded and clad in mail, and, on the lighted dais where Ayesha had given judgment, a man standing, robed, and surrounded by the symbols of his priestly office. And up the cave there came one clad in purple, and before him and behind him came minstrels and fair-maidens, chanting a wedding song. White stood the maid against the altar, fairer than the fairest there – purer than a lily, and more cold than the dew that glistens in its heart. But as the man drew near she shuddered. Then out of the press and throng there sprang a dark-haired youth, and put his arm about this long-forgotten maid, and kissed her pale face

however, was made from the roots, and among the people of Kôr there was a law, which Ayesha showed me alluded to on some of the inscriptions, to the effect that under heavy penalties no one under a certain rank was to be embalmed with the drugs prepared from the roots. The object and effect of this was, of course, to preserve the trees from extermination. The sale of the leaves and roots was a government monopoly, and from it the kings of Kôr derived a large proportion of their private revenue. – L. H. H.

in which the blood shot up like lights of the red dawn across the silent sky. And next there was turmoil and uproar, and a flashing of swords, and they tore the youth from her arms, and stabbed him, but with a cry she snatched the dagger from his belt, and drove it into her snowy breast, home to the heart, and down she fell, and then, with cries and wailing, and every sound of lamentation, the pageant rolled away from the arena of my vision, and once more the past shut to its book.

Let him who reads forgive the intrusion of a dream into a history of fact. But it came so home to me – I saw it all so clear in a moment, as it were; and, besides, who shall say what proportion of fact, past, present, or to come, may lie in the imagination? What is imagination? Perhaps it is the shadow of the intangible truth, perhaps it is the soul's thought.

In an instant the whole thing had passed through my brain, and *She* was addressing me.

"Behold the lot of man," said the veiled Ayesha, as she drew the winding sheets back over the dead lovers, speaking in a solemn, thrilling voice, which accorded well with the dream that I had dreamed. "To the tomb, and to the forgetfulness that hides the tomb, must we all come at last! Ay, even I who live so long. Even for me, O Holly, thousands upon thousands of years hence; thousands of years after thou hast gone through the gate and been lost in the mists, a day will dawn whereon I shall die, and be even as thou art and these are. And then what will it avail that I have lived a little longer, holding off death by the knowledge I have wrung from Nature, since at last I too must die? What is a span of ten thousand years, or ten times ten thousand years, in the history of time? It is as naught – it is as the mists that roll up in the sunlight; it fleeth away like an hour of sleep or a breath of the Eternal Spirit. Behold the lot of man! Certainly it shall overtake us, and we shall sleep. Certainly, too, we shall awake, and live again and again shall sleep, and so on and on, through periods, spaces, and times, from eon unto eon, till the world is dead, and the worlds beyond the world are dead, and, naught liveth save the Spirit that is Life. But for us twain and for these dead ones shall the end of ends be Life, or shall it be Death? As yet Death is but Life's Night, but out of the night is the Morrow born again, and doth again beget the Night. Only when Day and Night, and Life and Death, are ended and swallowed up in that from which they came, what shall be our fate, O Holly? Who can see so far? Not even I!"

And then, with a sudden change of tone and manner: "Hast thou seen enough, my stranger guest, or shall I show thee more of the wonders of these tombs that are my palace halls? If thou wilt, I can lead thee to where Tisno, the mightiest and most valorous king of Kôr, in whose day these caves were ended, lies in a pomp that seems to mock at nothingness, and bid the empty shadows of the past do homage to his sculptured vanity!"

"I have seen enough, O Queen," I answered. "My heart is overwhelmed by the power of the present Death. Mortality is weak, and easily broken down by a sense of the companionship that waits upon its end. Take me hence, O Ayesha!"

Chapter 17

The Balance Turns

In a few minutes, following the lamps of the mutes, which, held out from the body as a bearer holds water in a vessel, had the appearance of floating down the darkness by themselves, we came to a stair which led us to *She*'s anteroom, the same that Billali had crept up upon all fours on the previous day. Here I would have bid the Queen adieu, but she would not.

"Nay," she said, "enter with me, O Holly, for of a truth thy conversation pleaseth me. Think, O Holly: for two thousand years have I had none to converse with save slaves and my own thoughts, and though of all this thinking hath much wisdom come, and many secrets been made plain, yet am I weary of my thoughts, and have come to loathe mine own society, for surely the food that memory gives to eat is bitter to the taste, and it is only with the teeth of hope that we can bear to bite it. Now though thy thoughts are green and tender, as becometh one so young, yet are they those of a thinking brain, and in truth thou dost bring back to my mind certain of those old philosophers with whom in days bygone I have disputed at Athens, and at Becca in Arabia, for thou hast the same crabbed air and dusty look, as though thou hadst passed thy days in reading ill-writ Greek, and been stained dark with the grime of manuscripts. So draw the curtain, and sit here by my side, and we will eat fruit, and talk of pleasant things. See, I will again unveil to thee. Thou hast brought it on thyself, O Holly; fairly have I warned thee – and thou shalt call me beautiful as even those old philosophers were wont to do. Fie upon them, forgetting their philosophy!"

And without more ado she stood up and shook the white wrappings from her, and came forth shining and splendid like some glittering snake when she has cast her slough; ay, and fixed her wonderful eyes upon me – more deadly than any Basilisk's – and pierced me through and through with their beauty, and sent her light laugh ringing through the air like chimes of silver bells.

A new mood was on her, and the very color of her mind seemed to change beneath it. It was no longer torture-torn and hateful, as I had seen it when she was cursing her dead rival by the leaping flames, no longer icily terrible as in the judgment hall, no longer rich, and somber, and splendid, like a Tyrian cloth, as in the dwellings of the dead. No, her mood now was that of Aphrodite triumphing. Life – radiant, ecstatic, wonderful – seemed to flow from her and round her. Softly she laughed and sighed, and swift her glances flew. She shook her heavy tresses, and their perfume filled the place; she struck her little sandaled foot upon the floor, and hummed a snatch of some old Greek epithalamium. All the majesty was gone, or did but lurk and faintly flicker through her laughing eyes, like lightning seen through sunlight. She had cast off the terror of the leaping flame, the cold power of judgment that was even now being done, and the wise sadness of the tombs – cast them off and put them behind her, like the white shroud she wore, and now stood out the incarnation of lovely tempting womanhood, made more perfect – and in a way more spiritual – than ever woman was before.

"There, my Holly, sit there where thou canst see me. It is by thine own wish, remember – again I say, blame me not if thou dost spend the rest of thy little span with such a sick pain at the heart that thou wouldst fain have died before ever thy curious eyes were set upon me. There, sit so, and tell me, for in truth I am inclined for praises – tell me, am I not beautiful? Nay, speak not so hastily; consider well the point; take me feature by feature, forgetting not my form, and my hands and feet, and my hair, and the whiteness of my skin, and then tell me truly hast thou ever known a woman who in aught, ay, in one little portion of her beauty, in the curve of an eyelash even, or the modeling of a shell-like ear, is justified to hold a light before my loveliness?

Now, my waist! Perchance thou thinkest it too large, but of a truth it is not so; it is this golden snake that is too large, and doth not bind it as it should. It is a wise snake, and knoweth that it is ill to tie in the waist. But see, give me thy hands – so – now press them round me, there, with but a little force, thy fingers touch, O Holly."

I could bear it no longer. I am but a man, and she was more than a woman. Heaven knows what she was – I do not! But then and there I fell upon my knees before her, and told her in a sad mixture of languages – for such moments confuse the thoughts – that I worshiped her as never woman was worshiped, and that I would give my immortal soul to marry her, which at that time I certainly would have done, and so, indeed, would any other man, or all the race of men rolled into one. For a moment she looked a little surprised, and then she began to laugh, and clap her hands in glee.

"Oh, so soon, O Holly!" she said. "I wondered how many minutes it would need to bring thee to thy knees. I have not seen a man kneel before me for so many days, and, believe me, to a woman's heart the sight is sweet, ay, wisdom and length of days take not from that dear pleasure which is our sex's only right.

"What wouldst thou? What wouldst thou? Thou dost not know what thou doest. Have I not told thee that I am not for thee? I love but one, and thou art not the man. Ah, Holly, for all thy wisdom – and in a way thou art wise – thou art but a fool running after folly. Thou wouldst look into mine eyes – thou wouldst kiss me! Well, if it pleaseth thee, *look*," and she bent herself towards me, and fixed her dark and thrilling orbs upon my own; "ay, and *kiss* too, if thou wilt, for, thanks be given to the scheme-of things, kisses leave no marks, except upon the heart. But if thou dost kiss, I tell thee of a surety wilt thou eat out thy breast with love of me, and die!" and she bent yet further towards me till her soft hair brushed my brow, and her fragrant breath played upon my face, and made me faint and weak. Then of a sudden, even as I stretched out my arms to clasp, she straightened herself, and a quick change passed over her. Reaching out her hand, she held it over my head, and it seemed to me that something flowed from it that chilled me back to common sense, and a knowledge of propriety and the domestic virtues.

"Enough of this wanton play," she said with a touch of sternness. "Listen, Holly. Thou art a good and honest man, and I fain would spare thee; but, oh, it is so hard for a woman to be merciful. I have said I am not for thee, therefore let thy thoughts pass by me like an idle wind, and the dust of thy imagination sink again into the depths – well, of despair, if thou wilt. Thou dost not know me, Holly. Hadst thou seen me but ten hours past when my passion seized me, thou hadst shrunk from me in fear and trembling. I am a woman of many moods, and, like the water in that vessel, I reflect many things; but they pass, my Holly; they pass, and are forgotten. Only the water is the water still, and I still am I, and that which maketh the water maketh it, and that which maketh me maketh me, nor can my quality be altered. Therefore, pay no heed to what I seem, seeing that thou canst not know what I am. If thou troublest me again I will veil myself, and thou shalt behold my face no more."

I rose, and sank on the cushioned couch beside her, yet quivering with emotion, though for a moment my mad passion had left me, as the leaves of a tree quiver still, although the gust be gone that stirred them. I did not dare to tell her that I *had* seen her in that deep and hellish mood, muttering incantations to the fire in the tomb.

"So," she went on, "now eat some fruit; believe me, it is the only true food for man. Oh, tell me of the philosophy of that Hebrew Messiah, who came after me, and whom thou sayest doth now rule Rome, and Greece, and Egypt, and the barbarians beyond. It must have been a strange philosophy that He taught, for in my day the peoples would have naught of our philosophies. Revel and lust and drink, blood and cold steel, and the shock of men gathered in the battle – these were the canons of their creeds."

I had recovered myself a little by now, and, feeling bitterly ashamed of the weakness into which I had been betrayed, I did my best to expound to her the doctrines of Christianity, to which, however, with the single exception of our conception of Heaven and Hell, I found that she paid but faint attention, her interest being all directed towards the Man who taught them. Also, I told her that among her own people, the Arabs, another prophet, one Mohammed, had arisen and preached a new faith to which many millions of mankind now adhered.

"Ah!" she said. "I see – two new religions! I have known so many, and doubtless there have been many more since I knew aught beyond these caves of Kôr. Mankind asks ever of the skies to vision out what lies behind them. It is terror for the end, and but a subtler form of selfishness – this it is that breeds religions. Mark, my Holly, each religion claims the future for its followers; or, at the least, the good thereof. The evil is for those benighted ones who will have none of it, seeing the light the true believers worship as the fishes see the stars, but dimly. The religions come and the religions pass, and the civilizations come and pass, and naught endures but the world and human nature. Ah, if man would but see that hope is from within and not from without – that he himself must work out his own salvation! He is there, and within him is the breath of life and a knowledge of good and evil as good and evil is to him. Thereon let him build and stand erect, and not cast himself before the image of some unknown God, modeled like his poor self, but with a bigger brain to think the evil thing; and a longer arm to do it."

I thought to myself, which shows how old such reasoning is, being, indeed, one of the recurring quantities of theological discussion, that her argument sounded very like some that I have heard in the nineteenth century, and in other places than the caves of Kôr, and with which, by the way, I totally disagree, but I did not care to try and discuss the question with her. To begin with, my mind was too weary with all the emotions through which I had passed, and, in the second place, I knew that I should get the worst of it. It is weary work enough to argue with an ordinary materialist, who hurls statistics and whole strata of geological facts at your head, while you can only buffet him with deductions and instincts and the snowflakes of faith, that are, alas, so apt to melt in the hot embers of our troubles. How little chance, then, should I have against one whose brain was supernaturally sharpened, and who had two thousand years of experience, besides all manner of knowledge of the secrets of Nature at her command! Feeling that she would be more likely to convert me than I should to convert her, I thought it best to leave the matter alone, and so sat silent. Many a time since then have I bitterly regretted that I did so, for thereby I lost the only opportunity I can remember having had of ascertaining what Ayesha *really* believed, and what her "philosophy" was.

"Well, my Holly," she continued, "and so those people of mine have also found a prophet, a false prophet, thou sayest, for he is not thine own, and, indeed, I doubt it not. Yet in my day was it otherwise, for then we Arabs had many gods. Allât there was, and Saba, the Host of Heaven, Al Uzza, and Manah the stony one, for whom the blood of victims flowed, and Wadd and Sawa, and Yaghuth the Lion of the dwellers in Yaman, and Yäûk the Horse of Morad, and Nasr the Eagle of Hamyar; ay, and many more. Oh, the folly of it all, the shame and the pitiful folly! Yet when I rose in wisdom and spoke thereof, surely they would have slain me in the name of their outraged gods. Well, so hath it ever been – but, my Holly, art thou weary of me already, that thou dost sit so silent? Or dost thou fear lest I should teach thee my philosophy? For know I have a philosophy. What would a teacher be without her own philosophy? And if thou dost vex me overmuch, beware, for I will have thee learn it, and thou shalt be my disciple, and we twain will found a faith that shall swallow up all others. Faithless man! And but half an hour since thou wast upon thy knees – the posture does not suit thee. Holly – swearing that thou didst love me. What shall we do? Nay, I have it. I will come and see this youth, the Lion, as the old man Billali calls him, who came with thee, and who is so sick. The fever must have run its course by now, and if he is about to die I will recover him. Fear not, my Holly, I shall use no magic. Have I not told thee that there is no such thing as magic, though there is such a thing as understanding and applying the forces which are in Nature? Go now, and presently when I have made the drug ready I will follow thee."[1]

Accordingly I went, only to find Job and Ustane in a great state of grief, declaring that Leo was in the throes of death, and that they had been searching for me everywhere. I rushed to the couch and glanced at him: clearly he was dying. He was senseless, and breathing heavily, but his lips were quivering, and every now and again a little shudder ran down his frame. I knew enough of doctoring to see that in another hour he would be beyond the reach of earthly help – perhaps in another five minutes. How I cursed my selfishness and the folly that had kept me lingering by Ayesha's side while my dear boy lay dying! Alas and alas! How easily the best of us are lighted down to evil by the gleam of a woman's eyes! What a wicked wretch was I! Actually, for the last half hour I had scarcely thought of Leo, and this, be it remembered, of the man who for twenty years had been my dearest companion, and the chief interest of my existence. And now, perhaps it was too late!

I wrung my hands, and glanced round. Ustane was sitting by the couch, and in her eyes burned the dull light of despair. Job was blubbering – I am sorry I cannot name his distress by any more delicate word – audibly in the corner. Seeing my eye fixed upon him he went outside to give way to his grief in the passage. Obviously the only hope lay in Ayesha. She, and she alone – unless, indeed, she was an impostor, which I could not believe – could save him. I would go and implore her to come. As I started to do so, however, Job came flying into the room, his hair literally standing on end with terror.

1 Ayesha was a great chemist, indeed, chemistry appears to have been her only amusement and occupation. She had one of the caves fitted up as a laboratory, and, although her appliances were necessarily crude, the results that she attained were, as will become clear in the course of this narrative, sufficiently surprising. – L. H. H.

"Oh, God help us, sir!" he ejaculated in a frightened whisper. "Here's a corpse acoming sliding down the passage!"

For a moment I was puzzled, but presently, of course, it struck me that he must have seen Ayesha, wrapped in her gravelike garment, and been deceived by the extraordinary undulating smoothness of her walk into a belief that she was a white ghost gliding towards him. Indeed, at that very moment the question was settled, for Ayesha herself was in the apartment, or rather cave. Job turned and saw her sheeted form, and then, with a convulsive howl of "Here it comes!" sprang into a corner and jammed his face against the wall, and Ustane, guessing whose the dread presence must be, prostrated herself upon her face.

"Thou comest in a good time, Ayesha," I said, "for my boy lies at the point of death."

"So," she said softly; "provided he be not dead, it is no matter, for I can bring him back to life, my Holly. Is that man there thy servant, and is that the method wherewith thy servants greet strangers in thy country?"

"He is frightened of thy garb – it hath a deathlike air," I answered.

She laughed. "And the girl? Ah, I see now. It is her of whom thou didst speak to me. Well, bid them both to leave us, and we will see to this sick Lion of thine. I love not that underlings should perceive my wisdom."

Thereon I told Ustane in Arabic and Job in English both to leave the room; an order which the latter obeyed readily enough, and was glad to obey, for he could not in any way subdue his fear. But it was otherwise with Ustane.

"What does *She* want?" she whispered, divided between her fear of the terrible queen and her anxiety to remain near Leo. "It is surely the right of a wife to be near her husband when he dieth. Nay, I will not go, my lord, the Baboon."

"Why doth not that woman leave us, my Holly?" asked Ayesha from the other end of the cave, where she was engaged in carelessly examining some of the sculptures on the wall.

"She is not willing to leave Leo," I answered, not knowing what to say. Ayesha wheeled round, and, pointing to the girl Ustane, said one word, and one only, but it was quite enough, for the tone in which it was said meant volumes.

"Go!"

And then Ustane crept past her on her hands and knees, and went.

"Thou seest, my Holly," said Ayesha with a little laugh, "it was needful that I should give these people a lesson in obedience. That girl went nigh to disobeying me, but then she did not learn this morn how I treat the disobedient. Well, she has gone; and now let me see the youth," and she glided towards the couch on which Leo lay, with his face in the shadow and turned toward the wall.

"He hath a noble shape," she said, as she bent over him to look upon his face.

Next second her tall and willowy form was staggering back across the room, as though she had been shot or stabbed, staggering back till at last she struck the cavern wall, and then there burst from her lips the most awful and unearthly scream that I ever heard in all my life.

"What is it, Ayesha?" I cried. "Is he dead?"

She turned and sprang towards me like a tigress.

"Thou dog!" she said in her terrible whisper, which sounded like the hiss of a snake, "why didst thou hide this from me?" And she stretched out her arm, and I thought that she was about to slay me.

"What?" I ejaculated in the most lively terror. "What?"

"Ah," she said, "perchance thou didst not know. Learn, my Holly, learn: there lies – there lies my lost Kallikrates. Kallikrates, who has come back to me at last, as I knew he would, as I knew he would." And she began to sob and to laugh, and generally to conduct herself like any other lady who is a little upset, murmuring

"Kallikrates, Kallikrates!"

"Nonsense," thought I to myself, but I did not like to say it; and, indeed, at that moment I was thinking of Leo's life, having forgotten everything else in that terrible anxiety. What I feared now was that he should die while she was "carrying on."

"Unless thou art able to help him, Ayesha," I put in by way of a reminder, "thy Kallikrates will soon be far beyond thy calling. Surely he dieth even now."

"True," she said with a start. "Oh, why did I not come before! I am unnerved – my hand trembles, even mine – and yet it is very easy. Here, thou Holly, take this phial," and she produced a tiny jar of pottery from the folds of her garment, "and pour the liquid in it down his throat. It will cure him if he be not dead. Swift, now! Swift! The man dies!"

I glanced towards him; it was true enough, Leo was in his death struggle. I saw his poor face turning ashen, and heard the breath begin to rattle in his throat. The phial was stoppered with a little piece of wood. I drew it with my teeth, and a drop of the fluid within flew out upon my tongue. It had a sweet flavor, and for a second made my head swim, and a mist gather before my eyes, but happily the effect passed away as swiftly as it had arisen.

When I reached Leo's side he was plainly expiring – his golden head was slowly fuming from side to side, and his mouth was slightly open. I called to Ayesha to hold his head, and this she managed to do, though the woman was quivering from head to foot, like an aspen leaf or a startled horse. Then, forcing the jaw a little more open, I poured the contents of the phial into his mouth. Instantly a little vapor arose from it, as happens when one disturbs nitric acid, and this sight did not increase my hopes, already faint enough, of the efficacy of the treatment.

One thing, however, was certain, the death throes ceased – at first I thought because he had got beyond them, and crossed the awful river. His face turned to a livid pallor, and his heartbeats, which had been feeble enough before, seemed to die away altogether – only the eyelid still twitched a little. In my doubt I looked up at Ayesha, whose head wrapping had slipped back in her excitement when she went reeling across the room. She was still holding Leo's head, and, with a face as pale as his own, watching his countenance with such an expression of agonized anxiety as I have never seen before. Clearly she did not know if he would live or die. Five minutes slowly passed, and I saw that she was abandoning hope; her lovely oval face seemed to fall in and grow visibly thinner Beneath the pressure of a mental agony whose, pencil drew black lines about the hollows of her eyes. The coral faded even from her lips, till they were as white as Leo's face, and quivered pitifully. It was shocking to see her: even in my own grief I felt for hers.

"Is it too late?" I gasped.

She hid her face in her hands, and made no answer, and I too turned away. But as I did so I heard a deep-drawn breath, and looking down perceived a line of color creeping up Leo's face, then another and another, and then, wonder of wonders, the man we had thought dead turned over on his side.

"Thou seest," I said in a whisper.

"I see," she answered hoarsely. "He is saved. I thought we were too late – another moment – one little moment more – and he had been gone!" And she burst into an awful flood of tears, sobbing as though her heart would break, and yet looking lovelier than ever as she did it. At last she ceased.

"Forgive me, my Holly – forgive me for my weakness," she said. "Thou seest after all I am a very woman. Think – now think of it! This morning didst thou speak of the place of torment appointed by this new religion of thine. Hell or Hades thou didst call it – a place where the vital essence lives and retains an individual memory, and where all the errors and faults of judgment, and unsatisfied passions and the unsubstantial terrors of the mind wherewith it hath at any time had to do, come to mock and haunt and gibe and wring the heart forever and forever with the vision of its own hopelessness. Thus, even thus, have I lived for full two thousand years – for some six and sixty generations, as ye reckon time – in a hell, as thou callest it – tormented by the memory of a crime, tortured day and night with an unfulfilled desire – without companionship, without comfort, without death, and led on down my dreary road only by the marsh lights of hope, which though they nickered here and there, and now glowed strong, and now were not, yet, as my skill told me, would one day lead unto my deliverer.

"And then – think of it still, O Holly, for never shalt thou hear such another tale, or see such another scene, nay, not even if I give thee ten thousand years of life – and thou shalt have it in payment if thou wilt – think: at last my deliverer came – he for whom I had watched and waited through the generations – at the appointed time he came to seek me, as I knew that he must come, for my wisdom could not err, though I knew not when or how. Yet see how ignorant I was! See how small my knowledge, and how faint my strength! For hours he lay here sick unto death, and I felt it not – I who had waited for him for two thousand years – I knew it not. And then at last I see him, and behold, my chance is gone but by a hair's breadth even before I have it, for he is in the very jaws of death; whence no power of mine can draw him. And if he die, surely must the hell be lived through once more – once more must I face the weary centuries, and wait, and wait till the time in its fullness shall bring my beloved back to me. And then thou gavest him the medicine, and that five minutes dragged along before I knew if he would live or die, and I tell thee that all the sixty generations that are gone were not so long as that five minutes. But they passed at length, and still he showed no sign, and I knew that if the drug works not then, so far as I have had knowledge, it works not at all. Then thought I that he was once more dead, and all the tortures of all the years gathered themselves into a single venomed spear, and pierced me through and through, because once again I had lost Kallikrates! And then, when all was done, behold! he sighed, behold! he lived, and I knew that he would live, for none die on whom the drug takes hold. Think of it now, my Holly – think of the wonder of it! He will sleep for twelve hours, and then the fever will have left him!"

She stopped, and laid her hand upon the golden head, and then bent down and kissed the brow with a chastened abandonment of tenderness that would have been beautiful to behold had not the sight cut me to the heart – for I was jealous!

Chapter 18

Go, Woman!

THEN FOLLOWED a silence of a minute or so, during which *She* appeared, if one might judge from the almost angelic rapture of her face – for she looked angelic sometimes – to be plunged in a happy ecstasy. Suddenly, however, a new thought struck her, and her expression became the very reverse of angelic.

"Almost had I forgotten," she said, "that woman, Ustane. What is she to Kallikrates – his servant, or –" and she paused, and her voice trembled.

I shrugged my shoulders. "I understand that she is wed to him according to the custom of the Amahagger," I answered; "but I know not."

Her face grew dark as a thunder cloud. Old as she was, Ayesha had not outlived jealousy.

"Then there is an end," she said; "she must die, even now!"

"For what crime?" I asked, horrified. "She is guilty of naught that thou art not guilty of thyself, oh Ayesha. She loves the man, and he has been pleased to accept her love; where, then, is her sin?"

"Truly, O Holly, thou art foolish," she answered, almost petulantly. "Where is her sin? Her sin is that she stands between me and my desire. Well, I know that I can take him from her – for dwells there a man upon this earth, O Holly, who could resist me if I put out my strength? Men are faithful for so long only as temptations pass them by. If the temptation be but strong enough, then will the man yield, for every man, like every rope, hath his breaking strain, and passion is to men what gold and power are to women – the weight upon their weakness. Believe me, ill will it go with mortal women in that heaven of which thou speakest, if only the spirits be more fair, for their lords will never turn to look upon them, and their heaven will become their hell. For man can be bought with woman's beauty, if it be but beautiful enough; and woman's beauty can be ever bought with gold, if only there be gold enough. So was it in my day, and so it will be to the end of time. The world is a great mart, my Holly, where all things are for sale to him who bids the highest in the currency of oar desires."

These remarks, which were as cynical as might have been expected from a woman of Ayesha's age and experience, jarred upon me, and I answered testily that in our heaven there was no marriage or giving in marriage.

"Else would it not be heaven, dost thou mean?" she put in. "Fie upon thee. Holly, to think so ill of us poor women! Is it, then, marriage that marks the line between thy heaven and thy hell? But enough of this. This is no time for disputing and the challenge of our wits. Why dost thou always dispute? Art thou also a philosopher of these latter days? As for this woman, she must die; for though I can take her lover from her, yet, while she lived, might he think tenderly of her, and that I could not away with. No other woman shall dwell in my lord's thoughts; my empire shall be all my own. She hath had her day, let her be content; for better is an hour with love than a century of loneliness – now the night shall swallow her."

"Nay, nay," I cried, "it would be a wicked crime; and from a crime naught comes but what is evil. For thine own sake do not this deed."

"Is it, then, a crime, O foolish man, to put away that which stands between us and our ends? Then is our life one long crime, my Holly; for day by day we destroy that we may live, since in this world none save the strongest can endure. Those who are weak must perish; the earth is to the strong, and the fruits thereof. For every tree that grows a score shall wither, that the strong ones may take their share. We run to place and power over the dead bodies or those who fail and fall; ay, we win the food we eat from out the mouths of starving babes. It is the scheme of things. Thou sayest, too, that a crime breeds evil, but therein thou dost lack experience; for out of crimes come many good things, and out of good grows much evil. The cruel rage of the tyrant may prove a blessing to thousands who come after him, and the sweet-heartedness of a holy man may make a nation slaves. Man doeth this and doeth that from the good or evil of his heart; but he knoweth not to what end his moral sense doth prompt him; for when he striketh he is blind to where the blow shall fall, nor can he count the airy threads that weave the web of circumstance. Good and evil, love and hate, night and day, sweet and bitter, man and woman, heaven above and the earth beneath – all these things are necessary one to the other, and who knows the end of each? I tell thee that there is a hand of Fate that twines them up to bear the burden of its purpose, and all things are gathered in that great rope to which all things are needful. Therefore doth it not become us to say this thing is evil and this good, or the dark is hateful and the light lovely; for to other eyes than ours the evil may be the good and the darkness more beautiful than the day, or all alike be fair. Hearest thou, my Holly?"

I felt it was hopeless to argue against casuistry of this nature, which, if it were carried to its logical conclusion, would absolutely destroy all morality, as we understand it. But her talk gave me a fresh thrill of fear; for what may not be possible to a being who, unconstrained by human law, is also absolutely unshackled by a moral sense of right and wrong, which, however partial and conventional it may be, is yet based, as our conscience tells us, upon the great wall of individual responsibility that marks off mankind from the beasts?

But I was deeply anxious to save Ustane, whom I liked and respected, from the dire fate that overshadowed her at the hands of her mighty rival. So I made one more appeal.

"Ayesha," I said, "thou art too subtle for me; but thou thyself hast told me that each man should be a law unto himself, and follow the teaching of his heart. Hath thy heart no mercy towards her whose place thou wouldst take? Bethink thee, as thou sayest – though to me the thing is incredible – him whom thou desirest has returned to thee after many ages, and but now thou hast, as thou sayest also, wrung him from the jaws of death. Wilt thou celebrate his coming by the murder of one who loved him, and whom perchance he loved – one, at the least, who saved his life for thee when the spears of thy slaves would have made an end thereof? Thou sayest also that in past days thou didst grievously wrong this man, that with thine own hand thou didst slay him because of the Egyptian Amenartas whom he loved."

"How knowest thou that, O stranger? How knowest thou that name? I spoke it not to thee," she broke in with a cry, catching at my arm.

"Perchance I dreamed it," I answered; "strange dreams do hover about these caves of Kôr. It seems that the dream was, indeed, a shadow of the truth. What came to thee of thy mad crime? Two thousand years of waiting, was it not? And now wouldst thou repeat the history? Say what thou wilt, I tell thee that evil will come of it; for to him who doeth, at the least, good breeds good and evil evil, even though in after days out of evil cometh good. Offenses must needs come; but woe to him by whom the offense cometh. So said that Messiah of whom I spoke to thee, and it was truly said. If thou slayest this innocent woman, I say unto thee that thou shalt be accursed, and pluck no fruit from thine ancient tree of love. Also, what thinkest thou? How will this man take thee red-handed from the slaughter of her who loved and tended him?"

"As to that," she answered, "I have already answered thee. Had I slain thee as well as her, yet should he love me. Holly, because he could not save himself therefrom any more than thou couldst save thyself from dying, if by chance I slew thee, O Holly. And yet maybe there is truth in what thou dost say; for in some way it presseth on my mind. If it may be, I will spare this woman; for have I not told thee that I am not cruel for the sake of cruelty? I love not to see suffering, or to cause it. Let her come before me – quick now, before my mood changes," and she hastily covered her face with its gauzy wrapping.

Well pleased to have succeeded even to this extent, I passed out into the passage and called to Ustane, whose white garment I caught sight of some yards away, huddled up against one of the earthenware lamps that were placed at intervals along the tunnel. She rose and ran towards me.

"Is my lord dead? Oh, say not he is dead," she cried, lifting her noble-looking face, all stained as it was with tears, up to me with an air of infinite beseeching that went straight to my heart.

"Nay, he lives," I answered. "*She* hath saved him. Enter."

She sighed deeply, entered, and fell upon her hands and knees, after the custom of the Amahagger people, in the presence of the dread *She*.

"Stand," said Ayesha in her coldest voice, "and come hither."

Ustane obeyed, standing before her with bowed head.

Then came a pause, which Ayesha broke.

"Who is this man?" she said, pointing to the sleeping form of Leo.

"The man is my husband," she answered in a low voice.

"Who gave him to thee for a husband?"

"I took him according to the custom of our country, O *She*."

"Thou hast done evil, woman, in taking this man, who is a stranger. He is not a man of thine own race, and the custom fails. Listen: perchance thou didst this thing through ignorance, therefore, woman, do I spare thee, otherwise hadst thou died. Listen again. Go from hence back to thine own place, and never dare to speak to or set thine eyes upon this man again. He is not for thee. Listen a third time. If thou breakest this my law, that moment thou diest. Go,"

But Ustane did not move.

"Go, woman!"

Then she looked up, and I saw that her face was torn with passion.

"Nay, O *She*, I will not go," she answered in a choked voice. "The man is my husband, and I love him – I love him, and I will not leave him. What right hast thou to command me to leave my husband?"

I saw a little quiver pass down Ayesha's frame, and shuddered myself, fearing the worst.

"Be pitiful," I said in Latin; "it is but Nature working."

"I am pitiful," she answered coldly in the same language; "had I not been pitiful she had been dead even now." Then addressing Ustane: "Woman, I say to thee, go before I destroy thee where thou art!"

"I will not go! He is mine – mine!" she cried in anguish. "I took him, and I saved his life! Destroy me, then, if thou hast the power! I will not give thee my husband – never-never!"

Ayesha made a movement so swift that I could scarcely

follow it, but it seemed to me that she lightly struck the poor girl upon the head with her hand. I looked at Ustane, and then staggered back in horror, for there upon her hair, right across her bronzelike tresses, were three fingermarks *white as snow*. As for the girl herself, she had put her hands to her head, and was looking dazed.

"Great heavens!" I said, perfectly aghast at this dreadful manifestation of inhuman power; but *She* did but laugh a little.

"Thou thinkest, poor ignorant fool," she said to the bewildered woman, "that I have not power to slay. Stay, there lies a mirror," and she pointed to Leo's round shaving glass that had been arranged by Job with other things upon his portmanteau. "Give it to this woman, my Holly, and let her see that which lies across her hair, and whether or no I have power to slay."

I picked up the glass and held it before Ustane's eyes.

She gazed, then felt at her hair, then gazed again, and then sank upon the ground with a sort of sob.

"Now, wilt thou go, or must I strike a second time?" asked Ayesha, in mockery. "Look, I have set my seal upon thee so that I may know thee till thy hair is all as white as it. If I see thy face here again, be sure, too, that thy bones shall soon be whiter than my mark upon thy hair."

Utterly awed and broken down, the poor creature rose, and, marked with that awful mark, crept from the room sobbing bitterly.

"Look not so frightened, my Holly," said Ayesha when she had gone. "I tell thee I deal not in magic – there is no such thing. 'Tis only a force that thou dost not understand. I marked her to strike terror to her heart, else must I have slain her. And now I will bid my servants bear my lord Kallikrates to a chamber near mine own, that I may watch over him, and be ready to greet him when he wakes; and thither, too, shalt thou come, my Holly, and the white man, thy servant. But one thing remember at thy peril. Naught shalt thou say to Kallikrates as to how this woman went, and as little as may be of me. Now, I have warned thee!" and she slid away to give her orders, leaving me more absolutely confounded than ever. Indeed, so bewildered was I, and racked and torn with such a succession of various emotions, that I began to think that I must be going mad. However, perhaps fortunately, I had but little time to reflect, for presently the mutes arrived to carry the sleeping Leo and our possessions across the central cave, so for a while all was bustle. Our new rooms were situated immediately behind what we used to call Ayesha's boudoir – the curtained space where I had first seen her. Where she herself slept I did not then know, but it was somewhere quite close.

That night I passed in Leo's room, but he slept through it like the dead, never once stirring. I also slept fairly well, as, indeed, I needed to do, but my sleep was full of dreams of all the horrors and wonders I had undergone. Chiefly, however, I was haunted by that frightful piece of *diablerie* by which Ayesha left her fingermarks upon her rival's hair. There was something so terrible about the swift, snakelike movement, and the instantaneous blanching of that threefold line, that, if the results to Ustane had been much more tremendous, I doubt if they would have impressed me so deeply. To this day I often dream of that awful scene, and see the weeping woman, bereaved, and marked like Cain, cast a last look at her lover, and creep from the presence of her dread Queen.

Another dream that troubled me originated in the huge pyramid of bones. I dreamed that they all stood up and marched past me in thousands and tens of thousands – in squadrons, companies, and armies – with the sunlight shining through their hollow ribs. On they rushed across the plain to Kôr, their imperial home; I saw the drawbridges fall before them, and heard their bones clank through the brazen gates. On they went, up the splendid streets, on past fountains, palaces, and temples such as the eye of man never saw. But there was no man to greet them in the market place, and no woman's face appeared at the windows – only a bodiless voice went before them, calling: *"Fallen is Imperial Kôr! Fallen! Fallen! Fallen!"* On, right through the city, marched those gleaming phalanxes, and the rattle of their bony tread echoed through the silent air as they pressed grimly on. They passed through the city and climbed the wall, and marched along the great roadway that was made upon the wall, till at length they once more reached the drawbridge. Then, as the sun was sinking, they returned again towards their sepulcher, and luridly his light shone in the sockets of their empty eyes, throwing gigantic shadows of their bones that stretched away, and crept and crept like huge spider's legs as their armies wound across the plain. Then they came to the cave, and once more one by one flung themselves in unending files through the hole into the pit of bones, and I awoke, shuddering, to see *She*, who had evidently been standing between my couch and Leo's, glide like a shadow from the room.

After this I slept again, soundly this time, till morning, when I awoke much refreshed, and got up. At last the hour drew near at which, according to Ayesha, Leo was to awake, and with it came *She* herself, as usual, veiled.

"Thou shalt see, O Holly," she said; "presently shall he awake in his right mind, the fever having left him."

Hardly were the words out of her mouth when Leo turned round and stretched out his arms, yawned, opened his eyes, and, perceiving a female form bending over him, threw his arms round her and kissed her, mistaking her for Ustane. He said in Arabic, "Hullo, Ustane, why have you tied your head up like that? Have you got the toothache?" and then, in English, "I say, I'm awfully hungry. Why, Job, you old son of a gun, where the deuce have we got to now – eh?"

"I am sure I wish I knew, Mr. Leo," said Job, edging suspiciously past Ayesha, whom he still regarded with the utmost disgust and horror, being by no means sure that she was not an animated corpse; "but you mustn't talk, Mr. Leo, you've been very ill, and given us a great deal of hanxiety, and, if this lady" –

looking at Ayesha – "would be so kind as to move. I'll bring you your soup."

This turned Leo's attention to the "lady," who was standing by in perfect silence. "Hullo!" he said; "that is not Ustane – where is Ustane?"

Then, for the first time, Ayesha spoke to him, and her first words were a lie. "She has gone from hence upon a visit," she said; "and, behold, in her place am I here as thine handmaiden."

Ayesha's silver notes seemed to puzzle Leo's half-awakened intellect, as also did her corpselike wrappings. However, he said nothing at the time, but drank off his soup greedily enough, and then turned over and slept again till the evening. When he woke for the second time he saw me, and began to question me as to what had happened, but I had to put him off as best I could till the morrow, when he awoke almost miraculously better. Then I told him something of his illness and of my doings, but as Ayesha was present I could not tell him much except that she was the queen of the country, and well disposed towards us, and that it was her pleasure to go veiled; for, though of course I spoke in English, I was afraid that she might understand what we were saying from the expression of our faces, and besides, I remembered her warning.

On the following day Leo got up almost entirely recovered. The flesh wound in his side was healed, and his constitution, naturally a vigorous one, had shaken off the exhaustion consequent on his terrible fever with a rapidity that I can only attribute to the effects of the wonderful drug which Ayesha had given to him, and also to the fact that his illness had been too short to reduce him very much. With his returning health came back full recollection of all his adventures up to the time when he had lost consciousness in the marsh, and of course of Ustane also, to whom I had discovered he had grown considerably attached. Indeed, he overwhelmed me with questions about the poor girl, which I did not dare to answer, for after Leo's first wakening *She* had sent for me, and again warned me solemnly that I was to reveal nothing of the story to him, delicately hinting that if I did it would be the worse for me. She also, for the second time, cautioned me not to tell Leo anything more than I was obliged about herself, saying that she would reveal herself to him in her own time.

Indeed, her whole manner changed. After all that I had seen I had expected that she would take the earliest opportunity of claiming the man she believed to be her old-world lover, but this, for some reason of her own, which was at the time quite inscrutable to me, she did not do. All that she did was to attend to his wants quietly, and with a humility which was in striking contrast with her former imperious bearing, addressing him always in a tone of something very like respect, and keeping him with her as much as possible. Of course his curiosity was as much excited about this mysterious woman as my own had been, and he was particularly anxious to see her face, which I had, without entering into particulars, told him was as lovely as her form and voice. This in itself was enough to raise the expectations of any young man to a dangerous pitch, and had it not been that he had not as yet completely shaken off the effects of illness, and was much troubled in his mind about Ustane, of whose affection and brave devotion he spoke in touching terms, I have no doubt that he would have entered into her plans, and fallen in love with her by anticipation. As it was, however, he was simply wildly curious, and also, like myself, considerably awed, for though no hint had been given to him by Ayesha of her extraordinary age, he not unnaturally came to identify her with the woman spoken of on the potsherd. At last, quite driven into a corner by his continual questions, which he showered on me while he was dressing on this third morning, I referred him to Ayesha, saying, with perfect truth, that I did not know where Ustane was. Accordingly, after Leo had eaten a hearty breakfast, we adjourned into *She*'s presence, for her mutes had orders to admit us at all hours.

She was, as usual, seated in what, for want of a better term, we called her boudoir, and on the curtains being drawn she rose from her couch and, stretching out both hands, came forward to greet us, or rather Leo; for I, as may be imagined, was now quite left in the cold. It was a pretty sight to see her veiled form gliding towards the sturdy young Englishman, dressed in his gray flannel suit; for though he is half a Greek in blood, Leo is, with the exception of his hair, one of the most English-looking men I ever saw. He has nothing of the supple form or slippery manner of the modern Greek about him, though I presume that he got his remarkable personal beauty from his foreign mother, whose portrait he resembles not a little. He is very tall and big-chested, and yet not awkward, as so many big men are, and his head is set upon him in such a fashion as to give him a proud and vigorous air, which was well translated in his Amahagger name of the "Lion."

"Greeting to thee, my young stranger lord," she said in her softest voice. "Right glad am I to see thee upon thy feet. Believe me, had I not saved thee at the last, never wouldst thou have stood upon those feet again. But the danger is done, and it shall be my care" – and she flung a world of meaning into the words – "that it doth return no more."

Leo bowed to her, and then, in his best Arabic, thanked her for all her kindness and courtesy in caring for one unknown to her.

"Nay," she answered softly, "ill could the world spare such a man. Beauty is too rare upon it. Give me no thanks, who am made happy by thy coming."

"Humph! Old fellow," said Leo aside to me in English, "the lady is very civil. We seem to have tumbled into clover. I hope that you have made the most of your opportunities. By Jove, what a pair of arms she has got!"

I nudged him in the ribs to make him keep quiet, for I caught sight of a gleam from Ayesha's veiled eyes, which were regarding me curiously.

"I trust," went on Ayesha, "that my servants have attended well upon thee; if there can be comfort in this poor place, be sure it waits on thee. Is there aught that I can do for thee more?"

"Yes, O *She*," answered Leo hastily. "I would fain know whither the young lady who was looking after me has gone to."

"Ah," said Ayesha. "The girl – yes, I saw her. Nay, I know not; she said that she would go, I know not whither. Perchance she will return, perchance not. It is wearisome waiting on the sick, and these savage women are fickle."

Leo looked both sulky and distressed at this intelligence.

"It's very odd," he said to me in English; and then addressing *She*, "I cannot understand," he said; "the young lady and I – well – in short, we had a regard for each other."

Ayesha laughed a little, very musically, and then turned the subject.

Chapter 19

"Give Me a Black Goat!"

THE CONVERSATION after this was of such a desultory order that I do not quite recollect it. For some reason, perhaps from a desire to keep her identity and character in reserve, Ayesha did not talk freely, as she usually did. Presently, however, she informed Leo that she had arranged a dance that night for our amusement. I was astonished to hear this, as I fancied that the Amahagger were much too gloomy a folk to indulge in any such frivolity; but, as will presently more clearly appear, it turned out that an Amahagger dance has little in common with such fantastic festivities in other countries, savage or civilized. Then, as we were about to withdraw, she suggested that Leo might like to see some of the wonders of the caves, and as he gladly assented thither we departed, accompanied by Job and Billali. To describe our visit would only be to repeat a great deal of what I have already said. The tombs we entered were indeed different, for the whole rock was a honeycomb of sepulchers,[1] but the contents were nearly always similar. Afterwards we visited the pyramid of bones that had haunted my dreams on the previous night, and from thence went down a long passage to one of the great vaults occupied by the bodies of the poorer citizens of Imperial Kôr. These bodies were not nearly so well preserved as were those of the wealthier classes. Many of them had no linen covering on them, also they were buried from five hundred to one thousand in a single large vault, the corpses in some instances being thickly piled one upon another, like a heap of slain.

Leo was of course intensely interested in this stupendous and unequaled sight, which was, indeed, enough to awake all the imagination a man had in him into the most active life. But to poor Job it did not prove attractive. His nerves – already seriously shaken by what he had undergone since we had arrived in this terrible country – were, as may be imagined, still further disturbed by the spectacle of these masses of departed humanity, whereof the forms still remained perfect before his eyes, though their voices were forever lost in the eternal silence of the tomb. Nor was he comforted when old Billali, by way of soothing his evident agitation, informed him that he should not be frightened of these dead things, as he would soon be like them himself.

"There's a nice thing to say of a man, sir," he ejaculated, when I translated this little remark; "but there, what can one expect of an old man-eating savage? Not but what I dare say he's right," and Job sighed.

When we had finished inspecting the caves, we returned and had our meal, for it was now past four in the afternoon, and we all – especially Leo – needed some food and rest. At six o'clock we, together with Job, waited on Ayesha, who set to work to

1 For a long while it puzzled me to know what could have been done with the enormous quantities of rock that must have been dug out of these vast caves; but I afterwards discovered that it was for the most part built into the walls and palaces of Kôr, and also used to line the reservoirs and sewers. – L. H. H.

terrify our poor servant still further by showing him pictures on the pool of water in the fontlike vessel. She learned from me that he was one of seventeen children, and then bade him think of all his brothers and sisters, or as many of them as he could, gathered together in his father's cottage. Then she told him to look in the water, and there, reflected from its stilly surface, was that dead scene of many years gone by, as it was recalled to our retainer's brain. Some of the faces were clear enough, but some were mere blurs and splotches, or with one feature grossly exaggerated; the fact being that, in these instances, Job had been unable to recall the exact appearances of the individuals, or remembered them only by a peculiarity of his tribe, and the water could only reflect what he saw with his mind's eye. For it must be remembered that *She*'s power in this matter was strictly limited; she could apparently, except in very rare instances, only photograph upon the water what was actually in the mind of someone present, and then only by his will. But if she was personally acquainted with a locality, she could, as in the case of ourselves and the whaleboat, throw its reflection upon the water, and also it seems the reflection of anything extraneous that was passing there at the time. This power, however, did not extend to the minds of others. For instance, she could show me the interior of my college chapel, as I remembered it, but not as it was at the moment of reflection; for, where other people were concerned, her art was strictly limited to the facts or memories present to *their* consciousness at the moment. So much was this so, that when we tried, for her amusement, to show her pictures of noted buildings, such as St. Paul's or the Houses of Parliament, the result was most imperfect; for, of course, though we had a good general idea of their appearance, we could not recall all the architectural details, and therefore the minutiae necessary to a perfect reflection were wanting. But Job could not be got to understand this, and far from accepting a natural explanation of the matter, which was after all, though strange enough in all conscience, nothing more than an instance of glorified and perfected telepathy, he set the whole thing down as a manifestation of the blackest magic. I shall never forget the howl of terror which he uttered when he saw the more or less perfect portraits of his long-scattered brethren staring at him from the quiet water, or the merry peal of laughter with which Ayesha greeted his consternation. As for Leo, he did not altogether like it either, but ran his fingers through his yellow curls, and remarked that it gave him the creeps.

After about an hour of this amusement, in the latter part of which Job did *not* participate, the mutes by signs indicated that Billali was waiting for an audience. Accordingly he was told to "crawl up," which he did as awkwardly as usual, and announced that the dance was ready to begin if *She* and the white strangers would be pleased to attend. Shortly afterwards we all rose, and Ayesha having thrown a dark cloak (the same, by the way, that she had worn when I saw her cursing by the fire) over her white wrappings, we started. The dance was to be held in the open air, on the smooth rocky plateau in front of the great cave, and thither we made our way. About fifteen paces from the mouth of the cave we found three chairs placed, and here we sat and waited, for as yet no dancers were to be seen. The night was almost, but not quite, dark, the moon not having risen as yet, which made us wonder how we should be able to see the dancing.

"Thou wilt presently understand," said Ayesha, with a little laugh, when Leo asked her; and we certainly did. Scarcely were the words out of her mouth when from every point we saw dark forms rushing up, each bearing with him what we at first took to be an enormous flaming torch. Whatever they were they were burning furiously, for the flames stood out a yard or more behind each bearer. On they came, fifty or more of them, carrying their flaming burdens and looking like so many devils from hell. Leo was the first to discover what these burdens were.

"Great heavens!" he said. "They are corpses on fire!"

I stared and stared again. He was perfectly right – the torches that were to light our entertainment were human mummies from the caves!

On rushed the bearers of the flaming corpses, and, meeting at a spot about twenty paces in front of us, built their ghastly burdens crossways into a huge bonfire. Heavens, how they roared and flared! No tar barrel could have burned as those mummies did. Nor was this all. Suddenly I saw one great fellow seize a flaming human arm that had fallen from its parent frame, and rush off into the darkness. Presently he stopped, and a tall streak of fire shot up into the air, illumining the gloom, and also the lamp from which it sprang. That lamp was the mummy of a woman tied to a stout stake let into the rock, and he had fired her hair. On he went a few paces and touched a second, then a third, and a fourth, till at last we were surrounded on ill three sides by a great ring of bodies flaring furiously, the material with which they were preserved having rendered them so inflammable that the flames would literally spout out of the ears and mouth in tongues of fire a foot or more in length.

Nero illuminated his gardens with live Christians soaked in tar, and we were now treated to a similar spectacle, probably for the first time since his day, only happily our lamps were not living ones.

But although this element of honor was fortunately wanting, to describe the awful and hideous grandeur of the spectacle thus presented to us is, I feel, so absolutely beyond my poor powers, that I scarcely dare attempt it. To begin with, it appealed to the moral as well as the physical susceptibilities. There was something very terrible, and yet very fascinating, about the employment of the remote dead to illumine the orgies of the living; in itself the thing was a satire on both the living and the dead. Caesar's dust – or is it Alexander's? – may stop a bunghole, but the functions of these dead Caesars of the past was to light up a savage fetish dance. To such base uses may we come, of so little account may we be in the minds of the eager multitudes that we shall breed, many of whom, so far from revering our memory, will live to curse us for begetting them into such a world of woe.

Then there was the physical side of the spectacle, and a weird and splendid one it was. Those old citizens of Kôr burned as, to judge from their sculptures and inscriptions, they had lived, very fast, and with the utmost liberality. What is more, there were plenty of them. As soon as ever a mummy had burned down to the ankles, which it did in about twenty minutes, the feet were kicked away, and another one put in its place. The bonfire was kept going on the same generous scale, and its flames shot up, with a hiss and a crackle, twenty or thirty feet into the air, throwing great flashes of light far out into the gloom, through which the dark forms of the Amahagger flitted to and fro like devils replenishing the infernal fires. We all stood and stared aghast – shocked, and yet fascinated at so strange a spectacle, and half-expecting to see the spirits those flaming forms had once enclosed come creeping from the shadows to work vengeance on their desecrators.

"I promised thee a strange sight, my Holly," laughed Ayesha, whose nerves alone did not seem to be affected; "and, behold, I have not failed thee. Also, it hath its lesson. Trust not to the future, for who knows what the future may bring! Therefore, live for the day, and endeavor not to escape the dust which seems to be man's end. What thinkest thou those long-forgotten nobles and ladies would have felt had they known that they should one day flare to light the dance or boil the pot of savages? But see, here come the dancers; a merry crew, are they not? The stage is lit – now for the play."

As she spoke, we perceived two lines of figures, one male and the other female, to the number of about a hundred, each advancing round the human bonfire, arrayed only in the usual leopard and buck skins. They formed up, in perfect silence, in two lines, facing each other between us and the fire, and then the dance – a sort of infernal and fiendish cancan – began. To describe it is quite impossible, but, though there was a good deal of tossing of legs and double-shuffling, it seemed to our untutored minds to be more of a play than a dance, and, as usual with this dreadful people, whose minds seem to have taken their color from the caves in which they live, and "whose jokes and amusements are drawn from the inexhaustible stores of preserved mortality with which they share their homes, the subject appeared to be a most ghastly one. I know that it represented an attempted murder first of all, and then the burial alive of the victim and his struggling from the grave; each act of the abominable drama, which was carried on in perfect silence, being rounded off and finished with a furious and most revolting dance round the supposed victim, who writhed upon the ground in the red light of the bonfire.

Presently, however, this pleasing piece was interrupted: Suddenly there was a slight commotion, and a large powerful woman, whom I had noted as one of the most vigorous of the dancers, came, made mad and drunken with unholy excitement, bounding and staggering towards us, shrieking out as she came: "I want a black goat, I must have a black goat, bring me a black goat!" and down she fell upon the rocky floor foaming and writhing, and shrieking for a black goat, about as hideous a spectacle as can well be conceived.

Instantly most of the dancers came up and got round her, though some still continued their capers in the background.

"She has got a Devil," called out one of them. "Run and get a black goat. There, Devil, keep quiet! Keep quiet! You shall have the goat presently. They have gone to fetch it, Devil."

"I want a black goat, I must have a black goat!" shrieked the foaming rolling creature again.

"All right. Devil, the goat will be here presently; keep quiet, there's a good Devil!"

And so on till the goat taken from a neighboring kraal did at last arrive, being dragged bleating onto the scene by its horns.

"Is it a black one, is it a black one?" shrieked the possessed.

"Yes, yes, Devil, as black as night." Then, aside, "Keep it

behind thee, don't let the Devil see that it has got a white spot on its rump and another on its belly. In one minute, Devil. There, cut his throat quick. Where is the saucer?"

"The goat! The goat! The goat! Give me the blood of my black goat! I must have it, don't you see I must have it? Oh! Oh! Oh! Give me the blood of the goat."

At this moment a terrified *bah*! announced that the poor goat had been sacrificed, and the next minute a woman ran up with a saucer full of the blood. This the possessed creature, who was then raving and foaming her wildest, seized and drank, and was instantly recovered, and without a trace of hysteria, or fits, or being possessed, or whatever dreadful thing it was she was suffering from. She stretched her arms, smiled faintly, and walked quietly back to the dancers, who presently withdrew in a double line as they had come, leaving the space between us and the bonfire deserted.

I thought that the entertainment was now over, and, feeling rather queer, was about to ask *She* if we could rise, when suddenly what at first I took to be a baboon came hopping round the fire, and was instantly met upon the other side by a lion, or rather a human being dressed in a lion's skin. Then came a goat, then a man wrapped in an ox's hide, with the horns wobbling about in a ludicrous way. After him followed a blesbok, then an impala, then a koodoo, then more goats, and many other animals, including a girl sewn up in the shining scaly hide of a boa constrictor, several yards of which trailed along the ground behind her. When all the beasts had collected they began to dance about in a lumbering, unnatural fashion, and to imitate the sounds produced by the respective animals they represented, till the whole air was alive with roars and bleating and the hissing of snakes. This went on for a long time, till, getting tired of the pantomime, I asked Ayesha if there would be any objection to Leo and myself walking round to inspect the human torches, and, as she had nothing to say against it, we started, striking round to the left. After looking at one or two of the flaming bodies, we were about to return, thoroughly disgusted with the grotesque weirdness of the spectacle, when our attention was attracted by one of the dancers, a particularly active leopard, that had separated itself from its fellow-beasts, and was whisking about in our immediate neighborhood, but gradually drawing into a spot where the shadow was darkest, equidistant between two of the flaming mummies. Drawn by curiosity, we followed it, when suddenly it darted past us into the shadows beyond, and as it did so erected self and whispered, "Come," in a voice that we both recognized as that of Ustane. Without waiting to consult me Leo turned and followed her into the outer darkness, and I, feeling sick enough at heart, went after them. The leopard and crawled on for about fifty paces – a sufficient distance to be quite beyond the light of the fire and torches – and then Leo came up with it, or, rather, with Ustane.

"Oh, my lord," I heard her whisper, "so I have found thee! Listen. I am in peril of my life from *'She-who-must-be-obeyed.'* Surely the Baboon has told thee how she drove me from thee? I love thee, my lord, and thou art mine according to the custom of the country. I saved thy life! My lion, wilt thou cast me off now?"

"Of course not," ejaculated Leo; "I have been wondering whither thou hadst gone. Let us go and explain matters to the Queen."

"Nay, nay, she would slay us. Thou knowest not her power – the Baboon there, he knoweth, for he saw. Nay, there is but one way: if thou wilt cleave to me, thou must flee with me across the marshes even now, and then perchance we may escape."

"For heaven's sake, Leo," I began, but she broke in. "Nay, listen not to him. Swift – be swift – death is in the air we breathe. Even now, mayhap, *She* heareth us," and without more ado she proceeded to back her arguments by throwing herself into his arms. As she did so the leopard's head slipped from her hair, and I saw the three white fingermarks upon it, gleaming faintly in the starlight. Once more, realizing the desperate nature of our position, I was about to interpose, for I knew that Leo was not too strong-minded where women were concerned, when – oh, honor! – I heard a little silvery laugh behind me. I turned round, and there was *She* herself, and with her Billali and two male mutes. I gasped and nearly sank to the ground, for I knew that such a situation must result in some dreadful tragedy, of which it seemed exceedingly probable to me that I should be the first victim. As for Ustane, she untwined her arms and covered her eyes with her hands, while Leo, not knowing the full terror of the position, merely colored up, and looked as foolish as a man caught in such a trap would naturally do.

Chapter 20

Triumph

THEN FOLLOWED a moment of the most painful silence that I ever endured. It was broken by Ayesha, who addressed herself to Leo.

"Nay, now my lord and guest," she said in her softest tones, which yet had the ring of steel about them, "look not so bashful. Surely the sight was a pretty one – the leopard and the lion!"

"Oh, hang it all!" said Leo in English.

"And thou, Ustane," she went on, "surely I should have passed thee by had not the light fallen on the white across thy hair," and she pointed to the bright edge of the rising moon which was now appearing above the horizon. "Well, well! The dance is done – see, the tapers have burned down, and all things end in silence and in ashes. So thou thoughtest it a fit time for love,

Ustane, my servant – and I, dreaming not that I could be disobeyed, thought thee already far away."

"Play not with me," moaned the wretched woman; "slay me, and let there be an end."

"Nay, why? It is not well to go so swift from the hot lips of love down to the cold mouth of the grave," and she made a motion to the mutes, who instantly stepped up and caught the girl by either arm. With an oath Leo sprang upon the nearest, and hurled him to the ground, and then stood over him with his face set, and his fist ready.

Again Ayesha laughed. "It was well thrown, my guest; thou hast a strong arm for one who so late was sick. But now out of thy courtesy I pray thee let that man live and do my bidding. He shalt not harm the girl; the night air grows chill, and I would welcome her in mine own place. Surely she whom thou dost favor shall be favored of me also."

I took Leo by the arm, and pulled him from the prostrate mute, and he, half bewildered, obeyed the pressure. Then we all set out for the cave across the plateau, where a pile of white human ashes was all that remained of the fire that had lit the dancing, for the dancers had vanished.

In due course we gained Ayesha's boudoir – all too soon it seemed to me, having a sad presage of what was to come lying heavy on my heart.

Ayesha seated herself upon her cushions, and, having dismissed Job and Billali, by signs bade the mutes tend the lamps and retire, all save one girl, who was her favorite personal attendant. We three remained standing, the unfortunate Ustane a little to the left of the rest of us.

"Now, O Holly," Ayesha began, "how came it that thou who didst hear my words bidding this evildoer" – and she pointed to Ustane – "to go from hence – thou at whose prayer I did weakly spare her life – how came it, I say, that thou wast a sharer in what I saw tonight? Answer, and for thine own sake, I say, speak all the truth, for I am not minded to hear lies upon this matter!"

"It was by accident, O Queen," I answered. "I knew naught of it."

"I do believe thee, O Holly," she answered coldly, "and well it is for thee that I do – then does the whole guilt rest upon her."

"I do not find any guilt therein," broke in Leo. "She is not another man's wife, and it appears that she has married me according to the custom of this awful place, so who is the worse? Anyway, madam," he went on, "whatever she has done I have done too, so if she is to be punished let me be punished also; and I tell thee," he went on, working himself up into a fury, "that if thou biddest one of those deaf and dumb villains to touch her again I will tear him to pieces!" And he looked as though he meant it.

Ayesha listened in icy silence, and made no remark. When he had finished, however, she addressed Ustane.

"Hast thou aught to say, woman? Thou silly straw, thou feather, who didst think to float towards thy passion's petty ends, even against the great wind of my will! Tell me, for I fain would understand. Why didst thou this thing?"

And then I think I saw the most tremendous exhibition of moral courage and intrepidity that it is possible to conceive. For the poor doomed girl, knowing what she had to expect at the hands of her terrible queen, knowing, too, from bitter experience how great was her adversary's power, yet gathered herself together, and out of the very depths of her despair drew materials to defy her.

"I did it, O *She*," she answered, drawing herself up to the full of her stately height, and throwing back the panther skin from her head, "because my love is stronger than the grave. I did it because my life without this man whom my heart chose would be but a living death. Therefore did I risk my life, and now that I know that it is forfeit to thine anger, yet am I glad that I did risk it, and pay it away in the risking, ay, because he embraced me once, and told me that he loved me yet."

Here Ayesha half rose from her couch, and then sank down again.

"I have no magic," went on Ustane, her rich voice ringing strong and full, and I am not a queen, nor do I live forever, but a woman's heart is heavy to sink through waters, however deep, O Queen, and a woman's eyes are quick to see, even through thy veil, O Queen!

"Listen: I know it, thou dost love this man thyself, and therefore wouldst thou destroy me who stand across thy path. Ay, I die – I die, and go into the darkness, nor know I whither I go. But this I know. There is a light shining in my breast, and by that light, as by a lamp, I see the truth, and the future that I shall not share unroll itself before me like a scroll. When first I knew my lord" – and she pointed to Leo – "I knew also that death would be the bridal gift he gave me – it rushed upon me of a sudden, but I turned not back, being ready to pay the price, and, behold, death is here! And now, even as I knew that, so do I, standing on the steps of doom, know that thou shalt not reap the profits of thy crime. Mine he is, and, though thy beauty shine like a sun among the stars, mine shall he remain for thee. Never here in this life shall he look thee in the eyes and call thee spouse. Thou too art doomed, I see" – and her voice rang like the cry of an inspired prophetess – "ah, I see – "

Then came an answering cry of mingled rage and terror. I turned my head. Ayesha had risen, and was standing with her outstretched hand pointing at Ustane, who had suddenly stopped speaking. I gazed at the poor woman, and as I gazed there came upon her face that same woeful, fixed expression of terror that I had seen once before when she had broken out into her wild chant. Her eyes grew large, her nostrils dilated, and her lips blanched.

Ayesha said nothing, she made no sound, she only drew

herself up, stretched out her arm, and, her tall veiled frame quivering like an aspen leaf, appeared to look fixedly at her victim. Even as she did so Ustane put her hands to her head, uttered one piercing scream, turned round twice, and then fell backwards with a thud – prone upon the floor. Both Leo and myself rushed to her – she was stone dead – blasted into death by some mysterious electric agency or overwhelming will force whereof the dread *She* had command.

For a moment Leo did not quite realize what had happened. But when he did, his face was awful to see. With a savage oath he rose from beside the corpse, and, turning, literally sprang at Ayesha. But she was watching, and, seeing him come, stretched out her hand again, and he went staggering back towards me, and would have fallen, had I not caught him. Afterwards he told me that he felt as though he had suddenly received a violent blow in the chest, and, what is more, felt utterly cowed, as if all the manhood had been taken out of him.

Then Ayesha spoke. "Forgive me, my guest," she said softly, addressing him, "if I have shocked thee with my justice."

"Forgive thee, thou fiend," roared poor Leo, wringing his hands in his rage and grief. "Forgive thee, thou murderess! By heaven I will kill thee if I can!"

"Nay, nay," she answered in the same soft voice, "thou dost not understand – the time has come for thee to learn. *Thou* art my love, my Kallikrates, my Beautiful, my Strong? For two thousand years, Kallikrates, have I waited for *thee*, and now at length thou hast come back to me; and as for this woman" – pointing to the corpse – "she stood between me and thee, and therefore have I removed her, Kallikrates."

"It is an accursed lie!" said Leo. "My name is not Kallikrates! I am Leo Vincey; my ancestor was Kallikrates – at least, I believe he was."

"Ah, thou sayest it – thine ancestor was Kallikrates, and

thou, even thou, art Kallikrates reborn, come back – and mine own dear lord!"

"I am not Kallikrates, and as for being thy lord, or having aught to do with thee, I had sooner be the lord of a fiend from hell, for she would be better than thou."

"Sayest thou so – sayest thou so, Kallikrates? Nay, but thou hast not seen me for so long a time that no memory remains. Yet am I very fair, Kallikrates!"

"I hate thee, murderess, and I have no wish to see thee. What is it to me how fair thou art? I hate thee, I say."

"Yet within a very little space shalt thou creep to my knee, and swear that thou dost love me," answered Ayesha, with a sweet, mocking laugh. "Come, there is no time like the present time, here before this dead girl who loved thee, let us put it to the proof.

"Look now on me, Kallikrates!" and with a sudden motion she shook her gauzy covering from her, and stood forth in her low kirtle and her snaky zone, in her glorious radiant beauty and her imperial grace, rising from her wrappings, as it were, like Venus from the wave, or Galatea from her marble, or a beatified spirit from the tomb. She stood forth, and fixed her deep and glowing eyes upon Leo's eyes, and I saw his clenched fists unclasp, and his set and quivering features relax beneath her gaze. I saw his wonder and astonishment grow into admiration, and then into fascination, and the more he struggled the more I saw the power of her dread beauty fasten on him and take possession of his senses, drugging them, and drawing the heart out of him. Did I not know the process? Had not I, who was twice his age, gone through it myself? Was I not going through it afresh even then, although her sweet and passionate gaze was not for me? Yes, alas, I was! Alas, that I should have to confess that at that very moment I was rent by mad and furious jealousy. I could have flown at him, shame upon me! The woman had confounded and almost destroyed my moral sense, as she was bound to confound all who looked upon her superhuman loveliness. But – I do not quite know how – I got the better of myself, and once more turned to see the climax of the tragedy.

"Oh, great heaven!" gasped Leo; "art thou a woman?"

"A woman in truth – in very truth – and thine own spouse, Kallikrates!" she answered, stretching out her rounded ivory arms towards him, and smiling, ah, so sweetly!

He looked and looked, and slowly I perceived that he was drawing nearer to her. Suddenly his eye fell upon the corpse of poor Ustane, and he shuddered and stopped.

"How can I?" he said hoarsely. "Thou art a murderess; she loved me."

Observe, he was already forgetting that he had loved her.

"It is naught," she murmured, and her voice sounded as sweet as the night wind passing through the trees. "It is naught at all. If I have sinned, let my beauty answer for my sin. If I have sinned, it is for love of thee: let my sin, therefore, be put away and forgotten." And once more she stretched out her arms and whispered "*Come*," and then in another few seconds it was over. I saw him struggle – I saw him even turn to fly; but her eves drew him more strongly than iron bonds, and the magic of her beauty and concentrated will and passion entered into him and overpowered him – ay, even there, in the presence of the body of the woman who had loved him well enough to die for him. It sounds horrible and wicked enough, but he cannot be blamed too much, and be sure his sin will find him out. The temptress who drew him into evil was more than human, and her beauty was greater than the loveliness of the daughters of men.

I looked up again, and now her perfect form lay in his arms, and her lips were pressed against his own; and thus, with the corpse of his dead love for an altar, did Leo Vincey plight his troth to her red-handed murderess – plight it forever and a day. For those who sell themselves into a like dominion, paying down the price of their own honor, and throwing their soul into the balance to sink the scale to the level of their lusts, can hope for no deliverance here or hereafter. As they have sown, so shall they reap and reap, even when the poppy flowers of passion have withered in their hands, and their harvest is but bitter tares, garnered in satiety.

Suddenly, with a snakelike motion, she seemed to slip from his embrace, and then again broke out into her low laugh of triumphant mockery.

"Did I not tell thee that within a little space thou wouldst creep to my knee, O Kallikrates? And surely the space has not been a great one!"

Leo groaned in shame and misery; for though he was overcome and stricken down, he was not so lost as to be unaware of the depth of the degradation to which he had sunk. On the contrary, his better nature rose up in arms against his fallen self, as I saw clearly enough later on.

Ayesha laughed again, and then quickly veiled herself, and made a sign to the girl mute, who had been watching the whole scene with curious startled eyes. The girl left, and presently returned, followed by two male mutes, to whom the Queen made another sign. Thereon they all three seized the body of poor Ustane by the arms, and dragged it heavily down the cavern and away through the curtains at the end. Leo watched it for a little while, and then covered his eyes with his hand, and it too, to my excited fancy, seemed to watch us as it went.

"There passes the dead past," said Ayesha solemnly, as the curtains shook and fell back into their places, when the ghastly procession had vanished behind them. And then, with one of those extraordinary transitions of which I have already spoken, she again threw off her veil, and broke out, after the ancient and poetic fashion of the dwellers in Arabia,[1] into a paean of triumph

1 Among the ancient Arabians the power of poetic declamation, either in verse or prose, was held in the highest honor and esteem, and he who excelled in it was known as 'Khâteb' or Orator. Every year a general assembly was held at which the rival poets repeated their compositions, when those poems which were judged to be the best were, so soon as the knowledge of the art of writing became

(contd. on the next pg.)

or epithalamium, which, wild and beautiful as it was, is exceedingly difficult to render into English, and ought by rights to be sung to the music of a cantata, rather than written and read. It was divided into two parts – one descriptive or definitive, and the other personal; and, as nearly as I can remember, on as follows:

Love is like a flower in the desert.

It is like the aloe of Arabia that blooms but once and dies; it blooms in the salt emptiness of Life, and the brightness of its beauty is set upon the waste as a star is set upon a storm.

It hath the sun above that is the spirit, and above is blows the air of its divinity.

At the echoing of a step. Love blooms, I say; I say Love blooms, and bends her beauty down to him who passeth by.

He plucketh it, yea, he plucketh the red cup that is full of honey, and beareth it away; away across the desert, away till the flower be withered, away till the desert be done.

There is only one perfect flower in the wilderness of Life.

That flower is Love!

There is only one fixed star in the mists of our wandering.

That star is Love!

There is only one hope in our despairing night.

That hope is Love!

All else is false. All else is shadow moving upon water.

All else is wind and vanity.

Who shall say what is the weight or the measure of Love?

general, inscribed on silk in letters of gold, and publicly exhibited, being known as 'Al Modhahabât,' or golden verses. In the poem given above by Mr. Holly, Ayesha evidently followed the traditional poetic manner of her people, which was to embody their thoughts in a series of somewhat disconnected sentences, each remarkable for its beauty and the grace of its expression. – EDITOR.

It is born of the flesh, it dwelleth in the spirit. From each doth it draw its comfort.

For beauty it is as a star.

Many are its shapes, but all are beautiful, and none know where the star rose, or the horizon where it shall set.

Then, turning to Leo, and laying her hand upon his shoulder, she went on in a fuller and more triumphant tone, speaking in balanced sentences that gradually grew and swelled from idealized prose into pure and majestic verse:

Long have I loved thee, oh, my love; yet has my love not lessened.

Long have I waited for thee, and behold my reward is at hand – is here!

Far away I saw thee once, and thou wast taken from me.

Then in a grave sowed I the seed of patience, and shone upon it with the sun of hope, and watered it with tears of repentance, and breathed on it with the breath of my knowledge. And now, lo! it hath sprung up, and borne fruit. Lo! out of the grave hath it sprung. Yea, from among the dry bones and ashes of the dead.

I have waited and my reward is with me.

I have overcome Death, and Death brought back to me him that was dead.

Therefore do I rejoice, for fair is the future.

Green are the paths that we shall tread across the everlasting meadows.

The hour is at hand. Night hath fled away into the valleys.

The dawn kisseth the mountain tops.

Soft shall we lie, my love, and easy shall we go.

Crowned shall we be with the diadem of kings.
Worshiping and wonder-struck, all peoples of the world,
Blinded shall fall before our beauty and our might.
From time unto times shall our greatness thunder on,
Rolling like a chariot through the dust of endless days.
Laughing shall we speed in our victory and pomp,
Laughing like the Daylight as he leaps along the hills.
Onward, still triumphant, to a triumph ever new!
Onward, in our power, to a power unattained!
Onward, never weary, clad with splendor for a robe!
Till accomplished be our fate, and the night is rushing down.

She paused in her strange and most thrilling allegorical chant, of which I am, unfortunately, only able to give the burden, and that feebly enough, and then said, "Perchance thou dost not believe my word, Kallikrates – perchance thou thinkest that I do delude thee, and that I have not lived these many years, and that thou hast not been born again to me. Nay, look not so – put away that pale cast of doubt, for oh be sure herein can error find no foothold! Sooner shall the suns forget their course and the swallow miss her nest, than my soul shall swear a lie and be led astray from thee, Kallikrates. Blind me, take away mine eyes, and let the darkness utterly fence me in, and still mine ears would catch the tone of thine unforgotten voice, striking more loud against the portals of my sense than can the call of brazen-throated clarions: stop up mine hearing also, and let a thousand touch me on the brow, and I would name thee out of all: yea, rob me of every sense, and see me stand deaf and blind, and dumb, and with nerves that cannot weigh the value of a touch, yet would my spirit leap within me like a quickening child and cry unto my heart, behold Kallikrates! Behold, thou watcher, the watches of thy night are ended! Behold, thou who seekest in the night season, thy morning Star ariseth."

She paused awhile and then continued, "But stay, if thy heart is yet hardened against the mighty truth and thou dost require a further pledge of that which thou dost find too deep to understand, even now shall it be given to thee, and to thee also, O my Holly. Bear each one of you a lamp, and follow after me whither I shall lead you."

Without stopping to think – indeed, speaking for myself, I had almost abandoned the function in circumstances under which to think seemed to be absolutely useless, since thought fell hourly helpless against a black wall of wonder – we took the lamps and followed her. Going to the end of her "boudoir," she raised a curtain and revealed a little stair of the sort that was so common in these dim caves of Kôr. As we hurried down the stair I observed that the steps were worn in the center to such an extent that some of them had been reduced from seven and a half inches, at which I guessed their original height, to about three and a half. Now, all the other steps that I had seen in the caves had been practically unworn, as was to be expected, seeing that the only traffic which ever passed upon them was that of those who bore a fresh burden to the tomb. Therefore this fact struck my notice with that curious force with which little things do strike us when our minds are absolutely overwhelmed by a sudden rush of powerful sensations; beaten flat, as it were, like a sea beneath the first burst of a hurricane, so that every little object on the surface starts into an unnatural prominence.

At the bottom of the staircase I stood and stared at the worn steps, and Ayesha, turning, saw me.

"Wonderest thou whose are the feet that have worn away the rock, my Holly?" she asked. "They are mine – even mine own light feet! I can remember when these stairs were fresh and level, but for two thousand years and more have I gone down hither day by day, and see, my sandals have worn out the solid rock!"

I made no answer, but I do not think that anything that I had heard or seen brought home to my limited understanding so clear a sense of this being's overwhelming antiquity as that hard rock hollowed out by her soft white feet. How many millions of times must she have passed up and down that stair to bring about such a result?

The stair led to a tunnel, and a few paces down the tunnel was one of the usual curtain-hung doorways, a glance at which told me that it was the same where I had been a witness of that terrible scene by the leaping flame. I recognized the pattern of the curtain, and the sight of it brought the whole event vividly before my eyes, and made me tremble even at its memory. Ayesha entered the tomb (for it was a tomb), and we followed her – I, for one, rejoicing that the mystery of the place was about to be cleared up, and yet afraid to face its solution.

Chapter 21

The Dead and Living Meet

"SEE NOW the place where I have slept for these two thousand years," said Ayesha, taking the lamp from Leo's hand and holding it above her head. Its rays fell upon a little hollow in the floor, where I had seen the leaping flame, but the fire was out now. They fell upon the white form stretched there beneath its wrappings upon its bed of stone, upon the fretted carving of the tomb, and upon another shelf of stone opposite the one on which the body lay, and separated from it by the breadth of the cave.

"Here," went on Ayesha, laying her hand upon the rock, "here have I slept night by night for all these generations, with but a cloak to cover me. It did not become me that I should lie soft when my spouse yonder" – and she pointed to the rigid form – "lay stiff in death. Here night by night have I slept in his cold company – till, thou seest, this thick slab, like the stairs down which we passed, has worn thin with the tossing of my form – so faithful have I been to thee even in thy space of sleep. Kallikrates. And now, mine own, thou shalt see a wonderful thing – living, thou shalt behold thyself dead – for well have I tended thee during all these years, Kallikrates. Art thou prepared?"

We made no answer, but gazed at each other with frightened eyes, the whole scene was so dreadful and so solemn. Ayesha advanced, and laid her hand upon the corner of the shroud, and once more spoke.

"Be not affrighted," she said; "though the thing seem wonderful to thee – all we who live have thus lived before; nor is the very shape that holds us a stranger to the sun! Only we know it not, because memory writes no record, and earth hath gathered in the earth she lent us, for none have saved our glory from the grave. But I, by my arts and by the arts of those dead men of Kôr which I have learned, have held thee back, O Kallikrates, from the dust, that the waxen stamp of beauty on thy face should ever rest before mine eye. 'Twas a mask that memory might fill, serving to fashion out thy presence from the past, and give it strength to wander in the habitations of my thought, clad in a mummery of life that stayed my appetite with visions of dead days.

"Behold now, let the Dead and Living meet! Across the gulf of Time they still are one. Time hath no power against Identity, though sleep the merciful hath blotted out the tablets of our mind, and with oblivion sealed the sorrows that else would hound us from life to life, stuffing the brain with gathered griefs till it burst in the madness of uttermost despair. Still are they one, for the wrappings of our sleep shall roll away as thunderclouds before the wind; the frozen voices of the past shall melt in music like mountain snows beneath the sun; and the weeping and the laughter of the lost hours shall be heard once more most sweetly echoing up the cliffs of immeasurable time.

"Ay, the sleep shall roll away, and the voices shall be heard, when down the completed chain, whereof our each existence is a link, the lightning of the Spirit hath passed to work out the purpose of our being; quickening and fusing those separated days of life, and shaping them to a staff whereon we may safely lean as we wend to our appointed fate.

"Therefore, have no fear, Kallikrates, when thou – living, and but lately born – shalt look upon thine own departed self, who breathed and died so long ago. I do but turn one page in thy Book of Being, and show thee what is writ thereon.

"*Behold*!"

With a sudden motion she drew the shroud from the cold form, and let the lamplight play upon it. I looked, and then shrank back terrified; since, say what she might in explanation, the sight was an uncanny one – for her explanations were beyond the grasp of our finite minds, and when they were stripped from the mists of vague esoteric philosophy, and brought into conflict with the cold and horrifying fact, did not do much to break its force. For there, stretched upon the stone bier before us, robed in white and perfectly preserved, was what appeared to be the body of Leo Vincey. I stared from Leo, standing *there* alive, to Leo lying *there* dead, and could see no difference; except, perhaps, that the body on the bier looked older. Feature for feature they were the same, even down to the crop of little golden curls, which was Leo's most uncommon beauty. It even seemed to me, as I looked, that the expression on the dead man's face resembled that which I had sometimes seen upon Leo's when he was plunged into profound sleep. I can only sum up the closeness of the resemblance by saying that I never saw twins so exactly similar as that dead and living pair.

I turned to see what effect was produced upon Leo by

this sight of his dead self, and found it to be one of partial stupefaction. He stood for two or three minutes staring and said nothing, and when at last he spoke it was only to ejaculate, "Cover it up and take me away."

"Nay, wait, Kallikrates," said Ayesha, who, standing with the lamp raised above her head, flooding with its light her own rich beauty and the cold wonder of the death-clothed form upon the bier, resembled an inspired sibyl rather than a woman, as she rolled out her majestic sentences with a grandeur and a freedom of utterance which I am, alas, quite unable to reproduce.

"Wait; I would show thee something, that no tittle of my crime may be hidden from thee. Do thou, O Holly, open the garment on the breast of the dead Kallikrates, for perchance my lord may fear to touch himself."

I obeyed with trembling hands. It seemed a desecration and an unhallowed thing to touch that sleeping image of the live man by my side. Presently his broad chest was bare, and there upon it, right over the heart, was a wound, evidently inflicted with a spear.

"Thou seest, Kallikrates," she said. "Know then that it was *I* who slew thee: in the Place of Life *I* gave thee death. I slew thee because of the Egyptian Amenartas, whom thou didst love, for by her wiles she held thy heart, and her I could not smite as but now I smote the woman, for she was too strong for me. In my haste and bitter anger I slew thee, and now for all these days have I lamented thee, and waited for thy coming. And thou hast come, and none can stand between thee and me, and of a truth now for death I will give thee life – not life eternal, for that none can give, but life and youth that shall endure for thousands upon thousands of years, and with it pomp, and power, and wealth, and all things that are good and beautiful, such as have been to no man before thee, nor shall be to any man who comes after. And now one thing more, and thou shalt rest and make ready for the day of thy new birth. Thou seest this body, which was thine own. For all these centuries it hath been my cold comfort and my companion, but now I need it no more, for I have thy living presence, and it can but serve to stir up memories of that which I would fain forget. Let it therefore go back to the dust from which I held it.

"Behold! I have prepared against this happy hour!" and going to the other shelf, or stone ledge, which, she said, had served her for a bed, she took from it a large vitrified double-handed vase, the mouth of which was tied up with a bladder. This she loosed, and then, having bent down and gently kissed the white forehead of the dead man, she undid the vase, and sprinkled its contents carefully over the form, taking, I observed, the greatest precautions against any drop of them touching us or herself, and then poured out what remained of the liquid upon the chest and head. Instantly a dense vapor arose, and the cave was filled with choking fumes that prevented us from seeing anything while the deadly acid (for I presume it was some tremendous preparation of that sort) did its work. From the spot where the body lay came a fierce fizzing and cracking sound, which ceased, however, before the fumes had cleared away. At last they were all gone, except a little cloud that still hung over the corpse. In a couple of minutes more this too had vanished, and, wonderful as it may seem, it is a fact that on the stone bench that had supported the mortal remains of the ancient Kallikrates for so many centuries there was now nothing to be seen but a few handfuls of smoking white powder. The acid had utterly destroyed the body, and even in places eaten into the stone.

Ayesha stooped down, and, taking a handful of this powder in her grasp, threw it into the air, saying at the same time, in a voice of calm solemnity, "Dust to dust! The past to the past! The dead to the dead! Kallikrates is dead, and is born again!"

The ashes floated noiselessly to the rocky floor, and we stood in awed silence and watched them fall, too overcome for words.

"Now leave me," she said, "and sleep if ye may. I must watch and think, for tomorrow night we go hence, and the time is long since I trod the path that we must follow."

Accordingly we bowed and left her.

As we passed to our own apartment I peeped into Job's sleeping place, to see how he fared, for he had one away just before our interview with the murdered Ustane, quite prostrated by the terrors of the Amahagger festivity. He was sleeping soundly, good honest fellow that he was, and I rejoiced to think that his nerves, which, like those of most uneducated people, were far from strong, had been spared the closing scenes of this dreadful day. Then we entered our own chamber, and here at last poor Leo, who, ever since he had looked upon that frozen image of his living self, had been in a state not far removed from stupefaction, burst out into a torrent of grief. Now that he was no longer in the presence of the dread *She*, his sense of the awfulness of all that had happened, and more especially of the wicked murder of Ustane, who was bound to him by ties so close, broke upon him like a storm, and lashed him into an agony of remorse and terror which was painful to witness. He cursed himself – he cursed the hour when we had first seen the writing on the sherd, which was being so mysteriously verified, and bitterly he cursed his own weakness. Ayesha he dared not curse – who dared speak evil of such a woman, whose consciousness for aught we knew was watching us at the very moment?

"What am I to do, old fellow?" he groaned, resting his head against my shoulder in the extremity of his grief. "I let her be killed – not that I could help that, out within five minutes I was kissing her murderess over her body. I am a degraded brute, but I cannot resist that" – and here his voice sank – "that awful sorceress. I know I shall do it again tomorrow; I know that I am in her power for always; if I never saw her again I should never think of anybody else during all my life; I must follow her as a needle follows a magnet; I would not go away now if I could; I could not leave her, my legs would not carry me, but my mind is still clear enough, and in my mind I hate her – at least, I think so. It is all so horrible; and that – that body! What can I make of it? It was *me*! I am sold into bondage, old fellow, and she will take my soul as the price of herself!"

Then, for the first time, I told him that I was in a but very little better position; and I am bound to say that, notwithstanding his own infatuation, he had the decency to sympathize with me. Perhaps he did not think it worth while being jealous, realizing that he had no cause so far as the lady was concerned. I went on to suggest that we should try to run away, but we soon rejected the project as futile, and, to be perfectly honest, I do not believe that either of us would really have left Ayesha even if some superior power had suddenly offered to convey us from these gloomy caves and set us down in Cambridge. We could no more have left her than a moth can leave the light that destroys it. We were like confirmed opium eaters: in our moments of reason we well knew the deadly nature of our pursuit, but we certainly were not prepared to abandon its terrible delights.

No man who once had seen *She* unveiled, and heard the music of her voice, and drunk in the bitter wisdom of her words, would willingly give up the sight for a whole sea of placid joys. How much more, then, was this likely to be so when, as in Leo's case, to put myself out of the question, this extraordinary creature declared her utter and absolute devotion, and gave what appeared to be proofs of its having lasted for some two thousand years?

No doubt she was a wicked person, and no doubt she had murdered Ustane when she stood in her path, but then she was very faithful, and by a law of nature man is apt to think but lightly of a woman's crimes, especially if that woman be beautiful, and the crime be committed for the love of him.

And then for the rest, when had such a chance ever come to a man before as that which now lay in Leo's hand? True, in uniting himself to this dread woman, he would place his life under the influence of a mysterious creature of evil tendencies,[1] but

1 After some months of consideration of this statement I am bound to confess that I am not quite satisfied of its truth. It is perfectly true that Ayesha committed a murder, but I shrewdly suspect that, were we endowed with the same absolute power, and if we had the same tremendous interest at stake, we should be very apt to do likewise under parallel circumstances. Also, it must be remembered that she looked on it as an execution for disobedience under a system which made the slightest disobedience punishable by death. Putting

(contd. on the next pg.)

then that would be likely enough to happen to him in any ordinary marriage. On the other hand, however, no ordinary marriage could bring him such awful beauty – for awful is the only word that can describe it – such divine devotion, such wisdom, and command over the secrets of nature, and the place and power that they must win, or lastly the royal crown of unending youth, if indeed she could give that. No, on the whole, it is not wonderful that though Leo was plunged in bitter shame and grief, such as any gentleman would have felt under the circumstances, he was not ready to entertain the idea of running away from his extraordinary fortune.

My own opinion is that he would have been mad if he had done so. But then I confess that my statement on the matter must be accepted with qualifications. I am in love with Ayesha myself to this day, and I would rather have been the object of her affection for one short week than that of any other woman in the world for a whole lifetime. And let me add that if anybody who doubts this statement, and thinks me foolish for making it, could have seen Ayesha draw her veil and flash out in beauty on his gaze, his view would exactly coincide with my own. Of course, I am speaking of any *man*. We never had the advantage of a lady's opinion of Ayesha, but I think it quite possible that she would have regarded the Queen with dislike, would have expressed her disapproval in some more or less pointed manner, and ultimately have got herself blasted.

For two hours or more Leo and I sat with shaken nerves and frightened eyes, and talked over the miraculous events through which we were passing. It seemed like a dream or a fairy tale, instead of the solemn, sober fact. Who would have believed that the writing on the potsherd was not only true, but that we should live to verify its truth, and that we two seekers

aside this question of the murder, her evildoing resolves itself into the expression of views and the acknowledgment of motives which are contrary to our preaching if not to our practice. Now at first sight this might be fairly taken as a proof of an evil nature, but when we come to consider the great antiquity of the individual it becomes doubtful if it was anything more than the natural cynicism which arises from age and bitter experience, and the possession of extraordinary powers of observation. It is a well-known fact that very often,

(contd. on the next pg.)

should find her who was sought, patiently awaiting our coming in the tombs of Kôr? Who would have thought that in the person of Leo this mysterious woman should, as she believed, discover the being whom she awaited from century to century, and whose former earthly habitation she had till this very night preserved? But so it was. In the face of all we had seen it was difficult for us as ordinary reasoning men any longer to doubt its truth, and therefore at last, with humble hearts and a deep sense of the impotence of human knowledge, and the insolence of its assumption that denies that which it has no experience of to be possible, we laid ourselves down to sleep leaving our fates in the hands of that watching Providence which had thus chosen to allow us to draw the veil of human ignorance, and reveal to us for good or evil some glimpse of the possibilities of life.

putting the period of boyhood out of the question, the older we grow the more cynical and hardened we get, indeed, many of us are only saved by timely death from utter moral petrifaction if not moral corruption. No one will deny that a young man is on the average better than an old one, for he is without that experience of the order of things that in certain thoughtful dispositions can hardly fail to produce cynicism, and that disregard of acknowledged methods and established custom which we call evil. Now the oldest man upon the earth was but a babe compared to Ayesha, and the wisest man upon the earth was not one-third as wise. And the fruit of her wisdom was this, that there was but one thing worth living for, and that was Love in its highest sense, and to gain that good thing she was not prepared to stop at trifles. This is really the sum of her evil doings, and it must be remembered on the other hand that whatever may be thought of them she had some virtues developed to a degree very uncommon in either sex – constancy, for instance. – L. H. H.

Chapter 22

Job has a Presentiment

It was nine o'clock on the following morning when Job, who still looked scared and frightened, came in to call me, and at the same time breathe his gratitude at finding us alive in our beds, which it appeared was more than he had expected. When I told him of the awful end of poor Ustane he was even more grateful at our survival, and much shocked, though Ustane had been no favorite of his, or he of hers, for the matter of that. She had called him 'pig' in bastard Arabic, and he had called her 'hussy' in good English, but these amenities were forgotten in the face of the catastrophe that had overwhelmed her at the hands of her queen.

"I don't want to say anything as mayn't be agreeable, sir," said Job, when he had finished exclaiming at my tale, "but it's my opinion that that there *She* is the Old Gentleman himself, or perhaps his wife, if he has one, which I suppose he has, for he couldn't be so wicked all by himself. The Witch of Endor was a fool to her, sir: bless you, she Would make no more of raising every gentleman in the Bible out of these here beastly tombs than I should of growing cress on an old flannel. It's a country of devils, this is, sir, and she's the master one of the lot; and if ever we get out of it it will be more than I expect to do. I don't see no way out of it. That witch isn't likely to let a fine young man like Mr. Leo go."

"Come," I said, "at any rate she saved his life."

"Yes, and she'll take his soul to pay for it. She'll make him a witch, like herself. I say it's wicked to have anything to do with those sort of people. Last night, sir, I lay awake and read in my little Bible that my poor old mother gave me about what is going to happen to sorceresses and them sort till my hair stood on end. Lord, how the old lady would stare if she saw where her Job had got to!"

"Yes, it's a queer country, and a queer people too. Job," I answered with a sigh, for, though I am not superstitious like Job, I admit to a natural shrinking (which will not bear investigation) from the things that are above Nature.

"You are right, sir," he answered, "and if you won't think me very foolish, I should like to say something to you now that Mr. Leo is out of the way" – Leo had got up early and gone for a stroll – "and that is that I know it is the last country as ever I shall see in this world. I had a dream last night, and I dreamed that I saw my old father with a kind of nightshirt on him, something like these folks wear when they want to be in particular full-dress, and a bit of that feathery grass in his hand, which he may have gathered on the way, for I saw lots of it yesterday about three hundred yards from the mouth of this beastly cave.

" 'Job,' he said to me, solemn like, and yet with a kind of satisfaction shining through him, more like a Methody parson when he has sold a neighbor a marked horse for a sound one and cleared twenty pounds by the job than anything I can think on – ' Job, time's up. Job; but I never did expect to have to come and hunt you out in this 'ere place, Job. Such ado as I have had to nose you up; it wasn't friendly to give your poor old father such a run, let alone that a wonderful lot of bad characters hail from this place Kôr.' "

"Regular cautions," I suggested.

"Yes, sir – of course, sir, that's just what he said they was – 'cautious, downright scorchers,' sir – and I'm sure I don't doubt it, seeing what I know of them and their hot-potting ways," went on Job sadly. "Anyway, he was sure that time was up, and went away saying that we should see more than we cared for of each other soon, and I suppose he was a-thinking of the fact that Father and I never could hit it off together for longer nor three days, and I dare say that things will be similar when we meet again."

"Surely," I said, "you don't think that you are going to die because you dreamed you saw your old father; if one dies because one dreams of one's father, what happens to a man who dreams of his mother in law?"

"Ah, sir, you're laughing at me," said Job; "but, you see, you didn't know my old father. If it had been anybody else – my Aunt Mary, for instance, who never made much of a job – I should not have thought so much of it; but my father was that idle, which he shouldn't have been with seventeen children, that he would never have put himself out to come here just to see the place. No, sir; I know that he meant business. Well, sir, I can't help it; I suppose every man must go some time or other, though it is a hard thing to die in a place like this, where Christian burial isn't to be had for its weight in gold. I've tried to be a good man, sir, and do my duty honest, and if it wasn't for the supercilus kind of way in which Father carried on last night – a sort of sniffing at me as it were, as though he hadn't no opinion of my references and testimonials – I should feel easy enough in my mind. Anyway, sir, I've been a good servant to you and Mr. Leo, bless him! Why, it seems but the other day that I used to lead him about the streets with a penny whip; and if ever you get out of this place – which, as Father didn't allude to you, perhaps you may – I hope you will think kindly of my whitened bones, and never have anything more to do with Greek writing on flower pots, sir, if I may make so bold as to say so."

"Come, come, Job," I said seriously, "this is all nonsense, you know. You mustn't be silly enough to go getting such ideas into your head. We've lived through some queer things, and I hope that we may go on doing so."

"No, sir," answered Job, in a tone of conviction that jarred on me unpleasantly, "it isn't nonsense. I'm a doomed man, and I feel it, and a wonderful uncomfortable feeling it is, sir, for one can't help wondering how it's going to come about. If you are eating your dinner you think of poison and it goes against your stomach, and if you are walking along these dark rabbit burrows you think of knives, and Lord, don't you just shiver about the back! I ain't particular, sir, provided it's sharp, like that poor girl, who, now that she's gone, I am sorry to have spoke hard on, though I don't approve of her morals in getting married, which I considered too quick to be decent. Still, sir," and poor Job turned a shade paler as he said it, "I do hope it won't be that hot-pot game."

"Nonsense," I broke in angrily, "nonsense!"

"Very well, sir," said Job, "it isn't my place to differ from you, sir, but if you happen to be going anywhere, sir, I should be obliged if you could manage to take me with you, seeing that I shall be glad to have a friendly face to look at when the time comes, just to help one through, as it were. And now, sir, I'll be getting the breakfast," and he went, leaving me in a very uncomfortable state of mind. I was deeply attached to old Job, who was one of the best and most honest men I have ever had to do with in any class of life, and really more of a friend than a servant, and the mere idea of anything happening to him brought a lump into my throat. Beneath all his ludicrous talk I could see that he himself was quite convinced that something was going to happen, and though in most cases these convictions turn out to be utter moonshine – and this particular one especially was to be amply accounted for by the gloomy and unaccustomed surroundings in which its victim was placed – still it did more or less carry a chill to my heart, as any dread that is obviously a genuine object of belief is apt to do, however absurd the belief may be. Presently the breakfast arrived, and with it Leo, who had been taking a walk outside the cave – to clear his mind, he said – and very glad I was to see both, for they gave me a respite from my gloomy thoughts. After breakfast we went for another walk, and watched some of the Amahagger sowing a plot of ground with the grain from which they make their beer. This they did in Scriptural fashion – a man with a bag made of goat's hide fastened round his waist walking up and down the plot and scattering the seed as he went. It was a positive relief to see one of these dreadful people do anything so homely and pleasant as sow a field, perhaps because it seemed to link them, as it were, with the rest of humanity.

As we were returning Billali met us, and informed us that it was *She*'s pleasure that we should wait upon her, and accordingly we entered her presence, not without trepidation, for Ayesha was certainly an exception to the rule. Familiarity with her might and did breed passion and wonder and horror, but it certainly did *not* breed contempt.

We were as usual shown in by the mutes, and after these had retired Ayesha unveiled, and once more bade Leo embrace her, which, notwithstanding his heart-searchings of the previous night, he did with more alacrity and fervor than in strictness courtesy required.

She laid her white hand on his head, and looked him fondly in the eyes. "Dost thou wonder, my Kallikrates," she said, "when thou shalt call me all thine own, and when we shall of a truth be for one another and to one another? I will tell thee. First, must thou be even as I am, not immortal indeed, for that I am not, but so cased and hardened against the attacks of Time that his arrows shall glance from the armor of thy vigorous life as the sunbeams glance from water. As yet I may not mate with thee, for thou and I are different, and the very brightness of my being would burn thee up, and perchance destroy thee. Thou couldst not even endure to look upon me for too long a time lest thine eyes should ache, and thy senses swim, and therefore" – with a little coquettish nod – "shall I presently veil myself again." (This by the way she did not do.) "No: listen, thou shalt not be tried beyond endurance, for this very evening, an hour before the sun goes down, shall we start hence, and by tomorrow's dark, if all goes well, and the road is not lost to me, which I pray it may not be, shall we stand in the place of Life, and thou shalt bathe in the fire, and come forth glorified, as no man ever was before thee, and then, Kallikrates, shalt thou call me wife, and I will call thee husband."

Leo muttered something in answer to this astonishing statement, I do not know what, and she laughed a little at his confusion, and went on.

"And thou, too, O Holly; on thee also will I confer this boon, and then of a truth shalt thou be an evergreen tree, and this will I do – well, because thou hast pleased me. Holly, for thou art not altogether a fool, like most of the sons of men, and because, though thou hast a school of philosophy as full of nonsense as those of the old days, yet hast thou not forgotten how to turn a pretty phrase about a lady's eyes."

"Hullo, old fellow!" whispered Leo, with a return of his old cheerfulness. "Have you been paying compliments? I should never have thought it of you!"

"I thank thee, O Ayesha," I replied, with as much dignity as I could command, "but if there be such a place as thou dost describe, and if in this strange place there may be found a fiery virtue that can hold off Death when he comes to pluck us by the hand, yet would I none of it. For me, O Ayesha, the world has not proved so soft a nest that I would lie in it forever. A stony-hearted mother is our earth, and stones are the bread she gives her children for their daily food. Stones to eat and bitter water for their thirst, and stripes for tender nurture. Who would endure this for many lives? Who would so load up his back with memories of lost hours and loves, and of his neighbor's sorrows that he cannot lessen, and wisdom that brings not consolation? Hard is it to die, because our delicate flesh doth shrink back from the worm it will not feel, and from that unknown which the winding sheet doth curtain from our view. But harder still, to my fancy, would it be to live on, green in the leaf and fair, but dead and rotten at the core, and feel that other secret worm of recollection gnawing ever at the heart."

"Bethink thee, Holly," she said; "yet doth long life and strength and beauty beyond measure mean power and all things that are dear to man."

"And what, O Queen," I answered, "are those things that are dear to man? Are they not bubbles? Is not ambition but an endless ladder by which no height is ever climbed till the last unreachable rung is mounted? For height leads on to height, and there is no resting place upon them, and rung doth grow upon rung, and there is no limit to the number. Doth not wealth satiate and become nauseating, and no longer serve to satisfy or pleasure, or to buy an hour's ease of mind? And is there any end to wisdom that we may hope to reach it? Rather, the more we learn shall we not thereby be able only to better compass out our ignorance? Did we live ten thousand years could we hope to solve the secrets of the suns, and of the space beyond the suns, and of the Hand that hung them in the heavens? Would not our wisdom be but as a gnawing hunger calling our consciousness day by day to a knowledge of the empty craving of our souls? Would it not be but as a light in one of these great caverns, that though bright it burn, and brighter yet, doth but the more serve to show the depths of the gloom around it? And what good thing is there beyond that we may gain by length of days?"

"Nay, my Holly, there is love – love which makes all things beautiful, and doth breathe divinity into the very dust we tread. With love shall life roll gloriously on from year to year, like the voice of some great music that hath power to hold the hearer's heart poised on eagle's wings above the sordid shame and folly of the earth."

"It may be so," I answered; "but if the loved one prove a broken reed to pierce us, or if the love be loved in vain – what then? Shall a man grave his sorrows upon a stone when he hath but need to write them on the water? Nay, O *She*, I will live my day and grow old with my generation, and die my appointed death, and be forgotten. For I do hope for an immortality to which the little span that perchance thou canst confer will be but as a finger's length laid against the measure of the great world; and, mark this: the immortality to which I look, and which my faith doth promise to me, shall be free from the bonds that here must tie my spirit down. For, while the flesh endures, sorrow and evil and the scorpion whips of sin must endure also; but when the flesh hath fallen from us, then shall the spirit shine forth clad in the brightness of eternal good, and for its common air shall breathe so rare an ether of most noble thoughts, that the highest aspiration of our manhood, or the purest incense of a maiden's prayer, would prove too earthly gross to float therein."

"Thou lookest high," answered Ayesha, with a little laugh, "and speakest clearly as a trumpet and with no uncertain sound. And yet methinks that but now didst thou talk of 'that Unknown' from which the winding sheet doth curtain us. But perchance, thou seest with the eye of Faith, gazing on this brightness that is to be, through the painted glass of thy imagination. Strange are the pictures of the future that mankind can thus draw with this brush of faith and this many-colored pigment of imagination! Strange, too, that no one of them doth agree with another! I could tell thee – but there, what is the use? Why rob a fool of his bauble? Let it pass, and I pray, O Holly, that when thou dost feel old age creeping slowly towards thyself, and the confusion of senility making havoc, in thy brain, thou mayest not bitterly regret that thou didst cast away the imperial boon I would have given to thee. But so it hath ever been; man can never be content with that which his hand can pluck. If a lamp be in his reach to light him through the darkness, he must needs cast it down because it is no star. Happiness danceth ever a pace before him, like the marsh fires in the swamps, and he must catch the fire, and he must hold the star! Beauty is naught to him, because there are lips more honey-sweet; and wealth is naught, because others can weigh him down with heavier shekels; and fame is naught, because there have been greater men than he. Thyself thou saidst it, and I turn thy words against thee. Well, thou dreamest that thou shalt pluck the star. I believe it not, and I think thee a fool, my Holly, to throw away the lamp."

I made no answer, for I could not – especially before Leo – tell her that since I had seen her face I knew that it would always be before my eyes, and that I had no wish to prolong an existence which must always be haunted and tortured by her memory, and by the last bitterness of unsatisfied love. But so it was, and so, alas, is it to this hour!

"And now," went on *She*, changing her tone and the subject together, "tell me, my Kallikrates, for as yet I know it not, how came ye to seek me here? Yesternight thou didst say that Kallikrates – him whom thou sawest – was thine ancestor. How was it? Tell me – thou dost not speak overmuch!"

Thus adjured, Leo told her the wonderful story of the casket and of the potsherd that, written on by his ancestress, the Egyptian Amenartas, had been the means of guiding us to her. Ayesha listened intently, and, when he had finished, spoke to me.

"Did I not tell thee one day, when we did talk of good and evil, O Holly – it was when my beloved lay so ill – that out of good came evil, and out of evil good – that they who sowed knew not what the crop should be, nor he who struck where the blow should fall? See, now: this Egyptian Amenartas, this royal child of the Nile who hated me, and whom even now I hate, for in a way she did prevail against me – see, now, she herself hath been the very means to bring her lover to mine arms! For her sake I slew him, and now, behold, through her he hath come back to me! She would have done me evil, and sowed her seeds that I might reap tares, and behold she hath given me more than all the world can give, and there is a strange square for thee to fit into thy circle of good and evil, O Holly!

"And so," she went on after a pause, "and so she bade her son destroy me if he might, because I slew his father. And thou, my Kallikrates, art the father, and in a sense thou art likewise the son; and wouldst thou avenge thy wrong, and the wrong of that far-off mother of thine upon me, O Kallikrates? See," – and she slid to her knees, and drew the white corsage still farther down her ivory bosom – "see, here beats my heart, and there by thy side is a knife, heavy, and long, and sharp, the very knife to slay an erring woman with. Take it now, and be avenged. Strike, and strike home! So shalt thou be satisfied, Kallikrates, and go through life a happy man, because thou hast paid back the wrong, and obeyed the mandate of the past."

He looked at her, and then stretched out his hand and lifted her to her feet.

"Rise, Ayesha," he said sadly; "well thou knowest that I cannot strike thee, no, not even for the sake of her whom thou slewest but last night. I am in thy power, and a very slave to thee. How can I kill thee? Sooner should I slay myself."

"Almost dost thou begin to love me, Kallikrates," she answered, smiling. "And now tell me of thy country – 'tis a great people, is it not? With an empire like that of Rome! Surely thou wouldst return thither, and it is well, for I mean not that thou shouldst dwell in these caves of Kôr. Nay, when once thou art even as I am, we will go hence – fear not but that I shall find a path – and then shall we cross to this England of thine, and live as it becometh us to live. Two thousand years have I waited for the day when I should see the last of these hateful caves and this gloomy-visaged folk, and now it is at hand, and my heart bounds up to meet it like a child's towards its holiday. For thou shalt rule this England – "

"But we have a queen already," broke in Leo hastily. "It is naught, it is naught," said Ayesha; "she can be overthrown."

At this we both broke out into an exclamation of dismay, and explained that we should as soon think of overthrowing ourselves.

"But here is a strange thing," said Ayesha in astonishment; "a queen whom her people love! Surely the world must have changed since I have dwelt in Kôr."

Again we explained that it was the character of monarchs that had changed, and that the one under whom we lived was venerated and beloved by all right-thinking people in her vast realms. Also, we told her that real power in our country rested in the hands of the people, and that we were in fact ruled by the votes of the lower and least educated classes of the community.

"Ah," she said, "a democracy – then surely there is a tyrant, for I have long since seen that democracies, having no clear will of their own, in the end set up a tyrant, and worship him."

"Yes," I said, "we have our tyrants."

"Well," she answered resignedly, "we can at any rate destroy these tyrants, and Kallikrates shall rule the land."

I instantly informed Ayesha that in England "blasting" was not an amusement that could be indulged in with impunity, and that any such attempt would meet with the consideration of the law and probably end upon a scaffold.

"The law," she laughed with scorn, "the law! Canst thou not understand; O Holly, that I am above the law, and so shall my Kallikrates be also? All human law will be to us as the north wind to a mountain. Does the wind bend the mountain, or the mountain the wind?

"And now leave me, I pray thee, and thou too, my own Kallikrates, for I would get me ready against our journey, and so must ye both, and your servant also. But bring no great quantity of things with thee, for I trust that we shall be but three days gone. Then shall we return hither, and I will make a plan whereby we can bid farewell forever to these sepulchers of Kôr. Yes, surely thou mayst kiss my hand!"

So we went, I, for one, meditating deeply on the awful nature of the problem that now opened out before us. The terrible *She* had evidently made up her mind to go to England, and it made me absolutely shudder to think what would be the result of her arrival there. What her powers were I knew, and I could not doubt but that she would exercise them to the full. It might be possible to control her for a while, but her proud, ambitious spirit would be certain to break loose and avenge itself for the long centuries of its solitude. She would, if necessary, and if the power of her beauty did not unaided prove equal to the occasion, blast her way to any end she set before her, and as she could not die, and for aught I knew could not even be killed,[1] what was there to stop her? In the end she would, I had little doubt, assume absolute rule over the British dominions, and probably over the whole earth, and, though I was sure that she would speedily make ours the most glorious and prosperous empire that the world has ever seen, it would be at the cost of a terrible sacrifice of life.

The whole thing sounded like a dream of some extraordinary invention of a speculative brain, and yet it was a fact – a wonderful fact – of which the whole world would soon be called on to take notice. What was the meaning of it all? After much thinking I could only conclude that this wonderful creature, whose passion had kept her for so many centuries chained; as it were, and comparatively harmless, was now about to be used by Providence as a means to change the order of the world, and possibly, by the building up of a power that could no more be rebelled against or questioned than the decrees of Fate, to change it materially for the better.

1 I regret to say that I was never able to ascertain if She was invulnerable against the accidents of life. Presumably this was so, else some misadventure would have been sure to put an end to her in the course of so many centuries. True, she offered to let Leo slay her, but very probably this was only an experiment to try his temper and mental attitude towards her. Ayesha never gave way to impulse without some valid object. – L. H. H.

Chapter 23

The Temple of Truth

OUR PREPARATIONS did not take us very long. We put a change of clothing apiece and some spare boots into my Gladstone bag, also we took our revolvers and an express rifle each, together with a good supply of ammunition, a precaution to which, under Providence, we subsequently owed our lives over and over again. The rest of our gear, together with our heavy rifles, we left behind us.

A few minutes before the appointed time we once more attended in Ayesha's boudoir, and found her also ready, her dark cloak thrown over her winding sheet like wrappings.

"Are ye prepared for the great venture?" she said.

"We are," I answered, "though for my part, Ayesha, I have no faith in it."

"Ah, my Holly," she said, "thou art of a truth like those old Jews – of whom the memory vexes me so sorely – unbelieving, and hard to accept that which they have not known. But thou shalt see; for unless my mirror yonder lies" – and she pointed to the font of crystal water – "the path is yet open as it was of old time. And now let us start upon the new life which shall end – who knoweth where?"

"Ah," I echoed, "who knoweth where?" and we passed down into the great central cave, and out into the light of day. At the mouth of the cave we found a single litter with six bearers, all of them mutes, waiting, and with them I was relieved to see our old friend Billali, for whom I had conceived a sort of affection. It appeared that, for reasons not necessary to explain at length, Ayesha had thought it best that, with the exception of herself, we should proceed on foot, and this we were nothing loath to do, after our long confinement in these caves, which, however suitable they might be for sarcophagi – a singularly inappropriate word, by the way, for these particular tombs, which certainly did not consume the bodies given to their keeping – were depressing habitations for breathing mortals like ourselves. Either by accident or by the orders of *She*, the space in front of the cave where we had beheld that awful dance was perfectly clear of spectators. Not a soul was to be seen, and consequently I do not believe that our departure was known to anybody, except perhaps the mutes who waited on *She*, and they were, of course, in the habit of keeping what they saw to themselves.

In a few minutes' time we were stepping out sharply – across the great cultivated plain or lake bed, framed like a vast emerald in its setting of frowning cliff, and had another opportunity of wondering at the extraordinary nature of the site chosen by these old people of Kôr for their capital, and at the marvelous amount of labor, ingenuity, and engineering skill that must have been brought into requisition by the founders of the city to drain so huge a sheet of water, and to keep it clear of subsequent accumulations. It is, indeed, so far as my experience goes, an unequaled instance of what man can do in the face of nature, for in my opinion such achievements as the Suez Canal or even the Mont Cenis Tunnel do not approach this ancient undertaking in magnitude and grandeur of conception.

When we had been walking for about half an hour, enjoying ourselves exceedingly in the delightful cool which about this time of the day always appeared to descend upon the great plain of Kôr, and which in some degree atoned for the want of any land or sea breeze – for all wind was kept off by the rocky mountain wall – we began to get a clear view of what Billali had informed us were the ruins of the great city. And even from that distance we could see how wonderful those ruins were, a fact which with every step we took became more evident. The city was not very large if compared to Babylon or Thebes, or other cities of remote antiquity; perhaps its outer wall contained some twelve square miles of ground, or a little more. Nor had the walls, so far as we could judge when we reached them, been very high, probably not more than forty feet, which was about their present height where they had not through the sinking of the ground, or some such cause, fallen into ruin. The reason of this, no doubt, was that the people of Kôr, being protected from any outside attack by far more tremendous ramparts than any that the hand of man could rear, only required them for show and to guard against civil discord. But on the other hand they were as broad as they were high, built entirely of dressed stone, hewn, no doubt, from the vast caves, and surrounded by a great moat about sixty feet in width, some reaches of which were still filled with water. About ten minutes before the sun finally sank we reached this moat, and passed down and through it, clambering across what evidently were the piled-up fragments of a great bridge in order to do to, and then with some little difficulty up the slope of the wall to its summit. I wish that it lay within the power of my pen to give some idea of the grandeur of the sight that then met our view. There, all bathed in the red glow of the sinking sun, were miles upon miles of ruins – columns, temples, shrines, and the palaces of kings, varied with patches of green bush. Of course, the roofs of these buildings had long since fallen into decay and vanished, but owing to the extreme massiveness of the style of building, and to the hardness and durability of the rock employed, most of the party walls and great columns still remained standing.[1]

Straight before us stretched away what had evidently been the main thoroughfare of the city, for it was very wide, wider than the Thames Embankment, and regular. Being, as we afterwards discovered, paved, or rather built, throughout of

1 In connection with the extraordinary state of preservation of these ruins after so vast a lapse of time – at least six thousand years – it must be remembered that Kôr was not burned or destroyed by an enemy or an earthquake, but deserted, owing to the action of a terrible plague. Consequently the houses were left unharmed; also, the climate of the plain is remarkably fine and dry, and there is very little rain or wind; as a result of which these relics have only to contend against the unaided action of time, which works but slowly upon such massive blocks of masonry. – L. H. H.

blocks of dressed stone, such as were employed in the walls, it was but little overgrown even now with grass and shrubs that could get no depth of soil to live in. What had been the parks and gardens, on the contrary, were now dense jungle. Indeed, it was easy even from a distance to trace the course of the various roads by the burnt-up appearance of the scanty grass that grew upon them. On either side of this great thoroughfare were vast blocks of ruins, each block, generally speaking, being separated from its neighbor by a space of what had once, I suppose, been garden ground, but was now dense and tangled bush. They were all built of the same colored stone, and most of them had pillars, which was as much as we could make out in the fading light as we passed swiftly up the main road, which I believe I am right in saying no living foot had pressed for thousands of years.[1]

Presently we came to an enormous pile, which we rightly took to be a temple covering at least four acres of ground, and apparently arranged in a series of courts, each one enclosing another of smaller size, on the principle of a Chinese nest of boxes, which were separated one from the other by rows of huge columns. And, while I think of it, I may as well state a remarkable thing about the shape of these columns, which resembled none that I have ever seen or heard of, being fashioned with a kind of waist in the center, and swelling out above and below. At first we thought that this shape was meant to roughly symbolize or suggest the female form, as was a common habit amongst the ancient religious architects of many creeds. On the following day, however, as we went up the slopes of the mountain, we discovered a large quantity of the most stately-looking palms, of which the trunks grew exactly in this shape, and I have now no doubt but that the first designer of these columns drew his

1 Billali told me that the Amahagger believe that the site of the city is haunted, and could not be persuaded to enter it upon any consideration. Indeed, I could see that he himself did not at all like doing so, and was only consoled by the reflection that he was under the direct protection of *She*. It struck Leo and myself as very curious that a people which has no objection to living amongst the dead, with whom their familiarity has perhaps bred contempt, and even using their bodies for purposes of fuel, should be terrified at approaching the habitations that these very departed had occupied when alive. After all, however, it is only a savage inconsistency. – L. H. H.

inspiration from the graceful bends of those very palms, or rather of their, ancestors, which then, some eight or ten thousand years ago," as now, beautified the slopes of the mountain that had once formed the shores of the volcanic lake.

At the façade of this huge temple, which, I should imagine, is almost as large as that of El-Karnac, at Thebes, some of the largest columns, which I measured, being between eighteen to twenty feet in diameter at the base, by about seventy feet in height, our little procession was halted, and Ayesha descended from her litter.

"There used to be a spot here, Kallikrates," she said to Leo, who had run up to help her down, "where one might sleep. Two thousand years ago did thou and I and that Egyptian asp rest therein, but since then have I not set foot here, nor any man, and perchance it has fallen," and, followed by the rest of us, she passed up a vast flight of broken and ruined steps into the outer court, and looked round into the gloom. Presently she seemed to recollect, and, walking a few paces along the wall to the left, halted.

"It is here," she said, and at the same time beckoned to the two mutes, who were loaded with provisions and our little belongings, to advance. One of them came forward, and, producing a lamp, lit it from his brazier (for the Amahagger when on a journey nearly always carried with them a little lighted brazier, from which to provide fire). The tinder of this brazier was made of broken fragments of mummy carefully damped, and, if the admixture of moisture was properly managed, this unholy compound would smolder away for hours.[1] As soon as the lamp was lit we entered the place before which Ayesha had halted. It turned out to be a chamber hollowed in the thickness of the wall, and, from the fact of there still being a massive stone table in it, I should think that it had probably served as a living room, perhaps for one of the doorkeepers of the great temple.

Here we stopped, and after cleaning the place out and making

1 After all, we are not much in advance of the Amahagger in these matters. 'Mummy,' that is, pounded ancient Egyptian, is, I believe, a pigment much used by artists, and especially by those of them who direct their talents to the reproduction of the works of the old masters. – EDITOR.

it as comfortable as circumstances and the darkness would permit, we ate some cold meat, at least Leo, Job, and I did, for Ayesha, as I think I have said elsewhere, never touched anything except cakes of flour, fruit, and water. While we were still eating, the moon, which was at her full, rose above the mountain wall, and began to flood the place with silver.

"Wot ye why I have brought you here tonight, my Holly?" said Ayesha, leaning her head upon her hand and watching the great orb as she rose, like some heavenly queen, above the solemn pillars of the temple. "I brought you – nay, it is strange, but knowest thou, Kallikrates, that thou liest at this moment upon the very spot where thy dead body lay when I bore thee back to those caves of Kôr so many years ago? It all returns to my mind now. I can see it, and horrible is it to my sight!" and she shuddered.

Here Leo jumped up and hastily changed his seat. However the reminiscence might affect Ayesha, it clearly had few charms for him.

"I brought you," went on Ayesha presently, "that ye might look upon the most wonderful sight that ever the eye of man beheld – the full moon shining over ruined Kôr. When ye have done your eating – I would that I could teach thee to eat naught but fruit, Kallikrates, but that will come after thou hast laved in the fire, once I, too, ate flesh like a brute beast – when ye have done we will go out, and I will show you this great temple and the God whom men once worshiped therein."

Of course we got up at once, and started. And here again my pen fails me. To give a string of measurements and details of the various courts of the temple would only be wearisome, supposing that I had them, and yet I know not how I am to describe what we saw, magnificent as it was even in its ruin, almost beyond the power of realization. Court upon dim court, row upon row of mighty pillars – some of them (especially at the gateways) sculptured from pedestal to capital – space upon space of empty chambers that spoke more eloquently to the imagination than any crowded streets. And over all, the dead silence of the dead, the sense of utter loneliness, and the brooding spirit of the Past! How beautiful it was, and yet how drear! We did not dare to speak aloud. Ayesha herself was awed in the presence of an antiquity compared to which even her length of days was but a little thing; we only whispered, and our whispers seemed to run from column to column, till they were lost in the quiet air. Bright fell the moonlight on pillar and court and shattered wall, hiding all their rents and imperfections in its silver garment, and clothing their hoar majesty with the peculiar glory of the night. It was a wonderful sight to see the full moon looking down on the ruined fane of Kôr. It was a wonderful thing to think for how many thousands of years the dead orb above and the dead city below had gazed thus upon each other, and in the utter solitude of space poured forth each to each the tale of their lost life and long-departed glory. The white light fell, and minute by minute the quiet shadows crept across the grass-grown courts like the spirits of old priests haunting the habitations of their worship – the white light fell, and the long shadows grew till the beauty and grandeur of the scene and the untamed majesty of its present Death seemed to sink into our very souls, and speak more loudly than the shouts of armies concerning the pomp and splendor that the grave had swallowed, and even memory had forgotten.

"Come," said Ayesha, after we had gazed and gazed, I know not for how long, "and I will show you the stony flower of Loveliness and Wonder's very crown, if yet it stands to mock time with its beauty and fill the heart of man with longing for that which is behind the veil," and, without waiting for an answer, she led us through two more pillared courts into the inner shrine of the old fane.

And there, in the center of the inmost court, which might have been some fifty yards square, or a little more, we stood face to face with what is perhaps the grandest allegorical work of art that the genius of her children has ever given to the world. For in the exact center of the court, placed upon a thick square slab of rock, was a huge round ball of dark stone, some forty feet in diameter, and standing on the ball was a colossal winged figure of a beauty so entrancing and divine that when I first gazed upon it, illuminated and shadowed as it was by the soft light of the moon, my breath stood still, and for an instant my heart ceased its beating.

The statue was hewn from marble so pure and white that even now, after all those ages, it shone as the moonbeams danced upon it, and its height was, I should say, a trifle under twenty feet. It was the winged figure of a woman of such marvelous loveliness and delicacy of form that the size seemed rather to add to than to detract from its so human and yet more spiritual beauty. She was bending forward and poising herself upon her half-spread wings as though to preserve her balance as she leaned. Her arms were outstretched like those of some woman about to embrace one she dearly loved, while her whole attitude gave an impression of the tenderest beseeching. Her perfect and most gracious form was naked, save – and here came the extraordinary thing – the face, which was thinly veiled, so that we could only trace the marking of her features. A gauzy veil was thrown round and about the head, and of its two ends one fell down across her left breast, which was outlined beneath it, and one, now broken, streamed away upon the air behind her.

"Who is she?" I asked, as soon as I could take my eyes off the statue.

"Canst thou not guess, O Holly?" answered Ayesha. "Where then is thy imagination? It is Truth standing on the World, and calling to its children to unveil her face. See what is writ upon the pedestal. Without doubt it is taken from the book of the scriptures of these men of Kôr," and she led the way to the foot of the statue, where an inscription of the usual Chinese-looking hieroglyphics was so deeply graven as to be still quite legible, at least to Ayesha. According to her translation it ran thus:

> *"Is there no man that will draw my veil and look upon my face, for it is very fair? Unto him who draws my veil shall I be, and peace will I give him, and sweet children of knowledge and good works."*
>
> *And a voice cried, "Through all those who seek after thee desire thee, behold! Virgin art thou, and Virgin shall thou go till Time be done. No man is there born of woman who may draw thy veil and live, nor shall be. By Death only can thy veil be drawn, oh Truth!"*
>
> *And Truth stretched out her arms and wept, because those who sought her might not find her, nor look upon her face to face.*

"Thou seest," said Ayesha, when she had finished translating, "Truth was the goddess of the people of old Kôr, and to her they built their shrines, and her they sought; knowing that they should never find, still sought they."

"And so," I added sadly, "do men seek to this very hour, but they find not; and, as this scripture saith, nor shall they, for in Death only is Truth found."

Then with one more look at this veiled and spiritualized loveliness – which was so perfect and so pure that one might almost fancy that the light of a living spirit shone through the marble prison to lead man on to high and ethereal thoughts – this poet's dream of beauty frozen into stone, which I never shall forget while I live, though I find myself so helpless when I attempt to describe it, we turned and went back through the vast moonlit courts to the spot whence we had started. I never saw the statue again, which I the more regret, because on the great ball of stone representing the world whereon the figure stood, lines were drawn that probably, had there been light enough, we should have discovered to be a map of the universe as it was known to the people of Kôr. It is at any rate suggestive of some scientific knowledge that these long-dead worshipers of Truth had recognized the fact that the globe is round.

Chapter 24

Walking the Plank

NEXT DAY the mutes woke us before the dawn; and by the time that we had got the sleep out of our eyes, and gone through a perfunctory wash at a spring which still welled up into the remains of a marble basin in the center of the north quadrangle of the vast outer court, we found *She* standing by the litter ready to start, while old Billali and the two bearer mutes were busy collecting the baggage. As usual, Ayesha was veiled like the marble Truth, (by the way, I wonder if she originally got the idea of covering up her beauty from that statue?). I noticed, however, that she seemed very depressed, and had none of that proud and buoyant bearing which would have betrayed her among a thousand women of the same stature, even if they had been veiled like herself. She looked up as we came – for her head was bowed – and greeted us. Leo asked her how she had slept.

"Ill, my Kallikrates," she answered, "ill. This night have strange and hideous dreams come creeping through my brain, and I know not what they may portend. Almost do I feel as though some evil overshadowed me; and yet how can evil touch me? I wonder," she went on with a sudden outbreak of womanly tenderness, "I wonder if, should aught happen to me, so that I slept awhile and left thee waking, thou wouldst think gently of me? I wonder, my Kallikrates, it thou wouldst tarry till I came again, as for so many centuries I have tarried for thy coming?"

Then, without waiting for an answer, she went on:

"Come, let us be setting forth, for we have far to go, and before another day is born in yonder blue should we stand in the place of Life."

In another five minutes we were once more on our way through the vast ruined city, which loomed at us on either side in the gray dawning in a way that was at once grand and oppressive. Just as the first ray of the rising sun shot like a golden arrow athwart this storied desolation we gained the farther gateway of the outer wall, and having given one more glance at the hoar and pillared majesty through which we had passed, and (with the exception of Job, for whom ruins had no charms) breathed a sigh of regret that we had not had more time to explore it, passed through the great moat, and on to the plain beyond.

As the sun rose so did Ayesha's spirits, till by breakfast-time they had regained their normal level, and she laughingly set down her previous depression to the associations of the spot where she had slept.

"These barbarians declare that Kôr is haunted," she said, "and of a truth I do believe their saying, for never did I know so ill a night save once. I remember it now. It was on that very spot when thou didst lie dead at my feet, Kallikrates. Never will I visit it again; it is a place of evil omen."

After a very brief halt for breakfast we pressed on with such good will that by two o'clock in the afternoon we were at the foot of the vast wall of rock that formed the lip of the volcano, and which at this point towered up precipitously above us for fifteen hundred or two thousand feet. Here we halted, certainly not to my astonishment, for I did not see how it was possible that we should go any farther.

"Now," said Ayesha, as she descended from her litter, "doth our labor but commence, for here do we part with these men, and henceforward must we bear ourselves." And then, addressing Billali: "Do thou and these slaves remain here, and abide our coming. By tomorrow at the midday shall we be with thee – if not, wait."

Billali bowed humbly, and said that her august bidding, should be obeyed if they stopped there till they grew old.

"And this man, O Holly," said *She*, pointing to Job; "best is it that he should tarry also, for if his heart be not high and his courage great, perchance some evil might overtake him. Also, the secrets of the place whither we go are not fit for common eyes."

I translated this to Job, who instantly and earnestly entreated me, almost with tears in his eyes, not to leave him behind. He said he was sure that he could see nothing worse than he had already seen, and that he was terrified to death at the idea of being left alone with those "dumb folk," who, he thought, would probably take the opportunity to hot-pot him.

I translated what he said to Ayesha, who shrugged her shoulders, and answered, "Well, let him come, it is naught to me; on his own head be it, and he will serve to bear the lamp and this," and she pointed to a narrow plank, some sixteen feet in length, which had been bound above the long bearing pole of her hammock, as I had thought to make the curtains spread out better, but, as it now appeared, for some unknown purpose connected with our extraordinary undertaking.

Accordingly, the plank, which, though tough, was very light, was given to Job to carry, and also one of the lamps. I slung the other onto my back, together with a spare jar of oil, while Leo loaded himself with the provisions and some water in a kid's skin. When this was done *She* bade Billali and the six bearer mutes to retreat behind a grove of flowering magnolias about a hundred yards away, and remain there under pain of death till we had vanished. They bowed humbly, and went, and, as he departed, old Billali gave me a friendly shake of the hand, and whispered that he had rather that it was I than he who was going on this wonderful expedition with "*She-who-must-be-obeyed*," and upon my word I felt inclined to agree with him. In another minute they were gone, and then, having briefly asked us if we were ready, Ayesha turned, and gazed up the towering cliff.

"Goodness me, Leo," I said, "surely we are not going to climb that precipice!"

Leo shrugged his shoulders, being in a condition of half-fascinated, half-expectant mystification, and as he did so, Ayesha with a sudden move began to climb the cliff, and of course we had to follow her. It was perfectly marvelous to see the ease and grace with which she sprang from rock to rock, and swung herself along the ledges. The ascent was not, however, so difficult as it seemed, although there were one or two nasty places where it did not do to look behind you, the fact being that the rock still sloped here, and was not absolutely precipitous as it was higher up. In this way we, with no great labor, mounted to the height of some fifty feet above our last standing place, the only really troublesome thing to manage being Job's board, and in doing so drew some fifty or sixty paces to the left of our starting point, for we went up like a crab, sideways. Presently we reached a ledge, narrow enough at first, but which widened as we followed it, and moreover sloped inwards like the petal of a flower, so that as we followed it we gradually got into a kind of rut or fold of rock that grew deeper and deeper, till at last it resembled a Devonshire lane in stone, and hid us perfectly from the gaze of anybody on the slope below, if there had been anybody to gaze. This lane (which appeared to be a natural formation) continued for some fifty or sixty paces, and then suddenly ended in a cave, also natural, running at right angles to it. I am sure that it was a natural cave, and not hollowed by the hand of man, because of its irregular and contorted shape and course, which gave it the appearance of having been blown bodily in the mountain by some frightful eruption of gas following the line of the least resistance. All the caves hollowed by the ancients of Kôr, on the contrary, were cut out with the most perfect regularity and symmetry. At the mouth of this cave Ayesha halted, and bade us light the two lamps, which I did, giving one to her and keeping the other myself. Then, taking the lead, she advanced down the cavern, picking her way with great care, as indeed it was necessary to do, for the floor was most irregular – strewn with boulders like the bed of a stream, and in some places pitted with deep holes, in which it would have been easy to break one's leg.

This cavern we pursued for twenty minutes or more, it being, so far as I could form a judgment – owing to its numerous twists and turns no easy task – about a quarter of a mile long.

At last, however, we halted at its farther end, and while I was still trying to pierce the gloom a great gust of air came tearing down it, and extinguished both the lamps. Ayesha called to us, and we crept up to her, for she was a little in front, and were rewarded with a view that was positively appalling in its gloom and grandeur. Before us was a mighty chasm in the black rock, jagged and torn and splintered through it in a far past age by some awful convulsion of Nature, as though it had been cleft by stroke upon stroke of the lightning. This chasm, which was bounded by a precipice on the hither, and presumably, though we could not see it, on the farther side also, may have measured any width across, but from its darkness I do not think that it can have been very broad. It was impossible to make out much of its outline, or how far it ran, for the simple reason that the point where we were standing was so far from the upper surface of the cliff, at least fifteen hundred or two thousand feet, that only a very dim light struggled down to us from above. The mouth of the cavern that we had been following gave onto a most curious and tremendous spur of rock, which jutted out in midair into the gulf before us, for a distance of some fifty yards, coming to a sharp point at its termination, and resembling nothing that I can think of so much as the spur upon the leg of a cock in shape. This huge spur was attached only to the parent precipice at its base, which was, of course, enormous, just as the cock's spur is attached to its leg. Otherwise it was utterly unsupported.

"Here must we pass," said Ayesha. "Be careful lest giddiness overcome you, or the wind sweep you into the gulf beneath, for of a truth it hath no bottom." And, without giving us any further time to get scared, she started walking along the spur, leaving us to follow her as best we might. I was next to her, then came Job, painfully dragging his plank, while Leo brought up the rear. It was a wonderful sight to see this intrepid woman gliding fearlessly along that dreadful place. For my part, when I had gone but a very few yards, what between the pressure of the air and the awful sense of the consequences that a slip would entail, I found it necessary to go down on my hands and knees and crawl, and so did the other two.

But Ayesha never condescended to this. On she went, leaning her body against the gusts of wind, and never seeming to lose her head or her balance.

In a few minutes we had crossed some twenty paces of this awful bridge, which got narrower at every step, and then all of a sudden a great gust came tearing along the gorge. I saw Ayesha lean herself against it, but the strong draft got under her dark cloak, and tore it from her, and away it went down the wind flapping like a wounded bird. It was dreadful to see it go, till it was lost in the blackness. I clung to the saddle of rock, and looked round, while the great spur vibrated with a humming sound beneath us, like a living thing. The sight was a truly awesome one. There we were poised in the gloom between earth and heaven. Beneath us were hundreds upon hundreds of feet of emptiness that gradually grew darker, till at last it was absolutely black, and at what depth it ended is more than I can guess. Above were space upon space of giddy air, and far, far away a line of blue sky. And down this vast gulf upon which we were pinnacled the great draft dashed and roared, driving clouds and misty wreaths of vapor before it, till we were nearly blinded, and utterly confused.

The whole position was so tremendous and so absolutely unearthly that I believe it actually lulled our sense of terror, but to this hour I often see it in my dreams, and wake up covered with cold perspiration at its mere fantasy.

"On! On!" cried the white form before us, for now the cloak had gone *She* was robed in white, and looked more like a spirit riding down the gale than a woman. "On, or ye will fall and be dashed to pieces. Keep your eyes fixed upon the ground, and closely hug the rock."

We obeyed her, and crept painfully along the quivering Path against which the wind shrieked and wailed as it shook it, causing it to murmur like a vast tuning fork. On we went, I do not know for how long, only gazing round now and again, when it was absolutely necessary, until at last we saw that we were on the very tip of the spur, a slab of rock, little larger than an ordinary table, that throbbed and jumped like any over-engined steamer. There we lay on our stomachs, clinging to the ground, and looked about us, while Ayesha stood leaning out against the wind, down which her long hair streamed, and, absolutely heedless of the hideous depth that yawned beneath, pointed before her. Then we saw why the narrow plank, which Job and I had painfully dragged along between us, had been provided. Before us was an empty space. On the other side of which was something, as yet we could not see what, for here – either owing to the shadow of the opposite cliff, or from some other cause – the gloom was that of night.

"We must wait awhile," called Ayesha; "soon there will be light."

At the moment I could not imagine what she meant. How could more light than there was ever come to this dreadful spot? While I was still debating in my mind, suddenly, like a great sword of flame, a beam from the setting sun pierced the Stygian gloom, and smote upon the point of rock whereon we lay; illumining Ayesha's lovely form with an unearthly splendor. I only wish that

I could describe the wild and marvelous beauty of that sword of fire, laid across the darkness and rushing mist wreaths of the gulf. How it got there I do not to this moment know, but I presume that there was some cleft or hole in the opposing cliff, through which it pierced when the setting orb was in a direct line therewith. All I can say is that the effect was the most wonderful that I ever saw.

Right through the heart of the darkness that flaming sword was stabbed, and where it lay there was the most surpassingly vivid light, so vivid that even at a distance one could see the grain of the rock, while, outside of it – yes, within a few inches of its keen edge – was naught but clustering shadows.

And now, by this ray of light, for which *She* had been waiting, and timed our arrival to meet, knowing that at this season for thousands of years it had always struck thus at sunset, we saw what was before us. Within eleven or twelve feet of the very tip of the tonguelike rock whereon we stood there arose, presumably from the far bottom of the gulf, a sugarloaf-shaped cone, of which the summit was exactly opposite to us. But had there been a summit only it would not have helped us much, for the nearest point of its circumference was some forty feet from where we were. On the lip of this summit, however, which was circular and hollow, rested a tremendous flat stone, something like a glacier stone – perhaps it was one, for all I know to the contrary – and the end of this stone approached to within twelve feet or so of us. This huge boulder was nothing more or less than a gigantic rocking stone, accurately balanced upon the edge of the cone or miniature crater, like a half-crown on the rim of a wine glass; for, in the fierce light that played upon it and us, we could see it oscillating in the gusts of wind.

"Quick!" said Ayesha. "The plank – we must cross while the light endures; presently it will be gone."

"Oh, Lord, sir!" groaned Job. "Surely she don't mean us to walk across that there place on that there thing," as in obedience to my direction he pushed the long board towards me.

"That's it. Job," I halloed in ghastly merriment, though the idea of walking the plank was no pleasanter to me than to him.

I pushed the board on to Ayesha, who deftly ran it across the gulf so that one end of it rested on the rocking stone, the other remaining on the extremity of the trembling spur. Then, placing her foot upon it to prevent it from being blown away, she turned to me.

"Since last I was here, O Holly," she called, "the support of the moving stone hath lessened somewhat, so that I am not sure if it will bear our weight or no. Therefore will I cross the first, because no harm will come unto me," and, without further ado, she trod lightly but firmly across the frail bridge, and in another second was standing safe upon the heaving stone.

"It is safe," she called. "See, hold thou the plank! I will stand on the farther side of the stone so that it may not overbalance with your greater weights. Now come, O Holly, for presently the light will fail us."

I struggled to my knees, and if ever I felt sick in my life I felt sick then, and I am not ashamed to say that I hesitated and hung back.

"Surely thou art not afraid," called this strange creature in a lull of the gale, from where she stood, poised like a bird on the highest point of the rocking stone. "Make then way for Kallikrates."

This settled me; it is better to fall down a precipice and die than be laughed at by such a woman; so I clenched my teeth, and in another instant I was on that horrible, narrow, bending plank, with bottomless space beneath and around me. I have always hated a great height, but never before did I realize the full honors of which such a position is capable. Oh, the sickening sensation of that yielding board resting on the two moving supports. I grew dizzy, and thought that I must fall; my spine *crept*; it seemed to me that I was falling, and my delight at finding myself sprawling upon that stone, which rose and fell beneath me like a boat in a swell, cannot be expressed in words. All I know is that briefly, but earnestly enough, I thanked Providence for preserving me so far.

Then came Leo's turn, and, though he looked rather queer, he came across like a rope dancer. Ayesha stretched out her hand to clasp his own, and I heard her say, "Bravely done, my love – bravely done! The old Greek spirit lives in thee yet!"

And now only poor Job remained on the farther side of the gulf. He crept up to the plank, and yelled out, "I can't do it, sir. I shall fall into that beastly place."

"You must," I remember saying with inappropriate facetiousness, "you must, Job, it's as easy as catching flies." I suppose that I said it to satisfy my conscience, because although the expression conveys a wonderful idea of facility, as a matter of fact I know no more difficult operation in the whole world than catching flies – that is, in warm weather, unless, indeed, it is catching mosquitoes.

"I can't, sir – I can't, indeed."

"Let the man come, or let him stop and perish there. See, the light is dying! In a moment it will be gone!" said Ayesha.

I looked. She was right. The sun was passing below the level of the hole or cleft in the precipice through which the ray reached us.

"If you stop there, Job, you will die alone," I called; "the light is going."

"Come, be a man, Job," roared Leo; "it's quite easy."

Thus adjured, the miserable Job, with a most awful yell, precipitated himself face downwards on the plank – he did not dare, small blame to him, to try to walk it, and commenced to draw himself across in little jerks, his poor legs hanging down on either side into the nothingness beneath.

His violent jerks at the frail board made the great stone, which was only balanced on a few inches of rock, oscillate in a most sickening manner, and, to make matters worse, when he was halfway across, the flying ray of lurid light suddenly went out, just as though a lamp had been extinguished in a curtained room, leaving the whole howling wilderness of air black with darkness.

"Come on, Job, for God's sake!" I shouted in an agony of fear, while the stone, gathering motion with every swing, rocked so violently that it was difficult to hang on to it. It was a truly awful position.

"Lord have mercy on me!" cried poor Job from the darkness. "Oh, the plank's slipping!" and I heard a violent struggle, and thought that he was gone.

But at that moment his outstretched hand, clasping in agony at the air, met my own, and I hauled – ah, how I did haul, putting out all the strength that it has pleased Providence to give me in such abundance – and to my joy in another minute Job was gasping on the rock beside me. But the plank! I felt it slip, and heard it knock against a projecting knob of rock, and it was gone.

"Great Heavens!" I exclaimed. "How are we going to get back?"

"I don't know," answered Leo out of the gloom. "Sufficient to the day is the evil thereof. I am thankful enough to be here."

But Ayesha merely called to me to take her hand and creep after her.

Chapter 25

The Spirit of Life

I DID as I was bid, and in fear and trembling felt myself guided over the edge of the stone. I sprawled my legs out, but could touch nothing.

"I am going to fall!" I gasped.

"Nay, let thyself go, and trust to me," answered Ayesha.

Now, if the position is considered, it will be easily understood that this was a greater demand upon my confidence than was justified by my knowledge of Ayesha's character. For all I knew she might be in the very act of consigning me to a horrible doom. But in life we sometimes have to lay our faith upon strange altars, and so it was now.

"Let thyself go!" she cried, and, having no choice, I did.

I felt myself slide a pace or two down the sloping surface of the rock, and then pass into the air, and the thought flashed through my brain that I was lost. But no! In another instant my feet struck against a rocky floor, and I felt that I was standing on something solid, and out of reach of the wind, which I could hear singing away overhead. As I stood there thanking Heaven for these small mercies, there was a slip and a scuffle, and down came Leo alongside of me.

"Hullo, old fellow!" he called out. "Are you there? This is getting interesting, is it not?"

Just then, with a terrific yell. Job arrived right on top of us, knocking us both down. By the time that we had struggled to our feet again Ayesha was standing among us, and bidding us light the lamps, which fortunately remained uninjured, as also did the spare jar of oil.

I got out my box of Bryant and May's wax matches, and they struck as merrily there, in that awful place, as they could have done in a London drawing room.

In a couple of minutes both the lamps were alight; and a curious scene they revealed. We were huddled together in a rock chamber, some ten feet square, and scared enough we looked; that is, except Ayesha, who was standing calmly with her arms folded, and waiting for the lamps to burn up. The chamber appeared to be partly natural and partly hollowed out of the top of the cone. The roof of the natural part was formed of the swinging stone, and that of the back part of the chamber, which sloped downwards, was hewn from the live rock. For the rest, the place was warm and dry – a perfect haven of rest compared to the giddy pinnacle above, and the quivering spur that shot out to meet it in midair.

"So!" said *She*. "Safely have we come, though once I feared that the rocking stone would fall with you, and precipitate you into the bottomless deeps beneath, for I do believe that the cleft goeth down to the very womb of the world. The rock whereon the stone resteth hath crumbled beneath the swinging weight. And now that he" – nodding towards Job, who was sitting on the floor, feebly wiping his forehead with a red cotton pocket handkerchief – "whom they rightly called the 'Pig,' for as a pig is he stupid, hath let fall the plank, it will not be easy to return across the gulf, and to that end must I make a plan. But now rest awhile, and look upon this place. What think ye that it is?"

"We know not," I answered.

"Wouldst thou believe, O Holly, that once a man did choose this airy nest for a daily habitation, and did here endure for many years; leaving it only but one day in every twelve to seek food and water and oil that the people brought, more than he could carry, and laid as an offering in the mouth of the tunnel through which we passed hither?"

We looked up wonderingly, and she continued, "Yet so it was. There was a man – Noot, he named himself – who, though he lived in the latter days, had all of the wisdom of the sons of Kôr. A hermit was he, and a philosopher, and skilled in the secrets of Nature, and he it was who discovered the Fire that I shall show you, which is Nature's blood and life, and also that he who bathed therein, and breathed thereof, should live while Nature lives. But like unto thee, O Holly, this man, Noot, would not turn his knowledge to account. Ill, he said, was it for man to live, for man was born to die. Therefore did he tell his secret to none, and therefore did he come and live here, where the seeker after Life must pass, and was revered of the Amahagger of the day as holy, and a hermit. And when first I came to this country – knowest thou how I came, Kallikrates? Another time will I tell thee, it is a strange tale – I heard of this philosopher, and waited for him when he came to fetch his food, and returned with him hither, though greatly did I fear to tread the gulf. Then did I beguile him with my beauty and my wit, and flatter him with my tongue, so that he led me down and showed me the Fire, and told me the secrets of the Fire, but he would not suffer me to step therein, and, fearing lest he should slay me, I refrained, knowing that the man was very old, and soon would die. And I returned, having learned from him all that he knew of the wonderful Spirit of the World, and that was much, for the man was wise and very ancient, and by purity and abstinence, and the contemplations of his innocent mind, had worn thin the veil between that which we see and the great invisible truths, the whisper of whose wings at times we hear as they sweep through the gross air of the world. Then – it was but a very few days after – I met thee, my Kallikrates, who hadst wandered hither with the beautiful Egyptian Amenartas, and I learned to love for the first and last time, once and forever, so that it entered into my mind to come hither with thee, and receive the gift of Life for thee and me. Therefore came we, with that Egyptian who would not be left behind, and, behold, we found the old man Noot lying but newly dead. *There* he lay, and his white beard covered him like a garment," – and she pointed to a spot near where I was sitting – "but surely he hath long since crumbled into dust, and the wind hath borne his ashes hence."

Here I put out my hand and felt in the dust, and presently my fingers touched something. It was a human tooth, very yellow, but sound. I held it up and showed it to Ayesha, who laughed.

"Yes," she said, "it is his without a doubt. Behold what remaineth of Noot and the wisdom of Noot – one little tooth! And yet that man had all life at his command, and for his conscience's sake would have none of it. Well, he lay there newly dead, and we descended whither I shall lead you, and then, gathering up all my courage, and courting death that I might perchance win so glorious a crown of life, I stepped into the flames, and behold, life such as ye can never know until ye feel it also flowed into me, and I came forth undying, and lovely beyond imagining. Then did I stretch out mine arms to thee, Kallikrates, and bid thee take thine immortal bride, and behold, as I spoke, thou, blinded by my beauty, didst turn from me, and throw thine arms about the neck of Amenartas. And then a great fury filled me, and made me mad, and I seized the javelin that thou didst bear, and stabbed thee, so that there, at my very feet, in the place of Life, thou didst groan and go down into death. I knew not then that I had strength to slay with mine eyes and by the power of my will, therefore in my madness slew I with the javelin.[1]

"And when thou wast dead, ah, I wept, because I was undying and thou wast dead. I wept there in the place of Life so that had I been mortal any more my heart had surely broken. And

1 It will be observed that Ayesha's account of the death of Kallikrates differs materially from that written on the potsherd by Amenartas. The writing on the sherd says, "Then in her rage did she smite him by her magic, and he died." We never ascertained which was the correct version, but it will be remembered that the body of Kallikrates had a spear wound in the breast, which seems conclusive, unless, indeed, it was inflicted after death. Another thing that we never ascertained was how the two women – She and the Egyptian Amenartas – managed to beat the corpse of the man they both loved across the dread gulf and along the shaking spur. What a spectacle the two distracted creatures must have presented in their grief and loveliness as they toiled along that awful place with the dead man between them! Probably, however, the passage was easier then. – L. H. H.

she, the swart Egyptian – she cursed me by her gods. By Osiris did she curse me and by Isis, by Nephthys and by Hekt, by Sekhet, the lion-headed, and by Set, calling down evil on me, evil and everlasting desolation. Ah! I can see her dark face now lowering o'er me like a storm, but she could not hurt me, and I – I know not if I could hurt her. I did not try; it was naught to me then; so together we bore thee hence. And afterwards I sent her – the Egyptian – away through the swamps, and it seems that she lived to bear a son and to write the tale that should lead thee, her husband, back to me, her rival and thy murderess.

"Such is the tale, my love, and now is the hour at hand that shall set a crown upon it. Like all things on the earth, it is compounded of evil and of good – more of evil than of good, perchance; and writ in letters of blood. It is the truth; naught have I hidden from thee, Kallikrates. And now one thing before the final moment of thy trial. We go down into the presence of Death, for Life and Death are very near together, and – who knoweth? – that might happen which should separate us for another space of waiting. I am but a woman, and no prophetess, and I cannot read the future. But this I know – for I learned it from the lips of the wise man Noot – that my life is but prolonged and made more bright. It cannot live for aye. Therefore, before we go, tell me, oh Kallikrates, that of a truth thou dost forgive me, and dost love me from thy heart. See, Kallikrates: much evil have I done – perchance it was evil but two nights gone to strike that girl who loved thee cold in death – but she disobeyed me and angered me, prophesying misfortune to me, and I smote. Be careful when power comes to thee also, lest thou too shouldst smite in thine anger or thy jealousy, for unconquerable strength is a sore weapon in the hands of erring man. Yea, I have sinned – out of the bitterness born of a great love have I sinned – but yet do I know the good from the evil, nor is my heart altogether hardened. Thy love, O Kallikrates, shall be the gate of my redemption, even as aforetime my passion was the path down which I ran to evil. For deep love unsatisfied is the hell of noble hearts and a portion for the accursed, but love that is mirrored back more perfect from the soul of our desired doth fashion wings to lift us above ourselves, and make us what we might be. Therefore, Kallikrates, take me by the hand, and lift my veil with no more fear than though I were some peasant girl, and not the wisest and most beauteous woman in this wide world, and look me in the eyes, and tell me that thou dost forgive me with all thine heart, and that with all thine heart thou dost worship me."

She paused, and the strange tenderness in her voice seemed to hover round us like a memory. I know that the sound of it moved me more even than her words, it was so very human – so very womanly. Leo, too, was strangely touched. Hitherto he had been fascinated against his better judgment, something as a bird is fascinated by a snake, but now I think that all this passed away, and he realized that he really loved this strange and glorious creature, as, alas! I loved her also. At any rate, I saw his eyes fill with tears, and he stepped swiftly to her and undid the gauzy veil, and then took her by the hand, and, gazing into her deep eyes, said aloud, "Ayesha, I love thee with all my heart, and so far as forgiveness is possible I forgive thee the death of Ustane. For the rest, it is between thee and thy Maker; I know naught of it. I only know that I love thee as I never loved before, and that I will cleave to thee to the end."

"Now," answered Ayesha, with proud humility, "now when my lord doth speak thus royally and give with so free a hand, it cannot become me to lag behind in words, and be beggared of my generosity. Behold!" – and she took his hand and placed it upon her shapely head, and then bent herself slowly down till one knee for an instant touched the ground – "Behold! In token of submission do I bow me to my lord! Behold!" – and she kissed him on the lips – "In token of my wifely love do I kiss my lord. Behold!" – and she laid her hand upon his heart – "By the sin I sinned, by my lonely centuries of waiting wherewith it was wiped out, by the great love wherewith I love, and by the Spirit – the Eternal Thing that doth beget all life, from whom it ebbs, to whom it doth return again – I swear:

"I swear, even in this first most holy hour of completed womanhood, that I will abandon Evil and cherish Good. I sweat that I will be ever guided by thy voice in the straightest path of Duty. I swear that I will eschew Ambition, and through all my length of endless days set Wisdom over me as a guiding star to lead me unto Truth and a knowledge of the Right. I swear also that I will honor and will cherish thee, Kallikrates, who hast been swept by the wave of time back into my arms, ay, till the very end, come it soon or late. I swear – nay, I will swear no more, for what are words? Yet shalt thou learn that Ayesha hath no false tongue.

"So I have sworn, and thou, my Holly, art witness to my oath. Here, too, are we wed, my husband, with the gloom for bridal canopy – wed till the end of all things; here do we write our marriage vows upon the rushing winds which shall bear them up to heaven, and round and continually round this rolling world.

"And for a bridal gift I crown thee with my beauty's starry crown, and enduring life, and wisdom without measure, and wealth that none can count. Behold! The great ones of the earth shall creep about thy feet, and their fair women shall cover up their eyes because of the shining glory of thy countenance, and their wise ones shall be abased before thee. Thou shalt read the hearts of men as an open writing, and hither and thither shalt thou lead them as thy pleasure listeth. Like that old Sphinx of Egypt shalt thou sit aloft from age to age, and ever shall they cry to thee to solve the riddle of thy greatness that doth not pass away, and ever shalt thou mock them with thy silence!

"Behold! Once more I kiss thee, and by that kiss I give to thee dominion over sea and earth, over the peasant in his hovel, over the monarch in his palace halls, and cities crowned with towers, and those who breathe therein. Where'er the sun shakes out his spears, and the lonesome waters mirror up the moon, where'er storms roll, and Heaven's painted bows arch in the sky – from the pure North clad in snows, across the middle spaces of the world, to where the amorous South, lying like a bride upon her blue couch of seas, breathes in sighs made sweet with the odor of myrtles – there shall thy power pass and thy dominion find a home. Nor sickness, nor icy-fingered fear, nor sorrow, and pale waste of form and mind hovering ever o'er humanity, shall so much as shadow thee with the shadow of their wings. As a God shalt thou be, holding good and evil in the hollow of thy hand, and I, even I, I humble myself before thee. Such is the power of Love, and such is the bridal gift I give unto thee, Kallikrates, beloved of Râ, my Lord and Lord of All.

"And now it is done, and come storm, come shine, come good, come evil, come life, come death, it never, never can be undone. For, of a truth, that which is, is, and, being done, is done for aye, and cannot be altered. I have said – Let us hence, that all things may be accomplished in their order." And, taking one of the lamps, she advanced towards the end of the chamber that was roofed in by the swaying stone, where she halted.

We followed her, and perceived that in the wall of the cone there was a stair, or, to be more accurate, that some projecting knobs of rock had been so shaped as to form a good imitation of a stair. Down this Ayesha began to climb, springing from step to step, like a chamois, and after her we followed with less grace. When we had descended some fifteen or sixteen steps we found that they ended in a tremendous rocky slope, running first outwards and then inwards – like the slope of an inverted cone, or tunnel. The slope was very steep, and often precipitous, but it was nowhere impassable, and by the light of the lamps we went down it with no great difficulty, though it was gloomy work enough traveling on thus, no one of us knew whither, into the dead heart of a volcano. As we went, however, I took the precaution of noting our route as well as I could; and this was not difficult, owing to the extraordinary and most fantastic shape of the rocks that were strewn about, many of which in that dim light looked more like the grim faces carven upon medieval gargoyles than ordinary boulders.

For a long period we traveled on thus, half an hour I should say, till, after we had descended for many hundreds of feet, I perceived that we were reaching the point of the inverted cone. In another minute we were there, and found that at the very apex of the funnel was a passage, so low and narrow that we had to stoop as we crept along it in Indian file. After some fifty yards of this creeping, the passage suddenly widened into a cave, so huge that we could see neither the roof nor the sides. We only knew that it was a cave by the echo of our tread and the perfect quiet of the heavy air. On we went for many minutes in absolute awed silence, like lost souls in the depths of Hades, Ayesha's white and ghostlike form flitting in front of us, till once more the cavern ended in a passage which opened into a second cavern much smaller than the first. Indeed, we could, clearly make out the arch and stony banks of this second cave, and, from their rent and jagged appearance, discovered that, like the first long passage down which we had passed through the cliff before we reached the quivering spur, it had to all appearance been torn in the bowels of the rock by the terrific force of some explosive gas. At length this cave ended in a third passage, through which gleamed a faint glow of light.

I heard Ayesha give a sigh of relief as this light dawned upon us.

"It is well," she said; "prepare to enter the very womb of the Earth, wherein she doth conceive the Life that ye see brought forth in man and beast – ay, and in every tree and flower."

Swiftly she sped along, and after her we stumbled as best we might, our hearts filled like a cup with mingled dread and curiosity. What were we about to see? We passed down the tunnel; stronger and stronger the light beamed, reaching us in great flashes like the rays from a lighthouse, as one by one they are thrown wide upon the darkness of the waters. Nor was this all, for with the flashes came a soul-shaking sound like that of thunder and of crashing trees. Now we were through it, and – oh heavens!

We stood in a third cavern, some fifty feet in length by perhaps as great a height, and thirty wide. It was carpeted with fine white sand, and its walls had been worn smooth by the action of I know not what. The cavern was not dark like the others, it was filled with a soft glow of rose-colored light, more beautiful to look on than anything that can be conceived. But at first we saw no flashes, and heard no more of the thunderous sound. Presently, however, as we stood in amaze, gazing at the wonderful sight, and wondering whence the rosy radiance flowed, a dread and beautiful thing happened. Across the far end of the cavern, with a grinding and crashing noise – a noise so dreadful and awe-inspiring that we all trembled, and Job actually sank to his knees – there flamed out an awful cloud or pillar of fire, like a rainbow many-colored, and like the lightning bright. For a space, perhaps forty seconds, it flamed and roared thus, turning slowly round and round, and then by degrees the terrible noise ceased, and with the fire it passed away – I know not where – leaving behind it the same rosy glow that we had first seen.

"Draw near, draw near!" cried Ayesha with a voice of thrilling exultation. "Behold the very Fountain and Heart of Life as it beats in the bosom of the great world. Behold the substance from which all things draw their energy, the bright Spirit of the Globe, without which it cannot live, but must grow cold and dead as the dead moon. Draw near, and wash you in the living flames, and take their virtue into your poor frames in all its virgin strength – not as it now feebly glows within your bosoms, filtered thereto through all the fine strainers of a thousand intermediate lives, but as it is here in the very fount and seat of earthly Being."

We followed her through the rosy glow up to the head of the cave, till at last we stood before the spot where the great pulse beat and the great flame passed. And as we went we became sensible of a wild and splendid exhilaration, of a glorious sense of such a fierce intensity of Life that the most buoyant moments of our strength seemed flat and tame and feeble beside it. It was the mere effluvium of the flame, the subtle ether that it cast off as it passed, working on us, and making us feel strong as giants and swift as eagles.

We reached the head of the cave, and gazed at each other in the glorious glow, and laughed aloud – even Job laughed, and he had not laughed for a week – in the lightness of our hearts and the divine intoxication of our brains. I know that I felt as though all the varied genius of which the human intellect is capable had descended upon me. I could have spoken in blank verse of Shakespearean beauty, all sorts of great ideas flashed through my mind; it was as though the bonds of my flesh had been loosened, and left the spirit free to soar to the empyrean of its native power. The sensations that poured in upon me are indescribable. I seemed to live more keenly, to reach to a higher joy, and sip the goblet of a subtler thought than ever it had been my lot to do before. I was another and most glorified self, and all the avenues of the Possible were for a space laid open to the footsteps of the Real.

Then, suddenly, while I rejoiced in this splendid vigor of a new-found self, from far, far away there came a dreadful muttering noise that grew and grew to a crash and a roar, which combined in itself all that is terrible and yet splendid in the possibilities of sound. Nearer it came, and nearer yet, till it was dose upon us, rolling down like all the thunder wheels of heaven behind the horses of the lightning. On it came, and with it came the glorious blinding cloud of many-colored light, and stood before us for a space, turning, as it seemed to us, slowly round and round, and then, accompanied by its attendant pomp of sound, passed away I know not whither.

So astonishing was the wondrous sight that one and all of us, save *She*, who stood up and stretched her hands towards the fire, sank down before it, and hid our faces in the sand.

When it was gone, Ayesha spoke.

"Now, Kallikrates," she said, "the mighty moment is at hand.

When the great flame comes again thou must stand in it. First throw aside thy garments, for it will burn them, though thee it will not hurt. Thou must stand in the flame while thy senses will endure, and when it embraces thee suck the fire down into thy very heart, and let it leap and play around thy every part, so that thou lose no moiety of its virtue. Hearest thou me, Kallikrates?"

"I hear thee, Ayesha," answered Leo, "but, of a truth – I am no coward – but I doubt me of that raging flame. How know I that it will not utterly destroy me, so that I lose myself and lose thee also? Nevertheless will I do it," he added.

Ayesha thought for a minute, and then said, "It is not wonderful that thou shouldst doubt. Tell me, Kallikrates: if thou seest me stand in the flame and come forth unharmed, wilt thou enter also?"

"Yes," he answered, "I will enter even if it slay me. I have said that I will enter now."

"And that will I also," I cried.

"What, my Holly!" She laughed aloud. "Methought that thou wouldst naught of length of days. Why, how is this?"

"Nay, I know not," I answered, "but there is that in my heart that calleth to me to taste of the name, and live."

"It is well," she said. "Thou art not altogether lost in folly. See now, I will for the second time bathe me in this living bath. Fain would I add to my beauty and my length of days if that be possible. If it be not possible, at the least it cannot harm me.

"Also," she continued, after a momentary pause, "is there another and a deeper cause why I would once again dip me in the flame. When first I tasted of its virtue full was my heart of passion and of hatred of that Egyptian Amenartas, and therefore, despite my strivings to be rid thereof, have passion and hatred been stamped upon my soul from that sad hour to this. But now it is otherwise. Now is my mood a happy mood, and filled am I with the purest part of thought, and so would I ever be. Therefore, Kallikrates, will I once more wash and make me pure and clean, and yet more fit for thee. Therefore also, when thou dost in turn stand in the fire, empty all thy heart of evil, and let sweet contentment hold the balance of thy mind. Shake loose thy spirit's wings, and take thy stand upon the utter verge of holy contemplation; ay, dream upon thy mother's kiss, and turn thee towards the vision of the highest good that hath ever swept on silver wings across the silence of thy dreams. For from the germ of what thou art in that dread moment shall grow the fruit of what thou shalt be for all unreckoned time.

"Now prepare thee, prepare! Even as though thy last hour were at hand, and thou wast about to cross to the land of shadows, and not through the gates of glory into the realms of Life made beautiful. Prepare, I say!"

Chapter 26

What We Saw

THEN CAME a few moments' pause, during which Ayesha seemed to be gathering up her strength for the fiery trial, while we clung to each other, and waited in utter silence.

At last, from far far away, came the first murmur of sound, which grew and grew till it began to crash and bellow in the distance. As she heard it, Ayesha swiftly threw off her gauzy wrapping, loosened the golden snake from her kirtle, and then, shaking her lovely hair about her like a garment, beneath its cover slipped the kirtle off and replaced the snaky belt around her and outside the masses of falling hair. There she stood before us as Eve might have stood before Adam, clad in nothing but her abundant locks, held round her by the golden band; and no words of mine can tell how sweet she looked – and yet how divine. Nearer and nearer came the thunder wheels of fire, and as they came she pushed one ivory arm through the dark masses of her hair and flung it round Leo's neck.

"Oh, my love, my love!" she murmured. "Wilt thou ever know how I have loved thee?" And she kissed him on the forehead, and then went and stood in the pathway of the flame of Life.

There was, I remember, to my mind something very touching about her words and that kiss upon the forehead. It was like a mother's kiss, and seemed to convey a benediction with it.

On came the crashing, rolling noise, and the sound thereof was as the sound of a forest being swept flat by a mighty wind, and then tossed up by it like so much grass, and thundered down a mountainside. Nearer and nearer it came; now flashes of light, forerunners of the revolving pillar of flame, were passing like arrows through the rosy air; and now the edge of the pillar itself appeared. Ayesha turned towards it, and stretched out her arms to greet it. On it came very slowly, and lapped her round with flame. I saw the fire run up her form. I saw her lift it with both hands as though it were water, and pour it over her head. I even saw her open her mouth and draw it down into her lungs, and a dread and wonderful sight it was.

Then she paused, and stretched out her arms, and stood there quite still, with a heavenly smile upon her face, as though she were the very Spirit of the Flame.

The mysterious fire played up and down her dark and rolling locks, twining and twisting itself through and around them like threads of golden lace; it gleamed upon her ivory breast and shoulder, from which the hair had slipped aside; it slid along her pillared throat and delicate features, and seemed to find a home in the glorious eyes that shone and shone, more brightly even than the spiritual essence.

Oh, how beautiful she looked there in the flame! No angel

out of heaven could have worn a greater loveliness. Even now my heart faints before the recollection of it, as she stood and smiled at our awed faces, and I would give half my remaining time upon this earth to see her once like that again.

But suddenly – more suddenly than I can describe – a kind of change came over her face, a change which I could not define or explain on paper, but none the less a change. The smile vanished, and in its place there came a dry, hard look; the rounded face seemed to grow pinched, as though some great anxiety were leaving its impress upon it. The glorious eyes, too, lost their light, and, as I thought, the form its perfect shape and erectness.

I rubbed my eyes, thinking that I was the victim of some hallucination, or that the refraction from the intense light produced an optical delusion; and, as I did so, the flaming pillar slowly twisted and thundered off whithersoever it passes to in the bowels of the great earth, leaving Ayesha standing where it had been.

As soon as it was gone, she stepped forward to Leo's side – it seemed to me that there was no spring in her step – and stretched out her hand to lay it on his shoulder. I gazed at her arm. Where was its wonderful roundness and beauty? It was getting thin and angular. And her face – by heaven! – *her face was growing old before my eyes!* I suppose that Leo saw it also; certainly he recoiled a step or two.

"What is it, my Kallikrates?" she said, and her voice – what was the matter with those deep and thrilling notes? They were quite high and cracked.

"Why, what is it – what is it?" she said confusedly. "I feel dazed Surely the quality of the fire hath not altered. Can the principle of Life alter? Tell me, Kallikrates, is there aught wrong with my eyes? I see not clear," and she put her hand to her head and touched her hair – and oh, *horror of horrors*! – it all fell upon the floor.

"Oh, *look! Look! Look!*" shrieked Job, in a shrill falsetto of terror, his eyes nearly dropping out of his head, and foam upon his lips. *"Look! Look! Look!* She's shriveling up! She's turning into a monkey!" And down he fell upon the ground, foaming and gnashing in a fit.

True enough – I faint even as I write it in the living presence of that terrible recollection – she *was* shriveling up; the golden snake that had encircled her gracious form slipped over her hips and to the ground; smaller and smaller she grew; her skin changed color and in place of the perfect whiteness of its luster it turned dirty brown and yellow, like an old piece of withered parchment. She felt at her head: the delicate hand was nothing but a claw now, a human talon like that of a badly preserved Egyptian mummy, and then she seemed to realize what kind of change was passing over her, and she shrieked – ah, she shrieked! – she rolled upon the floor and shrieked!

Smaller she grew, and smaller yet, till she was no larger than a baboon. Now the skin was puckered into a million wrinkles, and on the shapeless face was the stamp of unutterable age. I never saw anything like it; nobody ever saw anything like the frightful age that was graven on that fearful countenance, no bigger now than that of a two-month-old child, though the skull remained the same size, or nearly so; and let all men pray to God they never may, if they wish to keep their reason.

At last she lay still, or only feebly moving. She, who but two minutes before had gazed upon us the loveliest, noblest, most splendid woman the world has ever seen, she lay still before us, near the masses of her own dark hair, no larger than a big monkey, and hideous – ah, too hideous for words. And yet, think of this – at that very moment I thought of it – it was the *same* woman!

She was dying: we saw it, and thanked God – for while she lived she could feel, and what must she have felt? She raised herself upon her bony hands, and blindly gazed around her, swaying her head slowly from side to side as a tortoise does. She could not see, for her whitish eyes were covered with a horny film. Oh, the horrible pathos of the sight! But she could still speak.

"Kallikrates," she said in husky, trembling notes. "Forget me not, Kallikrates. Have pity on my shame; I shall come again, and shall once more be beautiful, I swear it – it is true! *Oh – h – h –*" And she fell upon her face, and was still.

On the very spot where more than twenty centuries before she had slain Kallikrates the priest, she herself fell down and died.

Overcome with the extremity of horror, we too fell on the sandy floor of that dread place, and swooned away.

I know not how long we remained thus. Many hours, I suppose. When at last *I* opened my eyes, the other two were still outstretched upon the floor. The rosy light yet beamed like a celestial dawn, and the thunder wheels of the Spirit of Life yet rolled upon their accustomed track, for as I awoke the great pillar was passing away. There, too, lay the hideous little monkey frame, covered with crinkled yellow parchment, that once had been the glorious *She*. Alas! it was no hideous dream – it was an awful and unparalleled fact!

What had happened to bring this shocking change about? Had the nature of the life-giving Fire changed? Did it, perhaps, from time to time send forth an essence of Death instead of an essence of Life? Or was it that the frame once charged with its marvelous virtue could bear no more, so that were the process repeated – it mattered not at what lapse of time – the two impregnations neutralized each other, and left the body on which they acted as it was before it ever came into contact with the very essence of life? This, and this alone would account for the sudden and terrible aging of Ayesha, as the whole length of her two thousand years took effect upon her. I have not the slightest doubt myself but that the frame now lying before me was just what the frame of a woman would be if by any extraordinary means life could be preserved in her till she at length died at the age of two-and-twenty centuries.

But who can tell what had happened? There was the fact. Often since that awful hour I have reflected that it requires no great stretch of imagination to see the finger of Providence in the matter. Ayesha locked up in her living tomb waiting from age to age for the coming of her lover worked but a small change in the order of the World. But Ayesha strong and happy in her love, clothed in immortal youth and godlike beauty, and the wisdom of the centuries, would have revolutionized society, and even perchance have changed the destiny of Mankind. Thus she opposed herself against the eternal Law, and, strong though she was, by it was swept back to nothingness – swept back with shame and hideous mockery!

For some minutes I lay faintly turning these terrors over in my mind, while my physical strength came back to me, which it quickly did in that buoyant atmosphere. Then I bethought me of the others, and staggered to my feet, to see if I could arouse them. But first I took up Ayesha's kirtle and the gauzy scarf with which she had been wont to hide her dazzling loveliness from the eyes of men, and, averting my head so that I might not look upon it, covered up that dreadful relic of the glorious dead, that shocking epitome of human beauty and human life. I did this hurriedly, fearing lest Leo should recover, and see it again.

Then, stepping over the perfumed masses of dark hair that lay upon the sand, I stooped down by Job, who was lying upon his face, and turned him over. As I did so his arm fell back in a way that I did not like, and which sent a chill through me, and I glanced sharply at him. One look was enough. Our old and faithful servant was dead. His nerves, already shattered by all he had seen and undergone, had utterly broken down beneath this last dire sight, and he had died of terror, or in a fit brought on by terror. One had only to look at his face to see it.

It was another blow; but perhaps it may help people to understand how overwhelmingly awful was the experience through which we had passed – we did not feel it much at the time. It seemed quite natural that the poor old fellow should be dead. When Leo came to himself, which he did with a groan and trembling of the limbs about ten minutes afterwards, and I told him that Job was dead, he merely said, "Oh!" And, mind you, this was from no heartlessness, for he and Job were much attached to each other; and he often talks of him now with the deepest regret and affection. It was only that his nerves would bear no more. A harp can give out but a certain quantity of sound, however heavily it is smitten.

Well, I set myself to recovering Leo; who, to my infinite relief, I found was not dead, but only fainting, and in the end I succeeded, as I have said, and he sat up; and then I saw another dreadful thing. When we entered that awful place his curling hair had been of the ruddiest gold; now it was turning gray, and by the time we gained the outer air it was snow-white. Besides, he looked twenty years older.

"What is to be done, old fellow?" he said in a hollow, dead sort of voice, when his mind had cleared a little, and a recollection of what had happened forced itself upon it.

"Try and get out, I suppose," I answered; "that is, unless you would like to go in there," and I pointed to the column of fire that was once more rolling by.

"I would go in if I were sure that it would kill me," he said with a little laugh. "It was my cursed hesitation that did this. If I had not been doubtful she might never have tried to show me the road. But I am not sure. The fire might have the opposite effect upon me. It might make me immortal; and, old fellow, I have not the patience to wait a couple of thousand years for her to come back again as she did for me. I had rather die when my hour comes – and I should fancy that it isn't far off either – and go my ways to look for her. Do you go in if you like."

But I merely shook my head, my excitement was as dead as ditchwater, and my distaste for the prolongation of my mortal span had come back upon me more strongly than ever. Besides, we neither of us knew what the effects of the fire might be. The result upon *She* had not been of an encouraging nature, and of the exact causes that produced that result we were, of course, ignorant.

"Well, my boy," I said, "we cannot stop here till we go the way of those two," and I pointed to the little heap under the white garment and to the stiffening corpse of poor Job. "If we are going we had better go. But, by the way, I expect that the lamps have burned out," and I took one up and looked at it, and sure enough it had.

"There is some more oil in the vase," said Leo indifferently, "if it is not broken, at least."

I examined the vessel in question – it was intact. With a trembling hand I filled the lamps – luckily there was still some of the linen wick unburned. Then I lit them with one of our wax matches. While I did so we heard the pillar of fire approaching once more as it went on its never ending journey, if, indeed, it was the same pillar that passed and repassed in a circle.

"Let's see it come once more," said Leo; "we shall never look upon its like again in this world."

It seemed a bit of idle curiosity, but somehow I shared it, and so we waited till, turning slowly round upon its own axis, it had flamed and thundered by; and I remember wondering for how many thousands of years this same phenomenon had been taking place in the bowels of the earth, and for how many more thousands it would continue to take place. I wondered also if any mortal eyes would ever again mark its passage, or any mortal ears be thrilled and fascinated by the swelling volume of its majestic sound. I do not think that they will. I believe that we are the last human beings who will ever see that unearthly sight. Presently it had gone, and we too turned to go.

But before we did so we each took Job's cold hand in ours and shook it. It was a rather ghastly ceremony, but it was the only means in our power of showing our respect to the faithful dead and of celebrating his obsequies. The heap beneath the white garment we did not uncover. We had no wish to look upon that terrible sight again. But we went to the pile of rippling hair that had fallen from her in the agony of that hideous change which was worse than a thousand natural deaths, and each of us drew from it a shining lock, and these locks we still have, the sole memento that is left to us of Ayesha as we knew her in the fullness of her grace and glory. Leo pressed the perfumed hair to his lips.

"She called to me not to forget her," he said hoarsely, "and swore that we should meet again. By heaven! I never will forget her. Here I swear that, if we live to get out of this, I will not for all my days have anything to say to another living woman, and that wherever I go I will wait for her as faithfully as she waited for me."

"Yes" I thought to myself, "if she comes back as beautiful as we knew her. But supposing she came back like that!"[1]

Well, and then we went. We went, and left those two in the presence of the very well and spring of Life, but gathered to the cold company of Death. How lonely they looked as they lay there, and how ill assorted! That little heap had been for two thousand years the wisest, loveliest, proudest creature – I can hardly call her woman – in the whole universe. She had been wicked, too, in her way; but, alas, such is the frailty of the human heart, her wickedness had not detracted from her charm. Indeed, I am by no means certain that it did not add to it. It was after all of a grand order, there was nothing mean or small about Ayesha.

And poor Job, too! His presentiment had come true, and there was an end of him. Well, he has a strange burial place – no Norfolk hind ever had a stranger, or ever will; and it is something to lie in the same sepulcher with the poor remains of the imperial *She*.

We looked our last upon them and the indescribable rosy glow in which they lay, and then with hearts far too heavy for

1 What a terrifying reflection it is, by the way, that nearly all our deep love for women who are not our kindred depends – at any rate, in the first instance – upon their personal appearance. If we lost them, and found them again dreadful to look on, though otherwise they were the very same, should we still love them? – L. H. H.

words we left them, and crept thence broken down men – so broken down that we even renounced the chance of practically immortal life, because all that made life valuable had gone from us, and we knew even then that to prolong our days indefinitely would only be to prolong our sufferings. For we felt – yes, both of us – that having once looked Ayesha in the eyes, we could not forget her forever and ever while memory and identity remained. We both loved her now and for always, she was stamped and carven on our hearts, and no other woman or interest could ever raze that splendid die. And I – there lies the sting – I had and have no right to think thus of her. As she told me, I was naught to her, and never shall be through the un-fathomed depth of Time, unless, indeed, conditions alter, and a day comes at last when two men may love one woman, and all three be happy in the fact. It is the only hope of my broken-heartedness, and a rather faint one. Beyond it I have nothing. I have paid down this heavy price, all that I am worth here and hereafter, and that is my sols reward. With Leo it is different, and often and often I bitterly envy him his happy lot, for if *She* was right, and her wisdom and knowledge did not fail her at the last, which, arguing from the precedent of her own case, I think most unlikely, he has some future to look forward to. But I have none, and yet – mark the folly and the weakness of the human heart, and let him who is wise learn wisdom from it – yet I would not have it otherwise. I mean that I am content to give what I have given and must always give, and take in payment those crumbs that fall from my mistress's table, the memory of a few kind words, the hope one day in the far undreamed future of a sweet smile or two of recognition, a little gentle friendship, and a little show of thanks for my devotion to her – and Leo.

If that does not constitute true love, I do not know what does, and all I have to say is that it is a very bad state of mind for a man on the wrong side of middle age to fall into.

Chapter 27

We Leap

WE PASSED through the caves without trouble, but when we came to the slope of the inverted cone two difficulties stared us in the face. The first of these was the laborious nature of the ascent, and the next the extreme difficulty of finding our way. Indeed, had it not been for the mental notes that I had fortunately taken of the shape of various rocks, etc., I am sure that we never should have managed it at all, but have wandered about in the dreadful womb of the volcano – for I suppose it must once have been something of the sort – until we died of exhaustion and despair. As it was we went wrong several times, and once nearly fell into a huge crack or crevasse. It was terrible work creeping about in the dense gloom and awful stillness from boulder to boulder, and examining it by the feeble light of the lamps to see if I could recognize its shape. We rarely spoke – our hearts were too heavy for speech – we simply stumbled about, falling sometimes and cutting ourselves, in a rather dogged sort of way. The fact was that our spirits were utterly crushed, and we did not greatly care what happened to us. Only we felt bound to try and save our lives while we could, and indeed a natural instinct prompted us to it. So for some three or four hours, I should think – I cannot tell exactly how long, for we had no watch left that would go – we blundered on. During the last two hours we were completely lost, and I began to fear that we had got into the funnel of some subsidiary cone, when at last I suddenly recognized a very large rock which we had passed in descending but a little way from the top. It is a marvel that I should have recognized it, and, indeed, we had already passed it going at right angles to the proper path, when something about it struck me, and I turned back and examined it in an idle sort of way, and, as it happened, this proved our salvation.

After this we gained the rocky natural stair without much further trouble, and in due course found ourselves back in the little chamber where the benighted Noot had lived and died.

But now a fresh terror stared us in the face. It will be remembered that owing to Job's fear and awkwardness, the plank upon which we had crossed from the huge spur to the rocking stone had been whirled off into the tremendous gulf below.

How were we to cross without the plank?

There was only one answer – we must try and *jump* it, or else stop there till we starved. The distance in itself was not so very great, between eleven and twelve feet I should think, and I have seen Leo jump over twenty when he was a young fellow at college; but then, think of the conditions. Two weary, worn-out men, one of them on the wrong side of forty, a rocking stone to take off from, a trembling point of rock some few feet across to land upon, and a bottomless gulf to be cleared in a raging gale! It was bad enough. God knows, but when I pointed out these things to Leo, he put the whole matter in a nutshell by replying that, merciless as the choice was, we must choose between the certainty of a lingering death in the chamber and the risk of a swift one in the air. Of course, there was no arguing against this, but one thing was clear, we could attempt that leap in the dark; the only thing to do was to wait for the ray of light which pierced through the gulf at sunset. How near to or how far from sunset we might be, neither of us had the faintest notion; all we did know was that when at last the light came it would not endure more than a couple of minutes at the outside, so that we must be prepared to meet it. Accordingly, we made up our minds to creep onto the top of the rocking stone and lie there in readiness. We were the more easily reconciled to this course by the fact that our lamps were once more nearly exhausted – indeed, one had gone out bodily, and the other was jumping up and down as the flame of a lamp does when the oil is done. So, by the aid of its dying light, we hastened to crawl out of the little chamber and clamber up the side of the great stone.

As we did so the light went out.

The difference in our position was a sufficiently remarkable one. Below, in the little chamber, we had only heard the roaring of the gale overhead – here, lying on our faces on the swinging stone, we were exposed to its full force and fury, as the great draft drew first from this direction and then from that, howling against the mighty precipice and through the rocky cliffs like ten thousand despairing souls. We lay there hour after hour in terror and misery of mind so deep that I will not attempt to describe it, and listened to the wild storm voices of that Tartarus, as, set to the deep undertone of the spur opposite against which the wind hummed like some awful harp, they called to each other from precipice to precipice. No nightmare dreamed by man, no wild invention of the romancer, can ever equal the living horror of that place, and the weird crying of those voices of the night, as we clung like shipwrecked mariners to a raft, and tossed on the black, unfathomed wilderness of air. Fortunately the temperature was not a low one – indeed, the wind was warm – or we should have perished. So we clung and listened, and while we were stretched out upon the rock a thing happened which was so curious and suggestive in itself, though doubtless a mere coincidence, that, if anything, it added to, rather than deducted from, the burden on our nerves.

It will be remembered that when Ayesha was standing on the spur, before we crossed to the stone, the wind tore her cloak from her, and whirled it away into the darkness of the gulf, we could not see whither. Well – I hardly like to tell the story; it is so strange. As we lay there upon the rocking stone, this very cloak came floating out of the black space, like a memory from the dead, and fell on Leo – so that it covered him nearly from head to foot. We could not at first make out what it was, but soon discovered by its feel, and then poor Leo, for the first time, gave way, and I heard him sobbing there upon the stone. No doubt the cloak had been caught upon some pinnacle of the cliff, and was thence blown hither by a chance gust; but still, it was a most curious and touching incident.

Shortly after this, suddenly, without the slightest previous warning, the great red knife of light came stabbing the darkness through and through – struck the swaying stone on which we were, and rested its sharp point upon the spur opposite.

"Now for it," said Leo, "now or never."

We rose and stretched ourselves, and looked at the cloud wreaths stained the color of blood by that red ray as they tore through the sickening depths beneath, and then at the empty space between the swaying stone and the quivering rock, and, in our hearts, despaired, and prepared for death. Surely we could not clear it – desperate though we were.

"Who is to go first?" said I.

"Do you, old fellow," answered Leo. "I will sit upon the other side of the stone to steady it. You must take as much run as you can, and jump high; and God have mercy on us, say I."

I acquiesced with a nod, and then I did a thing I had never done since Leo was a little boy. I turned and put my arm round him, and kissed him on the forehead. It sounds rather French, but as a fact I was taking my last farewell of a man whom I could not have loved more if he had been my own son twice over.

"Good-by, my boy," I said, "I hope that we shall meet again, wherever it is that we go to."

The fact was I did not expect to live another two minutes.

Next I retreated to the far side of the rock, and waited till one of the chopping gusts of wind got behind me, and then, commending my soul to God, I ran the length of the huge stone, some three- or four-and-thirty feet, and sprang wildly out into the dizzy air. Oh, the sickening terrors that I felt as I launched myself at that little point of rock, and the horrible sense of despair that shot through my brain as I realized that I had *jumped short*! But so it was, my feet never touched the point, they went down into space, only my hands and body came in contact with it. I gripped at it with a yell, but one hand slipped, and I swung right round, holding by the other, so that I faced the stone from which I had sprung. Wildly I stretched up with my left hand, and this time managed to grasp a knob of rock, and there I hung in the fierce red light, with thousands of feet of empty air beneath me. My hands were holding to either side of the under part of the spur, so that its point was touching my head. Therefore, even if I could have found the strength, I could not pull myself up. The most that I could do would be to hang for about a minute, and then drop down, down into the bottomless pit. If any man can imagine a more hideous position, let him speak! All I know is that the torture of that half minute nearly turned my brain.

I heard Leo give a cry, and then suddenly saw him in midair springing up and out like a chamois. It was a splendid leap that he took under the influence of his terror and despair, clearing the horrible gulf as though it were nothing, and, landing well onto the rocky point, he threw himself upon his face, to prevent his pitching off into the depths. I felt the spur above me shake beneath the shock of his impact, and as it did so I saw the huge rocking stone, which had been violently depressed by him as he sprang, fly back when relieved of his weight till, for the first time during all these centuries, it got beyond its balance, and fell with a most awful crash right into the rocky chamber which had once served the philosopher Noot for a hermitage, as I have no doubt, forever hermetically sealing the passage that leads to the place of Life with some hundreds of tons of rock.

All this happened in a second, and curiously enough, notwithstanding my terrible position, I noted it involuntarily, as it were. I even remember thinking that no human being would go down that dread path again.

Next instant I felt Leo seize me by the right wrist with both hands. By lying flat on the point of rock he could just reach me.

"You must let go and swing yourself clear," he said in a

calm and collected voice, "and then I will try and pull you up, or we will both go together. Are you ready?"

By way of answer I let go, first with my left land and then with the right, and swayed out as a consequence clear of the overshadowing rock, my weight hanging upon Leo's arms. It was a dreadful moment. He was a very powerful man, I knew, but would his strength be equal to lifting me up till I could get a hold on the top of the spur, when owing to his position he had so little purchase?

For a few seconds I swung to and fro, while he gathered himself for the effort, and then I heard his sinews cracking above me, and felt myself lifted up as though I were a little child, till I got my left arm round the rock, and my chest was resting on it. The rest was easy; in two or three more seconds I was up, and we were lying panting side by side, trembling like leaves, and with the cold perspiration of terror pouring from our skins.

And then, as before, the light went out like a lamp.

For perhaps a half hour we lay thus without speaking a word, and then at length began to creep along the great spur as best we might in the dense gloom. As we drew towards the face of the cliff, however, from which the spur sprang out like a spike from a wall, the light increased, though only a very little, for it was night overhead. After that the gusts of wind decreased, and we got along rather better, and at last reached the mouth of the first cave or tunnel. But now a fresh trouble stared us in the face: our oil was gone, and the lamps were, no doubt, crushed to powder beneath the fallen rocking stone. We were even without a drop of water to stay our thirst, for we had drunk the last in the chamber of Noot. How were we to see to make our way through this last boulder-strewn tunnel? Clearly all that we could do was to trust to our sense of feeling, and attempt the passage in the dark, so in we crept, fearing that if we delayed to do so our exhaustion would overcome us, and we should probably lie down and die where we were.

Oh, the horrors of that last tunnel! The place was strewn with rocks, and we fell over them, and knocked ourselves up against them till we were bleeding from a score of wounds. Our only guide was the side of the cavern, which we kept touching, and so bewildered did we grow in the darkness that we were several times seized with the terrifying thought that we had turned, and were traveling the wrong way. On we went, feebly, and still more feebly, for hour after hour, stopping every few minutes to rest, for our strength was spent. Once we fell asleep, and, I think, must have slept for some hours, for, when we woke, our limbs were quite stiff, and the blood from our blows and scratches had caked, and was hard and dry upon our skin. Then we dragged ourselves on again, till at last, when despair was entering into our hearts, we once more saw the light of day, and found ourselves outside the tunnel in the rocky fold on the outer surface of the cliff that, it will be remembered, led into it.

It was early morning – that we could tell by the feel of the sweet air and the look of the blessed sky, which we had never hoped to see again. It was, so near as we knew, an hour after sunset when we entered the tunnel, so it followed that it had taken us the entire night to crawl through that dreadful place.

"One more effort, Leo," I gasped, "and we shall reach the slope where Billali is, if he hasn't gone. Come, don't give way," for he had cast himself upon his face. He got up, and, leaning on each other, we got down that fifty feet or so of cliff – somehow, I have not the least notion how.

I only remember that we found ourselves lying in a heap at the bottom, and then once more began to drag ourselves along on our hands and knees towards the grove where *She* had told Billali to wait her rearrival, for we could not walk another foot. We had not gone fifty yards in this fashion when suddenly one of the mutes emerged from some trees on our left, through which, I presume, he had been taking a morning stroll, and came running up to see what sort of strange animals we were. He stared, and stared, and then held up his hands in horror, and nearly fell to the ground. Next, he started off as hard as he could for the grove some two hundred yards away. No wonder that he was horrified at our appearance, for we must have been a shocking sight. To begin, Leo, with his golden curls turned a snowy white, his clothes nearly rent from his body, his worn face and his hands a mass of bruises, cuts, and blood-encrusted filth, was a sufficiently alarming spectacle, as he painfully dragged himself along the ground, and I have no doubt that I was little better to look on. I know that two days afterwards when I looked at my face in some water I scarcely recognized myself. I have never been famous for beauty, but there was something beside ugliness stamped upon my features that I have never got rid of until this day, something resembling that wild look with which a startled person wakes from deep sleep more than anything else that I can think of. And really it is not to be wondered at. What I do wonder at is that we escaped at all with our reason.

Presently, to my intense relief, I saw old Billali hurrying towards us, and even then I could scarcely help smiling at the expression of consternation on his dignified countenance.

"Oh, my Baboon, my Baboon!" he cried. "My dear son, is it indeed thee and the Lion? Why, his mane that was ripe as corn is white like the snow. Whence come ye? And where is the Pig, and where too *'She-who-must-be-obeyed'!*"

"Dead, both dead," I answered; "but ask no questions; help us, and give us food and water, or we too shall die before thine eyes. Seest thou not that our tongues are black for want of water? How can we talk, then?"

"Dead!" he gasped. "Impossible. *She* who never dies – dead, how can it be?" and then, perceiving, I think, that his face was being watched by the mutes who had come running up, he checked himself, and motioned to them to carry us to the camp, which they did.

Fortunately when we arrived some broth was boiling on the fire, and with this Billali fed us, for we were too weak to feed ourselves, thereby I firmly believe saving us from death by exhaustion. Then he bade the mutes wash the blood and grime from us with wet cloths, and after that we were laid down upon piles of aromatic grass, and instantly fell into the dead sleep of absolute exhaustion of mind and body.

Chapter 28

Over the Mountain

THE NEXT THING I recollect is a feeling of the most dreadful stiffness, and a sort of vague idea passing through my half-awakened brain that I was a carpet that had just been beaten. I opened my eyes, and the first thing they fell on was the venerable countenance of our old friend Billali, who was seated by the side of the improvised bed upon which I was sleeping, and thoughtfully stroking his long beard. The sight of him at once brought back to my mind a recollection of all that we had recently passed through, which was accentuated by the vision of poor Leo lying opposite to me, his face knocked almost to a jelly, and his beautiful crowd of curls turned from yellow to white,[1] and I shut my eyes again and groaned.

"Thou hast slept long, my Baboon," said old Billali.

"How long, my father?" I asked.

"A round of the sun and a round of the moon, a day and a night hast thou slept, and the Lion also. See, he sleepeth yet."

1 Curiously enough, Leo's hair has lately been to some extent regaining its color – that is to say, it is now a yellowish gray – and I am not without hopes that it will in time come quite right. – L. H. H.

"Blessed is sleep," I answered, "for it swallows up recollection."

"Tell me," he said, "what hath befallen ye, and what is this strange story of the death of *She* who, dieth not. Bethink thee, my son: if this be true, then is thy danger and the danger of the Lion very great – nay, almost is the pot red wherewith ye shall be potted, and the stomachs of those who shall eat ye are already hungry for the feast. Knowest thou not that these Amahagger, my children, these dwellers in the caves, hate ye? They hate ye as strangers, they hate ye more because of their brethren whom *She* put to the torment for your sake. Assuredly, if once they learn that there is naught to fear from Hiya, from the terrible One-who-must-be-obeyed, they will slay ye by the pot. But let me hear thy tale, my poor Baboon."

Thus adjured, I set to work and told him – not everything, indeed, for I did not think it desirable to do so, but sufficient for my purpose, which was to make him understand that *She* was really no more, having fallen into some fire, and, as I put it – for the real thing would have been incomprehensible to him – been burned up. I also told him some of the horrors we had undergone in effecting our escape, and these produced a great impression on him. But I clearly saw that he did not believe in the report of Ayesha's death. He believed indeed that we thought that she was dead, but his explanation was that it had suited her to disappear for a while. Once, he said, in his father's time, she had done so for twelve years, and there was a tradition in the country that many centuries back no one had seen her for a whole generation, when she suddenly reappeared, and destroyed a woman who had assumed the position of queen. I said nothing to this, but only shook my head sadly. Alas! I knew too well that Ayesha would appear no more, or at any rate that Billali would never see her again.

"And now," concluded Billali, "what wouldst thou do, my Baboon?"

"Nay," I said, "I know not, my rather. Can we not escape from this country?"

He shook his head.

"It is very difficult. By Kôr ye cannot pass, for ye would be seen, and as soon as those fierce ones found that ye were alone, well" – and he smiled significantly, and made a movement as though he were placing a hat on his head – "but there is a way over the cliff whereof I once spake to thee, where they drive the cattle out to pasture. Then beyond the pastures are three days' journey through the marshes, and after that I know not, but I have heard that seven days' journey from thence is a mighty river, which floweth to the black water. If ye could come thither, perchance ye might escape, but how can ye come thither?"

"Billali," I said, "once, thou knowest, I did save thy life. Now pay back the debt, my father, and save me mine and my friend's, the Lion's. It shall be a pleasant thing for thee to think of when thine hour comes, and something to set-in the scale against the evildoing of thy days, if perchance thou hast done any evil. Also, if thou be right, and if *She* doth but hide herself, surely when she comes again she shall reward thee."

"My son the Baboon," answered the old man, "think not that I have an ungrateful heart. Well do I remember how thou didst rescue me when those dogs stood by to see me drown. Measure for measure will I give thee, and if thou canst be saved, surely I will save thee. Listen: by dawn tomorrow be prepared, for litters shall be here to bear ye away across the mountains, and through the marshes beyond. This will I do, saying that it is the word of *She* that it be done, and he who obeyeth not the word of *She* food is he for the hyenas. Then when ye have crossed the marshes, ye must strike with your own hands, so that perchance, if good fortune go with you, ye may live to come to that black water whereof ye told me. And now, see, the Lion wakes, and ye must eat the food I have made ready for you."

Leo's condition when once he was fairly aroused proved not to be so bad as might have been expected from his appearance, and we both of us managed to eat a hearty meal, which indeed we needed sadly enough. After this we limped down to the spring and bathed, and then came back and slept again till evening, when we once more ate enough for five. Billali was all that day, no doubt making arrangements about litters and bearers, for we were awakened in the middle of the night by the arrival of a considerable number of men in the little camp.

At dawn the old man himself appeared, and told us that he had by using *She*'s dreaded name, though with some difficulty, succeeded in getting the necessary men and two guides to conduct us across the swamps, and that he urged us to start at once, at the same time announcing his intention of accompanying us so as to protect us against treachery. I was much touched by this act of kindness on the part of that wily old barbarian towards two utterly defenseless strangers. A three – or in his case, for he would have to return, six – days' journey through those deadly swamps was no light undertaking for a man of his age, but he consented to do it cheerfully in order to promote our safety. It shows that even among those dreadful Amahagger – who are certainly with their gloom and their devilish and ferocious rites by far the most terrible savages that I ever heard of – there are people with kindly hearts. Of course self-interest may have had something to do with it. He may have thought that *She* would suddenly reappear and demand an account of us at his hands, but still, allowing for all deductions, it was a great deal more than we could expect under the circumstances, and I can only say that I shall for as long as I live cherish a most affectionate remembrance of my nominal parent, old Billali.

Accordingly, after swallowing some food, we started in the litters, feeling, so far as our bodies went, wonderfully like our old selves after our long rest and sleep. I must leave the condition of our minds to the imagination.

Then came a terrible pull up the cliff. Sometimes the ascent was natural, more often it was a zigzag roadway cut, no doubt, in the first instance by the old inhabitants of Kôr. The Amahagger say they drive their spare cattle over it once a year to pasture outside; all I know is that those cattle must be uncommonly active on their feet. Of course the litters were useless here, so we had to walk.

By midday, however, we reached the great flat top of that mighty wall of rock, and grand enough the view was from it, with the plain of Kôr, in the center of which we could clearly make out the pillared ruins of the Temple of Truth to the one side, and the boundless and melancholy marsh on the other. The wall of rock, which had no doubt once formed the lip of the crater, was about a mile and a half thick, and still covered with clinker. Nothing grew there, and the only thing to relieve our eyes were occasional pools of rainwater (for rain had lately fallen) wherever there was a little hollow. Over the flat crest of this mighty rampart we went, and then came the descent, which, if not so difficult a matter as the getting up, was still sufficiently breakneck, and took us till sunset. That night, however, we camped in safety upon the mighty slopes that rolled away to the marsh beneath.

On the following morning, about eleven o'clock, began our dreary journey across those awful seas of swamps which I have already described.

For three whole days, through stench and mire, and the all-prevailing flavor of fever, did our bearers struggle along, till at length we came to open rolling ground quite uncultivated, and mostly treeless, but covered with game of all sorts, which lies beyond that most desolate, and without guides utterly impracticable, district. And here on the following morning we bade farewell, not without some regret, to old Billali, who stroked his white beard and solemnly blessed us.

"Farewell, my son the Baboon," he said, "and farewell to thee too, O Lion. I can do no more to help you. But if ever ye come to your country, be advised, and venture no more into lands that ye know not, lest ye come back no more, but leave your white bones to mark the limit of your journeyings. Farewell once more; often shall I think of you, nor wilt thou forget me, my Baboon, for though thy face is ugly thy heart is true." And then he turned and went, and with him went the tall and sullen-looking bearers, and that was the last that we saw of the Amahagger. We watched them winding away with the empty litters like a procession bearing dead men from a battle, till the mists from the marsh gathered round them and hid them, and then, left utterly desolate in the vast wilderness, we turned and gazed around us and at each other.

Three weeks or so before four men had entered the marshes of Kôr, and now two of us were dead, and the other two had gone through adventures and experiences so strange and terrible that death himself hath not a more fearful countenance. Three weeks – and only three weeks! Truly time should be measured by events, and not by the lapse of hours. It seemed like thirty years since we saw the last of our whaleboat.

"We must strike out for the Zambesi, Leo," I said, "but God knows if we shall ever get there."

Leo nodded – he had become very silent of late – and we started with nothing but the clothes we stood in, a compass, our revolvers and express rifles, and about two hundred rounds of ammunition, and so ended the history of our visit to the ancient ruins of mighty and imperial Kôr.

As for the adventures that subsequently befell us, strange and varied as they were, I have, after deliberation, determined not to record them here. In these pages I have only tried to give a short and clear account of an occurrence which I believe to be unprecedented, and this I have done, not with a view to immediate publication, but merely to put on paper while they are yet fresh in our memories the details of our journey and its result, which will, I believe, prove interesting to the world if ever we determine to make them public. This, as at present advised, we do not intend should be done during our joint lives.

For the rest, it is of no public interest, resembling as it does the experience of more than one Central African traveler. Suffice it to say that we did, after incredible hardships and privations, reach the Zambesi, which proved to be about a hundred and seventy miles south of where Billali left us. There we were for six months imprisoned by a savage tribe, who believed us to be supernatural beings, chiefly on account of Leo's youthful face and snow-white hair. From these people we ultimately escaped, and, crossing the Zambesi, wandered off southwards, where, when on the point of starvation, we were sufficiently fortunate to fall in with a half-caste Portuguese elephant hunter who had followed a troop of elephants farther inland than he had ever been before. This man treated us most hospitably, and ultimately through his assistance we, after innumerable sufferings and adventures, reached Delagoa Bay, more than eighteen months from the time when we emerged from the marshes of Kôr, and the very next day managed to catch one of the steamboats that run round the Cape to England. Our journey home was a prosperous one, and we set our foot on the quay at Southampton exactly two years from the date of our departure upon our wild and seemingly ridiculous quest, and I now write these last words with Leo leaning over my shoulder in my old room in my college, the very same into which some two-and-twenty years ago my poor friend Vincey came stumbling on the memorable night of his death, bearing the iron chest with him.

And that is the end of this history so far as it concerns science and the outside world. What its end will be as regards Leo and myself is more than I can guess at. But we feel that is not reached yet. A story that began more than two thousand years ago may stretch a long way into the dim and distant future.

Is Leo really a reincarnation of the ancient Kallikrates of whom the inscription tells? Or was Ayesha deceived by some strange hereditary resemblance? The reader must form his own opinion on this as on many other matters. I have mine, which is that she made no such mistake.

Often I sit alone at night, staring with the eyes of the mind into the blackness of unborn time, and wondering in what shape and form the great drama will be finally developed, and where the scene of its next act will be laid. And when that *final* development ultimately occurs, as I have no doubt it must and will occur, in obedience to a fate that never swerves and a purpose that cannot be altered, what will be the part played therein by that beautiful Egyptian Amenartas, the princess of the royal race of the Pharaohs, for the love of whom the priest Kallikrates broke his vows to Isis, and, pursued by the inexorable vengeance of the outraged goddess, fled down the coast of Libya to meet his doom at Kôr?

THE END

AYESHA THE RETURN OF SHE

INTRODUCTION

VERILY AND indeed it is the unexpected that happens! Probably if there was one person upon the earth from whom the Editor of this, and of a certain previous history, did not expect to hear again, that person was Ludwig Horace Holly. This, too, for a good reason; he believed him to have taken his departure from the earth.

When Mr. Holly last wrote, many, many years ago, it was to transmit the manuscript of *She,* and to announce that he and his ward, Leo Vincey, the beloved of the divine Ayesha, were about to travel to Central Asia in the hope, I suppose, that there she would fulfil her promise and appear to them again.

Often I have wondered, idly enough, what happened to them there; whether they were dead, or perhaps droning their lives away as monks in some Thibetan Lamasery, or studying magic and practising asceticism under the tuition of the Eastern Masters, trusting that thus they would build a bridge by which they might pass to the side of their adored Immortal.

Now at length, when I had not thought of them for months, without a single warning sign, out of the blue as it were, comes the answer to these wonderings!

To think – only to think – that I, the Editor aforesaid, from its appearance suspecting something quite familiar and without interest, pushed aside that dingy, unregistered, brown-paper parcel directed in an unknown hand, and for two whole days let it lie forgotten. Indeed there it might be lying now, had not another person been moved to curiosity, and opening it, found within a bundle of manuscript badly burned upon the back, and with this two letters addressed to myself.

Although so great a time had passed since I saw it, and it was shaky now because of the author's age or sickness, I knew the writing at once – nobody ever made an "H" with that peculiar twirl under it except Mr. Holly. I tore open the sealed envelope, and sure enough the first thing my eye fell upon was the signature, *L. H. Holly.* It is long since I read anything so eagerly as I did that letter. Here it is: –

MY DEAR SIR, – I have ascertained that you still live, and strange to say I still live also – for a little while.

He saw me looking at the last sheets, which had been burned away, and said (I repeat his exact words) –

Yes, yes, that can't be helped now, it must go as it is. You see I made up my mind to destroy it after all, and it was already on the fire when the command came – the clear, unmistakable command – and I snatched it off again.'

What Mr. Holly meant by this 'command' I do not know, for he would speak no more of the matter.

I pass on to the last-scene. One night about eleven o'clock, knowing that my patient's end was near, I went up to see him, proposing to inject some strychnine to keep the heart going a little longer. Before I reached the house I met the caretaker coming to seek me in a great fright, and asked her if her master was dead. She answered 'No; but he was *gone* – had got out of bed and, just as he was, barefooted, left the house, and was last seen by her grandson among the very Scotch firs where we were talking. The lad, who was *terrified* out of his wits, for he thought that he beheld a ghost, had told her so.

The moonlight was very brilliant that night, especially as fresh snow had fallen, which reflected its rays. I was on foot, and began to search among the firs, till presently just outside of them I found the track of naked feet in the snow. Of course I followed, calling to the housekeeper to go and wake her husband, for no one else lives near by. The spoor proved very easy to trace across the clean sheet of snow. It ran up the slope of a hill behind the house.

Now, on the crest of this hill is an ancient monument of upright monoliths set there by some primeval people, known locally as the Devil's Ring – a sort of miniature Stonehenge in fact. I had seen it several times, and happened to have been present not long ago at a meeting of an archaeological society when its origin and purpose were discussed. I remember that one learned but somewhat eccentric gentleman read a short paper upon a rude, hooded bust and head that are cut within the chamber of a tall, flat-topped cromlech, or dolmen, which stands alone in the centre of the ring.

He said that it was a representation of the Egyptian goddess, Isis, and that this place had once been sacred to some form of her worship, or at any rate to that of a Nature goddess with like attributes, family for generations. The housekeeper who summoned me told me that her master had but just returned from abroad, somewhere in Asia, she said, and that he was very ill with his heart – dying, she believed; both of which suppositions proved to be accurate.

I found the patient sitting up in bed (to ease his heart), and a strange-looking old man he was. He had dark eyes, small but full of fire and intelligence, a magnificent and snowy-white beard that covered a chest of extraordinary breadth, and hair also white, which encroached upon his forehead and face so much that it met the whiskers upon his cheeks. His arms were remarkable for their length and strength, though one of them seemed to have been much torn by some animal. He told me that a dog had done this, but if so it must have been a dog of unusual power. He was a very ugly man, and yet, forgive the bull, beautiful. I cannot describe what I mean better than by saying that his face was not like the face of any ordinary mortal whom I have met in my limited experience. Were I art artist who wished to portray a wise and benevolent but rather grotesque spirit, I should take that countenance as a model.

Mr. Holly was somewhat vexed at my being called in, which had been done without his knowledge. Soon we became friendly enough, however, and he expressed gratitude for the relief that I was able to give him, though I could not hope to do more. At different times he talked a good deal of the various countries in which he had travelled, apparently for very many years, upon some strange quest that he never clearly defined to me. Twice also he became light-headed, and spoke, for the most part in languages that I identified as Greek and Arabic; occasionally in English also, when he appeared to be addressing himself to a being who was the object of his veneration, I might almost say of his worship. What he said then, however, I prefer not to repeat, for I heard it in my professional capacity.

One day he pointed to a rough box made of some foreign wood (the same that I have now duly despatched to you by train), and, giving me your name and address, said that without fail it was to be forwarded to you after his death. Also he asked me to do up a manuscript, which, like the box, was to be sent to you.

a suggestion which the other learned gentlemen treated as absurd. They declared that Isis had never travelled into Britain, though for my part I do not see why the Phoenicians, or even the Romans, who adopted her cult, more or less, should not have brought it here. But I know nothing of such matters and will not discuss them.

I remembered also that Mr. Holly was acquainted with this place, for he had mentioned it to me on the previous day, asking if the stones were still uninjured as they used to be when he was young. He added also, and the remark struck me, that yonder was where he would wish to die. When I answered that I feared he would never take so long a walk again, I noted that he smiled a little.

Well, this conversation gave me a due, and without troubling more about the footprints I went on as fast as I could to the Ring, half a mile or so away. Presently I reached it, and there – yes, there – standing by the cromlech, bareheaded, and clothed in his night-things only, stood Mr. Holly in the snow, the strangest figure, I think, that ever I beheld.

Indeed never shall I forget that wild scene. The circle of rough, single stones pointing upwards to the star-strewn sky, intensely lonely and intensely solemn: the tall trilithon towering above them in the centre, its shadow, thrown by the bright moon behind it, lying long and black upon the dazzling sheet of snow, and, standing clear of this shadow so that I could distinguish his every motion, and even the rapt look upon his dying face, the white-draped figure of Mr. Holly. He appeared to be uttering some invocation – in Arabic, I think – for long before I reached him I could catch the tones of his full, sonorous voice, and see his waving, outstretched arms. In his right hand he held the looped sceptre which, by his express wish I send to you with the drawings. I could see the flash of the jewels strung upon the wires, and in the great stillness, hear the tinkling of its golden bells.

Presently, too, I seemed to become aware of another presence, and now you will understand why I desire, and must ask that my identity should be suppressed. Naturally enough I do not wish to be mixed up with a superstitious tale which is, on the face of it, impossible and absurd. Yet under all the circumstances I think it right to tell you that I saw, or thought I saw, something gather in the shadow of the

INTRODUCTION

As soon as I came into touch with civilization again I found a copy of your book *She,* or rather of my book, and read it – first of all in a Hindostani translation. My host – he was a minister of some religious body, a man of worthy but prosaic mind – expressed surprise that a 'wild romance' should absorb me so much. I answered that those who have wide experience of the hard facts of life often find interest in romance. Had he known what were the hard facts to which I alluded, I wonder what that excellent person would have said?

I see that you carried out your part of the business well and faithfully. Every instruction has been obeyed, nothing has been added or taken away. Therefore, to you, to whom some twenty years ago I entrusted the beginning of the history, I wish to entrust its end also. You were the first to learn of *She-Who-Must-Be-Obeyed,* who from century to century sat alone, clothed with unchanging loveliness in the sepulchres of Kôr, waiting till her lost love was born again, and Destiny brought him back to her.

It is right, therefore, that you should be the first to learn also of Ayesha, Hesea and Spirit of the Mountain, the priestess of that Oracle which since the time of Alexander the Great has reigned between the naming pillars in the Sanctuary, the last holder of the sceptre of Hes or Isis upon the earth. It is right also that to you first among men I should reveal the mystic consummation of the wondrous tragedy which began at Kôr, or perchance far earlier in Egypt and elsewhere.

I am very ill; I have struggled back to this old house of mine to die, and my end is at hand. I have asked the doctor here, after all is over, to send you the Record, that is unless I change my mind and bum it first. You will also receive, if you receive anything at all, a case containing several rough sketches which may be of use to you, and a *sistrum,* the instrument that has been always used in the worship of the Nature goddesses of the old Egyptians, Isis and Hathor, which you will see is as beautiful as it is ancient. I give it to you for two reasons; as a token of my gratitude and regard, and as the only piece of evidence that is left to me of the literal truth of what I have written in the accompanying manuscript, where you will find it often, mentioned. Perhaps also you will value it as a souvenir of, I suppose, the strangest and loveliest being who ever was, or rather, is. It was central dolmen, or emerge from its rude chamber – I know not which for certain – something bright and glorious which gradually took the form of a woman upon whose forehead burned a star-like fire.

At any rate the vision or reflection, or whatever it was, startled me so much that I came to a halt under the lee of one of the monoliths, and found myself unable even to call to the distraught man whom I pursued.

Whilst I stood thus it became clear to me that Mr. Holly also saw something. At least he turned towards the Radiance in the shadow, uttered one cry; a wild, glad cry, and stepped forward; then seemed to fall *through it* on to his face.

When I reached the spot the light had vanished, and all I found was Mr. Holly, his arms still out-stretched, and the sceptre gripped tightly in his hand, lying quite dead in the shadow of the trilithon.

The rest of the doctor's letter need not be quoted as it deals only with certain very improbable explanations of the origin of this Figure of light, the details of the removal of Holly's body, and of how he managed to satisfy the coroner that no inquest was necessary.

The box of which he speaks arrived safely. Of the drawings in it I need say nothing, and of the *sistrum* or sceptre only a few words. It was fashioned of crystal to the well-known shape of the *Crux-ansata,* or the emblem of life of the Egyptians; the rod, the cross and the loop combined in one. From side to side of this loop ran golden wires, and on these were strung gems of three colours, glittering diamonds, sea-blue sapphires, and blood-red rubies, while to the fourth wire, that at the top, hung four little golden bells.

When I took hold of it first my arm shook slightly with excitement, and those bells began to sound; a sweet, faint music like to that of chimes heard far away at night in the silence of the sea. I thought too, but perhaps this was fancy, that a thrill passed from the hallowed and beautiful thing into my body.

On the mystery itself, as it is recorded in the manuscript, I make no comment. Of it and its inner significations every reader must form his or her own judgment. One thing alone is clear to me – on the her sceptre, the rod of her power, with which I saw her salute the Shadows in the Sanctuary, and her gift to me.

It has virtues also; some part of Ayesha's might yet haunts the symbol to which even spirits bowed, but if you should discover them, beware how they are used.

I have neither the strength nor the will to write more, The Record must speak for itself. Do with it what you like, and believe it or not as you like. I care nothing who know that it is true.

Who and what was Ayesha, nay, what is Ayesha? An incarnate essence, a materialized spirit of Nature the unforeseeing, the lovely, the cruel and the immortal; ensouled alone, redeemable only by Humanity and its piteous sacrifice? Say you! I have done with speculations who depart to solve these mysteries.

I wish you happiness and good fortune. Farewell to you and to all.

L. HORACE HOLLY.

I laid the epistle down, and, filled with sensations that it is useless to attempt to analyse or describe, opened the second envelope, of which I also print the contents, omitting only certain irrelevant portions, and the name of the writer as, it will be noted, he requests me to do.

This epistle, that was dated from a remote place upon the shores of Cumberland, ran as follows: –

DEAR SIR, – As the doctor who attended Mr. Holly in his last illness I am obliged, in obedience to a promise that I made to him, to become an intermediary in a somewhat strange business, although in truth it is one of which I know very little, however much it may have interested me. Still I do so only on the strict understanding that no mention is to be made of my name in connexion with the matter, or of the locality in which I practise.

About ten days ago I was called in to see Mr. Holly at an old house upon the Cliff that for many years remained untenanted except by the caretakers, which house was his property, and had been in his hypothesis that Mr. Holly tells the truth as to what he and Leo Vincey saw and experienced, which I at least believe – that though sundry interpretations of this mystery were advanced by Ayesha and others, none of them are quite satisfactory.

Indeed, like Mr. Holly, I incline to the theory that *She,* if I may still call her by that name although it is seldom given to her in these pages, put forward some of them, such as the vague Isis-myth, and the wondrous picture-story of the Mountain-fire, as mere veils to hide the truth which it was her purpose to reveal at last in that song she never sang.

THE EDITOR.

CONTENTS

CHAPTER 1

THE DOUBLE SIGN

HARD ON twenty years have gone by since that night of Leo's Vision – the most awful years, perhaps, which were ever endured by men – twenty years of search and hardship ending in soul-shaking wonder and amazement.

My death is very near to me, and of this I am glad, for I desire to pursue the quest in other realms, as it has been promised to me that I shall do. I desire to learn the beginning and the end of the spiritual drama of which it has been my strange lot to read some pages upon earth.

I, Ludwig Horace Holly, have been very ill; they carried me, more dead than alive, down those mountains whose lowest slopes I can see from my window, for I write this on the northern frontiers of India. Indeed any other man had long since perished, but Destiny kept my breath in me, perhaps that a record might remain. I must bide here a month or two till I am strong enough to travel homewards, for I have a fancy to die in the place where I was born. So while I have strength I will put the story down, or at least those parts of it that are most essential, for much can, or at any rate must be omitted. I shrink from attempting too long a book, though my notes and memory would furnish me with sufficient material for volumes.

I will begin with the Vision.

After Leo Vincey and I came back from Africa in 1885, desiring solitude, which indeed we needed sorely to recover from the fearful shock we had experienced, and to give us time and opportunity to think, we went to an old house upon the shores of Cumberland that has belonged to my family for many generations. This house, unless somebody has taken it believing me to be dead, is still my property and thither I travel to die.

Those whose eyes read the words I write, if any should ever read them, may ask – What shock?

Well, I am Horace Holly, and my companion, my beloved friend, my son in the spirit whom I reared from infancy was – nay, is – Leo Vincey.

We are those men who, following an ancient due, travelled to the Caves of Kôr in Central Africa, and there discovered her whom we sought, the immortal *She-who-must-be-obeyed.* In Leo she found her love, that re-born Kallikrates, the Grecian priest of Isis whom some two thousand years before she had slain in her jealous rage, thus executing on him the judgment of the angry goddess. In her also I found the divinity whom I was doomed to worship from afar, not with the flesh, for that is all lost and gone from me, but, what is sorer still, because its burden is undying, with the will and soul which animate a man throughout the countless æons of his being. The flesh dies, or at least it changes, and its passions pass, but that other passion of the spirit – that longing for oneness – is undying as itself.

What crime have I committed that this sore punishment should be laid upon me? Yet, in truth, is it a punishment? May it not prove to be but that black and terrible Gate which leads to the joyous palace of Rewards? She swore that I should ever be her friend and his and dwell with them eternally, and I believe her.

For how many winters did we wander among the icy hills and deserts! Still, at length, the Messenger came and led us to the Mountain, and on the Mountain we found the Shrine, and in the Shrine the Spirit. May not these things be an allegory prepared for our instruction? I will take comfort. I will hope that it is so. Nay, I am sure that it is so.

It will be remembered that in Kôr we found the immortal woman. There before the flashing rays and vapours of the Pillar of Life she declared her mystic love, and then in our very sight was swept to a doom so horrible that even now, after all which has been and gone, I shiver at its recollection. Yet what were Ayesha's last words? "*Forget me not . . . have pity on my shame. I die not. I shall come again and shall once more be beautiful. I swear it – it is true.*"

Well, I cannot set out that history afresh. Moreover it is written; the man whom I trusted in the matter did not fail me, and the book he made of it seems to be known throughout the world, for I have found it here in English, yes, and read it first translated into Hindostani. To it then I refer the curious.

In that house upon the desolate sea-shore of Cumberland, we dwelt a year, mourning the lost, seeking an avenus by which it might be found again and discovering none. Here our strength came back to us, and Leo's hair, that had been whitened in the horror of the Caves, grew again from grey to golden.

His beauty returned to him also, so that his face was as it had been, only purified and saddened.

Well I remember that night – and the hour of illumination. We were heart-broken, we were in despair. We sought signs and could find none. The dead remained dead to us and no answer came to all our crying.

It was a sullen August evening, and after we had dined we walked upon the shore, listening to the slow surge of the waves and watching the lightning flicker from the bosom of a distant cloud. In silence we walked, till at last Leo groaned – it was more of a sob than a groan – and clasped my arm.

"I can bear it no longer, Horace," he said – for so he called me now – "I am in torment. The desire to see Ayesha once more saps my brain. Without hope I shall go quite mad. And I am strong, I may live another fifty years."

"What then can you do?" I asked.

"I can take a short road to knowledge – or to peace," he answered solemnly. "I can die, and die I will – yes, to-night."

I turned upon him angrily, for his words filled me with fear.

"Leo, you are a coward!" I said. "Cannot you bear your part of pain as – others do?"

"You mean as you do, Horace," he answered with a dreary laugh, "for on you also the curse lies – with less cause. Well, you are stronger than I am, and more tough; perhaps because you have lived longer. No, I cannot bear it. I will die."

"It is a crime," I said, "the greatest insult you can offer to the Power that made you, to cast back its gift of life as a thing outworn, contemptible and despised. A crime, I say, which will bring with it worse punishment than any you can dream; perhaps even the punishment of everlasting separation."

"Does a man stretched in some torture-den commit a crime if he snatches a knife and kills himself, Horace? Perhaps; but surely that sin should find forgiveness – if torn flesh and quivering nerves may plead for mercy. I am such a man, and I will use that knife and take my chance. She is dead, and in death at least I shall be nearer her."

"Why so, Leo? For aught you know Ayesha may be living."

"No; for then she would have given me some sign. My mind is made up, so talk no more, or, if talk we must, let it be of other things."

Then I pleaded with him, though with little hope, for I saw that what I had feared for long was come to pass. Leo was mad: shock and sorrow had destroyed his reason. Were it not so, he, in his own way a very religious man, one who held, as I knew, strict opinions on such matters, would never have purposed to commit the wickedness of suicide.

"Leo," I said, "are you so heartless that you would leave me here alone? Do you pay me thus for all my love and care, and wish to drive me to my death? Do so if you will, and my blood be on your head."

"Your blood! Why your blood, Horace?"

"Because that road is broad and two can travel it. We have lived long years together and together endured much; I am sure that we shall not be long parted."

Then the tables were turned and be grew afraid for me. But I only answered, "If you die I tell you that I shall die also. It will certainly kill me."

So Leo gave way. "Well," he exclaimed suddenly, "I promise you it shall not be to-night. Let us give Life another chance."

"Good," I answered; but I went to my bed full of fear. For I was certain that this desire of death, having once taken hold of him, would grow and grow, until at length it became too strong, and then – then I should wither and die who could not live on alone. In my despair I threw out my soul towards that of her who was departed.

"Ayesha!" I cried, "if you have any power, if in any way it is permitted, show that you still live, and save your lover from this sin and me from a broken heart. Have pity on his sorrow and breathe hope into his spirit, for without hope Leo cannot live; and without him I shall not live."

Then, worn out, I slept.

I was aroused by the voice of Leo speaking to me in low, excited tones through the darkness.

"Horace," he said, "Horace, my friend, my father, listen"

In an instant I was wide awake, every nerve and fibre of me, for the tones of his voice told me that something had happened which bore upon our destinies.

"Let me light a candle first," I said.

"Never mind the candle, Horace; I would rather speak in the dark. I went to sleep, and I dreamed the most vivid dream that ever came to me. I seemed to stand under the vault of heaven, it was black, black, not a star shone in it, and a great loneliness possessed me. Then suddenly high up in the vault, miles and miles away, I saw a little light and thought that a planet had appeared to keep me company. The light began to descend slowly, like a floating flake of fire. Down it sank, and down and down, till it was but just above me, and I perceived that it was shaped like a tongue or fan of flame. At the height of my head from the ground it stopped and stood steady, and by its ghostly radiance I saw that beneath was the shape of a woman and that the flame burned upon her forehead. The radiance gathered strength and now I saw the woman.

"Horace, it was Ayesha herself, her eyes, her lovely face, her cloudy hair, and she looked at me sadly, reproachfully, I thought, as one might who says, 'Why did you doubt?'

"I tried to speak to her but my lips were dumb. I tried to advance and to embrace her, my arms would not move. There was a barrier between us. She lifted her hand and beckoned as though bidding me to follow her.

"Then she glided away, and, Horace, my spirit seemed to loose itself from the body and to be given the power to follow. We passed swiftly eastward, over lands and seas, and – I knew the road. At one point she paused and I looked downwards. Beneath, shining in the moonlight, appeared the ruined palaces of Kôr, and there not far away was the gulf we trod together.

"Onward above the marshes, and now we stood upon the Ethiopian's Head, and gathered round, watching us earnestly, were the faces of the Arabs, our companions who drowned in the sea beneath. Job was among them also, and he smiled at me sadly and shook his head, as though he wished to accompany us and could not.

"Across the sea again, across the sandy deserts, across more sea, and the shores of India lay beneath us. Then northward, ever northward, above the plains, till we reached a place of mountains capped with eternal snow. We passed them and stayed for an instant above a building set upon the brow of a plateau. It was a monastery, for old monks droned prayers upon its terrace. I shall know it again, for it is built in the shape of a half-moon and in front of it sits the gigantic, ruined statue of a god who gazes everlastingly across the desert. I knew, how I cannot say, that now we were far past the furthest borders of Thibet and that in front of us lay untrodden lands. More mountains stretched beyond that desert, a sea of snowy peaks, hundreds and hundreds of them.

"Near to the monastery, jutting out into the plain like some rocky headland, rose a solitary hill, higher than all behind. We stood upon its snowy crest and waited, till presently, above the mountains and the desert at our feet shot a sudden beam of light, that beat upon us like some signal flashed across the sea. On we went, floating down the beam – on over the desert and the mountains, across a great flat land beyond, in which were many villages and a city on a mound, till we lit upon a towering peak. Then I saw that this peak was loop-shaped like the symbol of Life of the Egyptians – the *crux-ansata* – and supported by a lava stem hundreds of feet in height. Also I saw that the fire which shone through it rose from the crater of a volcano beyond. Upon the very crest of this loop we rested a while, till the Shadow of Ayesha pointed downward with its hand, smiled and vanished. Then I awoke.

"Horace, I tell you that the sign has come to us."

His voice died away in the darkness, but I sat still, brooding over what I had heard. Leo groped his way to me and, seizing my arm, shook it.

"Are you asleep?" he asked angrily. "Speak, man, speak!"

"No," I answered, "never was I more awake. Give me time."

Then I rose, and going to the open window, drew up the blind and stood there staring at the sky, which grew pearl-hued with the first faint tinge of dawn. Leo came also and leant upon the window-sill, and I could feel that his body was trembling as though with cold. Clearly he was much moved.

"You talk of a sign," I said to him, "but in your sign I see nothing but a wild dream."

"It was no dream," he broke in fiercely; "it was a vision."

"A vision then if you will, but there are visions true and false, and how can we know that this is true? Listen, Leo. What is there in all that wonderful tale which could not have been fashioned in your own brain, distraught as it is almost to madness with your sorrow and your longings? You dreamed that you were alone in the vast universe. Well, is not every living creature thus alone? You dreamed that the shadowy shape of Ayesha came to you. Has it ever left your side? You dreamed that she led you over sea and land, past places haunted by your memory, above the mysterious mountains of the Unknown to an undiscovered peak. Does she not thus lead you through life to that peak which lies beyond the Gates of Death? You dreamed – "

"Oh! no more of it," he exclaimed. "What I saw, I saw, and that I shall follow. Think as you will, Horace, and do what you will. To-morrow I start for India, with you if you choose to come; if not, without you."

"You speak roughly, Leo," I said. "You forget that *I* have had no sign, and that the nightmare of a man so near to insanity that but a few hours ago he was determined upon suicide, will be a poor staff to lean on when we are perishing in the snows of Central Asia. A mixed vision, this of yours, Leo, with its mountain peak shaped like a *crux-ansata* and the rest. Do you suggest that Ayesha is re-incarnated in Central Asia – as a female Grand Lama or something of that sort?"

"I never thought of it, but why not?" asked Leo quietly. "Do you remember a certain scene in the Caves of Kôr yonder, when the living looked upon the dead, and dead and living were the same? And do you remember what Ayesha swore, that she would come again – yes, to this world; and how could that be except by re-birth, or, what is the same thing, by the transmigration of the spirit?"

I did not answer this argument. I was struggling with myself.

"No sign has come to me," I said, "and yet I have had a part in the play, humble enough, I admit, and I believe that I have still a part."

"No," he said, "no sign has come to you. I wish that it had. Oh! how I wish you could be convinced as I am, Horace!"

Then we were silent for a long while, silent, with our eyes fixed upon the sky.

It was a stormy dawn. Clouds in fantastic masses hung upon the ocean. One of them was like a great mountain, and we watched it idly. It changed its shape, the crest of it grew hollow like a crater. From this crater sprang a projecting cloud, a rough pillar with a knob or lump resting on its top. Suddenly the rays of the risen sun struck upon this mountain and the column and they turned white like snow. Then as though melted by those fiery arrows, the centre of the excrescence above the pillar thinned out and vanished, leaving an enormous loop of inky cloud.

"Look," said Leo, in a low, frightened voice, "that is the shape of the mountain which I saw in my vision. There upon it is the black loop, and there through it shines the fire. *It would seem that the sign is for both of us, Horace.*"

I looked and looked again till presently the vast loop vanished into the blue of heaven. Then I turned and said –

"I will come with you to Central Asia, Leo."

CHAPTER 2

THE LAMASERY

SIXTEEN YEARS had passed since that night vigil in the old Cumberland house, and, behold! we two, Leo and I, were still travelling, still searching for that mountain peak shaped like the Symbol of Life which never, never could be found.

Our adventures would fill volumes, but of what use is it to record them? Many of a similar nature are already written of in books; those that we endured were more prolonged, that is all. Five years we spent in Thibet, for the most part as guests of various monasteries, where we studied the law and traditions of the Lamas. Here we were once sentenced to death in punishment for having visited a forbidden city, but escaped through the kindness of a Chinese official.

Leaving Thibet, we wandered east and west and north, thousands and thousands of miles, sojourning amongst many tribes in Chinese territory and elsewhere, learning many tongues, enduring much hardship. Thus we would hear a legend of a place, say nine hundred miles away, and spend about two years in reaching it, to find when we came there, nothing.

And so the time went on. Yet never once did we think of giving up the quest and returning, since, before we started, we had sworn an oath that we would achieve or die. Indeed we ought to have died a score of times, yet always were preserved, most mysteriously preserved.

Now we were in country where, so far as I could learn, no European had ever set a foot. In a part of the vast land called Turkestan there is a great lake named Balhkash, of which we visited the shores. Two hundred miles or so to the westward is a range of mighty mountains marked on the maps as Arkarty – Tau, on which we spent a year, and five hundred or so to the eastward are other mountains called Cherga, whither we journeyed at last, having explored the triple ranges of the Tau.

Here it was that at last our true adventures began. On one of the spurs of these awful Cherga mountains – it is unmarked on any map – we well-nigh perished of starvation. The winter was coming on and we could find no game. The last traveller we had met, hundreds of miles south, told us that on that range was a monastery inhabited by Lamas of surpassing holiness. He said that they dwelt in this wild land over which no power claimed dominion and where no tribes lived, to acquire "merit," with no other company than that of their own pious contemplations. We did not believe in its existence, still we were searching for that monastery, driven onward by the blind fatalism which was our only guide through all these endless wanderings. As we were starving and could find no "argals," that is fuel with which to make a fire, we walked all night by the light of the moon, driving between us a single yak – for now we had no attendant, the last having died a year before.

He was a noble beast, that yak, and had the best constitution of any animal I ever knew, though now, like his masters, he was near his end. Not that he was over-laden, for a few rifle cartridges, about a hundred and fifty, the remnant of a store which we had fortunately been able to buy from a caravan two years before, some money in gold and silver, a little tea and a bundle of skin rugs and sheepskin garments were his burden. On, on we trudged across a plateau of snow, having the great mountains on our right, till at length the yak gave a sigh and stopped. So we stopped also, because we must, and wrapping ourselves in the skin rugs, sat down in the snow to wait for daylight.

"We shall have to kill him and eat his flesh raw," I said, patting the poor yak that lay patiently at our side.

"Perhaps we may find game in the morning," answered Leo, still hopeful.

"And perhaps we may not, in which case we must die."

"Very good," he replied, "then let us die. It is the last resource of failure. We shall have done our best."

"Certainly, Leo, we shall have done our best, if sixteen years of tramping over mountains and through eternal snows in pursuit of a dream of the night can be called best."

"You know what I believe," he answered stubbornly, and there was silence between us, for here arguments did not avail. Also even then I could not think that all our toils and sufferings would be in vain.

The dawn came, and by its light we looked at one another anxiously, each of us desiring to see what strength was left to his companion. Wild creatures we should have seemed to the eyes of any civilized person. Leo was now over forty years of age, and certainly his maturity had fulfilled the promise of his youth, for a more magnificent man I never knew. Very tall, although he seemed spare to the eye, his girth matched his height, and those many years of desert life had turned his muscles to steel. His hair had grown long, like my own, for it was a protection from sun and cold, and hung upon his neck, a curling, golden mane, as his great beard hung upon his breast, spreading outwards almost to the massive shoulders. The face, too – what could be seen of it – was beautiful though burnt brown with weather; refined and full of thought, sombre almost, and in it, clear as crystal, steady as stars, shone his large grey eyes.

And I – I was what I have always been – ugly and hirsute, iron – grey now also, but in spite of my sixty odd years, still wonderfully strong, for my strength seemed to increase with time, and my health was perfect. In fact, during all this period of rough travels, although now and again we had met with accidents which laid us up for awhile, neither of us had known a day of sickness. Hardship seemed to have turned our constitutions to iron and made them impervious to every human ailment. Or was this because we alone amongst living men had once inhaled the breath of the Essence of Life?

Our fears relieved – for notwithstanding our foodless night, as yet neither of us showed any signs of exhaustion – we turned to contemplate the landscape. At our feet beyond a little belt of fertile soil, began a great desert of the sort with which we were familiar – sandy, salt-encrusted, treeless, waterless, and here and there streaked with the first snows of winter. Beyond it, eighty or a hundred miles away – in that lucent atmosphere it was impossible to say how far exactly – rose more mountains, a veritable sea of them, of which the white peaks soared upwards by scores.

As the golden rays of the rising sun touched their snows to splendour, I saw Leo's eyes become troubled. Swiftly he turned and looked along the edge of the desert.

"See there!" he said, pointing to something dim and enormous. Presently the light reached it also. It was a mighty mountain not more than ten miles away, that stood out by itself among the sands. Then he turned once more, and with his back to the desert stared at the slope of the hills, along the base of which we had been travelling. As yet they were in gloom, for the sun was behind them, but presently light began to flow over their crests like a flood. Down it crept, lower, and yet lower, till it reached a little plateau not three hundred yards above us. There, on the edge of the plateau, looking out solemnly across the waste, sat a great ruined idol, a colossal Buddha, while to the rear of the idol, built of yellow stone, appeared the low crescent-shaped mass of a monastery.

"At last!" cried Leo, "oh, Heaven! at last!" and, flinging himself down, he buried his face in the snow as though to hide it there, lest I should read something written on it which he did not desire that even I should see.

I let him lie a space, understanding what was passing in his heart, and indeed in mine also. Then going to the yak that, poor brute, had no share in these joyous emotions but only lowed and looked round with hungry eyes, I piled the sheepskin rugs on to its back. This done, I laid my hand on Leo's shoulder, saying, in the most matter-of-fact voice I could command –

"Come. If that place is not deserted, we may find food and shelter there, and it is beginning to storm again."

He rose without a word, brushed the snow from his beard and garments and came to help me to lift the yak to its feet, for the worn-out beast was too stiff and weak to rise of itself. Glancing at him covertly, I saw on Leo's face a very strange and happy look; a great peace appeared to possess him.

We plunged upwards through the snow slope, dragging the yak with us, to the terrace whereon the monastery was built. Nobody seemed to be about there, nor could I discern any footprints. Was the place but a ruin? We had found many such; indeed this ancient land is full of buildings that had once served as the homes of men, learned and pious enough after their own fashion, who lived and died hundreds, or even thousands, of years ago, long before our Western civilization came into being.

My heart, also my stomach, which was starving, sank at the thought, but while I gazed doubtfully, a little coil of blue smoke sprang from a chimney, and never, I think, did I see a more joyful sight. In the centre of the edifice was a large building, evidently the temple, but nearer to us I saw a small door, almost above which the smoke appeared. To this door I went and knocked, calling aloud –

"Open! open, holy Lamas. Strangers seek your charity." After awhile there was a sound of shuffling feet and the door creaked upon its hinges, revealing an old, old man, clad in tattered, yellow garments.

"Who is it? Who is it?" he exclaimed, blinking at me through a pair of horn spectacles. "Who comes to disturb our solitude, the solitude of the holy Lamas of the Mountains?"

"Travellers, Sacred One, who have had enough of solitude," I answered in his own dialect, with which I was well acquainted. "Travellers who are starving and who ask your charity, which," I added, "by the Rule you cannot refuse."

He stared at us through his horn spectacles, and, able to make nothing of our faces, let his glance fall to our garments which were as ragged as his own, and of much the same pattern. Indeed, they were those of Thibetan monks, including a kind of quilted petticoat and an outer vestment not unlike an Eastern burnous. We had adopted them because we had no others. Also they protected us from the rigours of the climate and from remark, had there been any to remark upon them.

"Are you Lamas?" he asked doubtfully, "and if so, of what monastery?"

"Lamas sure enough," I answered, "who belong to a monastery called the World, where, alas! one grows hungry."

The reply seemed to please him, for he chuckled a little, then shook his head, saying –

"It is against our custom to admit strangers unless they be of our own faith, which I am sure you are not."

"And much more is it against your Rule, holy Khubilghan," for so these abbots are entitled, "to suffer strangers to starve"; and I quoted a well-known passage from the sayings of Buddha which fitted the point precisely.

"I perceive that you are instructed in the Books," he exclaimed with wonder on his yellow, wrinkled face, "and to such we cannot refuse shelter. Come in, brethren of the monastery called the World. But stay, there is the yak, who also has claims upon our charity," and, turning, he struck upon a gong or bell which hung within the door.

At the sound another man appeared, more wrinkled and to all appearance older than the first, who stared at us open-mouthed.

"Brother," said the abbot, "shut that great mouth of yours lest an evil spirit should fly down it; take this poor yak and give it fodder with the other cattle."

So we unstrapped our belongings from the back of the beast, and the old fellow whose grandiloquent title was "Master of the Herds," led it away.

When it had gone, not too willingly – for our faithful friend disliked parting from us and distrusted this new guide – the abbot, who was named Kou-en led us into the living room or rather the kitchen of the monastery, for it served both purposes. Here we found the rest of the monks, about twelve in all, gathered round the fire of which we had seen the smoke, and engaged, one of them in preparing the morning meal, and the rest in warming themselves.

They were all old men; the youngest could not have been less than sixty-five. To these we were solemnly introduced as "Brethren of the Monastery called the World, where folk grow hungry," for the abbot Kou-en could not make up his mind to part from this little joke.

They stared at us, they rubbed their thin hands, they bowed and wished us well and evidently were delighted at our arrival. This was not strange, however, seeing that ours were the first new faces which they had seen for four long years.

Nor did they stop at words, for while they made water hot for us to wash in, two of them went to prepare a room and others drew off our rough hide boots and thick outer garments and brought us slippers for our feet. Then they led us to the guest chamber, which they informed us was a "propitious place," for once it had been slept in by a noted saint. Here a fire was lit, and, wonder of wonders! clean garments, including linen, all of them ancient and faded, but of good quality, were brought for us to put on.

So we washed – yes, actually washed all over – and having arrayed ourselves in the robes, which were somewhat small for Leo, struck the bell that hung in the room and were conducted by a monk who answered it back to the kitchen, where the meal was now served. It consisted of a kind of porridge, to which was added new milk brought in by the

"Master of the Herds," dried fish from a lake, and buttered tea, the last two luxuries produced in our special honour. Never had food tasted more delicious to us, and, I may add, never did we eat more. Indeed, at last I was obliged to request Leo to stop, for I saw the monks staring at him and heard the old abbot chuckling to himself.

"Oho! The Monastery called the World, where folk grow *hungry*" to which another monk, who was called the "Master of the Provisions," replied uneasily, that if we went on like this, their store of food would scarcely last the winter. So we finished at length, feeling, as some book of maxims which I can remember in my youth said all polite people should do – that we could eat more, and much impressed our hosts by chanting a long Buddhist grace.

"Their feet are in the Path! Their feet are in the Path!" they said, astonished.

"Yes," replied Leo, "they have been in it for sixteen years of our present incarnation. But we are only beginners, for you, holy Ones, know how star-high, how ocean-wide and how desert-long is that path. Indeed it is to be instructed as to the right way of walking therein that we have been miraculously directed by a dream to seek you out, as the most pious, the most saintly and the most learned of all the Lamas in these parts."

"Yes, certainly we are that," answered the abbot Kou-en, "seeing that there is no other monastery within five months' journey," and again he chuckled, "though, alas!" he added with a pathetic little sigh, "our numbers grow few."

After this we asked leave to retire to our chamber in order to rest, and there, upon very good imitations of beds, we slept solidly for four and twenty hours, rising at last perfectly refreshed and well.

Such was our introduction to the Monastery of the Mountains – for it had no other name – where we were destined to spend the next six months of our lives. Within a few days – for they were net long in giving us their complete confidence – those good-hearted and simple old monks told us all their history.

It seemed that of old time there was a Lamasery here, in which dwelt several hundred brethren. This, indeed, was obviously true, for the place was enormous, although for the most part ruined, and, as the weather-worn statue of Buddha showed, very ancient. The story ran, according to the old abbot, that two centuries or so before, the monks had been killed out by some fierce tribe who lived beyond the desert and across the distant mountains, which tribe were heretics and worshippers of fire. Only a few of them escaped to bring the sad news to other communities, and for five generations no attempt was made to re-occupy the place.

At length it was revealed to him, our friend Kou-en, when a young man, that he was a reincarnation of one of the old monks of this monastery, who also was named Kou-en, and that it was his duty during his present life to return thither, as by so doing he would win much merit and receive many wonderful revelations. So he gathered a band of zealots and, with the blessing and consent of his superiors, they started out, and after many hardships and losses found and took possession of the place, repairing it sufficiently for then needs.

This happened about fifty years before, and here they had dwelt ever since, only communicating occasionally with the outside world. At first their numbers were recruited from time to time by new brethren, but at length these ceased to come, with the result that the community was dying out.

"And what then?" I asked.

"And then," the abbot answered, "nothing. We have acquired much merit; we have been blest with many revelations, and, after the repose we have earned in Devachan, our lots in future existences will be easier. What more can we ask or desire, removed as we are from all the temptations of the world?"

For the rest, in the intervals of their endless prayers, and still more endless contemplations, they were husbandmen, cultivating the soil, which was fertile at the foot of the mountain, and tending their herd of yaks. Thus they wore away their blameless lives until at last they died of old age, and, as they believed – and who shall say that they were wrong – the eternal round repeated itself elsewhere.

Immediately after, indeed on the very day of our arrival at the monastery the winter began in earnest with bitter cold and snow-storms so heavy and frequent that all the desert was covered deep. Very soon it became obvious to us that here we must stay until the spring, since to attempt to move in any direction would be to perish. With some misgivings we explained this to the abbot Kou-en, offering to remove to one of the empty rooms in the ruined part of the building, supporting ourselves with fish that we could catch by cutting a hole in the ice of the lake above the monastery, and if we were able to find any, on game, which we might trap or shoot in the scrub-like forest of stunted pines and junipers that grew around its border. But he would listen to no such thing. We had been sent to be their guests, he said, and their guests we should remain for so long as might be convenient to us. Would we lay upon them the burden of the sin of inhospitality? Besides, he remarked with his chuckle –

"We who dwell alone like to hear about that other great monastery called the World, where the monks are not so favoured as we who are set in this blessed situation, and where folk even go hungry in body, and," he added, "in soul."

Indeed, as we soon found out, the dear old man's object was to keep our feet in the Path until we reached the goal of Truth, or, in other words, became excellent Lamas like himself and his flock.

So we walked in the Path, as we had done in many another Lamasery, and assisted at the long prayers in the ruined temple and studied the *Kandjur,* or "Translation of the Words" of Buddha, which is their bible and a very long one, and generally showed that our "minds were open." Also we expounded to them the doctrines of our own faith, and greatly delighted were they to find so many points of similarity between it and theirs. Indeed, I am not certain but that if we could have stopped there long enough, say ten years, we might have persuaded some of them to accept a new revelation of which we were the prophets. Further, in spare hours we told them many tales of "the Monastery called the World," and it was really delightful, and in a sense piteous, to see the joy with which they listened to these stories of wondrous countries and new races of men; they who knew only of Russia and China and some semi-savage tribes, inhabitants of the mountains and the deserts.

"It is right for us to learn all this," they declared, "for, who knows, perhaps in future incarnations we may become inhabitants of these places."

But though the time passed thus in comfort and indeed, compared to many of our experiences, in luxury, oh! our hearts were hungry, for in them burned the consuming fire of our quest. We felt that we were on the threshold – yes, we knew it, we knew it, and yet our wretched physical limitations made it impossible for us to advance by a single step. On the desert beneath fell the snow, moreover great winds arose suddenly that drove those snows like dust, piling them in heaps as high as trees, beneath which any unfortunate traveller would be buried.

Here we must wait, there was nothing else to be done.

One alleviation we found, and only one. In a ruined room of the monastery was a library of many volumes, placed there, doubtless, by the monks who were massacred in times bygone. These had been more or less cared for and re-arranged by their successors, who gave us liberty to examine them as often as we pleased. Truly it was a strange collection, and I should imagine of priceless value, for among them were to be found Buddhistic, Sivaistic and Shamanistic writings that we had never before seen or heard of, together with the lives of a multitude of Bodhisatvas, or distinguished saints, written in various tongues, some of which we did not understand.

What proved more interesting to us, however, was a diary in many tomes that for generations had been kept by the Khubilghans or abbots of the old Lamasery, in which every event of importance was recorded in great detail. Turning over the pages of one of the last volumes of this diary, written apparently about two hundred and fifty years earlier, and shortly before the destruction of the monastery, we came upon an entry of which the following – for I can only quote from memory – is the substance –

"In the summer of this year, after a very great sandstorm, a brother (the name was given, but I forget it) found in the desert a man of the people who dwell beyond the Far Mountains, of whom rumours have reached this Lamasery from time to time. He was living, but beside him were the bodies of two of his companions who had been overwhelmed by sand and thirst. He was very fierce looking. He refused to say how he came into the desert, telling us only that he had followed the road known to the ancients before communication between his people and the outer world ceased. We gathered, however, that his brethren with whom he fled had committed some crime for which they had been condemned to die, and that he had accompanied them in their flight. He told us that there was a fine country beyond the mountains, fertile, but plagued with droughts and earthquakes, which latter, indeed, we often feel here.

"The people of that country were, he said, warlike and very numerous but followed agriculture. They had always lived there, though ruled by Khans who were descendants of the Greek king called Alexander, who conquered much country to the south-west of us. This may be true, as our records tell us that about two thousand years ago an army sent by that invader penetrated to these parts, though of his being with them nothing is said.

"The stranger-man told us also that his people worship a priestess called Hes or the Hesea, who is said to reign from generation to generation. She lives in a great mountain, apart, and is feared and adored by all, but is not the queen of the country, in the government of which she seldom interferes. To her, however, sacrifices are offered, and he who incurs her vengeance dies, so that even the chiefs of that land are afraid of her. Still their subjects often fight, for they hate each other.

"We answered that he lied when he said that this woman was immortal – for that was what we supposed he meant – since nothing is immortal; also we laughed at his tale of her power. This made the man very angry. Indeed he declared that our Buddha was not so strong as this priestess, and that she would show it by being avenged upon us.

"After this we gave him food and turned him out of the Lamasery, and he went, saying that when he returned we should learn who spoke the truth. We do not know what became of him, and he refused to reveal to us the road to his country, which lies beyond the desert and the Far Mountains. We think that perhaps he was an evil spirit sent to frighten us, in which he did not succeed."

Such is a *précis* of this strange entry, the discovery of which, vague as it was, thrilled us with hope and excitement. Nothing more appeared about the man or his country, but within a little over a year from that date the diary of the abbot came to a sudden end without any indication that unusual events had occurred or were expected.

Indeed, the last item written in the parchment book mentioned the preparation of certain new lands to be used for the sowing of grain in future seasons, which suggested that the brethren neither feared nor expected disturbance. We wondered whether the man from beyond the mountains was as good as his word and had brought down the vengeance of that priestess called the Hesea upon the community which sheltered him. Also we wondered – ah! how we wondered – who and what this Hesea might be.

On the day following this discovery we prayed the abbot, Kou-en, to accompany us to the library, and having read him the passage, asked if he knew anything of the matter. He swayed his wise old head, which always reminded me of that of a tortoise, and answered –

"A little. Very little, and that mostly about the army of the Greek king who is mentioned in the writing."

We inquired what he could possibly know of this matter, whereon Kou-en replied calmly –

"In those days when the faith of the Holy One was still young, I dwelt as a humble brother in this very monastery, which was one of the first built, and I saw the army pass, that is all. That," he added meditatively," was in my fiftieth incarnation of this present Round – no, I am thinking of another army – in my seventy-third."*

* As students of their lives and literature will be aware, it is common for Buddhist priests to state positively that they remember events which occurred during their previous incarnations. – ED.

Here Leo began a great laugh, but I managed to kick him beneath the table and he turned it into a sneeze. This was fortunate, as such ribald merriment would have hurt the old man's feelings terribly. After all, also, as Leo himself had once said, surely we were not the people to mock at the theory of re-incarnation, which, by the way, is the first article of faith among nearly one quarter of the human race, and this not the most foolish quarter.

"How can that be – I ask for instruction, learned One – seeing that memory perishes with death?"

"Ah!" he answered, "Brother Holly, it may seem to do so, but oftentimes it comes back again, especially to those who are far advanced upon the Path. For instance, until you read this passage I had forgotten all about that army, but now I see it passing, passing, and myself with other monks standing by the statue of the big Buddha in front yonder, and watching it go by. It was not a very large army, for most of the soldiers had died, or been killed, and it was being pursued by the wild people who lived south of us in those days, so that it was in a great hurry to put the desert between it and them. The general of the army was a swarthy man – I wish that I could remember his name, but I cannot.

"Well," he went on, "that general came up to the Lamasery and demanded a sleeping place for his wife and children, also provisions and medicines, and guides across the desert. The abbot of that day told him it was against our law to admit a woman under our roof, to which he answered that if we did not, we should have no roof left, for he would burn the place and kill every one of us with the sword. Now, as you know, to be killed by violence means that we must pass sundry incarnations in the forms of animals, a horrible thing, so we chose the lesser evil and gave way, and afterwards obtained absolution for our sins from the Great

Lama. Myself I did not see this queen, but I saw the priestess of their worship – alas! alas!" and Kou-en beat his breast.

"Why, alas?" I asked, as unconcernedly as I could, for this story interested me strangely.

"Why? Oh! because I may have forgotten the army, but I have never forgotten that priestess, and she has been a great hindrance to me through many ages, delaying me upon my journey for the Other Side, to the Shore of Salvation. I, as a humble Lama, was engaged in preparing her apartment when she entered and threw aside her veil; yes, and perceiving a young man, spoke to me, asking many questions, and even if I was not glad to look again upon a woman."

"What – what was she like?" said Leo, anxiously.

"What was she like? Oh! she was all loveliness in one shape; she was like the dawn upon the snows; she was like the evening star above the mountains; she was like the first flower of the spring. Brother, ask me not what she was like, nay, I will say no more. Oh! my sin, my sin. I am slipping backward and you draw my black shame out into the light of day. Nay, I will confess it that you may know how vile a thing I am – I whom perhaps you have thought holy – like yourselves. That woman, if woman she were, lit a fire in my heart which will not burn out, oh! and more, more," and Kou-en rocked himself to and fro upon his stool while tears of contrition trickled from beneath his horn spectacles, "*she made me worship her!* For first she asked me of my faith and listened eagerly as I expounded it, hoping that the light would come into her heart; then, after I had finished she said –

"'So your Path is Renunciation and your Nirvana a most excellent Nothingness which some would think it scarce worth while to strive so hard to reach. Now I will show you a more joyous way and a goddess more worthy of your worship.'

"What way, and what goddess?' I asked of her.

" 'The way of Love and Life,' she answered, 'that makes all the world to be, that made *you,* O seeker of Nirvana, and the goddess called Nature.'

"Again I asked where is that goddess, and behold! she drew herself up, looking most royal, and touching her ivory breast, she said, 'I am She. Now kneel you down and do me homage.'

"My brethren, I knelt, yes, I kissed her foot, and then I fled away shamed and broken-hearted, and as I went she laughed, and cried: 'Remember me when you reach Devachan, O servant of the Buddha-saint, for though I change, I do not die, and even there I shall be with you who once have given me worship.'

"And it is so, my brethren, it is so; for though I obtained absolution for my sin and have suffered much for it through this, my next incarnation yet I cannot be rid of her, and for me the Utter Peace is far, far away," and Kou-en placed his withered hands before his face and sobbed outright.

A ridiculous sight, truly, to see a holy Khublighan well on the wrong side of eighty, weeping like a child over a dream of a beautiful woman which he imagined he had once dreamt in his last life more than two thousand years ago. So the reader will say. But I, Holly, for reasons of my own, felt deep sympathy with that poor old man, and Leo was also sympathetic. We patted him on the back; we assured him that he was the victim of some evil hallucination which could never be brought up against him in this or any future existence, since, if sin there were, it must have been forgiven long ago, and so forth. When his calm was somewhat restored we tried also to extract further information from him, but with poor results, so far as the priestess was concerned.

He said that he did not know to what religion she belonged, and did not care, but thought that it must be an evil one. She went away the next morning with the army, and he never saw or heard of her any more, though it came into his mind that he was obliged to be locked in his cell for eight days to prevent himself from following her. Yes, he had heard one thing, for the abbot of that day had told the brethren. This priestess was the real general of the army, not the king or the queen, the latter of whom hated her. It was by her will that they pushed on northwards across the desert to some country beyond the mountains, where she desired to establish herself and her worship.

We asked if there really was any country beyond the mountains, and Kou-en answered wearily that he believed so. Either in this or in a previous life he had heard that people lived there who worshipped fire. Certainly also it was true that about thirty years ago a brother who had climbed the great peak yonder to spend some days in solitary meditation, returned and reported that he had seen a marvellous thing, namely, a shaft of fire burning in the heavens beyond those same mountains, though whether this were a vision, or what, he could not say. He recalled, however, that about that time they had felt a great earthquake.

Then the memory of that fancied transgression again began to afflict Kou-en's innocent old heart and he crept away lamenting and was seen no more for a week. Nor would he ever speak again to us of this matter.

But we spoke of it much with hope and wonder, and made up our minds that we would at once ascend this mountain.

CHAPTER 3

THE BEACON LIGHT

A WEEK later came our opportunity of making this ascent of the mountain, for now in midwinter it ceased storming, and hard frost set in, which made it possible to walk upon the surface of the snow. Learning from the monks that at this season *ovis poli* and other kinds of big-horned sheep and game descended from the hills to take refuge in certain valleys, where they scraped away the snow to find food, we announced that we were going out to hunt. The excuse we gave was that we were suffering from confinement and needed exercise, having by the teaching of our religion no scruples about killing game.

Our hosts replied that the adventure was dangerous, as the weather might change at any moment. They told us, however, that on the slopes of this very mountain which we desired to climb, there was a large natural cave where, if need be, we could take shelter, and to this cave one of them, somewhat younger and more active than the rest, offered to guide us. So, having manufactured a rough tent from skins, and laden our old yak, now in the best of condition, with food and garments, on one still morning we started as soon as it was light. Under the guidance of the monk, who, notwithstanding his years walked very well, we reached the northern slope of the peak before mid-day. Here, as he had said, we found a great cave of which the opening was protected by an over-hanging ledge of rock.

Evidently this cave was the favourite place of shelter for game at certain seasons of the year, since in it were heaped vast accumulations of their droppings, which removed any fear of a lack of fuel.

The rest of that short day we spent in setting up our tent in the cave, in front of which we lit a large fire, and in a survey of the slopes of the mountain, for we told the monk that we were searching for the tracks of wild sheep. Indeed, as it happened, on our way back to the cave we came across a small herd of ewes feeding upon the mosses in a sheltered spot where in summer a streamlet ran. Of these we were so fortunate as to kill two, for no sportsman had ever come here, and they were tame enough, poor things. As meat would keep for ever in that temperature, we had now sufficient food to last us for a fortnight, and dragging the animals down the snow slopes to the cave, we skinned them by the dying light.

That evening we supped upon fresh mutton, a great luxury, which the monk enjoyed as much as we did, since, whatever might be his views as to taking life, he liked mutton. Then we turned into the tent and huddled ourselves together for warmth, as the temperature must have been some degrees below zero. The old monk rested well enough, but neither Leo nor I slept over much, for wonder as to what we might see from the top of that mountain banished sleep.

Next morning at the dawn, the weather being still favourable, our companion returned to the monastery, whither we said we would follow him in a day or two.

Now at last we were alone, and without wasting an instant began our ascent of the peak. It was many thousand feet high and in certain places steep enough, but the deep, frozen snow made climbing easy, so that by midday we reached the top. Hence the view was magnificent. Beneath us stretched the desert, and beyond it a broad belt of fantastically shaped, snow-clad mountains, hundreds and hundreds of them; in front, to the right, to the left as far as the eye could reach.

"They are just as I saw them in my dream so many years ago," muttered Leo? "the same the very same."

"And where was the fiery light?" I asked.

"Yonder, I think;" and he pointed north by east.

"Well, it is not there now." I answered, "and this place is cold."

So, since it was dangerous to linger, lest the darkness should overtake us on our return journey, we descended the peak again, reaching the cave about sunset. The next four days we spent in the same way. Every morning we crawled up those wearisome banks of snow, and every afternoon we slid and tobogganed down them again, till I grew heartily tired of the exercise.

On the fourth night, instead of coming to sleep in the tent Leo sat himself down at the entrance to the cave. I asked him why he did this, but he answered impatiently; because he wished it, so I left him alone. I could see, indeed, that he was in a strange and irritable mood, for the failure of our search oppressed him. Moreover, we knew, both of us, that it could not be much prolonged, since the weather might break at any moment, when ascents of the mountain would become impossible.

In the middle of the night I was awakened by Leo shaking me and saying –

"Come here, Horace, I have something to show you."

Reluctantly enough I crept from between the rugs and out of the tent. To dress there was no need, for we slept in all our garments. He led me to the mouth of the cave and pointed northward. I looked. The night was very dark; but far, far away appeared a faint patch of light upon the sky, such as might be caused by the reflection of a distant fire.

"What do you make of it?" he asked anxiously.

"Nothing in particular," I answered, "it may he anything. The moon – no, there is none, dawn – no, it is too northerly, and it does not break for three hours. Something burning, a house, or a funeral pyre, but how can there be such things here? I give it up."

"I think it is a reflection, and that if we were on the peak we should see the light which throws it." said Leo slowly.

"Yes, but we are not, and cannot get there in the dark."

"Then, Horace, we must spend a night there."

"It will be our last in this incarnation," I answered with a laugh, "that is if it comes on to snow."

"We must risk it, or I will risk it. Look, the light has faded;" and there at least he was right, for undoubtedly it had. The night was as black as pitch.

"Let's talk it over to-morrow," I said, and went back to the tent, for I was sleepy and incredulous, but Leo sat on by the mouth of the cave.

At dawn I awoke and found breakfast already cooked.

"I must start early," Leo explained.

"Are you mad?" I asked. "How can we camp on that place?"

"I don't know, but I am going. I must go, Horace."

"Which means that we both must go. But how about the yak?"

"Where we can climb, it can follow," he answered.

So we strapped the tent and other baggage, including a good supply of cooked meat, upon the beast's back, and started. The tramp was long since we were obliged to make some detours to avoid slopes of frozen snow in which, on our previous ascents, we had cut footholds with an axe, for up these the laden animal could not clamber. Reaching the summit at length, we dug a hole, and there pitched the tent, piling the excavated snow about its sides. By this time it began to grow dark, and having descended into the tent, yak and all, we ate our food and waited.

Oh! what cold was that. The frost was fearful, and at this height a wind blew whose icy breath passed through all our wrappings, and seemed to burn our flesh beneath as though with hot irons. It was fortunate that we had brought the yak, for without the warmth from its shaggy body I believe that we should have perished, even in our tent. For some hours we watched, as indeed we must, since to sleep might mean to die, yet saw nothing save the lonely stars, and heard nothing in that awful silence, for here even the wind made no noise as it slid across the snows. Accustomed as I was to such exposure, my faculties began to grow numb and my eyes to shut, when suddenly Leo said –

"Look, below the red star!"

I looked, and there high in the sky was the same curious glow which we had seen upon the previous night. There was more than this indeed, for beneath it, almost on a line with us and just above the crests of the intervening peaks, appeared a faint sheet of fire and revealed against it something black. Whilst we watched, the fire widened, spread upwards and grew in power and intensity. Now against its flaming background the black object became clearly visible, and lo! it was the top of a soaring pillar surmounted by a loop. Yes, we could see its every outline. It was the *crux ansata,* the Symbol of Life itself.

The symbol vanished, the fire sank. Again it blazed up more fiercely than before and the loop appeared afresh, then once more disappeared. A third time the fire shone, and with such intensity, that no lightning could surpass its brilliance. All around the heavens were lit up, and through the black needle-shaped eye of the symbol, as from the flare of a beacon, or the search-light of a ship, one fierce ray shot across the sea of mountain tops and the spaces of the desert, straight as an arrow to the lofty peak on which we lay. Yes, it lit upon the snow, staining it red, and upon the wild, white faces of us who watched, though to the right and left of us spread thick darkness. My compass lay before me on the snow, and I could even see its needle; and beyond us the shape of a white fox that had crept near, scenting food. Then it was gone as swiftly as it came. Gone too were the symbol and the veil of flame behind it, only the glow lingered a little on the distant sky.

For awhile there was silence between us, then Leo said –

"Do you remember, Horace, when we lay upon the Rocking Stone where *her* cloak fell upon me – " as he said the words the breath caught in his throat – "how the ray of light was sent to us in farewell, and to show us a path of escape from the Place of Death? Now I think that it has been sent again in greeting to point out the path to the Place of Life where Ayesha dwells, whom we have lost awhile."

"It may be so," I answered shortly, for the matter was beyond speech or argument, beyond wonder even. But I knew then, as I know now, that we were players in some mighty, predestined drama; that our parts were written and we must speak them, as our path was prepared and we must tread it to the end unknown. Fear and doubt were left behind, hope was sunk in certainty; the fore-shadowing visions of the night had found an actual fulfillment and the pitiful seed of the promise of her who died, growing unseen through all the cruel, empty years, had come to harvest.

No, we feared no more, not even when with the dawn rose the roaring wind, through which we struggled down the mountain slopes, as it would seem in peril of our lives at every step; not even as hour by hour we fought our way onwards through the whirling snow-storm, that made us deaf and blind. For we knew that those lives were charmed. We could not see or hear, yet we were led. Clinging to the yak, we struggled downward and homewards, till at length out of the turmoil and the gloom its instinct brought us unharmed to the door of the monastery, where the old abbot embraced us in his joy, and the monks put up prayers of thanks. For they were sure that we must be dead. Through such a storm, they said, no man had ever lived before.

It was still mid-winter, and oh! the awful weariness of those months of waiting. In our hands was the key, yonder amongst those mountains lay the door, but not yet might we set that key within its lock. For between us and these stretched the great desert, where the snow rolled like billows, and until that snow melted we dared not attempt its passage. So we sat in the monastery, and schooled our hearts to patience.

Still even to these frozen wilds of Central Asia spring comes at last. One evening the air felt warm, and that night there were only a few degrees of frost. The next the clouds banked up, and in the morning not snow was falling from them, but rain, and we found the old monks preparing their instruments of husbandry, as they said that the season of sowing was at hand. For three days it rained, while the snows melted before our eyes. On the fourth torrents of water were rushing down the mountain and the desert was once more brown and bare, though not for long, for within another week it was carpeted with flowers. Then we knew that the time had come to start.

"But whither go you? Whither go you?" asked the old abbot in dismay. "Are you not happy here? Do you not make great strides along the Path, as may be known by your pious conversation? Is not everything that we have your own? Oh! why would you leave us?"

"We are wanderers," we answered, "and when we see mountains in front of us we must cross them."

Kou-en looked at us shrewdly, then asked –

"What do you seek beyond the mountains? And, my brethren, what merit is gathered by hiding the truth from an old man, for such concealments are separated from falsehoods but by the length of a single barleycorn. Tell me, that at least my prayers may accompany you."

"Holy abbot," I said, "awhile ago yonder in the library you made a certain confession to us."

"Oh! remind me not of it," he said, holding up his hands. "Why do you wish to torment me?"

"Far be the thought from us, most kind friend and virtuous man." I answered. "But, as it chances, your story is very much our own, and we think that we have experience of this same priestess."

"Speak on," he said, much interested.

So I told him the outlines of our tale; for an hour or more I told it while, he sat opposite to us swaying his head like a tortoise and saying nothing. At length it was done.

"Now," I added, "let the lamp of your wisdom shine upon our darkness. Do you not find this story wondrous, or do you perchance think that we are liars?"

"Brethren of the great monastery called the World," Kou-en answered with his customary chuckle, "why should I think you liars who, from the moment my eyes fell upon you, knew you to be true men? Moreover, why should I hold this tale so very wondrous? You have but stumbled upon the fringe of a truth with which we have been acquainted for many, many ages.

"Because in a vision she showed you this monastery, and led yon to a spot beyond the mountains where she vanished, you hope that this woman whom you saw die is re-incarnated yonder. Why not? In this there is nothing impossible to those who are instructed in the truth, though the lengthening of her last life was strange and contrary to experience. Doubtless you will find her there as you expect, and doubtless her *khama,* or identity, is the same as that which in some earlier life of hers once brought me to sin.

"Only be not mistaken, she is no immortal; nothing is immortal. She is but a being held back by her own pride, her own greatness if you will, upon the path towards Nirvana. That pride will be humbled, as already it has been humbled; that brow of majesty shall be sprinkled with the dust of change and death, that sinful spirit must be purified by sorrows and by separations. Brother Leo, if you win her, it will be but to lose, and then the ladder must be reclimbed. Brother Holly, for you as for me loss is our only gain, since thereby we are spared much woe. Oh! bide here and pray with me. Why dash yourselves against a rock? Why labour to pour water into a broken jar whence it must sink into the sands of profitless experience, and there be wasted, whilst you remain athirst?"

"Water makes the sand fertile," I answered. "Where water falls life comes, and sorrow is the seed of joy."

"Love is the law of life," broke in Leo; "with out love there is no life. I seek love that I may live. I believe that all these things are ordained to an end which we do not know. Fate draws me on – fulfil my fate – "

"And do but delay your freedom. Yet I will not argue with you, brother, who must follow your own road. See now, what has this woman, this priestess of a false faith if she be so still, brought you in the past? Once in another life, or so I understand your story, you were sworn to a certain nature-goddess, who was named Isis, were you not, and to her alone? Then a woman tempted you, and you fled with her afar. And there what found you? The betrayed and avenging goddess who slew you, or if not the goddess, one who had drunk of her wisdom and was the minister of her vengeance. Having that wisdom this minister – woman or evil spirit – refused to die because she had learned to love you, but waited knowing that in your next life she would find you again, as indeed she would have done more swiftly in Devachan had she died without living on alone in so much misery. And she found you, and she died, or seemed to die, and now she is re-born, as she must be, and doubtless you will meet once more, and again there must come misery. Oh! my friends, go not across the mountains; bide here with me and lament your sins."

"Nay," answered Leo, "we are sworn to a tryst, and we do not break our word."

"Then, brethren, go keep your tryst, and when you have reaped its harvest think upon my sayings for I am sure that the wine you crush from the vintage of your desire will run red like blood, and that in its drinking you shall find neither forgetfulness nor peace. Made blind by a passion of which well I know the sting and power, you seek to add a fair-faced evil to your lives, thinking that from this unity there shall be born all knowledge and great joy.

"Rather should you desire to live alone in holiness until at length your separate lives are merged and lost in the Good Unspeakable, the eternal bliss that lies in the last Nothingness. Ah! you do not believe me now; you shake your heads and smile; yet a day will dawn, it may be after many incarnations, when you shall bow them in the dust and weep, saying to me, 'Brother Kou-en, yours were the words of wisdom, ours the deeds of foolishness;' " and with a deep sigh the old man turned and left us.

"A cheerful faith, truly," said Leo, looking after him, "to dwell through æons in monotonous misery in order that consciousness may be swallowed up at last in some void and formless abstraction called the 'Utter Peace.' I would rather take my share of a bad world and keep my hope of a better. Also I do not think that he knows anything of Ayesha and her destiny."

"So would I," I answered, "though perhaps he is right after all. Who can tell? Moreover, what is the use of reasoning? Leo, we have no choice; we follow our fate. To what that fate may lead us we shall learn in due season."

Then we went to rest, for it was late, though I found little sleep that night. The warnings of the ancient abbot, good and learned man as he was, full also of ripe experience and of the foresighted wisdom that is given to such as he, oppressed me deeply. He promised us sorrow and bloodshed beyond the mountains, ending in death and re-births full of misery. Well, it might be so, but no approaching sufferings could stay our feet. And even if they could, they should not, since to see her face again I was ready to brave them all. And if this was my case what must be that of Leo!"

A strange theory that of Kou-en's, that Ayesha was the goddess in old Egypt to whom Kallikrates was priest, or at the least her representative. That the royal Amenartas, with whom he fled, seduced him from the goddess to whom he was sworn. That this goddess incarnate in Ayesha – or using the woman Ayesha and her passions as her instruments – was avenged upon them both at Kôr, and that there in an after age the bolt she shot fell back upon her own head.

Well, I had often thought as much myself. Only I was sure that *She* herself could be no actual divinity, though she might be a manifestation of one, a priestess, a messenger, charged to work its will, to avenge or to reward, and yet herself a human soul, with hopes and passions to be satisfied, and a destiny to fulfil. In truth, writing now, when all is past and done with, I find much to confirm me in, and little to turn me from that theory, since life and powers of a quality which are more than human do not alone suffice to make a soul divine. On the other hand, however, it must be borne in mind that on one occasion at any rate, Ayesha did undoubtedly suggest that in the beginning she was "a daughter of Heaven," and that there were others, notably the old Shaman Simbri, who seemed to take it for granted that her origin was supernatural. But of all these things I hope to speak in their season.

Meanwhile what lay beyond the mountains? Should we find her there, who held the sceptre and upon earth wielded the power of the outraged Isis, and with her, that other woman who wrought the wrong? And if so, would the dread, inhuman struggle reach its climax around the person of the sinful priest? In a few months, a few days even, we might begin to know.

Thrilled by this thought at length I fell asleep.

CHAPTER 4

THE AVALANCHE

ON THE morning of the second day from that night the sunrise found us already on our path across the desert. There, nearly a mile behind us, we could see the ruined statue of Buddha seated in front of the ancient monastery, and in that clear atmosphere could even distinguish the bent form of our friend, the old abbot, Kou-en, leaning against it until we were quite lost to sight. All the monks had wept when we parted from them, and Kou-en even more bitterly than the rest, for he had learned to love us.

"I am grieved," he said, "much grieved, which indeed I should not 'be, for such emotion partakes of sin. Yet I find comfort, for I know well that although I must soon leave this present life, yet we shall meet again in many future incarnations, and after you have put away these follies, together tread the path to perfect peace. Now take with you my blessings and my prayers and begone, forgetting not that should you live to return" – and he shook his head doubtfully – "here you will be ever welcome."

So we embraced him and went sorrowfully.

It will be remembered that when the mysterious light fell upon us on the peak I had my compass with me and was able roughly to take its bearings. For lack of any better guide we now followed these bearings, travelling almost due northeast, for in that direction had shone the fire. All day in the must beautiful weather we marched across the flower-strewn desert, seeing nothing except bunches of game and one or two herds of wild asses which had come down from the mountains to feed upon the new grass. As evening approached we shot an antelope and made our camp – for we had brought the yak and a tent with us – among some tamarisk scrub, of which the dry stems furnished us with fuel. Nor did we lack for water, since by scraping in the sand soaked with melted snow, we found plenty of fair quality. So that night we supped in luxury upon tea and antelope meat, which indeed we were glad to have, as it spared our little store of dried provisions.

The next morning we ascertained our position as well as we could, and estimated that we had crossed about a quarter of the desert, a guess which proved very accurate, for on the evening of the fourth day of our journey we reached the bottom slopes of the opposing mountains, without having experienced either accident or fatigue. As Leo said, things were "going like clockwork," but I reminded him that a good start often meant a bad finish. Nor was I wrong, for now came our hardships. To begin with, the mountains proved to be exceeding high; it took us two days to climb their lower slopes. Also the heat of the sun had softened the snow, which made walking through it laborious, whilst, accustomed though we were to such conditions through long years of travelling, its continual glitter affected our eyes.

The morning of the seventh day found us in the mouth of a defile which wound away into the heart of the mountains. As it seemed the only possible path, we followed it, and were much cheered to discover that here must once have run a road. Not that we could see any road, indeed, for everything was buried in snow. But that one lay beneath our feet we were certain, since, although we marched along the edge of precipices, our path, however steep, was always flat; moreover, the rock upon one side of it had often been scarped by the hand of man. Of this there could be no doubt, for as the snow did not cling here, we saw the tool marks upon its bare surface.

Also we came to several places where galleries had been built out from the mountain side, by means of beams let into it, as is still a common practice in Thibet. These beams of course had long since rotted away, leaving a gulf between us and the continuation of the path. When we met with such gaps we were forced to go back and make a detour round or over some mountain; but although much delayed thereby, as it happened, we always managed to regain the road, if not without difficulty and danger.

What tried us more – for here our skill and experience as mountaineers could not help us – was the cold at night, obliged as we were to camp in the severe frost at a great altitude, and to endure through the long hours of darkness penetrating and icy winds, which soughed ceaselessly down the pass.

At length on the tenth day we reached the end of the defile, and as night was falling, camped there in the most bitter cold. Those were miserable hours, for now we had no fuel with which to boil water, and must satisfy our thirst by eating frozen snow, while our eyes smarted so sorely that we could not sleep, and notwithstanding all our wraps and the warmth that we gathered from the yak in the little tent, the cold caused our teeth to chatter like castanets.

The dawn came, and, after it, the sunrise. We crept from the tent, and leaving it standing awhile, dragged our stiffened limbs a hundred yards or so to a spot where the defile took a turn, in order that we might thaw in the rays of the sun, which at that hour could not reach us where we had camped.

Leo was round it first, and then I heard him utter an exclamation. In a few seconds I reached his side, and lo! before us lay our Promised Land.

Far beneath us, ten thousand feet at least – for it must be remembered that we viewed it from the top of a mountain – it stretched away and away till its distances met the horizon. In character it was quite flat, an alluvial plain that probably, in some primeval age, had been the bottom of one of the vast lakes of which a number exist in Central Asia, most of them now in process of desiccation. One object only relieved this dreary flatness, a single, snow-clad, and gigantic mountain, of which even at that distance – for it was very far from us – we could clearly see the outline. Indeed we could see more, for from its rounded crest rose a great plume of smoke, showing that it was an active volcano, and on the hither lip of the crater an enormous pillar of rock, whereof the top was formed to the shape of a loop.

Yes, there it stood before us, that symbol of our vision which we had sought these many years, and at the sight of it our hearts beat fast and our breath came quickly. We noted at once that although we had not seen it during our passage of the mountains, since the peaks ahead and the rocky sides of the defile hid it from view, so great was its height that it overtopped the tallest of them. This made it clear to us how it came to be possible that the ray of light passing through the loop could fall upon the highest snows of that towering pinnacle which we had climbed upon the further side of the desert.

Also now we were certain of the cause of that ray, for the smoke behind the loop explained this mystery. Doubtless, at times when the volcano was awake, that smoke must be replaced by flame, emitting light of fearful intensity, and this light it was that reached us, concentrated and directed by the loop.

For the rest we thought that about thirty miles away we could make out a white-roofed town set upon a mound, situated among trees upon the banks of a wide river, which flowed across the plain. Also it was evident that this country had a large population who cultivated the soil, for by the aid of a pair of field glasses, one of our few remaining and most cherished possessions, we could see the green of springing crops pierced by irrigation canals and the lines of trees that marked the limits of the fields.

Yes, there before us stretched the Promised Land, and there rose the mystic Mount, so that all we had to do was to march down the snow slopes and enter it where we would.

Thus we thought in our folly, little guessing what lay before us, what terrors and weary suffering we must endure before we stood at length beneath the shadow of the Symbol of Life.

Our fatigues forgotten, we returned to the tent, hastily swallowed some of our dried food, which we washed down with lumps of snow that gave us toothache and chilled us inside, but which thirst compelled us to eat, dragged the poor yak to its feet, loaded it up, and started.

All this while, so great was our haste and so occupied were each of us with our own thoughts that, if my memory serves me, we scarcely interchanged a word. Down the snow slopes we marched swiftly and without hesitation, for here the road was marked for us by means of pillars of rock set opposite to one another at intervals. These pillars we observed with satisfaction, for they told us that we were still upon a highway which led to the Promised Land.

Yet, as we could not help noting, it was one which seemed to have gone out of use, since with the exception of a few wild-sheep tracks and the spoor of some bears and mountain foxes, not a single sign of beast or man could we discover. This, however, was to be explained, we reflected, by the fact that doubtless the road was only used in the summer season, Or perhaps the inhabitants of the country were now stay-at-home people who never travelled it at all.

Those slopes were longer than we thought; indeed, when darkness dosed in we had not reached the foot of them. So we were obliged to spend another night in the snow, pitching our tent in the shelter of an over-hanging rock. As we had descended many thousand feet, the temperature proved, fortunately, a little milder; indeed, I do not think that there were more than eighteen or twenty degrees of frost that night. Also here and there the heat of the sun had melted the snow in secluded places, so that we were able to find water to drink, while the yak could fill its poor old stomach with dead-looking mountain mosses, which it seemed to think better than nothing.

Again, the still dawn came, throwing its red garment over the lonesome, endless mountains, and we dragged ourselves to our numbed feet, ate some of our remaining food, and started onwards. Now we could no longer see the country beneath, for it and even the towering volcano were hidden from us by an intervening ridge that seemed to be pierced by a single narrow gulley, towards which we headed. Indeed, as the pillars showed us, thither ran the buried road. By mid-day it appeared quite close to us, and we tramped on in feverish haste. As it chanced, however, there was no need to hurry, for an hour later we learned the truth.

Between us and the mouth of the gulley rose, or rather sank, a sheer precipice that was apparently three or four hundred feet in depth, and at its foot we could hear the sound of water.

Right to the edge of this precipice ran the path, for one of the stone pillars stood upon its extreme brink, and yet how could a road descend such a place as that? We stared aghast; then a possible solution occurred to us.

"Don't you see," said Leo, with a hollow laugh, "the gulf has opened since this track was used: volcanic action probably."

"Perhaps, or perhaps there was a wooden bridge or stairway which has rotted. It does not matter. We must find another path, that is all," I answered as cheerfully as I could.

"Yes, and soon," he said, "if we do not wish to stop here for ever."

So we turned to the right and marched along the edge of the precipice till, a mile or so away, we came to a small glacier, of which the surface was sprinkled with large stones frozen into its substance. This glacier hung down the face of the cliff like a petrified waterfall, but whether or no it reached the foot we could not discover. At any rate, to think of attempting its descent seemed out of the question. From this point onwards we could see that the precipice increased in depth and far as the eye could reach was absolutely sheer.

So we went back again and searched to the left of our road. Here the mountains receded, so that above us rose a mighty, dazzling slope of snow and below us lay that same pitiless, unclimbable gulf. As the light began to fade we perceived, half a mile or more in front a bare-topped hillock of rock, which stood on the verge of the precipice, and hurried to it, thinking that from its crest we might be able to discover a way of descent.

When at length we had struggled to the top, it was about a hundred and fifty feet high; what we did discover was that, here also, as beyond the glacier, the gulf was infinitely deeper than at the spot where the road ended, so deep indeed that we could not see its bottom, although from it came the sound of roaring water. Moreover, it was quite half a mile in width.

Whilst we stared round us the sinking sun vanished behind a mountain and, the sky being heavy, the light went out like that of a candle. Now the ascent of this hillock had proved so steep, especially at one place, where we were obliged to climb a sort of rock ladder, that we scarcely cared to attempt to struggle down it again in that gloom. Therefore, remembering that there was little to choose between the top of this knoll and the snow plain at its foot in the matter of temperature or other conveniences, and being quite exhausted, we determined to spend the night upon it, thereby, as we were to learn, saving our lives.

Unloading the yak, we pitched our tent under the lee of the topmost knob of rock and ate a couple of handfuls of dried fish and corn-cake. This was the last of the food that we had brought with us from the Lamasery, and we reflected with dismay that unless we could shoot something, our commissariat was now represented by the carcase of our old friend the yak. Then we wrapped ourselves up in our thick rugs and fur garments and forgot our miseries in sleep.

It cannot have been long before daylight when we were awakened by a sudden and terrific sound like the boom of a great cannon, followed by thousands of other sounds, which might be compared to the fusillade of musketry.

"Great Heaven! What is that?" I said.

We crawled from the tent, but as yet could see nothing, whilst the yak began to low in a terrified manner. But if we could not see we could hear and feel. The booming and cracking had ceased, and was followed by a soft, grinding noise, the most sickening sound, I think, to which I ever listened. This was accompanied by a strange, steady, unnatural wind, which seemed to press upon us as water presses. Then the dawn broke and we saw.

The mountain-side was moving down upon us in a vast avalanche of snow.

Oh! what a sight was that. On from the crest of the precipitous slopes above, two miles and more away, it came, a living thing, rolling, sliding, gliding; piling itself in long, leaping waves, hollowing itself into cavernous valleys, like a tempest-driven sea, whilst above its surf ace hung a powdery cloud of frozen spray.

As we watched, clinging to each other terrified, the first of these waves struck our hill, causing the mighty mass of solid rock to quiver like a yacht beneath the impact of an ocean roller, or an aspen in a sudden rush of wind. It struck and slowly separated, then with a majestic motion flowed like water over the edge of the precipice on either side, and fell with a thudding sound into the unmeasured depths beneath. And this was but a little thing, a mere forerunner, for after it, with a slow, serpentine movement, rolled the body of the avalanche.

It came in combers, it came in level floods. It piled itself against our hill, yes, to within fifty feet of the head of it, till we thought that even that rooted rock must be torn from its foundations and hurled like a pebble to the deeps beneath.

And the turmoil of it all! The screaming of the blast caused by the compression of the air, the dull, continuous thudding of the fall of millions of tons of snow as they rushed through space and ended their journey in the gulf.

Nor was this the worst of it, for as the deep snows above thinned, great boulders that had been buried beneath them, perhaps for centuries, were loosened from their resting-places and began to thunder down the hill. At first they moved slowly, throwing up the hard snow around them as the prow of a ship throws foam. Then gathering momentum, they sprang into the air with leaps such as those of shells ricocheting upon water, till in the end, singing and hurtling, many of them rushed past and even over us to vanish far beyond. Some indeed struck our little mountain with the force of shot fired from the great guns of a battle-ship, and shattered there, or if they fell upon its side, tore away tons of rock and passed with them into the chasm like a meteor surrounded by its satellites. Indeed, no bombardment devised and directed by man could have been half so terrible or, had there been anything to destroy, half so destructive.

The scene was appalling in its unchained and resistless might evolved suddenly from the completest calm. There in the lap of the quiet mountains, looked down upon by the peaceful, tender sky, the powers hidden in the breast of Nature were suddenly set free, and, companioned by whirlwinds and all the terrifying majesty of sound, loosed upon the heads of us two human atoms.

At the first rush of snow we had leapt back behind our protecting peak and, lying at full length upon the ground, gripped it and clung there, fearing lest the wind should whirl us to the abyss. Long ago our tent had gone like a dead leaf in an autumn gale, and at times it seemed as if we must follow.

The boulders hurtled over and past us; one of them fell full upon the little peak, shattering its crest and bursting into fragments, which fled away, each singing its own wild song. We were not touched, but when we looked behind us it was to see the yak, which had risen in its terror, lying dead and headless. Then in our fear we lay still, waiting for the end, and wondering dimly whether we should be buried in the surging snow or swept away with the hill, or crushed by the flying rocks, or lifted and lost in the hurricane.

How long did it last? We never knew. It may have been ten minutes or two hours, for in such a scene time loses its proportions. Only we became aware that the wind had fallen, while the noise of grinding snow and hurtling boulders ceased. Very cautiously we gained our feet and looked.

In front of us the sheer mountain side, for a depth of two miles, by the width of about a thousand yards, which had been covered with many feet of snow, was now bare rock. Piled up against the face of our hill, almost to its summit, lay a tongue of snow, pressed to the consistency of ice and spotted with boulders that had lodged there. The peak itself was torn and shattered, so that it revealed great gleaming surfaces and pits, in which glittered mica, or some other mineral. The vast gulf behind was half filled with the avalanche and its debris. But for the rest, it seemed as though nothing had happened, for the sun shone sweetly overhead and the solemn snows reflected its rays from the sides of a hundred hills. And we had endured it all and were still alive; yes, and unhurt.

But what a position was ours! We dared not attempt to descend the mount, lest we should sink into the loose snow and be buried there. Moreover, all along the breadth of the path of the avalanche boulders from time to time still thundered down the rocky slope, and with them came patches of snow that had been left behind by the big slide, small in themselves it is true, but each of them large enough to kill a hundred men. It was obvious, therefore, that until these conditions changed, or death released us, we must abide where we were upon the crest of the hillock.

So there we sat, foodless and frightened, wondering what our old friend Kou-en would say if he could see us now. By degrees hunger mastered all our other sensations and we began to turn longing eyes upon the headless body of the yak.

"Let's skin him," said Leo, "it will be something to do, and we shall want his hide to-night."

So with affection, and even reverence, we performed this office for the dead companion of our journeyings, rejoicing the while that it was not we who had brought him to his end. Indeed, long residence among peoples who believed fully that the souls of men could pass into, or were risen from, the bodies of animals, had made us a little superstitious on this matter. It would be scarcely pleasant, we reflected, in some future incarnation to find our faithful friend clad in human form and to hear him bitterly reproach us for his murder.

Being dead, however, these arguments aid not apply to eating him, as we were sure he would himself acknowledge. So we cut off little bits of his flesh and, rolling them in snow till they looked as though they were nicely floured, hunger compelling us, swallowed them at a gulp. It was a disgusting meal and we felt like cannibals: but what could we do?

CHAPTER 5

THE GLACIER

EVEN THAT day came to an end at last, and after a few more lumps of yak, our tent being gone, we drew his hide over us and rested as best we could, knowing that at least we had no more avalanches to fear. That night it froze sharply, so that had it not been for the yak's hide and the other rugs and garments, which fortunately we were wearing when the snow-slide began, it would, I think, have gone hard with us. As it was, we suffered a great deal.

"Horace," said Leo at the dawn, "I am going to leave this. If we have to die, I would rather do so moving; but I don't believe that we shall die."

"Very well," I said, "let us start. If the snow won't bear us now, it never will."

So we tied up our rugs and the yak's hide in two bundles and, having cut off some more of the frozen meat, began our descent. Now, although the mount was under two hundred feet high, its base, fortunately for us – for otherwise it must have been swept away by the mighty pressure of the avalanche – was broad, so that there was a long expanse of piled-up snow between us and the level ground.

Since, owing to the overhanging conformation of the place, it was quite impossible for us to descend in front where pressure had made the snow hard as stone, we were obliged to risk a march over the looser material upon its flank. As there was nothing to be gained by waiting, off we went, Leo leading and step by step trying the snow. To our joy we discovered that the sharp night frost had so hardened its surface that it would support us. About half way down, however, where the pressure had been less, it became much softer, so that we were forced to lie upon our faces, which enabled us to distribute our weight over a larger surface, and thus slither gently down the hill.

All went well until we were within twenty paces of the bottom, where we must cross a soft mound formed of the powdery dust thrown off by the avalanche in its rush. Leo slipped over safely, but I, following a yard or two to his right, of a sudden felt the hard crust yield beneath me. An ill-judged but quite natural flounder and wriggle, such as a newly-landed flat-fish gives upon the sand, completed the mischief, and with one piercing but swiftly stifled yell, I vanished.

Any one who has ever sunk in deep water will know that the sensation is not pleasant, but I can assure him that to go through the same experience in soft snow is infinitely worse; mud alone could surpass its terrors. Down I went, and down, till at length I seemed to reach a rock which alone saved me from disappearing for ever. Now I felt the snow closing above me and with it came darkness and a sense of suffocation. So soft was the drift, however, that before I was overcome I contrived with my arms to thrust away the powdery dust from about my head, thus forming a little hollow into which air filtered slowly. Getting my hands upon the stone, I strove to rise, but could not, the weight upon me was too great.

Then I abandoned hope and prepared to die. The process proved not altogether unpleasant. I did not see visions from my past life as drowning men are supposed to do, but – and this shows how strong was her empire over me – my mind flew back to Ayesha. I seemed to behold her and a man all her side, standing over me in some dark, rocky gulf, She was wrapped in a long travelling cloak, and her lovely eyes were wild with fear. I rose to salute her, and make report, but she cried in a fierce, concentrated voice –

"What evil thing has happened here? Thou livest; then where is my lord Leo? Speak, man, and say where thou hast hid my lord – or die."

The vision was extraordinarily real and vivid, I remember, and, considered in connection with a certain subsequent event, in all ways most remarkable, but it passed as swiftly as it came.

Then my senses left me.

I saw light again. I heard a voice, that of Leo! "Horace," he cried, "Horace, hold fast to the Stock of the rifle." Something was thrust against my outstretched hand. I gripped it despairingly, and there came a strain. It was useless, I did not move. Then, bethinking me, I drew up my legs and by chance or the mercy of Heaven, I know not, got my feet against a ridge of the rock on which I was lying. Again I felt the strain, and thrust with all my might. Of a sudden the snow gave, and out of that hole I shot like a fox from its earth.

I struck something. It was Leo straining at the gun, and I knocked him backwards. Then down the steep slope we rolled, landing at length upon the very edge of the precipice. I sat up, drawing in the air with great gasps, and oh! how sweet it was. My eyes fell upon my hand, and I saw that the veins stood out on the back of it, black as ink and large as cords. Clearly I must have been near my end.

"How long was I in there?" I gasped to Leo, who sat at my side, wiping off the sweat that ran from his face in streams.

"Don't know. Nearly twenty minutes, I should think."

"Twenty minutes! It seemed like twenty centuries. How did you get me out? You could not stand upon the drift dust."

"No: I lay upon the yak skin where the snow was harder and tunnelled towards you through the powdery stuff with my hands, for I knew where you had sunk and it was not far off. At last I saw your finger tips; they were so blue that for a few seconds I took them for rock; and thrust the butt of the rifle against them. Luckily you still had life enough to catch hold of it, and you know the rest. Were we not both very strong, it could never have been done."

"Thank you; old fellow," I said simply.

Why should you thank me?" he asked with one of his quick smiles. "Do you suppose that I wished to continue this journey alone? Come, if you have got your breath, let us be getting on. You have been sleeping in a cold bed and want exercise. Look, my rifle is broken and yours is lost in the snow. Well, it will save us the trouble of carrying the cartridges," and he laughed drearily.

Then we began our march, heading for the spot where the road ended four miles or so away, for to go forward seemed useless. In due course we reached it safely. Once a mass of snow as large as a church swept down just in front of us, and once a great boulder loosened from the mountain rushed at us suddenly like an attacking lion, or the stones thrown by Polyphemus at the ship of Odysseus, and, leaping over our heads, vanished with an angry scream into the depths beneath. But we took little heed of these things: our nerves, were deadened, and no danger seemed to affect them.

There was the end of the road, and there were our own footprints and the impress of the yak's hoofs in the snow. The sight of them affected me for it seemed strange that we should have lived to look upon them again. We stared over the edge of the precipice. Yes, it was sheer and absolutely unclimbable.

"Come to the glacier," said Leo.

So we went on to it, and scrambling a little way down its root, made an examination. Here, so far as we could judge, the cliff was about four hundred feet deep. But whether or no the tongue of ice reached to the foot of it we were unable to tell, since about two thirds of the way down it arched inwards, like the end of a bent bow, and the conformation of the overhanging rocks on either side was such that we could not see where it terminated. We climbed back again and sat down, and despair took hold of us, bitter, black despair.

"What are we to do?" I asked. "In front of us death. Behind us death, for how can we re-cross those mountains without food or guns to shoot it with? Here death, for we must sit and starve. We have striven and failed. Leo, our end is at hand. Only a miracle can save us."

"A miracle," he answered. "Well, what was it that led us to the top of the mount so that we were able to escape the avalanche. And what was it which put that rock in your way as you sank into the bed of dust, and gave me wit and strength to dig you out of your grave of snow? And what is it that has preserved us through seventeen years of dangers such as few men have known and lived? Some directing Power. Some Destiny that will accomplish itself in us. Why should the Power cease to guide? Why should the Destiny be baulked at last?"

He paused, then added fiercely, "I tell you Horace, that even if we had guns, food, and yaks, I would not turn back upon our spoor, since to do so would prove me a coward and unworthy of her. I will go on."

"How?" I asked.

"By that road," and he pointed to the glacier.

"It is a road to death!"

"Well, if so, Horace, it would seem that in this land men find life in death, or so they believe. If we die now, we shall die travelling our path, and in the country where we perish we may be born again. At least I am determined, so you must choose."

"I have chosen long ago. Leo, we began this journey together and we will end it together. Perhaps Ayesha knows and will help us," and I laughed drearily. "If not – come, we are wasting time."

Then we took counsel, and the end of it was that we cut a skin rug and the yak's tough hide into strips and knotted these together into two serviceable ropes, which we fastened about our middles, leaving one end loose, for we thought that they might help us in our descent.

Next we bound fragments of another skin rug about our legs and knees to protect them from the chafing of the ice and rocks, and for the same reason put on our thick leather gloves. This done, we took the remainder of our gear and heavy robes and, having placed stones in them, threw them over the brink of the precipice, trusting to find them again, should we ever reach its foot. Now our preparations were complete, and it was time for us to start upon perhaps one of the most desperate journeys ever undertaken by men of their own will.

Yet we stayed a little, looking at each other in a piteous fashion, for we could not speak. Only we embraced, and I confess, I think I wept a little. It all seemed so sad and hopeless, these longings endured through many years, these perpetual, weary travellings, and now – the end. I could not bear to think of that splendid man, my ward, my most dear friend, the companion of my life, who stood before me so full of beauty and of vigour, but who must within a few short minutes be turned into a heap of quivering, mangled flesh. For myself it did not matter. I was old, it was time that I should die. I had lived innocently, if it were innocent to follow this lovely image, this Siren of the caves, who lured us on to doom.

No, I don't think that I thought of myself then, but I thought a great deal of Leo, and when I saw his determined face and flashing eyes as he nerved himself to the last endeavour, I was proud of him. So in broken accents I blessed him and wished him well through all the æons, praying that I might be his companion to the end of time. In few words and short he thanked me and gave me back my blessing. Then he muttered –

"Come."

So side-by-side we began the terrible descent. At first it was easy enough, although a slip would have hurled us to eternity. But we were strong and skilful, accustomed to such places moreover, and made none. About a quarter of the way down we paused, standing upon a great boulder that was embedded in the ice, and, turning round cautiously, leaned our backs against the glacier and looked about us. Truly it was a horrible place, almost sheer, nor did we learn much, for beneath us, a hundred and twenty feet or more, the projecting bend cut off our view of what lay below.

So, feeling that our nerves would not bear a prolonged contemplation of that dizzy gulf, once more we set our faces to the ice and proceeded on the downward climb. Now matters were more difficult, for the stones were fewer and once or twice we must slide to reach them, not knowing if we should ever stop again. But the ropes which we threw over the angles of the rocks, or salient points of ice, letting ourselves down by their help and drawing them after us when we reached the next foothold, saved us from disaster.

Thus at length we came to the bend, which was more than half way down the precipice, being, so far as I could judge, about two hundred and fifty feet from its lip, and say one hundred and fifty from the darksome bottom of the narrow gulf. Here were no stones, but only some rough ice, on which we sat to rest.

"We must look," said Leo presently.

But the question was, how to do this. Indeed, there was only one way, to hang over the bend and discover what lay below. We read each other's thought without the need of words, and I made a motion as though I would start.

"No," said Leo, "I am younger and stronger than you. Come, help me," and he began to fasten the end of his rope to a strong, projecting point of ice. "Now," he said, "hold my ankles."

It seemed an insanity, but there was nothing else to be done, so, fixing my heels in a niche, I grasped them and slowly he slid forward till his body vanished to the middle. What he saw does not matter, for I saw it all afterwards, but what happened was that suddenly all his great weight came upon my arms with such a jerk that his ankles were torn from my grip.

Or, who knows? perhaps in my terror I loosed them, obeying the natural impulse which prompts a man to save his own life. If so, may I be forgiven, but had I held on, I must have been jerked into the abyss. Then the rope ran out and remained taut.

"Leo!" I screamed, "Leo!" and I heard a muffled voice saying, as I thought, "Come." What it really said was – "Don't come." But indeed – and may it go to my credit – I did not pause to think, but face outwards, just as I was sitting, began to slide and scramble down the ice.

In two seconds I had reached the curve, in three I was over it. Beneath was what I can only describe as a great icicle broken off short, and separated from the cliff by about four yards of space. This icicle was not more than fifteen feet in length and sloped outwards, so that my descent was not sheer. Moreover, at the end of it the trickling of water, or some such accident, had worn away the ice, leaving a little ledge as broad, perhaps, as a man's hand. There were roughnesses on the surface below the curve, upon which my clothing caught, also I gripped them desperately with my fingers. Thus it came about that I slid down quite gently and, my heels landing upon the little ledge, remained almost upright, with outstretched arms – like a person crucified to a cross of ice.

Then I saw everything, and the sight curdled the blood within my veins. Hanging to the rope, four or five feet below the broken point, was Leo, out of reach of it, and out of reach of the cliff; as he hung turning slowly round and round, much as – for in a dreadful, inconsequent fashion the absurd similarity struck me even then – a joint turns before the fire. Below yawned the black gulf, and at the bottom of it, far, far beneath, appeared a faint, white sheet of snow. That is what I saw.

Think of it! Think of it! I crucified upon the ice, my heels resting upon a little ledge; my fingers grasping excrescences on which a bird could scarcely have found a foothold; round and below me dizzy space. To climb back whence I came was impossible, to stir even was impossible, since one slip and I must be gone.

And below me, hung like a spider to its cord, Leo turning slowly round and round!

I could see that rope of green hide stretch beneath his weight and the double knots in it slip and tighten, and I remember wondering which would give first, the hide or the knots, or whether it would hold till he dropped from the noose limb by limb.

Oh! I have been in many a perilous place, I who sprang from the Swaying Stone to the point of the Trembling Spur, and missed my aim, but never, never in such a one as this. Agony took hold of me; a cold sweat burst from every pore. I could feel it running down my face like tears; my hair bristled upon my head. And below, in utter silence, Leo turned round and round, and each time he turned his up-cast eyes met mine with a look that was horrible to see.

The silence was the worst of it, the silence and the helplessness. If he had cried out, if he had struggled, it would have been better. But to know that he was alive there, with every nerve and perception at its utmost stretch. Oh! my God! Oh! my God!

My limbs began to ache, and yet I dared not stir a muscle. They ached horribly, or so I thought, and beneath this torture, mental and physical, my mind gave. I remembered things: remembered how, as a child, I had climbed a tree and reached a place whence I could move neither up nor down, and what I suffered then. Remembered how once in Egypt a foolhardy friend of mine had ascended the Second Pyramid alone, and become thus crucified upon its shining cap, where he remained for a whole half hour with four hundred feet of space beneath him. I could see him now stretching his stockinged foot downwards in a vain attempt to reach the next crack, and drawing it back again; could see his tortured face, a white blot upon the red granite.

Then that face vanished and blackness gathered round me, and in the blackness visions of the living, resistless avalanche, of the snow-grave into which I had sunk – oh! years and years ago; of Ayesha demanding Leo's life at my hands. Blackness and silence, through which I could only hear the cracking of my muscles.

Suddenly in the blackness a flash, and in the silence a sound. The flash was the flash of a knife which Leo had drawn. He was hacking at the cord with it fiercely, fiercely, to make an end. And the sound was that of the noise he made, a ghastly noise, half shout of defiance and half yell of terror, as at the third stroke it parted.

I saw it part. The tough hide was half cut through, and its severed portion curled upwards and downwards like the upper and lower lips of an angry dog, whilst that which was unserved stretched out slowly, slowly, till grew quite thin. Then it snapped, so that the rope flew upwards and struck me across the face like the lash of a whip.

Another instant and I heard a crackling, thudding sound. Leo had struck the ground below. Leo was dead a mangled mass of flesh and bone as I had pictured him. I could not bear it. My nerve and human dignity came back. I would not wait until my strength exhausted, I slid from my perch as a wounded bird falls from a tree. No, I would follow him at once, of my own act.

I let my arms fall against my sides, and rejoiced in the relief from pain that the movement gave me. Then balanced upon my heels, I stood upright, took my last look at the sky, muttered my last prayer. For an instant I remained thus poised.

Shouting, "I come," I raised my hands above my head and dived as a bather dives, dived into the black gulf beneath.

CHAPTER 6

IN THE GATE

OH! THAT rush through space! Folk falling thus are supposed to lose consciousness, but I can assert that this is not true. Never were my wits and perceptions more lively than while I travelled from that broken glacier to the ground, and never did a short journey seem to take a longer time. I saw the white floor, like some living thing, leaping up through empty air to meet me, then – *finis!*

Crash! Why, what was this? I still lived. I was in water, for I could feel its chill, and going down, down, till I thought I should never rise again. But rise I did, though my lungs were nigh to bursting first. As I floated up towards the top I remembered the crash, which told me that I had passed through ice. Therefore I should meet ice at the surface again. Oh! to think that after surviving so much I must be drowned like a kitten and beneath a sheet of ice. My hands touched it. There it was above me shining white like glass. Heaven be praised! My head broke through; in this low and sheltered gorge it was but a film no thicker than a penny formed by the light frost of the previous night. So I rose from the deep and stared about me, treading water with my feet.

Then I saw the gladdest sight that ever my eyes beheld, for on the right, not ten yards away, the water running from his hair and beard, was Leo. Leo alive, for he broke the thin ice with his arms as he struggled towards the shore from the deep river.* He saw me also, and his grey eyes seemed to start out of his head.

"Still living, both of us, and the precipice passed!" he shouted in a ringing, exultant voice. "I told you we were led."

"Aye, but whither?" I answered, as I too fought my way through the film of ice.

Then it was I became aware that we were no longer alone, for on the bank of the river, some thirty yards from us, stood two figures, a man leaning upon a long staff and a woman. He was a very old man, for his eyes were horny, his snow-white hair and beard hung upon the bent breast and shoulders, and his sardonic, wrinkled features were yellow as wax. They might have been those of a death mask cut in marble. There, clad in an ample, monkish robe, and leaning upon the staff, he stood still as a statue and watched us. I noted it all, every detail, although at the time I did not know that I was doing so, as we broke our way through the ice towards them and afterwards the picture came back to me. Also I saw that the woman, who was very tall, pointed to us.

Nearer the bank, or rather to the rock edge of the river, its surface was free of ice, for here the stream ran very swiftly. Seeing this, we drew close together and swam on side by side to help each other if need were. There was much need, for in the fringe of the torrent the strength that had served me so long seemed to desert me, and I became helpless; numbed, too, with the biting coldness of the water. Indeed, had not Leo grasped my clothes I think that I should have been swept away by the current to perish. Thus aided I fought on a while, till he said –

"I am going under. Hold to the rope end."

* Usually, as we learned afterwards, the river at this spot was quite shallow; only a foot or two in depth. It was the avalanche that by damming it with fallen heaps of snow had raised its level very many feet. Therefore, to this avalanche, which had threatened to destroy us, we in reality owed our lives, for had the stream stood only at its normal height we must have been dashed to pieces upon the stones. – L.H.H.

So I gripped the strip of yak's hide that was still fast about him, and, his hand thus freed, Leo made a last splendid effort to keep us both, cumbered as we were with the thick, soaked garments that dragged us down like lead, from being sucked beneath the surface. Moreover, he succeeded where any other swimmer of less strength must have failed. Still, I believe that we should have drowned, since here the water ran like a mill-race, had not the man upon the shore, seeing our plight and urged thereto by the woman, run with surprising swiftness in one so aged, to a point of rock that jutted some yards into the stream, past which we were being swept, and seating himself, stretched out his long stick towards us.

With a desperate endeavour, Leo grasped it as we went by, rolling over and over each other, and held on. Round we swung into the eddy, found our feet, were knocked down again, rubbed and pounded on the rocks. But still gripping that staff of salvation, to his end of which the old man clung like a limpet to a stone, while the woman clung to him, we recovered ourselves, and, sheltered somewhat by the rock, floundered towards the shore. Lying on his face – for we were still in great danger – the man extended his arm. We could not reach it; and worse, suddenly the staff was torn from him; we were being swept away.

Then it was that the woman did a noble thing, for springing into the water – yes, up to her armpits – and holding fast to the old man by her left hand, with the right she seized Leo's hair and dragged him shorewards. Now he found his feet for a moment, and throwing one arm about her slender form, steadied himself thus, while with the other he supported me. Next followed a long confused struggle, but the end of it was that three of us, the old man, Leo and I, rolled in a heap upon the bank and lay there gasping.

Presently I looked up. The woman stood over us, water streaming from her garments, staring like one in a dream at Leo's face, smothered as it was with blood running from a deep cut in his head. Even then I noticed how stately and beautiful she was. Now she seemed to awake and, glancing at the robes that clung to her splendid shape, said something to her companion, then turned and ran towards the cliff.

As we lay before him, utterly exhausted, the old man, who had risen, contemplated us solemnly with his dim eyes. He spoke, but we did not understand. Again he tried another language and without success. A third time and our ears were opened, for the tongue he used was Greek; yes, there in Central Asia he addressed us in Greek, not very pure, it is true, but still Greek.

"Are you wizards," he said, "that you have lived to reach this land?"

"Nay." I answered in the same tongue, though in broken words – since of Greek I had thought little for many a year – "for then we should have come otherwise," and I pointed to our hurts and the precipice behind us.

"They know the ancient speech; it is as we were told from the Mountain," he muttered to himself. Then he asked –

"Strangers, what seek you?"

Now I grew cunning and did not answer, fearing lest, should he learn the truth, he would thrust us back into the river. But Leo had no such caution, or rather all reason had left him; he was lightheaded.

"We seek," he stuttered out – his Greek, which had always been feeble, now was simply barbarous and mixed with various Thibetan dialects – "we seek the land of the Fire Mountain that is crowned with the Sign of Life."

The man stared at us. "So you know," he said, then broke off and added, "and *whom* do you seek? "

"Her," answered Leo wildly, "the Queen." I think that he meant to say the priestess, or the goddess, but could only think of the Greek for Queen, or rather something resembling it. Or perhaps it was because the woman who had gone looked like a queen.

"Oh!" said the man, "you seek a queen – then you *are* those for whom we were bidden to watch. Nay, how can I be sure?"

"Is this a time to put questions?" I gasped angrily. "Answer me one rather: who are you?"

"I? Strangers, my title is Guardian of the Gate, and the lady who was with me is the Khania of Kaloon."

At this point Leo began to faint.

"That man is sick," said the Guardian, "and now that you have got your breath again, you must have shelter, both of you, and at once. Come, help me."

So, supporting Leo on either side, we dragged ourselves away from that accursed cliff and Styx-like river up a narrow, winding gorge. Presently it opened out, and there, stretching across the glade, we saw the Gate. Of this all I observed then, for my memory of the details of this scene and of the conversation that passed is very weak and blurred, was that it seemed to be a mighty wall of rock in which a pathway had been hollowed where doubtless once passed the road. On one side of this passage was a stair, which we began to ascend with great difficulty, for Leo was now almost senseless and scarcely moved his legs. Indeed at the head of the first flight he sank down in a heap, nor did our strength suffice to lift him.

While I wondered feebly what was to be done, I heard footsteps, and looking up, saw the woman who had saved him descending the stair, and after her two robed men with a Tartar cast of countenance, very impassive; small eyes and yellowish skin. Even the sight of us did not appear to move them to astonishment. She spoke some words to them, whereon they lifted Leo's heavy frame, apparently with ease, and carried him up the steps.

We followed, and reached a room that seemed to be hewn from the rock above the gateway, where the woman called Khania left us. From it we passed through other rooms, one of them a kind of kitchen, in which a fire burned, till we came to a large chamber, evidently a sleeping place, for in it were wooden bedsteads, mattresses and rugs. Here Leo was laid down, and with the assistance of one of his servants, the old Guardian undressed him, at the same time motioning me to take off my own garments. This I did gladly enough, for the first time during many days though with great pain and difficulty, to find that I was a mass of wounds and bruises.

Presently our host blew upon a whistle, and the other servant appeared bringing hot water in a jar, with which we were washed over. Then the Guardian dressed our hurts with some soothing ointment, and wrapped us round with blankets. After this broth was brought, into which he mixed medicine, and giving me a portion to drink where I lay upon one of the beds, he took Leo's head upon his knee and poured the rest of it down his throat. Instantly a wonderful warmth ran through me, and my aching brain began to swim. Then I remembered no more.

After this we were very, very ill. What may be the exact medical definition of our sickness I do not know, but in effect it was such as follows loss of blood, extreme exhaustion of body, paralysing shock to the nerves and extensive cuts and contusions. These taken together produced a long period of semi-unconsciousness, followed by another period of fever and delirium. All that I can recall of those weeks while we remained the guests of the Guardian of the Gate, may be summed up in one word – dreams, that is until at last I recovered my senses.

The dreams themselves are forgotten, which is perhaps as well, since they were very confused, and for the most part awful; a hotch-potch of nightmares, reflected without doubt from vivid memories of our recent and fearsome sufferings. At times I would wake up from them a little, I suppose when food was administered to me, and receive impressions of whatever was passing in the place. Thus I can recollect that yellow-faced old Guardian standing over me like a ghost in the moonlight, stroking his long beard, his eyes fixed upon my face, as though he would search out the secrets of my soul.

"They are the men," he muttered to himself, "without doubt they are the men," then walked to the window and looked up long and earnestly, like one who studies the stars.

After this I remember a disturbance in the room, and dominating it, as it were, the rich sound of a woman's voice and the rustle of a woman's silks sweeping the stone floor. I opened my eyes and saw that it was she who had helped to rescue us, who *had* rescued us in fact, a tall and noble-looking lady with a beauteous, weary face and liquid eyes which seemed to burn. From the heavy cloak she wore I thought that she must have just returned from a journey.

She stood above me and looked at me, then turned away with a gesture of indifference, if not of disgust, speaking to the Guardian in a low voice. By way of answer he bowed, pointing to the other bed where Leo lay asleep, and thither she passed with slow, imperious movements. I saw her bend down and lift the corner of a wrapping which covered his wounded head, and heard her utter some smothered words before she turned round to the Guardian as though to question him further.

But he had gone, and being alone, for she thought me senseless, she drew a rough stool to the side of the bed, and seating herself studied Leo, who lay thereon, with an earnestness that was almost terrible, for her soul seemed to be concentrated in her eyes, and to find expression through them. Long she gazed thus, then rose and began to walk swiftly up and down the chamber, pressing her hands now to her bosom and now to her brow, a certain passionate perplexity stamped upon her face, as though she struggled to remember something and could not.

"Where and when?" she whispered. "Oh! where and when?"

Of the end of that scene I know nothing, for although I fought hard against it, oblivion mastered me. After this I became aware that the regal-looking woman called Khania, was always in the room, and that she seemed to be nursing Leo with great care and tenderness. Sometimes even she nursed me when Leo did not need attention, and she had nothing else to do, or so her manner seemed to suggest. It was as though I excited her curiosity, and she wished me to recover that it might be satisfied.

Again I awoke, how long afterwards I cannot say. It was night, and the room was lighted by the moon only, now shining in a clear sky. Its steady rays entering at the window-place fell on Leo's bed, and by them I saw that the dark, imperial woman was watching at his side. Some sense of her presence must have communicated itself to him, for he began to mutter in his sleep, now in English, now in Arabic. She became intensely interested; as her every movement showed. Then rising suddenly she glided across the room on tiptoe to look at me. Seeing her coming I feigned to be asleep, and so well that she was deceived.

For I was also interested. Who was this lady whom the Guardian had called the Khania of Kaloon? Could it be she whom we sought? Why not? And yet if I saw Ayesha, surely I should know her, surely there would be no room for doubt.

Back she went again to the bed, kneeling down beside Leo, and in the intense silence which followed – for he had ceased his mutterings – I thought that I could hear the beating of her heart. Now she began to speak, very low and in that same bastard Greek tongue, mixed here and there with Mongolian words such as are common to the dialects of Central Asia. I could not hear or understand all she said, but some sentences I did understand, and they frightened me not a little.

"Man of my dreams,' she murmured, "whence come you? Who are you? Why did the Hesea bid me to meet you?" Then some sentences I could not catch. "You sleep; in sleep the eyes are opened. Answer, I bid you; say what is the bond between you and me? Why have I dreamt of you? Why do I know you? Why –?" and the sweet, rich voice died slowly from a whisper into silence, as though she were ashamed to utter what was on her tongue.

As she bent over him a lock of her hair broke loose from its jewelled fillet and fell across his face. At its touch Leo seemed to wake, for he lifted his gaunt, white hand and touched the hair, then said in English –

"Where am I? Oh! I remember; "and their eyes met as he strove to lift himself and could not. Then he spoke again in his broken, stumbling Greek, "You are the lady who saved me from the water. Say, are you also that queen whom I have sought so long and endured so much to find?"

"I know not," she answered in a voice as sweet as honey, a low, trembling voice; "but true it is I am a queen – if a Khania be a queen."

"Say then. Queen, do you remember me?"

"We have met in dreams," she answered, "I think that we have met in a past that is far away. Yes; I knew it when first I saw you there by the river. Stranger with the well-remembered face, tell me, I pray you, how you are named?"

"Leo Vincey."

She shook her head, whispering –

"I know not the name, yet you I know."

"You know me! How do you know me?" he said heavily, and seemed to sink again into slumber or swoon.

She watched him for awhile very intently. Then as though some force that she could not resist drew her, I saw her bend down her head over his sleeping face. Yes; and I saw her kiss him swiftly on the lips, then spring back crimson to the hair, as though overwhelmed with shame at this victory of her mad passion.

Now it was that she discovered me.

Bewildered, fascinated, amazed, I had raised myself upon my bed, not knowing it; I suppose that I might see and hear the better. It was wrong, doubtless, but no common curiosity over-mastered me, who had my share in all this story. More, it was foolish, but illness and wonder had killed my reason.

Yes, she saw me watching them, and such fury seemed to take hold of her that I thought my hour had come.

"Man, have you dared – ?" she said in an intense whisper, and snatching at her girdle. Now in her hand shone a knife, and I knew that it was destined for my heart. Then in this sore danger my wit came back to me, and as she advanced I stretched out my shaking hand, saying –

"Oh! of your pity, give me to drink. The fever burns me, it burns," and I looked round like one bewildered who sees not, repeating, "Give me drink, you who are called Guardian," and I fell back exhausted.

She stopped like a hawk in its stoop, and swiftly sheathed the dagger. Then taking a bowl of milk that stood on a table near her, she held it to my lips, searching my face the while with her flaming eyes, for indeed passion, rage, and fear had lit them till they seemed to flame. I drank the milk in great gulps, though never in my life did I find it more hard to swallow.

"You tremble," she said; "have dreams haunted you?"

"Aye, friend," I answered, "dreams of that fearsome precipice and of the last leap."

"Aught else?" she asked.

"Nay; is it not enough? Oh! what a journey to have taken to befriend a queen."

"To befriend a queen," she repeated puzzled. "What means the man? You swear you have had no other dreams?"

"Aye, I swear by the Symbol of Life and the Mount of the Wavering Flame, and by yourself, O Queen from the ancient days."

Then I sighed and pretended to swoon, for I could think of nothing else to do. As I closed my eyes I saw her face that had been red as dawn turn pale as eve, for my words and all which might lie behind them, had gone home. Moreover, she was in doubt, for I could hear her fingering the handle of the dagger. Then she spoke aloud, words for my ears if they still were open.

"I am glad," she said, "that he dreamed no other dreams, since had he done so and babbled of them it would have been ill-omened, and I do not wish that one who has travelled far to visit us should be hurled to the death-dogs for burial; one, moreover, who although old and hideous, still has the air of a wise and silent man."

Now while I shivered at these unpleasant hints – though what the "death-dogs" in which people were buried might be, I could not conceive – to my intense joy I heard the foot of the Guardian on the stair, heard him too enter the room and saw him bow before the lady.

"How go these sick men, niece?"* he said in his cold voice.

"They swoon, both of them," she answered.

"Indeed, is it so? I thought otherwise. I thought they woke."

"What have you heard, Shaman (i.e. wizard)?" she asked angrily.

"I? Oh! I heard the grating of a dagger in its sheath and the distant baying of the death-hounds."

"And what have you seen, Shaman?" she asked again, "looking through the Gate you guard?"

"Strange sights, Khania, my niece. But – men awake from swoons."

"Aye," she answered, "so while this one sleeps, bear him to another chamber, for he needs change, and the lord yonder needs more space and untainted air."

The Guardian, whom she called "Shaman" or Magician, held a lamp in his hand, and by its light it was easy to see his face, which I watched out of the corner of my eye. I thought that it wore a very strange expression, one moreover that alarmed me somewhat, From the beginning I had misdoubted me of this old man, whose cast of countenance was vindictive as it was able; now I was afraid of him.

"To which chamber, Khania?" he said with meaning.

* I found later that the Khania, Atene, was not Simbri's niece but his great-niece, on the mother's side. – L. H. H.

"I think," she answered slowly, "to one that is healthful, where he will recover. The man has wisdom, she added as though in explanation, "moreover, having the word from the Mountain, to harm him would be dangerous. But why do you ask?"

He shrugged his shoulders.

"I tell you I heard the death-hounds bay, that is all. Yes, with you I think that he has wisdom, and the bee which seeks honey should suck the flower – before it fades! Also, as you say, there are commands with which it is ill to trifle, even if we cannot guess their meaning."

Then going to the door he blew upon his whistle, and instantly I heard the feet of his servants upon the stairs. He gave them an order, and gently enough they lifted the mattress on which I lay and followed him down sundry passages and past some had into, another chamber shaped like that we had left, but not so large, where they placed me upon a bed.

The Guardian watched me awhile to see that I did not wake, Next he stretched out his hand and felt my heart and pulse; an examination the results of which seemed to puzzle him, for he uttered a little exclamation and shook his head. After this he left the room, and I heard him bolt the door behind him. Then, being still very weak, I fell asleep in earnest.

When I awoke it was broad daylight. My mind was clear and I felt better than I had done for many a day, signs by which I knew that the fever had left me and that I was on the high road to recovery. Now I remembered all the events of the previous night and was able to weigh them carefully. This, to be sure, I did for many reasons, among them that I knew I had been and still was, in great danger.

I had seen and heard too much, and this woman called Khania guessed that I had seen and heard. Indeed, had it not been for my hints about the Symbol of Life and the Mount of Flame, after I had disarmed her first rage by my artifice, I felt sure that she would have ordered the old Guardian or Shaman to do me to death in this way or the other; sure also that he would not have hesitated to obey her. I had been spared partly because, for some unknown reason, she was afraid to kill me, and partly that she might learn how much I knew, although the "death-hounds had bayed," whatever that might mean. Well, up to the present I was safe, and for the rest I must take my chance. Moreover it was necessary to be cautious, and, if need were, to feign ignorance. So, dismissing the matter of my own fate from my mind, I fell to considering the scene which I had witnessed and what might be its purport.

Was our quest at an end? Was this woman Ayesha? Leo had so dreamed, but be was still delirious, therefore here was little on which to lean. What seemed more to the point was that the herself evidently appeared to think that there existed some tie between her and this sick man. Why had she embraced him? I was sure that she could be no wanton, nor indeed would any woman indulge for its own sake in such folly with a stranger who hung between life and death. What she had done was done because irresistible impulse, born of knowledge, or at least of memories, drove her on, though mayhap the knowledge was imperfect and the memories were undefined. Who save Ayesha could have known anything of Leo in the past? None who lived upon the earth to-day.

And yet, why not; if what Kou-en the abbot and tens of millions of his fellow-worshippers believed were true? If the souls of human beings were in fact strictly limited in number and became the tenants of an endless succession of physical bodies which they change from time to time as we change our worn-out garments, why should not others have known him? For instance that daughter of the Pharaohs who "caused him through love to break the vows that he had vowed" knew a certain Kallikrates, a priest of "Isis whom the gods cherish and the demons obey"; even Amenartas, the mistress of magic.

Oh! now a light seemed to break upon me, a wonderful light. What if Amenartas and this Khania, this woman with royalty stamped on every feature, should be the same? Would not that "magic of my own people that I have" of which she wrote upon the Sherd, enable her to pierce the darkness of the Past and recognize the priest whom she had bewitched to love her, snatching him out of the very hand of the goddess? What if it were not Ayesha, but Amenartas re-incarnate who ruled this hidden land and once more sought to make the man she loved break through his vows? If so, knowing the evil that must come, I shook even at its shadow. The truth must be learned, but how?

Whilst I wondered the door opened, and the sardonic, inscrutable-old-faced man, whom this Khania had called Magician, and who called the Khania niece, entered and stood before me.

CHAPTER 7

THE FIRST ORDEAL

THE SHAMAN advanced to my side and asked me courteously how I fared.

I answered, "Better. Far better, oh, my host – but how are you named?"

"Simbri," he answered, "and, as I told you by the water, my title is Hereditary Guardian of the Gate. By profession I am the royal Physician in this land."

"Did you say physician or magician?" I asked carelessly, as though I had not caught the word. He gave me a curious look.

"I *said* physician, and it is well for you and your companion that I have some skill in my art. Otherwise I think, perhaps, you would not have been alive to-day, O my guest – but how are *you* named?"

"Holly," I said.

"O my guest, Holly."

"Had it not been for the foresight that brought you and the lady Khania to the edge of yonder darksome river, certainly we should *not* have been alive, venerable Simbri, a foresight that seems to me to savour of magic in such a lonely place. That is why I thought you might have described yourself as a magician, though it is true that you may have been but fishing in those waters."

"Certainly I was fishing, stranger Holly – or men, and I caught two."

"Fishing by chance, host Simbri?"

"Nay, by design, guest Holly. My trade of physician includes the study of future events, for I am the chief of the Shamans or Seers of this land, and, having been warned of your coming quite recently, I awaited your arrival."

"Indeed, that is strange, most courteous also. So here physician and magician mean the same."

"You say it," he answered with a grave bow; "but tell me, if you will, how did you find your way to a land whither visitors do not wander?"

"Oh!" I answered, "perhaps we are but travellers, or perhaps we also have studied – medicine."

"I think that you must have studied it deeply, since otherwise you would not have lived to cross those mountains in search of – now, what did you seek? Your companion, I think, spoke of a queen – yonder, on the banks of the torrent."

"Did he? Did he, indeed? Well, that is strange since he seems to have found one, for surely that royal-looking lady, named Khania, who sprang into the stream and saved us, must be a queen."

"A queen she is, and a great one, for in our land Khania means queen, though how, friend Holly, a man who has lain senseless can have learned this, I do not know. Nor do I know how you come to speak our language."

"That is simple, for the tongue you talk is very ancient, and as it chances in my own country it has been my lot to study and to teach it. It is Greek, but although it is still spoken in the world, how it reached these mountains I cannot say."

"I will tell you," he answered. "Many generations ago a great conqueror born of the nation that spoke this tongue fought his way through the country to the south of us. He was driven back, but a general of his of another race advanced and crossed the mountains, and overcame the people of this land, bringing with him his master's language and his own worship. Here he established his dynasty, and here it remains, for being ringed in with deserts and with pathless mountain snows, we hold no converse with the outer world."

"Yes, I know something of that story; the conqueror was named Alexander, was he not?" I asked.

"He was so named, and the name of the general was Rassen, a native of a country called Egypt, or so our records tell us. His descendants hold the throne to this day, and the Khania is of his blood."

"Was the goddess whom he worshipped called Isis?"

"Nay," he answered, "she was called Hes."

"Which," I interrupted, "is but another title for Isis. Tell me, is her worship continued here? I ask because it is now dead in Egypt, which was its home."

"There is a temple on the Mountain yonder," he replied indifferently, "and in it are priests and priestesses who practise some ancient cult. But the real god of this people now, as long before the day of Rassen their conqueror, is the fire that dwells in this same Mountain, which from time to time breaks out and slays them."

"And does a goddess dwell in the fire?" I asked.

Again he searched my face with his cold eyes, then answered –

"Stranger Holly, I know nothing of any goddess. That Mountain is sacred, and to seek to learn its secrets is to die. Why do you ask such questions?"

"Only because I am curious in the matter of old religions, and seeing the symbol of Life upon yonder peak, came hither to study yours, of which indeed a tradition still remains among the learned."

"Then abandon that study, friend Holly, for the road to it runs through the jaws of the death-hounds, and the spears of savages. Nor indeed is there anything to learn."

"And what, Physician, are the death-hounds?"

"Certain dogs to which, according to our ancient custom, all offenders against the law or the will of the Khan, are cast to be torn to pieces."

"The will of the Khan! Has this Khania of yours a husband then?"

"Aye," he answered, "her cousin, who was the ruler of half the land. Now they and the land are one. But you have talked enough; I am here to say that your food is ready," and he turned to leave the room.

"One more question, friend Simbri. How came I to this chamber, and where is my companion?"

"You were borne hither in your sleep, and see, the change has bettered you. Do you remember nothing?"

"Nothing, nothing at all," I answered earnestly. "But what of my friend?"

"He also is better. The Khania Atene nurses him."

"Atene?" I said. "That is an old Egyptian name. It means the Disk of the Sun, and a woman who bore it thousands of years ago was famous for her beauty."

"Well, and is not my niece Atene beautiful?"

"How can I tell, O uncle of the Khania," I answered wearily, "who have scarcely seen her?"

Then he departed, and presently his yellow-faced, silent servants brought me my food.

Later in the morning the door opened again, and through it, unattended, came the Khania Atene, who shut and bolted it behind her. This action did not reassure me, still, rising in my bed, I saluted her as best I could, although at heart I was afraid. She seemed to read my doubts for she said –

"Lie down, and have no fear. At present you will come by no harm from me. Now, tell me what is the man called Leo to you? Your son? Nay it cannot be, since – forgive me – light is not born of darkness."

"I have always thought that it was so born, Khania. Yet you are right; he is but my adopted son, and a man whom I love."

"Say, what seek you here?" she asked.

"We seek, Khania, whatsoever Fate shall bring us on yonder Mountain, that which is crowned with flame."

Her face paled at the words, but she answered in a steady voice –

"Then there you will find nothing but doom, if indeed you do not find it before you reach its slopes, which are guarded by savage men. Yonder is the College of Hes, and to violate its Sanctuary is death to any man, death in the ever-burning fire."

And who rules this college, Khania – a priestess?"

"Yes, a priestess, whose face I have never seen, for she is so old that she veils herself from curious eyes."

"Ah! she veils herself, does she?" I answered, as the blood went thrilling through my veins, I who remembered another who also was so old that she veiled herself from curious eyes. "Well, veiled or unveiled, we would visit her, trusting to find that we are welcome."

"That you shall not do," she said, "for it is unlawful, and I will not have your blood upon my hands."

"Which is the stronger," I asked of her, "you, Khania, or this priestess of the Mountain?"

"I am the stronger, Holly, for so you are named, are you not? Look you, at my need I can summon sixty thousand men in war, while she has naught but her priests and the fierce, untrained tribes."

"The sword is not the only power in the world," I answered. "Tell me, now, does this priestess ever visit the country of Kaloon?"

"Never, never, for by the ancient pact, made after the last great struggle long centuries ago between the College and the people of the Plain, it was decreed and sworn to that should she set her foot across the river, this means war to the end between us, and rule for the victor over both. Likewise, save when unguarded they bear their dead to burial, or for some such high purpose, no Khan or Khania of Kaloon ascends the Mountain."

"Which then is the true master – the Khan of Kaloon or the head of the College of Hes?" I asked again.

"In matters spiritual, the priestess of Hes, who is our Oracle and the voice of Heaven. In matters temporal, the Khan of Kaloon."

"The Khan. Ah! you are married, lady, are you not? "

"Aye," she answered, her face flushing. "And I will tell you what you soon must learn, if you have not learned it already, I am the wife of a madman, and he is – hateful to me."

"I *have* learned the last already, Khania."

She looked at me with her piercing eyes.

"What! Did my uncle, the Shaman, he who is called Guardian, tell you? Nay, you saw, as I knew you saw, and it would have been best to slay you for, oh! what must you think of me?"

I made no answer, for in truth I did not know what to think, also I feared lest further rash admissions should be followed by swift vengeance.

"You must believe," she went on, "that I, who have ever hated men, that I – I swear that it is true – whose lips are purer than those mountain snows, I, the Khania of Kaloon, whom they name Heart-of-Ice, am but a shameless thing." And, covering her face with her hand, she moaned in the bitterness of her distress.

"Nay," I said, "there may be reasons, explanations, if it pleases you to give them."

"Wanderer, there are such reasons; and since you know so much, you shall learn them also. Like that husband of mine, I have become mad. When first I saw the face of your companion, as I dragged him from the river, madness entered me, and I – I – "

"Loved him," I suggested. "Well, such things have happened before to people who were not mad."

"Oh!" she went on, "it was more than love; I was possessed, and that night I knew not what I did. A Power drove me on; a Destiny compelled me, and to the end I am his, and his alone. Yes, I am his, and I swear that he shall be mine" and with this wild declaration, dangerous enough under the conditions, she turned and fled the room.

She was gone, and after the struggle, for such it was, I sank back exhausted. How came it that this sudden passion had mastered her? Who and what was this Khania, I wondered again, and – this was more to the point, who and what would Leo believe her to be? If only I could be with him before he said words or did deeds impossible to recall.

* * * * *

Three days went by, during which time I saw no more of the Khania, who, or so I was informed by Simbri, the Shaman, had returned to her city to make ready for us, her guests. I begged him to allow me to rejoin Leo, but he answered politely, though with much firmness, that my foster-son did better without me. Now, I grew suspicious, fearing lest some harm had come to Leo, though how to discover the truth I knew not. In my anxiety I tried to convey a note to him, written upon a leaf of a water-stained pocket-book, but the yellow-faced servant, refused to touch it, and Simbri said drily that he would have naught to do with writings which he could not read. At length, on the third night I made up my mind that whatever the risk, with leave or without it, I would try to find him.

By this time I could walk well, and indeed was almost strong again. So about midnight, when the moon was up, for I had no other light, I crept from my bed, threw on my garments, and taking a knife, which was the only weapon I possessed, opened the door of my room and started.

Now, when I was carried from the rock-chamber where Leo and I had been together, I took note of the way. First, reckoning from my sleeping-place, there was a passage thirty paces long, for I had counted the footfalls of my bearers. Then came a turn to the left, and ten more paces of passage, and lastly near certain steps running to some place unknown, another sharp turn to the right which led to our old chamber.

Down the long passage I walked stealthily, and although it was pitch dark, found the turn to the left, and followed it till I came to the second sharp turn to the right, that of the gallery from which rose the stairs. I crept round it only to retreat hastily enough, as well I might, for at the door of Leo's room, which she was in the act of locking on the outside, as I could see by the light of the lamp that she held in her hand, stood the Khania herself.

My first thought was to fly back to my own chamber, but I abandoned it, feeling sure that I should be seen. Therefore I determined, if she discovered me, to face the matter out and say that I was trying to find Leo and to learn how he fared. So I crouched against the wall, and waited with a beating heart. I heard her sweep down the passage, and – yes – begin to mount the stair.

Now, what should I do? To try to reach Leo was useless, for she had locked the door with the key she held. Go back to bed? No, I would follow her, and if we met would make the same excuse. Thus I might get some tidings, or perhaps – a dagger thrust.

So round the corner and up the steps I went, noiselessly as a snake. They were many and winding, like those of a church tower, but at length I came to the head of them, where was a little landing, and opening from it a door. It was a very ancient door; the light streamed through cracks where its panels had rotted, and from the room beyond came the sound of voices, those of the Shaman Simbri and the Khania.

"Have you learned aught, my niece?" I heard him say, and also heard her answer –

"A little. A very little."

Then in my thirst for knowledge I grew bold, and stealing to the door, looked through one of the cracks in its wood. Opposite to me, in the full flood of light thrown by a hanging lamp, her hand resting on a table at which Simbri was seated, stood the Khania. Truly she was a beauteous sight, for she wore robes of royal purple, and on her brow a little coronet of gold, beneath which her curling hair streamed down her shapely neck and bosom. Seeing her I guessed at once that she had arrayed herself thus for some secret end, enhancing her loveliness by every art and grace that is known to woman. Simbri was looking at her earnestly, with fear and doubt written on even his cold, impassive features.

"What passed between you, then?" he asked, peering at her.

"I questioned him closely as to the reason of his coming to this land, and wrung from him the answer that it was to seek some beauteous woman – he would say no more. I asked him if she were more beauteous than I am, and he replied with courtesy – nothing else, I think – that it would be hard to say, but that she had been different. Then I said that though it behoved me not to speak of such a matter, there was no lady in Kaloon whom men held to be so fair as I; moreover, that I was its ruler, and that I and no other had saved him from the water. Aye, and I added that my heart told me I was the woman whom he sought."

"Have done, niece," said Simbri impatiently, "I would not hear of the arts you used – well enough, doubtless. What then?"

"Then he said that it might be so, since he thought that this woman was born again, and studied me a while, asking me if I had ever 'passed through fire.' To this I replied that the only fires I had passed were those of the spirit, and that I dwelt in them now. He said, 'Show me your hair,' and I placed a lock of it in his hand. Presently he let it fall and from that satchel which he wears about his neck drew out another tress of hair – oh! Simbri, my uncle, the loveliest hair that ever eyes beheld, for it was soft as silk, and reached from my coronet to the ground. Moreover, no raven's wing in the sunshine ever shone as did that fragrant tress.

" 'Yours is beautiful,' he said, 'but see, they are not the same.'

" 'Mayhap,' I answered, 'since no woman ever wore such locks.'

" 'You are right,' he replied, 'for she whom I seek was more than a woman.'

"And then – and then – though I tried him in many ways he would say no more, so, feeling hate against this Unknown rising in my heart, and fearing lest I should utter words that were best unsaid, I left him. Now I bid you, search the books which are open to your wisdom and tell me of this woman whom he seeks, who she is, and where she dwells. Oh! search them swiftly, that I will find her and – kill her if I can."

"Aye, if you can," answered the Shaman, "and if she lives to kill. But say, where shall we begin our quest? Now, this letter from the Mountain that the head-priest Oros sent to your court a while ago?" – and he selected a parchment from a pile which lay upon the table and looked at her.

"Read," she said, "I would hear it again."

So he read:

> "From the Hesea of the House of Fire, to Atene, Khania of Kaloon.
>
> MY SISTER – Warning has reached me that two strangers of a western race journey to your land, seeking my Oracle, of which they would ask a question. On the first day of the next moon, I command that you

and with you Simbri, your great-uncle, the wise Shaman, Guardian of the Gate, shall be watching the river in the gulf at the foot of the ancient road, for by that steep path the strangers travel. Aid them in all things and bring them safely to the Mountain, knowing that in this matter I shall hold him and you to account. Myself I will not meet them, since to do so would be to break the pact between our powers, which says that the Hesea of the Sanctuary visits not the territory of Kaloon, save in war. Also their coming is otherwise appointed."

"It would seem," said Simbri, laying down the parchment, "that these are no chance wanderers, since Hes awaits them."

"Aye, they are no chance wanderers, since my heart awaited one of them also. Yet the Hesea cannot be that woman, for reasons which are known to you."

"There are many women on the Mountain," suggested the Shaman in a dry voice, "if indeed any woman has to do with this matter."

"I at least have to do with it, and he shall not go to the Mountain."

"Hes is powerful, my niece, and beneath these smooth words of hers lies a dreadful threat. I say that she is mighty from of old and has servants in the earth and air who warned her of the coming of these men, and will warn her of what befalls them. I know it, who hate her, and to your royal house of Rassen it has been known for many a generation. Therefore thwart her not lest ill befall us all, for she is a spirit and terrible. She says that it is appointed that they shall go – "

"And I say it is appointed that he shall not go. Let the other go if he desires."

"Atene, be plain, what will you with the man called Leo – that he should become your lover?" asked the Shaman.

She stared him straight in the eyes, and answered boldly –

"Nay, I will that he should become my husband."

"First he must will it too, who seems to have no mind that way. Also, how can a woman have two husbands?"

She laid her hand upon his shoulder and said –

"I have no husband. You know it well, Simbri. I charge you by the close bond of blood between us, brew me another draught — "

"That we may be bound yet closer in a bond of murder! Nay, Atene, I will not; already your sin lies heavy on my head. You are very fair; take the man in your own net, if yon may, or let him be, which is better far."

"I cannot let him be. Would that I were able. I must love him as I must hate the other whom he loves, yet some power hardens his heart against me. Oh! great Shaman, you that peep and mutter, you who can read the future and the past, tell me what you have learned from your stars and divinations."

"Already I have sought through many a secret, toilsome hour and learned this, Atene," he answered. "You are right, the fate of yonder man is intertwined with yours, but between you and him there rises a mighty wall that my vision cannot pierce nor my familiars climb. Yet I am taught that in death you and he – aye, and I also, shall be very near together."

"Then come death," she exclaimed with sullen pride, "for thence at least I'll pluck out my desire."

"Be not so sure," he answered, "for I think that the Power follows us even down this dark gulf of death. I think also that I feel the sleepless eyes of Hes watching our secret souls."

"Then blind them with the dust of illusions – as you can. To-morrow, also, saying nothing of their sex, send a messenger to the Mountain and tell the Hesea that two old strangers have arrived – mark you, *old* – but that they are very sick, that their limbs were broken in the river, and that when they have healed again, I will send them to ask the question of her Oracle – that is, some three moons hence. Perchance she may believe you, and be content to wait; or if she does not, at least no more words. I must sleep or my brain will burst. Give me that medicine which brings dreamless rest, for never did I need it more, who also feel eyes upon me," and she glanced towards the door.

Then I left, and not too soon, for as I crept down the darksome passage, I heard it open behind me.

CHAPTER 8

THE DEATH-HOUNDS

IT MAY have been ten o'clock on the following morning, or a little past it, when the Shaman Simbri came into my room and asked me how I had slept.

"Like a log," I answered, "like a log. A drugged man could not have rested more soundly."

"Indeed, friend Holly, and yet you look fatigued."

"My dreams troubled me somewhat," I answered. "I suffer from such things. But surely by your face, friend Simbri, you cannot have slept at all, for never yet have I seen you with so weary an air."

"I am weary," he said, with a sigh. "Last night I spent upon my business – watching at the Gates."

"What gates?" I asked. "Those by which we entered this kingdom, for, if so, I would rather watch than travel them."

"The Gates of the Past and of the Future. Yes, those by which you entered, if you will; for did you not travel out of a wondrous Past towards a Future that you cannot guess?"

"But both of which interest you," I suggested.

"Perhaps," he answered, then added, "I come to tell you that within an hour you are to start for the city, whither the Khania has but now gone on to make ready for you."

"Yes; only you told me that she had gone some days ago. Well, I am sound again and prepared to march, but say, how is my foster-son?"

"He mends, he mends. But you shall see him for yourself. It is the Khania's will. Here come the slaves bearing your robes, and with them. I leave you."

So with their assistance I dressed myself, first in good, clean under-linen, then in wide woollen trousers and vest, and lastly in a fur-lined camel hair robe dyed black that was very comfortable to wear, and in appearance not unlike a long overcoat. A flat cap of the same material and a pair of boots made of untanned hide completed my attire.

Scarcely was I ready when the yellow-faced servants, with many bows, took me by the hand and led me down the passages and stairs of the Gatehouse to its door. Here, to my great joy, I found Leo, looking pale and troubled, but otherwise as well as I could expect after his sickness. He was attired like myself, save that his garments were of a finer quality, and the overcoat was white, with a hood to it, added, I suppose, to protect the wound in his head from cold and the sun. This white dress I thought became him very well, also about it there was nothing grotesque or even remarkable. He sprang to me and seized my hand, asking how I fared and where I had been hidden away, a greeting of which, as I could see, the warmth was not lost upon Simbri, who stood by.

I answered, well enough now that we were together again, and for the rest I would tell him later.

Then they brought us palanquins, carried, each of them, by two ponies, one of which was harnessed ahead and the other behind between long shaft-like poles. In these we seated ourselves, and at a sign from Simbri slaves took the leading ponies by the bridle and we started, leaving behind us that grim old Gate-house through which we were the first strangers to pass for many a generation.

For a mile or more our road ran down a winding, rocky gorge, till suddenly it took a turn, and the country of Kaloon lay stretched before us. At our feet was a river, probably the same with which we had made acquaintance in the gulf, where, fed by the mountain snows, it had its source. Here it flowed rapidly, but on the vast, alluvial lands beneath became a broad and gentle stream that wound its way through the limitless plains till it was lost in the blue of the distance.

To the north, however, this smooth, monotonous expanse was broken by that Mountain which had guided us from afar, the House of Fire. It was a great distance from us, more than a hundred miles, I should say, yet even so a most majestic sight in that clear air. Many leagues from the base of its peak the ground began to rise in brown and rugged hillocks, from which sprang the holy Mountain itself, a white and dazzling point that soared full twenty thousand feet into the heavens.

Yes, and there upon the nether lip of its crater stood the gigantic pillar, surmounted by a yet more gigantic loop of virgin rock, whereof the blackness stood out grimly against the blue of the sky beyond and the blinding snow beneath.

We gazed at it with awe, as well we might, this beacon of our hopes that for aught we knew might also prove their monument, feeling even then that yonder our fate would declare itself. I noted further that all those with us did it reverence by bowing their heads as they caught sight of the peak, and by laying the first finger of the right hand across the first finger of the left, a gesture, as we afterwards discovered, designed to avert its evil influence. Yes, even Simbri bowed, a yielding to inherited superstition of which I should scarcely have suspected him.

"Have you ever journeyed to that Mountain?" asked Leo of him.

Simbri shook his head and answered evasively.

"The people of the Plain do not set foot upon the Mountain. Among its slopes beyond the river which washes them, live hordes of brave and most savage men, with whom we are oftentimes at war; for when they are hungry they raid our cattle and our crops. Moreover, there, when the Mountain labours, run red streams of molten rock, and now and again hot ashes fall that slay the traveller."

"Do the ashes ever fall in your country?" asked Leo.

"They have been known to do so when the Spirit of the Mountain is angry, and that is why we fear her."

"Who is this Spirit?" said Leo eagerly.

"I do not know, lord," he answered with impatience. "Can men see a spirit?"

"*You* look as though you might, and had, not so long ago," replied Leo, fixing his gaze on the old man's waxen face and uneasy eyes. For now their horny calm was gone from the eyes of Simbri, which seemed as though they had beheld some sight that haunted him.

"You do me too much honour, lord," he replied; "my skill and vision do not reach so far. But see, here is the landing-stage, where boats await us, for the rest of our journey is by water."

These boats proved to be roomy and comfortable, having flat bows and stems, since, although sometimes a sail was hoisted, they were designed for towing, not to be rowed with oars. Leo and I entered the largest of them, and to our joy were left alone except for the steersman.

Behind us was another boat, in which were attendants and slaves, and some men who looked like soldiers, for they carried bows and swords. Now the ponies were taken from the palanquins, that were packed away, and ropes of green hide, fastened to iron rings in the prows of the boats, were fixed to the towing tackle with which the animals had been re-harnessed. Then we started, the ponies, two arranged tandem fashion to each punt, trotting along a well-made towing path that was furnished with wooden bridges wherever canals or tributary streams entered the main river.

"Thank Heaven," said Leo, "we are together again at last! Do you remember, Horace, that when we entered the land of Kôr it was thus, in a boat? The tale repeats itself."

"I can quite believe it," I answered. "I can believe anything. Leo, I say that we are but gnats meshed in a web, and yonder Khania is the spider and Simbri the Shaman guards the net. But tell me all you remember of what has happened to you, and be quick, for I do not know how long they may leave us alone."

"Well," he said, "of course I remember our arrival at that Gate after the lady and the old man had pulled us out of the river, and, Horace, talking of spiders reminds me of hanging at the end of that string of yak's hide. Not that I need much reminding, for I am not likely to forget it. Do you know I cut the rope because I felt that I was going mad, and wished to die sane. What happened to you? Did you slip?"

"No; I jumped after you. It seemed best to end together, so that we might begin again together."

"Brave old Horace!" he said affectionately, the tears starting to his grey eyes.

"Well, never mind all that," I broke in; "you see you were right when you said that we should get through, and we have. Now for your tale."

"It is interesting, but not very long," he answered, colouring. "I went to sleep, and when I woke it was to find a beautiful woman leaning over me, and Horace – at first I thought that it was – you know who, and that she kissed me; but perhaps it was all a dream."

"It was no dream," I answered. "I saw it."

"I am sorry to hear it – very sorry. At any rate there was the beautiful woman – the Khania – for I saw her plenty of times afterwards, and talked to her in my best modern Greek – by the way, Ayesha knew the old Greek; that's curious."

"She knew several of the ancient tongues, and so did other people. Go on."

"Well, she nursed me very kindly, but, so far as I know, until last night there was nothing more affectionate, and I had sense enough to refuse to talk about our somewhat eventful past. I pretended not to understand, said that we were explorers, etc., and kept asking her where you were, for I forgot to say I found that you had gone. I think that she grew rather angry with me, for she wanted to know something, and, as you can guess, I wanted to know a good deal. But I could get nothing out of her except that she was the Khania – a person in authority. There was no doubt about that, for when one of those slaves or servants came in and interrupted her while she was trying to draw the facts out of me, she called to some of her people to throw him out of the window, and he only saved himself by going down the stairs very quickly.

"Well, I could make nothing of her, and she could make little of me, though why she should be so tenderly interested in a stranger, I don't know – unless, unless – oh! who is she, Horace?"

"If you will go on I will tell you what I think presently. One tale at a time."

"Very good. I got quite well and strong, comparatively speaking, till the climax last night, which upset me again. After that old prophet, Simbri, had brought me my supper, just as I was thinking of going to sleep, the Khania came in alone, dressed like a queen. I can tell you she looked really royal, like a princess in a fairy book, with a crown on, and her chestnut black hair flowing round her.

"Well, Horace, then she began to make love to me in a refined sort of way, or so I thought, looked at me and sighed, saying that we had known each other in the past – very well indeed I gathered – and implying that she wished to continue our friendship. I fenced with her as best I could; but a man feels fairly helpless lying on his back with a very handsome and very imperial-looking lady standing over him and paying him compliments.

"The end of it was that, driven to it by her questions and to stop that sort of thing, I told her that I was looking for my wife, whom I had lost, for, after all, Ayesha is my wife, Horace. She smiled and suggested that I need not look far; in short, that the lost wife was already found – in herself, who had come to save me from death in the river. Indeed, she spoke with such conviction that I grew sure that she was not merely amusing herself, and felt very much inclined to believe her, for, after all, Ayesha may be changed now.

"Then while I was at my wits' end I remembered the lock of hair – all that remains to us of *her,*" and Leo touched his breast. "I drew it out and compared it with the Khania's, and at the sight of it she became quite different, jealous, I suppose, for it is longer than hers, and not in the least like.

"Horace, I tell you that the touch of that lock of hair – for she did touch it – appeared to act upon her nature like nitric acid upon sham gold. It turned it black; all the bad in her came out. In her anger her voice sounded coarse; yes, she grew almost vulgar, and, as you know, when Ayesha was in a rage she might be wicked as we understand it, and was certainly terrible, but she was never either coarse or vulgar, any more than lightning is.

"Well, from that moment I was sure that whoever this Khania may be, she has nothing to do with Ayesha; they are so different that they never could have been the same – like the hair. So I lay quiet and let her talk, and coax, and threaten on, until at length she drew herself up and marched from the room, and I heard her lock the door behind her. That's all I have to tell you, and quite enough too, for I don't think that the Khania has done with me, and to say the truth, I am afraid of her."

"Yes," I said, "quite enough. Now sit still, and don't start or talk loud, for that steersman is probably a spy, and I can feel old Simbri's eyes fixed upon our backs. Don't interrupt either, for our time alone may be short."

Then I set to work and told him everything I knew, while he listened in blank astonishment.

"Great Heavens! what a tale," he exclaimed as I finished. "Now, who is this Hesea who sent the letter from the Mountain? And who, who is the Khania?"

"Who does your instinct tell you that she is, Leo?"

"Amenartas?" he whispered doubtfully. "The woman who wrote the *Sherd,* whom Ayesha said was the Egyptian princess – my wife two thousand years ago? Amenartas re-born?"

I nodded. "I think so. Why not? As I have told you again and again, I have always been certain of one thing, that if we were allowed to see the next act of the piece, we should find Amenartas, or rather the spirit of Amenartas, playing a leading part in it; you will remember I wrote as much in that record.

"If the old Buddhist monk Kou-en could remember *his* past, as thousands of them swear that they do, and be sure of his identity continued from that past, why should not this woman, with so much at stake, helped as she is by the wizardry of the Shaman, her uncle, faintly remember hers?

"At any rate, Leo, why should she not still be sufficiently under its influence to cause her, without any fault or seeking of her own, to fall madly in love at first sight with a man whom, after all, she has always loved?"

"The argument seems sound enough, Horace, and if so I am sorry for the Khania, who hasn't much choice in the matter – been forced into it, so to speak."

"Yes, but meanwhile your foot is in a trap again. Guard yourself, Leo, guard yourself. I believe that this is a trial sent to you, and doubtless there will be more to follow. But I believe also that it would be better for you to die than to make any mistake."

"I know it well," he answered; "and you need not be afraid. Whatever this Khania may have been to me in the past – if she was anything at all – that story is done with. I seek Ayesha, and Ayesha alone, and Venus herself shall not tempt me from her."

Then we began to speak with hope and fear of that mysterious Hesea who had sent the letter from the Mountain, commanding the Shaman Simbri to meet us: the priestess or spirit whom he declared was "mighty from of old" and had "servants in the earth and air."

Presently the prow of our barge bumped against the bank of the river, and looking round I saw that Simbri had left the boat in which he sat and was preparing to enter ours. This he did, and, placing himself gravely on a seat in front of us, explained that nightfall was coining on, and he wished to give us his company and protection through the dark.

"And to see that we do not give him the slip in it," muttered Leo.

Then the drivers whipped up their ponies, and we went on again.

"Look behind you," said Simbri presently, "and you will see the city where you will sleep to-night."

We turned ourselves, and there, about ten miles away, perceived a flat-roofed town of considerable, though not of very great size. Its position was good, for it was set upon a large island that stood a hundred feet or more above the level of the plain, the river dividing into two branches at the foot of it, and, as we discovered afterwards, uniting again beyond.

The vast mound upon which this city was built had the appearance of being artificial, but very possibly the soil whereof it was formed had been washed up in past ages during times of flood, so that from a mudbank in the centre of the broad river it grew by degrees to its present proportions. With the exception of a columned and towered edifice that crowned the city and seemed to be encircled by gardens, we could see no great buildings in the place.

"How is the city named?" asked Leo of Simbri.

"Kaloon," he answered, "as was all this land even when my fore-fathers, the conquerors, marched across the mountains and took it more than two thousand years ago. They kept the ancient title, but the territory of the Mountain they called Hes, because they said that the too? upon yonder peak was the symbol of a goddess of this name whom their general worshipped."

"Priestesses still live there, do they not?" said Leo, trying in his turn to extract the truth.

"Yes, and priests also. The College of them was established by the conquerors, who subdued all the land. Or rather, it took the place of another College of those who fashioned the Sanctuary and the Temple, whose god was the fire in the Mountain, as it is that of the people of Kaloon to-day."

"Then who is worshipped there now?"

"The goddess Hes, it is said; but we know little of the matter, for between us and the Mountain folk there has been enmity for ages. They kill us and we kill them, for they are jealous of their shrine, which none may visit save by permission, to consult the Oracle and to make prayer or offering in times of calamity, when a Khan dies, or the waters of the river sink and the crops fail, or when ashes fall and earthquakes shake the land, or great sickness comes. Otherwise, unless they attack us, we leave them alone, for though every man is trained to arms, and can fight if need be, we are a peaceful folk, who cultivate the soil from generation to generation, and thus grow rich. Look round you. Is it not a scene of peace?"

We stood up in the boat and gazed about us at the pastoral prospect. Everywhere appeared herds of cattle feeding upon meadow lands, or troops of mules and horses, or square fields sown with corn and outlined by trees. Village folk, also, clad; in long, grey gowns, were labouring on the land, or, their day's toil finished, driving their beasts homewards along roads built upon the banks of the irrigation dykes, towards the hamlets that were placed on rising knolls amidst tall poplar groves.

In its sharp contrast with the arid deserts and fearful mountains amongst which we had wandered for so many years, this country struck us as most charming, and indeed, seen by the red light of the sinking sun on that spring day, even as beautiful with the same kind of beauty which is to be found in Holland. One could understand too that these landowners and peasant-farmers would by choice be men of peace, and what a temptation their wealth must offer to the hungry, half-savage tribes of the mountains.

Also it was easy to guess when the survivors of Alexander's legions under their Egyptian general burst through the iron band of snow-clad hills and saw this sweet country, with its homes, its herds, and its ripening grain, that they must have cried with one voice, "We will march and fight and toil no more. Here we will sit us down to live and die." Thus doubtless they did, taking them wives from among the women of the people of the land which they had conquered – perhaps after a single battle.

Now as the light faded the wreaths of smoke which hung over the distant Fire-mountain began to glow luridly. Redder and more angry did they become while the darkness gathered, till at length they seemed to be charged with pulsing sheets of flame propelled from the womb of the volcano, which threw piercing beams of light through the eye of the giant loop that crowned its brow. Far, far fled those beams, making a bright path across the land, and striking the white crests of the bordering wall of mountains. High in the air ran that path, over the dim roofs of the city of Kaloon, over the river, yes, straight above us, over the mountains, and doubtless – though there we could not follow them – across the desert to that high eminence on its farther side where we had lain bathed in their radiance. It was a wondrous and most impressive sight, one too that filled our companions with fear, for the steersmen in our boats and the drivers on the towing-path groaned aloud and began to utter prayers.

"What do they say?" asked Leo of Simbri.

"They say, lord, that the Spirit of the Mountain is angry, and passes down yonder flying light that is called 'the Road of Hes' to work some evil to our land. Therefore they pray her not to destroy them."

"Then does that light not always shine thus?" he asked again.

"Nay, but seldom. Once about three months ago, and now to-night, but before that not for years. Let us pray that it portends no misfortune to Kaloon and its inhabitants."

For some minutes this fearsome illumination continued, then it ceased as suddenly as it had begun, and there remained of it only the dull glow above the crest of the peak.

Presently the moon rose, a white, shining ball, and by its rays we perceived that we drew near to the city. But there was still something left for us to see before we reached its shelter. While we sat quietly in the boat – for the silence was broken only by the lapping of the still waters against its sides and the occasional splash of the slackened tow-line upon their surface – we heard a distant sound as of a hunt in full cry.

Nearer and nearer it came, its volume swelling every moment, till it was quite close at last. Now echoing from the trodden earth of the towing-path – not that on which our ponies travelled, but the other on the west bank of the river – was heard the beat of the hoofs of a horse galloping furiously. Presently it appeared, a fine, white animal, on the back of which sat a man. It passed us like a flash, but as he went by the man lifted himself and turned his head, so that we saw his face in the moonlight; Saw also the agony of fear that was written on it and in his eyes.

He had come out of the darkness. He was gone into the darkness, but after him swelled that awful music. Look! a dog appeared, a huge red dog, that dropped its foaming muzzle to the ground as it galloped, then lifted it and uttered a deep-throated, bell-like bay. Others followed, and yet others:

in all there must have been a hundred of them, every one baying as it took the scent.

"*The death-hounds!*" I muttered, clasping Leo by the arm.

"Yes," he answered, "they are running that poor devil. Here comes the huntsman."

As he spoke there appeared a second figure, splendidly mounted, a cloak streaming from his shoulders, and in his hand a long whip, which he waved. He was big but loosely jointed, and as he passed he turned his face also, and we saw that it was that of a madman. There could be no doubt of it; insanity blazed in those hollow eyes and rang in that savage, screeching laugh.

"The Khan! The Khan!" said Simbri, bowing, and I could see that he was afraid.

Now he too was gone, and after him came his guards. I counted eight of them, all carrying whips, with which they flogged their horses.

"What does this mean, friend Simbri?" I asked, as the sounds grew faint in the distance.

"It means, friend Holly,' he answered. "that the Khan does justice in his own fashion – hunting to death one that has angered him."

"What then is his crime? And who is that poor man?"

"He is a great lord of this land, one of the royal kinsmen, and the crime for which he has been condemned is that he told the Khania he loved tier, and offered to make war upon her husband and kill him, if she would promise herself to him in marriage. But she hated the man, as she hates all men, and brought the matter before the Khan. That is all the story."

"Happy is that prince who has so virtuous a wife!" I could not help saying unctuously, but with meaning, and the old wretch of a Shaman turned his head at my words and began to stroke his white beard.

It was but a little while afterwards that once more we heard the baying of the death-hounds. Yes, they were heading straight for us, this time across country. Again the white horse and its rider appeared, utterly exhausted, both of them, for the poor beast could scarcely struggle on to the towing-path. As it gained it a great red hound with a black ear gripped its flank, and at the touch of the fangs it screamed aloud in terror as only a horse can. The rider sprang from its back, and, to our horror, ran to the river's edge, thinking evidently to take refuge in our boat. But before ever he reached the water the devilish brutes were upon him.

* * * * *

What followed I will not describe, but never shall I forget the scene of those two heaps of worrying wolves, and of the maniac Khan, who yelled in his fiendish joy, and cheered on his death-hounds to finish their red work.

CHAPTER 9

THE COURT OF KALOON

HORRIFIED, SICK at heart, we continued our journey. No wonder that the Khania hated such a mad despot. And this woman was in love with Leo, and this lunatic Khan, her husband, was a victim to jealousy, which he avenged after the very unpleasant fashion that we had witnessed. Truly an agreeable prospect for all of us! Yet, I could not help rejecting, as an object lesson that horrid scene had its advantages.

Now we reached the place where the river forked at the end of the island, and disembarked upon a quay. Here a guard of men commanded by some Household officer, was waiting to receive us. They led us through a gate in the high wall, for the town was fortified, up a narrow, stone-paved street which ran between houses apparently of the usual Central Asian type, and, so far as I could judge by moonlight, with no pretensions to architectural beauty, and not large in size.

Clearly our arrival was expected and excited interest, for people were gathered in knots about the street to watch us pass; also at the windows of the houses and even on their flat roofs. At the top of the long street was a sort of market place, crossing which, accompanied by a curious crowd who made remarks about us that we could not understand, we reached a gate in an inner wall. Here we were challenged, but at a word from Simbri it opened, and we passed through to find ourselves in gardens. Following a road or drive, we came to a large, rambling house or palace, surmounted by high towers and very solidly built of stone in a heavy, bastard Egyptian style.

Beyond its doorway we found ourselves in a courtyard surrounded by a kind of verandah, from which short passages led to different rooms. Down one of these passages we were conducted by the officer to an apartment, or rather a suite, consisting of a sitting and two bed-chambers, which were panelled, richly furnished in rather barbaric fashion, and well-lighted with primitive oil lamps.

Here Simbri left us, saying that the officer would wait in the outer room to conduct us to the dining-hall as soon as we were ready. Then we entered the bed-chambers, where we found servants, or slaves, quiet-mannered, obsequious men. These valets changed our foot-gear, and taking off our heavy travelling robes, replaced them with others fashioned like civilized frock-coats, but made of some white material and trimmed with a beautiful ermine fur.

Having dressed us in these they bowed to show that our toilette was finished, and led us to the large outer room where the officer awaited us. He conducted us through several other rooms, all of them spacious and apparently unoccupied, to a great hall lit with many lamps and warmed – for the nights were still cold – with large peat fires, The roof of this hall was flat and supported by thick stone columns with carved capitals, and its walls were hung with worked tapestries, that gave it an air of considerable comfort.

At the head of the hall on a dais stood a long, narrow table, spread with a cloth and set with platters and cups of silver. Here we waited till butlers with wands appeared through some curtains which they drew. Then came a man beating a silver gong, and after him a dozen or more courtiers, all dressed in white robes like ourselves, followed by perhaps as many ladies, some of them young and good-looking, and for the most part of a fair type, with well-cut features, though others were rather yellow-skinned. They bowed to us and we to them.

Then there was a pause while we studied one another, till a trumpet blew and heralded by footmen in a kind of yellow livery, two figures were seen advancing down the passage beyond the curtains, preceded by the Shaman Simbri and followed by other officers. They were the Khan and the Khania of Kaloon.

No one looking at this Khan as he entered his dining-hall clad in festal white attire would have imagined him to be the same raving human brute whom we had just seen urging on his devilish hounds to tear a fellow-creature and a helpless horse to fragments and devour them. Now he seemed a heavy, loutish man, very strongly built and not ill-looking, but with shifty eyes, evidently a person of dulled intellect, whom one would have thought incapable of keen emotions of any kind. The Khania need not be described. She was as she had been in the chambers of the Gate, only more weary looking; indeed her eyes had a haunted air and it was easy to see that the events of the previous night had left their mark upon her mind. At the sight of us she flushed a little, then beckoned to us to advance, and said to her husband –

"My lord, these are the strangers of whom I have told you."

His dull eyes fell upon me first, and my appearance seemed to amuse him vaguely, at any rate he laughed rudely, saying in barbarous Greek mixed with words from the local patois –

"What a curious old animal! I have never seen you before, have I?"

"No, great Khan," I answered, "but I have seen you out hunting this night. Did you have good sport?"

Instantly he became wide awake, and answered, rubbing his hands –

"Excellent. He gave us a fine run, but my little dogs caught him at last, and then – " and he snapped his powerful jaws together.

"Cease your brutal talk," broke in his wife fiercely, and he slunk away from her and in so doing stumbled against Leo, who was waiting to be presented to him.

The sight of this great, golden-bearded man seemed to astonish him, for he stared at him, then asked –

"Are you the Khania's other friend whom she went to see in the mountains of the Gate? Then I could not understand why she took so much trouble, but now I do. Well, be careful, or I shall have to hunt you also."

Now Leo grew angry and was about to reply, but I laid my hand upon his arm and said in English –

"Don't answer; the man is mad."

"Bad, you mean," grumbled Leo; "and if he tries to set his cursed dogs on me, I will break his neck."

Then the Khania motioned to Leo to take a seat beside her, placing me upon her other hand, between herself and her uncle, the Guardian, while the Khan shuffled to a chair a little way down the table, where he called two of the prettiest ladies to keep him company.

Such was our introduction to the court of Kaloon. As for the meal that followed, it was very plentiful, but coarse, consisting for the most part of fish, mutton, and sweetmeats, all of them presented upon huge silver platters. Also much strong drink was served, a kind of spirit distilled from grain, of which nearly all present drank more than was good for them. After a few words to me about our journey, the Khania turned to Leo and talked to him for the rest of the evening, while I devoted myself to the old Shaman Simbri.

Put briefly, the substance of what I learned from him then and afterwards was as follows –

Trade was unknown to the people of Kaloon, for the reason that all communication with the south had been cut off for ages, the bridges that once existed over the chasm having been allowed to rot away. Their land, which was very large and densely inhabited, was ringed round with unclimbable mountains, except to the north, where stood the great Fire-peak. The slopes of this Peak, and an unvisited expanse of country behind that ran up to the confines of a desert, were the home of ferocious mountain tribes, untamable highlanders, who killed every stranger they caught. Consequently, although the precious and other metals were mined to a certain extent and manufactured into articles of use and ornament, money did not exist among the peoples either of the Plain or of the Mountain, all business being transacted on the principle of barter, and even the revenue collected in kind.

Amongst the tens of thousands of the aborigines of Kaloon dwelt a mere handful of a ruling class, who were said to be – and probably were – descended from the conquerors that appeared in the time of Alexander. Their blood, however, was now much mixed with that of the first inhabitants, who, to judge from their appearance and the yellow hue of their descendants must have belonged to some branch of the great

Tartar race. The government, if so it could be called, was on the whole, of a mild though of a very despotic nature, and vested in an hereditary Khan or Khania, according as a man or a woman might be in the most direct descent.

Of religions there were two, that of the people, who worshipped the Spirit of the Fire Mountain, and that of the rulers, who believed in magic, ghosts and divinations. Even this shadow of a religion, if so it can be called, was dying out, like its followers, for generation by generation, the white lords grew less in number or became absorbed in the bulk of the people.

Still their rule was tolerated. I asked Simbri why, seeing that they were so few. He shrugged his shoulders and answered, because it suited the country of which the natives had no ambition. Moreover, the present Khania, our hostess, was the last of the direct line of rulers, her husband and cousin having less of the blood royal in his veins, and as such the people were attached to her.

Also, as is commonly the case with bold and beautiful women, she was popular among them, especially as she was just and very liberal to the poor. These were many, as the country was over-populated, which accounted for its wonderful state of cultivation. Lastly they trusted to her skill and courage to defend them from the continual attacks of the Mountain tribes who raided their crops and herds. Their one grievance against her was that she had no child to whom the khanship could descend, which meant that after her death, as had happened after that of her father, there would be struggles for the succession.

"Indeed," added Simbri, with meaning, and glancing at Leo, out of the corners of his eyes, "the folk say openly that it would be a good thing if the Khan, who oppresses them and whom they hate, should die, so that the Khania might take another husband while she is still young. Although he is mad, he knows this, and that is why he is so jealous of any lord who looks at her, as, friend Holly you saw to-night. For should such an one gain her favour, Rassen thinks that it would mean his death."

"Also he may be attached to his wife," I suggested, speaking in a whisper.

"Perhaps so," answered Simbri; "but if, so, she loves not him, nor any of these men," and he glanced round the hall.

Certainly they did not look lovable, for by this time most of them were half drunk, while even the women seemed to have taken as much as was good for them. The Khan himself presented a sorry spectacle, for he was leaning back in his chair, shouting something about his hunting, in a thick voice. The arm of one of his pretty companions was round his neck, while the other gave him to drink from a gold cup: some of the contents of which had been spilt down his white robe.

Just then Atene looked round and saw him and an expression of hatred and contempt gathered on her beautiful face.

"See," I heard her say to Leo, "see the companion of my days, and learn what it is to be Khania of Kaloon."

"Then why do you not cleanse your court?" he asked.

"Because, lord, if I did so there would be no court left. Swine will to their mire and these men and women, who live in idleness upon the toil of the humble folk, will to their liquor and vile luxury. Well, the end is near, for it is killing them, and their children are but few; weakly also, for the ancient blood grows thin and stale. But yon are weary and would rest. To-morrow we will ride together" and calling to an officer, she bade him conduct us to our rooms.

So we rose, and, accompanied by Simbri, bowed to her and went, she standing and gazing after as, a royal and pathetic figure in the midst of all that dissolute revelry. The Khan rose also, and in his cunning fashion understood something of the meaning of it all.

"You think us gay," he shouted; "and why should we not be who do not know how long we have to live? But you yellow-haired fellow, you must not let Atene look at you like that. I tell you she is my wife, and if you do, I shall certainly have to hunt you."

At this drunken sally the courtiers roared with laughter, but taking Leo by the arm, Simbri hurried him from the hall.

"Friend," said Leo, when we were outside, "it seems to me that this Khan of yours threatens my life."

"Have no fear, lord," answered the Guardian; "so long as the Khania does not threaten it you are safe. She is the real ruler of this land, and I stand next to her."

"Then I pray you," said Leo, "keep me out of the way of that drunken man, for, look you, if I am attacked I defend myself."

"And who can blame you?" Simbri replied, with one of his slow, mysterious smiles.

Then we parted, and having placed both our beds in one chamber, slept soundly enough, for we were very tired, till we were awakened in the morning by the baying of those horrible death-hounds, being fed, I suppose, in a place near by.

Now in this city of Kaloon it was our weary destiny to dwell for three long months, one of the most hateful times, perhaps, that we ever passed in all our lives. Indeed, compared to it our endless wanderings amid the Central Asian snows and deserts were out pleasure pilgrimages, and our stay at the monastery beyond the mountains a sojourn in Paradise. To set out its record in full would be both tedious and useless, so I will only tell briefly of our principal adventures.

On the morrow of our arrival the Khania Atene sent us two beautiful white horses of pure and ancient blood, and at noon we mounted them and went out to ride with her accompanied by a guard of soldiers. First she led us to the kennels where the death-hounds were kept, great flagged courts surrounded by iron bars, in which were narrow, locked gates. Never have I seen brutes so large and fierce; the mastiffs of Thibet were but as lapdogs compared to them. They were red and black, smooth-coated and with a blood-hound head, and the moment they saw us they came ravening and leaping at the bars as an angry wave leaps against a rock.

These hounds were in the charge of men of certain families, who had tended them for generations. They obeyed their keepers and the Khan readily enough, but no stranger might venture near them. Also these brutes were the executioners of the land, for to them all murderers and other criminals were thrown, and with them, as we had seen, the Khan hunted any who had incurred his displeasure. Moreover, they were used for a more innocent purpose, the chasing of certain great bucks which were preserved in woods and swamps of reeds. Thus it came about that they were a terror to the country, since no man knew but what in the end he might be devoured by them. "Going to the dogs" is a term full of meaning in any land, but in Kaloon it had a significance that was terrible.

After we had looked at the hounds, not without a prophetic shudder, we rode round the walls of the town, which were laid out as a kind of boulevard, where the inhabitants walked and took their pleasure in the evenings. On these, however, there was not much to see except the river beneath and the plain beyond, moreover, though they were thick and high there were places in them that must be passed carefully, for, like everything else with which the effete ruling class had to do, they had been allowed to fall into disrepair.

The town itself was an uninteresting place also, for the most part peopled by hangers-on of the Court. So we were not sorry when we crossed the river by a high-pitched bridge, where in days to come I was destined to behold one of the strangest sights ever seen by mortal man, and rode out into the country. Here all was different, for we found ourselves among the husbandmen, who were the descendants of the original owners of the land and lived upon its produce. Every available inch of soil seemed to be cultivated by the aid of a wonderful system of irrigation. Indeed water was lifted to levels where it would not flow naturally, by means of wheels turned with mules, or even in some places carried up by the women, who bore poles on their shoulders to which were balanced buckets.

Leo asked the Khania what happened if there was a bad season. She replied grimly that famine happened, in which thousands of people perished, and that after the famine came pestilence. These famines were periodical, and were it not for them, she added, the people would long ago have been driven to kill each other like hungry rats, since having no outlet and increasing so rapidly, the land, large as it was, could not hold them all.

"Will this be a good year?" I asked.

"It is feared not," she answered, "for the river has not risen well and but few rains have fallen. Also the light that shone last night on the Fire-mountain is thought a bad omen, which means, they say, that the Spirit of the Mountain is angry and that drought will follow. Let us hope they will not say also that this is because strangers have visited the land, bringing with them bad luck."

"If so," said Leo with a laugh, "we shall have to fly to the Mountain to take refuge there."

"Do you then wish to take refuge in death?" she asked darkly. "Of this be sure, my guest, that never while I live shall you be allowed to cross the river which borders the slopes of yonder peak."

"Why not, Khania?"

"Because, my lord Leo – that is your name, is it not? – such is my will, and while I rule here my will is law. Come, let us turn homewards."

That night we did not eat in the great hall, but in the room which adjoined our bed-chambers. We were not left alone, however, for the Khania and her uncle, the Shaman, who always attended her, joined our meal. When we greeted them wondering, she said briefly that it was arranged thus because she refused to expose us to more insults. She added that a festival had begun which would last for a week, and that she did not wish us to see how vile were the ways of her people.

That evening and many others which followed it – we never dined in the central hall again – passed pleasantly enough, for the Khania made Leo tell her of England where he was born, and of the lands that he had visited, their peoples and customs. I spoke also of the history of Alexander, whose general Rassen, her far-off forefather, conquered the country of Kaloon, and of the land of Egypt, whence the latter came, and so it went on till midnight, while Atene listened to us greedily, her eyes fixed always on Leo's face.

Many such nights did we spend thus in the palace of the city of Kaloon where, in fact, we were close prisoners. But oh! the days hung heavy on our hands. If we went into the courtyard or reception rooms of the palace, the lords and their followers gathered round us and pestered us with questions, for, being very idle, they were also very curious.

Also the women, some of whom were fair enough, began to talk to us on this pretext or on that, and did their best to make love to Leo; for, in contrast with their slim, delicate-looking men, they found this deep-chested, yellow-haired stranger to their taste. Indeed they troubled him much with gifts of flowers and messages sent by servants or soldiers, making assignations with him, which of course he did not keep.

If we went out into the streets, matters were as bad, for then the people ceased from their business, such as it was, and followed us about, staring at us till we took refuge again in the palace gardens.

There remained, therefore, only our rides in the country with the Khania, but after three or four of them, these came to an end owing to the jealousy of the Khan, who vowed that if we went out together any more he would follow with the death-hounds. So we must ride alone, if at all, in the centre of a large guard of soldiers sent to see that we did not attempt to escape, and accompanied very often by a mob of peasants, who with threats and entreaties demanded that we should give back the rain which they said we had taken from them. For now the great drought had begun in earnest.

Thus it came about that at length our only resource was making pretence to fish in the river, where the water was so clear and low that we could catch nothing, watching the while the Fire-mountain, that loomed in the distance mysterious and unreachable, and vainly racking our brains for plans to escape thither, or at least to communicate with its priestess, of whom we could learn no more.

For two great burdens lay upon our souls. The burden of desire to continue our search and to meet with its reward which we were sure that we should pluck amid the snows of yonder peak, if we could but come there; and the burden of approaching catastrophe at the hands of the Khania Atene. She had made no love to Leo since that night in the Gateway, and, indeed, even if she had wished to, this would have been difficult, since I took care that he was never left for one hour alone. No duenna could have clung to a Spanish princess more closely than I did to Leo.

Yet I could see well that her passion was no whit abated; that it grew day by day, indeed, as the fire swells in the heart of a volcano, and that soon it must break loose and spread its ruin round. The omen of it was to be read in her words, her gestures, and her tragic eyes.

CHAPTER 10

IN THE SHAMAN'S CHAMBER

ONE night Simbri asked us to dine with him in his own apartments in the highest tower of the palace – had we but known it, for us a fateful place indeed, for here the last act of the mighty drama was destined to be fulfilled. So we went, glad enough of any change. When we had eaten, Leo grew very thoughtful, then said suddenly –

"Friend Simbri, I wish to ask a favour of you – that you will beg the Khania to let us go our ways."

Instantly the Shaman's cunning old face became like a mask of ivory.

"Surely you had better ask your favours of the lady herself, lord; I do not think that any in reason will be refused to you," he replied.

"Let us stop fencing," said Leo," and consider the facts. It has seemed to me that the Khania Atene is not happy with her husband."

"Your eyes are very keen, lord, and who shall say that they have deceived you?"

"It has seemed, further," went on Leo, reddening, "that she has been so good as to look on me with – some undeserved regard."

"Ah! perhaps you guessed that in the Gate-house yonder, it you have not forgotten what most men would remember."

"I remember certain things, Simbri, that have to do with her and you."

The Shaman only stroked his beard and said: "Proceed!"

"There is little to add, Simbri, except that I am not minded to bring scandal on the name of the first lady in your land."

"Nobly said, lord, nobly said, though here they do not trouble much about such things. But how if the matter could be managed without scandal? If, for instance, the Khania chose to take another husband the whole land would rejoice, for she is the last of her royal race."

"How can she take another husband when she has one living?"

"True; indeed that is a question which I have considered, but the answer to it is that men die. It is the common lot, and the Khan has been drinking very heavily of late."

"You mean that men can be murdered," said Leo angrily. "Well, I will have nothing to do with such a crime. Do you understand me?"

As the words passed his lips I heard a rustle and turned my head. Behind us were curtains beyond which the Shaman slept, kept his instruments of divination and worked out his horoscopes. Now they had been drawn, and between them, in her royal array, stood the Khania still as a statue.

"Who was it that spoke of crime?" she asked in a cold voice. "Was it you, my lord Leo?"

Rising from his chair, he faced her and said –

"Lady, I am glad that you have heard my words, even if they should vex you."

"Why should it vex me to learn that there is one honest man in this court who will have naught to do with murder? Nay, I honour you for those words. Know also that no such foul thoughts have come near to me. Yet, Leo Vincey, that which is written – is written."

"Doubtless, Khania; but what is written?"

"Tell him, Shaman."

Now Simbri passed behind the curtain and returned thence with a roll from which he read: "The heavens' have declared by their signs infallible that before the next new moon, the Khan Rassen will lie dead at the hands of the stranger lord who came to this country from across the mountains."

"Then the heavens have declared a lie," said Leo contemptuously.

"That is as you will," answered Atene; "but so it must befall, not by my hand or those of my servants, but by yours. And then?"

"Why by mine? Why not by Holly's? Yet, if so, then doubtless I shall suffer the punishment of my crime at the hands of his mourning widow," he replied exasperated.

"You are pleased to mock me, Leo Vincey, well knowing what a husband this man is to me."

Now I felt that the crisis had come, and so did Leo, for he looked her in the face and said –

"Speak on, lady, say all you wish; perhaps it will be better for us both."

"I obey you, lord. Of the beginning of this fate I know nothing, but I read from the first page that is open to me. It has to do with this present life of mine. Learn, Leo Vincey, that from my childhood onwards you have haunted me. Oh! when first I saw you yonder by the river, your face was not strange to me, for I knew it – I knew it well in dreams. When I was a little maid and slept one day amidst the flowers by the river's brim, it came first to me – ask my uncle here if this be not so, though it is true that your face was younger then. Afterwards again and again I saw it in my sleep and learned to know that you were mine, for the magic of my heart taught me this.

"Then passed the long years while I felt that you were drawing near to me, slowly, very slowly, but ever drawing nearer, wending onward and outward through the peoples of the world; across the hills, across the plains, across the sands, across the snows, on to my side. At length came the end, for one night not three moons ago, whilst this wise man, my uncle, and I sat together here studying the lore that he has taught me and striving to wring its secrets from the past, a vision came to me.

"Look you, I was lost in a charmed sleep which looses the spirit from the body and gives it strength to stray afar and to see those things that have been and that are yet to be. Then I saw you and your companion clinging to a point of broken ice, over the river of the gulf. I do not lie; it is written here upon the scroll. Yes, it was you, the man of my dreams, and no other, and we knew the place and hurried thither and waited by the water, thinking that perhaps beneath it you lay dead.

"Then, while we waited, lo! two tiny figures appeared far above upon the icy tongue that no man may climb, and oh! you know the rest. Spellbound we stood and saw you slip and hang, saw you sever the thin cord and rush downwards, yes and, saw that brave man, Holly, leap headlong after you.

"But mine was the hand that drew you from the torrent, where otherwise you must have drowned, you the love of the long past and of to-day, aye, and of all time. Yes, you and no other, Leo Vincey. It was this spirit that foresaw your danger and this hand which delivered you from death, and – and would you refuse them now – when I, the Khania of Kaloon, proffer them to you?"

So she spoke, and leaned upon the table, looking up into his face with lips that trembled and with appealing eyes.

"Lady," said Leo, "you saved me, and again I thank you, though perhaps it would have been better if you had let me drown. But, forgive me the question, if all this tale be true, why did you marry another man?"

Now she shrank back as though a knife had pricked her.

"Oh! blame me not," she moaned, "it was but policy which bound me to this madman, whom I ever loathed. They urged me to it; yes, even you, Simbri, my uncle, and for that deed accursed be your head – urged me, saying that it was necessary to end the war between Rassen's faction and my own. That I was the last of the true race, moreover, which must be carried on; saying also that my dreams and my rememberings were but sick phantasies. So, alas! alas! I yielded, thinking to make my people great."

"And yourself, the greatest of them, if all I hear is true," commented Leo bluntly, for he was determined to end this thing. "Well, I do not blame you, Khania, although now you tell me that I must cut a knot you tied by taking the life of this husband of your own choice, for so forsooth it is decreed by fate, that fate which *you* have shaped. Yes, I must do what you will not do, and kill him. Also your tale of the decree of the heavens and of that vision which led you to the precipice to save us is false. Lady, you met me by the river because the 'mighty' Hesea, the Spirit of the Mountain, so commanded you."

"How know you that?" Atene said, springing up and facing him, while the jaw of old Simbri dropped and the eyelids blinked over his glazed eyes:

"In the same way that I know much else. Lady, it would have been better if you had spoken all the truth."

Now Atene's face went ashen and her cheeks sank in.

"Who told you?" she whispered. "Was it you, Magician?" and she turned upon her uncle like a snake about to strike. "Oh! if so, be sure that I shall learn it, and though we are of one blood and have loved each other, I will pay you back in agony."

"Atene, Atene," Simbri broke in, holding up his claw-like hands, "you know well it was not I."

"Then it was you, you ape-faced wanderer, you messenger of the evil gods? Oh! why did I not kill you at the first? Well, that fault can be remedied."

"Lady," I said blandly, "am I also a magician?"

"Aye," she answered, "I think that you are, and that you have a mistress who dwells in fire."

"Then, Khania," I said, "such servants and such mistresses are ill to meddle with. Say, what answer has the Hesea sent to your report of our coming to this land?"

"Listen," broke in Leo before she could reply. "I go to ask a certain question of the Oracle on yonder mountain peak. With your will or without it I tell you that I go, and afterwards you can settle which is the stronger – the Khania of Kaloon or the Hesea of the House of Fire."

Atene listened and for a while stood silent, perhaps because she had no answer. Then she said with a little laugh –

"Is that your will? Well, I think that yonder are none whom you would wish to wed. There is fire and to spare, but no lovely, shameless spirit haunts it to drive men mad with evil longings;" and as though at some secret thought, a spasm of pain crossed her face and caught her breath. Then she went on in the same cold voice –

"Wanderers, this land has its secrets, into which no foreigner must pry. I say to you yet again that while I live you set no foot upon that Mountain. Know also, Leo Vincey, I have bared my heart to you, and I have been told in answer that this long quest of yours is not for me, as I was sure in my folly, but, as I think, for some demon wearing the shape of woman, whom you will never find. Now I make no prayer to you; it is not fitting, but you have learned too much.

"Therefore, consider well to-night and before next sundown answer. Having offered, I do not go back, and tomorrow you shall tell me whether you will take me when the time comes, as come it must, and rule this land and be great and happy in my love, or whether, you and your familiar together, you will – die. Choose then between the vengeance of Atene and her love, since I am not minded to be mocked in my own land as a wanton who sought a stranger and was – refused."

Slowly, slowly, in an intense whisper she spoke the words, that fell one by one from her lips like drops of blood from a death wound, and there followed silence. Never shall I forget the scene. There the old wizard watched us through his horny eyes, that blinked like those of some night bird. There stood the imperial woman in her royal robes, with icy rage written on her face and vengeance in her glance. There, facing her, was the great form of Leo, quiet, alert, determined, holding back his doubts and fears with the iron hand of will. And there to the right was I, noting all things and wondering how long I, "the familiar," who had earned Atene's hate, would be left alive upon the earth.

Thus we stood, watching each other, till suddenly I noted that the flame of the lamp above us flickered and felt a draught strike upon my face. Then I looked round, and became aware of another presence. For yonder in the shadow showed the tall form of a man. See! it shambled forward silently, and I saw that its feet were naked. Now it reached the ring of the lamplight and burst into a savage laugh.

It was the Khan.

Atene, his wife, looked up and saw him, and never did I admire that passionate woman's boldness more, who admired little else about her save her beauty, for her face showed neither anger nor fear, but contempt only. And yet she had some cause to be afraid, as she well knew.

"What do you here, Rassen?" she asked, "creeping on me with your naked feet? Get you back to your drink and the ladies of your court."

But he still laughed on, a hyena laugh.

"What have you heard?" she said, "that makes you so merry?"

"What have I heard?" Rassen gurgled out between his screams of hideous glee. "Oho! I have heard the Khania, the last of the true blood, the first in the land, the proud princess who will not let her robes be soiled by those of the 'ladies of the court' and my wife, my wife, who asked me to marry her – mark that, you strangers – because I was her cousin and a rival ruler, and the richest lord in all the land, and thereby she thought she would increase her power – I have heard her offer herself to a nameless wanderer with a great yellow beard, and I have heard him, who hates and would escape from her" – here he screamed with laughter – "refuse her in such a fashion as I would not refuse the lowest woman in the palace.

"I have heard also – but that I always knew – that I am mad; for, strangers, I was made mad by a hate-philtre which that old Rat," and he pointed to Simbri, "gave me in my drink – yes, at my marriage feast. It worked well, for truly there is no one whom I hate more than the Khania Atene. Why, I cannot bear her touch, it makes me sick. I loathe to be in the same room with her; she taints the air; there is a smell of sorceries about her.

"It seems that it takes you thus also, Yellow-beard? Well, if so, ask the old Rat for a love drink; he can mix it, and then you will think her sweet and sound and fair, and spend some few months jollily enough. Man, don't be a fool, the cup that is thrust into your hands looks goodly. 'Drink, drink deep. You'll never guess the liquor's bad – till to-morrow – though it be mixed with a husband's poisoned blood," and again Rassen screamed in his unholy mirth.

To all these bitter insults, venomed with the sting of truth, Atene listened without a word. Then she turned to us and bowed.

"My guests," she said, "I pray you pardon me for all I cannot help. You have strayed to a corrupt and evil land, and there stands its crown and flower. Khan Rassen, your doom is written, and I do not hasten it, because once for a little while we were near to each other, though you have been naught to me for this many a year save a snake that haunts my house. Were it otherwise, the next cup you drank should still your madness, and that vile tongue of yours which gives its venom voice. My uncle, come with me. Your hand, for I grow weak with shame and woe."

The old Shaman hobbled forward, but when he came face to face with the Khan he stopped and looked him up and down with his dim eyes. Then he said –

"Rassen, I saw you born, the son of an evil woman, and your father none knew but I. The flame flared that night upon the Fire-mountain, and the stars hid their faces, for none of them would own you, no, not even those of the most evil influence. I saw you wed and rise drunken from your marriage feast, your arm about a wanton's neck. I have seen you rule, wasting the land for your cruel pleasure, turning the fertile fields into great parks for your game leaving those who tilled them to starve upon the road or drown themselves in ditches for very misery. And soon, soon I shall see you die in pain and blood, and then the chain will fall from the neck of this noble lady whom you revile, and another more worthy shall take your place and rear up children to fill your throne, and the land shall have rest again."

Now I listened to these words – and none who did not hear them can guess the fearful bitterness with which they were spoken – expecting every moment that the Khan would draw the short sword at his side and cut the old man down. But he did not; he cowered before him like a dog before some savage master, the weight of whose whip he knows. Yes, answering nothing, he shrank into the corner and cowered there, while Simbri, taking Atene by the hand, went from the room. At its massive, iron-bound door he turned and pointing to the crouching figure with his staff, said –

"Khan Rassen, I raised you up, and now I cast you down. Remember me when you lie dying – in blood and pain."

Their footsteps died away, and the Khan crept from his corner, looking about him furtively.

"Have that Rat and the other gone?" he asked of us, wiping his damp brow with his sleeve; and I saw that fear had sobered him and that for awhile the madness had left his eyes.

I answered that they had gone.

"You think me a coward," he went on passionately, "and it is true, I am afraid of him and her – as you, Yellow-beard, will be afraid when your turn comes. I tell you that they sapped my strength and crazed me with their drugged drink, making me the thing I am, for who can war against their wizardries? Look you now. Once I was a prince, the lord of half this land, noble of form and upright of heart, and I loved her cursed beauty as all must love it on whom she turns her eyes. And she turned them on me, she sought *me* in marriage; it was that old Rat who bore her message.

"So I stayed the great war and married the Khania and became the Khan; but better had it been for me if I had crept into her kitchen as a scullion, than into her chamber as a husband. For from the first she hated me, and the more I loved, the more she hated, till at our wedding feast she doctored me with that poison which made me loathe her, and thus divorced us; which made me mad also, eating into my brain like fire."

"If she hated you so sorely, Khan," I asked, "why did she not mix a stronger draught and have done with you?"

"Why? Because of policy, for I ruled half the land. Because it suited her also that I should live on, a thing to mock at, since while I was alive no other husband could be forced upon her by the people. For she is not a woman, she is a witch, who desires to live alone, or so I thought until to-night" – and he glowered at Leo.

"She knew also that although I must shrink from her, I still love her in my heart, and can still be jealous, and therefore that I should protect her from all men. It was she who set me on that lord whom my dogs tore awhile ago, because he was powerful and sought her favour and would not be denied. But now," and again he glowered at Leo, "now I know why she has always seemed so cold. It is because there lived a man to melt whose ice she husbanded her fire."

Then Leo, who all this while had stood silent, stepped forward.

"Listen, Khan," he said. "Did the ice seem like melting a little while ago?"

"No – unless you lied. But that was only because the fire is not yet hot enough. Wait awhile until it burns up, and melt you must, for who can match his will against Atene?"

"And what if the ice desires to flee the fire? Khan, they said that I should kill you, but I do not seek your blood. You think that I would rob you of your wife, yet I have no such thought towards her. We desire to escape this town of yours, but cannot, because its gates are locked, and we are prisoners, guarded night and day. Hear me, then. You have the power to set us free and to be rid of us."

The Khan looked at him cunningly. "And if I set you free, whither would you go? You could tumble down yonder gorge, but only the birds can climb its heights."

"To the Fire-mountain, where we have business." Rassen stared at him.

"Is it I who am mad, or are you, who wish to visit the Fire-mountain? Yet that is nothing to me, save that I do not believe you. But if so you might return again and bring others with you. Perchance, having its lady, you wish this land also by right of conquest. It has foes up yonder."

"It is not so," answered Leo earnestly. "As one man to another, I tell you it is not so. I ask no smile of your wife and no acre of your soil. Be wise and help us to be gone, and live on undisturbed in such fashion as may please you."

The Khan stood still awhile, swinging his long arms vacantly, till something seemed to come into his mind that moved him to merriment, for he burst into one of his hideous laughs.

"I am thinking," he said, "what Atene would say if she woke up to find her sweet bird flown. She would search for you and be angry with me."

"It seems that she cannot be angrier than she is," I answered. "Give us a night's start and let her search never so closely, she shall not find us."

"You forget, Wanderer, that she and her old Rat have arts. Those who knew where to meet you might know where to seek you. And yet, and yet, it would be rare to see her rage. 'Oh, Yellow-beard, where are you, Yellow-beard?' he went on, mimicking his wife's voice. 'Come back and let me melt your ice. Yellow-beard.' "

Again he laughed; then said suddenly –

"When can you be ready? "

"In half an hour," I answered.

"Good. Go to your chambers and prepare will join you there presently."

So we went.

CHAPTER 11

THE HUNT AND THE KILL

WE REACHED our rooms, meeting no one in the passages, and there made our preparations. First we changed our festal robes for those warmer garments in which we had travelled to the city of Kaloon. Then we ate and drank what we could of the victuals which stood in the ante-chamber, not knowing when we should find more food, and filled two satchels such as these people sling about their shoulders, with the remains of the meat and liquor and a few necessaries. Also we strapped our big hunting knives about our middles and armed ourselves with short spears that were made for the stabbing of game.

"Perhaps he has laid a plot to murder us, and we may as well defend ourselves while we can," suggested Leo.

I nodded, for the echoes of the Khan's last laugh still rang in my ears. It was a very evil laugh.

"Likely enough," I said. "I do not trust that insane brute. Still, he wishes to be rid of us."

"Yes, but as he said, live men may return, whereas the dead do not."

"Atene thinks otherwise," I commented.

"And yet she threatened us with death," answered Leo.

"Because her shame and passion make her mad," I replied, after which we were silent.

Presently the door opened, and through it came the Khan, muffled in a great cloak as though to disguise himself.

"Come," he said, "if you are ready." Then catching sight of the spears we held, he added:

"You will not need those things. You do not go a-hunting."

"No," I answered, "but who can say – we might be hunted."

"If you believe that perhaps you had best stay where you are till the Khania wearies of Yellow-beard and opens the gates for you," he replied, eyeing me with his cunning glance.

"I think not," I said, and we started, the Khan leading the way and motioning us to be silent.

We passed through the empty rooms on to the verandah, and from the verandah down into the courtyard, where he whispered to us to keep in the shadow. For the moon shone very clearly that night, so clearly, I remember, that I could see the grass which grew between the joints of the pavement, and the little shadows thrown by each separate blade upon the worn surface of its stones. Now I wondered how we should pass the gate, for there a guard was stationed, which had of late been doubled by order of the Khania. But this gate we left upon our right, taking a path that led into the great walled garden, where Rassen brought us to a door hidden behind a clump of shrubs, which he unlocked with a key he carried.

Now we were outside the palace wall, and our road ran past the kennels. As we went by these, the great, sleepless death-hounds, that wandered to and fro like prowling lions, caught our wind and burst into a sudden chorus of terrific bays. I shivered at the sound, for it was fearful in that silence, also I thought that it would arouse the keepers. But the Khan went to the bars and showed himself, whereon the brutes, which knew him, ceased their noise.

"Fear not," he said as he returned, "the huntsmen know that they are starved to-night, for tomorrow certain criminals will be thrown to them."

Now we had reached the palace gates. Here the Khan bade us hide in an archway and departed. We looked at each other, for the same thought was in both our minds – that he had gone to fetch the murderers who were to make an end of us. But in this we did him wrong, for presently we heard the sound of horses' hoofs upon the stones, and he returned leading the two white steeds that Atene had given us.

"I saddled them with my own hands," he whispered. "Who can do more to speed the parting guest? Now mount, hide your faces in your cloaks as I do, and follow me."

So we mounted, and he trotted before us like a running footman, such as the great lords of Kaloon employed when they went about their business or their pleasure. Leaving the main street, he led us through a quarter of the town that had an evil reputation, and down its tortuous by-ways. Here we met a few revellers, while from time to time night-birds flitted from the doorways and, throwing aside their veils, looked at us, but as we made no sign drew back again, thinking that we passed to some assignation. We reached the deserted docks upon the river's edge and came to a little quay, alongside of which a broad ferry-boat was fastened.

"You must put your horses into it and row across," Rassen said, "for the bridges are guarded, and without discovering myself I cannot bid the soldiers to let you pass."

So with some little trouble we urged the horses into the boat, where I held them by their bridles while Leo took the oars.

"Now go your ways, accursed wanderers," cried the Khan as he thrust us from the quay, "and pray the Spirit of the Mountain that the old Rat and his pupil – your love, Yellow-beard, your love – are not watching you in their magic glass. For if so we may meet again."

Then as the stream caught us, sweeping the boat out towards the centre of the river, he began to laugh that horrible laugh of his, calling after us –

"Ride fast, ride fast for safety, strangers; there is death behind."

Leo put out his strength and backed water, so that the punt hung upon the edge of the stream.

"I think that we should do well to land again and kill that man, for he means mischief," he said.

He spoke in English, but Rassen must have caught the ring of his voice and guessed its meaning with the cunning of the mad. At least he shouted.

"Too late, fools," and with a last laugh turned, ran so swiftly up the quay that his cloak flew out upon the air behind him, and vanished into the shadows at its head.

"Row on," I said, and Leo bent himself to the oars.

But the ferry-boat was cumbersome and the current swift, so that we were swept down a long way before we could cross it. At length we reached still water near the further shore, and seeing a landing-place, managed to beach the punt and to drag our horses to the bank. Then leaving the craft to drift, for we had no time to scuttle her, we looked to our girths and bridles, and mounted, heading towards the far column of glowing smoke which showed like a beacon above the summit of the House of Fire.

At first our progress was very slow, for here there seemed to be no path, and we were obliged to pick our way across the fields, and to search for bridges that spanned such of the water-ditches as were too wide for us to jump. More than an hour was spent in this work, till we came to a village wherein none were stirring, and here struck a road which seemed to run towards the mountain, though, as we learned afterwards, it took us very many miles out of our true path. Now for the first time we were able to canter, and pushed on at some speed, though not too fast, for we wished to spare our horses and feared lest they might fall in the uncertain light.

A while before dawn the moon sank behind the Mountain, and the gloom grew so dense that we were forced to stop, which we did, holding the horses by their bridles and allowing them to graze a little on some young corn. Then the sky turned grey, the light faded from the column of smoke that was our guide, the dawn came, blushing red upon the vast snows of the distant peak, and shooting its arrows through the loop above the pillar. We let the horses drink from a channel that watered the corn, and, mounting them, rode onward slowly.

Now with the shadows of the night a weight of fear seemed to be lifted off our hearts and we grew hopeful, aye, almost joyous. That hated city was behind us. Behind us were the Khania with her surging, doom-driven passions and her stormy loveliness, the wizardries of her horny-eyed mentor, so old in years and secret sin, and the madness of that strange being, half-devil, half-martyr, at once cruel and a coward – the Khan, her husband, and his polluted court. In front lay the fire, the snow and the mystery they hid, sought for so many empty years. Now we would solve it or we would die. So we pressed forward joyfully to meet our fate, whatever it might be.

For many hours our road ran deviously through cultivated land, where the peasants at their labour laid down their tools and gathered into knots to watch us pass, and quaint, flat-roofed villages, whence the women snatched up their children and fled at the sight of us. They believed us to be lords from the court who came to work them some harm in person or in property, and their terror told us how the country smarted beneath the rod of the oppressor. By midday, although the peak seemed to be but little nearer, the character of the land had changed. Now it sloped gently upwards, and therefore could not be irrigated.

Evidently all this great district was dependent on the fall of timely rains, which had not come that spring. Therefore, although the population was still dense and every rod of the land was under the plough or spade, the crops were failing. It was pitiful to see the green, uneared corn already turning yellow because of the lack of moisture, the beasts searching the starved pastures for food and the poor husbandmen wandering about their fields or striving to hoe the iron soil.

Here the people seemed to know us as the two foreigners whose coming had been noised abroad, and, the fear of famine having made them bold, they shouted at us as we went by to give them back the rain which we had stolen, or so we understood their words. Even the women and the children in the villages prostrated themselves before us, pointing first to the Mountain and then to the hard, blue sky, and crying to us to send them rain. Once, indeed, we were threatened by a mob of peasants armed with spades and reaping-hooks, who seemed inclined to bar our path, so that we were obliged to put our horses to a gallop and pass through them with a rush. As we went forward the country grew ever more arid and its inhabitants more scarce, till we saw no man save a few wandering herds who drove their cattle from place to place in search of provender.

By evening we guessed that we had reached that border tract which was harried by the Mountain tribes, for here strong towers built of stone were dotted about the heaths, doubtless to serve as watch-houses or places of refuge. Whether they were garrisoned by soldiers I do not know, but I doubt it, for we saw none. It seems probable indeed that these forts were relics of days when the land of Kaloon was guarded from attack by rulers of a very different character to that of the present Khan and his immediate predecessors.

At length even the watch-towers were left behind, and by sundown we found ourselves upon a vast uninhabited plain, where we could see no living thing. Now we made up our minds to rest our horses awhile, proposing to push forward again with the moon, for having the wrath of the Khania behind us we did not dare to linger. By this evening doubtless she would have discovered our escape, since before sundown, as she had decreed, Leo must make his choice and give his answer. Then, as we were sure, she would strike swiftly. Perhaps her messengers were already at their work rousing the country to capture us, and her soldiers following on our path.

We unsaddled the horses and let them refresh themselves by rolling on the sandy soil, and graze after a fashion upon the coarse tufts of withering herbage which grew around. There was no water here; but this did not so much matter, for both they and we had drunk at a little muddy pool we found not more than an hour before. We were finishing our meal of the food that we had brought with us, which, indeed, we needed sorely after our sleepless night and long day's journey, when my horse, which was knee-haltered close at hand, lay down to roll again. This it could not do with ease because of the rope about its fore-leg, and I watched its efforts idly, till at length, at the fourth attempt, after hanging for a few seconds upon its back, its legs sticking straight into the air, it fell over slowly towards me as horses do.

"Why are its hoofs so red? Has it cut itself?" asked Leo in an indifferent voice.

As it chanced I also had just noticed this red tinge, and for the first time, since it was most distinct about the animal's frogs, which until it rolled thus I had not seen. So I rose to look at them, thinking that probably the evening light had deceived us, or that we might have passed through some ruddy-coloured mud. Sure enough they *were* red, as though a dye had soaked into the horn and the substance of the frogs. What was more, they gave out a pungent, aromatic smell that was unpleasant, such a smell as might arise from blood mixed with musk and spices.

"It is very strange," I said. "Let us look at your beast, Leo."

So we did, and found that its hoofs had been similarly treated.

"Perhaps it is a native mixture to preserve the horn," suggested Leo.

I thought awhile, then a terrible idea struck me.

"I don't want to frighten you," I said, "but I think that we had better saddle up and get on."

"Why?" he asked.

"Because I believe that villain of a Khan has doctored our horses."

"What for? To make them go lame?"

"No, Leo, to make them leave a strong scent upon dry ground."

He turned pale. "Do you mean – those hounds?"

I nodded. Then wasting no more time in words we saddled up in frantic haste. Just as I fastened the last strap of my saddle I thought that a faint sound reached my ear.

"Listen," I said. Again it came, and now there was no doubt about it. It was the sound of baying dogs.

"By Heaven! the death-hounds," said Leo.

"Yes," I answered quietly enough, for at this crisis my nerves hardened and all fear left me, "our friend the Khan is out a-hunting. That is why he laughed."

"What shall we do?" asked Leo. "Leave the horses?"

I looked at the Peak. Its nearest flanks were miles and miles away.

"Time enough to do that when we are forced. We can never reach that mountain on foot, and after they had run down the horses, they would hunt us by spoor or gaze. No, man ride as you never rode before."

We sprang to our saddles, but before we gave rein I turned and looked behind me. It will be remembered that we had ridden up a long slope which terminated in a ridge, about three miles away, the border of the great plain whereon we stood. Now the sun had sunk behind that ridge so that although it was still light the plain had fallen into shadow. Therefore, while no distant object could be seen upon the plain, anything crossing the ridge remained visible enough in that clear air, at least to persons of keen sight.

This is what we saw. Over the ridge poured a multitude of little objects, and amongst the last of these galloped a man mounted on a great horse, who led another horse by the bridle.

"All the pack are out," said Leo grimly, "and Rassen has brought a second mount with him. Now I see why he wanted us to leave the spears, and I think," he shouted as we began to gallop, "that before all is done the Shaman may prove himself a true prophet."

Away we sped through the gathering darkness, heading straight for the Peak. While we went I calculated our chances. Our horses, as good as any in the land, were still strong and fresh, for although we had ridden far we had not over-pressed them, and their condition was excellent. But doubtless the death-hounds were fresh also, for, meaning to run us down at night when he thought that he might catch us sleeping, Rassen would have brought them along easily, following us by inquiry among the peasants and only laying them on our spoor after the last village had been left behind.

Also he had two mounts, and for aught we knew – though afterwards this proved not to be the case, for he wished to work his wickedness alone and unseen – he might be followed by attendants with relays. Therefore it would appear that unless we reached some place whither he did not dare to follow, before him – that is the slopes of the Peak many miles away, he must run us down. There remained the chance also that the dogs would tire and refuse to pursue the chase.

This, however, seemed scarcely probable, for they were extraordinarily swift and strong, and so savage that when once they had scented blood, in which doubtless our horse's hoofs were steeped, they would fall dead from exhaustion sooner than abandon the trail. Indeed, both the Khania and Simbri had often told us as much. Another chance – they might lose the scent, but seeing its nature, again this was not probable. Even an English pack will carry the trail of a red herring breast high without a fault for hours, and here was something stronger – a cunning compound of which the tell-tale odour would hold for days. A last chance. If we were forced to abandon our horses, we, their riders, might possibly escape, could we find any place to hide in on that great plain. If not, we should be seen as well as scented, and then –

No, the odds were all against us, but so they had often been before; meanwhile we had three miles start, and perhaps help would come to us from the Mountain, some help unforeseen. So we set our teeth and sped away like arrows while the light lasted.

Very soon it failed, and whilst the moon was hidden behind the mountains the night grew dark.

Now the hounds gained on us, for in the gloom, which to them was nothing, we did not dare to ride full speed, fearing lest our horses should stumble and lame themselves, or fall. Then it was for the second time since we had dwelt in this land of Kaloon that of a sudden the fire flamed upon the Peak. When we had seen it before, it had appeared to flash across the heavens in one great lighthouse ray, concentrated through the loop above the pillar, and there this night also the ray ran far above us like a lance of fire. But now that we were nearer to its fount we found ourselves bathed in a soft, mysterious radiance like that of the phosphorescence on a summer sea, reflected downwards perhaps from the clouds and massy rock roof of the column loop and diffused by the snows beneath.

This unearthly glimmer, faint as it was, helped us much, indeed but for it we must have been overtaken, for here the ground was very rough, full of holes also made by burrowing marmots. Thus in our extremity help did come to us from the Mountain, until at length the moon rose, when as quickly as they had appeared the volcanic fires vanished, leaving behind them nothing but the accustomed pillar of dull red smoke.

It is a commonplace to speak of the music of hounds at chase, but often I have wondered how that music sounds in the ears of the deer or the fox fleeing for its life. Now, when we filled the place of the quarry, it was my destiny to solve this problem, and I assert with confidence that the progeny of earth can produce no more hideous noise. It had come near to us, and in the desolate silence of the night the hellish harmonies of its volume seemed terrific, yet I could discern the separate notes of which it was composed, especially one deep, bell-like bay.

I remembered that I had heard this bay when we sat in the boat upon the river and saw that poor noble done to death for the crime of loving the Khania. As the hunt passed us then I observed that it burst from the throat of the leading hound, a huge brute, red in colour, with a coal-black ear, fangs that gleamed like ivory, and a mouth which resembled a hot oven. I even knew the name of the beast, for afterwards the Khan, whose peculiar joy it was, had pointed it out to me. He called it Master, because no dog in the pack dared fight it, and told me that it could kill an armed man alone.

Now, as its baying warned us, Master was not half a mile away!

The coming of the moonlight enabled us to gallop faster, especially as here the ground was smooth, being covered with a short, dry turf, and for the next two hours we gained upon the pack. Yes, it was only two hours, or perhaps less, but it seemed a score of centuries. The slopes of the Peak were now not more than ten miles ahead, but our horses were giving out at last. They had borne us nobly, poor beasts, though we were no lightweights, yet their strength had its limits. The sweat ran from them, their sides panted like bellows, they breathed in gasps, they stumbled and would scarcely answer to the flogging of our spear-shafts. Their gallop sank to a jolting canter, and I thought that soon they must come to a dead stop.

We crossed the brow of a gentle rise, from which the ground, that was sprinkled with bush and rocks, sloped downwards to where, some miles below us, the river ran, bounding the enormous flanks of the Mountain. When we had travelled a little way down this slope we were obliged to turn in order to pass between two heaps of rock, which brought us side on to its brow. And there, crossing it not more than three hundred yards away, we saw the pack. There were fewer of them now; doubtless many had fallen out of the hunt, but many still remained. Moreover, not far behind them rode the Khan, though his second mount was gone, or more probably he was riding it, having galloped the first to a standstill.

Our poor horses saw them also, and the sight lent them wings, for all the while they knew that they were running for their lives. This we could tell from the way they quivered whenever the baying came near to them, not as horses tremble with the pleasure-able excitement of the hunt, but in an extremity of terror, as I have often seen them do when a prowling tiger roars close to their camp. On they went as though they were fresh from the stable, nor did they fail again until another four miles or so were covered and the river was but a little way ahead, for we could hear the rush of its waters.

Then slowly but surely the pack overtook us. We passed a clump of bush, but when we had gone a couple of hundred yards or so across the open plain beyond, feeling that the horses were utterly spent, I shouted to Leo –

"Ride round back to the bush and hide there."

So we did, and scarcely had we reached it and dismounted when the hounds came past. Yes, they went within fifty yards of us, lolloping along upon our spoor and running all but mute, for now they were too weary to waste their breath in vain. "Run for it," I said to Leo as soon as they had gone by, "for they will be back on the scent presently," and we set off to the right across the line that the hounds had taken, so as not to cut our own spoor.

About a hundred yards away was a rock, which fortunately we were able to reach before the pack swung round upon the horses' tracks, and therefore they did not view us. Here we stayed until, following the loop, they came to the patch of bush and passed behind it. Then we ran forward again as far as we could go. Glancing backwards as we went, I saw our two poor, foundered beasts plunging away across the plain, happily almost in the same line along which we had ridden from the rise. They were utterly done, but freed from our weights and urged on by fear, could still gallop and keep ahead of the dogs, though we knew that this would not be for very long. I saw also that the Khan, guessing what we had done in our despair, was trying to call his hounds off the horses, but as yet without avail, for they would not leave the quarry which they had viewed.

All this came to my sight in a flash, but I remember the picture well. The mighty, snow-clad Peak surmounted by its column of glowing smoke and casting its shadow for mile upon mile across the desert flats; the plain with its isolated rocks and grey bushes; the doomed horses struggling across it with convulsive bounds; the trailing line of great dogs that loped after them, and amongst these, looking small and lonely in that vast place, the figure of the Khan and his horse, of which the black hide was beflecked with foam. Then above, the blue and tender sky, where the round moon shone so clearly that in her quiet, level light no detail, even the smallest, could escape the eye.

Now youth and even middle age were far behind me, and although a very strong man for my years, I could not run as I used to do. Also I was most weary, and my limbs were stiff and chafed with long riding, so I made but slow progress, and to worsen matters I struck my left foot against a stone and hurt it much. I implored Leo to go on and leave me, for we thought that if we could once reach the river our scent would be lost in the water; at any rate that it would give us a chance of life. Just then, too, I heard the belling bay of the hound Master, and waited for the next. Yes, it was nearer to us. The Khan had made a cast and found our line. Presently we must face the end.

"Go, go!" I said. "I can keep them back for a few minutes and you may escape. It is your quest, not mine. Ayesha awaits you, not me, and I am weary of life. I wish to die and have done with it."

Thus I gasped, not all at once, but in broken words, as I hobbled along clinging to Leo's arm. But he only answered in a low voice –

"Be quiet, or they will hear you," and on he went, dragging me with him.

We were quite near the water now, for we could see it gleaming below us, and oh! how I longed for one deep drink. I remember that this was the uppermost desire in my mind, to drink and drink. But the hounds were nearer still to us, so near that we could hear the pattering of their feet on the dry ground mingled with the thud of the hoofs of the Khan's galloping horse. We had reached some rocks upon a little rise, just where the bank began, when Leo said suddenly –

"No use, we can't make it. Stop and let's see the thing through."

So we wheeled round, resting our backs against the rock. There, about a hundred yards off, were the death-hounds, but Heaven be praised! *only three of them.* The rest had followed the flying horses, and doubtless when they caught them at last, which may have been far distant, had stopped to gorge themselves upon them. So they were out of the fight. Only three, and the Khan, a wild figure who galloped with them; but those three, the black and red brute. Master and two others were almost as fierce and big.

"It might be worse," said Leo. "If you will try to tackle the dogs, I'll do my best with the Khan," and stooping down he rubbed his palms in the grit, for they were wet as water, an example which I followed. Then we gripped the spears in our right hands and the knives in our left, and waited.

The dogs had seen us now and came on, growling and baying fearfully. With a rush they came, and I am not ashamed to own that I felt terribly afraid, for the brutes seemed the size of lions and fiercer. One, it was the smallest of them, outstripped the others, and, leaping up the little rise, sprang straight at my throat.

Why or how I do not know, but on the impulse of the moment I too sprang to meet it, so that its whole weight came upon the point of my spear, which was backed by my weight. The spear entered between its forelegs, and such was the shock that I was knocked backwards. But when I regained my feet I saw the dog rolling on the ground before me and gnashing at the spear shaft, which had been twisted from my hand.

The other two had jumped at Leo, but failed to get hold, though one of them tore away a large fragment from his tunic. Foolishly enough, he hurled his spear at it but missed, for the steel passed just under its belly and buried itself deep in the ground. The pair of them did not come on again at once. Perhaps the sight of their dying companion made them pause. At any rate, they stood at a little distance snarling, where, as our spears were gone, they were safe from us.

Now the Khan had ridden up and sat upon his horse glowering at us, and his face was like the face of a devil. I had hoped that he might fear to attack, but the moment I saw his eyes, I knew that this would not be. He was quite mad with hate, jealousy, and the long-drawn excitement of the hunt, and had come to kill or be killed. Sliding from the saddle, he drew his short sword – for either he had lost his spear or had brought none – and made a hissing noise to the two dogs, pointing at me with the sword. I saw them spring and I saw him rush at Leo, and after that who can tell exactly what happened?

My knife went home to the hilt in the body of one dog and it came to the ground, and lay there – for its hind-quarters were paralysed, howling, snarling and biting at me. But the other, the fiend called Master, got me by the right arm beneath the elbow, and I felt my bones crack in its mighty jaws, and the agony of it, or so I suppose, caused me to drop the knife, so that I was weaponless. The brute dragged me from the rock and began to shake and worry me, although I kicked it in the stomach with all my strength. I fell to my knees and, as it chanced, my left hand came upon a stone of about the size of a large orange, which I gripped. I gained my feet again and pounded at its skull with the stone, but still it did not leave go, and this was well for me, for its next hold would have been on my throat.

We twisted and tumbled to and fro, man and dog together. At one turn I thought that I saw Leo and the Khan rolling over and over each other upon the ground; at another, that he, the Khan, was sitting against a stone looking at me, and it came into my mind that he must have killed Leo and was watching while the dog worried me to death.

Then just as things began to grow black, something sprang forward and I saw the huge hound lifted, from the earth. Its jaws opened, my arm came free and fell against my side. Yes! the brute was whirling round in the air. Leo held it by its hind legs and with all his great strength whirled it round and round.

Thud! He had dashed its head against the rock, and it fell and lay still, a huddled heap of black and red.

Oddly enough, I did not faint; I suppose that the pain and the shock to my nerves kept me awake, for I heard Leo say in a matter-of-fact voice between his gasps for breath –

"Well, that's over, and I think that I have fulfilled the Shaman's prophecy. Let's look and make sure."

Then he led me with him to one of the rocks, and there, resting supinely against it, sat the Khan, still living but unable to move hand or foot. The madness had quite left his face and he looked at us with melancholy eyes, like the eyes of a sick child.

"You are brave men," he said slowly, "strong also, to have killed those hounds and broken my back. So it has come about as was foretold by the old Rat. After all, I should have hunted Atene, not you, though now she lives to avenge me, for her own sake, not mine. Yellow-beard, she hunts you too and with deadlier hounds than these, those of her thwarted passions. Forgive me and fly to the Mountain, Yellow-beard, whither I go before you, for there one dwells who is stronger than Atene."

Then his jaw dropped and he was dead.

CHAPTER 12

THE MESSENGER

"HE IS gone." I panted, "and the world hasn't lost much."

"Well, it didn't give him much, did it, poor devil, so don't let's speak ill of him," answered Leo, who had thrown himself exhausted to the ground. "Perhaps he was all right before they made him mad. At any rate he had pluck, for I don't want to tackle such another."

"How did you manage it?" I asked.

"Dodged in beneath his sword, closed with him, threw him and smashed him up over that lump of stone. Sheer strength, that's all. A cruel business, but it was his life or mine, and there you are. It's lucky I finished it in time to help you before that oven-mouthed brute tore your throat out. Did you ever see such a dog? It looks as large as a young donkey. Are you much hurt, Horace?"

"Oh, my forearm is chewed to a pulp, but nothing else, I think. Let us get down to the water; if I can't drink soon I shall faint. Also the rest of the pack is somewhere about, fifty or more of them."

"I don't think they will trouble us, they have got the horses, poor beasts. Wait a minute and I will come."

Then he rose, found the Khan's sword, a beautiful and ancient weapon, and with a single cut of its keen edge, killed the second dog that I had wounded, which was still yowling and snarling at us. After this he collected the two spears and my knife, saying that they might be useful, and without trouble caught the Khan's horse, which stood with hanging head close by, so tired that even this desperate fight had not frightened it away.

"Now," he said, "up you go, old fellow. You are not fit to walk any farther;" and with his help I climbed into the saddle.

Then slipping the rein over his arm he led the horse, which walked stiffly, on to the to the river, that ran within a quarter of a mile of us, though to me, tortured as I was by pain and half delirious with exhaustion, the journey seemed long enough.

Still we came there somehow, and, forgetting my wounds, I tumbled from the horse, threw myself flat and drank and drank, more, I think, than ever I did before. Not in all my life have I tasted anything so delicious as was that long draught of water. When I had satisfied my thirst, I dipped my head and made shift to jerk my wounded arm into it, for its coolness seemed to still the pain. Presently Leo rose, the water running from his face and beard, and said –

"What shall we do now? The river seems to be wide, over a hundred yards, and it is low, but there may be deep water in the middle. Shall we try to cross, in which case we might drown, or stop where we are till daylight and take our chance of the death-hounds?"

"I can't go another foot," I murmured faintly, "much less try to ford an unknown river."

Now, about thirty yards from the shore was an island covered with reeds and grasses.

"Perhaps we could reach that," he said. "Come, get on to my back, and we will try."

I obeyed with difficulty, and we set out, he feeling his way with the handle of the spear. The water proved to be quite shallow; indeed, it never came much above his knees, so that we reached the island without trouble. Here Leo laid me down on the soft rushes, and, returning to the mainland, brought over the black horse and the remaining weapons, and having unsaddled the beast, knee-haltered and turned it loose, whereon it immediately lay down, for it was too spent to feed.

Then he set to work to doctor my wounds. Well it proved for me that the sleeve of my garment was so thick, for even through it the flesh of my forearm was torn to ribbons, moreover a bone seemed to be broken. Leo collected a double handful of some soft wet moss and, having washed the arm, wrapped it round with a handkerchief, over which he laid the moss. Then with a second handkerchief and some strips of linen torn from our under-garments he fastened a couple of split reeds to serve as rough splints to the wounded limb. While he was doing this I suppose that I slept or swooned. At any rate, I remember no more.

Sometime during that night Leo had a strange dream, of which he told me the next morning. I suppose that it must have been a dream as certainly I saw or was aware of nothing. Well, he dreamed – I use his own words as nearly as possible – that again he heard those accursed death-hounds in full cry. Nearer and nearer they came, following our spoor to the edge of the river – all the pack that had run down the horses. At the water's brink they halted and were mute. Then suddenly a puff of wind brought the scent of us upon the island to one of them which lifted up its head and uttered a single bay. The rest clustered about it, and all at once they made a dash at the water.

Leo could see and hear everything. He felt that after all our doom was now at hand, and yet, held in the grip of nightmare, if nightmare it were, he was quite unable to stir or even to cry out to wake and warn me.

Now followed the marvel of this vision. Giving tongue as they came, half swimming and half plunging, the hounds drew near to the island where we slept. Then suddenly Leo saw that we were no longer alone. In front of us, on the brink of the water, stood the figure of a woman clad in some dark garment. He could not describe her face or appearance, for her back was towards him. All he knew was that she stood there, like a guard, holding some object in her raised hand, and that suddenly the advancing hounds caught sight of her. In an instant it was as though they were paralysed by fear – for their bays turned to fearful howlings. One or two of those that were nearest to the island seemed to lose their footing and be swept away by the stream. The rest struggled back to the bank, and fled wildly like whipped curs.

Then the dark, commanding figure, which in his dream Leo took to be the guardian Spirit of the Mountain, vanished. That it left no footprints behind it I can vouch, for in the morning we looked to see.

When, awakened by the sharp pangs in my arm, I opened my eyes again, the dawn was breaking. A thin mist hung over the river and the island, and through it I could see Leo sleeping heavily at my side and the shape of the black horse, which had risen and was grazing close at hand. I lay still for a while remembering all that we had undergone and wondering that I should live to wake, till presently above the murmuring of the water I heard a sound which terrified me, the sound of voices. I sat up and peered through the reeds, and there upon the bank, looking enormous in the mist, I saw two figures mounted upon horses, those of a woman and a man.

They were pointing to the ground as though they examined spoor in the sand. I heard the man say something about the dogs not daring to enter the territory of the Mountain, a remark which came back to my mind again after Leo had told me his dream. Then I remembered how we were placed.

"Wake!" I whispered to Leo. "Wake, we are pursued."

He sprang to his feet, rubbing his eyes and snatching at a spear. Now those upon the bank saw him, and a sweet voice spoke through the mist, saying –

"Lay down that weapon, my guest, for we are not come to harm you."

It was the voice of the Khania Atene, and the man with her was the old Shaman Simbri.

"What shall we do now, Horace?" asked Leo with something like a groan, for in the whole world there were no two people whom he less wished to see.

"Nothing," I answered, "it is for them to play."

"Come to us," called the Khania across the water. "I swear that we mean no harm. Are we not alone?"

"I do not know," answered Leo, "but it seems unlikely. Where we are we stop until we are ready to march again."

Atene spoke to Simbri. What she said we could not hear, for she whispered, but she appeared to be arguing with him and persuading him to some course of which he strongly disapproved. Then suddenly both of them put their horses at the water and rode to us through the shallows. Reaching the island, they dismounted, and we stood staring at each other. The old man seemed very weary in body and oppressed in mind, but the Khania was strong and beautiful as ever, nor had passion and fatigue left any trace upon her inscrutable face. It was she who broke the silence, saying –

"You have ridden fast and far since last we met, my guests, and left an evil token to mark the path you took. Yonder among the rocks one lies dead.

Say, how came he to his end, who has no wound upon him?"

"By these," answered Leo, stretching out his hands.

"I knew it," she answered, "and I blame you not, for fate decreed that death for him, and now it is fulfilled. Still, there are those to whom you must answer for his blood, and I only can protect you from them."

"Or betray me to them," said Leo. "Khania, what do you seek?"

"That answer which you should have given me this twelve hours gone. Remember, before you speak, that I alone can save your life – aye, and will do it and clothe you with that dead madman's crown and mantle."

"You shall have your answer on yonder Mountain," said Leo, pointing to the peak above us, "where I seek mine."

She paled a little and replied, "To find that it is death, for, as I have told you, the place is guarded by savage folk who know no pity."

"So be it. Then Death is the answer that we seek. Come, Horace, let us go to meet him."

"I swear to you," she broke in, "that there dwells not the woman of your dreams. I am that woman, yes, even I, as you are the man of mine."

"Then, lady, prove it yonder upon the Mountain," Leo answered.

"There dwells there no woman," Atene went on hurriedly, "nothing dwells there. It is the home of fire and – a Voice."

"What voice?"

"The Voice of the Oracle that speaks from the fire. The Voice of a spirit whom no man has ever seen, or shall see."

"Come, Horace," said Leo, and he moved towards the horse.

"Men," broke in the old Shaman, "would you rush upon your doom? Listen; I have visited yonder haunted place, for it was I who according to custom brought thither the body of the Khan Atene's father for burial, and I warn you to set no foot within its temples."

"Which your mistress said that we should never reach," I commented, but Leo only answered –

"We thank you for your warning," and added, "Horace, watch them while I saddle the horse, lest they do us a mischief."

So I took the spear in my uninjured hand and stood ready. But they made no attempt to hurt us, only fell back a little and began to talk in hurried whispers. It was evident to me that they were much perturbed. In a few minutes the horse was saddled and Leo assisted me to mount it. Then he said –

"We go to accomplish our fate, whatever it may be, but before we part, Khania, I thank you for the kindness you have shown us, and pray you to be wise and forget that we have ever been. Through no will of mine your husband's blood is on my hands, and that alone must separate us for ever. We are divided by the doors of death and destiny. Go back to your people, and pardon me if most unwillingly I have brought you doubt and trouble. Farewell."

She listened with bowed head, then replied, very sadly –

"I thank you for your gentle words, but, Leo Vincey, we do not part thus easily. You have summoned me to the

Mountain, and even to the Mountain I shall follow you. Aye, and there I will meet its Spirit, as I have always known I must and as the Shaman here has always known I must. Yes, I will match my strength and magic against hers, as it is decreed that I shall do. To the victor be that crown for which we have warred for ages."

Then suddenly Atene sprang to her saddle, and turning her horse's head rode it back through the water to the shore, followed by old Simbri, who lifted up his crooked hands as though in woe and fear, muttering as he went –

"You have entered the forbidden river and now, Atene, the day of decision is upon us all – upon us and her – that predestined day of ruin and of war."

"What do they mean?" asked Leo of me.

"I don't know," I answered; "but I have no doubt we shall find out soon enough and that it will be something unpleasant. Now for this river."

Before we had struggled through it I thought more than once that the day of drowning was upon us also, for in places there were deep rapids which nearly swept us away. But Leo, who waded, leading the Khan's horse by the bridle, felt his path and supported himself with the spear shaft, so that in the end we reached the other bank safely.

Beyond it lay a breadth of marshy lands, that doubtless were overflowed when the torrent was in flood. Through these we pushed our way as fast as we could, for we feared lest the Khania had gone to fetch her escort, which we thought she might have left behind the rise, and would return with it presently to hunt us down. At that time we did not know what we learned afterwards, that with its bordering river the soil of the Mountain was absolutely sacred and, in practice, inviolable. True, it had been invaded by the people of Kaloon in several wars, but on each occasion their army was destroyed or met with terrible disaster. Little wonder then they had come to believe that the House of Fire was under the protection of some unconquerable Spirit.

Leaving the marsh, we reached a bare, rising plain, which led to the first slope of the Mountain three or four miles away. Here we expected every moment to be attacked by the savages of whom we had heard so much, but no living creature did we see. The place was a desert streaked with veins of rock that once had been molten lava. I do not remember, much else about it; indeed, the pain in my arm was so sharp that I bad no eyes for physical features. At length the rise ended in a bare, broad donga, quite destitute of vegetation, of which the bottom was buried in lava and a debris of rocks washed down by the rain or melting snows from slopes above. This donga was bordered on the farther side by a cliff, perhaps fifty feet in height, in which we could see no opening.

Still we descended the place, that was dark and rugged; pervaded, moreover, by an extraordinary gloom, and as we went perceived that its lava floor was sprinkled over with a multitude of white objects. Soon we came to the first of these and found that it was the skeleton of a human being. Here was a veritable Valley of Dead Bones, thousands upon thousands of them; a gigantic graveyard. It seemed as though some great army had perished here.

Indeed, we found afterwards that this was the case, for on one of those occasions in the far past when the people of Kaloon had attacked the Mountain tribes, they were trapped and slaughtered in this gully, leaving their bones as a warning and a token. Among these sad skeletons we wandered disconsolately, seeking a path up the opposing cliff, and finding none, until at length we came to a halt, not knowing which way to turn. Then it was that we met with our first strange experience on the Mountain.

The gulf and its mouldering relics depressed us, so that for awhile we were silent, and, to tell the truth, somewhat afraid. Yes, even the horse seemed afraid, for it snorted a little, hung its head and shivered. Close by us lay a pile of bones, the remains evidently of a number of wretched creatures that, dead or living, had been hurled down from the cliff above, and on the top of the pile was a little huddled heap, which we took for more bones.

"Unless we can find a way out of this accursed charnel-house before long, I think that we shall add to its company," I said, staring round me.

As the words left my lips it seemed to me that from the corner of my eye I saw the heap on the top of the bones stir. I looked round. Yes, it was stirring. It rose, it stood up, a human figure, apparently that of a woman – but of this I could not be sure – wrapped from head to foot in white and wearing a hanging veil over its face, or rather a mask with cut eye-holes. It advanced towards us while we stared at it, till the horse, catching sight of the thing, shied violently and nearly threw me. When at a distance of about ten paces it paused and beckoned with its hand, that was also swathed in white like the arm of a mummy.

"What the devil are you?" shouted Leo, and his voice echoed drearily among those naked rocks. But the creature did not answer, it only continued to beckon.

Leo walked up to it to assure himself that we were not the victims of some hallucination. As he came it glided back to its heap of bones and stood there like a ghost of one dead arisen from amidst these grinning evidences of death, or rather a swathed corpse, for that is what it resembled. Leo followed with the intention of touching it to assure himself of its reality, whereon it lifted its white-wrapped arm and struck him lightly on the breast. Then as he recoiled it pointed with its hand, first upwards as though to the Peak or the sky, and next at the wall of rock which faced us.

He returned to me saying, "What shall we do?"

"Follow, I suppose. It may be a messenger from above;" and I nodded toward the mountain crest.

"From below, more likely," Leo muttered, "for I don't like the look of this guide."

Still he motioned with his hand to the creature to proceed. Apparently it understood, for it turned to the left and began to pick its way amongst the stones and skeletons swiftly and without noise. We followed for several hundred yards till it reached a shallow cleft in the rock. This cleft we had seen already, but as it appeared to end at a depth of about thirty feet, we passed on. The figure entered here and vanished.

"It must be a shadow," said Leo doubtfully.

"Nonsense," I answered, "shadows don't strike one. Go on."

So he led the horse up the cleft, to find that at the end it turned sharply to the right and that the form was standing there awaiting us. Forward it went again and we after it down a little gorge that grew ever gloomier till it terminated in what might have been a cave, or a gallery cut in the rock.

Here our guide came back to us apparently with the intention of taking the horse by the bridle, but at this nearer sight of it the brute snorted and reared up, so that it almost fell backwards upon me. As it found its feet again the figure struck it on the head in the same passionless, inhuman way that it had struck Leo, whereon the horse trembled and burst into a sweat as though with fear, making no further attempt to escape or to disobey. Then it took one side of the bridle in its swathed hand and, Leo clinging to the other, we plunged into the tunnel.

Our position was not pleasant, for we knew not whither we were being led by this horrible conductor, and suspected that it might be to meet our deaths in the darkness. Moreover, I guessed that the path was narrow and bordered by some gulf, for as we went I heard stones fall, apparently to a considerable depth, while the poor horse lifted its feet gingerly and snorted in abject fear. At length we saw daylight, and never was I more glad of its advent, although it showed us that there was a gulf on our right, and that the path we travelled could not measure more than ten feet in width.

Now we are out of the tunnel, that evidently had saved us a wide detour, and standing for the first time upon the actual slope of the Mountain, which stretched upwards for a great number of miles till it reached the snow-line above. Here also we saw evidences of human life, for the ground was cultivated in patches and herds of mountain sheep and cattle were visible in the distance.

Presently we entered a gully, following a rough path that led along the edge of a raging torrent. It was a desolate place, half a mile wide or more, having hundreds of fantastic lava boulders strewn about its slopes. Before we had gone a mile I heard a shrill whistle, and suddenly from behind these boulders sprang a number of men, quite fifty of them. All we could note at the time was that they were brawny, savage-looking fellows, for the most part red haired and bearded, although their complexions were rather dark, who wore cloaks of white goat skins and carried spears and shields. I should imagine that they were not unlike the ancient Picts and Scots as they appeared to the invading Romans. At us they came uttering their shrill, whistling cries, evidently with the intention of spearing us on the spot.

"Now for it," said Leo, drawing his sword, for escape was impossible; they were all round us. "Good-bye, Horace."

"Good-bye," I answered rather faintly, understanding what the Khania and the old Shaman had meant when they said that we should be killed before we ascended the first slope of the Mountain.

Meanwhile our ghastly-looking guide had slipped behind a great boulder, and even then it occurred to me that her part in the tragedy being played, she, if it were a woman at all, was withdrawing herself while we met our miserable fate. But here I did her injustice, for she had, I suppose, come to save us from this very fate which without her presence we must most certainly have suffered. When the savages were within a few yards suddenly she appeared on the top of the boulder, looking like a second Witch of Endor, and stretched out her arm. Not a word did she speak, only stretched out her draped arm, but the effect was remarkable and instantaneous.

At the sight of her down on to their faces went those wild men, every one of them, as though a lightning stroke had in an instant swept them out of existence. Then she let her arm fall and beckoned, whereon a great fellow who, I suppose, was the leader of the band, rose and crept towards her with bowed head, submissive as a beaten dog. To him she made signs, pointing to us, pointing to the far-off Peak, crossing and uncrossing her white-wrapped arms, but so far as I could hear, speaking no word. It was evident that the chief understood her, however, for he said something in a guttural language. Then he uttered his shrill whistle, whereon the band arose and departed thence at full speed, this way and the other so that in another minute they had vanished as quickly as they came.

Now our guide motioned to us to proceed, and led the way upward as calmly as though nothing had happened.

For over two hours we went on thus till our path brought us from the ravine on to a grassy declivity, across which it wound its way. Here, to our astonishment, we found a fire burning, and hanging above the fire an earthenware pot, which was on the boil, although we could see no man tending it. The figure signalled to me to dismount, pointing to the pot in token that we were to eat the food which doubtless she had ordered the wild men to prepare for us, and very glad was I to obey her. Provision had been made for the horse also, for near the fire lay a great bundle of green forage.

While Leo off-saddled the beast and spread the provender for it, taking with me a spare earthen vessel that lay ready, I went to the edge of the torrent to drink and steep my wounded arm in its ice-cold stream. This relieved it greatly, though by now I was sure from various symptoms that the brute Master's fangs had fortunately only broken or injured the small bone, a discovery for which I was thankful enough. Having finished attending to it as well as I was able, I filled the jar with water.

On my way back a thought struck me, and going to where our mysterious guide stood still as Lot's wife after she had been turned into a pillar of salt, I offered it to her, hoping that she would unveil her face and drink. Then for the first time she showed some sign of being human, or so I thought, for it seemed to me that she bowed ever so little in acknowledgment of the courtesy. If so – and I may have been mistaken – this was all, for the next instant she turned her back on me to show that it was declined. So she would not, or for aught I knew, could not drink. Neither would she eat, for when Leo tried her afterwards with food she refused it in like fashion.

Meanwhile he had taken the pot off the fire, and as soon as its contents grew cool enough we fell on them eagerly, for we were starving. After we had eaten and drunk, Leo re-dressed my arm as best he could and we rested awhile. Indeed, I think that, being very tired, we began to doze, for I was awakened by a shadow falling on us and looked up to see our corpse-like guide standing dose by and pointing first to the sun, then at the horse, as though to show us that we had far to travel. So we saddled up and went on again somewhat refreshed, for at least we were no longer ravenous.

All the rest of that day we journeyed on up the grassy slopes, seeing no man, although occasionally we heard the wild whistle which told us that we were being watched by the Mountain savages. By sundown the character of the country had changed, for the grass was replaced with rocks, amongst which grew stunted firs. We had left the lower slopes and were beginning to climb the Mountain itself.

The sun sank and we went on through the twilight. The twilight died and we went on through the dark, our path lit only by the stars and the faint radiance of the glowing pillar of smoke above the Peak, which was reflected on to us from the mighty mantle of its snows. Forward we toiled, whilst a few paces ahead of us walked our unwearying guide. If she had seemed weird and inhuman before, now she appeared a very ghost, as, clad in her graveyard white, upon which the faint light shimmered, never speaking, never looking back, she glided on noiselessly between the black rocks and the twisted, dark-green firs and junipers.

Soon we lost all count of the road. We turned this way and turned that way, we passed an open patch and through the shadows of a grove, till at length as the moon rose we entered a ravine, and following a path that ran down it, came to a place which is best described as a large amphitheatre cut by the hand of nature out of the rock of the Mountain. Evidently it was chosen as a place of defence, for its entrance was narrow and tortuous, built up at the end also, so that only one person could pass its gateway at a time. Within an open space and at its farther side stood low, stone houses built against the rock. In front of these houses, the moonlight shining full upon them, were gathered several hundred men and women arranged in a semi-circle and in alternate companies, who appeared to be engaged in the celebration of some rite.

It was wild enough. In front of them, and in the exact centre of the semi-circle, stood a gigantic, red-bearded man, who was naked except for a skin girdle about his loins. He was swinging himself backwards and forwards, his hands resting upon his hips, and as he swung, shouting something like "*Ho, haha, ho!*" When he bent towards the audience it bent towards him, and every time he straightened himself it echoed his final shout of "*Ho!*" in a volume of sound that made the precipices ring. Nor was this all, for perched upon his hairy head, with arched back and waving tail, stood a great white cat.

Anything stranger, and indeed more fantastic than the general effect of this scene, lit by the bright moonlight and set in that wild arena, it was never my lot to witness. The red-haired, half-naked men and women, the gigantic priest, the mystical white cat, that, gripping his scalp with its claws, waved its tail and seemed to take a part in the performance; the unholy chant and its volleying chorus, all helped to make it extraordinarily impressive. This struck us the more, perhaps, because at the time we could not in the least guess its significance, though we imagined that it must be preliminary to some sacrifice or offering. It was like the fragment of a nightmare preserved by the awakened senses in all its mad, meaningless reality.

Now round the open space where these savages were celebrating their worship, or whatever it might be, ran a rough stone wall about six feet in height, in which wall was a gateway. Towards this we advanced quite unseen, for upon our side of the wall grew many stunted pines. Through these pines our guide led us, till in the thickest of them, some few yards from the open gateway and a little to the right of it, she motioned to as to stop.

Then she went to a low place in the wall and stood there as though she were considering the scene beyond. It seemed to us, indeed, that she saw what she had not expected and was thereby perplexed or angered. Presently she appeared to make up her mind, for again she motioned to us to remain where we were, enjoining silence upon us by placing her swathed hand upon the mask that hid her face. Next moment she was gone. How she went, or whither, I cannot say; all we knew was that she was no longer there.

"What shall we do now?" whispered Leo to me.

"Stay where we are till she comes back again or something happens," I answered.

So there being nothing else to be done, we stayed, hoping that the horse would not betray us by neighing, or that we might not be otherwise discovered, since we were certain that if so we should be in danger of death. Very soon, however, we forgot the anxieties of our own position in the study of the wild scene before us, which now began to develop a fearful interest.

It would seem that what has been described was but preliminary to the drama itself, and that this drama was the trial of certain people for their lives. This we could guess, for after a while the incantation ceased and the crowd in front of the big man with the cat upon his head opened out, while behind him a column of smoke rose into the air, as though light had been set to some sunk furnace.

Into the space that had thus been cleared were now led seven persons, whose hands were tied behind them. They were of both sexes and included an old man and a woman with a tall and handsome figure, who appeared to be quite young, scarcely more than a girl indeed. These seven were ranged in a line where they stood, clearly in great fear, for the old man fell upon his knees and one of the women began to sob. Thus they were left awhile, perhaps to allow the fire behind them to burn up, which it soon did with great fierceness, throwing a vivid light upon every detail of the spectacle.

Now all was ready, and a man brought a wooden tray to the red-bearded priest, who was seated on a stool, the white cat upon his knees, whither we had seen it leap from his head a little while before. He took the tray by its handles and at a word from him the cat jumped on to it and sat there. Then amidst the most intense silence he rose and uttered some prayer, apparently to the cat, which sat facing him. This done he turned the tray round so that the creature's back was now towards him, and, advancing to the line of prisoners, began to walk up and down in front of them, which he did several times, at each turn drawing a little nearer.

Holding out the tray, he presented it at the face of the prisoner on the left, whereon the cat rose, arched its back and began to lift its paws up and down. Presently he moved to the next prisoner and held it before him awhile, and so on till he came to the fifth, that young woman of whom I have spoken. Now the cat grew very angry, for in the death-like stillness we could hear it spitting and growling. At length it seemed to lift its paws and strike the girl upon the face, whereon she screamed aloud, a terrible scream. Then all the audience broke out into a shout, a single word, which we understood, for we had heard one very like it used by the people of the Plain. It was "Witch! Witch! *Witch!*"

Executioners who were waiting for the victim to be chosen in this ordeal by cat, rushed forward and seizing the girl began to drag her towards the fire. The prisoner who was standing by her and whom we rightly guessed to be her husband, tried to protect her, but his arms being bound, poor fellow, he could do nothing. One of the executioners knocked him down with a stick. For a moment his wife escaped and threw herself upon him, but the brutes lifted her up again, haling her towards the fire, whilst all the audience shouted wildly.

"I can't stand this," said Leo, "it's murder – cold-blooded murder," and he drew his sword.

"Best leave the beasts alone," I answered doubtfully, though my own blood was boiling in my veins.

Whether he heard or not I do not know, for the next thing I saw was Leo rushing through the gate waving the Khan's sword and shouting at the top of his voice. Then I struck my heels into the ribs of the horse and followed after him. In ten seconds we were among them. As we came the savages fell back this way and that, staring at us amazed, for at first I think they took us for apparitions. Thus Leo on foot and I galloping after him, we came to the place.

The executioners and their victim were near the fire now – a very great fire of resinous pine logs built in a pit that measured about eight feet across. Close to it sat the priest upon his stool, watching the scene with a cruel smile, and rewarding the cat with little gobbets of raw meat, that he took from a leathern pouch at his side, occupations in which he was so deeply engaged that he never saw us until we were right on to him.

Shouting, "Leave her alone, you blackguards," Leo rushed at the executioners, and with a single blow of his sword severed the arm of one of them who gripped the woman by the nape of the neck.

With a yell of pain and rage the man sprang back and stood waving the stump towards the people and staring at it wildly. In the confusion that followed I saw the victim slip from the hands of her astonished would-be murderers and run into the darkness, where she vanished. Also I saw the witch-doctor spring up, still holding the tray on which the cat was sitting, and heard him begin to shout a perfect torrent of furious abuse at Leo, who in reply waved his sword and cursed him roundly in English and many other languages.

Then of a sudden the cat upon the tray, infuriated, I suppose, by the noise and the interruption of its meal, sprang straight at Leo's face. He appeared to catch it in mid-air with his left hand and with all his strength dashed it to the ground, where it lay writhing and screeching. Then, as though by an afterthought, he stooped, picked the devilish creature up again and hurled it into the heart of the fire, for he was mad with rage and knew not what he did.

At the sight of that awful sacrilege – for such it was to them who worshipped this beast – a gasp of horror rose from the spectators, followed by a howl of execration. Then, like a wave of the sea, they rushed at us. I saw Leo cut one man down, and next instant I was off the horse and being dragged towards the furnace. At the edge of it I met Leo in like plight, but fighting furiously, for his strength was great and they were half afraid of him.

"Why couldn't you leave the cat alone?" I shouted at him in idiotic remonstrance, for my brain had gone, and all I knew was that we were about to be thrown into the fiery pit. Already I was over it; I felt the flames singe my hair and saw its red caverns awaiting me, when of a sudden the brutal hands that held me were unloosed and I fell backwards to the ground, where I lay staring upwards.

This was what I saw. Standing in front of the fire, her draped form quivering as though with rage, was our ghostly-looking guide, who pointed with her hand at the gigantic, red-headed witch-doctor. But she was no longer alone, for with her were a score or more of men clad in white robes and armed with swords; black-eyed, ascetic-looking men, with clean-shaved heads and faces, for their scalps shone in the firelight.

At the sight of them terror had seized that multitude which, mad as goaded bulls but a few seconds before, now fled in every direction like sheep frightened by a wolf. The leader of the white-robed priests, a man with a gentle face, which when at rest was clothed in a perpetual smile, was addressing the medicine-man, and I understood something of his talk.

"Dog," he said in effect, speaking in a smooth, measured voice that yet was terrible, "accursed dog, beast-worshipper, what were you about to do to the guests of the mighty Mother of the Mountain? Is it for this that you and your idolatries have been spared so long? Answer, if you have anything to say. Answer quickly, for your time is short."

With a groan of fear the great fellow flung himself upon his knees, not to the head-priest who questioned him, but before the quivering shape of our guide, and to her put up half-articulate prayers for mercy.

"Cease," said the high-priest, "she is the Minister who judges and the Sword that strikes. I am the Ears and the Voice. Speak and tell me – were you about to cast those men, whom you were commanded to receive hospitably, into yonder fire because they saved the victim of your devilries and killed the imp you cherished? Nay, I saw it all. Know that it was but a trap set to catch you, who have been allowed to live too long."

But still the wretch writhed before the draped form and howled for mercy.

"Messenger," said the high-priest, "with thee the power goes. Declare thy decree."

Then our guide lifted her hand slowly and pointed to the fire. At once the man turned ghastly white, groaned and fell back, as I think, quite dead, slain by his own terror.

Now many of the people had fled, but some remained, and to these the priest called in cold tones, bidding them approach. They obeyed, creeping towards him.

"Look," he said, pointing to the man, "look and tremble at the justice of Hes the Mother. Aye, and be sure that as it is with him, so shall it be with every one of you who dares to defy her and to practise sorcery and murder. Lift up that dead dog who was your chief."

Some of them crept forward and did his bidding.

"Now, cast him into the bed which he had made ready for his victims."

Staggering forward to the edge of the flaming pit, they obeyed, and the great body fell with a crash amongst the burning boughs and vanished there.

"Listen, you people," said the priest, "and learn that this man deserved his dreadful doom. Know you why he purposed to kill that woman whom the strangers saved? Because his familiar marked her as a witch, you think. I tell you it was not so. It was because she being fair, he would have taken her from her husband, as he had taken many another, and she refused him. But the Eye saw, the Voice spoke, and the Messenger did judgment. He is caught in his own snare, and so shall you be, every one of you who dares to think evil in his heart or to do it with his hands.

"Such is the just decree of the Hesea, spoken by her from her throne amidst the fires of the Mountain."

CHAPTER 13

BENEATH THE SHADOWING WINGS

ONE BY one the terrified tribesmen crept away. When the last of them were gone the priest advanced to Leo and saluted him by placing his hand upon his forehead.

"Lord," he said, in the same corrupt Grecian dialect which was used by the courtiers of Kaloon, "I will not ask if you are hurt, since from the moment that you entered the sacred river and set foot within this land you and your companion were protected by a power invisible and could not be harmed by man or spirit, however great may have seemed your danger. Yet vile hands have been laid upon you, and this is the command of the Mother whom I serve, that, if you desire it, every one of those men who touched you shall die before your eyes. Say, is that your will?"

"Nay," answered Leo; "they are mad and blind, let no blood be shed for us. All we ask of you, friend – but, how are you called?"

"Name me Oros," he answered.

"Friend Oros – a good title for one who dwells upon the Mountain – all we ask is food and shelter, and to be led swiftly into the presence of her whom you name Mother, that Oracle whose wisdom we have travelled far to seek."

He bowed and answered: "The food and shelter are prepared, and to-morrow, when you have rested, I am commanded to conduct you whither you desire to be. Follow me, I pray you"; and he preceded us past the fiery pit to a building that stood about fifty yards away against the rock wall of the amphitheatre.

It would seem that it was a guest-house, or at least had been made ready to serve that purpose, as in it lamps were lit and a fire burned, for here the air was cold. The house was divided into two rooms, the second of them a sleeping place, to which he led us through the first.

"Enter," he said, "for you will need to cleanse yourselves, and you" – here he addressed himself to me – "to be treated for that hurt to your arm which you had from the jaws of the great hound."

"How know you that?" I asked.

"It matters not if I do know and have made ready," Oros answered gravely.

This second room was lighted and warmed like the first, moreover, heated water stood in basins of metal and on the beds were laid clean linen garments and dark-coloured hooded robes, lined with rich fur. Also upon a little table were ointments, bandages, and splints, a marvellous thing to see, for it told me that the very nature of my hurt had been divined. But I asked no more questions; I was too weary; moreover, I knew that it would be useless.

Now the priest Oros helped me to remove my tattered robe, and, undoing the rough bandages upon my arm, washed it gently with warm water, in which he mixed some spirit, and examined it with the skill of a trained doctor.

"The fangs rent deep," he said, "and the small bone is broken, but you will take no harm, save for the scars which must remain." Then, having treated the wounds with ointment, he wrapped the limb with such a delicate touch that it scarcely pained me, saying that by the morrow the swelling would have gone down and he would set the bone. This indeed happened.

After it was done he helped me to wash and to clothe myself in the clean garments, and put a sling about my neck to serve as a rest for my arm. Meanwhile Leo had also dressed himself, so that we left the chamber together very different men to the foul, blood-stained wanderers who had entered there. In the outer room we found food prepared for us, of which we ate with a thankful heart and without speaking. Then, blind with weariness, we returned to the other chamber and, having removed our outer garments, flung ourselves upon the beds and were soon plunged in sleep.

At some time in the night I awoke suddenly, at what hour I do not know, as certain people wake, I among them, when their room is entered, even without the slightest noise. Before I opened my eyes I felt that some one was with us in the place. Nor was I mistaken. A little lamp still burned in the chamber, a mere wick floating in oil, and by its light I saw a dim, ghost-like form standing near the door. Indeed I thought almost that it was a ghost, till presently I remembered, and knew it for our corpse-like guide, who appeared to be looking intently at the bed on which Leo lay, or so I thought, for the head was bent in that direction.

At first she was quite still, then she moaned aloud, a low and terrible moan, which seemed to well from the very heart.

So the thing was not dumb, as I had believed. Evidently it could suffer, and express its suffering in a human fashion. Look! it was wringing its padded hands as in an excess of woe. Now it would seem that Leo began to feel its influence also, for he stirred and spoke in his sleep, so low at first that I could only distinguish the tongue he used, which was Arabic. Presently I caught a few words.

"Ayesha," he said, "*Ayesha!*"

The figure glided towards him and stopped. He sat up in the bed still fast asleep, for his eyes were shut. He stretched out his arms as though seeking one whom he would embrace, and spoke again in a low and passionate voice –

"Ayesha, through life and death I have sought thee long. Come to me, my goddess, my desired."

The figure glided yet nearer, and I could see that it was trembling and now its arms were extended also.

At the bedside she halted, and Leo laid himself down again. Now the coverings had fallen back, exposing his breast, where lay the leather satchel he always wore, that which contained the lock of Ayesha's hair. He was fast asleep, and the figure seemed to fix its eyes upon this satchel. Presently it did more, for, with surprising deftness those white-wrapped fingers opened its clasp, yes, and drew out the long tress of shining hair. Long and earnestly she gazed at it, then gently replaced the relic, closed the satchel and for a little while seemed to weep. While she stood thus the dreaming Leo once more stretched out his arms and spoke, saying, in the same passion-laden voice –

"Come to me, my darling, my beautiful, my beautiful!"

At those words, with a little muffled scream, like that of a scared night-bird, the figure turned and flitted through the doorway.

When I was quite certain that she had gone, I gasped aloud.

What might this mean, I wondered, in a very agony of bewilderment. This could certainly be no dream: it was real, for I was wide awake. Indeed, what did it all mean? Who was the ghastly, mummy-like thing which had guided us unharmed through such terrible dangers; the Messenger that all men feared, who could strike down a brawny savage with a motion of its hand? Why did it creep into the place thus at dead of night, like a spirit revisiting one beloved? Why did its presence cause me to awake and Leo to dream? Why did it draw out the tress; indeed, how knew it that this tress was hidden there? And why – oh! why, at those tender and passionate words did it flit away at last like some scared bat?

The priest Oros had called our guide Minister, and Sword, that is, one who carries out decrees. But what if they were its own decrees? What if this thing should be she whom we sought, *Ayesha herself?* Why should I tremble at the thought, seeing that if so, our quest was ended, we had achieved? Oh! it must be because about this being there was something terrible, something unhuman and appalling. If Ayesha lived within those mummy-cloths, then it was a different Ayesha whom we had known and worshipped. Well could I remember the white-draped form of *She-Who-Must-Be-Obeyed,* and how, long before she revealed her glorious face to us, we guessed the beauty and the majesty hidden beneath that veil by which her radiant life and loveliness incarnate could not be disguised.

But what of this creature? I would not pursue the thought. I was mistaken. Doubtless she was what the priest Oros had said – some half-supernatural being to whom certain powers were given, and, doubtless, she had come to spy on us in our rest that she might make report to the giver of those powers.

Comforting myself thus I fell asleep again, for fatigue overcame even such doubts and fears. In the morning, when they were naturally less vivid, I made up my mind that, for various reasons, it would be wisest to say nothing of what I had seen to Leo, Nor, indeed, did I do so until some days had gone by.

When I awoke the full light was pouring into the chamber, and by it I saw the priest Oros standing at my bedside. I sat up and asked him what time it was, to which he answered with a smile, but in a low voice, that it lacked but two hours of mid-day, adding that he had come to set my arm. Now I saw why he spoke low, for Leo was still fast asleep.

"Let him rest on," he said, as he undid the wrappings on my arm, for he has suffered much, and," he continued significantly, "may still have more to suffer."

"What do you mean, friend Oros?" I asked sharply. "I thought you told us that we were safe upon this Mountain."

"I told you, friend – " and he looked at me.

"Holly is my name – "

" – friend Holly, that your bodies are safe. I said nothing of all the rest of you. Man is more than flesh and blood. He is mind and spirit as well, and these can be injured also."

"Who is there that would injure them?" I asked.

"Friend," he answered, gravely, "you and your companion have come to a haunted land, not as mere wanderers, for then you would be dead ere now, but of set purpose, seeking to lift the veil from mysteries which have been hid for ages. Well, your aim is known and it may chance that it will be achieved. But if this veil is lifted, it may chance also that you will find what shall send your souls shivering to despair and madness. Say, are you not afraid?"

"Somewhat," I answered. "Yet my foster-son and I have seen strange things and lived. We have seen the very Light of Life roll by in majesty; we have been the guests of an Immortal, and watched Death seem to conquer her and leave us untouched.

Think you then that we will turn cowards now? Nay, we march on to fulfil our destinies."

At these words Oros showed neither curiosity nor surprise; it was as though I told him only what he knew.

"Good," he replied, smiling, and with a courteous bow of his shaven head, "within an hour you shall march on – to fulfil your destinies. If I have warned you, forgive me, for I was bidden so to do, perhaps to try your mettle. Is it needful that I should repeat this warning to the lord – " and again he looked at me.

"Leo Vincey," I said.

"Leo Vincey, yes, Leo Vincey," he repeated, as though the name were familiar to him but had slipped his mind. "But you have not answered my question. Is it needful that I should repeat the warning?"

"Not in the least; but you can do so if you wish when he awakes."

"Nay, I think with you, that it would be but waste of words, for – forgive the comparison – what the wolf dares" – and he looked at me – "the tiger does not flee from," and he nodded towards Leo.

"There, see how much better are the wounds upon your arm, which is no longer swollen. Now I will bandage it, and within some few weeks the bone will be as sound again as it was before you met the Khan Rassen hunting in the Plains. By the way, you will see him again soon, and his fair wife with him."

"See him again? Do the dead, then, come to life upon this Mountain?"

"Nay, but certain of them are brought hither for burial. It is the privilege of the rulers of Kaloon; also, I think, that the Khania has questions to ask of its Oracle."

"Who is its Oracle?" I asked with eagerness.

"The Oracle," he replied darkly, "is a Voice. It was ever so, was it not?"

"Yes; I have heard that from Atene, but a voice implies a speaker. Is this speaker she whom you name Mother?"

"Perhaps, friend Holly."

"And is this Mother a spirit?"

"It is a point that has been much debated. They told you so in the Plains, did they not? Also the Tribes think it on the Mountain. Indeed, the thing seems reasonable, seeing that all of us who live are flesh and spirit. But you will form your own judgment and then we can discuss the matter. There, your arm is finished. Be careful now not to strike it or to fall, and look, your companion awakes."

Something over an hour later we started upon our upward journey. I was again mounted on the Khan's horse, which having been groomed and fed was somewhat rested, while to Leo a litter had been offered. This he declined, however, saying that he had now recovered and would not be carried like a woman. So he walked by the side of my horse, using his spear as a staff. We passed the fire-pit – now full of dead, white ashes, among which were mixed those of the witch-finder and his horrible cat – preceded by our dumb guide, at the sight of whom, in her pale wrappings, the people of the tribe who had returned to their village prostrated themselves, and so remained until she was gone by.

One of them, however, rose again and, breaking through our escort of priests, ran to Leo, knelt before him and kissed his hand. It was that young woman whose life he had saved, a noble-looking girl, with masses of red hair, and by her was her husband, the marks of his bonds still showing on his arms. Our guide seemed to see this incident, though how she did so I do not know. At any rate she turned and made some sign which the priest interpreted.

Calling the woman to him he asked her sternly how she dared to touch the person of this stranger with her vile lips. She answered that it was because her heart was grateful. Oros said that for this reason she was forgiven; moreover, that in reward for what they had suffered he was commanded to lift up her husband to be the ruler of that tribe during the pleasure of the Mother. He gave notice, moreover, that all should obey the new chief in his place, according to their customs, and if he did any evil, make report that he might suffer punishment. Then waving the pair aside, without listening to their thanks or the acclamations of the crowd, he passed on.

As we went down the ravine by which we had approached the village on the previous night, a sound of chanting struck our ears. Presently the path turned, and we saw a solemn procession advancing up that dismal, sunless gorge. At the head of it rode none other than the beautiful Khania, followed by her great-uncle, the old Shaman, and after these came a company of shaven priests in their white robes, bearing between them a bier, upon which, its face uncovered, lay the body of the Khan, draped in a black garment. Yet he looked better thus than he had ever done, for now death had touched this insane and dissolute man with something of the dignity which he lacked in life.

Thus then we met. At the sight of our guide's white form, the horse which the Khania rode reared up so violently that I thought it would have thrown her. But she mastered the animal with her whip and voice, and called out –

"Who is this draped hag of the Mountain that stops the path of the Khania Atene and her dead lord? My guests, I find you in ill company, for it seems that you are conducted by an evil spirit to meet an evil fate. That guide of yours must surely be something hateful and hideous, for were she a wholesome woman she would not fear to show her face."

Now the Shaman plucked his mistress by the sleeve, and the priest Oros, bowing to her, prayed her to be silent and cease to speak such ill-omened words into the air, which might carry them she knew not whither. But some instinctive hate seemed to bubble up in Atene, and she would not be silent, for she addressed our guide using the direct "thou," a manner of speech that we found was very usual on the Mountain though rare upon the Plains.

"Let the air carry them whither it will," she cried. "Sorceress, strip off thy rags, fit only for a corpse too vile to view. Show us what thou art, thou flitting night-owl, who thinkest to frighten me with that livery of death, which only serves to hide the death within."

"Cease, I pray lady, cease," said Oros, stirred for once out of his imperturbable calm. "She is the Minister, none other, and with her goes the Power."

"Then it goes not against Atene, Khania of Kaloon," she answered, "or so I think. Power, forsooth! Let her show her power. If she has any it is not her own, but that of the Witch of the Mountain, who feigns to be a spirit, and by her sorceries has drawn away my guests" – and she pointed to us – "thus bringing my husband to his death."

"Niece, be silent!" said the old Shaman, whose wrinkled face was white with terror, whilst Oros held up his hands as though in supplication to some unseen Strength, saying –

"O thou that hearest and seest, be merciful, I beseech thee, and forgive this woman her madness lest the blood of a guest should stain the hands of thy servants, and the ancient honour of our worship be brought low in the eyes of men."

Thus he prayed, but although his hands were uplifted, it seemed to me that his eyes were fixed upon our guide, as ours were. While he spoke, I saw her hand raised, as she had raised it when she slew or rather sentenced the witch-doctor. Then she seemed to reflect, and stayed it in mid air, so that it pointed at the Khania. She did not move, she made no sound, only she pointed, and the angry words died upon Atene's lips, the fury left her eyes, and the colour her face. Yes, she grew white, and silent as the corpse upon the bier behind her. Then, cowed by that invisible power, she struck her horse so fiercely that it bounded by us onward towards the village, at which the funeral company were to rest awhile.

As the Shaman Simbri followed the Khania, the priest Oros caught his horse's bridle and said to him –

"Magician, we have met before, for instance, when your lady's father was brought to his funeral. Warn her, then, you that know something of the truth and of her power to speak more gently of the ruler of this land. Say to her, from me, that had she not been the ambassadress of death, and, therefore, inviolate, surely ere now she would have shared her husband's bier. Farewell, to-morrow we will speak again," and, loosing the Shaman's bridle, Oros passed on.

Soon we had left the melancholy procession behind us and, issuing from the gorge, turned up the Mountain slope towards the edge of the bright snows that lay not far above. It was as we came out of this darksome valley, where the overhanging pine trees almost eclipsed the light that suddenly we missed our guide.

"Has she gone back to – to reason with the Khania?" I asked of Oros.

"Nay!" he answered, with a slight smile, "I think that she has gone forward to give warning that the Hesea's guests draw near."

"Indeed," I answered, staring hard at the bare slope of mountain, up which not a mouse could have passed without being seen. "I understand – she has gone forward," and the matter dropped. But what I did *not* understand was – how she had gone. As the Mountain was honeycombed with caves and galleries, I suppose, however, that she entered one of them.

All the rest of that day we marched upwards, gradually drawing nearer to the snow-line, as we went gathering what information we could from the priest Oros. This was the sum of it –

From the beginning of the world, as he expressed it, that is, from thousands and thousands of years ago, this Mountain had been the home of a peculiar fire-worship, of which the head heirophant was a woman. About twenty centuries before, however, the invading general named Rassen, had made himself Khan of Kaloon. Rassen established a new priestess on the Mountain, a worshipper of the Egyptian goddess, Hes, or Isis. This priestess had introduced certain modifications in the ancient doctrines, superseding the cult of fire, pure and simple, by a new faith, which, while holding to some of the old ceremonies, revered as its head the Spirit of Life or Nature, of whom they looked upon their priestess as the earthly representative.

Of this priestess Oros would only tell us that she was "ever present," although we gathered that when one priestess died or was "taken to the fire," as he put it, her child, whether in fact or by adoption, succeeded her and was known by the same names, those of "Hes" or the "Hesea" and "Mother." We asked if we should see this Mother, to which he answered that she manifested herself very rarely. As to her appearance and attributes he would say nothing, except that the former changed from time to time and that when she chose to use it she had "all power."

The priests of her College, he informed us, numbered three hundred, never more nor less, and there were also three hundred priestesses. Certain of those who desired it were allowed to marry, and from among their children were reared up the new generation of priests and priestesses. Thus they were a people apart from all others, with distinct racial characteristics. This, indeed, was evident, for our escort were all exceedingly like to each other, very handsome and refined in appearance, with dark eyes, clean-cut features and olive-hued skins; such a people as might well have descended from Easterns of high blood, with a dash of that of the Egyptians and Greeks thrown in.

We asked him whether the mighty looped pillar that towered from the topmost cup of the Mountain was the work of men. He answered, No; the hand of Nature had fashioned it, and that the light shining through it came from the fires which burned in the crater of the volcano. The first priestess, having recognized in this gigantic column the familiar Symbol of Life of the Egyptian worship, established her altars beneath its shadow.

For the rest, the Mountain with its mighty slopes and borderlands was peopled by a multitude of half-savage folk, who accepted the rule of the Hesea, bringing her tribute of all things necessary, such as food and metals. Much of the meat and grain however the priests raised themselves on sheltered farms, and the metals they worked with their own hands. This rule, however, was of a moral nature, since for centuries the College had sought no conquests and the

Mother contented herself with punishing crime in some such fashion as we had seen. For the petty wars between the Tribes and the people of the Plain they were not responsible, and those chiefs who carried them on were deposed, unless they had themselves been attacked. All the Tribes, however, were sworn to the defence of the Hesea and the College, and, however much they might quarrel amongst themselves, if need arose, were ready to die for her to the last man. That war must one day break out again between the priests of the Mountain and the people of Kaloon was recognized; therefore they endeavoured to be prepared for that great and final struggle.

Such was the gist of his history, which, as we learned afterwards, proved to be true in every particular.

Towards sundown we came to a vast cup extending over many thousand acres, situated beneath the snow-line of the peak and filled with rich soil washed down, I suppose, from above. So sheltered was the place by its configuration and the over-hanging mountain that, facing south-west as it did, notwithstanding its altitude it produced corn and other temperate crops in abundance. Here the College had its farms, and very well cultivated these seemed to be. This great cup, which could not be seen from below, we entered through a kind of natural gateway, that might be easily defended against a host.

There were other peculiarities, but it is not necessary to describe them further than to say that I think the soil benefited by the natural heat of the volcano, and that when this erupted, as happened occasionally, the lava streams always passed to the north and south of the cup of land. Indeed, it was these lava streams that had built up the protecting cliffs.

Crossing the garden-like lands, we came to a small town beautifully built of lava rock. Here dwelt the priests, except those who were on duty, no man of the Tribes or other stranger being allowed to set foot within the place.

Following the main street of this town, we arrived at the face of the precipice beyond, and found ourselves in front of a vast archway, closed with massive iron gates fantastically wrought. Here, taking my horse with them, our escort left us alone with Oros. As we drew near the great gates swung back upon their hinges. We passed them – with what sensations I cannot describe – and groped our way down a short corridor which ended in tall, iron-covered doors. These also rolled open at our approach, and next instant we staggered back amazed and half-blinded by the intense blaze of light within.

Imagine, you who read, the nave of the vastest cathedral with which you are acquainted. Then double or treble its size, and you will have some conception of that temple in which we found ourselves. Perhaps in the beginning it had been a cave, who can say? but now its sheer walls, its multitudinous columns springing to the arched roof far above us, had all been worked on and fashioned by the labour of men long dead; doubtless the old fire-worshippers of thousands of years ago.

You will wonder how so great a place was lighted, but I think that never would you guess. Thus – by twisted columns of living flame! I counted eighteen of them, but there may have been others. They sprang from the floor at regular intervals along the lines of what in a cathedral would be the aisles. Right to the roof they sprang, of even height and girth, so fierce was the force of the natural gas that drove them, and there were lost, I suppose, through chimneys bored in the thickness of the rock. Nor did they give off smell or smoke, or in that great, cold place, any heat which could be noticed, only an intense white light like that of molten iron, and a sharp hissing noise as of a million angry snakes.

The huge temple was utterly deserted, and, save for this sybilant, pervading sound, utterly silent; an awesome, an overpowering place.

"Do these candles of yours ever go out?" asked Leo of Oros, placing his hand before his dazzled eyes.

"How can they," replied the priest, in his smooth, matter-of-fact voice, "seeing that they rise from the eternal fire which the builders of this hall worshipped? Thus they have burned from the beginning, and thus they will burn for ever, though, if we wish it, we can shut off their light.* Be pleased to follow me: you will see greater things."

So in awed silence we followed, and, oh! how small and miserable we three human beings looked alone in that vast temple illuminated by this lightning radiance. We reached the end of it at length, only to find that to right and left ran transepts on a like gigantic scale and lit in the same amazing fashion. Here Oros bade us halt, and we waited a little while, till presently, from either transept arose a sound of chanting, and we perceived two white-robed processions advancing towards us from their depths.

On they came, very slowly, and we saw that the procession to the right was a company of priests, and that to the left a company of priestesses, a hundred or so of them in all.

Now the men ranged themselves in front of us, while the women ranged themselves behind, and at a signal from Oros,

* This, as I ascertained afterwards, was done by thrusting a broad stone of great thickness over the apertures through which the gas or fire rushed and thus cutting off the air. These stones were worked to and fro by means of pulleys connected with iron rods. – L. H. H.

all of them still chanting some wild and thrilling hymn, once more we started forward, this time along a narrow gallery closed at the end with double wooden doors. As our procession reached these they opened, and before us lay the crowning wonder of this marvellous fane, a vast, ellipse-shaped apse. Now we understood. The plan of the temple was the plan of the looped pillar which stood upon the brow of the Peak, and as we rightly guessed, its dimensions were the same.

At intervals around this ellipse the fiery columns flared, but otherwise the place was empty.

No, not quite, for at the head of the apse, almost between two of the flame columns, stood a plain, square altar of the size of a small room, in front of which, as we saw when we drew nearer, were hung curtains of woven silver thread. On this altar was placed a large statue of silver, that, backed as it was by the black rock, seemed to concentrate and reflect from its burnished surface the intense light of the two blazing pillars.

It was a lovely thing, but to describe it is hard indeed. The figure, which was winged, represented a draped woman of mature years, and pure but gracious form, half hidden by the forward-bending wings. Sheltered by these, yet shown between them, appeared the image of a male child, clasped to its bearer's breast with her left arm, while the right was raised toward the sky. A study of Motherhood, evidently, but how shall I write of all that was conveyed by those graven faces?

To begin with the child. It was that of a sturdy boy, full of health and the joy of life. Yet he had been sleeping, and in his sleep some terror had overshadowed him with the dark shades of death and evil. There was fear in the lines of his sweet mouth and on the lips and cheeks, that seemed to quiver. He had thrown his little arm about his mother's neck, and, pressing close against her breast, looked up to her for safety, his right hand and outstretched finger pointing downwards and behind him, as though to indicate whence the danger came. Yet it was passing, already half-forgotten, for the upturned eyes expressed confidence renewed, peace of soul attained.

And the mother. She did not seem to mock or chide his fears, for her lovely face was anxious and alert. Yet upon it breathed a very atmosphere of unchanging tenderness and power invincible; care for the helpless, strength to shelter it from every harm. The great, calm eyes told their story, the parted lips were whispering some tale of hope, sure and immortal; the raised hand revealed whence that hope arose. All love seemed to be concentrated in the brooding figure, so human, yet so celestial; all heaven seemed to lie an open path before those quivering wings. And see, the arching instep, the upward-springing foot, suggested that thither those wings were bound, bearing their God-given burden far from the horror of the earth, deep into the bosom of a changeless rest above.

The statue was only that of an affrighted child in its mother's arms; its interpretation made clear even to the dullest by the simple symbolism of some genius – Humanity saved by the Divine.

While we gazed at its enchanting beauty, the priests and priestesses, filing away to right and left, arranged themselves alternately, first a man and then a woman, within the ring of the columns of fire that burned around the loop-shaped shrine. So great was its circumference that the whole hundred of them must stand wide apart one from another, and, to our sight, resembled little lonely children clad in gleaming garments, while their chant of worship reached us only like echoes thrown from a far precipice. In short, the effect of this holy shrine and its occupants was superb yet overwhelming, at least I know that it filled me with a feeling akin to fear.

Oros waited till the last priest had reached his appointed place. Then he turned and said, in his gentle, reverent tones –

"Draw nigh, now, O Wanderers well-beloved, and give greeting to the Mother," and he pointed towards the statue.

"Where is she?" asked Leo, in a whisper, for here we scarcely dared to speak aloud. "I see no one."

"The Hesea dwells yonder," he answered, and, taking each of us by the hand, he led us forward across the great emptiness of the apse to the altar at its head.

As we drew near the distant chant of the priests gathered in volume, assuming a glad, triumphant note, and it seemed to me – though this, perhaps was fancy – that the light from the twisted columns of flame grew even brighter.

At length we were there, and, Oros, loosing our hands, prostrated himself thrice before the altar. Then he rose again, and, falling behind us, stood in silence with bent head and folded fingers. We stood silent also, our hearts filled with mingled hope and fear like a cup with wine.

Were our labours ended? Had we found her whom we sought, or were we, perchance, but enmeshed in the web of some marvellous mummery and about to make acquaintance with the secret of another new and mystical worship? For years and years we had searched, enduring every hardness of flesh and spirit that man can suffer, and now we were to learn whether we had endured in vain. Yes, and Leo would learn if the promise was to be fulfilled to him, or whether she whom he adored had become but a departed dream to be sought for only beyond the gate of Death. Little wonder that he trembled and turned white in the agony of that great suspense.

Long, long was the time. Hours, years, ages, æons, seemed to flow over us as we stood there before glittering silver curtains that hid the front of the black altar beneath the mystery of the sphinx-like face of the glorious image which was its guardian, clothed with that frozen smile of eternal love and pity. All the past went before us as we struggled in those dark waters of our doubt. Item by item, event by event, we rehearsed the story which began in the Caves of Kôr, for our thoughts, so long attuned, were open to each other and flashed from soul to soul.

Oh! now we knew, they were open also to *another* soul. We could see nothing save the Altar and the Effigy, we could only hear the slow chant of the priests and priestesses and the snake-like hiss of the rushing fires. Yet we knew that our hearts were as an open book to One who watched beneath the Mother's shadowing wings.

CHAPTER 14

THE COURT OF DEATH

NOW THE curtains were open. Before us appeared a chamber hollowed from the thickness of the altar, and in its centre a throne, and on the throne a figure clad in waves of billowy white flowing from the head over the arms of the throne down to its marble steps. We could see no more in the comparative darkness of that place, save that beneath the folds of the drapery the Oracle held in its hand a loop-shaped, jewelled sceptre.

Moved by some impulse, we did as Oros had done prostrating ourselves, and there remained upon our knees. At length we heard a tinkling as of little bells, and, looking up, saw that the sistrum-shaped sceptre was stretched towards us by the draped arm which held it. Then a thin, clear voice spoke, and I thought that it trembled a little. It spoke in Greek, but in a much purer Greek than all these people used.

"I greet you, Wanderers, who have journeyed so far to visit this most ancient shrine, and although doubtless of some other faith, are not ashamed to do reverence to that unworthy one who is for this time its Oracle and the guardian of its mysteries. Rise now and have no fear of me; for have I not sent my Messenger and servants to conduct you to this Sanctuary?"

Slowly we rose, and stood silent, not knowing what to say.

"I greet you, Wanderers," the voice repeated.

"Tell me thou" – and the sceptre pointed towards Leo – "how art thou named?"

"I am named Leo Vincey," he answered.

"Leo Vincey! I like the name, which to me well befits a man so goodly. And thou, the companion of – Leo Vincey?"

"I am named Horace Holly."

"So. Then tell me, Leo Vincey and Horace Holly, what came ye so far to seek?"

We looked at each other, and I said –

"The tale is long and strange. O – but by what title must we address thee?"

"By the name which I bear here, Hes."

"O Hes," I said, wondering what name she bore elsewhere.

"Yet I desire to hear that tale," she went on, and to me her voice sounded eager. "Nay, not all to-night, for I know that you both are weary; a little of it only. In sooth, Strangers, there is a sameness in this home of contemplations, and no heart can feed only on the past, if such a thing there be. Therefore I welcome a new history from the world without. Tell it me, thou, Leo, as briefly as thou wilt, so that thou tell the truth, for in the Presence of which I am a Minister, may nothing else be uttered."

"Priestess," he said, in his curt fashion," I obey. "Many years ago when I was young, my friend and foster-father and I, led by records of the past, travelled to a wild land, and there found a certain divine woman who had conquered time."

"Then that woman must have been both aged and hideous."

"I said, Priestess, that she had conquered time, not suffered it, for the gift of immortal youth was hers. Also she was not hideous; she was beauty itself."

"Therefore, stranger, thou didst worship her for her beauty's sake, as a man does."

"I did not worship her. I loved her, which is another thing. The priest Oros here worships thee, whom he calls Mother. I loved that immortal woman."

"Then thou shouldst love her still. Yet, not so, since love is very mortal."

"I love her still," he answered, "although she died."

"Why, how is that? Thou saidst she was immortal,"

"Perchance she only seemed to die; perchance she changed. At least I lost her, and what I lost I seek, and have sought this many a year."

"Why dost thou seek her in my Mountain, Leo Vincey?"

"Because a vision led me to ask counsel of its Oracle. I am come hither to learn tidings of my lost love, since here alone these may be found."

"And thou. Holly, didst thou also love an immortal woman whose immortality, it seems, must bow to death?"

"Priestess," I answered, "I am sworn to this quest, and where my foster-son goes I follow. He follows beauty that is dead – "

"And thou dost follow him. Therefore both of you follow beauty as men have ever done, being blind and mad."

"Nay," I answered, "if they were blind, beauty would be naught to them who could not see it, and if they were mad, they would not know it when it was seen. Knowledge and vision belong to the wise, O Hes."

"Thou art quick of wit and tongue. Holly, as – " and she checked herself, then of a sudden, said, "Tell me, did my servant the Khania of Kaloon entertain both of you hospitably in her city, and speed you on your journey hither, as I commanded her?"

"We knew not that she was thy servant," I replied. "Hospitality we had and to spare, but we were sped from her Court hitherward by the death-hounds of the Khan, her husband. Tell us, Priestess, what thou knowest of this journey of ours."

"A little," she answered carelessly. "More than three moons ago my spies saw you upon the far mountains, and, creeping very dose to you at night, heard you speak together of the object of your wanderings, then, returning thence swiftly, made report to me. Thereon I bade the Khania Atene, and that old magician her great-uncle, who is Guardian of the Gate, go down to the ancient gates of Kaloon to receive you and bring you hither with all speed. Yet for men who burned to learn the answer to a riddle, you have been long in coming."

"We came as fast as we might, O Hes," said Leo; "and if thy spies could visit those mountains where no man was, and find a path down that hideous precipice, they must have been able also to tell thee the reason of our delay. Therefore I pray, ask it not of us."

"Nay, I will ask it of Atene herself, and she shall surely answer me, for she stands without," replied the Hesea in a cold voice. "Oros, lead the Khania hither and be swift."

The priest turned and walking quickly to the wooden doors by which we had entered the shrine, vanished there.

"Now," said Leo to me nervously in the silence that followed, and speaking in English, "now I wish we were somewhere else for I think that there will be trouble."

"I don't think, I am sure," I answered; "but the more the better, for out of trouble may come the truth, which we need sorely." Then I stopped, reflecting that the strange woman before us said that her spies had overheard our talk upon the mountains, where we had spoken nothing but English.

As it proved, I was wise, for quite quietly the Hesea repeated after me –

"Thou hast experience. Holly, for out of trouble comes the truth, as out of wine."

Then she was silent, and, needless to say, I did not pursue the conversation.

The doors swung open, and through them came a procession clad in black, followed by the Shaman Simbri, who walked in front of a bier, upon which lay the body of the Khan, carried by eight priests. Behind it was Atene, draped in a black veil from head to foot, and after her marched another company of priests. In front of the altar the bier wag set down and the priests fell back, leaving Atene and her uncle standing alone before the corpse.

"What seeks my vassal, the Khania of Kaloon?" asked the Hesea in a cold voice.

Now Atene advanced and bent the knee, but with little graciousness.

"Ancient Mother, Mother from of old, I do reverence to thy holy Office, as my forefathers have done for many a generation," and again she curtseyed. "Mother, this dead man asks of thee that right of sepulchre in the fires of the holy Mountain which from the beginning has been accorded to the royal departed who went before him."

"It has been accorded as thou sayest," answered the Hesea, "by those priestesses who filled my place before me, nor shall it be refused to thy dead lord, – or to thee Atene – when thy time comes."

"I thank thee, O Hes, and I pray that this decree may be written down, for the snows of age have gathered on thy venerable head and soon that must save us for awhile. Therefore bid thy scribes that it be written down, so that the Hesea who rules after thee may fulfil it in its season."

"Cease," said the Hesea, "cease to pour out thy bitterness at that which should command thy reverence, oh! thou foolish child, who dost not know but that to-morrow the fire shall claim the frail youth and beauty which are thy boast. I bid thee cease, and tell me how did death find this lord of thine?"

"Ask those wanderers yonder, that were his guests, for his blood is on their heads and cries for vengeance at thy hands."

"I killed him," said Leo, "to save my own life. He tried to hunt us down with his dogs, and there are the marks of them," and he pointed to my arm. "The priest Oros knows, for he dressed the hurts."

"How did this chance?" asked the Hesea of Atene.

"My lord was mad," she answered boldly, "and such was his cruel sport."

"So. And was thy lord jealous also? Nay, keep back the falsehood I see rising to thy lips. Leo Vincey, answer thou me. Yet, I will not ask thee to lay bare the secrets of a woman who has offered thee her love. Thou, Holly, speak, and let it be the truth."

"It is this, O Hes," I answered. "Yonder lady and her uncle the Shaman Simbri saved us from death in the waters of the river that bounds the precipices of Kaloon. Afterwards we were ill, and they treated us kindly, but the Khania became enamoured of my foster-son."

Here the figure of the Priestess stirred beneath its gauzy wrappings, and the Voice asked –

"And did thy foster-son become enamoured of the Khania, as being a man he may well have done, for without doubt she is fair?"

"He can answer that question for himself, O Hes. All I know is that he strove to escape from her, and that in the end she gave him a day to choose between death and marriage with her, when her lord should be dead. So, helped by the Khan, her husband, who was jealous of him, we fled towards this Mountain, which we desired to reach. Then the Khan set his hounds upon us, for he was mad and false-hearted. We killed him and came on in spite of this lady, his wife, and her uncle, who would have prevented us, and were met in a Place of Bones by a certain veiled guide, who led us up the Mountain and twice saved us from death. That is all the story."

"Woman, what hast thou to say?" asked the Hesea in a menacing voice.

"But little," Atene answered, without flinching. "For years I have been bound to a madman and a brute, and if my fancy wandered towards this man and his fancy wandered towards me – well, Nature spoke to us, and that is all. Afterwards it seems that he grew afraid of the vengeance of Rassen, or this Holly, whom I would that the hounds had torn bone from bone, grew afraid. So they strove to escape the land, and perchance wandered to thy Mountain. But I weary of this talk, and ask thy leave to rest before to-morrow's rite."

"Thou sayest, Atene," said the Hesea, "that Nature spoke to this man and to thee, and that his heart is thine; but that, fearing thy lord's vengeance, he fled from thee, he who seems no coward. Tell me, then, is that tress he hides in the satchel on his breast thy gage of love to him?"

"I know nothing of what he hides in the satchel," answered the Khania sullenly.

"And yet, yonder in the Gatehouse when he lay so sick he set the lock against thine own – ah, dost remember now?"

"So, O Hes, already he has told thee all our secrets, though they be such as most men hide within their breasts;" and she looked contemptuously at Leo.

"I told her nothing of the matter, Khania," Leo said in an angry voice.

"Nay, *thou* toldest me nothing; Wanderer my watching spirit told me. Oh, didst thou think, Atene, that thou couldst hide the truth from the all-seeing Hesea of the Mountain? If so, spare thy breath, for I know all, and have known it from the first. I passed thy disobedience by; of thy false messages I took no heed. For my own purposes I, to whom time is naught, suffered even that thou shouldst hold these, my guests, thy prisoners whilst thou didst strive by threats and force to win a love denied."

She paused, then went on coldly: "Woman, I tell thee that, to complete thy sin, thou hast even dared to lie to me here, in my very Sanctuary."

"If so, what of it?" was the bold answer. "Dost thou love the man thyself? Nay, it is monstrous. Nature would cry aloud at such a shame. Oh! tremble not with rage. Hes, I know thy evil powers, but I know also that I am thy guest, and that in this hallowed place, beneath yonder symbol of eternal Love, thou may'st shed no blood. More, thou canst not harm me, Hes, who am thy equal."

"Atene," replied the measured Voice, "did I desire it, I could destroy thee where thou art. Yet thou art right, I shall not harm thee, thou faithless servant. Did not my writ bid thee through yonder searcher of the stars, thy uncle, to meet these guests of mine and bring them straight to my shrine? Tell me, for I seek to know, how comes it that thou didst disobey me?"

"Have then thy desire," answered Atene in a new and earnest voice, devoid now of bitterness and falsehood. "I disobeyed because that man is not thine, but mine, and no other woman's; because I love him and have loved him from of old. Aye, since first our souls sprang into life I have loved him, as he has loved me. My own heart tells me so; the magic of my uncle here tells me so, though how and where and when these things have been I know not. Therefore I come to thee, Mother of Mysteries, Guardian of the secrets of the past, to learn the truth. At least *thou* canst not lie at thine own altar, and I charge thee, by the dread name of that Power to which thou also must render thy account, that thou answer now and here.

"Who is this man to whom my being yearns? What has he been to me? What has he to do with thee? Speak, O Oracle and make the secret clear. Speak, I command, even though afterwards thou dost slay me – if thou canst."

"Aye, speak! speak!" said Leo, "for know I am in sore suspense. I also am bewildered by memories and rent with hopes and fears."

And I too echoed, "Speak!"

"Leo Vincey," asked the Hesea, after she had thought awhile, "whom dost thou believe me to be?"

"I believe," he answered solemnly, "that thou art that Ayesha at whose hands I died of old in the Caves of Kôr in Africa. I believe thou art that Ayesha whom not twenty years ago I found and loved in those same Caves of Kôr, and there saw perish miserably, swearing that thou wouldst return again."

"See now, how madness can mislead a man," broke in Atene triumphantly. " 'Not twenty years ago', he said, whereas I know well that more than eighty summers have gone by since my grandsire in his youth saw this same priestess sitting on the Mother's throne."

"And whom dost thou believe me to be, O Holly?" the Priestess asked, taking no note of the Khania's words.

"What he believes I believe," I answered. "The dead come back to life – sometimes. Yet alone thou knowest the truth, and by thee only it can be revealed."

"Aye," she said, as though musing, "the dead come back to life – sometimes – and in strange shape, and, mayhap, I know the truth. To-morrow when yonder body is borne on high for burial we will speak of it again. Till then rest you all, and prepare to face that fearful thing – the Truth."

While the Hesea still spoke the silvery curtains swung to their place as mysteriously as they had opened. Then, as though at some signal, the black-robed priests advanced. Surrounding Atene, they led her from the Sanctuary, accompanied by her uncle the Shaman, who, as it seemed to me, either through fatigue or fear, could scarcely stand upon his feet, but stood blinking his dim eyes as though the light dazed him. When these were gone, the priests and priestesses, who all this time had been ranged round the walls, far out of hearing of our talk, gathered themselves into their separate companies, and still chanting, departed also, leaving us alone with Oros and the corpse of the Khan, which remained where it had been set down.

Now the head-priest Oros beckoned to us to follow him, and we went also. Nor was I sorry to leave the place, for its death-like loneliness – enhanced, strangely enough, as it was, by the flood of light that filled it; a loneliness which was concentrated and expressed in the awful figure stretched upon the bier, oppressed and overcame us, whose nerves were broken by all that we had undergone. Thankful enough was I when, having passed the transepts and down the length of the vast nave, we came to the iron doors, the rock passage, and the outer gates, which, as before, opened to let us through, and so at last into the sweet, cold air of the night at that hour which precedes the dawn.

Oros led us to a house well-built and furnished, where at his bidding, like men in a dream, we drank of some liquor which he gave us. I think that drink was drugged, at least after swallowing it I remembered no more till I awoke to find myself lying on a bed and feeling wonderfully strong and well. This I thought strange, for a lamp burning in the room showed me that it was still dark, and therefore that I could have rested but a little time.

I tried to sleep again, but was not able, so fell to thinking till I grew weary of the task. For here thoughts would not help me; nothing could help, except the truth, "that fearful thing," as the veiled Priestess had called it.

Oh! what if she should prove not the Ayesha whom we desired, but some "fearful thing"? What were the meaning of the Khania's hints and of her boldness, that surely had been inspired by the strength of a hidden knowledge? What if – nay, it could not be – I would rise and dress my arm. Or I would wake Leo and make him dress it – anything to occupy my mind until the appointed hour, when we must learn – the best – or the worst.

I sat up in the bed and saw a figure advancing towards me. It was Oros, who bore a lamp in his hand.

"You have slept long, friend Holly," he said, "and now it is time to be up and doing."

"Long?" I answered testily. "How can that be, when it is still dark?"

"Because, friend, the dark is that of a new night. Many hours have gone by since you lay down upon this bed. Well, you were wise to rest you while you may, for who knows when you will sleep again! Come, let me bathe your arm."

"Tell me," I broke in –

"Nay, friend," he interrupted firmly, "I will tell you nothing, except that soon you must start to be present at the funeral of the Khan, and, perchance, to learn the answer to your questions."

Ten minutes later he led me to the eating-chamber of the house, where I found Leo already dressed, for Oros had awakened him before he came to me and bidden him to prepare himself. Oros told us here that the Hesea had not suffered us to be disturbed until the night came again since we had much to undergo that day. So presently we started.

Once more we were led through the flame-lit hall till we came to the loop-shaped apse. The place was empty now, even the corpse of the Khan had gone, and no draped Oracle sat in the altar shrine, for its silver curtains were drawn, and we saw that it was untenanted.

"The Mother has departed to do honour to the dead, according to the ancient custom," Oros explained to us.

Then we passed the altar, and behind the statue found a door in the rock wall of the apse, and beyond the door a passage, and a hall as of a house, for out of it opened other doors leading to chambers. These, our guide told us, were the dwelling-places of the Hesea and her maidens. He added that they ran to the side of the Mountain and had windows that opened on to gardens and let in the light and air. In this hall six priests were waiting, each of whom carried a bundle of torches beneath his arm and held in his hand a lighted lamp.

"Our road runs through the dark," said Oros, "though were it day we might climb the outer snows, but this at night it is dangerous to do."

Then taking torches, he lit them at a lamp and gave one to each of us.

Now our climb began. Up endless sloping galleries we went, hewn with inconceivable labour by the primeval fire-worshippers from the living rock of the Mountain. It seemed to me that they stretched for miles, and indeed this was so, since, although the slope was always gentle, it took us more than an hour to climb them. At length we came to the foot of a great stair.

"Rest awhile here, my lord," Oros said, bowing to Leo with the reverence that he had shown him from the first, "for this stair is steep and long. Now we stand upon the Mountain's topmost lip, and are about to climb that tall looped column which soars above."

So we sat down in the vault-like place and let the sharp draught of air rushing to and from the passages play upon us, for we were heated with journeying up those close galleries. As we sat thus I heard a roaring sound and asked Oros what it might be. He answered that we were very near to the crater of the volcano, and that what we heard through the thickness of the rock was the rushing of its everlasting fires. Then the ascent commenced.

It was not dangerous though very wearisome, for there were nearly six hundred of those steps. The climb of the passages had reminded me of that of the gallery of the Great Pyramid drawn out for whole furlongs; that of the pillar was like the ascent of a cathedral spire, or rather of several spires piled one upon another.

Resting from time to time, we dragged ourselves up the steep steps, each of them quite a foot in height, till the pillar was climbed and only the loop remained. Up it we went also, Oros leading us, and glad was I that the stairway still ran within the substance of the rock, for I could feel the needle's mighty eye quiver in the rush of the winds which swept about its sides.

At length we saw light before us, and in another twenty steps emerged upon a platform. As Leo, who went in front of me, walked from the stairway I saw Oros and another priest seize him by the arms, and called to him to ask what they were doing.

"Nothing," he cried back, "except that this is a dizzy place and they feared lest I should fall. Mind how you come, Horace," and he stretched out his hand to me.

Now I was clear of the tunnel, and I believe that had it not been for that hand I should have sunk to the rocky floor, for the sight before me seemed to paralyse my brain. Nor was this to be wondered at, for I doubt whether the world can show such another.

We stood upon the very apex of the loop, a flat space of rock about eighty yards in length by some thirty in breadth, with the star-strewn sky above us. To the south, twenty thousand feet or more below, stretched the dim Plain of Kaloon, and to the east and west the snow-clad shoulders of the peak and the broad brown slopes beneath. To the north was a different sight, and one more awesome. There, right under us as it seemed, for the pillar bent inwards, lay the vast crater of the volcano, and in the centre of it a wide lake of fire that broke into bubbles and flowers of sudden flame, or spouted, writhed and twisted like an angry sea.

From the surface of this lake rose smoke and gases that took fire as they floated upwards, and, mingling together, formed a gigantic sheet of living light. Right opposite to us burned this sheet and, the flare of it passing through the needle-eye of the pillar under us, sped away in one dazzling beam across the country of Kaloon, across the mountains beyond, till it was lost on the horizon.

The wind blew from south to north, being sucked in towards the hot crater of the volcano, and its fierce breath, that screamed through the eye of the pillar and against its rugged surface, bent the long crest of the sheet of flame, as an ocean roller is bent over by the gale, and tore from it fragments of fire, that floated away to leeward like the blown-out sails of a burning ship.

Had it not been for this strong and steady wind indeed, no creature could have lived upon the pillar, for the vapours would have poisoned him, but its unceasing blast drove these all away towards the north. For the same reason, in the thin air of that icy place the heat was not too great to be endured.

Appalled by that terrific spectacle, which seemed more appropriate to the terrors of the Pit than to this earth of ours, and fearful lest the blast should whirl me like a dead leaf into the glowing gulf beneath, I fell on to my sound hand and my knees, shouting to Leo to do likewise, and looked about me. Now I observed lines of priests wrapped in great capes, kneeling upon the face of the rock and engaged apparently in prayer, but of Hes the Mother, or of Atene, or of the corpse of the dead Khan I could see nothing.

Whilst I wondered where they might be, Oros, upon whose nerves this dread scene appeared to have no effect, and some of our attendant priests surrounded us and led us onwards by a path that ran perilously near to the rounded edge of the rock. A few downward steps and we found that we were under shelter, for the gale was roaring over us. Twenty more paces and we came to a recess cut, I suppose, by man in the face of the loop, in such fashion that a lava roof was left projecting half across its width.

This recess, or rock chamber, which was large enough to shelter a great number of people, we reached safely, to discover that it was already tenanted. Seated in a chair hewn from the rock was the Hesea, wearing a broidered, purple mantle above her gauzy wrappings that enveloped her from head to foot. There, too, standing near to her were the Khania Atene and her uncle the old Shaman, who looked but ill at ease, and lastly, stretched upon his funeral couch, the fiery light beating upon his stark form and face, lay the dead Khan, Rassen.

We advanced to the throne and bowed to her who sat thereon. The Hesea lifted her hooded head, which seemed to have been sunk upon her breast as though she were overcome by thought or care, and addressed Oros the priest. For in the shelter of those massive walls by comparison there was silence and folk could hear each other speak.

"So thou hast brought them safely, my servant," she said, "and I am glad, for to those that know it not this road is fearful. My guests, what say you of the burying-pit of the Children of Hes?"

"Our faith tells us of a hell, lady," answered Leo, "and I think that yonder cauldron looks like its mouth."

"Nay," she answered, "there is no hell, save that which from life to life we fashion for ourselves within the circle of this little star. Leo Vincey, I tell thee that hell is here, aye, *here"* and she struck her hand upon her breast, while once more her head drooped forward as though bowed down beneath some load of secret misery.

Thus she stayed awhile, then lifted it and spoke again, saying –

"Midnight is past, and much must be done and suffered before the dawn. Aye, the darkness must be turned to light, or perchance the light to eternal darkness."

"Royal woman," she went on, addressing Atene, "as is his right, thou hast brought thy dead lord hither for burial in this consecrated place; where the ashes of all who went before him have become fuel for the holy fires. Oros, my priest, summon thou the Accuser and him who makes defence, and let the books be opened that I may pass my judgment on the dead, and call his soul to live again, or pray that from it the breath of life may be withheld.

"Priest, I say the Court of Death is open."

CHAPTER 15

THE SECOND ORDEAL

OROS BOWED and left the place, whereon the Hesea signed to us to stand upon her right and to Atene to stand upon her left. Presently from either side the hooded priests and priestesses stole into the chamber, and to the number of fifty or more ranged themselves along its walls. Then came two figures draped in black and masked, who bore parchment books in their hands, and placed themselves on either side of the corpse, while Oros stood at its feet, facing the Hesea.

Now she lifted the sistrum that she held, and in obedience to the signal Oros said –

"Let the books be opened."

Thereon the masked Accuser to the right broke the seal of his book and began to read its pages. It was a tale of the sins of this dead man entered as fully as though that officer were his own conscience given life and voice. In cold and horrible detail it told of the evil doings of his childhood, of his youth, and of his riper years, and thus massed together the record was black indeed.

I listened amazed, wondering what spy had been set upon the deeds of yonder man throughout his days; thinking also with a shudder of how heavy would be the tale against any one of us, if such a spy should companion him from the cradle to the grave; remembering too that full surely this count is kept by scribes even more watchful than the ministers of Hes.

At length the long story drew to its dose. Lastly it told of the murder of that noble upon the banks of the river; it told of the plot against our lives for no just cause; it told of our cruel hunting with the death-hounds, and of its end. Then the Accuser shut his book and cast it on the ground, saying –

"Such is the record, O Mother. Sum it up as thou hast been given wisdom."

Without speaking, the Hesea pointed with her sistrum to the Defender, who thereon broke the seal of his book and began to read.

Its tale spoke of all the good that the dead man had done; of every noble word that he had said, of every kind action; of plans which he had made for the welfare of his vassals; of temptations to ill that he had resisted; of the true love that he had borne to the woman who became his wife; of the prayers which he had made and of the offerings which he had sent to the temple of Hes.

Making no mention of her name, it told of how that wife of his had hated him, of how she and the magician, who had fostered and educated her, and was her relative and guide, had set other women to lead him astray that she might be free of him. Of how too they had driven him mad with a poisonous drink which took away his judgment, unchained all the evil in his heart, and caused him by its baneful influence to shrink unnaturally from her whose love he still desired.

Also it set out that the heaviest of his crimes were inspired by this wife of his, who sought to befoul his name in the ears of the people whom she led him to oppress, and how bitter jealousy drove him to cruel acts, the last and worst of which caused him foully to violate the law of hospitality, and in attempting to bring about the death of blameless guests, at their hands to find his own.

Thus the Defender read, and having read, closed the book and threw it on the ground, saying –

"Such is the record, O Mother, sum it up as thou hast been given wisdom.

Then the Khania, who all this time had stood cold and impassive, stepped forward to speak, and with her her uncle, the Shaman Simbri, But before a word passed Atene's lips the Hesea raised her sceptre and forbade them, saying –

"Thy day of trial is not yet, nor have we aught to do with thee. When thou liest where he lies and the books of thy deeds are read aloud to her who sits in judgment, then let thine advocate make answer for these things."

"So be it," answered Atene haughtily and fell back.

Now it was the turn of the high-priest Ores.

"Mother," he said, "thou hast heard. Balance the writings, assess the truth, and according to thy wisdom, issue thy commands. Shall we hurl him who was Rassen feet first into the fiery gulf, that he may walk again in the paths of life, or head first, in token that he is dead indeed?"

Then while all waited in a hushed expectancy, the great Priestess delivered her verdict.

"I hear, I balance, I assess, but judge I do not, who claim no such power. Let the Spirit who sent him forth, to whom he is returned again, pass judgment on his spirit. This dead one has sinned deeply, yet has he been more deeply sinned against. Nor against that man can be reckoned the account of his deeds of madness. Cast him then to his grave feet first that his name may be whitened in the ears of those unborn, and that thence he may return again at the time appointed. It is spoken."

Now the Accuser lifted the book of his accusations from the ground and, advancing, hurled it into the gulf in token that it was blotted out. Then he turned and vanished from the chamber; while the Advocate, taking up his book, gave it into the keeping of the priest Oros, that it might be preserved in the archives of the temple for ever. This done, the priests began a funeral chant and a solemn invocation to the great Lord of the Under-world that he would receive this spirit and acquit it there as here it had been acquitted by the Hesea, his minister.

Ere their dirge ended certain of the priests, advancing with slow steps, lifted the bier and carried it to the edge of the gulf; then at a sign from the Mother, hurled it feet foremost into the fiery lake below, whilst all watched to see how it struck the flame. For this they held to be an omen, since should the body turn over in its descent it was taken as a sign that the judgment of mortal men had been refused in the Place of the Immortals. It did not turn; it rushed downwards straight as a plummet and plunged into the fire hundred; of feet below, and there for ever vanished. This indeed was not strange since, as we discovered afterwards, the feet were weighted.

In fact this solemn rite was but a formula that, down to the exact words of judgment and committal, had been practised here from unknown antiquity over the bodies of the priests and priestesses of the Mountain, and of certain of the great ones of the Plain. So it was in ancient Egypt, whence without doubt this ceremony of the trial of the dead was derived, and so it continued to be in the land of Hes, for no priestess ever ventured to condemn the soul of one departed.

The real interest of the custom, apart from its solemnity and awful surroundings, centred in the accurate knowledge displayed by the masked Accuser and Advocate of the life-deeds of the deceased. It showed that although the College of Hes affected to be indifferent to the doings and politics of the people of the Plain that they once ruled and over which, whilst secretly awaiting an opportunity of re-conquest, they still claimed a spiritual authority, the attitude was assumed rather than real. Moreover it suggested a system of espionage so piercing and extraordinary that it was difficult to believe it unaided by the habitual exercise of some gift of clairvoyance.

The service, if I may call it so, was finished; the dead man had followed the record of his sins into that lurid sea of fire, and by now was but a handful of charred dust. But if his book had closed, ours remained open and at its strangest chapter. We knew it, all of us, and waited, our nerves thrilled, with expectancy.

The Hesea sat brooding on her rocky throne. She also knew that the hour had come. Presently she sighed, then motioned with her sceptre and spoke a word or two, dismissing the priests and priestesses, who departed and were seen no more. Two of them remained however, Oros and the head priestess who was called Papave, a young woman of a noble countenance.

"Listen, my servants," she said. "Great things are about to happen, which have to do with the coming of yonder strangers, for whom I have waited these many years as is well known to you. Nor can I tell the issue since to me, to whom power is given so freely, foresight of the future is denied. It well may happen, therefore, that this seat will soon be empty and this frame but food for the eternal fires. Nay, grieve not, grieve not, for I do not die, and if so, the spirit shall return again.

"Hearken, Papave. Thou art of the blood, and to thee alone have I opened all the doors of wisdom. If I pass now or at any time, take thou the ancient power, fill thou my place, and in all things do as I have instructed thee, that from this Mountain light may shine upon the world. Further I command thee, and thee also, Oros my priest, that if I be summoned hence you entertain these strangers hospitably until it is possible to escort them from the land, whether by the road they came or across the northern hills and deserts. Should the Khania Atene attempt to detain them against their will, then raise the Tribes upon her in the name of the Hesea; depose her from her seat, conquer her land and hold it. Hear and obey."

"Mother, we hear and we will obey," answered Oros and Papave as with a single voice.

She waved her hand to show that this matter was finished; then after long thought spoke again, addressing herself to the Khania.

"Atene, last night thou didst ask me a question – why thou dost love this man," and she pointed to Leo. "To that the answer would be easy, for is he not one who might well stir passion in the breast of a woman such as thou art? But thou didst say also that thine own heart and the wisdom of yonder magician, thy uncle, told thee that since thy soul first sprang to life thou hadst loved him, and didst adjure me by the Power to whom I must give my account to draw the curtain from the past and let the truth be known.

"Woman, the hour has come, and I obey thy summons – not because thou dost command but because it is my will. Of the beginning I can tell thee nothing, who am still human and no goddess. I know not why we three are wrapped in this coil of fate; I know not the destinies to which we journey up the ladder of a thousand lives, with grief and pain climbing the endless stair of circumstance, or, if I know, I may not say. Therefore I take up the tale where my own memory gives me light."

The Hesea paused, and we saw her frame shake as though beneath some fearful inward effort of the will.

"Look now behind you," she cried, throwing her arms wide.

We turned, and at first saw nothing save the great curtain of fire that rose from the abyss of the volcano, whereof, as I have told, the crest was bent over by the wind like the crest of a breaking billow. But presently, as we watched, in the depths of this red veil, Nature's awful lamp-flame, a picture began to form as it forms in the seer's magic crystal.

Behold! a temple set amid sands and washed by a wide, palm-bordered river, and across its pyloned court processions of priests, who pass to and fro with flaunting banners. The court empties; I could see the shadow of a falcon's wings that fled across its sunlit floor. A man clad in a priest's white robe, shaven-headed, and bare-footed, enters through the southern pylon gate and walks slowly towards a painted granite shrine, in which sits the image of a woman crowned with the double crown of Egypt, surmounted by a lotus bloom, and holding in her hand the sacred sistrum. Now, as though he heard some sound, he halts and looks towards us, and by the heaven above me, his face is the face of Leo Vincey in his youth, the face too of that Kallikrates whose corpse we had seen in the Caves of Kôr!

"Look, look!" gasped Leo, catching me by the arm; but I only nodded my head in answer.

The man walks on again, and kneeling before the goddess in the shrine, embraces her feet and makes his prayer to her. Now the gates roll open, and a procession enters, headed by a veiled, noble-looking woman, who bears offerings, which she sets on the table before the shrine, bending her knee to the effigy of the goddess. Her oblations made, she turns to depart, and as she goes brushes her hand against the hand of the watching priest, who hesitates, then follows her.

When all her company have passed the gate she lingers alone in the shadow of the pylon, whispering to the priest and pointing to the river and the southern land beyond. He is disturbed; he reasons with her, till, after one swift glance round, she lets drop her veil, bending towards him and – their lips meet.

As she flies her face is turned towards us, and lo! it is the very face of Atene, and amid her dusky hair the uræus rears itself in jewelled gold, the symbol of her royal rank. She looks at the shaven priest; she laughs as though in triumph; she points to the westering sun and to the river, and is gone.

Aye, and that laugh of long ago is echoed by Atene at our side, for she also laughs in triumph and cries aloud to the old Shaman –

"True diviners were my heart and thou! Behold how I won him in the past."

Then, like ice on fire fell the cold voice of the Hesea.

"Be silent, woman, and see how thou didst lose him in the past."

Lo! the scene changes, and on a couch a lovely shape lies sleeping. She dreams; she is afraid; and over her bends and whispers in her ear a shadowy form clad with the emblems of the goddess in the shrine, but now wearing upon her head the vulture cap. The woman wakes from her dream and looks round, and oh! the face is the face of Ayesha as it was seen of us when first she loosed her veil in the Caves of Kôr.

A sigh went up from us; we could not speak who thus fearfully once more beheld her loveliness.

Again she sleeps, again the awful form bends over her and whispers. It points, the distance opens. Lo! on a stormy sea a boat, and in the boat two wrapped in each other's arms, the priest and the royal woman, while over them like a Vengeance, raw-necked and ragged-pinioned, hovers a following vulture, such a vulture as the goddess wore for headdress.

That picture fades from its burning frame, leaving the vast sheet of fire empty as the noonday sky. Then another forms. First a great, smooth-walled cave carpeted with sand, a cave that we remembered well. Then lying on the sand, now no longer shaven, but golden-haired, the corpse of the priest staring upwards with his glazed eyes, his white skin streaked with blood, and standing over him two women. One holds a javelin in her hand and is naked except for her flowing hair, and beautiful, beautiful beyond imagining. The other, wrapped in a dark cloak, beats the air with her hands, casting up her eyes as though to call the curse of Heaven upon her rival's head. And those women are she into whose sleeping ear the shadow had whispered, and the royal Egyptian who had kissed her lover beneath the pylon gate.

Slowly all the figures faded; it was as though the fire ate them up, for first they became thin and white as ashes; then vanished. The Hesea, who had been leaning forward, sank backwards in her chair, as if weary with the toil of her own magic.

For a while confused pictures flitted rapidly to and fro across the vast mirror of the flame, such as might be reflected from an intelligence crowded with the memories of over two thousand years which it was too exhausted to separate and define.

Wild scenes, multitudes of people, great caves, and in them faces, amongst others our own, starting up distorted and enormous, to grow tiny in an instant and depart; stark imaginations of Forms towering and divine; of Things monstrous and inhuman; armies marching, illimitable battle-fields, and corpses rolled in blood, and hovering over them the spirits of the slain.

These pictures died as the others had died, and the fire was blank again.

Then the Hesea spoke in a voice very faint at first, that by slow degrees grew stronger.

"Is thy question answered, O Atene?"

"I have seen strange sights, Mother, mighty limnings worthy of thy magic, but how know I that they are more than vapours of thine own brain cast upon yonder fire to deceive and mock us?"*

"Listen then," said the Hesea, in her weary voice, "to the interpretation of the writing, and cease to trouble me with thy doubts. Many an age ago, but shortly after I began to live this last, long life of mine, Isis, the great goddess of Egypt, had her Holy House at Behbit, near the Nile. It is a ruin now, and Isis has departed from Egypt, though still under the Power that fashioned it and her: she rules the world, for she is Nature's self. Of that shrine a certain man, a Greek, Kallikrates by name, was chief priest, chosen for her service by the

* Considered in the light of subsequent revelations, vouchsafed to us by Ayesha herself, I am inclined to believe that Atene's shrewd surmise was accurate, and that these fearful pictures, although founded on events that had happened in the past, were in the main 'vapours' cast upon the crater fire; visions raised in our minds to 'deceive and mock us.' – L. H. H.

favour of the goddess, vowed to her eternally and to her alone, by the dreadful oath that might not be broken without punishment as eternal.

"In the flame thou sawest that priest, and here at thy side he stands, re-born, to fulfil his destiny and ours.

"There lived also a daughter of Pharaoh's house, one Amenartas, who cast eyes of love upon this Kallikrates, and, wrapping him in her spells – for then as now she practised witcheries, – caused him to break Iris oaths and fly with her, as thou sawest written in the flame. Thou, Atene, wast that Amenartas.

"Lastly there lived a certain Arabian, named Ayesha, a wise and lovely woman, who, in the emptiness of her heart, and the sorrow of much knowledge, had sought refuge in the service of the universal Mother, thinking there to win the true wisdom which ever fled from her. That Ayesha, as thou sawest also, the goddess visited in a dream, bidding her to follow those faithless ones, and work Heaven's vengeance on them, and promising her in reward victory over death upon the earth and beauty such as had not been known in woman.

She followed far; she awaited them where they wandered. Guided by a sage named Noot, one who from the beginning had been appointed to her service and that of another – thou, O Holly, wast that man – she found the essence in which to bathe is to outlive Generations, Faiths, and Empires, saying –

" 'I will slay these guilty ones. I will slay them presently, as I am commanded.'

"Yet Ayesha slew not, for now their sin was her sin, since she who had never loved came to desire this man. She led them to the Place of Life, purposing there to clothe him and herself with immortality, and let the woman die. But it was not so fated, for then the goddess smote. The life was Ayesha's as had been sworn, but in its first hour, blinded with jealous rage because he shrank from her unveiled glory to the mortal woman at his side, this Ayesha brought him to his death, and alas! alas! left herself undying.

"Thus did the angry goddess work woe upon her faithless ministers, giving to the priest swift doom to the priestess Ayesha long remorse and misery, and to the royal Amenartas jealousy more bitter than life or death, and the fate of unending effort to win back that love which, defying Heaven, she had dared to steal, but to be bereft thereof again.

"Lo! now the ages pass, and, at the time appointed, to that undying Ayesha who, whilst awaiting his re-birth, from century to century mourned his loss, and did bitter penance for her sins, came back the man, her heart's desire. Then, whilst all went well for her and him, again the goddess smote and robbed her of her reward. Before her lover's living eyes, sunk in utter shame and misery, the beautiful became hideous, the undying seemed to die.

"Yet, O Kallikrates, I tell thee that she died not. Did not Ayesha swear to thee yonder in the caves of Kôr that she would come again? for even in that awful hour this comfort kissed her soul. Thereafter, Leo Vincey, who art Kallikrates, did not her spirit lead thee in thy sleep and stand with thee upon this very pinnacle which should be thy beacon light to guide thee back to her? And didst thou not search these many years, not knowing that she companioned thy every step and strove to guard thee in every danger, till at length in the permitted hour thou earnest back to her?"

She paused, and looked towards Leo, as though awaiting his reply.

"Of the first part of the tale, except from the writing on the sherd, I know nothing, Lady," he said; "of the rest I, or rather we, know that it is true. Yet I would ask a question, and I pray thee of thy charity let thy answer be swift and short. Thou sayest that in the permitted hour I came back to Ayesha. Where then is Ayesha? Art thou Ayesha? And if so why is thy voice changed? Why art thou less in stature? Oh! in the name of whatever god thou dost worship, tell me art thou Ayesha?"

"I am Ayesha" she answered solemnly, "that very Ayesha to whom thou didst pledge thyself eternally."

"She lies, she lies," broke in Atene. "I tell thee, husband – for such with her own lips she declares thou art to me – that yonder woman who says that she parted from thee young and beautiful, less than twenty years ago, is none other than the aged priestess who for a century at least has borne rule in these halls of Hes. Let her deny it if she can."

"Oros," said the Mother, "tell thou the tale of the death of that priestess of whom the Khania speaks."

The priest bowed, and in his usual calm voice, as though he were narrating some event of every day, said mechanically, and in a fashion that carried no conviction to my mind.

"Eighteen years ago, on the fourth night of the first month of winter in the year 2333 of the founding of the worship of Hes on this Mountain, the priestess of whom the Khania Atene speaks died of old age in my presence in the hundred and eighth year of her rule. Three hours later we went to lift her from the throne on which she died, to prepare her corpse for burial in this fire, according to the ancient custom. Lo! a miracle, for she lived again, the same, yet very changed.

"Thinking this a work of evil magic, the Priests and Priestesses of the College rejected her, and would have driven her from the throne. Thereon the Mountain blazed and thundered, the light from the fiery pillars died, and great terror fell upon the souls of men. Then from the deep darkness above the altar where stands the statue of the Mother of Men, the voice of the living goddess spoke, saying –

" 'Accept ye her whom I have set to rule over you, that my judgments and my purposes may be fulfilled.'

"The Voice ceased, the fiery torches burnt again, and we bowed the knee to the new Hesea, and named her Mother in the ears of all. That is the tale to which hundreds can bear witness."

"Thou hearest, Atene," said the Hesea. "Dost thou still doubt?"

"Aye," answered the Khania, "for I hold that Oros also lies, or if he lies not, then he dreams, or perchance that voice he heard was thine own. Now if thou art this undying woman, this Ayesha, let proof be made of it to these two men who knew thee in the past. Tear away those wrappings that guard thy loveliness thus jealously. Let thy shape divine, thy beauty incomparable, shine out upon our dazzled sight. Surely thy lover will not forget such charms; surely he will know thee, and bow the knee, saying, 'This is my Immortal, and no other woman.'

"Then, and not till then, will I believe that thou art even what thou declarest thyself to be, an evil spirit, who bought undying life with murder and used thy demon loveliness to bewitch the souls of men."

Now the Hesea on the throne seemed to be much troubled, for she rocked herself to and fro, and wrung her white-draped hands.

"Kallikrates," she said in a voice that sounded like a moan, "is this thy will? For if it be, know that I must obey. Yet I pray thee command it not, for the time is not yet come; the promise unbreakable is not yet fulfilled. *I am somewhat changed,* Kallikrates, since I kissed thee on the brow and named thee mine, yonder in the Caves of Kôr."

Leo looked about him desperately, till his eyes fell upon the mocking face of Atene, who cried –

"Bid her unveil, my lord. I swear to thee I'll not be jealous."

At that taunt he took fire.

"Aye," he said, "I bid her unveil, that I may learn the best of worst, who otherwise must die of this suspense. Howsoever changed, if she be Ayesha I shall know her, and if she be Ayesha. I shall love her."

"Bold words, Kallikrates," answered the Hesea; "yet from my very heart I thank thee for them: those sweet words of trust and faithfulness to thou knowest not what. Learn now the truth, for I may keep naught back from thee. When I unveil it is decreed that thou must make thy choice for the last time on this earth between yonder woman, my rival from the beginning, and that Ayesha to whom thou art sworn. Thou canst reject me if thou wilt, and no ill shall come to thee, but many a blessing, as men reckon them – power and wealth and love. Only then thou must tear my memory from thy heart, for then I leave thee to follow thy fate alone, till at the last the purpose of these deeds and sufferings is made clear.

"Be warned. No light ordeal lies before thee. Be warned. I can promise thee naught save such love as woman never gave to man, love that perchance – I know not – must yet remain unsatisfied upon the earth."

Then she turned to me and said: "Oh! thou. Holly, thou true friend, thou guardian from of old, thou, next to him most beloved by me, to thy clear and innocent spirit perchance wisdom may be given that is denied to us, the little children whom thine arms protect. Counsel thou him, my Holly, with the counsel that is given thee, and I will obey thy words and his, and, whatever befalls, will bless thee from my soul. Aye, and should he cast me off, then in the Land beyond the lands, in the Star appointed, where all earthly passions fade, together will we dwell eternally in a friendship glorious, thou and I alone."

"For *thou* wilt not reject; thy steel, forged in the furnace of pure truth and power, shall not lose its temper in these small fires of temptation and become a rusted chain to bind thee to another woman's breast – until it canker to her heart and thine."

"Ayesha, I thank thee for thy words," I answered simply, "and by them and that promise of thine, I, thy poor friend – for more I never thought to be – am a thousandfold repaid for many sufferings. This I will add, that for my part I know that thou art She whom we have lost, since, whate'er the lips that speak them, those thoughts and words are Ayesha's and hers alone."

Thus I spoke, not knowing what else to say, for I was filled with a great joy, a calm and ineffable satisfaction, which broke thus feebly from my heart. For now I knew that I was dear to Ayesha as I had always been dear to Leo; the closest of friends, from whom she never would be parted. What more could I desire?"

We fell back; we spoke together, whilst they watched us silently. What we said I do not quite remember, but the end of it was that, as the Hesea had done, Leo bade me judge and choose. Then into my mind there came a clear command, from my own conscience or otherwhere, who can say? This was the command, that I should bid her to unveil, and let fate declare its purposes.

"Decide," said Leo, "I cannot bear much more. Like that woman, whoever she may be, whatever happens, I will not blame you, Horace."

"Good," I answered, "I have decided," and, stepping forward, I said: "We have taken counsel, Hes, and it is our will, who would learn the truth and be at rest, that thou shouldst unveil before us, here and now."

"I hear and obey," the Priestess answered, in a voice like to that of a dying woman, "only, I beseech you both, be pitiful to me, spare me your mockeries; add not the coals of your hate and scorn to the fires of a soul in hell, for whate'er I am, I became it for thy sake, Kallikrates. Yet, yet I also am athirst for knowledge; for though I know all wisdom, although I wield much power, one thing remains to me to learn – what is the worth of the love of man, and if, indeed, it can live beyond the horrors of the grave?"

Then, rising slowly, the Hesea walked, or rather tottered to the unroofed open space in front of the rock chamber, and stood there quite near to the brink of the flaming gulf beneath.

"Come hither, Papave, and loose these veils," she cried in a shrill, thin voice.

Papave advanced, and with a look of awe upon her handsome face began the task. She was not a tall woman, yet as she bent over her I noted that she seemed to tower above her mistress, the Hesea.

The outer veils fell revealing more within. These fell also, and now before us stood the mummy-like shape, although it seemed to be of less stature, of that strange being who had met us in the Place of Bones. So it would seem that our mysterious guide and the high priestess Hes were the same.

Look! Length by length the wrappings sank from her. Would they never end? How small grew the frame within? She was very short now, unnaturally short for a full-grown woman, and oh! I grew sick at heart. The last bandages uncoiled themselves like shavings from a stick; two wrinkled hands appeared, if hands they could be called. Then the feet – once I had seen such on the mummy of a princess of Egypt, and even now by some fantastic play of the mind, I remembered that on her coffin this princess was named "The Beautiful."

Everything was gone now, except a shift and a last inner veil about the head. Hes waved back the priestess Papave, who fell half fainting to the ground and lay there covering her eyes with her hand. Then uttering something like a scream she gripped this veil in her thin talons, tore it away, and with a gesture of uttermost despair, turned and faced us.

Oh! she was – nay, I will not describe her. I knew her at once, for thus had I seen her last before the Fire of Life, and, strangely enough, through the mask of unutterable age, through that cloak of humanity's last decay, still shone some resemblance to the glorious and superhuman Ayesha: the shape of the face, the air of defiant pride that for an instant bore her up – I know not what.

Yes, there she stood, and the fierce light of the heartless fires beat upon her, revealing every shame.

There was a dreadful silence. I saw Leo's lips turn white and his knees begin to give; but by some effort he recovered himself, and stayed still and upright like a dead man held by a wire. Also I saw Atene – and this is to her credit – turn her head away. She had desired to see her rival humiliated, but that horrible sight shocked her; some sense of their common womanhood for the moment touched her pity. Only Simbri, who, I think, knew what to expect, and Oros remained quite unmoved; indeed, in that ghastly silence the latter spoke, and ever afterwards I loved him for his words.

"What of the vile vessel, rotted in the grave of time? What of the flesh that perishes?" he said. "Look through the ruined lamp to the eternal light which burns within. Look through its covering carrion to the inextinguishable soul."

My heart applauded these noble sentiments. I was of one mind with Oros, but oh. Heaven! I felt that my brain was going, and I wished that it would go, so that I might hear and see no more.

That look which gathered on Ayesha's mummy face! At first there had been a little hope, but the hope died, and anguish, anguish, *anguish* took its place.

Something must be done, this could not endure. My lips clave together, no word would come; my feet refused to move.

I began to contemplate the scenery. How wonderful were that sheet of flame, and the ripples which ran up and down its height. How awesome its billowy crest. It would be warm lying in yonder red gulf below with the dead Rassen, but oh! I wished that I shared his bed and had finished with these agonies.

Thank Heaven, Atene was speaking. She had stepped to the side of the naked-headed Thing, and stood by it in all the pride of her rich beauty and perfect womanhood.

"Leo Vincey, or Kallikrates," said Atene, "take which name thou wilt; thou thinkest ill of me perhaps, but know that at least I scorn to mock a rival in her mortal shame. She told us a wild tale but now, a tale true or false, but more false than true, I think, of how I robbed a goddess of a votary, and of how that goddess – Ayesha's self perchance – was avenged upon me for the crime of yielding to the man I loved. Well, let goddesses – if such indeed there be – take their way and work their will upon the helpless, and I, a mortal, will take mine until the clutch of doom doses round my throat and chokes out life and memory, and I too am a goddess – or a clod.

"Meanwhile, thou man, I shame not to say it before all these witnesses, I love thee, and it seems that this – this woman or goddess – loves thee also, and she has told us that now, *now* thou must choose between us once and for ever. She has told us too that if I sinned against Isis, whose minister be it remembered she declares herself, herself she sinned yet more. For she would have taken thee both from a heavenly mistress and from an earthly bride, and yet snatch that guerdon of immortality which is hers to-day. Therefore if I am evil, she is worse, nor does the flame that burns within the casket whereof Oros spoke shine so very pure and bright.

"Choose thou then Leo Vincey, and let there be an end. I vaunt not myself; thou knowest what I have been and seest what I am. Yet I can give thee love and happiness and, mayhap, children to follow after thee, and with them some place and power. What yonder witch can give thee thou canst guess. Tales of the past, pictures on the flame, wise maxims and honeyed words, and after thou art dead once more, promises perhaps, of joy to come when that terrible goddess whom she serves so closely shall be appeased. I have spoken. Yet I will add a word:

"O thou for whom, if the Hesea's tale be true, I did once lay down my royal rank and dare the dangers of an unsailed sea; O thou whom in ages gone I would have sheltered with my frail body from the sorceries of this cold, self-seeking witch; O thou whom but a little while ago at my own life's risk I drew from death in yonder river, choose, choose!"

To all this speech, so moderate yet so cruel, so well – reasoned and yet so false, because of its glosses and omissions, the huddled Ayesha seemed to listen with a fierce intentness. Yet she made no answer, not a single word, not a sign even; she who had said her say and scorned to plead her part.

I looked at Leo's ashen face. He leaned towards Atene, drawn perhaps by the passion shining in her beauteous eyes, then of a sudden straightened himself, shook his head and sighed. The colour flamed to his brow, and his eyes grew almost happy.

"After all," he said, thinking aloud rather than speaking. "I have to do not with unknowable pasts or with mystic futures, but with the things of my own life. Ayesha waited for me through two thousand years; Atene could marry a man she hated for power's sake, and then could poison him, as perhaps she would poison me when I wearied her. I know not what oaths I swore to Amenartas, if such a woman lived. I remember the oaths I swore to Ayesha. If I shrink from her now, why then my life is a lie and my belief a fraud; then love will not endure the touch of age and never can survive the grave.

"Nay, remembering what Ayesha was I take her as she is, in faith and hope of what she shall be. At least love is immortal and if it must, why let it feed on memory alone till death sets free the soul."

Then stepping to where stood the dreadful, shrivelled form, Leo knelt down before it and kissed her on the brow.

Yes, he kissed the trembling horror of that wrinkled head, and I think it was one of the greatest, bravest acts ever done by man.

"Thou hast chosen," said Atene in a cold voice, "and I tell thee, Leo Vincey, that the manner of thy choice makes me mourn my loss the more. Take now thy – thy bride and let me hence."

But Ayesha still said no word and made no sign, till presently she sank upon her bony knees and began to pray aloud. These were the words of her prayer, as I heard them, though the exact Power to which it was addressed is not very easy to determine, as I never discovered who or what it was that she worshipped in her heart –

"O Thou minister of the almighty Will, thou sharp sword in the hand of Doom, thou inevitable Law that art named Nature; thou who wast crowned as Isis of the Egyptians, but art the goddess of all climes and ages; thou that leadest the man to the maid and layest the infant on his mother's breast, that bringest our dust to its kindred dust, that givest life to death, and into the dark of death breathest the light of life again; thou who causest the abundant earth to bear, whose smile is Spring, whose laugh is the ripple of the sea, whose noontide rest is drowsy Summer, and whose sleep is

Winter's night, hear thou the supplication of thy chosen child and minister:

"Of old thou gavest me thine own strength with deathless days, and beauty above every daughter of this Star. But I sinned against thee sore, and for my sin I paid in endless centuries of solitude, in the vileness that makes me loathsome to my lover's eyes, and for its diadem of perfect power sets upon my brow this crown of naked mockery. Yet in thy breath, the swift essence that brought me light, that brought me gloom, thou didst vow to me that I who cannot die should once more pluck the lost flower of my immortal loveliness from this foul slime of shame.

"Therefore, merciful Mother that bore me, to thee I make my prayer. Oh, let his true love atone my sin; or, if it may not be, then give me death, the last and most blessed of thy boons!"

CHAPTER 16

THE CHANGE

SHE CEASED, and there was a long, long silence. Leo and I looked at each other in dismay. We had hoped against hope that this beautiful and piteous prayer, addressed apparently to the great, dumb spirit of Nature, would be answered. That meant a miracle, but what of it? The prolongation of the life of Ayesha was a miracle, though it is true that some humble reptiles are said to live as long as she had done.

The transference of her spirit from the Caves of Kôr to this temple was a miracle, that is, to our western minds, though the dwellers in these parts of Central Asia would not hold it so. That she should re-appear with the same hideous body was a miracle. But was it the same body? Was it not the body of the last Hesea? One very ancient woman is much like another, and eighteen years of the working of the soul or identity within might well wear away their trivial differences and give to the borrowed form some resemblance to that which it had left.

At least the figures on that mirror of the flame were a miracle. Nay, why so? A hundred clairvoyants in a hundred cities can produce or see their like in water and in crystal, the difference being only one of size. They were but reflections of scenes familiar to the mind of Ayesha, or perhaps not so much as that. Perhaps they were only phantasms called up in *our* minds by her mesmeric force.

Nay, none of these things were true miracles, since all, however strange, might be capable of explanation. What right then had we to expect a marvel now?

Such thoughts as these rose in our minds as the endless minutes were born and died and – nothing happened.

Yes, at last one thing did happen. The light from the sheet of flame died gradually away as the flame itself sank downwards into the abysses of the pit. But about this in itself there was nothing wonderful, for as we had seen with our own eyes from afar this fire varied much, and indeed it was customary for it to die down at the approach of dawn, which now drew very near.

Still that onward-creeping darkness added to the terrors of the scene. By the last rays of the lurid light we saw Ayesha rise and advance some few paces to that little tongue of rock at the edge of the pit off which the body of Rassen had been hurled; saw her standing on it also, looking like some black, misshapen imp against the smoky glow which still rose from the depths beneath.

Leo would have gone forward to her, for he believed that she was about to hurl herself to doom, which indeed I thought was her design. But the priest Oros, and the priestess Papave, obeying, I suppose, some secret command that reached them I know not how, sprang to him and seizing his arms, held him back. Then it became quite dark, and through the darkness we could hear Ayesha chanting a dirge-like hymn in some secret, holy tongue which was unknown to us.

A great flake of fire floated through the gloom, rocking to and fro like some vast bird upon its pinions. We had seen many such that night, torn by the gale from the crest of the blazing curtain as I have described. But – but –

"Horace," whispered Leo through his chattering teeth, "that flame is coming up *against the wind!*"

"Perhaps the wind has changed," I answered, though I knew well that it had not; that it blew stronger than ever from the south.

Nearer and nearer sailed the rocking flame, two enormous wings was the shape of it, with something dark between them. It reached the little promontory. The wings appeared to fold themselves about the dwarfed figure that stood thereon – illuminating it for a moment. Then the light went out of them and they vanished – everything vanished.

A while passed, it may have been one minute or ten, when suddenly the priestess Papave, in obedience to some summons which we could not hear, crept by me. I knew that it was she because her woman's garments touched me as she went. Another space of silence and of deep darkness, during which I heard Papave return, breathing in short, sobbing gasps like one who is very frightened.

Ah! I thought, Ayesha has cast herself into the pit. The tragedy is finished!

Then it was that the wondrous music came. Of course it *may* have been only the sound of priests chanting beyond us, but I do not think so, since its quality was quite different to any that I heard in the temple before or afterwards: to any indeed that ever I heard upon the earth.

I cannot describe it, but it was awful to listen to, yet most entrancing. From the black, smoke-veiled pit where the fire had burned it welled and echoed – now a single heavenly voice, now a sweet chorus, and now an air-shaking thunder as of a hundred organs played to time.

That diverse and majestic harmony seemed to include, to express every human emotion, and I have often thought since then that in its all-embracing scope and range, this, the song or pæan of her rebirth was symbolical of the infinite variety of Ayesha's spirit. Yet like that spirit it had its master notes; power, passion, suffering, mystery and loveliness. Also there could be no doubt as to the general significance of the chant by whomsoever it was sung. It was the changeful story of a mighty soul; it was worship, worship, worship of a queen divine!

Like slow clouds of incense fading to the bannered roof of some high choir, the bursts of unearthly melodies grew faint; in the far distance of the hollow pit they wailed themselves away.

Look! from the east a single ray of upward-springing light.

"Behold the dawn," said the quiet voice of Oros.

That ray pierced the heavens above our heads, a very sword of flame. It sank downwards, swiftly. Suddenly it fell, not upon us, for as yet the rocky walls of our chamber warded it away, but on to the little promontory at its edge.

Oh! and there – a Glory covered with a single garment – stood a shape celestial. It seemed to be asleep, since the eyes were shut. Or was it dead, for at first that face was a face of death? Look, the sunlight played upon her, shining through the thin veil, the dark eyes opened like the eyes of a wondering child; the blood of life flowed up the ivory bosom into the pallid cheeks; the raiment of black and curling tresses wavered in the wind; the head of the jewelled snake that held them sparkled beneath her breast.

Was it an illusion, or was this Ayesha as she had been when she entered the rolling flame in the caverns of Kôr? Our knees gave way beneath us, and down, our arms about each other's necks, Leo and I sank till we lay upon the ground. Then a voice sweeter than honey, softer than the whisper of a twilight breeze among the reeds, spoke near to us, and these were the words it said –

"*Come hither to me, Kallikrates, who would pay thee back that redeeming kiss of faith and love thou gavest me but now!*"

Leo struggled to his feet. Like a drunken man he staggered to where Ayesha stood, then overcome, sank before her on his knees.

"Arise," she said, "it is I who should kneel to thee," and she stretched out her hand to raise him, whispering in his ear the while.

Still he would not, or could not rise, so very slowly she bent over him and touched him with her lips upon the brow. Next she beckoned to me. I came and would have knelt also, but she suffered it not.

"Nay," she said, in her rich, remembered voice, "thou art no suitor; it shall not be. Of lovers and worshippers henceforth as before, I can find a plenty if I will, or even if I will it not. But where shall I find another friend like to thee, O Holly, whom thus I greet?" and leaning towards me, with her lips she touched me also on the brow – just touched me, and no more.

Fragrant was Ayesha's breath as roses, the odour of roses clung to her lovely hair; her sweet body gleamed like some white sea-pearl; a faint but palpable radiance crowned her head; no sculptor ever fashioned such a marvel as the arm with which she held her veil about her; no stars in heaven ever shone more purely bright than did her calm, entranced eyes.

Yet it is true, even with her lips upon me, all I felt for her was a love divine into which no human passion entered. Once, I acknowledge to my shame, it was otherwise, but I am an old man now and have done with such frailties. Moreover, had not Ayesha named me Guardian, Protector, Friend, and sworn to me that with her and Leo I should ever dwell where all earthly passions fail. I repeat; what more could I desire? Taking Leo by the hand Ayesha returned with him into the shelter of the rock-hewn chamber and when she entered its shadows, shivered a little as though with cold. I rejoiced at this I remember, for it seemed to show me that she still was human, divine as she might appear. Here her priest and priestess prostrated themselves before her new-born splendour, but she motioned to them to rise, laying a hand upon the head of each as though in blessing.

"I am a' cold," she said, "give me my mantle," and Papave threw the purple-broidered garment upon her shoulders, whence now it hung royally, like a coronation robe.

"Nay," she went on, "it is not this long-lost shape of mine, which in his kiss my lord gave back to me, that shivers in the icy wind, it is my spirit's self bared to the bitter breath of Destiny. O my love, my love, offended Powers are not easily appeased, even when they appear to pardon, and though I shall no more be made a mockery in thy sight, how long is given us together upon the world I know not but a little hour perchance. Well, ere we pass otherwhere, we will make it glorious, drinking as deeply of the cup of joy as we have drunk of those of sorrows and of shame. This place is hateful to me, for here I have suffered more than ever woman did on earth or phantom in the deepest hell. It is hateful, it is ill-omened. I pray that never again may I behold it.

"Say, what is it passes in thy mind, magician?" and of a sudden she turned fiercely upon the Shaman Simbri who stood near, his arms crossed upon his breast.

"Only, thou Beautiful," he answered, "a dim shadow of things to come. "I have what thou dost lack with all thy wisdom, the gift of foresight, and here I see a dead man lying – "

"Another word," she broke in with fury born of some dark fear," and thoushalt be that man. Fool, put me not in mind that now I have strength again to rid me of the ancient foes I hate, lest I should use a sword thou thrustest to my hand," and her eyes that had been so calm and happy, blazed upon him like fire.

The old wizard felt their fearsome might and shrank from it till the wall stayed him.

"Great One! now as ever I salute thee. Yes, now as at the first beginning whereof we know alone," he stammered. "I had no more to say; the face of that dead man was not revealed to me. I saw only that some crowned Khan of Kaloon to be shall lie here, as he whom the flame has taken lay an hour ago."

"Doubtless many a Khan of Kaloon will lie here," she answered coldly. "Fear not, Shaman, my wrath is past, yet be wise, mine enemy, and prophesy no more evil to the great. Come, let us hence."

So, still led by Leo, she passed from that chamber and stood presently upon the apex of the soaring pillar. The sun was up now, flooding the Mountain flanks, the plains of

Kaloon far beneath and the distant, misty peaks with a sheen of gold. Ayesha stood considering the mighty prospect, then addressing Leo, she said –

"The world is very fair; I give it all to thee."

Now Atene spoke for the first time.

"Dost thou mean Hes – if thou art still the Hesea and not a demon arisen from the Pit – that thou offerest my territories to this man as a love-gift? If so, I tell thee that first thou must conquer them."

"Ungentle are thy words and mien," answered Ayesha, "yet I forgive them both, for I also can scorn to mock a rival in my hour of victory. When thou wast the fairer, thou didst proffer him these very lands, but say, who is the fairer now? Look at us, all of you, and judge," and she stood by Atene and smiled.

The Khania was a lovely woman. Never to my knowledge have I seen one lovelier, but oh! how coarse and poor she showed beside the wild, ethereal beauty of Ayesha born again. For that beauty was not altogether human, far less so indeed than it had been in the Caves of Kôr; now it was the beauty of a spirit.

The little light that always shone upon Ayesha's brow; the wide-set, maddening eyes which were filled sometimes with the fire of the stars and sometimes with the blue darkness of the heavens wherein they float; the curved lips, so wistful yet so proud; the tresses fine as glossy silk that still spread and rippled as though with a separate life; the general air, not so much of majesty as of some secret power hard to be restrained, which strove in that delicate body and proclaimed its presence to the most careless; that flame of the soul within whereof Oros had spoken, shining now through no "vile vessel." but in a vase of alabaster and of pearl – none of these things and qualities were altogether human. I felt it and was afraid, and Atene felt it also, for she answered –

"I am but a woman. What thou art, thou knowest best. Still a taper cannot shine midst yonder fires or a glow-worm against a fallen star; nor can my mortal flesh compare with the glory thou hast earned from hell in payment for thy gifts and homage to the lord of Ill. Yet as woman I am thy equal, and as spirit I shall be thy mistress, when robbed of these borrowed beauties thou, Ayesha, standest naked and ashamed before the Judge of all whom thou hast deserted and defied; yes, as thou stoodest but now upon yonder brink above the burning pit where thou yet shalt wander wailing thy lost love. For this I know, mine enemy, that *man and spirit cannot mate,*" and Atene ceased, choking in her bitter rage and jealousy.

Now watching Ayesha, I saw her wince a little beneath these evil-omened words, saw also a tinge of grey touch the carmine of her lips and her deep eyes grow dark and troubled. But in a moment her fears had gone and she was asking in a voice that rang clear as silver bells –

"Why ravest thou, Atene, like some short-lived summer torrent against the barrier of a seamless cliff? Dost think, poor creature of an hour, to sweep away the rock of my eternal strength with foam and bursting bubbles? Have done and listen. I do not seek thy petty rule, who, if I will it, can take the empire of the world. Yet learn, thou boldest it of my hand. More – I purpose soon to visit thee in thy city – choose thou if it shall be in peace or war!

"Therefore, Khania, purge thy court and amend thy laws, that when I come I may find contentment in the land which now it lacks, and confirm thee in thy government. My counsel to thee also is that thou choose some worthy man to husband, let him be whom thou wilt, if only he is just and upright and one upon whom thou mayest rest, needing wise guidance as thou dost, Atene.

"Come, now, my guests, let us hence," and she walked past the Khania, stepping fearlessly upon the very edge of the wind-swept, rounded peak.

In a second the attempt had been made and failed, so quickly indeed that it was not until Leo and I compared our impressions afterwards that we could be sure of what had happened. As Ayesha passed her, the maddened Khania drew a hidden dagger and struck with all her force at her rival's back. I saw the knife vanish to the hilt in her body, as I thought, but this cannot have been so since it fell to the ground, and she who should have been dead, took no hurt at all.

Feeling that she had failed, with a movement like the sudden lurch of a ship, Atene thrust at Ayesha, proposing to hurl her to destruction in the depths beneath. Lo! her outstretched arms went past her although Ayesha never seemed to stir. Yes it was Atene who would have fallen, Atene who already fell, had not Ayesha put out her hand and caught her by the wrist, bearing all her backward-swaying weight as easily as though she were but an infant, and without effort drawing her to safety.

"Foolish woman!" she said in pitying tones. "Wast thou so vexed that thou wouldst strip thyself of the pleasant shape which heaven has given thee? Surely this is madness, Atene, for how knowest thou in what likeness thou mightest be sent to tread the earth again? As no queen perhaps, but as a peasant's child, deformed, unsightly; for such reward, it is said, is given to those that achieve self-murder. Or even, as many think, shaped like a beast – a snake, a cat, a tigress! Why, see," and she picked the dagger from the ground and cast it into the air, "that point was poisoned. Had it but pricked thee now!" and she smiled at her and shook her head.

But Atene could bear no more of this mockery, more venomed than her own steel.

"Thou art not mortal," she wailed. "How can I prevail against thee? To Heaven I leave thy punishment," and there upon the rocky peak Atene sank down and wept.

Leo stood nearest to her, and the sight of this royal woman in her misery proved too much for him to bear. Stepping to her side he stooped and lifted her to her feet, muttering some kind words. For a moment she rested on his arm, then shook herself free of him and took the proffered hand of her old uncle Simbri.

"I see," said Ayesha, "that as ever, thou art courteous, my lord Leo, but it is best that her own servant should take charge of her, for – she may hide more daggers. Come, the day grows, and surely we need rest."

CHAPTER 17

THE BETROTHAL

"'TOGETHER WE descended the multitudinous steps and passed the endless, rock-hewn passages till we came to the door of the dwelling of the high-priestess and were led through it into a hall beyond. Here Ayesha parted from us saying that she was outworn, as indeed she seemed to be with an utter weariness, not of the body, but of the spirit. For her delicate form drooped like a rain-laden lily, her eyes grew dim as those of a person in a trance, and her voice came in a soft, sweet whisper, the voice of one speaking in her sleep.

"Good-bye," she said to us, "Oros will guard you both, and lead you to me at the appointed time. Rest you well."

So she went and the priest led us into a beautiful apartment that opened on to a sheltered garden. So overcome were we also by all that we had endured and seen, that we could scarcely speak, much less discuss these marvellous events.

"My brain swims," said Leo to Oros, "I desire to sleep."

He bowed and conducted us to a chamber where were beds, and on these we flung ourselves down and slept, dreamlessly, like little children.

When we awoke it was afternoon. We rose and bathed, then saying that we wished to be alone, went together into the garden where even at this altitude, now, at the end of August, the air was still mild and pleasant. Behind a rock by a bed of campanulas and other mountain flowers and ferns, was a bench near to the banks of a little stream, on which we seated ourselves.

"What have you to say, Horace?" asked Leo laying his hand upon my arm.

"Say?" I answered. "That things have come about most marvellously; that we have dreamed aright and laboured not in vain; that you are the most fortunate of men and should be the most happy."

He looked at me somewhat strangely, and answered –

"Yes, of course; she is lovely, is she not – but," and his voice dropped to its lowest whisper, "I wish, Horace, that Ayesha were a little more human, even as human as she was in the Caves of Kôr. I don't think she is quite flesh and blood, I felt it when she kissed me – if you can call it a kiss – for she barely touched my hair. Indeed how can she be who changed thus in an hour? Flesh and blood are not born of flame, Horace."

"Are you sure that she was so born?" I asked. "Like the visions on the fire, may not that hideous shape have been but an illusion of our minds? May she not be still the same Ayesha whom we knew in Kôr, not re-born, but wafted hither by some mysterious agency?"

"Perhaps. Horace, we do not know – I think that we shall never know. But I admit that to me the thing is terrifying. I am drawn to her by an infinite attraction, her eyes set my blood on fire, the touch of her hand is as that of a wand of madness laid upon my brain. And yet between us there is some wall, invisible, still present. Or perhaps it is only fancy. But, Horace, I think that she is afraid of Atene. Why, in the old days the Khania would have been dead and forgotten in an hour – you remember Ustane?"

"Perhaps she may have grown more gentle, Leo, who, like ourselves, has learned hard lessons."

"Yes," he answered," I hope that is so. At any rate she has grown more divine – only, Horace, what kind of a husband shall I be for that bright being, if ever I get so far?"

"Why should you not get so far?" I asked angrily, for his words jarred upon my tense nerves.

"I don't know," he answered, "but on general principles do you think that such fortune will be allowed to a man? Also, what did Atene mean when she said that man and spirit cannot mate – and – other things?"

"She meant that she *hoped* they could, not, I imagine, and, Leo, it is useless to trouble yourself with forebodings that are more fitted to my years than yours, and probably are based on nothing. Be a philosopher, Leo. You have striven by wonderful ways such as are unknown in the history of the world; you have attained. Take the goods the gods provide you – the glory, the love and the power – and let the future look to itself."

Before he could answer Oros appeared from round the rock, and, bowing with more than his usual humility to Leo, said that the Hesea desired our presence at a service in the Sanctuary. Rejoiced at the prospect of seeing her again before he had hoped to do so, Leo sprang up and we accompanied him back to our apartment.

Here priests were waiting, who, somewhat against his will, trimmed his hair and beard, and would have done the same for me had I not refused their offices. Then they placed gold-embroidered sandals on our feet and wrapped Leo in a magnificent white robe, also richly worked with gold and purple; a somewhat similar robe, but of less ornate design, being given to me. Lastly, a silver sceptre was thrust into his hand and into my mine a plain wand. This sceptre was shaped like a crook, and the sight of it gave me some clue to the nature of the forthcoming ceremony.

"The crook of Osiris!" I whispered to Leo.

"Look here," he answered, "I don't want to impersonate any Egyptian god, or to be mixed up in their heathen idolatries; in fact, I won't."

"Better go through with it," I suggested, "probably it is only something symbolical."

But Leo, who, notwithstanding the strange circumstances connected with his life, retained the religious principles in which I had educated him very strongly indeed, refused to move an inch until the nature of this service was made clear to him. Indeed he expressed himself upon the subject with vigour to Oros. At first the priest seemed puzzled what to do, then explained that the forthcoming ceremony was one of betrothal.

On learning this Leo raised no farther objections, asking only with some nervousness whether the Khania would be present. Oros answered "No," as she had already departed to Kaloon, vowing war and vengeance.

Then we were led through long passages, till finally we emerged into the gallery immediately in front of the great wooden doors of the apse. At our approach these swung open and we entered it, Oros going first, then Leo, then myself, and following us, the procession of attendant priests.

As soon as our eyes became accustomed to the dazzling glare of the naming pillars, we saw that some great rite was in progress in the temple, for in front of the divine statue of Motherhood, white-robed and arranged in serried ranks, stood the company of the priests to the number of over two hundred, and behind these the company of the priestesses. Facing this congregation and a little in advance of the two pillars of fire that flared on either side of the shrine, Ayesha herself was seated in a raised chair so that she could be seen of all, while to her right stood a similar chair of which I could guess the purpose.

She was unveiled and gorgeously apparelled, though save for the white beneath, her robes were those of a queen rather than of a priestess. About her radiant brow ran a narrow band of gold, whence rose the head of a hooded asp cut out of a single crimson jewel, beneath which in endless profusion the glorious waving hair flowed down and around, hiding even the folds of her purple cloak.

This cloak, opening in front, revealed an under-tunic of white silk cut low upon her bosom and kept in place by a golden girdle, a double-headed snake, so like to that which She had worn in Kôr that it might have been the same. Her naked arms were bare of ornament, and in her right hand she held the jewelled sistrum set with its gems and bells.

No empress could have looked more royal and no woman was ever half so lovely, for to Ayesha's human beauty was added a spiritual glory, her heritage alone. Seeing her we could see naught else. The rhythmic movement of the bodies of the worshippers, the rolling grandeur of their chant of welcome echoed from the mighty roof, the fearful torches of living flame; all these things were lost on us. For there re-born, enthroned, her arms stretched out in gracious welcome, sat that perfect and immortal woman, the appointed bride of one of us, the friend and lady of the other, her divine presence breathing power, mystery and love.

On we marched between the ranks of hierophants, till Oros and the priests left us and we stood alone face to face with Ayesha. Now she lifted her sceptre and the chant ceased. In the midst of the following silence, she rose from her seat and gliding down its steps, came to where Leo stood and touched him on the forehead with her sistrum, crying in a loud, sweet voice –

"Behold the Chosen of the Hesea!" whereon all that audience echoed in a shout of thunder –

"Welcome to the Chosen of the Hesea!"

Then while the echoes of that glad cry yet rang round the rocky walls. Ayesha motioned to me to stand at her side, and taking Leo by the hand drew him towards her, so that now he faced the white-robed company. Holding him thus she began to speak in clear and silvery tones.

"Priests and priestesses of Hes, servants with her of the Mother of the world, hear me. Now for the first time I appear among you as I am, you who heretofore have looked but on a hooded shape, not knowing its form or fashion. Learn now the reason that I draw my veil. Ye see this man, whom ye believed a stranger that with his companion had wandered to our shrine. I tell you that he is no stranger; that of old, in lives forgotten, he was my lord who now comes to seek his love again. Say, is it not so, Kallikrates?"

"It is so," answered Leo.

"Priests and priestesses of Hes, as ye know, from the beginning it has been the right and custom of her who holds my place to choose one to be her lord. Is it not so?"

"It is so, O Hes," they answered.

She paused a while, then with a gesture of infinite sweetness turned to Leo, bent towards him thrice and slowly sank upon her knee.

"Say thou," Ayesha said, looking up at him with her wondrous eyes, "say before these here gathered, and all those witnesses whom thou canst not see, dost thou again accept me as thy affianced bride?"

"Aye, Lady," he answered, in a deep but shaken voice, "now and for ever."

Then while all watched, in the midst of a great silence. Ayesha rose, cast down her sistrum sceptre that rang upon the rocky floor, and stretched out her aims towards him.

Leo also bent towards her, and would have kissed her upon the lips. But I who watched, saw his face grow white as it drew near to hers. While the radiance crept from her brow to his, turning his bright hair to gold, I saw also that this strong man trembled like a reed and seemed as though he were about to fall.

I think that Ayesha noted it too, for ere ever their lips met she thrust him from her, and again that grey mist of fear gathered on her face.

In an instant it passed. She had slipped from him and with her hand held his hand as though to support him. Thus they stood till his feet grew firm and his strength returned.

Oros restored the sceptre to her, and lifting it she said –

"O love and lord, take thou the place prepared for thee, where thou shalt sit for ever at my side, for with myself I give thee more than thou canst know or than I will tell thee now. Mount thy throne, O Affianced of Hes, and receive the worship of thy priests."

"Nay," he answered with a start as that word fell upon his ears. "Here and now I say it once and for all. I am but a man who know nothing of strange gods, their attributes and ceremonials. None shall bow the knee to me and on earth, Ayesha, I bow mine to thee alone."

Now at this bold speech some of those who heard it looked astonished and whispered to each other, while a voice called –

"Beware, thou Chosen, of the anger of the Mother!"

Again for a moment Ayesha looked afraid, then with a little laugh, swept the thing aside, saying –

"Surely with that I should be content. For me, O Love, thy adoration; for thee the betrothal song, no more."

So, having no choice, Leo mounted the throne, where notwithstanding his splendid presence, enhanced as it was by those glittering robes, he looked ill enough at ease, as indeed must any man of his faith and race. Happily however, if some act of semi-idolatrous homage had been proposed. Ayesha found a means to prevent its celebration, and soon all such matters were forgotten both by the singers who sang, and we who listened to the majestic chant that followed.

Of its words unfortunately we were able to understand but little, both because of the volume of sound and of the secret priestly language in which it was given, though its general purport could not be mistaken.

The female voices began it, singing very low, and conveying a strange impression of time and distance. Now followed bursts of gladness alternating with melancholy chords suggesting sighs and tears and sorrows long endured, and at the end a joyous, triumphant pæan thrown to and fro between the men and women singers, terminating in one united chorus repeated again and again, louder and yet louder, till it culminated in a veritable crash of melody, then of a sudden ceased.

Ayesha rose and waved her sceptre, whereon all the company bowed thrice, then turned and breaking into some sweet, low chant that sounded like a lullaby, marched, rank after rank, across the width of the Sanctuary and through the carven doors, which closed behind the last of them.

When all had gone, leaving us alone, save for the priest Oros and the priestess Papave, who remained in attendance on their mistress. Ayesha, who sat gazing before her with dreaming, empty eyes, seemed to awake, for she rose and said –

"A noble chant, is it not, and an ancient? It was the wedding song of the feast of Isis and Osiris at Behbit in Egypt, and there I heard it before ever I saw the darksome Caves of Kôr. Often have I observed, my Holly, that music lingers longer than aught else in this changeful world, though it is rare that the very words should remain unvaried. Come, beloved – tell me, by what name shall I call thee? Thou art Kallikrates and yet – "

"Call me Leo, Ayesha," he answered, "as I was christened in the only life of which I have any knowledge. This Kallikrates seems to have been an unlucky man, and the deeds he did, if in truth he was aught other than a tool in the hand of destiny, have bred no good to the inheritors of his body – or his spirit, whichever it may be – or to those women with whom his life was intertwined. Call me Leo, then, for of

Kallikrates I have had enough since that night when I looked upon the last of him in Kôr."

"Ah! I remember," she answered, "when thou sawest thyself lying in that narrow bed, and I sang thee a song, did I not, of the past and of the future? I can recall two lines of it; the rest I have forgotten –

Onward, never weary, clad with splendour for a robe!
Till accomplished be our fate, and the night is rushing down."

Yes, my Leo, now indeed we are 'clad with splendour for a robe,' and now our fate draws near to its accomplishment. Then perchance will come the down-rushing of the night"; and she sighed, looked up tenderly, and said, "See, I am talking to thee in Arabic. Hast thou forgotten it?"

"No."

"Then let it be our tongue, for I love it best of all, who lisped it at my mother's knee. Now leave me here alone awhile; I would think. Also," she added thoughtfully, and speaking with a strange and impressive inflexion of the voice, "there are some to whom I must give audience."

So we went, all of us, supposing that Ayesha was about to receive a deputation of the Chiefs of the Mountain Tribes who came to felicitate her upon her betrothal.

CHAPTER 18

THE THIRD ORDEAL

AN HOUR, two hours passed, while we strove to rest in our sleeping place, but could not, for some influence disturbed us.

"Why does not Ayesha come?" asked Leo at length, pausing in his walk up and down the room. "I want to see her again; I cannot bear to be apart from her. I feel as though she were drawing me to her."

"How can I tell you? Ask Oros; he is outside the door."

So he went and asked him, but Oros only smiled, and answered that the Hesea had not entered her chamber, so doubtless she must still remain in the Sanctuary.

"Then I am going to look for her. Come, Oros, and yon too, Horace."

Oros bowed, but declined, saying that he was bidden to bide at our door, adding that we, "to whom all the paths were open," could return to the Sanctuary if we thought well.

"I do think well" replied Leo sharply. "Will you come, Horace, or shall I go without you?"

I hesitated. The Sanctuary was a public place, it is true, but Ayesha had said that she desired to be alone there for awhile. Without more words, however, Leo shrugged his shoulders and started.

"You will never find your way." I said, and followed him.

We went down the long passages that were dimly lighted with lamps and came to the gallery. Here we found no lamps; still we groped our way to the great wooden doors. They were shut, but Leo pushed upon them impatiently, and one of them swung open a little, so that we could squeeze ourselves between them. As we passed it closed noiselessly behind us.

Now we should have been in the Sanctuary, and in the full blaze of those awful columns of living fire. But they were out, or we had strayed elsewhere; at least the darkness was intense. We tried to work our way back to the doors again, but could not. We were lost.

More, something oppressed us; we did not dare to speak. We went on a few paces and stopped, for we became aware that we were not alone. Indeed, it seemed to me that we stood in the midst of a thronging multitude, but not of men and women. Beings pressed about us; we could feel their robes, yet could not touch them; we could feel their breath, but it was *cold.* The air stirred all round us as they passed to and fro, passed in endless numbers. It was as though we had entered a cathedral filled with the vast congregation of all the dead who once had worshipped there. We grew afraid – my face was damp with fear, the hair stood up upon my head. We seemed to have wandered into a hall of the Shades.

At length light appeared far away, and we saw that it emanated from the two pillars of fire which had burned on either side of the Shrine, that of a sudden became luminous. So we were in the Sanctuary, and still near to the doors. Now those pillars were not bright; they were low and lurid; the rays from them scarcely reached us standing in the dense shadow.

But if we could not be seen in them we still could see. Look! Yonder sat Ayesha on a throne, and oh! she was awful in her death-like majesty. The blue light of the sunken columns played upon her, and in it she sat erect, with such a face and mien of pride as no human creature ever wore. Power seemed to flow from her; yes, it flowed from those wide-set, glittering eyes like light from jewels.

She seemed a Queen of Death receiving homage from the dead. More, she *was* receiving homage from dead or living – I know not which – for, as I thought it, a shadowy Shape arose before the throne and bent the knee to her, then another, and another, and another.

As each vague Being appeared and bowed its starry head she raised her sceptre in answering salutation. We could hear the distant tinkle of the sistrum bells, the only sound in all that place, yes, and see her lips move, though no whisper reached us from them. Surely spirits were worshipping her!

We gripped each other. We shrank back and found the door. It gave to our push. Now we were in the passages again, and now we had reached our room.

At its entrance Oros was standing as we had left him. He greeted us with his fixed smile, taking no note of the terror written on our faces. We passed him, and entering the room stared at each other.

"What is she?" gasped Leo. "An angel?"

"Yes," I answered, "something of that sort." But to myself I thought that there are doubtless many kinds of angels.

"And what were those – those *shadows* – doing?" he asked again.

"Welcoming her after her transformation, I suppose. But perhaps they were not shadows – only priests disguised and conducting some secret ceremonial!"

Leo shrugged his shoulders but made no other answer.

At length the door opened, and Oros, entering, said that the Hesea commanded our presence in her chamber.

So, still oppressed with fear and wonder – for what we had seen was perhaps more dreadful than anything that had gone before – we went, to find Ayesha seated and looking somewhat weary, but otherwise unchanged. With her was the priestess Papave, who had just unrobed her of the royal mantle which she wore in the Sanctuary.

Ayesha beckoned Leo to her, taking his hand and searching his face with her eyes, not without anxiety as I thought.

Now I turned, purposing to leave them alone, but she saw, and said to me, smiling –

"Why wouldest thou forsake us. Holly? To go back to the Sanctuary once more?" and she looked at me with meaning in her glance." Hast thou questions to ask of the statue of the Mother yonder that thou lovest the place so much? They say it speaks, telling of the future to those who dare to kneel beside it uncompanioned from night till dawn. Yet I have often done so, but to me it has never spoken, though none long to learn the future more.'

I made no answer, nor did she seem to expect any, for she went on at once –

"Nay, bide here and let us have done with all sad and solemn thoughts. We three will sup together as of old, and for awhile forget our fears and cares, and be happy as children who know not sin and death, or that change which is death indeed. Oros, await my lord without. Papave, I will call thee later to disrobe me. Till then let none disturb us."

The room that Ayesha inhabited was not very large, as we saw by the hanging lamps with which it was lighted. It was plainly though richly furnished, the rock walls being covered with tapestries, and the tables and chairs inlaid with silver, but the only token that here a woman had her home was that about it stood several bowls of flowers. One of these, I remember, was filled with the delicate harebells I had admired, dug up roots and all, and set in moss.

"A poor place," said Ayesha, "yet better than that in which I dwelt those two thousand years awaiting thy coming, Leo, for, see, beyond it is a garden, wherein I sit," and she sank down upon a couch by the table, motioning to us to take our places opposite to her.

The meal was simple; for us, eggs boiled hard and cold venison; for her, milk, some little cakes of flour, and mountain berries.

Presently Leo rose and threw off his gorgeous, purple-broidered robe, which he still wore, and cast upon a chair the crook-headed sceptre that Oros had again thrust into his hand. Ayesha smiled as he did so, saying –

"It would seem that thou boldest these sacred emblems in but small respect."

"Very small," he answered. "Thou heardest my words in the Sanctuary, Ayesha, so let us make a pact. Thy religion I do not understand, but I understand my own, and not even for thy sake will I take part in what I hold to be idolatry."

Now I thought that she would be angered by this plain speaking, but she only bowed her head and answered meekly –

"Thy will is mine, Leo, though it will not be easy always to explain thy absence from the ceremonies in the temple. Yet thou hast a right to thine own faith, which doubtless is mine also."

"How can that be?" he asked, looking up.

"Because all great Faiths are the same, changed a little to suit the needs of passing times and peoples. What taught that of Egypt, which, in a fashion, we still follow here? That hidden in a multitude of manifestations, one Power great and good, rules all the universes: that the holy shall inherit a life eternal and the vile, eternal death: that men shall be shaped and judged by their own hearts and deeds, and here and hereafter drink of the cup which they have brewed: that their real home is not on earth, but beyond the earth, where all riddles shall be answered and all sorrows cease. Say, dost thou believe these things, as I do?"

"Aye, Ayesha, but Hes or Isis is thy goddess, for hast thou not told us tales of thy dealings with her in the past, and did we not hear thee make thy prayer to her? Who, then, is this goddess Hes?"

"Know, Leo, that she is what I named her – Nature's soul, no divinity, but the secret spirit of the world; that universal Motherhood, whose symbol thou hast seen yonder, and in whose mysteries lie hid all earthly life and knowledge."

"Does, then, this merciful Motherhood follow her votaries with death and evil, as thou sayest she has followed thee for thy disobedience, and me – and another – because of some unnatural vows broken long ago?" Leo asked quietly.

Resting her arm upon the table. Ayesha looked at him with sombre eyes and answered –

"In that Faith of thine of which thou speakest are there perchance two gods, each having many ministers: a god of good and a god of evil, an Osiris and a Set?"

He nodded.

"I thought it. And the god of ill is strong, is he not, and can put on the shape of good? Tell me, then, Leo, in the world that is to-day, whereof I know so little, hast thou ever heard of frail souls who for some earthly bribe have sold themselves to that evil one, or to his minister, and been paid their price in bitterness and anguish?"

"All wicked folk do as much in this form or in that," he answered.

"And if once there lived a woman who was mad with the thirst for beauty, for life, for wisdom, and for love, might she not – oh! might she not perchance – "

"Sell herself to the god called Set, or one of his angels? Ayesha, dost thou mean" – and Leo rose, speaking in a voice that was full of fear – "that thou art such a woman?"

"And if so?" she asked, also rising and drawing slowly near to him.

"If so," he answered hoarsely, "if so, I think that perhaps we had best fulfil our fates apart – "

"Ah!" she said, with a little scream of pain as though a knife had stabbed her, "wouldst thou away to Atene? I tell thee that thou canst not leave me. I have power – above all men thou shouldst know it, whom once I slew. Nay, thou hast no memory, poor creature of a breath, and I – I remember too well. I will not hold thee dead again, – I'll hold thee living. Look now on my beauty, Leo" – and she bent her swaying form towards him, compelling him with her glorious, alluring eyes – "and begone if thou canst. Why, thou drawest nearer to me. Man, that is not the path of flight.

"Nay, I will not tempt thee with these common lures. Go, Leo, if thou wilt. Go, my love, and leave me to my loneliness and my sin. Now – at once. Atene will shelter thee till spring, when thou canst cross the mountains and return to thine own world again, and to those things of common life which are thy joy. See, Leo, I veil myself that thou mayest not be tempted," and she flung the corner of her cloak about her head, then asked a sudden question through it –

"Didst thou not but now return to the Sanctuary with Holly after I bade thee leave me there alone? Methought I saw the two of you standing by its doors."

"Yes, we came to seek thee," he answered. "And found more than ye sought, as often chances to the bold – is it not so? Well, I willed that ye should come and see, and protected you where others might have died."

"What didst thou there upon the throne, and whose were those forms which we saw bending before thee?" he asked coldly.

"I have ruled in many shapes and lands, Leo. Perchance they were ancient companions and servitors of mine come to greet me once again and to hear my tidings. Or perchance they were but shadows of thy brain, pictures like those upon the fire, that it pleased me to summon to thy sight, to try thy strength and constancy.

"Leo Vincey, know now the truth; that all things are illusions, even that there exists no future and no past, that what has been and what shall be already is eternally. Know that I, Ayesha, am but a magic wraith, foul when thou seest me foul, fair when thou seest me fair; a spirit-bubble reflecting a thousand lights in the sunshine of thy smile, grey as dust and gone in the shadow of thy frown. Think of the throned Queen before whom the shadowy Powers bowed and worship, for that is I. Think of the hideous, withered Thing thou sawest naked on the rock, and flee away, for that is I. Or keep me lovely, and adore, knowing all evil centred in my spirit, for that is I. Now, Leo, thou hast the truth. Put me from thee for ever and for ever if thou wilt, and be safe; or clasp me, clasp me to thy heart, and in payment for my lips and love take my sin upon thy head! Nay, Holly, be thou silent, for now he must judge alone."

Leo turned, as I thought, at first, to find the door. But it was not so, for he did but walk up and down the room awhile. Then he came back to where Ayesha stood, and spoke quite simply and in a very quiet voice, such as men of his nature often assume in moments of great emotion.

"Ayesha," he said," when I saw thee as thou wast, aged and – thou knowest how – I clung to thee. Now, when thou hast told me the secret of this unholy pact of thine, when with my eyes, at least, I have seen thee reigning a mistress of spirits good or ill, yet I cling to thee. Let thy sin, great or little – whate'er it is – be my sin also. In truth, I feel its weight sink to my soul and become a part of me, and although I have no vision or power of prophecy, I am sure that I shall not escape its punishment. Well, though I be innocent, let me bear it for thy sake. I am content."

Ayesha heard, the cloak slipped from her head, and for a moment she stood silent like one amazed, then burst into a passion of sudden tears. Down she went before him, and clinging to his garments, she bowed her stately shape until her forehead touched the ground. Yes, that proud being, who was more than mortal, whose nostrils but now had drunk the incense of the homage of ghosts or spirits humbled herself at this man's feet.

With an exclamation of horror, half-maddened at the piteous sight, Leo sprang to one side, then stooping, lifted and led her still weeping to the couch.

"Thou knowest not what thou hast done," Ayesha said at last. "Let all thou sawest on the Mountain's crest or in the Sanctuary be but visions of the night; let that tale of an offended goddess be a parable, a fable, if thou wilt. This at least is true, that ages since I sinned for thee and against thee and another; that ages since I bought beauty and life indefinite wherewith I might win thee and endow thee at a cost which few would dare; that I have paid interest on the debt, in mockery, utter loneliness, and daily pain which scarce could be endured, until the bond fell due at last and must be satisfied.

"Yes, how I may not tell thee, thou and thou alone stoodst between me and the full discharge of this most dreadful debt – for know that in mercy it is given to us to redeem one another.

Now he would have spoken, but with a motion of her hand she bade him be silent, and continued –

"See now, Leo, three great dangers has thy body passed of late upon its journey to my side; the Death-hounds, the Mountains, and the Precipice. Know that these were but types and ordained fore-shadowings of the last threefold trial of thy soul. From the pursuing passions of Atene which must have undone us both, thou hast escaped victorious. Thou hast endured the desert loneliness of the sands and snows starving for a comfort that never came. Even when the avalanche thundered round thee thy faith stood fast as it stood above the Pit of flame, while after bitter years of doubt a rushing flood of horror swallowed up thy hopes. As thou didst descend the glacier's steep, not knowing what lay beneath that fearful path, so but now and of thine own choice, for very love of me, thou hast plunged headlong into an abyss that is deeper far, to share its terrors with my spirit. Dost thou understand at last?"

"Something, not all, I think," he answered slowly.

"Surely thou art wrapped in a double veil of blindness," she cried impatiently. "Listen again –

"Hadst thou yielded to Nature's crying and rejected me but yesterday, in that foul shape, I must perchance have lingered for uncounted time, playing the poor part of priestess of a forgotten faith. This was the first temptation, the ordeal of thy flesh – nay, not the first – the second, for Atene and her lurings were the first. But thou wast loyal, and in the magic of thy conquering love my beauty and my womanhood were re-born.

"Hadst thou rejected me to-night, when, as I was bidden to do, I showed thee that vision in the Sanctuary and confessed to thee my soul's black crime, then hopeless and helpless, unshielded by my earthly power, I must have wandered on into the deep and endless night of solitude. This was the third appointed test, the trial of thy spirit, and by thy steadfastness, Leo, thou hast loosed the hand of Destiny from about my throat. Now I am regenerate in thee – through thee may hope again for some true life beyond, which thou shalt share. And yet, and yet, if thou shouldst suffer, as well may chance – "

"Then I suffer, and there's an end," broke in Leo serenely. "Save for a few things my mind is clear, and there must be justice for us all at last. If I have broken the bond that bound thee if I have freed thee from some threatening, spiritual ill by taking a risk upon my head, well, I have not lived, and if need be, shall not die, in vain. So let us have done with all these problems, or rather first answer thou me one. Ayesha, how wast thou changed upon that peak? "

"In flame I left thee, Leo, and in flame I did return, as in flame, mayhap, we shall both depart. Or perhaps the change was in the eyes of all of you who watched, and not in this shape of mine. I have answered. Seek to learn no more."

"One thing I do still seek to learn. Ayesha, we were betrothed to-night. When wilt thou marry me?"

"Not yet, not yet," she answered hurriedly, her voice quivering as she spoke. "Leo, thou must put that hope from thy thoughts awhile, and for some few months, a year perchance, be content to play the part of friend and lover."

"Why so?" he asked, with bitter disappointment. "Ayesha, those parts have been mine for many a day; more, I grow no younger, and, unlike thee, shall soon be old. Also, life is fleeting, and sometimes I think that I near its end."

"Speak no such evil-omened words," she said, springing from the couch and stamping her sandalled foot upon the ground in anger born of fear. "Yet thou sayest truth; thou art unfortified against the accidents of time and chance. Oh! horrible, horrible; thou mightest die again, and leave me living."

"Then give me of thy life, Ayesha."

"That would I gladly, all of it, couldst thou but repay me with the boon of death to come.

"Oh! ye poor mortals," she went on, with a sudden burst of passion; "ye beseech your gods for the gift of many years, being ignorant that ye would sow a seed within your breasts whence ye must garner ten thousand miseries. Know ye not that this world is indeed the wide house of hell, in whose chambers from time to time the spirit tarries a little while, then, weary and aghast, speeds wailing to the peace that it has won.

"Think then what it is to live on here externally and yet be human; to age in soul and see our beloved die and pass to lands whether we may not hope to follow; to wait while drop by drop the curse of the long centuries falls upon our imperishable being, like water slow dripping on a diamond that it cannot wear, till they be born anew forgetful of us, and again sink from our helpless arms into the void unknowable.

"Think what it is to see the sins we sin, the tempting look, the word idle or unkind – aye, even the selfish thought or struggle, multiplied ten thousandfold and more external than ourselves, spring up upon the universal bosom of the earth to be the bane of a million destinies, whilst the everlasting Finger writes its endless count, and a cold voice of Justice cries in our conscience-haunted solitude, 'Oh! soul unshriven, behold the ripening harvest thy wanton hand did scatter, and long in vain for the waters of forgetfulness.'

"Think what it is to have every earthly wisdom, yet to burn unsatisfied for the deeper and forbidden draught; to gather up all wealth and power and let them slip again, like children weary of a painted toy; to sweep the harp of fame, and, maddened by its jangling music, to stamp it small beneath our feet; to snatch at pleasure's goblet and find its wine is sand, and at length, outworn, to cast us down and pray the pitiless gods with whose stolen garment we have wrapped ourselves, to take it back again, and suffer us to slink naked to the grave.

"Such is the life thou askest, Leo. Say, wilt thou have it now?"

"If it may be shared with thee," he answered. "These woes are born of loneliness, but then our perfect fellowship would turn them into joy."

"Aye," she said, "while it was permitted to endure. So be it, Leo. In the spring, when the snows melt, we will journey together to Libya, and there thou shalt be bathed in the Fount of Life, that forbidden Essence of which once thou didst fear to drink, afterwards I will wed thee."

"That place is closed for ever. Ayesha."

"Not to my feet and thine," she answered. "Fear not, my love, were this mountain heaped thereon, I would blast a path through it with mine eyes and lay its secret bare. Oh! would that thou wast as I am, for then before to-morrow's sun we'd watch the rolling pillar thunder by, and thou shouldst taste its glory.

"But it may not be. Hunger or cold can starve thee, and waters drown; swords can slay thee, or sickness sap away thy strength. Had it not been for the false Atene, who disobeyed my words, as it was foredoomed that she should do, by this day we were across the mountains, or had travelled northward through the frozen desert and the rivers. Now we must await the melting of the snows, for winter is at hand, and in it, as thou knowest, no man can live upon their heights."

"Eight months till April before we can start, and how long to cross the mountains and all the vast distances beyond, and the seas, and the swamps of Kôr? Why, at the best, Ayesha, two years must go by before we can even find the place;" and he fell to entreating her to let them be wed at once and journey afterwards.

But she said, Nay, and nay, and nay, it should not be, till at length, as though fearing his pleading, or that of her own heart, she rose and dismissed us.

"Ah! my Holly," she said to me as we three parted, "I promised thee and myself some few hours of rest and of the happiness of quiet, and thou seest how my desire has been fulfilled. Those old Egyptians; were wont to share their feasts with one grizzly skeleton, but here I counted four to-night that you both could see, and they are named Fear, Suspense, Foreboding, and Love-denied. Doubtless also, when these are buried others will come to haunt us, and snatch the poor morsel from our lips.

"So hath it ever been with me, whose feet misfortune dogs. Yet I hope on, and now many a barrier lies behind us; and Leo, thou hast been tried in the appointed triple fires and yet proved true. Sweet be thy slumbers, O my love, and sweeter still thy dreams, for know, my soul shall share them. I vow to thee that to-morrow we'll be happy, aye, to-morrow without fail."

"Why will she not marry me at once?" asked Leo, when we were alone in our chamber, "Because she is afraid," I answered.

CHAPTER 19

LEO AND THE LEOPARD

DURING THE weeks that followed these momentous days often and often I wondered to myself whether a more truly wretched being had ever lived than the woman, or the spirit, whom we knew as She, Hes, and Ayesha. Whether in fact also, or in our imagination only, she had arisen from the ashes of her hideous age into the full bloom of perpetual life and beauty inconceivable.

These things at least were certain: Ayesha had achieved the secret of an existence so enduring that for all human purposes it might be called unending. Within certain limitations – such as her utter inability to foresee the future – undoubtedly also, she was endued with powers that can only be described as supernatural.

Her rule over the strange community amongst whom she lived was absolute; indeed, its members regarded her as a goddess, and as such she was worshipped. After marvellous adventures, the man who was her very life, I might almost say her soul, whose being was so mysteriously intertwined with hers, whom she loved also with the intensest human passion of which woman can be capable, had sought her out in this hidden corner of the world.

More, thrice he had proved his unalterable fidelity to her. First, by his rejection of the royal and beautiful, if undisciplined, Atene. Secondly, by clinging to Ayesha when she seemed to be repulsive to every natural sense. Thirdly, after that homage scene in the Sanctuary – though with her unutterable perfections before his eyes this did not appear to be so wonderful – by steadfastness in the face of her terrible avowal, true or false, that she had won her gifts and him through some him, unholy pact with the powers of evil, in the unknown fruits and consequences of which he must be involved as the price of her possession.

Yet Ayesha was miserable. Even in her lightest moods it was clear to me that those skeletons at the feast of which she had spoken were her continual companions. Indeed, when we were alone she would acknowledge it in dark hints and veiled allegories or allusions. Crushed though her rival the Khania Atene might be, also she was still jealous of her.

Perhaps "afraid" would be a better word, for some instinct seemed to warn Ayesha that soon or late her hour would come to Atene again, and that then it would be her own turn to drink of the bitter waters of despair.

What troubled her more a thousandfold, however, were her fears for Leo. As may well be understood, to stand in his intimate relationship to this half divine and marvellous being, and yet not to be allowed so much as to touch her lips, did not conduce to his physical or mental well-being, especially as he knew that the wall of separation must not be climbed for at least two years. Little wonder that Leo lost appetite, grew thin and pale, and could not sleep, or that he implored her continually to rescind her decree and marry him.

But on this point Ayesha was immovable. Instigated thereto by Leo, and I may add my own curiosity, when we were alone I questioned her again as to the reasons of this self-denying ordinance. All she would tell me, however, was that between them rose the barrier of Leo's mortality, and that until his physical being had been impregnated with the mysterious virtue of the Vapour of Life, it was not wise that she should take him as a husband.

I asked her why, seeing that though a long-lived one, she was still a woman, whereon her face assumed a calm but terrifying smile, and she answered –

"Art so sure, my Holly? Tell me, do your women wear such jewels as that set upon my brow?" and she pointed to the faint but lambent light which glowed about her forehead.

More, she began slowly to stroke her abundant hair, then her breast and body. Wherever her fingers passed the mystic light was born, until in that darkened room – for the dusk was gathering – she shimmered from head to foot like the water of a phosphorescent sea, a being glorious yet fearful to behold. Then she waved her hand, and, save for the gentle radiance on her brow, became as she had been.

"Art so sure, my Holly?" Ayesha repeated "Nay, shrink not; that flame will not burn thee. Mayhap thou didst but imagine it, as I have noted thou dost imagine many things; for surely no woman could clothe herself in light and live, nor has so much as the smell of fire passed upon my garments."

Then at length my patience was outworn, and I grew angry.

"I am sure of nothing, Ayesha," I answered, "except that thou wilt make us mad with all these tricks and changes. Say, art thou a spirit then?"

"We are all spirits," she said reflectively, "and I, perhaps, more than some. Who can be certain?"

"Not I," I answered. "Yet I implore, woman or spirit, tell me one thing. Tell me the truth. In the beginning what wast thou to Leo, and what was he to thee?"

She looked at me very solemnly and answered –

"Does my memory deceive me. Holly, or is it written in the first book of the Law of the Hebrews, which once I used to study, that the sons of Heaven came down to the daughters of men, and found that they were fair?"

"It is so written," I answered.

"Then, Holly, might it not have chanced that once a daughter of Heaven came down to a man of Earth and loved him well? Might it not chance that for this her sin, she, this high fallen star, who had befouled her immortal state for him, was doomed to suffer till at length his love, made divine by pain and faithful even to a memory, was permitted to redeem her?"

Now at length I saw light and sprang up eagerly, but in a cold voice she added:

"Nay, Holly, cease to question me, for there are things of which I can but speak to thee in figures and in parables, not to mock and bewilder thee, but because I must. Interpret them as thou wilt. Still, Atene thought me no mortal, since she told us that man and spirit may not mate; and there are matters in which I let her judgment weigh with me, as without doubt now, as in other lives, she and that old Shaman, her uncle, have wisdom, aye, and foresight. So bid my lord press me no more to wed him, for it gives me pain to say him nay – ah! thou knowest not how much.

"Moreover, I will declare myself to thee, old friend; whatever else I be, at least I am too womanly to listen to the pleadings of my best beloved and not myself be moved. See, I have set a curb upon desire and drawn it until my heart bleeds; but if he pursues me with continual words – and looks of burning love, who knoweth but that I shall kindle in his flame and throw the reins of reason to the winds?

"Oh, then together we might race adown our passions' steep; together dare the torrent that rages at its foot, and there perchance be whelmed or torn asunder. Nay, nay, another space of journeying, but a little space, and we reach the bridge my wisdom found, and cross it safely, and beyond for ever ride on at ease through the happy meadows of our love."

Then she was silent, nor would she speak more upon the matter. Also – and this was the worst of it – even now I was not sure that she told me the truth, or, at any rate, all of it, for to Ayesha's mind truth seemed many coloured as are the rays of light thrown from the different faces of a cut jewel. We never could be certain which shade of it she was pleased to present, who, whether by preference or of necessity, as she herself had said, spoke of such secrets in figures of speech and parables.

It is a fact that to this hour I do not know whether Ayesha is spirit or woman, or, as I suspect, a blend of both. I do not know the limits of her powers, or if that elaborate story of the beginning of her love for Leo was true – which personally I doubt – or but a fable, invented by her mind, and through it, as she had hinted, pictured on the flame for her own hidden purposes.

I do not know whether when first we saw her on the Mountain she was really old and hideous, or did but put on that shape in our eyes in order to test her lover. I do not know whether, as the priest Oros bore witness – which he may well have been bidden to do – her spirit passed into the body of the dead priestess of Hes, or whether when she seemed to perish there so miserably, her body and her soul were wafted straightway from the caves of Kôr to this Central Asian peak.

I do not know why, as she was so powerful, she did not come to seek us, instead of leaving us to seek her through so many weary years, though I suggest that some superior force forbade her to do more than companion us unseen, watching our every act, reading our every thought, until at length we reached the predestined place and hour. Also, as will appear, there were other things of which this is not the time to speak, whereby I am still more tortured and perplexed.

In short, I know nothing, except that my existence has been intertangled with one of the great mysteries of the world; that the glorious being called Ayesha won the secret of life from whatever power holds it in its keeping; that she alleged – although of this, remember, we have no actual proof – such life was to be attained by bathing in a certain emanation, vapour or essence; that she was possessed by a passion not easy to understand, but terrific in its force and immortal in its nature, concentrated upon one other being and one alone. That through this passion also some angry fate smote her again, again, and yet again, making of her countless days a burden, and leading the power and the wisdom which knew all but could foreknow nothing, into abysses of anguish, suspense, and disappointment such as – Heaven be thanked! – we common men and women are not called upon to plumb.

For the rest, should human eyes ever fall upon it, each reader must form his own opinion of this history, its true interpretation and significance. These and the exact parts played by Atene and myself in its development I hope to solve shortly, though not here.

Well, as I have said, the upshot of it all was that Ayesha was devoured with anxiety about Leo. Except in this matter of marriage, his every wish was satisfied, and indeed forestalled. Thus he was never again asked to share in any of the ceremonies of the Sanctuary, though, indeed, stripped of its rites and spiritual symbols, the religion of the College of Hes proved pure and harmless enough. It was but a diluted version of the Osiris and Isis worship of old Egypt, from which it had been inherited, mixed with the Central Asian belief in the transmigration or reincarnation of souls and the possibility of drawing near to the ultimate Godhead by holiness of thought and life.

In fact, the head priestess and Oracle was only worshipped as a representative of the Divinity, while the temporal aims of the College in practice were confined to good works, although it is true that they still sighed for their lost authority over the country of Kaloon. Thus they had hospitals, and during the long and severe winters, when the Tribes of the Mountain slopes were often driven to the verge of starvation, gave liberally to the destitute from their stores of food.

Leo liked to be with Ayesha continually, so we spent each evening in her company, and much of the day also, until she found that this inactivity told upon him who for years had been accustomed to endure every rigour of climate in the open air. After this came home to her – although she was always haunted by terror lest any accident should befall him – Ayesha insisted upon his going out to kill the wild sheep and the ibex, which lived in numbers on the mountain ridges, placing him in the charge of the chiefs and huntsmen of the Tribes, with whom thus he became well acquainted. In this exercise, however, I accompanied him but rarely, as, if used too much, my arm still gave me pain.

Once indeed such an accident did happen. I was seated in the garden with Ayesha and watching her. Her head rested on her hand, and she was looking with her wide eyes, across which the swift thoughts passed like clouds over a windy sky, or dreams through the mind of a sleeper – looking out vacantly towards the mountain snows. Seen thus her loveliness was inexpressible, amazing; merely to gaze upon it was an intoxication. Contemplating it, I understood indeed that, like to that of the fabled Helen, this gift of hers alone – and it was but one of many – must have caused infinite sorrows, had she ever been permitted to display it to the world. It would have driven humanity to madness; the men with longings and the women with jealousy and hate.

And yet in what did her surpassing beauty lie? Ayesha's face and form were perfect, it is true; but so are those of some other women. Not in these then did it live alone, but rather, I think, especially while what I may call her human moods were on her, in the soft mystery that dwelt upon her features and gathered and changed in her splendid eyes. Some such mystery may be seen, however faintly, on the faces of certain of the masterpieces of the Greek sculptors, but Ayesha it clothed like an ever-present atmosphere, suggesting a glory that was not of earth, making her divine.

As I gazed at her and wondered thus, of a sudden she became terribly agitated, and, pointing to a shoulder of the Mountain miles and miles away, said –

"Look!"

I looked, but saw nothing except a sheet of distant snow.

"Blind fool, canst thou not see that my lord is in danger of his life?" she cried. "Nay, I forgot, thou hast no vision. Take it now from me and look again"; and laying her hand, from which a strange, numbing current seemed to flow, upon my head, she muttered some swift words.

Instantly my eyes were opened, and, not upon the distant Mountain, but in the air before me as it were, I saw Leo rolling over and over at grips with a great snow-leopard, whilst the chief and huntsmen with him ran round and round, seeking an opportunity to pierce the savage brute with their spears and yet leave him unharmed.

Ayesha, rigid with terror, swayed to and fro at my side, till presently the end came, for I could see Leo drive his long knife into the bowels of the leopard, which at once grew limp, separated from him, and after a struggle or two in the bloodstained snow, lay still. Then he rose, laughing and pointing to his rent garments, whilst one of the huntsmen came forward and began to bandage some wounds in his hands and thigh with strips of linen torn from his under-robe.

The vision vanished suddenly as it had come, and I felt Ayesha leaning heavily upon my shoulder like any other frightened woman, and heard her gasp –

"That danger also has passed by, but how many are there to follow? Oh! tormented heart, how long canst thou endure!"

Then her wrath flamed up against the chief and his huntsmen, and she summoned messengers and sent them out at speed with a litter and ointments, bidding them to bear back the lord Leo and to bring his companions to her very presence.

"Thou seest what days are mine, my Holly, aye, and have been these many years," she said; "but those hounds shall pay me for this agony."

Nor would she suffer me to reason with her.

Four hours later Leo returned, limping after the litter in which, instead of himself, for whom it was sent, lay a mountain sheep and the skin of the snow leopard that he had placed there to save the huntsmen the labour of carrying them. Ayesha was waiting for him in the hall of her dwelling, and gliding to him – I cannot say she walked – over-whelmed him with mingled solicitude and reproaches. He listened awhile, then asked "How dost thou know anything of this matter?

The leopard skin has not yet been brought to thee."

"I know because I saw," she answered. "The worst hurt was above thy knee; hast thou dressed it with the salve I sent?"

"Not I," he said. "But thou hast not left this Sanctuary; how didst thou see? By thy magic?"

"If thou wilt, at least I saw, and Holly also saw thee rolling in the snow with that fierce brute, while those curs ran round like scared children."

"I am weary of this magic," interrupted Leo crossly. "Cannot a man be left alone for an hour even with a leopard of the mountain? As for those brave men – "

At this moment Oros entered and whispered something, bowing low.

"As for those 'brave men,' I will deal with them," said Ayesha with bitter emphasis, and covering herself – for she never appeared unveiled to the people of the Mountain – she swept from the place.

"Where has she gone, Horace?" asked Leo.

"To one of her services in the Sanctuary?"

"I don't know," I answered; "but if so, I think it will be that chiefs burial service."

"Will it?" he exclaimed, and instantly limped after her.

A minute or two later I thought it wise to follow. In the Sanctuary a curious scene was in progress. Ayesha was seated in front of the statue. Before her, very much frightened, knelt a brawny, red-haired chieftain and five of his followers, who still carried their hunting spears, while with folded arms and an exceedingly grim look upon his face, Leo, who, as I learned afterwards, had already interfered and been silenced, stood upon one side listening to what passed. At a little distance behind were a dozen or more of the temple guards, men armed with swords and picked for their strength and stature.

Ayesha, in her sweetest voice, was questioning the men as to how the leopard, of which the skin lay before her, had come to attack Leo. The chief answered that they had tracked the brute to its lair between two rocks; that one of them had gone in and wounded it, whereon it sprang upon him and struck him down; that then the lord Leo had engaged it while the man escaped, and was also struck down, after which, rolling with it on the ground, he stabbed and slew the animal. That was all.

"No, not all," said Ayesha; "for you forget, cowards that you are, that, keeping yourselves in safety, you left my lord to the fury of this beast. Good. Drive them out on to the Mountain, there to perish also at the fangs of beasts, and make it known that he who gives them food or shelter dies."

Offering no prayer for pity or excuse, the chief and his followers rose, bowed, and turned to go.

"Stay a moment, comrades," said Leo, "and, chief, give me your arm; my scratch grows stiff; I cannot walk fast. We will finish this hunt together."

"What doest thou? Art mad?" asked Ayesha.

"I know not whether I am mad," he answered, "but I know that thou art wicked and unjust. Look now, than these hunters none braver ever breathed. That man" – and he pointed to the one whom the leopard had struck down – "took my place and went in before me because I ordered that we should attack the creature, and thus was felled. As thou seest all, thou mightest have seen this also. Then it sprang on me, and the rest of these, my friends, ran round waiting a chance to strike, which at first they could not do unless they would have killed me with it, since I and the brute rolled over and over in the snow. As it was, one of them seized it with his bare hands: look at the teeth marks on his arm. So if they are to perish on the Mountain, I, who am the man to blame, perish with them."

Now, while the hunters looked at him with fervent gratitude in their eyes. Ayesha thought a little, then said cleverly enough –

"In truth, my lord Leo, had I known all the tale, well mightest thou have named me wicked and unjust; but I knew only what I saw, and out of their own mouths did I condemn them. My servants, my lord here has pleaded for you, and you are forgiven; more, he who rushed in upon the leopard and he who seized it with his hands shall be rewarded and advanced. Go; but I warn you if you suffer my lord to come into more danger, you shall not escape so easily again."

So they bowed and went, still blessing Leo with their eyes, since death by exposure on the Mountain snows was the most terrible form of punishment known to these people, and one only inflicted by the direct order of Hes upon murderers or other great criminals.

When we had left the Sanctuary and were alone again in the hall, the storm that I had seen gathering upon Leo's face broke in earnest. Ayesha renewed her inquiries about his wounds, and wished to call Oros, the physician, to dress them, and as he refused this, offered to do so herself. He begged that she would leave his wounds alone, and then, his great beard bristling with wrath, asked her solemnly if he was a child in arms, a query so absurd that I could not help laughing.

Then he scolded her – yes, he scolded Ayesha! Wishing to know what she meant (1) by spying upon him with her magic, an evil gift that he had always disliked and mistrusted; (2) by condemning brave and excellent men, his good friends, to a death of fiendish cruelty upon such evidence, or rather out of temper, on no evidence at all; and (3) by giving him into charge of them, as though he were a little boy, and telling them that they would have to answer for it if he were hurt: he who, in his time, had killed every sort of big game known and passed through some perils and encounters?

Thus he beat her with his words, and, wonderful to say, Ayesha, this being more than woman, submitted to the chastisement meekly. Yet had any other man dared to address her with roughness even, I doubt not that his speech and his life would have come to a swift and simultaneous end, for I knew that now, as of old, she could slay by the mere effort of her will. But she did not slay; she did not even threaten, only, as any other loving woman might have done, she began to cry. Yes, great tears gathered in those lovely eyes of hers and rolling one by one down her face, fell – for her head was bent humbly forward – like heavy raindrops on the marble floor.

At the sight of this touching evidence of her human, loving heart all Leo's anger melted. Now it was he who grew penitent and prayed her pardon humbly. She gave him her hand in token of forgiveness, saying –

"Let others speak to me as they will." (sorry should I have been to try it)! "but from thee, Leo, I cannot bear harsh words. Oh, thou art cruel, cruel. In what have I offended?

Can I help it if my spirit keeps its watch upon thee, as indeed, though thou knewest it not, it has done ever since we parted yonder in the Place of Life? Can I help it if, like some mother who sees her little child at play upon a mountain's edge, my soul is torn with agony when I know thee in dangers that I am powerless to prevent or share? What are the lives of a few half-wild huntsmen that I should let them weigh for a single breath against thy safety, seeing that if I slew these, others would be more careful of thee? Whereas if I slay them not, they or their fellows may even lead thee into perils that would bring about – thy *death,"* and she gasped with horror at the word.

"Listen, beloved," said Leo. "The life of the humblest of those men is of as much value to him as mine is to me, and thou hast no more right to kill him than thou hast to kill me. It is evil that because thou carest for me thou shouldst suffer thy love to draw thee into cruelty and crime. If thou art afraid for me, then clothe me with that immortality of thine, which, although I dread it somewhat, holding it a thing unholy, and, on this earth, not permitted by my Faith, I should still rejoice to inherit for thy dear sake, knowing that then we could never more be parted. Or, if as thou sayest, this as yet thou canst not do, then let us be wed and take what fortune gives us. All men must die; but at least before I die I shall have been happy with thee for a while – yes, if only for a single hour."

"Would that I dared," Ayesha answered with a little piteous motion of her hand. "Oh! urge me no more, Leo, lest that at last I should take the risk and lead thee down a dreadful road. Leo, hast thou never heard of the love which slays, or of the poison that may lurk in a cup of joy too perfect?"

Then, as though she feared herself, Ayesha turned from him and fled.

Thus this matter ended. In itself it was not a great one, for Leo's hurts were mere scratches, and the hunters, instead of being killed, were promoted to be members of his bodyguard. Yet it told us many things. For instance, that whenever she chose to do so. Ayesha had the power of perceiving all Leo's movements from afar, and even of communicating her strength of mental vision to others, although to help him in any predicament she appeared to have no power, which, of course, accounted for the hideous and ever-present might of her anxiety.

Think what it would be to any one of us were we mysteriously acquainted with every open danger, every risk of sickness, every secret peril through which oar best-beloved must pass. To see the rock trembling to its fall and they loitering beneath it; to see them drink of water and know it full of foulest poison; to see them embark upon a ship and be aware that it was doomed to sink, but not to be able to warn them or to prevent them. Surely no mortal brain could endure such constant terrors, since hour by hour the arrows of death flit unseen and unheard past the breasts of each of us, till at length one finds its home there.

What then must Ayesha have suffered, watching with her spirit's eyes all the hair-breadth escapes of our journeyings? When, for instance, in the beginning she saw Leo at my house in Cumberland about to kill himself in his madness and despair, and by some mighty effort of her superhuman will, wrung from whatever Power it was that held her in its fearful thraldom, the strength to hurl her soul across the world and thereby in his sleep reveal to him the secret of the hiding-place where he would find her.

Or to take one more example out of many – when she saw him hanging by that slender thread of yak's hide from the face of the waterfall of ice and herself remained unable to save him, or even to look forward for a single moment and learn whether or no he was about to meet a hideous death, in which event she must live on alone until in some dim age he was born again.

Nor can her sorrows have ended with these more material fears, since others as piercing must have haunted her. Imagine, for instance, the agonies of her jealous heart when she knew her lover to be exposed to the temptations incident to his solitary existence, and more especially to those of her ancient rival Atene, who, by Ayesha's own account, had once been his wife. Imagine also her fears lest time and human change should do their natural work on him, so that by degrees the memory of her wisdom and her strength, and the image of her loveliness faded from his thought, and with them his desire for her company; thus leaving her, who had endured so long, forgotten and alone at last.

Truly, the Power that limited our perceptions did so in purest mercy, for were it otherwise with us, our race would go mad and perish raving in its terrors.

Thus it would seem that Ayesha, great tormented soul, thinking to win life and love eternal and most glorious, was in truth but another blind Pandora. From her stolen casket of beauty and super-human power had leapt into her bosom, there to dwell unceasingly, a hundred torturing demons, of whose wings mere mortal kind do but feel the far-off, icy shadowing.

Yes; and that the parallel might be complete, Hope alone still lingered in that rifled chest.

CHAPTER 20

AYESHA'S ALCHEMY

IT WAS shortly after this incident of the snow-leopard that one of these demon familiars of Ayesha's, her infinite ambition, made its formidable appearance. When we had dined with her in the evening, Ayesha's habit was to discuss plans for our mighty and unending future, that awful inheritance which she had promised to us.

Here I must explain, if I have not done so already, that she had graciously informed me that notwithstanding my refusal in past years of such a priceless opportunity, I also was to be allowed to bathe my superannuated self in the vital fires, though in what guise I should emerge from them, like Herodotus when he treats of the mysteries of old Egypt, if she knew, she did not think it lawful to reveal.

Secretly I hoped that my outward man might change for the better, as the prospect of being fixed for ever in the shape of my present and somewhat unpleasing personality, did not appeal to me as attractive. In truth, so far as I was concerned, the matter had an academic rather than an actual interest, such as we take in a fairy tale, since I did not believe that I should ever put on this kind of immortality. Nor, I may add, now as before, was I at all certain that I wished to do so.

These plans of Ayesha's were far reaching and indeed terrific. Her acquaintance with the modern world, its political and social developments, was still strictly limited; for if she had the power to follow its growth and activities, certainly it was one of which she, made no use. In practice her knowledge seemed to be confined to what she had gathered during the few brief talks which took place between us upon this subject in past time at Kôr. Now her thirst for information proved insatiable, although it is true that ours was scarcely up to date, seeing that ever since we lost touch with the civilized peoples, namely for the last fifteen years or so, we had been as much buried as she was herself.

Still we were able to describe to her the condition of the nations and their affairs as they were at the period when we bade them farewell, and, more or less incorrectly, to draw maps of the various countries and their boundaries, over which she pondered long.

The Chinese were the people in whom she proved to be most interested, perhaps because she was acquainted with the Mongolian type, and like ourselves, understood a good many of their dialects. Also she had a motive for her studies, which one night she revealed to us in the most matter-of-fact fashion.

Those who have read the first part of her history, which I left in England to be published, may remember that when we found her at Kôr, *She* horrified us by expressing a determination to possess herself of Great Britain, for the simple reason that we belonged to that country. Now, however, like her powers, her ideas had grown, for she purposed to make Leo the absolute monarch of the world. In vain did he assure her most earnestly that he desired no such empire. She merely laughed at him and said –

"If I arise amidst the Peoples, I must rule the Peoples, for how can Ayesha take a second place among mortal men?

And thou, my Leo, rulest me, yes, mark the truth, thou art my master! Therefore it is plain that thou wilt be the master of this earth, aye, and perchance of others which do not yet appear, for of these also I know something, and, I think, can reach them if I will, though hitherto I have had no mind that way. My true life has not yet begun. Its little space within this world has been filled with thought and care for thee; in waiting till thou wast born again, and during these last years of separation, until thou didst return.

"But now a few more months, and the days of preparation past, endowed with energy eternal, with all the wisdom of the ages, and with a strength that can bend the mountains or turn the ocean from its bed, and we begin to be. Oh! how I sicken for that hour when first, like twin stars new to the firmament of heaven, we break in our immortal splendour upon the astonished sight of men. It will please me, I tell thee, Leo, it will please me, to see Powers, Principalities and Dominions, marshalled by their kings and governors, bow themselves before our thrones and humbly crave the liberty to do our will. At least," she added, "it will please me for a little time, until we seek higher things."

So she spoke, while the radiance upon her brow increased and spread itself, gleaming above her like a golden fan, and her slumbrous eyes took fire from it till, to my thought, they became glowing mirrors in which I saw pomp enthroned and suppliant peoples pass.

"And how," asked Leo, with something like a groan – for this vision of universal rule viewed from afar did not seem to charm him – "how, Ayesha wilt thou bring these things about?"

"How, my Leo? Why, easily enough. For many nights I have listened to the wise discourses of our Holly here, at least he thinks them wise who still has so much to learn, and pored over his crooked maps, comparing them with those that are written in my memory, who of late have had no time for the study of such little matters. Also I have weighed and pondered your reports of the races of this world; their various follies, their futile struggling for wealth and small supremacies, and I have determined that it would be wise and kind to weld them to one whole, setting ourselves at the head of them to direct their destinies, and cause wars, sickness, and poverty to cease, so that these creatures of a little day (ephemeridæ was the word she used) may live happy from the cradle to the grave.

"Now, were it not because of thy strange shrinking from bloodshed, however politic and needful – for my Leo, as yet thou art no true philosopher – this were quickly done, since I can command a weapon which would crush their armouries and whelm their navies in the deep; yes, I, whom even the lightnings and Nature's elemental powers must obey. But thou shrinkest from the sight of death, and thou believest that Heaven would be displeased because I make myself – or am chosen – the instrument of Heaven. Well, so let it be, for thy will is mine, and therefore we will tread a gentler path."

"And how wilt thou persuade the kings of the earth to place their crowns upon thy head?" I asked, astonished.

"By causing their peoples to offer them to us," she answered suavely. "Oh! Holly, Holly, how narrow is thy mind, how strained the quality of thine imagination! Set its poor gates ajar, I pray, and bethink thee. When we appear among men, scattering gold to satisfy their want, clad in terrifying power, in dazzling beauty and in immortality of days will they not cry, 'Be ye our monarchs and rule over us!' "

"Perhaps," I answered dubiously, "but where wilt thou appear?"

She took a map of the eastern hemisphere which I had drawn and, placing her finger upon Pekin, said –

"There is the place that shall be our home for some few centuries, say three, or five, or seven, should it take so long to shape this people to my liking and our purposes. I have chosen these Chinese because thou tellest me that their numbers are uncountable, that they are brave, subtle, and patient, and though now powerless because ill-ruled and untaught, able with their multitudes to flood the little western nations. Therefore among them we will begin our reign and for some few ages be at rest while they learn wisdom from us, and thou, my Holly, makest their armies unconquerable and givest their land good government, wealth, peace, and a new religion."

What the new religion was to be I did not ask. It seemed unnecessary, since I was convinced that in practice it would prove a form of Ayesha-worship. Indeed, my mind was so occupied with conjectures, some of them quaint and absurd enough, as to what would happen at the first appearance of Ayesha in China that I forgot this subsidiary development of our future rule.

"And if the 'little western nations' will not wait to be flooded?" suggested Leo with irritation, for her contemptuous tone angered him, one of a prominent "western nation" of which he was very proud. "If they combine, for instance, and attack thee first?"

"Ah!" she said, with a flash of her eyes. "I have thought of it, and for my part hope that it will chance, since then thou canst not blame me if I put out my strength. Oh! then the East, that has slept so long, shall awake – shall awake, and upon battlefield after battlefield such as history cannot tell of, thou shalt see my flaming standards sweep on to victory. One by one thou shalt watch the nations fall and perish, until at length I build thy throne upon the hecatombs of their countless dead and crown thee emperor of a world regenerate in blood and fire."

Leo, whom this new gospel of regeneration seemed to appall, who was, in fact, a hater of absolute monarchies and somewhat republican in his views and sympathies, continued the argument, but I took no further heed. The thing was grotesque in its tremendous and fantastic absurdity; Ayesha's ambitions were such as no imperial-minded madman could conceive.

Yet – here came me rub – I had not the slightest doubt but that she was well able to put them into practice and carry them to some marvellous and awful conclusion. Why not? Death could not touch her; she had triumphed over death. Her beauty – that "cup of madness" in her eyes, as she named it once to me – and her reckless will would compel the hosts of men to follow her. Her piercing intelligence would enable her to invent new weapons with which the most highly-trained army could not possibly compete. Indeed, it might be as she said, and as I for one believed, with good reason, it proved, that she held at her command the elemental forces of Nature, such as those that lie hid in electricity, which would give all living beings to her for a prey.

Ayesha was still woman enough to have worldly ambitions, and the most dread circumstance about her superhuman powers was that they appeared to be unrestrained by any responsibility to God or man. She was, as we might well imagine a fallen angel to be, if indeed, as she herself once hinted and as Atene and the old Shaman believed, this were not her true place in creation. By only two things that I was able to discover could she be moved – her love for Leo and, in a very small degree, her friendship for myself.

Yet her devouring passion for this one man, inexplicable in its endurance and intensity, would, I felt sure even then, in the future as in the past, prove to be her heel of Achilles. When Ayesha was dipped in the waters of Dominion and Deathless-ness, this human love left her heart mortal, that through it she might be rendered harmless as a child, who otherwise would have devastated the universe.

I was right.

Whilst I was still indulging myself in these reflections and hoping that Ayesha would not take the trouble to read them in my mind, I became aware that Oros was bowing to the earth before her.

"Thy business, priest?" she asked sharply; for when she was with Leo Ayesha did not like to be disturbed.

"Hes, the spies are returned."

"Why didst thou send them out?" she asked indifferently. "What need have I of thy spies?"

"Hes, thou didst command me."

"Well, their report?"

"Hes, it is most grave. The people of Kaloon are desperate because of the drought which has caused their crops to fail, so that starvation stares them in the eyes, and this they lay to the charge of the strangers who came into their land and fled to thee. The Khania Atene also is mad with rage against thee and our holy College. Labouring night and day, she has gathered two great armies, one of forty, and one of twenty thousand men, and the latter of these she sends against the Mountain under the command of her uncle,

Simbri the Shaman. In case it should be defeated she purposes to remain with the second and greater army on the plains about Kaloon."

"Tidings indeed," said Ayesha with a scornful laugh. "Has her hate made this woman mad that she dares thus to match herself against me? My Holly, it crossed thy mind but now that it was I who am mad, boasting of what I have no power to perform. Well, within six days thou shalt learn – oh! verily thou shalt learn, and, though the issue be so very small, in such a fashion that thou wilt doubt no more for ever. Stay, I will look, though the effort of it wearies me, for those spies may be but victims to their own fears, or to the falsehoods of Atene."

Then suddenly, as was common with her when thus. Ayesha threw her sight afar, which either from indolence, or because, as she said, it exhausted her, she did but rarely, her lovely face grew rigid like that of a person in a trance; the light faded from her brow, and the great pupils of her eyes contracted themselves and lost their colour.

In a little while, five minutes perhaps, she sighed like one awakening from a deep sleep, passed her hand across her forehead and was as she had been, though somewhat languid, as though strength had left her.

"It is true enough," she said, "and soon I must be stirring lest many of my people should be killed. My lord, wouldst thou see war? Nay, thou shalt bide here in safety whilst I go forward – to visit Atene as I promised."

"Where thou goest, I go," said Leo angrily, his face flushing to the roots of his hair with shame.

"I pray thee not, I pray thee not," she answered, yet without venturing to forbid him. "We will talk of it hereafter.

Oros, away! Send round the Fire of Hes to every chief. Three nights hence at the moonrise bid the Tribes gather – nay, not all, twenty thousand of their best will be enough, the rest shall stay to guard the Mountain and this Sanctuary. Let them bring food with them for fifteen days. I join them at the following dawn. Go."

He bowed and went, whereon, dismissing the matter from her mind. Ayesha began to question me again about the Chinese and their customs.

It was in course of a somewhat similar conversation on the following night, of which, however, I forget the exact details, that a remark of Leo's led to another exhibition of Ayesha's marvellous powers.

Leo – who had been considering her plans for conquest, and again combating them as best he could, for they were entirely repugnant to his religious, social and political views – said suddenly that after all they must break down, since they would involve the expenditure of sums of money so vast that even Ayesha herself would be unable to provide them by any known methods of taxation. She looked at him and laughed a little.

"Verily, Leo," she said, "to thee, yes; and to Holly here I must seem as some madcap girl blown to and fro by every wind of fancy, and building me a palace wherein to dwell out of dew and vapours, or from the substance of the sunset fires. Thinkest thou then that I would enter on this war – one woman against all the world" – and as she spoke her shape grew royal and in her awful eyes there came a look that chilled my blood – "and make no preparation for its necessities? Why, since last we spoke upon this matter, foreseeing all, I have considered in my mind, and now thou shalt learn how, without cost to those we rule – and for that reason alone shall they love us dearly – I will glut the treasuries of the Empress of the Earth.

"Dost remember, Leo, how in Kôr I found but a single pleasure during all those weary ages – that of forcing my mother Nature one by one to yield me up her choicest secrets; I, who am a student of all things which are and of the forces that cause them to be born. Now follow me, both of you, and ye shall look on what mortal eyes have not yet beheld."

"What are we to see?" I asked doubtfully, having a lively recollection of Ayesha's powers as a chemist.

"That thou shalt learn, or shalt not learn if it pleases thee to stay behind. Come, Leo, my love, my love, and leave this wise philosopher first to find his riddle and next to guess it."

Then turning her back to me she smiled on him so sweetly that although really he was more loth to go than I, Leo would have followed her through a furnace door, as indeed, had he but known it, he was about to do.

So they started, and I accompanied them, since with Ayesha it was useless to indulge in any foolish pride, or to make oneself a victim to consistency. Also I was anxious to see her new marvel, and did not care to rely for an account of it upon Leo's descriptive skill, which at its best was never more than moderate.

She took us down passages that we had not passed before, to a door which she signed to Leo to open. He obeyed, and from the cave within issued a flood of light. As we guessed at once, the place was her laboratory, for about it stood metal flasks and various strange-shaped instruments. Moreover, there was a furnace in it, one of the best conceivable, for it needed neither fuel nor stoking, whose gaseous fires, like those of the twisted columns in the Sanctuary, sprang from the womb of the volcano beneath our feet.

When we entered two priests were at work there: one of them stirring a cauldron with an iron rod and the other receiving its molten contents into a mould of clay. They stopped to salute Ayesha, but she bade them to continue their task, asking them if all went well.

"Very well, O Hes," they answered; and we passed through that cave and sundry doors and passages to a little chamber cut in the rock. There was no lamp or flame of fire in it, and yet the place was filled with a gentle light which seemed to flow from the opposing wall.

"What were those priests doing?" I said, more to break the silence than for any other reason.

"Why waste breath upon foolish questions?" she replied. "Are no metals smelted in thy country, O Holly? Now hadst thou sought to know what I am doing – But that, without seeing, thou wouldst not believe, so, Doubter, thou shalt see."

Then she pointed to and bade us don, two strange garments that hung upon the wall, made of a material which seemed to be half cloth and half wood and having head-pieces not unlike a diver's helmet.

So under her directions Leo helped me into mine, lacing it up behind, after which, or so I gathered from the sounds – for no light came through the helmet – she did the same service for him.

"I seem very much in the dark," I said presently; for now there was silence again, and beneath this extinguisher I felt alarmed and wished to be sure that I was not left alone.

"Aye Holly," I heard Ayesha's mocking voice make answer, "in the dark, as thou wast ever, the thick dark of ignorance and unbelief. Well, now, as ever also, I will give thee light." As she spoke I heard something roll back; I suppose that it must have been a stone door.'

Then, indeed, there was light, yes, even through the thicknesses of that prepared garment, such light as seemed to blind me. By it I saw that the wall opposite to us had opened and that we were all three of us on the threshold of another chamber. At the end of it stood something like a little altar of hard, black stone, and on this altar lay a mass of substance of the size of a child's head, but fashioned, I suppose from fantasy, to the oblong shape of a human eye.

Out of this eye there poured that blistering and intolerable light. It was shut round by thick, funnel-shaped screens of a material that looked like fire-brick, yet it pierced them as though they were but muslin. More, the rays thus directed upwards struck full upon a lump of metal held in place above them by a massive frame-work.

And what rays they were! If all the cut diamonds of the world were brought together and set beneath a mighty burning-glass, the light flashed from them would not have been a thousandth part so brilliant. They scorched my eyes and caused the skin of my face and limbs to smart, yet Ayesha stood there unshielded from them. Aye, she even went down the length of the room and, throwing back her veil, bent over them, as it seemed a woman of molten steel in whose body the bones were visible, and examined the mass that was supported by the hanging cradle.

"It is ready and somewhat sooner than I thought," she said. Then as though it were but a feather weight, she lifted the lump in her bare hands and glided back with it to where we stood, laughing and saying –

"Tell me now, O thou well-read Holly, if thou hast ever heard of a better alchemist than this poor priestess of a forgotten faith?" And she thrust the glowing substance up almost to the mask that hid my face.

Then I turned and ran, or rather waddled, for in that gear I could not run, out of the chamber until the rock wall beyond stayed me, and there, with my back towards her, thrust my helmeted head against it, for I felt as though red hot bradawls had been plunged into my eyes. So I stood while she laughed and mocked behind me until at length I heard the door close, and the blessed darkness came like a gift from Heaven.

Then Ayesha began to loose Leo from his ray-proof armour, if so it can be called, and he in turn loosed me; and there in that gentle radiance we stood blinking at each other like owls in the sunlight, while the tears streamed down our faces.

"Well, art satisfied, my Holly?" she asked.

"Satisfied with what?" I answered angrily, for the smarting of my eyes was unbearable. "Yes, with burnings and bedevilments I am well satisfied."

"And I also," grumbled Leo, who was swearing softly but continuously to himself in the other corner of the place.

But Ayesha only laughed, oh! she laughed until she seemed the goddess of all merriment come to earth, laughed till she also wept, then said –

"Why, what ingratitude is this? Thou, my Leo, didst wish to see the wonders that I work, and thou, O Holly, didst come unbidden after I bade thee stay behind, and now both of you are rude and angry, aye, and weeping like a child with a burnt finger. Here take this," and she gave us some salve that stood upon a shelf, "and rub it on your eyes and the smart will pass away."

So we did, and the pain went from them, though, for hours afterwards, mine remained red as blood.

"And what are these wonders?" I asked her presently. "If thou meanest that unbearable flame – "

"Nay, I mean what is born of the name, as, in thine ignorance thou dost call that mighty agent. Look now;" and she pointed to the metallic lump she had brought with her, which, still gleaming faintly, lay upon the floor. "Nay, it has no heat. Thinkest thou that I would wish to burn my tender hands and so make them unsightly? Touch it, Holly."

But I would not, who thought to myself that Ayesha might be well accustomed to the hottest fires, and feared her impish mischief. I looked, however, long and earnestly.

"Well, what is it, Holly?"

"Gold," I said, then corrected myself and added, "Copper," for the dull, red glow might have been that of either metal.

"Nay, nay," she answered, "it is gold, pure gold."

"The ore in this place must be rich," said Leo, incredulously, for I would not speak any more.

"Yes, my Leo, the iron ore is rich."

"Iron ore?" and he looked at her.

"Surely," she answered, "for from what mine do men dig out gold in such great masses? Iron ore, beloved, that by my alchemy I change to gold, which soon shall serve us in our need."

Now Leo stared and I groaned, for I did not believe that it was gold, and still less that she could make that metal.

Then, reading my thought, with one of those sudden changes of mood that were common to her, Ayesha grew very angry.

"By Nature's self!" she cried; "wert thou not my friend. Holly, the fool whom it pleases me to cherish, I would bind that right hand of thine in those secret rays till the very bones within it were turned to gold. Nay, why should I be vexed with thee, who art both blind and deaf? Yet thou *shalt* be persuaded," and leaving us, she passed down the passages, called something to the priests who were labouring in the workshop, then returned to us.

Presently they followed her, carrying on a kind of stretcher between them an ingot of iron ore that seemed to be as much as they could lift.

"Now," she said, "how wilt thou that I mark this mass which as thou must admit is only iron? With the sign of Life? Good," and at her bidding the priests took cold-chisels and hammers and roughly cut upon its surface the symbol of the looped cross – the *crux ansata.*

"It is not enough," she said when they had finished. "Holly, lend me that knife of thine, tomorrow I will return it to thee, and of more value."

So I drew my hunting knife, an Indian-made thing, that had a handle of plated iron, and gave it her.

"Thou knowest the marks on it," and she pointed to various dents and to the maker's name upon the blade; for though the hilt was Indian work the steel was of Sheffield manufacture.

I nodded. Then she bade the priests put on the ray-proof armour that we had discarded, and told us to go without the chamber and lie in the darkness of the passage with our faces against the floor.

This we did, and remained so until, a few minutes later, she called us again. We rose and returned into the chamber to find the priests, who had removed the protecting garments, gasping and rubbing the salve upon their eyes; to find also that the lump of iron ore and my knife were gone. Next she commanded them to place the block of gold-coloured metal upon their stretcher and to bring it with them. They obeyed, and we noted that, although those priests were both of them strong men they groaned beneath its weight.

"How came it," said Leo, "that thou, a woman, couldst carry what these men find so heavy?"

"It is one of the properties of that force which thou callest fire," she answered sweetly, "to make what has been exposed to it, if for a little while only, as light as thistle-down. Else, how could I, who am so frail, have borne yonder block of gold?"

"Quite so! I understand now," answered Leo.

Well, that was the end of it. The lump of metal was hid away in a kind of rock pit, with an iron cover, and we returned to Ayesha's apartments.

"So all wealth is thine, as well as all power," said Leo, presently, for remembering Ayesha's awful threat I scarcely dared to open my mouth.

"It seems so," she answered wearily, "since centuries ago I discovered that great secret, though until ye came I had put it to no use. Holly here, after his common fashion, believes that this is magic, but I tell thee again that there is no magic, only knowledge which I have chanced to win."

"Of course," said Leo, "looked at in the right way, that is in thy way, the thing is simple." I think he would have liked to add. "as lying," but as the phrase would have involved explanations, did not. "Yet, Ayesha,' he went on, "hast thou thought that this discovery of thine will wreck the world?"

"Leo," she answered, "is there then nothing that I can do which will not wreck this world, for which thou hast such tender care, who shouldst keep all thy care-for me?"

I smiled, but remembering in time, turned the smile into a frown at Leo, then fearing lest that also might anger her, made my countenance as blank as possible.

"If so," she continued, "well, let the world be wrecked. But what meanest thou? Oh! my lord, Leo, forgive me if I am so dull that I cannot always follow thy quick thought – I who have lived these many years alone, without converse with nobler minds, or even those to which mine own is equal."

"It pleases thee to mock me," said Leo, in a vexed voice, "and that is not too brave."

Now Ayesha turned on him fiercely, and I looked towards the door. But he did not shrink, only folded his arms and stared her straight in the face. She contemplated him a little, then said –

"After that great ordained reason which thou dost not know, I think, Leo, that why I love thee so madly is that thou alone art not afraid of me. Not like Holly there, who, ever since I threatened to turn his bones to gold – which, indeed, I was minded to do," and she laughed – "trembles at my footsteps and cowers beneath my softest glance.

"Oh! my lord, how good thou art to me, how patient with my moods and woman's weaknesses," and she made as though she were about to embrace him. Then suddenly remembering herself, with a little start that somehow conveyed more that the most tragic gesture, she pointed to the couch in token that he should seat himself. When he had done so she drew a footstool to his feet and sank upon it, looking up into his face with attentive eyes, like a child who listens for a story.

"Thy reasons, Leo, give me thy reasons. Doubtless they are good, and, oh! be sure I'll weigh them well."

"Here they are in brief," he answered, "The world, as thou knewest in thy – " and he stopped.

"Thy earlier wanderings there," she suggested.

"Yes – thy earlier wanderings there, has set up gold as the standard of its wealth. On it all civilizations are founded. Make it as common as it seems thou canst, and these must fall to pieces. Credit will fail and, like their savage forefathers, men must once more take to barter to supply their needs as they do in Kaloon to-day."

"Why not?" she asked. "It would be more simple and bring them closer to the time when they were good and knew not luxury and greed."

"And smashed in each other's heads with stone axes," added Leo.

"Who now pierce each other's hearts with steel, or those leaden missiles of which thou hast told me. Oh! Leo, when the nations are beggared and their golden god is down; when the usurer and the fat merchant tremble and turn white as chalk because their hoards are but useless dross; when I have made the bankrupt Exchanges of the world my mock, and laugh across the ruin of its richest markets, why, then, will not true worth come to its heritage again?

"What of it if I do discomfort those who think more of pelf than of courage and of virtue; those who, as that Hebrew prophet wrote, lay field to field and house to house, until the wretched whom they have robbed find no place left whereon to dwell? What if I prove your sagest chapmen fools, and gorge your greedy money-changers with the gold that they desire until they loathe its very sight and touch? What if I uphold the cause of the poor and the oppressed against the ravening lusts of Mammon? Why, will not this world of yours be happier then?"

"I do not know," answered Leo. "All that I know is that it would be a different world, one shaped upon a new plan, governed by untried laws and seeking other ends. In so strange a place who can say what might or might not chance?"

"That we shall learn in its season, Leo. Or, rather, if it be against thy wish, we will not turn this hidden page. Since thou dost desire it, that old evil, the love of lucre, shall still hold its mastery upon the earth. Let the peoples keep their yellow king, I'll not crown another in his place, as I was minded – such as that living Strength thou sawest burning eternally but now; that Power whereof I am the mistress, which can give health to men, or even change the character of metals, and in truth, if I so desire, obedient to my word, destroy a city or rend this Mountain from its roots.

"But see, Holly is wearied with much wondering and needs his rest. Oh, Holly! thou wast born a critic of things done, not a doer of them. I know thy tribe, for even in my day the colleges of Alexandria echoed with their wranglings and already the winds blew thick with the dust of their forgotten bones. Holly, I tell thee that at times those who create and act are impatient of such petty doubts and cavulings. Yet fear not, old friend, nor take my anger ill. Already thy heart is gold without alloy, so what need have I to gild thy bones?"

I thanked Ayesha for her compliment, and went to my bed wondering which was real, her kindness or her wrath, or if both were but assumed. Also I wondered in what way she had fallen foul of the critics of Alexandria. Perhaps once she had published a poem or a system of philosophy and been roughly handled by them! It is quite possible, only if Ayesha had ever written poetry I think that it would have endured, like Sappho's.

In the morning I discovered that whatever else about her might be false. Ayesha was a true chemist, the very greatest, I suppose, who ever lived. For as I dressed myself, those priests whom we had seen in the laboratory, staggered into the room carrying between them a heavy burden, that was covered with a cloth, and, directed by Oros, placed it upon the floor.

"What is that?" I asked of Oros.

"A peace-offering sent by the Hesea," he said, "with whom, as I am told, you dared to quarrel yesterday."

Then he withdrew the cloth, and there beneath it shone that great lump of metal which, in the presence of myself and Leo, had been marked with the Symbol of Life, that still appeared upon its surface. Only now it was gold, not iron, gold so good and soft that I could write my name upon it with a nail. My knife lay with it also, and of that too the handle, though not the blade, had been changed from iron into gold.

Ayesha asked to see this afterwards and was but ill-pleased with the result of her experiment. She pointed out to me that lines and blotches of gold ran for an inch or more down the substance of the steel, which she feared that they might weaken or distemper, whereas it had been her purpose that the hilt only should be altered.*

* I proved in after days how real were Ayesha's alchemy, and the knowledge which enabled her to solve the secret that chemists have hunted for in vain, and, like Nature's self, to transmute the commonest into the most precious of the metals. At the first town that I reached on the frontiers of India, I took this knife to a jeweller, a native, who was as clever as he proved dishonest, and asked him to test the handle. He did so with acids and by other means, and told me that it was of very pure gold, *twenty-four carats*, I think he said. Also he pointed out that this gold became gradually merged into the steel of the blade in a way which was quite inexplicable to him, and asked me to clear up the matter. Of course I could not, but at his request I left the knife in his shop to give him an opportunity of examining it further. The next day I was taken ill with one of the heart-attacks to which I have been liable of late, and when I became able to move about again a while, afterwards, I found that this jeweller had gone, none knew whither. So had my knite. – L. H. H.

Often since that time I have marvelled how Ayesha performed this miracle, and from what substances she gathered or compounded the lightning-like material which was her servant in the work; also, whether or no it had been impregnated with the immortalizing fire of Life that burned in the caves of Kôr. Yet to this hour I have found no answer to the problem, for it is beyond my guessing.*

I suppose that, in preparation for her conquest of the inhabitants of this globe – to which, indeed, it would have sufficed unaided by any other power – the manufacture of gold from iron went on in the cave unceasingly.

However this may be, during the few days that we remained together Ayesha never so much as spoke of it again. It seemed to have served her purpose for the while, or in the press of other and more urgent matters to have been forgotten or thrust from her mind. Still, amongst others, of which I have said nothing, since it is necessary to select, I record this strange incident, and our conversations concerning it at length, for the reason that it made a great impression upon me and furnishes a striking example of Ayesha's dominion over the hidden forces of Nature whereof we were soon to experience a more fearful instance.

* Recent discoveries would appear to suggest that this mysterious 'Fire of Life,' which, whatever else it may have been, was evidently a force and no true fire, since it did not burn, owed its origin to the emanations from radium, or some kindred substance. Although in the year 1885, Mr. Holly would have known nothing of the properties of these marvellous rays or emanations, doubtless Ayesha was familiar with them and their enormous possibilities, of which our chemists and scientific men have, at present, but explored the fringe. – EDITOR.

CHAPTER 21

THE PROPHECY OF ATENE

ON THE day following this strange experience of the iron that was turned to gold some great service was held in the Sanctuary, as we understood, "to consecrate the war." We did not attend it, but that night we ate together as usual. Ayesha was moody at the meal, that is, she varied from sullen-ness to laughter.

"Know you," she said, "that to-day I was an Oracle, and those fools of the Mountain sent their medicine-men to ask of the Hesea how the battle would go, and which of them would be slain, and which gain honour. And I – I could not tell them, but juggled with my words, so that they might take them as they would. How the battle will go I know well, for I shall direct it, but the future – ah! that I cannot read better than thou canst, my Holly, and that is ill indeed. For me the past and all the present lie bathed in light reflected from that black wall – the future."

Then she fell to brooding, and looking up at length with an air of entreaty, said to Leo –

"Wilt thou not hear my prayer and bide where thou art for some few days, or even go a-hunting? Do so, and I will stay with thee, and send Holly and Oros to command the Tribes in this petty fray."

"I will not," answered Leo, trembling with indignation, for this plan of hers that I should be sent out to war, while he bided in safety in a temple, moved him, a man brave to rashness, who, although he disapproved of it in theory, loved fighting for its own sake also, to absolute rage.

"I say, Ayesha, that I will not," he repeated; "moreover, that if thou leavest me here I will find my way down the mountain alone, and join the battle."

"Then come," she answered, "and on thine own head be it. Nay, not on thine beloved, on mine, on mine."

After this, by some strange reaction, she became like a merry girl, laughing more than I have ever seen her do, and telling us many tales of the far, far past, but none that were sad or tragic. It was very strange to sit and listen to her while she spoke of people, one or two of them known as names in history and many others who never have been heard of, that had trod this earth and with whom she was familiar over two thousand years ago. Yet she told us anecdotes of their loves and hates, their strength or weaknesses, all of them touched with some tinge of humorous satire, or illustrating the comic vanity of human aims and aspirations.

At length her talk took a deeper and more personal note. She spoke of her searchings after truth; of how, aching for wisdom, she had explored the religions of her day and refused them one by one; of how she had preached in Jerusalem and been stoned by the Doctors of the Law. Of how also she had wandered back to Arabia and, being rejected by her own people as a reformer, had travelled on to Egypt, and at the court of the Pharaoh of that time met a famous magician, half charlatan and half seer who, because she was far-seeing, 'clairvoyante' we should call it, instructed her in his art so well that soon she became his master and forced him to obey her.

Then, as though she were unwilling to reveal too much, suddenly Ayesha's history passed from Egypt to Kôr. She spoke to Leo of his arrival there a wanderer who was named

Kallikrates, hunted by savages and accompanied by the Egyptian Amenartas, whom she appeared to have known and hated in her own country, and of how she entertained them. Yes, she even told of a supper that the three of them had eaten together on the evening before they started to discover the Place of Life, and of an evil prophecy that this royal Amenartas had made as to the issue of their journey.

"Aye," Ayesha said, "it was such a silent night as this and such a meal as this we ate, and Leo, not so greatly changed, save that he was beardless then and younger, was at my side. Where thou sittest, Holly, sat the royal Amenartas, a very fair woman; yes, even more beautiful than I before I dipped me in the Essence, fore-sighted also, though not so learned as I had grown. From the first we hated each other, and more than ever now, when she guessed how I had learned to look upon thee, her lover, Leo; for her husband thou never wast, who didst flee too fast for marriage. She knew also that the struggle between us which had begun of old and afar was for centuries and generations, and that until the end should declare itself neither of us could harm the other, who both had sinned to win thee, that wast appointed by fate to be the lodestone of our souls. Then Amenartas spoke and said –

" 'Lo! to my sight, Kallikrates, the wine in thy cup is turned to blood, and that knife in thy hand, O daughter of Yarâb' – for so she named me – 'drips red blood. Aye, and this place is a sepulchre, and thou, O Kallikrates, sleepest here, nor can she, thy murderers, kiss back the breath of life into those cold lips of thine.'

"So indeed it came about as was ordained," added Ayesha reflectively, "for I slew thee in yonder Place of Life, yes, in my madness I slew thee because thou wouldst not or couldst not understand the change that had come over me, and shrankest from my loveliness like a blind bat from the splendour of flame, hiding thy face in the tresses of her dusky hair – Why, what is it now, thou Oros? Can I never be rid of thee for an hour?"

"O Hes, a writing from the Khania Atene," the priest said with his deprecating bow.

"Break the seal and read," she answered carelessly. "Perchance she has repented of her folly and makes submission."

So he read –

> To the Hesea of the College on the Mountain, known as Ayesha upon earth, and in the household of the Over-world whence she has been permitted to wander, as 'Star-that-hath-fallen – '

"A pretty sounding name, forsooth," broke in Ayesha; "ah! but, Atene, set stars rise again – even from the Under-world. Read on, thou Oros."

> Greetings, O Ayesha. Thou who art very old, hast gathered much wisdom in the passing of the centuries, and with other powers, that of making thyself seem fair in the eyes of men blinded by thine arts. Yet one thing thou lackest that I have – vision of those happenings which are not yet. Know, O Ayesha, that I and my uncle, the great seer, have searched the heavenly books to learn what is written there of the issue of this war.
>
> This is written: – For me, death, whereat I rejoice. For thee a spear cast by thine own hand. For the land of Kaloon blood and ruin bred of thee!
>
> ATENE,
>
> Khania of Kaloon.

Ayesha listened in silence, but her lips did not tremble, nor her cheek pale. To Oros she said proudly –

"Say to the messenger of Atene that I have received her message, and ere long will answer it, face to face with her in her palace of Kaloon. Go, priest, and disturb me no more."

When Oros had departed she turned to us and said –

"That tale of mine of long ago was well fitted to this hour, for as Amenartas prophesied of ill, so does Atene prophesy of ill, and Amenartas and Atene are one. Well, let the spear fall, if fall it must, and I will not flinch from it who know that I shall surely triumph at the last. Perhaps the Khania does but think to frighten me with a cunning lie, but if she has read aright, then be sure, beloved, that it is still well with us, since none can escape their destiny, nor can our bond of union which was fashioned with the universe that bears us, ever be undone."

She paused awhile, then went on with a sudden outburst of poetic thought and imagery:

"I tell thee, Leo, that out of the confusions of our lives and deaths order shall yet be born. Behind the mask of cruelty shine Mercy's tender eyes; and the wrongs of this rough and twisted world are but hot blinding sparks which stream from the all-righting sword of pure, eternal Justice. The heavy lives we see and know are only links in a golden chain that shall draw us safe to the haven of our rest; steep and painful steps are they whereby we climb to the allotted palace of our joy. Henceforth I fear no more, and fight no more against that which must befall. For I say we are but winged seeds blown down the gales of fate and change to the appointed garden where we shall grow, filling its blest air with the immortal fragrance of our bloom.

"Leave me now, Leo, and sleep awhile, for we ride at dawn."

It was midday on the morrow when we moved down the mountain-side with the army of the Tribes, fierce and savage-looking men. The scouts were out before us, then came the great body of their cavalry mounted on wiry horses, while to right and left and behind, the foot soldiers marched in regiments, each under the command of its own chief.

Ayesha, veiled now – for she would not show her beauty to these wild folk – rode in the midst of the horsemen on a white mare of matchless speed and shape. With her went Leo and myself, Leo on the Khan's black horse, and I on another not unlike it, though thicker built. About us were a bodyguard of armed priests and a regiment of chosen soldiers, among them those hunters that Leo had saved from Ayesha's wrath, and who were now attached to his person.

We were merry, all of us, for in the crisp air of late autumn flooded with sunlight, the fears and forebodings that had haunted us in those gloomy, firelit caves were forgotten. Moreover, the tramp of thousands of armed men and the excitement of coming battle thrilled our nerves.

Not for many a day had I seen Leo look so vigorous and happy. Of late he had grown somewhat thin and pale, probably from causes that I have suggested, but now his cheeks were red and his eyes shone bright again. Ayesha also seemed joyous, for the moods of this strange woman were as fickle as those of Nature's self, and varied as a landscape varies under the sunshine or the shadow. Now she was noon and now dark night; now dawn, now evening, and now thoughts came and went in the blue depths of her eyes like vapours wafted across the summer sky, and in the press of them her sweet face changed and shimmered as broken water shimmers beneath the beaming stars.

"Too long," she said, with a little thrilling laugh, "have I been shut in the bowels of sombre mountains, companied only by mutes and savages or by melancholy, chanting priests, and now I am glad to look upon the world again. How beautiful are the snows above, and the brown slopes below, and the broad plains beyond that roll away to those bordering hills! How glorious is the sun, eternal as myself; how sweet the keen air of heaven.

"Believe me, Leo, more than twenty centuries have gone by since I was seated on a steed, and yet thou seest I have not forgot my horsemanship, though this beast cannot match those arabs that I rode in the wide deserts of Arabia. Oh! I remember how at my father's side I galloped down to war against the marauding Bedouins, and how with my own hand I speared their chieftain and made him cry for mercy. One day I will tell thee of that father of mine, for I was his darling, and though we have been long apart, I hold his memory dear and look forward to our meeting.

"See, yonder is the mouth of that gorge where lived the cat-worshipping sorcerer, who would have murdered both of you because thou, Leo, didst throw his familiar to the fire. It is strange, but several of the tribes of this Mountain and of the lands behind it make cats their gods or divine by means of them. I think that the first Rassen, the general of Alexander, must have brought the practice here from Egypt. Of this Macedonian Alexander I could tell thee much, for he was almost a contemporary of mine, and when I last was born the world still rang with the fame of his great deeds.

"It was Rassen who on the Mountain supplanted the primeval fire-worship whereof the flaming pillars which light its Sanctuary remain as monuments, by that of Hes, or Isis, or rather blended the two in one. Doubtless among the priests in his army were some of Pasht or Sekket the Cat-headed, and these brought with them their secret cult, that to-day has dwindled down to the vulgar divinations of savage sorcerers. Indeed I remember dimly that it was so, for I was the first Hesea of this Temple, and journeyed hither with that same general Rassen, a relative of mine."

Now both Leo and I looked at her wonderingly, and I could see that she was watching us through her veil. As usual, however, it was I whom she reproved, since Leo might think and do what he willed and still escape her anger.

"Thou, Holly," she said quickly, "who art ever of a cavilling and suspicious mind, remembering what I said but now, believest that I lie to thee."

I protested that I was only reflecting upon an apparent variation between two statements.

"Play not with words," she answered; "in thy heart thou didst write me down a liar, and I take that ill. Know, foolish man, that when I said that the Macedonian Alexander lived before me, I meant before this present life of mine. In the existence that preceded it, though I outlasted him by thirty years, we were born in the same summer, and I knew him well, for I was the Oracle whom he consulted most upon his wars, and to my wisdom he owed his victories. Afterwards we quarrelled, and I left him and pushed forward with Rassen. From that day the bright star of Alexander began to wane."

At this Leo made a sound that resembled a whistle. In a very agony of apprehension, beating back the criticisms and certain recollections of the strange tale of the old abbot, Kou-en, which would rise within me, I asked quickly –

"And dost thou, Ayesha, remember well all that befel thee in this former life?"

"Nay, not well," she answered, meditatively, "only the greater facts, and those I have for the most part recovered by that study of secret things which thou callest vision or magic. For instance, my Holly, I recall that thou wast living in that life. Indeed I seem to see an ugly philosopher clad in a dirty robe and filled both with wine and the learning of others, who disputed with Alexander till he grew wroth with him and caused him to be banished, or drowned: I forget which."

"I suppose that I was not called Diogenes?" I asked tartly, suspecting, perhaps not without cause, that Ayesha was amusing herself by fooling me.

"No," she replied gravely, "I do not think that was thy name. The Diogenes thou speakest of was a much more famous man, one of real if crabbed wisdom; moreover, he did not indulge in wine. I am mindful of very little of that life, however, not of more indeed than are many of the followers of the prophet Buddha, whose doctrines I have studied and of whom thou, Holly, hast spoken to me so much. Maybe we did not meet while it endured. Still I recollect that the Valley of Bones, where I found thee, my Leo, was the place where a great battle was fought between the Fire-priests with their vassals, the Tribes of the Mountain and the army of Rassen aided by the people of Kaloon. For between these and the Mountain, in old days as now, there was enmity, since in this present war history does but rewrite itself."

"So thou thyself wast our guide," said Leo, looking at her sharply.

"Aye, Leo, who else? though it is not wonderful that thou didst not know me beneath those deathly wrappings. I was minded to wait and receive thee in the Sanctuary, yet when I learned that at length both of you had escaped Atene and drew near, I could restrain myself no more, but came forth thus hideously disguised. Yes, I was with you even at the river's bank, and though you saw me not, there sheltered you from harm.

"Leo, I yearned to look upon thee and to be certain that thy heart had not changed, although until the allotted time thou mightest not hear my voice or see my face who wert doomed to undergo that sore trial of thy faith. Of Holly also I desired to learn whether his wisdom could pierce through my disguise, and how near he stood to truth. It was for this reason that I suffered him to see me draw the lock from the satchel on thy breast and to hear me wail over thee yonder in the Rest-house. Well he did not guess so ill, but thou, thou knewest me – in thy sleep – knewest me as I am, and not as I seemed to be, yes," she added softly, "and didst say certain sweet words which I remember well."

"Then beneath that shroud was thine own face," asked Leo again, for he was very curious on this point, "the same lovely face I see to-day?"

"Mayhap – as thou wilt," she answered coldly; "also it is the spirit that matters, not the outward seeming, though men in their blindness think otherwise. Perchance my face is but as thy heart fashions it, or as my will presents it to the sight and fancy of its beholders. But hark! The scouts have touched."

As Ayesha spoke a sound of distant shouting was borne upon the wind, and presently we saw a fringe of horsemen falling back slowly upon our foremost line. It was only to report, however, that the skirmishers of Atene were in full retreat. Indeed, a prisoner whom they brought with them, on being questioned by the priests, confessed at once that the Khania had no mind to meet us upon the holy Mountain. She proposed to give battle on the river's farther bank, having for a defence its waters which we must ford, a decision that showed good military judgment.

So it happened that on this day there was no fighting.

All that afternoon we descended the slopes of the Mountain, more swiftly by far than we had climbed them after our long flight from the city of Kaloon. Before sunset we came to our prepared camping ground, a wide and sloping plain that ended at the crest of the Valley of Dead Bones, where in past days we had met our mysterious guide. This, however, we did not reach through the secret mountain tunnel along which she had led us, the shortest way by miles, as Ayesha told us now, since it was unsuited to the passage of an army.

Bending to the left, we circled round a number of unclimbable koppies, beneath which that tunnel passed, and so at length arrived upon the brow of the dark ravine where we could sleep safe from attack by night.

Here a tent was pitched for Ayesha, but as it was the only one, Leo and I with our guard bivouacked among some rocks at a distance of a few hundred yards. When she found that this must be so, Ayesha was very angry and spoke bitter words to the chief who had charge of the food and baggage, although, he, poor man, knew nothing of tents.

Also she blamed Oros, who replied meekly that he had thought us captains accustomed to war and its hardships. But most of all she was angry with herself, who had forgotten this detail, and until Leo stopped her with a laugh of vexation, went on to suggest that we should sleep in the tent, since she had no fear of the rigours of the mountain cold.

The end of it was that we supped together outside, or rather Leo and I supped, for as there were guards around us Ayesha did not even lift her veil.

That evening Ayesha was disturbed and ill at ease, as though new fears which she could not overcome assailed her. At length she seemed to conquer them, by some effort of her will and announced that 'she was minded to sleep and thus refresh her soul; the only part of her, I think, which ever needed rest. Her last words to us were –

"Sleep you also, sleep sound, but be not astonished, my Leo, if I send to summon both of you during the night, since in my slumbers I may find new counsels and need to speak of them to thee ere we break camp at dawn."

Thus we parted, but ah! little did we guess how and where the three of us would meet again.

We were weary and soon fell fast asleep beside our camp-fire, for, knowing that the whole army guarded us, we had no fear. I remember watching the bright stars which shone in the immense vault above me until they paled in the pure light of the risen moon, now somewhat past her full, and hearing Leo mutter drowsily from beneath his fur rug that Ayesha was quite right, and that it was pleasant to be in the open air again, as he was tired of caves.

After that I knew no more until I was awakened by the challenge of a sentry in the distance; then after a pause, a second challenge from the officer of our own guard. Another pause, and a priest stood bowing before us, the flickering light from the fire playing upon his shaven head and face, which I seemed to recognise.

"I" – and he gave a name that was familiar to me, but which I forget – "am sent, my lords, by Oros, who commands me to say that the Hesea would speak with you both and at once."

Now Leo sat up yawning and asked what was the matter. I told him, whereon he said he wished that Ayesha could have waited till daylight, then added –

"Well, there is no help for it. Come on, Horace," and he rose to follow the messenger.

The priest bowed again and said –

"The commands of the Hesea are that my lords should bring their weapons and their guard."

"What," grumbled Leo, "to protect us for a walk of a hundred yards through the heart of an army?"

"The Hesea," explained the man, "has left her tent; she is in the gorge yonder, studying the line of advance."

"How do you know that?" I asked.

"I do not know it," he replied. "Oros told me so, that is all, and therefore the Hesea bade my lords bring their guard, for she is alone."

"Is she mad," ejaculated Leo, "to wander about in such a place at midnight? Well, it is like her."

I too thought it was like her, who did nothing that others would have done, and yet I hesitated. Then I remembered that Ayesha had said she might send for us; also I was sure that if any trick had been intended we should not have been warned to bring an escort. So we called the guard – there were twelve of them – took our spears and swords and started.

We were challenged by both the first and second lines of sentries, and I noticed that as we gave them the pass-word the last picket, who of course recognized us, looked astonished. Still, if they had doubts they did not dare to express them. So we went on.

Now we began to descend the sides of the ravine by a very steep path, with which the priest, our guide, seemed to be curiously familiar, for he went down it as though it were the stairway of his own house.

"A strange place to take us to at night," said Leo doubtfully, when we were near the bottom and the chief of the bodyguard, that great red-bearded hunter who had been mixed up in the matter of the snow-leopard also muttered some words of remonstrance. Whilst I was trying to catch what he said, of a sudden something white walked into the patch of moonlight at the foot of the ravine, and we saw that it was the veiled figure of Ayesha herself. The chief saw her also and said contentedly –

"Hes! Hes!"

"Look at her," grumbled Leo, "strolling about in that haunted hole as though it were Hyde Park;" and on he went at a run.

The figure turned and beckoned to us to follow her as she glided forward, picking her way through the skeletons which were scattered about upon the lava bed of the cleft. Thus she went on into the shadow of the opposing cliff that the moonlight did not reach. Here in the wet season a stream trickled down a path which it had cut through the rock in the course of centuries, and the grit that it had brought with it was spread about the lava floor of the ravine, so that many of the bones were almost completely buried in the sand.

These, I noticed, as we stepped into the shadow, were more numerous than usual just here, for on all sides I saw the white crowns of skulls, or the projecting ends of ribs and thigh bones. Doubtless, I thought to myself, that streamway made a road to the plain above, and in some past battle, the fighting around it was very fierce and the slaughter great.

Here Ayesha had halted and was engaged in the contemplation of this boulder-strewn path, as though she meditated making use of it that day. Now we drew near to her, and the priest who guided us fell back with our guard, leaving us to go forward alone, since they dared not approach the Hesea unbidden. Leo was somewhat in advance of me, seven or eight yards perhaps, and I heard him say –

"Why dost thou venture into such places at night, Ayesha, unless indeed it is not possible for any harm to come to thee?"

She made no answer, only turned and opened her arms wide, then let them fall to her side again. Whilst I wondered what this signal of hers might mean, from the shadows about us came a strange, rustling sound.

I looked, and lo! everywhere the skeletons were rising from their sandy beds. I saw their white skulls, their gleaming arm and leg bones, their hollow ribs. The long-slain army had come to life again, and look! in their hands were the ghosts of spears.

Of course I knew at once that this was but another manifestation of Ayesha's magic powers, which some whim of hers had drawn us from our beds to witness. Yet I confess that I felt frightened. Even the boldest of men, however free from superstition, might be excused should their nerve fail them if, when standing in a churchyard at midnight, suddenly on every side they saw the dead arising from their graves. Also our surroundings were wilder and more eerie than those of any civilized burying-place.

"What new devilment of thine is this?" cried Leo in a scared and angry voice. But Ayesha made no answer.

I heard a noise behind me and looked round. The skeletons were springing upon our body-guard, who for their part, poor men, paralysed with terror, had thrown down their weapons and fallen, some of them, to their knees. Now the ghosts began to stab at them with their phantom spears, and I saw that beneath the blows they rolled over. The veiled figure above me pointed with her hand at Leo and said –

"Seize him, but I charge you, harm him not."

I knew the voice; *it was that of Atene!*

Then too late I understood the trap into which we had fallen.

"Treachery!" I began to cry, and before the word was out of my lips, a particularly able-bodied skeleton silenced me with a violent blow upon the head. But though I could not speak, my senses still stayed with me for a little. I saw Leo fighting furiously with a number of men who strove to pull him down, so furiously, indeed that his frightful efforts caused the blood to gush out of his mouth from some burst vessel in the lungs.

Then sight and hearing failed me, and thinking that this was death, I fell and remembered no more.

Why I was not killed outright I do not know, unless in their hurry the disguised soldiers thought me already dead, or perhaps that my life was to be spared also. At least, beyond the knock upon the head I received no injury.

CHAPTER 22

THE LOOSING OF THE POWERS

WHEN I came to myself again, it was daylight. I saw the calm, gentle face of Oros bending over me as he poured some strong fluid down my throat that seemed to shoot through all my body, and melt a curtain in my mind. I saw also that beside him stood Ayesha.

"Speak, man, speak," she said in a terrible voice. "What has chanced here? Thou livest, then where is my lord? Where hast thou hid my lord? Tell me – or die."

It was the vision that I saw when my senses left me in the snow of the avalanche, fulfilled to the last detail!

"Atene has taken him," I answered.

"Atene has taken him and thou art left alive?"

"Do not be wrath with me," I answered, "it is no fault of mine. Little wonder we were deceived after thou hadst said that thou mightest summon us ere dawn."

Then, as briefly as I could, I told the story.

She listened, went to where our murdered guards lay with unstained spears, and looked at them.

"Well for these that they are dead," she exclaimed. "Now, Holly, thou seest what is the fruit of mercy. The men whose lives I gave my lord have failed him at his need."

Then she passed forward to the spot where Leo was captured. Here lay a broken sword – Leo's – that had been the Khan Rassen's, and two dead men. Both of these were clothed in some tight-fitting black garments; having their heads and faces whitened with chalk and upon their vests a rude imitation of a human skeleton, also daubed in chalk.

"A trick fit to frighten fools with," she said contemptuously. "But oh! that Atene should have dared to play the part of Ayesha, that she should have dared!" and she clenched her little hand. "See, surprised and overwhelmed, yet he fought well. Say! was he hurt, Holly? It comes upon me – no, tell me that I see amiss."

"Not much, I think," I answered doubtfully, "a little blood was running from his mouth, no more. Look, there go the stains of it upon that rock."

"For every drop I'll take a hundred lives. By myself I swear it," Ayesha muttered with a groan. Then she cried in a ringing voice:

"Back and to horse, for I have deeds to do this day. Nay, bide thou here, Holly; we go a shorter path while the army skirts the gorge. Oros, give him food and drink and bathe that hurt upon his head. It is but a bruise, for his hood and hair are thick."

So while Oros rubbed some stinging lotion on my scalp, I ate and drank as best I could till my brain ceased to swim, for the blow, though heavy, had not fractured the bone. When I was ready they brought the horses to us, and mounting them, slowly we scrambled up the steep bed of the water-course.

"See," Ayesha said, pointing to tracks and hoof-prints on the plain at its head, "there was a chariot awaiting him, and harnessed to it were four swift horses. Atene's scheme was clever and well laid, and I, grown oversure and careless, slept through it all!"

On this plain the army of the Tribes that had broken camp before the dawn was already gathering fast; indeed, the cavalry, if I may call them so, were assembled there to the number of about five thousand men, each of whom had a led horse. Ayesha summoned the chiefs and captains, and addressed them.

"Servants of Hes," she said, "the stranger lord, my bethrothed and guest, has been tricked by a false priest and, falling into a cunning snare, captured as a hostage. It is necessary that I follow him fast, before harm comes to him. We move down to attack the army of the Khania beyond the river. When its passage is forced I pass on with the horsemen, for I must sleep in the city of Kaloon to-night. What sayest thou, Oros? that a second and greater army defends its walls? Man, I know it, and if there is need, that army I will destroy. Nay, stare not at me. Already they are as dead. Horsemen, you accompany me.

"Captains of the Tribes, you follow, and woe be to that man who hangs back in the hour of battle, for death and eternal shame shall be his portion, but wealth and honour to those who bear them bravely. Yes, I tell you, theirs shall be the fair land of Kaloon. You have your orders for the passing of yonder river. I, with the horsemen, take the central ford. Let the wings advance."

The chiefs answered with a cheer, for they were fierce men whose ancestors had loved war for generations. Moreover, mad as seemed the enterprise, they trusted in their Oracle, the Hesea, and, like all hill peoples, were easily fired by the promise of rich plunder.

An hour's steady march down the slopes brought the army to the edge of the marsh lands. These, as it chanced, proved no obstacle to our progress, for in that season of great drought they were quite dry, and for the same reason the shrunken river was not so impassable a defence as I feared that it would be. Still, because of its rocky bottom and steep, opposing banks, it looked formidable enough, while on the crests of those banks, in squadrons and companies of horse and foot, were gathered the regiments of Atene.

While the wings of footmen deployed to right and left, the cavalry halted in the marshes and let their horses fill themselves with the long grass, now a little browned by frost, that grew on this boggy soil, and afterwards drink some water.

All this time Ayesha stood silent, for she also had dismounted, that the mare she rode and her two led horses might graze with the others. Indeed, she spoke but once, saying –

"Thou thinkest this adventure mad, my Holly? Say, art afraid? "

"Not with thee for captain," I answered. "Still, that second army – "

"Shall melt before me like mist before the gale," she replied in a low and thrilling voice. "Holly, I tell thee thou shalt see things such as no man upon the earth has ever seen. Remember my words when I *loose the Powers* and thou followest the rent veil of Ayesha through the smitten squadrons of Kaloon. Only – what if Atene should dare to murder him? Oh, if she should dare!"

"Be comforted," I replied, wondering what she might mean by this loosing of the Powers. "I think that she loves him too well."

"I bless thee for the words, Holly, yet – I know he will refuse her, and then her hate for me and her jealous rage may overcome her love for him. Should this be so, what will avail my vengeance? Eat and drink again. Holly – nay, I touch no food until I sit in the palace of Kaloon – and look well to girth and bridle, for thou ridest far and on a wild errand. Mount thee on Leo's horse, which is swift and sure; if it dies, the guards will bring thee others."

I obeyed her as best I could, and once more bathed my head in a pool, and with the help of Oros tied a rag soaked in the liniment on the bruise, after which I felt sound enough. Indeed, the mad excitement of those minutes of waiting, and some foreshadowing of the terrible wonders that were about to befall, made me forget my hurts.

Now, Ayesha was standing staring upwards, so that although I could not see her veiled face, I guessed that her eyes must be fixed on the sky above the mountain top. I was certain, also, that she was concentrating her fearful will upon an unknown object, for her whole frame quivered like a reed shaken in the wind.

It was a very strange morning – cold and clear, yet curiously still, and with a heaviness in the air such as precedes a great fall of snow, although for much snow the season was yet too early. Once or twice, too, in that utter calm, I thought that I felt everything shudder; not the ordinary trembling of earthquake, however, for the shuddering seemed to be of the atmosphere quite as much as of the land. It was as though all Nature around us were a living creature which is very much afraid.

Following Ayesha's earnest gaze, I perceived that thick, smoky clouds were gathering one by one in the clear sky above the peak, and that they were edged, each of them, with a fiery rim. Watching these fantastic and ominous clouds, I ventured to say to her that it looked as though the weather would change – not a very original remark, but one which the circumstances suggested.

"Aye," she answered, "ere night the weather will be wilder even than my heart. No longer shall they cry for water in Kaloon! Mount, Holly, mount! The advance begins!" and unaided she sprang to the saddle of the mare that Oros brought her.

Then, in the midst of the five thousand horsemen, we moved down upon the ford. As we reached its brink I noted that the two divisions of tribesmen were already entering the stream half a mile to the right and left of us. Of what befell them I can tell nothing from observation, although I learned later that they forced it after great slaughter on both sides.

In front of us was gathered the main body of the Khania's army, massed by regiments upon the further bank, while hundreds of picked men stood up to their middles in the water, waiting to spear or hamstring our horses as we advanced.

Now, uttering their wild, whistling cry, our leading companies dashed into the river, leaving us upon the bank, and soon were engaged hotly with the footmen in midstream. While this fray went on, Oros came to Ayesha and told her a spy had reported that Leo, bound in a two-wheeled carriage and accompanied by Atene, Simbri and a guard, had passed through the enemy's camp at night, galloping furiously towards Kaloon.

"Spare thy words, I know it," she answered, and he fell back behind her.

Our squadrons gained the bank, having destroyed most of the men in the water, but as they set foot upon it the enemy charged them and drove them back with loss. Thrice they returned to the attack, and thrice were repulsed in this fashion. At length Ayesha grew impatient.

"They need a leader, and I will give them one," she said. "Come with me, my Holly," and followed by the main body of the horsemen, she rode a little way into the river, and there waited until the shattered troops had fallen back upon us. Oros whispered to me –

"It is madness, the Hesea will be slain."

"Thinkest thou so?" I answered. "More like that we shall be slain," a saying at which he smiled a little more than usual and shrugged his shoulders, since, for all his soft ways, Oros was a brave man. Also I believe that he spoke to try me, knowing that his mistress would take no harm.

Ayesha held up her hand, in which there was no weapon, and waved it forwards. A great cheer answered that signal to advance, and in the midst of it this frail, white-robed woman spoke to her horse, so that it plunged deep into the water.

Two minutes later, and spears and arrows were flying about us so thickly that they seemed to darken the sky. I saw men and horses fall to right and left, but nothing touched me or the white Robes that floated a yard or two ahead. Five minutes and we were gaining the further bank, and there the worst fight began.

It was fierce indeed, yet never an inch did the white robes give back, and where they went men would follow, them or fall. We were up the bank and the enemy was packed about us, but through them we passed slowly, like a boat through an adverse sea that buffets but cannot stay it. Yes, further and further, till at last the lines ahead grew thin as the living wedge of horsemen forced its path between them – grew thin, broke and vanished.

We had passed through the heart of the host, and leaving the tribesmen who followed to deal with its flying fragments, rode on half a mile or so and mustered. Many were dead and more were hurt, but the command was issued that all sore-wounded men should fall out and give their horses to replace those that had been killed.

This was done, and presently we moved on, three thousand of us now, not more, heading for Kaloon. The trot grew to a canter, and the canter to a gallop, as we rushed forward across that endless plain, till at midday, or a little after – for this route was far shorter than that taken by Leo and myself in our devious flight from Rassen and his death-hounds – we dimly saw the city of Kaloon set upon its hill.

Now a halt was ordered, for here was a reservoir in which was still some water, whereof the horses drank, while the men ate of the food they carried with them; dried meat and barley meal. Here, too, more spies met us, who said that the great army of Atene was posted guarding the city bridges, and that to attack it with our little force would mean destruction. But Ayesha took no heed of their words; indeed, she scarcely seemed to hear them. Only she ordered that all wearied horses should be abandoned and fresh ones mounted.

Forward again for hour after hour, in perfect silence save for the thunder of our horses' hoofs. No word spoke Ayesha, nor did her wild escort speak, only from time to time they looked over their shoulders and pointed with their red spears at the red sky behind.

I looked also, nor shall I forget its aspect. The dreadful, fire-edged clouds had grown and gathered so that beneath their shadows the plain lay almost black. They marched above us like an army in the heavens, while from time to time vaporous points shot forward, thin like swords, or massed like charging horse.

Under them a vast stillness reigned. It was as though the earth lay dead beneath their pall.

Kaloon, lit in a lurid light, grew nearer. The pickets of the foe flew homeward before us, shaking their javelins, and their mocking laughter reached us in hollow echoes. Now we saw the vast array, posted rank on rank with silken banners drooping in that stirless air, flanked and screened by glittering regiments of horse.

An embassy approached us, and at the signal of Ayesha's uplifted arm we halted. It was headed by a lord of the court whose face I knew. He pulled rein and spoke boldly.

"Listen, Hes, to the words of Atene. Ere now the stranger lord, thy darling, is prisoner in her palace. Advance, and we destroy thee and thy little band; but if by any miracle thou shouldest conquer, then he dies. Get thee gone to thy Mountain fastness and the Khania gives thee peace, and thy people their lives. What answer to the words of the Khania?"

Ayesha whispered to Oros, who called aloud –

"There is no answer. Go, if ye love life, for death draws near to you."

So they went, fast as their swift steeds would carry them, but for a little while Ayesha still sat lost in thought.

Presently she turned, and through her thin veil I saw that her face was white and terrible, and that the eyes in it glowed like those of a lioness at night. She said to me – hissing the words between her clenched teeth –

"Holly, prepare thyself to look into the mouth of hell. I desired to spare them if I could, I swear it, but my heart bids me be bold, to put off human pity, and use all my secret might if I would see Leo living. Holly, I tell thee they are about *to murder him!*"

Then she cried aloud, "Fear nothing, Captains. Ye are but few, yet with you goes the strength of ten thousand

thousand. Now follow the Hesea, and whatever ye meet, be not dismayed. Repeat it to the soldiers, that fearing nothing they follow the Hesea through yonder host and across the bridge and into the city of Kaloon."

So the chiefs rode hither and thither, crying out her words, and the savage tribesmen answered –

"Aye, we who followed through the water, will follow across the plain. Onward, Hes, for darkness swallow us."

Now some orders were given, and the companies fell into a formation that resembled a great wedge. Ayesha herself being its very point and apex, for though Oros and I rode on either side of her, spur as we would, our horses' heads never passed her saddle bow. In front of that dark mass she shone a single spot of white – one snowy feather on a black torrent's breast.

A screaming bugle note – and, like giant arms, from the shelter of some groves of poplar trees, curved horns of cavalry shot out to surround us, while the broad bosom of the opposing army, shimmering with spears, rolled forward as a wave rolls crowned with sunlit foam, and behind it, line upon line, uncountable, lay a surging sea of men.

Our end was near. We were lost, or so it seemed.

Ayesha tore off her veil and held it on high, flowing from her like a pennon, and lo! upon her brow blazed that wide and mystic diadem of light which once only I had seen before.

Denser and denser grew the rushing clouds above; brighter and brighter gleamed the unearthly star of light beneath. Louder and louder beat the sound of the falling hoofs of ten thousand horses. From the Mountain peak behind us went up sudden sheets of flame; it spouted fire as a whale spouts foam.

The scene was dreadful. In front, the towers of Kaloon lurid in a monstrous sunset. Above, a gloom as of an eclipse. Around the darkling, sunburnt plain. On it Atene's advancing army, and our rushing wedge of horsemen destined, it would appear, to inevitable doom.

Ayesha let fall her rein. She tossed her arms, saving the torn, white veil as though it were a signal cast to heaven.

Instantly from the churning jaws of the unholy night above belched a blaze of answering flame, that also wavered like a rent and shaken veil in the grasp of a black hand of cloud.

Then did Ayesha roll the thunder of her might upon the Children of Kaloon. Then she called, and the Terror came, such as men had never seen and perchance never more will see. Awful bursts of wind tore past us, lifting the very stones and soil before them, and with the wind went hail and level, hissing rain, made visible by the arrows of perpetual lightnings that leapt downwards from the sky and upwards from the earth.

It was as she had warned me. It was as though hell had broken loose upon the world, yet through that hell we rushed on unharmed. For always these furies passed before us. No arrow flew, no javelin was stained. The jagged hail was a herald of our coming; the levens that smote and stabbed were our sword and spear, while ever the hurricane roared and screamed with a million separate voices which blended to one yell of sound, hideous and indescribable.

As for the hosts about us they melted and were gone.

Now the darkness was dense, like to that of thickest night; yet in the fierce flares of the lightnings I saw them run this way and that, and amidst the volleying, elemental voices I heard their shouts of horror and of agony. I saw horses and riders roll confused upon the ground; like storm-drifted eaves I saw their footmen piled in high and whirling heaps, while the brands of heaven struck and struck them till they sank together and grew still.

I saw the groves of trees bend, shrivel up and vanish. I saw the high walls of Kaloon blown in and flee away, while the houses within the walls took fire, to go out beneath the torrents of the driving rain, and again take fire. I saw blackness sweep over us with great wings, and when I looked, lo! those wide wings were flame, floods of pulsing flame that flew upon the tormented air.

Blackness, utter blackness: turmoil, doom, dismay! Beneath me the labouring horse; at my side the steady crest of light which sat on Ayesha's brow, and through the tumult a clear, exultant voice that sang –

"I promised thee wild weather! Now, Holly, dost thou believe that I can loose the prisoned Powers of the world? "

Lo! all was past and gone, and above us shone the quiet evening sky, and before us lay the empty bridge, and beyond it the flaming city of Kaloon. But the armies of Atene, where were they? Go, ask of those great cairns that hide their bones. Go ask it of her widowed land.

Yet of our wild company of horsemen not one was lost. After us they galloped trembling, white-lipped, like men who face to face had fought and conquered Death, but triumphant – ah, triumphant!

On the high head of the bridge Ayesha wheeled her horse, and so for one proud moment stood to welcome them. At the sight of her glorious, star-crowned countenance, which now her Tribes beheld for the first time and the last, there went up such a shout as men have seldom heard.

"*The Goddess!*" that shout thundered. "Worship the Goddess!"

Then she turned her horse's head again, and they followed on through the long strait street of the burning city, up to the palace on its crest.

As the sun set we sped beneath its gateway. Silence in the courtyard, silence everywhere, save for the distant roar of fire and the scared howlings of the death-hounds in their kennel.

Ayesha sprang from her horse, and waving back all save Oros and myself, swept through the open doors into the halls beyond.

They were empty, every one – all were fled or dead. Yet she never paused or doubted, but so swiftly that we scarce could follow her, flitted up the wide stone stair that led to the topmost tower. Up, still up, until we reached the chamber where had dwelt Simbri the Shaman, that same chamber whence he was wont to watch his stars, in which Atene had threatened us with death.

Its door was shut and barred; still, at Ayesha's coming, yes, before the mere breath of her presence, the iron bolts snapped like twigs, the locks flew back, and inward burst that massive portal.

Now we were within the lamp-lit chamber, and this is what we saw. Seated in a chair, pale-faced, bound, yet proud and defiant-looking, was Leo. Over him, a dagger in his withered hand – yes, about to strike, in the very act – stood the old Shaman, and on the floor hard by, gazing upward with wide-set eyes, dead and still majestic in her death, lay Atene, Khania of Kaloon.

Ayesha waved her arm and the knife fell from Simbri's hand, clattering on the marble, while in an instant he who had held it was smitten to stillness and became like a man turned to stone.

She stooped, lifted the dagger, and with a swift stroke severed Leo's bonds; then, as though overcome at last, sank on to a bench in silence. Leo rose, looking about him bewildered, and said in the strained voice of one who is weak with much suffering –

"But just in time, Ayesha. Another second, and that murderous dog" – and he pointed to the Shaman – "well, it was in time. But how went the battle, and how earnest thou here through that awful hurricane? And, oh, Horace, thank heaven they did not kill you after all!"

"The battle went ill for some," Ayesha answered, "and I came not through the hurricane, but on its wings. Tell me now, what has befallen thee since we parted?"

"Trapped, overpowered, bound, brought here, told that I must write to thee and stop thy advance, or die – refused, of course, and then – " and he glanced at the dead body on the floor.

"And then?" repeated Ayesha.

"Then that fearful tempest, which seemed to drive me mad. Oh! if thou couldst have heard the wind howling round these battlements, tearing off their stones as though they were dry leaves; if thou hadst seen the lightnings falling thick and fast as rain – "

"They were my messengers. I sent them to save thee," said Ayesha simply.

Leo stared at her, making no comment, but after a pause, as though he were thinking the matter over, he went on –

"Atene said as much, but I did not believe her. I thought the end of the world had come, that was all. Well, she returned just now more mad even than I was, and told me that her people were destroyed and that she could not fight against the strength of hell, but that she could send me thither, and took a knife to kill me.

"I said, 'Kill on,' for I knew that wherever I went thou wouldst follow, and I was sick with the loss of blood from some hurt I had in that struggle, and weary of it all. So I shut my eyes waiting for the stroke, but instead I felt her lips pressed upon my forehead, and heard her say –

"Nay, I will not do it. Fare thee well; fulfil thou thine own destiny, as I fulfil mine. For this cast the dice have fallen against me; elsewhere it may be otherwise. I go to load them if I may.'

"I opened my eyes and looked. There Atene stood, a glass in her hand – see, it lies beside her.

" 'Defeated, yet I win,' she cried, 'for I do but pass before thee to prepare the path that thou shalt tread, and to make ready thy place in the Under-world. Till we meet again I pledge thee, for I am destroyed. Ayesha's horsemen are in my streets, and, clothed in lightnings, at their head, rides Ayesha's avenging self.'

"So she drank, and fell dead – but now. Look, her breast still quivers. Afterwards, that old man would have murdered me, for, being roped, I could not resist him, but the door burst in and thou camest. Spare him, he is of her blood, and he loved her."

Then Leo sank back into the chair where we had discovered him bound, and seemed to fall into a kind of torpor, for of a sudden he grew to look like an old man.

"Thou art sick," said Ayesha anxiously. "Oros, thy medicine, the draught I bade thee bring! Be swift, I say."

The priest bowed, and from some pocket in his ample robe produced a phial which he opened and gave to Leo, saying –

"Drink, my lord; this stuff will give thee back thy health, for it is strong."

"The stronger the better," answered Leo, rousing himself, and with something like his old, cheerful laugh. "I am thirsty who have touched nothing since last night, and have fought hard and been carried far, yes – and lived through that hellish storm."

Then he took the draught and emptied it.

There must have been virtue in that potion; at least, the change which it produced in him was wonderful. Within a minute his eyes grew bright again, and the colour returned into his cheeks.

"Thy medicines are very good, as I have learned of old," he said to Ayesha; "but the best of all of them is to see thee safe and victorious before me, and to know that I, who looked for death, yet live to greet thee, my beloved. There is food," and he pointed to a board upon which were meats, "say, may I eat of them, for I starve?"

"Aye," she answered softly, "eat, and, my Holly, eat thou also."

So we fell to, yes, we fell to and ate even in the presence of that dead woman who looked so royal in her death; of the old magician who stood there powerless, like a man petrified, and of Ayesha, the wondrous being that could destroy an army with the fearful weapons which were servant to her will.

Only Oros ate nothing, but remained where he was, smiling at us benignantly, nor did Ayesha touch any food.

CHAPTER 23

THE YIELDING OF AYESHA

WHEN I had satisfied myself, Leo was still at his meal, for loss of blood or the effects of the tremendous nerve tonic which Ayesha ordered to be administered to him, had made him ravenous.

I watched his face and became aware of a curious change in it, no immediate change indeed, but one, I think, that had come upon him gradually, although I only fully appreciated it now, after our short separation. In addition to the thinness of which I have spoken, his handsome countenance had grown more ethereal; his eyes were full of the shadows of things that were to come.

His aspect pained me, I knew not why, it was no longer that whom I was familiar, the deep-chested, mighty-limbed, jovial, upright traveller, hunter and fighting-man who had chanced to love and be loved of a spiritual power incarnated in a mould of perfect womanhood and armed with all the might of Nature's self. These things were still present indeed, but the man was changed, and I felt sure that this change came from Ayesha, since the look upon his face had become exceeding like to that which often hovered upon hers at rest.

She also was watching him, with speculative, dreamy eyes, till presently, as some thought swept through her, I saw those eyes blaze up, and the red blood pour to cheek and brow. Yes, the mighty Ayesha who was dead, slain for him, lay strewn by the thousand on yonder plain, blushed and trembled like a maiden at her first lover's kiss.

Leo rose from the table. "I would that I had been with thee in the fray," he said.

"At the drift there was fighting," she answered, "afterwards none. My ministers of Fire, Earth and Air smote, no more; I waked them from their sleep and at my command they smote for thee and saved thee."

"Many lives to take for one man's safety," Leo said solemnly, as though the thought pained him.

"Had they been millions and not thousands, I would have spent them every one. On my head be their deaths, not on thine. Or rather on hers," and she pointed to the dead Atene. "Yes, on hers who made this war. At least she should thank me who have sent so royal a host to guard her through the darkness."

"Yet it is terrible," said Leo, "to think of thee, beloved, red to the hair with slaughter."

"What reck I?" she answered with a splendid pride. "Let their blood suffice to wash the stain of thy blood from on these cruel hands that once did murder thee."

"Who am I that I should blame thee?" Leo went on as though arguing with himself, "I who but yesterday killed two men – to save myself from treachery."

"Speak not of it," she exclaimed in cold rage. "I saw the place and, Holly, thou knowest how I swore that a hundred lives should pay for every drop of that dear blood of thine, and I, who lie not, have kept the oath. Look now on that man who stands yonder struck by my will to stone, dead yet living, and say again what was he about to do to thee when I entered here?"

"To take vengeance on me for the doom of his queen and of her armies," answered Leo, "and, Ayesha, how knowest thou that a Power higher than thine own will not demand it yet?"

As he spoke a pale shadow flickered on Leo's face, such a shadow as might fall from Death's advancing wing, and in the fixed eyes of the Shaman there shone a stony smile.

For a moment terror seemed to take Ayesha, then it was gone as quickly as it came.

"Nay," she said. "I ordain that it shall not be, and save One who listeth not, what power reigns in this wide earth that dare defy my will?"

So she spoke, and as her words of awful pride – for they were very awful – rang round that stone – built chamber, a vision came to me – Holly.

I saw illimitable space peopled with shining suns, and sunk in the infinite void above them one vast Countenance clad in a calm so terrific that at its aspect my spirit sank to nothingness. Yes, and I knew that this was Destiny enthroned above the spheres. Those lips moved and obedient worlds rushed upon their course. They moved again and these rolling chariots of the heavens were turned or stayed, appeared or disappeared. I knew also that against this calm Majesty the being, woman or spirit, at my side had dared to hurl her passion and her strength. My soul reeled. I was afraid.

The dread phantasm passed, and when my mind cleared again Ayesha was speaking in new, triumphant tones.

"Nay, nay," she cried. "Past is the night of dread; dawns the day of victory! Look!" and she pointed through the window-places shattered by the hurricane, to the flaming town beneath, whence rose one continual wail of misery, the wail of women mourning their countless slain while the fire reared through their homes like some unchained and rejoicing demon. "Look, Leo, on the smoke of the first sacrifice that I offer to thy royal state and listen to its music. Perchance thou deemst it naught. Why then I'll give thee others. Thou lovest war. Good! we will go down to war and the rebellious cities of the earth shall be the torches of our march."

She paused a moment, her delicate nostrils quivering, and her face alight with the prescience of ungarnered splendours; then like a swooping swallow flitted to where, by dead Atene, the gold circlet fallen from the Khania's hair lay upon the floor.

She stooped, lifted it, and coming to Leo held it high above his head. Slowly she let her hand fall until the glittering coronet rested for an instant on his brow. Then she spoke, in her glorious voice that rolled out rich and low, a very pæan of triumph and of power.

"By this poor, earthly symbol I create thee King of Earth; yea in its round for thee is gathered all her rule. Be thou its king, and mine!"

Again the coronet was held aloft, again it sank, and again she said or rather chanted –

"With this unbroken ring, token of eternity, I swear to thee the boon of endless days. Endure thou while the world endures, and be its lord, and mine."

A third time the coronet touched his brow.

"By this golden round I do endow thee with Wisdom's perfect gold uncountable, that is the talisman whereat all nature's secret paths shall open to thy feet. Victorious, victorious, tread thou her wondrous ways with me, till from her topmost peak at last she wafts us to our immortal throne whereof the columns twain are Life and Death."

Then Ayesha cast away the crown and lo! it fell upon the breast of the lost Atene and rested there.

"Art content with these gifts of mine, my lord?" she cried.

Leo looked at her sadly and shook his head.

"What more wilt thou then? Ask and I swear it shall be thine."

"Thou swearest; but wilt thou keep the oath?"

"Aye, by myself I swear; by myself and by me Strength that bred me. If it be ought that I can grant – then if I refuse it to thee, may such destruction fall upon me as will satisfy even Atene's watching soul."

I heard and I think that another heard also, at least once more the stony smile shone in the eyes of the Shaman.

"I ask of thee nothing that thou canst not give. Ayesha, I ask of thee thyself – not at some distant time when I have been bathed in a mysterious fire, but now, now this night."

She shrank back from him a little, as though dismayed.

"Surely," she said slowly, "I am like that foolish philosopher who, walking abroad to read the destinies of nations in the stars, fell down a pitfall dug by idle children and broke his bones and perished there. Never did I guess that with all these glories stretched before thee like mountain top on glittering mountain top, making a stairway for thy mortal feet to the very dome of heaven, thou wouldst still clutch at thy native earth and seek of it – but the common boon of woman's love.

"Oh! Leo, I thought that thy soul was set upon nobler aims, that thou wouldst pray me for wider powers, for a more vast dominion; that as though they were but yonder fallen door of wood and iron, I should break for thee the bars of Hades, and like the Eurydice of old fable draw thee living down the steeps of Death, or throne thee midst the fires of the furthest sun to watch its subject worlds at play.

"Or I thought that thou wouldst bid me reveal what no woman ever told, the bitter, naked truth – all my sins and sorrows, all the wandering fancies of my fickle thought; even what thou knowest not and perchance ne'er shalt know, *who I am and whence I came,* and how to thy charmed eyes I seemed to change from foul to fair, and what is the purpose of my love for thee, and what the meaning of that tale of an angry goddess – who never was except in dreams.

"I thought – nay, no matter what I thought, save that thou wert for other than thou art, my Leo, and in so high a moment that thou wouldst seek to pass the mystic gates my glory can throw wide and with me tread an air supernal to the hidden heart of things. Yet thy prayer is but the same that the whole world whispers beneath the silent moon, in the palace and the cottage, among the snows and on the burning desert's waste. 'Oh! my love, thy lips, thy lips. Oh! my love, be mine, now, now, beneath the moon, beneath the moon!'

"Leo, I thought better, higher, of thee."

"Mayhap, Ayesha, thou wouldest have thought worse of me had I been content with thy suns and constellations and spiritual gifts and dominations that I neither desire nor understand.

"If I had said to thee: Be thou my angel, not my wife; divide the ocean that I may walk its bed; pierce the firmament and show me how grow the stars; tell me the origins of being and of death and instruct me in their issues; give up the races of mankind to my sword, and the wealth of all the earth to fill my treasuries. Teach me also how to drive the hurricane as thou canst do, and to bend the laws of nature to my purpose: on earth make me half a god – as thou art.

"But, Ayesha, I am no god; I am a man, and as a man I seek the woman whom I love. Oh! divest thyself of all these wrappings of thy power – that power which strews thy path with dead and keeps me apart from thee. If only for one short night, forget the ambition that gnaws unceasingly at thy soul; I say forget thy greatness and be a woman and – my wife."

She made no answer, only looked at him and shook her head, causing her glorious hair to ripple like water beneath a gentle breeze.

"Thou deniest me," he went on with gathering strength, "and that thou canst not do, that thou mayest not do, for Ayesha, thou hast sworn, and I demand the fulfilment of thine oath.

"Hark thou. I refuse thy gifts; I will have none of thy rule who ask no Pharaoh's throne and wish to do good to men and not to kill them – that the world may profit. I will not go with thee to Kôr, nor be bathed in the breath of Life. I will leave thee and cross the mountains, or perish on them, nor with all thy strength canst thou bold me to thy side, who indeed needest me not. No longer will I endure this daily torment, the torment of thy presence and thy sweet words; thy loving looks, thy promises for next year, next year – next year. So keep thine oath or let me begone."

Still Ayesha stood silent, only now her head drooped and her breast began to heave. Then Leo stepped forward; he seized her in his arms and kissed her. She broke from his embrace, I know not how, for though unreturned it was close enough, and again stood before him but at a little distance.

"Did I not warn Holly," she whispered with a sigh, "to bid thee beware lest I should catch thy human fire? Man, I say to thee, it begins to smoulder in my heart, and should it grow to flame – "

"Why then," he answered laughing, "we will be happy for a little while."

"Aye, Leo, bat how long? Why, wert thou sole lord of this loveliness of mine and not set above their harming, night and day a hundred jealous daggers would seek thy heart and – find it."

"How long, Ayesha? A lifetime, a year, a month, a minute – I neither know nor care, and while thou art true to me I fear no stabs of envy."

"Is it so? Wilt take the risk? I can promise thee nothing. Thou mightest – yes, in this way or in that thou mightest – die."

"And if I die, what then? Shall we be separated?"

"Nay, nay, Leo, that is not possible. We never can be severed, of this I am sure; it is sworn to me. But then through other lives and other spheres, higher lives and higher spheres mayhap, our fates must force a painful path to their last goal of union."

"Why then I take the hazard, Ayesha. Shall the life that I can risk to slay a leopard or a lion in the sport of an idle hour, be too great a price to offer for the splendours of thy breast? Thine oath! Ayesha, I claim thine oath."

Then it was that in Ayesha there began the most mysterious and thrilling of her many changes. Yet how to describe it I know not, unless it be by simile.

Once in Thibet we were imprisoned for months by snows that stretched down from the mountain slopes into the valleys and oh! how weary did we grow of those arid, aching fields of purest white. At length rain set in, and blinding mists in which it was not safe to wander, that made the dark nights darker yet.

So it was, until there came a morning when, seeing the sun shine, we went to our door and looked out. Behold a miracle! Gone were the snows that choked the valley, and in the place of them appeared vivid springing grass, starred everywhere with flowers, and murmuring brooks and birds that sang and nested in the willows. Gone was the frowning sky, and all the blue firmament seemed one tender smile, Gone were, the austerities of winter with his harsh winds, and in their place spring, companioned by her zephyrs, glided down the vale singing her song of love and life.

There in this high chamber, in the presence of the living and the dead, while the last act of the great tragedy unrolled itself before me, looking on Ayesha, that forgotten scene sprang into my mind. For on her face just such a change had come. Hitherto, with all her loveliness, the heart of Ayesha had seemed like that winter mountain wrapped in its unapproachable snow and before her pure brow and icy self-command, aspirations sank abashed and desires died.

She swore she loved and her love fulfilled itself in death and many a mysterious way. Yet it was hard to believe that this passion of hers was more than a spoken part, for how can the star seek the moth although the moth may seek the star? Though the man may worship the goddess, for all her smiles divine, how can the goddess love the man?

But now everything was altered! Look! Ayesha grew human; I could see her heart beat beneath her robes and hear her breath come in soft, sweet sobs, while o'er her upturned face and in her alluring eyes there spread itself that look which is born of love alone. Radiant and more radiant did she seem to grow, sweeter and more sweet, no longer the veiled Hermit of the Caves, no longer the Oracle of the Sanctuary, no longer the Valkyrie of the battle-plain, but only the loveliest and most happy bride that ever gladdened a husband's eyes.

She spoke, and it was of little things, for thus Ayesha proclaimed the conquest of herself.

"Fie!" she said, showing her white robes torn with spears and stained by the dust and dew of war; "Fie, my lord, what marriage garments are these in which at last I come to thee, who would have been adorned in regal gems and raiment befitting to my state and thine?"

"I seek the woman, not her garment," said Leo, his burning eyes fixed upon her face.

"Thou seekest the woman. Ah! there it lies. Tell me, Leo, am I woman or spirit? Say that I am woman, for now the prophecy of this dead Atene lies heavy on my soul, Atene who said that mortal and immortal may not mate."

"Thou must be woman, or thou wouldst not have tormented me as thou hast done these many weeks."

"I thank thee for the comfort of thy words. Yet, was it *woman* whose breath wrought destruction upon yonder plain? Was it to a *woman* that Blast and Lightning bowed and said, 'We are here: Command us, we obey'? Did that dead thing (and she pointed to the shattered door) break inward at a *woman*'s will? Or could a *woman* charm this man to stone?

"Oh! Leo, would that I were woman! I tell thee that I'd lay all my grandeur down, a wedding offering at thy feet, could I be sure that for one short year I should be naught but *woman* and – thy happy wife.

"Thou sayest that I did torment thee, but it is I who have known torment, I who desired to yield and dared not. Aye, I tell thee, Leo, were I not sure that thy little stream of life is draining dry into the great ocean of my life, drawn thither as the sea draws its rivers, or as the sun draws mists, e'en now I would not yield. But I know, for my wisdom tells it me, ere ever we could reach the shores of Libya, the ill work would be done, and thou dead of thine own longing, thou dead and I widowed who never was a wife.

"Therefore see! like lost Atene I take the dice and cast them, not knowing how they shall fall. Not knowing how they shall fall, for good or ill I cast," and she made a wild motion as of some desperate gamester throwing his last throw.

"So," Ayesha went on, "the thing is done and the number summed for aye, though it be hidden from my sight. I have made an end of doubts and fears, and come death, come life, I'll meet it bravely.

"Say, how shall we be wed? I have it. Holly here must join our hands; who else? He that ever was our guide shall give me unto thee, and thee to me. This burning city is our altar, the dead and living are our witnesses on earth and heaven. In place of rites and ceremonials for this first time I lay my lips on thine, and when 'tis done, for music I'll sing thee a nuptial chant of love such as mortal poet has not written nor have mortal lovers heard.

"Come, Holly, do now thy part and give this maiden to this man."

Like one in a dream I obeyed her and took Ayesha's outstretched hand and Leo's. As I held them thus, I tell the truth – it was as though some fire rushed through my veins from her to him, shaking and shattering me with swift waves of burning and unearthly bliss. With the fire too came glorious visions and sounds of mighty music, and a sense as though my brain, filled with over-flowing life, must burst asunder beneath its weight.

I joined their hands; I know not how; I blessed them, I know not in what words. Then I reeled back against the wall and watched.

This is what I saw.

With an abandonment and a passion so splendid and intense that it seemed more than human, with a murmured cry of "Husband!" Ayesha cast her arms about her lover's neck and drawing down his head to hers so that the gold hair was mingled with her raven locks, she kissed him on the lips.

Thus they clung a little while, and as they clung the gentle diadem of light from her brow spread to his brow also, and through the white wrappings of her robe became visible her perfect shape shining with faint fire. With a little happy laugh she left him, saying:

"Thus, Leo Vincey, oh! thus for the second time do I give myself to thee, and with this flesh and spirit all I swore to thee, there in the dim Caves of Kôr and here in the palace of Kaloon. Know thou this, come what may, never, never more shall we be separate who are ordained one. Whilst thou livest I live at thy side, and when thou diest, if die thou must, I'll follow thee through worlds and firmaments, nor shall all the doors of heaven or hell avail against my love. Where thou goest, thither I will go. When thou sleepest, with thee will I sleep and it is my voice that thou shalt hear murmuring through the dreams of life and death; my voice that shall summon thee to awaken in the last hour of everlasting dawn, when all this night of misery hath furled her wings for aye.

"Listen now while I sing to thee and hear that song aright, for in its melody at length thou shalt learn the truth, which unwed I might not tell to thee. Thou shalt learn who and what *I* am, and who and what *thou* art, and of the high purposes of our love, and this dead woman's hate, and of all that I have hid from thee in veiled, bewildering words and visions.

"Listen then, my love and lord, to the burden of the Song of Fate."

She ceased speaking and gazed heavenwards with a rapt look as though she waited for some inspiration to fall upon her, and never, never – not even in the fires of Kôr had Ayesha seemed so divine as she did now in this moment of the ripe harvest of her love.

My eyes wandered from her to Leo, who stood before her pale and still, still as the death-like figure of the Shaman, still as the Khania's icy shape which stared upwards from the ground. What was passing in his mind, I wondered, that he could remain thus insensible while in all her might and awful beauty this proud being worshipped him.

Hark! she began to sing in a voice so rich and perfect that its honeyed notes seemed to cloy my blood and stop my breath.

The world was not, was not, and in the womb of
 Silence
 Slept the souls of men.
 Yet I was and thou –

Suddenly Ayesha stopped, and I felt rather than saw the horror on her face.

Look! Leo swayed to and fro as though the stones beneath him were but a rocking boat. To and fro he swayed, stretched out his blind arms to clasp her – then suddenly fell backwards, and lay still.

Oh! what a shriek was that she gave! Surely it must have wakened the very corpses upon the plain. Surely it must have echoed in the stars. One shriek only – then throbbing silence.

I sprang to him, and there, withered in Ayesha's kiss, slain by the fire of her love, Leo lay dead – lay dead upon the breast of dead Atene!

CHAPTER 24

THE PASSING OF AYESHA

I HEARD Ayesha say presently, and the words struck me as dreadful in their hopeless acceptance of a doom against which even she had no strength to struggle.

"It seems that my lord has left me for a while; I must hasten to my lord afar."

After that I do not quite know what happened. I had lost the man who was all in all to me, friend and child in one, and I was crushed as I had never been before. It seemed so sad that I, old and outworn, should still live on whilst he in the flower of his age, snatched from joy and greatness such as no man hath known, lay thus asleep.

I think that by an afterthought Ayesha and Oros tried to restore him, tried without result, for here her powers were of no avail. Indeed my conviction is that although some lingering life still kept him on his feet, Leo had really died at the moment of her embrace, since when I looked at him before he fell, his face was that of a dead man.

Yes, I believe that last speech of hers, although she knew it not, was addressed to his spirit, for in her burning kiss his flesh had perished.

When at length I recovered myself a little, it was to hear Ayesha in a cold, calm voice – her face I could not see, for she had veiled herself – commanding certain priests who had been summoned to "bear away the body of that accursed woman and bury her as befits her rank." Even then I bethought me, I remember, of the tale of Jehu and Jezebel.

Leo, looking strangely calm and happy, lay now upon a couch, the arms folded on his breast. When the priests had tramped away carrying their royal burden, Ayesha, who sat by his body brooding, seemed to awake, for she rose and said –

"I need a messenger, and for no common journey, since he must search out the habitations of the Shades," and she turned herself towards Oros and appeared to look at him.

Now, for the first time, I saw that priest change countenance a little, for the eternal smile, of which even this scene had not quite rid it, left his face and he grew pale and trembled.

"Thou art afraid," she said contemptuously. "Be at rest, Oros, I will not send one who is afraid. Holly, wilt thou go for me – and him?"

"Aye," I answered. "I am weary of life and desire no other end. Only let it be swift and painless."

She mused a while, then said –

"Nay, thy time is not yet, thou still hast work to do. Endure, my Holly, 'tis only for a breath."

Then she looked at the Shaman, the man turned to stone, who all this while had stood there as a statue stands, and cried –

"Awake!"

Instantly he seemed to thaw into life, his limbs relaxed, his breast heaved, he was as he had always been: ancient, gnarled, malevolent.

"I hear thee, mistress," he said, bowing as a man bows to the power that he hates.

"Thou seest, Simbri," and she waved her hand.

"I see. Things have befallen as Atene and I foretold, have they not? 'Ere long the corpse of a new-crowned Khan of Kaloon,' " and he pointed to the gold circlet that Ayesha had set on Leo's brow, " 'will lie upon the brink of the Pit of Flame' – as I foretold." An evil smile crept into his eyes and he went on –

"Hadst thou not smote me dumb, I who watched could have warned thee that they would so befall; but, great mistress, it pleased thee to smite me dumb. And so it seems, O Hes, that thou hast overshot thyself and liest broken at the foot of that pinnacle which step by step thou hast climbed for more than two thousand weary years. See what thou hast bought at the price of countless lives that now before the throne of Judgment bring accusations against thy powers misused, and cry out for justice on thy head," and he looked at the dead form of Leo.

"I sorrow for them; yet, Simbri, they were well spent," Ayesha answered reflectively, "who by their fore-written doom, as it was decreed, held thy knife from falling and thus won me my husband. Aye and I am happy – happier than such blind bats as thou can see or guess. For know that now with him I have re-wed my wandering soul divorced by sin from me, and that of our marriage kiss which burned his life away there shall still be born to us children of Forgiveness and eternal Grace and all things that are pure and fair.

"Look thou, Simbri, I will honour thee. Thou shalt be my messenger, and beware! beware I say how thou dost fulfil thine office, since of every syllable thou must render an account.

"Go thou down the dark paths of Death, and, since even my thought may not reach to where he sleeps to-night, search out my lord and say to him that the feet of his spouse Ayesha are following fast. Bid him have no fear for me who by this last sorrow have atoned my crimes and am in his embrace regenerate. Tell him that thus it was appointed, and thus is best, since now he is dipped, indeed, in the eternal Flame of Life; now for him the mortal night is done and the everlasting day arises. Command him that he await me in the Gate of Death, where it is granted that I greet him presently. Thou nearest?"

"I hear, O Queen, Mighty-from-of-Old."

"One message more. Say to Atene that I forgive her. Her heart was high and greatly did she play her part. There in the Gates we will balance our account. Thou hearest?"

"I hear, O Eternal Star that hath conquered Night."

"Then, man, *begone*!"

As the word left Ayesha's lips Simbri leapt from the floor, grasping at the air as though he would clutch his own departing soul, staggered back against the board where Leo and I had eaten, overthrowing it, and amid a ruin of gold and silver vessels, fell down and died.

She looked at him, then said to me –

"See, though he ever hated me, this magician who has known Ayesha from the first, did homage to my ancient majesty at last, when lies and defiance would serve his end no more. No longer now do I hear the name that his dead mistress gave to me. The 'Star-that-hath-fallen' in his lips and in very truth is become the 'Star-which-hath-burst-the bonds-of-Night,' and, re-arisen, shines for ever – shines with its twin immortal to set no more – my Holly. Well, he is gone, and ere now, those that serve me in the Under-world – dost remember? – thou sawest their captains in the Sanctuary – bend the head at great Ayesha's word and make her place ready near her spouse.

"But oh! what folly has been mine. When even here my wrath can show such power, how could I hope that my lord would outlive the fires of my love? Still it was better so, for he sought not the pomp I would have given him, nor desired the death of men. Yet such pomp must have been his portion in this poor shadow of a world, and the steps that encircle an usurper's throne are ever slippery with blood.

"Thou art weary, my Holly, go rest thee. Tomorrow night we journey to the Mountain, there to celebrate these obsequies."

I crept into the room adjoining – it had been Simbri's, and laid me down upon his bed, but to sleep I was not able. Its door was open, and in the light of the burning city that shone through the casements I could see Ayesha watching by her dead. Hour after hour she watched, her head resting on her hand, silent, stirless. She wept not, no sigh escaped her; only watched as a tender woman watches a-slumbering babe that she knows will awake at dawn.

Her face was unveiled and I perceived that it had greatly changed. All pride and anger were departed from it; it was grown soft, wistful, yet full of confidence and quietness. For a while I could not think of what it reminded me, till suddenly I remembered. Now it was like, indeed the counterpart almost, of the holy and majestic semblance of the statue of the Mother in the Sanctuary. Yes, with just such a look of love and power as that mother cast upon her frightened child new-risen from its dream of death, did Ayesha gaze upon her dead, while her parted lips also seemed to whisper "some tale of hope, sure and immortal."

At length she rose and came into my chamber.

"Thou thinkest me fallen and dost grieve for me, my Holly," she said in a gentle voice, "knowing my fears lest some such fate should overtake my lord."

"Ay, Ayesha, I grieve for thee as for myself."

"Spare then thy pity, Holly, since although the human part of me would have kept him on the earth, now my spirit doth rejoice that for a while he has burst his mortal bonds. For many an age, although I knew it not, in my proud defiance of the Universal Law, I have fought against his true weal and mine. Thrice have I and the angel wrestled, matching strength with strength, and thrice has he conquered me. Yet as he bore away his prize this night he whispered wisdom in my ear. This was his message: That in death is love's home, in death its strength; that from the charnel-house of life this love springs again glorified and pure, to reign a conqueror for ever. Therefore I wipe away my tears and, crowned once more a queen of peace, I go to join him whom we have lost, there where be awaits us, as it is granted to me that I shall do.

"But I am selfish, and forgot. Thou needest rest. Sleep, friend, I bid thee sleep."

And I slept, wondering as my eyes closed whence Ayesha drew this strange confidence and comfort. I know not, but it was there, real and not assumed. I can only suppose, therefore, that some illumination had fallen on her soul, and that, as she stated, the love and end of Leo, in a way unknown, did suffice to satisfy her count of sins.

At the least those sins and all the load of death that lay at her door never seemed to trouble her at all. She appeared to look upon them merely as events which were destined to occur; as inevitable fruits of a seed sowed long ago by the hand of Fate, for whose workings she was not responsible. The fears and considerations which weigh with mortals did not affect or oppress her. In this, as in other matters. Ayesha was a law unto herself.

When I awoke it was day, and through the window-place I saw the rain that the people of Kaloon had so long desired falling in one straight sheet. I saw also that Ayesha, seated by the shrouded form of Leo, was giving orders to her priests and captains and to some nobles, who had survived the slaughter of Kaloon, as to the new government of the land. Then I slept again.

It was evening, and Ayesha stood at my bedside.

"All is prepared," she said. "Awake and ride with me."

So we went, escorted by a thousand cavalry, for the rest stayed to occupy, or perchance to plunder, the land of Kaloon. In front the body of Leo was borne by relays of priests, and behind it rode the veiled Ayesha, I at her side.

Strange was the contrast between this departure, and our arrival.

Then the rushing squadrons, the elements that raved, the perpetual sheen of lightnings seen through the swinging curtains of the hail; the voices of despair from an army rolled in blood beneath the chariot wheels of thunder.

Now the white-draped corpse, the slow-pacing horses, the riders with their spears reversed, and on either side, seen in that melancholy moonlight, the women of Kaloon burying their innumerable dead.

And Ayesha herself, yesterday a Valkyrie crested with the star of flame, to-day but a bereaved woman humbly following her husband to the tomb.

Yet how they feared her! Some widow standing on the grave mould she had dug, pointed as we passed to the body of Leo, uttering bitter words which I could not catch. Thereon her companions flung themselves upon her and felling her with fist and spade, prostrated themselves upon the ground, throwing dust on their hair in token of their submission to the priestess of Death.

Ayesha saw them, and said to me with something of her ancient fire and pride –

"I tread the plain of Kaloon no more, yet as a parting gift have I read this high-stomached people a lesson that they needed long. Not for many a generation, O Holly, will they dare to lift spear against the College of Hes and its subject Tribes."

Again it was night, and where once lay that of the Khan, the man whom he had killed, flanked by the burning pillars, the bier of Leo stood in the inmost Sanctuary before the statue of the Mother whose gentle, unchanging eyes seemed to search his quiet face.

On her throne sat the veiled Hesea, giving commands to her priests and priestesses.

"I am weary," she said, "and it may be that I leave you for a while to rest – beyond the mountains. A year, or a thousand years – I cannot say. If so, let Papave, with Oros as her counsellor and husband and their seed hold my place till I return again.

"Priests and priestesses of the College of Hes, over new territories have I held my hand; take them as an heritage from me, and rule them well and gently. Henceforth let the Hesea of the Mountain be also the Khania of Kaloon.

"Priests and priestesses of our ancient faith, learn to look through its rites and tokens, outward and visible, to the informing Spirit. If Hes the goddess never ruled on earth, still pitying Nature rules. If the name of Isis never rang through the courts of heaven, still in heaven, with all love fulfilled, nursing her human children on her breast, dwells the mighty Motherhood whereof this statue is the symbol, that Motherhood which bore us, and, unforgetting, faithful, will receive us at the end.

"For of the bread of bitterness we shall not always eat, of the water of tears we shall not always drink. Beyond the night the royal suns ride on; ever the rainbow shines around the rain. Though they slip from our clutching hands like melted snow, the lives we lose shall yet be found immortal, and from the burnt-out fires of our human hopes will spring a heavenly star."

She paused and waved her hand as though to dismiss them, then added by an after-thought, pointing to myself –

"This man is my beloved friend and guest. Let him be yours also. It is my will that you tend and guard him here, and when the snows have melted and summer is at hand, that you fashion a way for him through the gulf and bring him across the mountains by which he came, till you leave him in safety. Hear and forget not, for be sure that to me you shall give account of him."

The night drew towards the dawn, and we stood upon the peak above the gulf of fire, four of us only – Ayesha and I, and Oros and Papave. For the bearers had laid down the body of Leo upon its edge and gone their way. The curtain of flame flared in front of us, its crest bent over like a billow in the gale, and to leeward, one by one, floated the torn-off clouds and pinnacles of fire. By the dead Leo knelt Ayesha, gazing at that icy, smiling face, but speaking no single word. At length she rose, and said –

"Darkness draws near, my Holly, that deep darkness which foreruns the glory of the dawn. Now fare thee well for one little hour. When thou art about to die, but not before, call me, and I will come to thee. Stir not and speak not till all be done, lest when I am no longer here to be thy guard some Presence should pass on and slay thee.

"Think not that I am conquered, for now my name is Victory! Think not that Ayesha's strength is spent or her tale is done, for of it thou readest but a single page. Think not even that I am to-day that thing of sin and pride, the Ayesha thou didst adore and fear, I who in my lord's love and sacrifice have again conceived my soul. For know that now once more as at the beginning, his soul and mine are *one.*"

She thought awhile and added:

"Friend take this sceptre in memory of me, but beware how thou usest it save at the last to summon me, for it has virtues," and she gave me the jewelled Sistrum that she bore – then said:

"So kiss his brow, stand back, and be still."

Now, as once before, the darkness gathered on the pit, and presently, although I heard no prayer, though now no mighty music broke upon the silence, through that darkness, beating up the gale, came the two-winged flame and hovered where Ayesha stood.

It appeared, it vanished, and one by one the long minutes crept away until the first spear of dawn lit upon the point of rock.

Lo! it was empty, utterly empty and lonesome. Gone was the corse of Leo and gone too was Ayesha the imperial, the divine.

Whither had she gone? I know not. But this I know, that as the light returned and the broad sheet of flame flared out to meet it, I seemed to see two glorious shapes sweeping, upward on its bosom, and the faces that they wore were those of Leo and of Ayesha.

Often and often during the weary months that followed, whilst I wandered through the temple or amid the winter snows upon the Mountain side, did I seek to solve this question – Whither had She gone? I asked it of my heart; I asked it of the skies; I asked it of the spirit of Leo which often was so near to me.

But no sure answer ever came, nor will I hazard one. As mystery wrapped Ayesha's origin and lives – for the truth of these things I never learned – so did mystery wrap her deaths, or rather her departings, for I cannot think her dead. Surely she still is, if not on earth, then in some other sphere?

So I believe; and when my own hour comes, and it draws near swiftly, I shall know whether I believe in vain, or whether she will appear to be my guide as, with her last words, she swore that she would do. Then, too, I shall learn what she was about to reveal to Leo when he died, the purposes of their being and of their love.

So I can wait in patience who must not wait for long, though my heart is broken and I am desolate.

Oros and all the priests were very good to me. Indeed, even had it been their wish, they would have feared to be otherwise, who remembered and were sure that in some time to come they must render an account of this matter to their dread queen. By way of return, I helped them as I was best able to draw up a scheme for the government of the conquered country of Kaloon, and with my advice upon many other questions.

And so at length the long months wore away, till at the approach of summer the snows melted. Then I said that I must be gone. They gave me of their treasures in precious stones, lest I should need money for my faring, since the gold of which I had such plenty was too heavy to be carried by one man alone. They led me across the plains of Kaloon, where now the husbandmen, those that were left of them, ploughed the land and scattered seed, and so on to its city. But amidst those blackened ruins over which Atene's palace still frowned unharmed, I would not enter, for to me it was, and always must remain, a home of death. So I camped outside the walls by the river just where Leo and I had landed after that poor mad Khan set us free, or rather loosed us to be hunted by his death-hounds.

Next day we took boat and rowed up the river, past the place where we had seen Atene's cousin murdered, till we came to the Gate-house. Here once again I slept, or rather did not sleep.

On the following morning I went down into the ravine and found to my surprise that the rapid torrent – shallow enough now – had been roughly bridged, and that in preparation for my coming rude but sufficient ladders were built on the lace of the opposing precipice. At the foot of these I bade farewell to Oros, who at our parting smiled benignantly as on the day we met.

"We have seen strange things together," I said to him, not knowing what else to say.

"Very strange," he answered.

"At least, friend Oros," I went on awkwardly enough, "events have shaped themselves to your advantage, for you inherit a royal mantle."

"I wrap myself in a mantle of borrowed royalty," he answered with precision, "of which doubtless one day I shall be stripped."

"You mean that the great Hesea is not dead?"

"I mean that Hes never dies. She changes, that is all. As the wind blows now hence, now hither, so she comes and goes, and who can tell at what spot upon the earth, or beyond it, for a while that wind lies sleeping? But at sunset or at dawn, at noon or at midnight, it will begin to blow again, and then woe to those who stand across its path.

'Remember the dead heaped upon the plains of Kaloon. Remember the departing of the Shaman Simbri with his message and the words that she spoke then. Remember the passing of the Hesea from the Mountain point. Stranger from the West, surely as to-morrow's sun must rise, as she went, so she will return again, and in my borrowed garment I await her advent."

"I also await her advent," I answered, and thus we parted.

Accompanied by twenty picked men bearing provisions and arms, I climbed the ladders easily enough, and now that I had food and shelter, crossed the mountains without mishap. They even escorted me through the desert beyond, till one night we camped within sight of the gigantic Buddha that sits before the monastery, gazing eternally across the sands and snows.

When I awoke next morning the priests were gone. So I took up my pack and pursued my journey alone, and walking slowly came at sunset to the distant lamasery. At its door an ancient figure, wrapped in a tattered cloak, was sitting, engaged apparently in contemplation of the skies. It was our old friend Kou-en. Adjusting his horn spectacles on his nose he looked at me.

"I was awaiting you, brother of the Monastery called the World," he said in a voice, measured, very ineffectually, to conceal his evident delight. "Have you grown hungry there that you return to this poor place?"

"Aye, most excellent Kou-en," I answered, "hungry for rest."

"It shall be yours for all the days of this incarnation. But say, where is the other brother?"

"Dead," I answered.

"And therefore re-born elsewhere, or perhaps, dreaming in Devachan for a while. Well, doubtless we shall meet him later on. Come, eat, and afterwards tell me your story."

So I ate, and that night I told him all. Kou-en listened with respectful attention, but the tale, strange as it might seem to most people, excited no particular wonder in his mind. Indeed, he explained it to me at such length by aid of some marvellous theory of re-incarnations, that at last I began to doze.

"At least," I said sleepily, "it would seem that we are all winning merit on the Everlasting Plane," for I thought that favourite catchword would please him.

"Yes, brother of the Monastery called the World," Kou-en answered in a severe voice, "doubtless you are all winning merit, but, if I may venture to say so, you are winning it very slowly, especially the woman – or the sorceress – or the mighty evil spirit – whose names I understand you to tell me are She, Hes, and Ayesha upon earth and in *Avitchi,* Star-that-hath-Fallen – "

(*Here Mr. Holly's manuscript ends, its outer sheets having been burnt when he threw it on to the fire at his house in Cumberland.*)

THE END

"[illegible] your brother of the Monastery called the World?" he said in a voice ... [illegible] ... Have you grown [illegible] [illegible] to this place?"

[illegible]

"[illegible] the [illegible] of this [illegible] ... [illegible] is the [illegible]?"

"Dead," I answered.

"And therefore [illegible] elsewhere, or perhaps [illegible] [illegible] [illegible] [illegible] ... [illegible] words tell me your story."

So [illegible] [illegible] [illegible] [illegible] [illegible] with [illegible] attention, but [illegible] [illegible] [illegible] [illegible] [illegible] [illegible] [illegible] [illegible] [illegible] [illegible] ... [illegible] to ... [illegible] [illegible] [illegible] began to [illegible].

At length [illegible] [illegible] [illegible] [illegible] [illegible] [illegible] the [illegible] [illegible] ... [illegible] [illegible] would [illegible] [illegible].

"Yes, brother of the Monastery called the World," [illegible] [illegible] [illegible] [illegible] [illegible] [illegible] ... [illegible] [illegible] [illegible] ... [illegible] [illegible] [illegible] [illegible] ... [illegible] [illegible] ... [illegible] [illegible] ... [illegible] [illegible] [illegible] [illegible] [illegible] ... [illegible] [illegible]."

[illegible] [illegible] [illegible] ... [illegible] [illegible] [illegible] [illegible] ... [illegible].

The End